MOUNT!

Also by Jilly Cooper

FICTION	Riders
	Rivals
	Polo
	The Man Who Made Husbands
	Jealous
	Appassionata
	Score!
	Pandora
	Wicked!
	Jump!

NON-FICTION	How to Stay Married
	How to Survive from Nine to Five
	Jolly Super
	Men and Supermen
	Jolly Super Too
	Women and Superwomen
	Work and Wedlock
	Jolly Superlative
	Super Men and Super Women
	Super Jilly
	Class
	Super Cooper
	Intelligent and Loyal
	Jolly Marsupial
	Animals in War
	The Common Years
	Hotfoot to Zabriskie Point (with
	Patrick Lichfield)
	How to Survive Christmas
	Turn Right at the Spotted Dog
	Angels Rush In
	Araminta's Wedding

CHILDREN'S BOOKS	Little Mabel
	Little Mabel's Great Escape
	Little Mabel Wins
	Little Mabel Saves the Day

ROMANCE	Emily
	Bella
	Harriet
	Octavia
	Prudence
	Imogen
	Lisa & Co

ANTHOLOGIES	The British in Love
	Violets and Vinegar

For more information on Jilly Cooper and her books, see her
website at www.jillycooper.co.uk

MOUNT!

JILLY COOPER

BANTAM PRESS

LONDON • TORONTO • SYDNEY • AUCKLAND • JOHANNESBURG

TRANSWORLD PUBLISHERS
61–63 Uxbridge Road, London W5 5SA
www.penguin.co.uk

Transworld is part of the Penguin Random House group of companies
whose addresses can be found at global.penguinrandomhouse.com

Penguin
Random House
UK

First published in Great Britain in 2016 by Bantam Press
an imprint of Transworld Publishers

A CIP catalogue record for this book
is available from the British Library.

ISBNs 9780593072905 (cased)
9780593072912 (tpb)

Typeset in 11.5/14pt New Baskerville by Falcon Oast Graphic Art Ltd.
Printed and bound by Clays Ltd, Bungay, Suffolk.

Penguin Random House is committed to a sustainable
future for our business, our readers and our planet. This book
is made from Forest Stewardship Council® certified paper.

MIX
Paper from
responsible sources
FSC® C018179

1 3 5 7 9 10 8 6 4 2

To dear Amanda Butler, who
by her sweet nature, sense of fun
and unbelievable efficiency has
transformed my life.

CAST OF CHARACTERS IN 1786

RUPERT BLACK	A bloodstock expert and awfully amusing adventurer.
THE FOURTH BARON RUTSHIRE	A lecherous old peer, owning much of the county, including Rutminster Racecourse.
THE HON. JAMES NORTHFIELD	Lord Rutshire's scholarly reclusive elder son.
THE HON. GISELA NORTHFIELD	Ex-kitchenmaid and James' very new wife.
THE HON. RUFUS NORTHFIELD	Lord Rutshire's younger son, hard man to hounds, hellraiser, inseparable crony of Rupert Black and far more suited to run the estate.

THE ANIMALS

SWEET AZURE   Rupert Black's blue roan mare.

SPARTAN   James Northfield's dark-brown
                            gelding.

SEEKER   James Northfield's white mastiff.

THIRD LEOPARD   A super-stallion, winner of the
                            St Leger and Leading Sire.

CAST OF PRINCIPAL CONTEMPORARY CHARACTERS

SHEIKH ABDUL BADDI

Qatari big hitter, newly obsessed with racing and snapping up star horses.

WOODY ADAMS

Delectable Willowwood tree surgeon. Live-in lover of Canon Niall Forbes.

EDDIE ALDERTON

Rupert Campbell-Black's American grandson, known as Young Eddie. Gilded brat, poster boy and former flat jockey trying his luck at jump racing, Eddie is also trying to stay faithful to his girlfriend, Trixie Macbeth.

PARIS ALVASTON

Dora Belvedon's boyfriend. Ice-cool Adonis simultaneously reading Classics at Cambridge and forging a highly successful acting career.

SETH BAINTON

Unscrupulous, drop-dead gorgeous, middle-aged actor known as Mr Bulging Crotchester and the estranged father of Trixie Macbeth's forthcoming baby.

MARTIN BANCROFT

An appalling fundraising creep.

BRUTE BARRACLOUGH

A dodgy racehorse trainer, who gets a lot of extra-marital sex.

ROSARIA BARRACLOUGH	Brute's sweet, bullied, endlessly cheated-on wife, whose hard work and gift with horses holds his yard together.
HARMONY BATES	Excellent but extremely large Valhalla stable lass, more adored by horses than the opposite sex.
DORA BELVEDON	Eighteen-year-old smart cookie, besotted with dogs, horses and Paris Alvaston. Multi-tasks as press officer for Mrs Wilkinson and ghost-writer for both Rupert Campbell-Black and a goat called Chisolm.
JAMES BENSON	A smooth and very expensive private doctor.
LESTER BOLTON	Internet tycoon specializing in porn, living in Willowwood and as short on inches as he is on charm.
CINDY BOLTON	Lester's child bride, an extremely successful porn star and sometime racehorse owner.
WALTER BRANDON	Rupert's Head Lad, in charge of Rupert's yard. Known as Walter Walter because he shoves his nose in everywhere.
SAM BRIDLINGTON	Chairman of Panel at the British Racing Association enquiry.
RUPERT CAMPBELL-BLACK	Hugely successful owner, trainer, breeder, who bestrides the racing world like a colossus. Despite being as bloody-minded as he is beautiful, still Nirvana for most women.

TAGGIE CAMPBELL-BLACK	His second wife, an angel.
BIANCA CAMPBELL-BLACK	Rupert and Taggie's ravishing Colombian adopted daughter, best friend of Dora Belvedon, girlfriend of rising football star, Feral Jackson.
XAVIER CAMPBELL-BLACK	Rupert and Taggie's adopted Colombian son – a point-to-point rider.
EDDIE CAMPBELL-BLACK	Rupert's increasingly dotty father, known as Old Eddie. Five times married and sexual buccaneer of the old school.
ADRIAN CAMPBELL-BLACK	Rupert's younger brother, who runs a New York art gallery. Boyfriend of Baby Spinosissimo.
JEMMY CARTER	Apprentice jockey and Penscombe stable lad, lacks ambition despite huge potential.
CELESTE	A lazy, malevolent, manipulative but extremely pretty Penscombe stable lass.
COLIN CHALFORD (Mr Fat and Happy)	A very nice rich man looking for love.
CLOVER	Penscombe's youngest stable lass.
MAJOR NORMAN CUNLIFFE	Retired bank manager and pompous ass, treasurer of Willowwood syndicate who formerly owned Mrs Wilkinson.
MANU DE LA TOUR	Charismatic French jockey.

VALENT EDWARDS	Etta Bancroft's brusque, but intensely kind and charismatic, new husband. Man of the people and ex-Premier League footballer, his hawk-like goalkeeper eyes have found gaps in every market, making him a major player on the world financial stage.
ETTA EDWARDS	A poppet – very newly married to Valent Edwards, and the original rescuer and now owner of Grand National winner, Mrs Wilkinson.
CANON NIALL FORBES	Formerly vicar of Willowwood and Woody Adams' boyfriend.
MRS FORD-WINTERS	Geoffrey's owner. Resident of Ashbourne House, a Rutshire care home.
GEE GEE	Gentle giantess and Junoesque Penscombe stud hand, worshipped by Meerkat.
GERALDINE	Rupert's PA who'd like to be the next Mrs Campbell-Black. A bitch.
MARTI GLUCKSTEIN	Rupert's lawyer.
CATHAL GOGAN	Rupert's travelling Head Lad, in charge of horses the moment they leave the yard.
SIMMY HALLIDAY	Rupert's Estate Manager.
DAME HERMIONE HAREFIELD	World-famous diva, and Cosmo Rannaldini's mother, seriously tiresome, brings out the Crippen in all.

LADY HAWKLEY (HELEN)	Mother of Marcus and Tabitha Campbell-Black. A nervy beauty. Having numbered Rupert and Roberto Rannaldini as former husbands, Helen hoped marriage to ex-headmaster and classical scholar, David Hawkley, would mean calmer waters but they seem to have drifted apart.
HANJI HIROSHI	Leading Japanese jockey.
PAT INGLIS	Penscombe's essentially kind and phlegmatic Stallion Master.
HAMMOND JOHNSON	Leading American jockey.
GAVIN LATTON	Rupert Campbell-Black's work rider, a genius with horses, marred by alcoholism exacerbated by the contemptuous infidelity of his wife, Bethany.
BETHANY LATTON	A beautiful bitchy nymphomaniac.
JANEY LLOYD-FOXE	Billy Lloyd-Foxe's widow, a totally unprincipled journalist on the hunt for a new husband.
ISA LOVELL	A brilliant obsessive trainer and ex-champion jockey – a Heathcliff of the gallops, now in sinister partnership with Cosmo Rannaldini, with a yard and a stud at Valhalla doing alarmingly well.
MARTY LOVELL	Isa's very boyish Australian second wife.
ROMAN LOVELL	Isa and Marty's eighteen-year-old son, a jockey.

ALAN MACBETH	Etta Edwards' beguiling son-in-law, author of *Wilkie*, a hugely successful biography of Mrs Wilkinson.
TRIXIE MACBETH	Extremely pretty and very bright teenage granddaughter of Etta Edwards. Estranged from Seth Bainton, the caddish middle-aged father of her forthcoming baby. Trixie is trying to form a relationship with the seriously wayward Eddie Alderton.
HEREWARD/HERRY MACBETH	Trixie's baby son, known as Hereward the Awake.
LOUISE MALONE	Very pretty Penscombe stable lass, known as Lou-easy because of her freedom with her favours.
MARKETA	A gorgeous, voluble, volatile, voluptuous Penscombe stable lass from the Czech Republic who adores horses and the opposite sex.
TEDDY MATTHEWS	Hong Kong jockey nearing retirement.
TARQUIN (TARQUI) McGALL	Joint First Jockey to Cosmo Rannaldini and Isa Lovell. The go-to jockey for the big occasion, Tarqui goes every which way sexually.
ASHLEY (ASH) McINTYRE	Isa Lovell's chillingly ruthless stable jockey, a post shared with Tarqui McGall. Rupert refers to the gay Ashley and the bisexual Tarqui as 'Sodom and Begorrah'.

MICHAEL MEAGAN	Penscombe work rider and some-time stud hand known as Roving Mike.
MEERKAT	Nickname for Stevie O'Dell. Rupert Campbell-Black's adorable second jockey.
GALA MILBURN	A Zimbabwean carer, employed to look after Old Eddie Campbell-Black.
THE HON. RODDY NORTHFIELD	Lord Rutshire's younger brother. A Stipendiary Steward and pillar of the British Racing Association, a self-important prat, nicknamed Famous Grouse because of his incessant nitpicking.
ENID NORTHFIELD	Roddy's wife, known as 'Damsire' because of her obsession with horses' pedigrees.
CHAS NORVILLE	Racehorse trainer, very reliant on charm and the ability to give his owners a good time.
LIONEL (LION) O'CONNOR	Rupert's workmanlike and conscientious stable jockey.
DERMIE O'DRISCOLL	Geoffrey's jockey.
LORD O'HARA (DECLAN)	Ex-television megastar and author. Rupert Campbell-Black's father-in-law.
LADY O'HARA (MAUD)	His feckless actress wife.
CHARLIE RADCLIFFE	An excellent vet.

COSMO RANNALDINI	Dame Hermione Harefield's son, a little fiend possessing the same lethal brand of sex appeal as his evil conductor father, the late Roberto Rannaldini. Forming a partnership with Isa Lovell, Cosmo has transformed the land round the haunted Abbey of Valhalla into a magnificent state-of-the-art racing yard and stud.
WOLFIE RANNALDINI	Cosmo's stepbrother, as straight and honourable as Cosmo is corrupt.
TABITHA RANNALDINI	Rupert Campbell-Black's tempestuous daughter, Olympic eventing gold medallist, married to Wolfie Rannaldini.
TIMON RANNALDINI	Tabitha and Wolfie's six-year-old son, bears an alarming resemblance to his Uncle Cosmo.
SAPPHIRE RANNALDINI	Timon's four-year-old sister.
LORD RUTSHIRE (RUFUS)	Chairman and owner of Rutshire Racecourse, whose estate borders that of Rupert Campbell-Black, causing many territorial skirmishes over the years.
SAUVIGNON SMITHSON	Cosmo Rannaldini's stunning but utterly ruthless PA. Used by Cosmo to lead up horses and lead on owners.
BABY SPINOSISSIMO	Dazzling Australian tenor and racehorse owner, ex-lover of Isa Lovell and current lover of Rupert Campbell-Black's New York gallery-owning brother Adrian.

CONSTANCE SPRIGHTLY	A rather pushy vicar's wife.
SALLY STONEHOUSE	Member of panel at the British Racing Association enquiry.
LARK TOLLAND	A sweet, hardworking, endlessly cheerful Penscombe stable lass, harbouring a hopeless passion for Eddie Alderton.
BAO TONG	Savvy Chinese teenager, who spends several months at Penscombe learning about training and breeding racehorses.
MR TONG (GENGHIS)	Bao's father, trillionaire manufacturer of aeroplanes.
MRS TONG (AIGUO)	Second wife of Genghis Tong and Bao's stepmother.
IONE TRAVIS-LOCK	Very green, bossy-boots, married to ex-ambassador Alban, and Willowwood 'Lady of the Manor'.
JAN VAN DEVENTER	A South African carer.
BOBBY WALKER	Rupert's lorry driver.
MRS WALTON (RUTH)	Cosmo Rannaldini's mature but stunning squeeze.
MR WANG (ZIXIN)	A corrupt Chinese mafia warlord who is cruelly colonizing Africa. Also sexual predator known as 'The Great Willy of China'.
MRS WANG (BINGWEN)	His second wife – a beauty.
TOMMY WESTERHAM	Another charming racehorse trainer who ensures his owners have even more of a nice time.

THE ANIMALS

PRICELESS   Etta Edwards' black greyhound.

BANQUO   Rupert Campbell-Black's black
                             Labrador.

CUTHBERT   Rupert Campbell-Black's Jack
                             Russell.

FORESTER   Taggie Campbell-Black's brindle
                             greyhound.

GROPIUS   Gala Milburn's Staffordshire Bull
                             Terrier.

CADBURY   Dora Belvedon's chocolate
                             Labrador.

GILCHRIST   Rupert Campbell-Black's other
                             Jack Russell.

GWENNY   Etta Edwards' black cat.

PURRPUSS   Another black cat – Master
                             Quickly's stable companion.

CHISOLM   A goat – Mrs Wilkinson's stable
                             companion and later Nanny to
                             Master Quickly.

RUPERT CAMPBELL-BLACK'S STALLIONS

LOVE RAT	Master Quickly's sire – Rupert's favourite.
PEPPY KOALA	A Super Star.
TITUS ANDRONICUS	A psychopath.
THANE OF FIFE	
HAMLET'S GHOST	
ENOBARBUS	
DARDANIUS	
BASSANIO	
BLOOD RIVER	A South African First Season Sire – in love with the vet.

RUPERT CAMPBELL-BLACK'S HORSES IN TRAINING

SAFETY CAR	Another one of Rupert's favourites.
PROMISCUOUS	Son of Love Rat.
LIBERTINE	Another son of Love Rat.

PETRUCHIO

FLEANCE   A real trier. Yet another son of
                            Love Rat.

NEW YEAR'S DAVE   An angel. And yet another son of
                            Love Rat.

TOUCHY FILLY   Whose stable name is PMT.

BLANK CHEKOV   Known as Chuck-Off.

BEIJING BERTIE   Ex-pat who likes lots of patting.

DELECTABLE   An appropriately named Chestnut
                            filly.

DICK THE SECOND

HELL BENT HAL

SEE YOU IN A BIT (BITSY)   A pacemaker.

HORSES IN RUPERT CAMPBELL-BLACK'S STUD

DOROTHY   The practice mare.

GLOUCESTER   The teaser.

MY CHILD CORDELIA   A favourite brood mare.

ISA LOVELL AND COSMO RANNALDINI'S ACE STALLION

ROBERTO'S REVENGE
(VENGIE)

ISA AND COSMO'S HORSES IN TRAINING

(All progeny of Roberto's Revenge)

FEUD FOR THOUGHT

I WILL REPAY

IVAN THE TERRORIST

NERO TOLERANCE

BONE TO PICK

BORIS BADENOUGH

EUMENIDES

VIOLETTA'S VENGEANCE

JEZEBELLA

OTHER HORSES INCLUDE

VERDI'S REQUIEM	Irish Triple Crown winner and a leading sire for past fifteen years.
MRS WILKINSON	Etta Edwards' Grand National winner.
MASTER QUICKLY	Son of Mrs Wilkinson and Love Rat – a piece of work, later trained by Rupert Campbell-Black.
WAGES OF CINDY	Cindy Bolton's brood mare.

GEOFFREY   Star colt of very humble origins,
                            trained by Brute Barraclough.

TRANS JENNIFER   Seductive filly trained by Chas
                            Norville, and fancied by Master
                            Quickly.

RED TROUSERS   Roddy Northfield's colt.

SIMONE DE BEAUVOIR   A mighty French mare.

TO DIE FOR   A mighty American mare.

NOONDAY SILENCE   A Japanese success story.

MOBILE CHARGER   Colt trained by Tommy
                            Westerham.

PROLOGUE

Rutshire, 1786

The last race should have been called off, as the twin saboteurs, night and fog, crept stealthily over the course. Rutminster Cathedral spire, a landmark for miles around, was no longer visible. The Bishop of Rutminster, battling to ban racing, could identify neither rabble nor runners as he peered furiously out of his palace window.

Nor had bitter cold nor relentless drizzle dispersed a vast crowd, swarming round the betting posts, clamouring to watch the most eagerly awaited race in years – despite there being only two contenders.

The first was Rupert Black, a young adventurer, hellraiser, hard drinker and womanizer, who possessed the hauteur of beauty, but not of birth. His father was a small Northern race-horse trainer, and in the late eighteenth century, trainers were regarded as no higher than grooms.

Rupert Black had no income and fewer principles, but was such an amusing fellow that a fast aristocratic set had taken him up, welcomed him into their houses and let him advise them on bloodstock – about which he was clearly an expert.

Rupert Black had been called 'Blackguard' and 'Black Sheep', but was more often nicknamed 'Rupert of the Roan' because of his dashing cavalry charges on the hunting field and his beautiful blue roan mare, Sweet Azure, whom he was riding in the race ahead.

Pitted against him on a vastly superior horse called Spartan was the Hon. James Northfield, elder son of the fourth Baron Northfield, who owned 2,000 Cotswold acres, which included Rutminster Racecourse.

The austere, scholarly James, who had hitherto shown little interest in the estate or in women, had then outraged his parents and scandalized society by impregnating one of his mother's kitchenmaids: a pretty Dutch girl called Gisela. Even more scandalously, he had then secretly married her.

The Hon. Rufus Northfield, except for having the same dark auburn hair, sallow complexion and close-set, fox-brown eyes, was a total contrast to his older brother James. A crack shot and rider, the inseparable crony of Rupert Black, Rufus loved the land and carousing with his father's tenants. Despite his profligate behaviour, Rufus was showing signs of calming down, having just become betrothed to a rich and well-born local beauty.

At the ball given by Lord and Lady Northfield to celebrate this engagement, James' new wife, Gisela, had nearly died of embarrassment after her husband had insisted she attend: only for her to be sneered at by the guests and served by the very servants on whom she had waited in the kitchen.

Worse was to come when the loathsome Rupert Black, already in his cups and having fluttered the pulses of all the ladies, had wandered up to her. Sliding a too-high hand around her thickening waist and squeezing her breast, he mockingly handed her a late wedding present. It turned out to be a copy of *Pamela*, Samuel Richardson's wildly popular novel about a servant girl fighting for her virtue in the house of a lecherous master.

'Richardson could have been writing about you,' drawled Rupert, causing a ripple of laughter to run through several female guests who'd gathered around.

To their disappointment, however, Rupert showed no desire to dance with any of them and instead retired to the gambling tables in an attempt to reduce his debts and finish paying for a colt called Third Leopard, whose owner was threatening to sell him elsewhere.

As he raked in his winnings – a pile of sovereigns as gold as his hair – Rupert Black was singing the praises of his mare Sweet Azure, whom he might have been forced to sell if things didn't pick up.

'Like all good fillies,' he said insolently, so a passing James Northfield could hear, 'she has the face of an angel and the posterior of a cook – not unlike your new wife, James.'

Looking down at Rupert's cruel, unsmiling face, its beauty hardly impaired by bloodshot, slightly crossing blue eyes, James, who loved his wife, upended the table; and, as coins scattered all over the floor, he challenged Rupert to a duel.

'A better idea,' suggested Rupert to noisy cheers, 'would be a match race between Spartan and Sweet Azure round Rutminster Racecourse on the old track through the woods, the loser giving the winner four thousand guineas.' And, as the Northfields owned the racecourse, it was arranged in front of witnesses that the contest would take place after the final race on the following Saturday.

Throughout that Saturday, rumours swirled round more thickly than the fog. Many of the gentry rolled up on horseback after a day's hunting and were instantly engulfed by pickpockets, drunkards, prostitutes, cutpurses and gypsies telling fortunes, crowding round the betting posts as the money poured in.

Northfield had the finer horse, Black was the finer rider. But, although lithe and lean, at six feet tall, Rupert was twelve pounds heavier than the weedy James – twelve pounds which Sweet Azure, far smaller and slighter than Spartan, would have to carry over four miles. Yet Black was still the favourite.

The fog was thickening, ghost-grey, suffocating and blurring everything. As James pulled on his boots, he was reminded of Leonardo da Vinci's treatise on painting, which claimed that objects seen through fog will loom larger than they are. In fact, James had been so busy writing his own treatise on Leonardo that, unlike Rupert Black, he hadn't bothered to walk the course.

The only person apart from the Bishop of Rutminster not at the races was Gisela Northfield, who, fighting all-day sickness, was in the cathedral praying for her husband's safe return.

Down at the start in the water meadows, oak trunks darkened by rain, like towers in the twisting vapours, were just distinguishable from the black wooded hillside beyond. Once again, the starter questioned whether the race should be run.

'I can see well enough,' mocked Rupert Black, who was already mounted, 'to notice the sweat of fear glistening on James Northfield's face and to have no difficulty recognizing the winning post.'

James didn't reply. He was having difficulty merely climbing aboard the plunging, insufficiently ridden Spartan. More so when Hibbert, his groom, let go of the reins in order to contain Seeker, James' white mastiff, who was fighting to join the race and follow his master.

The crowd huddled together, unwilling to lose their places on the rail, blowing on their fingers, drinking from bottles which they might later throw at a losing horse, and shouting to keep warm. Their roar could almost be heard in Newmarket, miles away, as the two riders splashed off across the water meadows and up on to a track that ran round the wooded bowl of hills, before dropping back down to the water meadows for the finish.

It was colder and more claustrophobic up in the woods. The going was as slippery as the fat from the roasting capon Gisela had spilled over the floor, the first time shy James had stolen a kiss.

Leaves blew into the horses' faces and lay in a treacherous carpet over arthritic roots, fallen twigs, Cotswold stones, rabbit holes and badger setts. Not to mention the sinister coils of Old Man's Beard hanging from overhead branches, waiting to garrotte a passing rider. As the track grew narrower from being little used, James Northfield cursed himself for not walking the course.

The bellow of the impatient crowd rose to a deafening climax, then turned to a groan as a horse and rider eventually emerged from the woods, parting the thick grey curtain of mist and splashing back across the water meadows. Both were so coated with dark-brown mud, they were assumed to be James Northfield and Spartan. But as they galloped up the straight, the groan became a thunderous cheer again, as the mob distinguished the flying gold curls of a rider, almost too big for his gallant little mare. Instantly the jubilant mounted spectators peeled off to follow the pair up the course to the winning post.

But as time ticked away there was no sign of the Honourable James.

'I lost him about two miles back, just above Walker's Mill,' Rupert told the stewards as he removed his saddle to weigh in.

Sweet Azure stood desperately panting with drooping head, steam pouring out of inflated red nostrils. From the wheals on her quarters and her bleeding flanks, it was clear that neither whip nor spur had been spared. Rufus Northfield, overjoyed because he'd backed his friend very heavily, ordered Rupert's groom to cover the damage with a rug.

Then everyone waited and waited for James Northfield and Spartan, until Seeker the mastiff broke away from Hibbert the groom and plunged back into the dark in search of his master. No one else left. The crowd had closed round the betting posts to stop any bookmaker doing a runner. Then over the shouting and celebration came the unearthly howl of a dog.

It took time to light torches, then stumbling and sliding through the darkening woods, a party of mounted stewards set out. After two miles, they at last identified the ghostly white form of Seeker, still howling on the side of the track. As the distraught animal refused to let anyone closer, he had to be shot before Spartan's body was discovered slumped at the bottom of a fifty-foot ravine. Beneath the horse, his back and neck broken, lay James Northfield.

Next day the fog cleared, but rumour writhed round more thickly and darkly, particularly when, by the ravine, two sets of hoof-prints were discovered side by side, accompanied by much skidding. Only the smaller set of footprints passed onwards.

But as Rupert Black, refusing to admit he had blue blood on his hands, pointed out, he and Sweet Azure must have passed the spot a good ten minutes before James and Spartan – and both riders must have taken an identical route to avoid a big sycamore branch that had fallen across the track.

Darker rumours suggested that Rupert could have been egged on by Rufus, whose extravagant tastes were hampered by the enforced poverty of a younger son. Any suggestions of foul play, however, were quashed by the Northfield family, who owned the racecourse and probably the local constabulary. Refusing to blame Rupert, they honourably paid him the four thousand guineas. This, added to his winnings from the vast sum he had wagered on himself and Sweet Azure, enabled him to complete the payments on Third Leopard.

Did the Northfields feel a secret relief? James had always been a difficult, introspective son. Rufus, particularly when guided by his sensible new wife, would run the estate far better. Privately, Lord Northfield had never forgiven James for stealing from him the fair Gisela, on whom he too had had designs. After a few weeks, nemesis struck and his Lordship was punished by a fatal heart attack.

The timid, heartbroken Gisela was speedily paid off and sent packing back to Holland. Although she wrote occasionally to Mrs Jenkins the cook, by the time she gave birth, the title had already passed to Rufus.

Gisela, who had never ceased to mourn James, sank into despair and took her own life. No one in Rutminster bothered to find out if she had given birth to a daughter or a son.

Meanwhile, Third Leopard, who was both a direct descendant of the Darley Arabian and grandson of the mighty Eclipse, was trained by Rupert Black into a great horse, winning numerous races including the oldest classic, the St Leger, which had been established in 1776.

At stud, Third Leopard was even more successful, siring 400 sons and daughters, who in turn won many classics, notching up 822 victories. This for several years made the stallion the country's Leading Sire, during which time his master Rupert was able to charge a massive stud fee of fifty guineas. With riches pouring in, Rupert Black became a grand gentleman, marrying, like Rufus Northfield, a rich, well-born beauty, a

Miss Campbell, whose ancestors had fought bravely for the Royalists in the Civil War, and who joined her name with his. The Campbell-Blacks bought a beautiful house in Penscombe overlooking a wooded Gloucestershire valley, where horses have thrived ever since.

The marriage was successful. If Mrs Campbell-Black corrected her husband Rupert's pronunciation a little too often, he could always find solace in the adulation of the neighbouring belles.

Such was his hubris, he and Third Leopard were even painted by Stubbs in a country landscape with a pale-gold house peering out of dark-green trees, with olive-green lawns flowing down to a lake on which floated swans.

Normally Stubbs immortalized legendary racehorses held by grooms identified by name. But Rupert Black insisted on aping the Prince Regent. Like Prinny he was dressed in tight white breeches and brown topped boots, with a wide-brimmed hat tipped over his Greek nose and flaxen curls flowing over the collar of a long, brass-buttoned riding coat, which emphasized his strong, lithe body. A frilled white shirt showed off the perfect jawline and a passionate but ruthless mouth. Rupert Black was also portrayed like Prinny, trotting past with a triumphant wave of his whip: 'Haven't I and this great horse done well.'

And yet to this day, no one – least of all Rupert Black's descendants – likes to ride or walk in Rutminster woods at dusk. There have been too many sightings of pale riders on dark horses and howling white mastiffs. Even hounds in full cry on late winter afternoons have always turned away, whimpering, if a fox has run into the woods.

1

On a stiflingly hot June evening, some 225 years later, Rupert Campbell-Black, the great-great-great-great-great-great-grandson of Rupert Black, looked out of his office in the west wing of the same pale-gold Queen Anne house at Penscombe.

The same lake still glittered as sweetly azure as his ancestor's blue roan mare in the June sun, but to the right of the olive-green lawns and down the valley sprawled a giant complex of a racing yard, entitled Rupert Campbell-Black Racing. This was surrounded by a tangle of gallops for all weathers and distances, a stud farm, Penscombe Stud, helicopter pad, hangar, lorry park, staff cottages, and lush paddocks, with plenty of shade to safeguard every kind of racehorse: stallions, visiting mares, mares in foal or with foal, yearlings and horses in training.

But Rupert Black's descendant didn't feel any great pride as he scrolled through the emails still congratulating him on his three-thousandth win, or his Grand National victory with a mare called Mrs Wilkinson back in April or the 2000 Guineas back in May. He was merely irritated not to have won the Derby earlier in the month.

Nor did he bother to read more emails pouring in to congratulate him on the speech he'd made at Billy Lloyd-Foxe's memorial service yesterday, a task he'd found harder than winning an Olympic Gold in Los Angeles with a trapped nerve years ago. He had never dreamed how wiped out he would be by Billy's death. Billy, his inseparable companion of fifty years, joined at the hip, finishing each other's jokes, rejoicing in every success.

Rupert looked down at his speech.

'This was the noblest rider of them all,' he had told a packed Rutminster Cathedral congregation which had spilled out over the water meadows. Then he had regaled them with stories about his and Billy's antics at prep school and Harrow, hell-raising on the showjumping circuit, fighting for a television franchise, moving on to Billy's career as equine correspondent for the BBC.

'Nothing in Billy's life became him like the leaving of it,' he had ended. 'He bore pain and illness with equal fortitude, but the happiest moment of his life came at the end, when his daughter Amber won the Grand National on a little one-eyed mare called Mrs Wilkinson.

'Billy had an equally marvellous little horse called The Bull on whom he'd won a silver medal. "I hope I see The Bull again," were his last words. I'm sure Billy's riding The Bull across the clouds. Lucky heaven, to have both of them.' Bloody mawkish that, Rupert thought wryly.

The party afterwards, most of which he'd paid for, resulted in him having a blazing row with Billy's widow Janey, who'd made a drunken and soppy speech, repeatedly quoting the line: 'That's the way for Billy and me', while boasting of the over 3,019 letters of sympathy she had received. She was furious Rupert hadn't praised her as a wonderful wife.

'You were a fucking awful wife,' Rupert had snarled back. 'Billy'd be alive today if he hadn't been permanently stressed by you squandering his money and fucking other men.'

This had also resulted in a rare screaming match between Rupert and his wife Taggie, who'd ticked him off before rushing away to comfort Janey.

Rupert was sure Janey would take the opportunity to solicit an invitation to move back into Lime Tree Cottage, the little seventeenth-century house in Rupert's woods nearby, which she and Billy had lived in rent-free when they were first married. If Janey returned, Rupert knew she'd be hanging round, playing the grieving widow, reminding him of Billy for the rest of his life.

Last night's row with Taggie had ended up with her sleeping in the spare room and their not speaking all day. He was tempted to ring her in the kitchen and make it up. Instead he poured himself another glass of whisky.

On the wall opposite were monitors on which he could watch his own horses and the progeny of his stallions and brood mares winning races all over the world. On the left wall, flanked by framed photographs of victorious horses, hung the Stubbs of Rupert Black and Third Leopard, winner of the St Leger and for five years Leading Sire.

Today there were two ways a horse could become Leading Sire: either if he were the stallion whose offspring had clocked up the most wins in a year, or, more importantly, if those off-spring had earned the most prize money. Verdi's Requiem, a dark-brown Irish Triple Crown winner, had topped the Leading Sire charts for Great Britain and Europe for fifteen years but now, aged twenty-five, his reign must be drawing to a close.

Opening the *Racing Post*, Rupert noted Bloodstock News had predicted a bloody battle to topple Verdi's Requiem between Rupert Campbell-Black's Love Rat and Isa Lovell's Roberto's Revenge. Rupert ground his teeth. Isa Lovell, ex-champion jockey and ex-son-in-law, had worked uneasily for Rupert for ten years, learning everything he could about training and breeding before defecting to start his own yard directly in competition with Rupert.

Even worse, Isa had joined forces with Cosmo Rannaldini, the fiendish little son of Rupert's arch enemy, the late, great conductor Roberto Rannaldini. Married to Rupert's first wife Helen, Roberto had not only tried to rape Rupert's daughter Tabitha, but had managed to batter to death Taggie's little mongrel Gertrude when she tried to protect Tabitha. In the Campbell-Black canon, it was arguable which was the greater crime.

Cosmo and Isa were proving maddeningly successful with the progeny of Roberto's Revenge, particularly with a colt called Feud for Thought, which had just beaten Rupert's colt Dardanius in the Derby. Cosmo had inherited a great deal of money from his father, but he and Isa were spending such a fortune on year-lings and two-year-olds that someone must be bankrolling them. Rupert would kill to stop them beating him to Leading Sire. Love Rat *must* topple Verdi's Requiem.

In the still-baking evening, out in the fields he could see foals lying flat and motionless except for their frantically waving tails. Rupert's four dogs: Jack Russells, Cuthbert and Gilchrist, a brindle greyhound called Forester and a black Labrador called Banquo, panted in their baskets.

Up on a monitor, evening racing had started at the Curragh, Ireland's greatest racecourse. Rupert hoped one of Love Rat's progeny, Promiscuous, would win a later race there.

Promiscuous had been trained by Rupert's old stable jockey, the also lascivious Bluey Charteris, who'd married an Irish trainer's daughter, and managed to stay faithful enough to take over his father-in-law's yard. Bluey and Isa Lovell doing so well made Rupert feel old. Overwhelmed with sadness and restless-ness, he rang Valent Edwards, who had just married Etta Bancroft, the owner of Grand National-winning Mrs Wilkinson, and who was now back from their honeymoon.

'We ought to discuss Mrs Wilkinson,' he said. 'Come over and have a drink.'

The moment he rang off, the telephone rang again: 'No, you can't have a discount on three mares,' said Rupert tersely, and poured himself another glass of whisky.

There was a knock on the door and a very pretty blonde, with an utterly deceptive air of innocence, walked in. Dora Belvedon was the eighteen-year-old daughter of Rupert's late friend, Raymond Belvedon, and his much younger second wife, Anthea. A gold-digger and an absolute bitch, Anthea had never given Dora enough pocket money. As a result, Dora had supported herself, her dog Cadbury and her pony Loofah by flogging stories to the tabloids.

For the past two years, as well as acting sporadically as Rupert's press officer, she had been ghosting his contentious, highly successful column in the *Racing Post*. She also wrote a column supposedly by Mrs Wilkinson's stable companion, a goat called Chisolm, in the *Daily Mirror*.

Missing her sweet father desperately, an itinerant Dora found comfort spending time at Penscombe, where she could always grab a bed if needs be. In addition, she often stayed in Willowwood, in the cottage of Miss Painswick, the former secretary of her old boarding school.

Fearing that Mrs Wilkinson might be homesick just before the Grand National, when she had been moved to Penscombe to be trained by Rupert, Dora, in an incredibly daring move, had smuggled the little mare into the mighty Love Rat's stallion paddock, and a joyful coupling had taken place.

Mrs Wilkinson's dam had been a successful flat horse called Usurper, and her sire was Rupert's most successful stallion: the Derby and St Leger-winning Peppy Koala. As Love Rat had been a champion sprinter, who would add his lightning speed to Mrs Wilkinson's stamina, any foal consequently should be a cracker. But as Dora had executed this move without Rupert's permission, she was extremely anxious to avoid the subject of stud fees. Now, brandishing an Italian phrasebook, she said, 'Poor Emilia was awfully low, but I've been talking to her in Italian and she's really perked up' – Emilia being a very good filly Rupert had bought cheap because of the collapsing Italian economy.

'I've also been playing her *La Traviata*,' babbled Dora, 'and she loved it, particularly the bit that goes, "Da dum dum da de dum, da dum, dum da, de, dum".'

'Where the hell have you been?' demanded Rupert, who adored Dora but felt she needed reining in.

Dora replied that she'd been in Sardinia with her actor boyfriend Paris, and housesitting Mrs Wilkinson while Etta her owner and her husband Valent were on their honeymoon.

'It's Mrs Wilkinson we've got to talk about,' Rupert said.

'I must get your *Racing Post* copy in by tomorrow afternoon,' Dora said hastily. 'I thought you might like to write about Roberto's Revenge's climb up the Leading Sire's chart. Isa Lovell's doing really well.'

'I'm not doing any favours for that moody, vindictive little shit, or that oily little toad Cosmo.'

'I quite like Cosmo,' confessed Dora. 'He's funny and we both have mothers who are embarrassingly bats about you.'

'Shut up, Dora,' snapped Rupert. 'We need to talk about Mrs Wilkinson.'

'Did you see Amanda Platell's piece in the *Mail*, about the doctors' surgeries teeming with women suffering from loss of libido, and suggesting the perfect cure was Rupert Campbell-Black?'

'Don't be even more fatuous,' said Rupert irritably. But he smirked slightly. 'Now about this stolen service.'

On cue, Dora's chocolate Labrador, Cadbury, wandered in from Taggie's kitchen, and all Rupert's dogs woke up and fell on him, barking joyously. 'Go back to your boxes. Stop that bloody awful din!' roared Rupert.

'Din, because they want their dinner, ha, ha. Can Cadbury have some too?'

'Shut up, Cuthbert.' Rupert pulled a Jack Russell on to his knee, shutting its yapping jaws with his hand and asked: 'Can you remember exactly what day Love Rat covered Mrs Wilkinson?'

'About a fortnight before the National.'

Rupert looked up at the calendar. 'Foal in February then.'

'Mrs Wilkinson's had a lovely day,' sighed Dora, edging off the subject again, 'opening a supermarket in Cotchester. Huge cheering crowds turned out to pat her and Chisolm. They do adore the attention.'

'With a valuable foal inside, she ought to be taking it easy.'

'Mares can run up to a hundred and twenty days,' chided Dora. 'Mrs Wilkinson's a working mother, has to earn her keep.' Then, deflecting Rupert's shaft of disapproval: 'And did you know that people are Skyping Chisolm from all over the world? She's got a website called Skypegoat. Isn't that a cool joke?'

'Quite,' said Rupert, who was then fortunately distracted by a monitor on which jockeys and horses were going down to the start of the Curragh. There was Promiscuous, son of Love Rat, looking really well.

Dora looked out of one window at the squirrels fighting in the angelic green of Rupert's beechwoods, which formed a great crescent round the rear of the house.

Turning back to Dora, Rupert said: 'Do you realize Love Rat's stud fee is £100,000?'

'Goodness,' she said, then gave a sigh of relief as Valent walked in. 'Hi, Valent, hope you had a lovely honeymoon. Mrs Wilkinson missed you both. Must go and counsel Emilia some more. Dum, da, da, dum de dum,' sang Dora as beaming, followed by five dogs, she sidled out of the room.

2

Rupert respected Valent Edwards. He couldn't push him around and, despite being strong, tough and hugely successful, Valent didn't take himself at all seriously; nor, although humble about his working-class origins, was he remotely chippy. An ex-Premier League footballer, whose legendary Cup Final-winning save was still remembered, Valent had been a great athlete who, like Rupert, on giving up had channelled his ambition and killer instinct into finding gaps in world markets. The fact that both men had made a huge amount of money didn't deter them from being hell bent on beating their rivals and making a great deal more.

In his late sixties, tall, handsome, hefty of shoulder and square of jaw, with black eyebrows and grey hair rising thickly without the aid of any product, Valent had been described by Louise Malone, one of Rupert's most comely stable lasses as: 'A cross between my dad and my granddad, but you still want to shag him.'

Having married Mrs Wilkinson's owner, Etta Bancroft, Valent had returned from a four-week honeymoon looking tanned and happy.

'How was it?' asked Rupert, handing him a can of beer.

'Grite, went by in a flash.'

'You were bloody lucky, it's been raining since you left.'

Glancing round the room, Valent caught sight of the Stubbs. 'Christ, that's you.'

'No, a distant ancestor, Rupert Black.'

Valent moved closer. 'But he's exactly like you,' he said incredulously. 'Where d'you get it from?'

'It somehow got handed down to some queer uncle, who left it to me. Should have left it to my brother, Adrian, who's an art dealer, but I'm better-looking. Adrian's livid. Stubbs was a leftie and usually painted racehorses held by their stable lads, but Rupert Black was so up himself, he insisted on riding the horse – a Leading Sire, no less, called Third Leopard. Perhaps I ought to start riding Love Rat.'

Valent shook his head. 'He is so like you.'

'Classic case of pre-potency,' explained Rupert. 'Some stallions (like some men) have genes so strong, they imprint their looks and temperaments on succeeding generations. So for generations, the offspring are far more like them than their immediate fathers or grandfathers.'

Rupert, who hadn't had any lunch, opened a tin of Pringles and handed them to Valent who, having put on ten pounds during his honeymoon, waved them away.

'For example, two hundred-odd years later,' went on Rupert, 'I look far more like Rupert Black than my own father, while Tabitha and Perdita, my daughters, and Eddie, my grandson, are all the image of Rupert Black. They have also inherited his brilliance as a rider, his arrogance, his tricky temperament and the same killer instinct.'

'And stooning looks.' Although as the sun fell on the indigo shadows beneath Rupert's eyes, Valent thought he looked desperately tired. 'What do you know about him?'

'Not a lot. His father was a trainer, and Rupert Black won a match race which apparently enabled him to buy Third Leopard. As I said, the horse became Leading Sire, making Rupert a fortune in stud fees. And talking of Leading Sires, one of Love Rat's colts is in this race . . .' Turning up the sound, Rupert became totally superglued to the television.

'Come on, little boy, come on, little boy . . . come on, come on, *come on!*' he yelled, giving a shout of joy as Promiscuous left the field for dead and romped home by three lengths.

Through the open window, cheers could be heard from

stable lads watching the race on television screens all over the yard and stud. Next moment, a bell rang to announce a winner, which always raised morale.

Looking out, Valent could see Rupert's beautiful wife Taggie crossing the yard on her way to the stud to reward the winner's sire Love Rat with a carrot.

'Bloody good result. That's two Group Ones and a Group Two won by Love Rat's progeny this week,' said Rupert happily. He picked up his mobile to share the news with Billy, who had also loved Promiscuous, then realized the futility. God, would it never stop hurting?

Valent, meanwhile, was thinking about Etta, his new wife, and dreading getting caught up in work again. They could have stayed away more than a month, but Etta couldn't bear to be parted any longer from Priceless, her greyhound, Gwenny her cat, Mrs Wilkinson and her stable companion, Chisolm the goat, and the garden in the growing season.

There were, in fact, few places abroad where some stray dog or cat wouldn't upset Etta. He longed to take her to China where he had been doing a huge amount of business, but felt a country where dogs were rammed into cages in the market-place on the way to the dinner-table would finish her off completely. So they had returned home and it was blissful to be back at his house, Badger's Court, in the nearby village of Willowwood. He had left Etta pruning roses and wailing at the bindweed toppling the delphiniums and the brown slugs, bigger than Dora's chocolate Labrador, eating everything.

Suddenly he noticed a large, dark-brown horse with only one ear wandering out of his box in the direction of the feed room.

'Loose horse,' he said in alarm. Rupert glanced out.

'No, that's Safety Car – got the run of the yard.'

'Why's he only got one ear?'

'Titus Andronicus, the yard sociopath, bit the other off and most of his tail.'

As Taggie came out of Love Rat's box, she apologized to Safety Car for giving away her last carrot, then glanced tentatively up at the window, waving shyly at Valent before disappearing back into the house, followed purposefully by Safety Car.

'We'd better talk about Mrs Wilkinson's foal,' said Valent.

Mrs Wilkinson had originally been rescued by Valent's new wife Etta. Nursed back to health, she had turned out to have an immaculate pedigree. To afford to put her into training, Etta had formed a syndicate of fellow villagers living in Willowwood.

Back in March, after Mrs Wilkinson fell in the Cheltenham Gold Cup, Valent had bought her to stop her being acquired by a very unpleasant rival owner. When Rupert suggested she had a crack at the National in three weeks' time, Mrs Wilkinson, when transferred to Rupert's yard, had detested the draconian regime. It was here, to cheer her up, that Dora had sneaked her into stallion Love Rat's paddock. Thus encouraged, Mrs Wilkinson had gone on to win the National.

Rupert, in fact, had been winding Dora up about stud fees, because Mrs Wilkinson actually belonged to Valent, who would own any foal born and therefore be responsible for stud fees. Having handed Valent another beer, Rupert foxily announced that foal shares were standard these days, and that if he and Valent shared ownership of the foal, he would train it for nothing.

Valent liked and admired Rupert, whom he was also aware he couldn't push around. He was also slightly edgy about him, not least because Rupert had been Etta's long-term pin-up. But although it would be most women's idea of heaven to share ownership of a potential superhorse with Rupert Campbell-Black, Valent knew that Etta felt Rupert was too rough on horses, regarding them as marketable stock rather than furry animals to be adored.

'I'd also be waiving Love Rat's £120,000 stud fee,' Rupert added.

'You told Dora £100,000.'

'Varies,' said Rupert airily. 'What's the state of play with that ghastly syndicate?'

'They still own ten per cent of Mrs Wilkinson.'

'Get rid of them, pay them off.'

'Here's the contract.' Valent had some difficulty extracting it from the pocket of his newly tight trousers before handing it to Rupert, who scanned it.

'Thank Christ, there's nothing about breeding rights, so the foal's ours.'

'I'll talk to Etta,' said Valent firmly. 'I gave Wilkie back to her as a wedding present.'

He then moved on to discuss China, where racing was almost entirely forbidden because the Communist regime, like the Bishop of Rutminster back in the eighteenth century, thought it a corrupting influence, particularly the betting side.

Hong Kong, however, which offered vast prize money, made more in tax on the day of the Hong Kong Cup than the country did in an entire year – money which also paid for all the hospitals. An impressed China was therefore seriously considering establishing an indigenous racing and breeding industry. There were already plans afoot to build two international racecourses, five training tracks and to provide stabling and facilities for 4,000 horses.

'The potential of this market is so vast,' said Valent, starting on the Pringles, 'with bloodstock agents all over the world salivating at the prospect of selling horses to China.'

'The Irish and the Arabs are already doing deals and sending stallions,' volunteered Rupert. 'Imagine *The Morning Line* with 400 million viewers.'

'I've got the contacts, but not the expert knowledge.'

'Then you'd better acquire some,' said Rupert.

3

Rupert whisked Valent through the racing yard, into Penscombe Stud and past a row of boxes, known as Billionaire's Row because it housed Rupert's finest stallions, and included the house of Pat Inglis the Stallion Master, so he could keep an eye on them all. Each stallion had a brass plate with his name on attached to the cheek-piece of his head collar.

'Much better than those name-badges at parties, when you have to surreptitiously glance down at a person's bosom to check who they are,' observed Valent. 'Here you can look your stallion in the eye.'

Rupert, a gambler like his ancestor Rupert Black, had a few years ago had a successful bet that he could get a GCSE in English Literature as a very mature student. Acquiring a fondness for the subject, he had named his more recent horses after characters in Shakespeare.

Valent proceeded to admire Thane of Fife, dark brown and workmanlike, who had no trouble covering three mares a day, with a strike rate of getting 90 per cent of them in foal.

'Didn't win that many big races,' explained Rupert, 'so his stud fee is a third of Love Rat's.'

Next Bassanio, who was very shy and could only perform if Dorothy the practice mare stood in the corner of the covering shed watching him.

Then prowling Titus Andronicus, a black brute who descended on mares like the Heavy Brigade, and who so terrified the stable lads, he was sometimes dispatched down a tunnel of cages to the covering shed.

'One day he'll have you against the wall, another he'll be sweet as pie. I hope his foals don't inherit his temperament,' said Rupert.

They had reached the box of Hamlet's Ghost, who only fancied greys.

'The only way to get him to mount a mare of any other colour,' Rupert told Valent, 'is to put a white sheet over her.'

Enobarbus's box was empty. He was spending a season in France and not enjoying it, because he couldn't get a grip on the quarters of those slim French mares.

Valent shook his head. 'They're all different.'

'And here's Mrs Wilkinson's sire, Peppy Koala,' went on Rupert as a wild-eyed chestnut darted out his head and took a nip at Rupert's sleeve. 'Winner of the Derby and the St Leger, contender for Leading Sire. Stud fee even higher than Love Rat's.

'And talk of the angel, here is Mrs Wilkinson's husband Love Rat,' he added fondly, as they reached the last box. Valent admired the big grey with a long blond mane and tail, who nickered at Rupert and rubbed a whiskery soft pink nose against his face.

'He's the gentlest horse in the yard; any child would be safe in his box, always offering to babysit. His only problem,' Rupert scratched Love Rat behind the ears, 'is laziness. Unless he really fancies a mare, he's a bit inclined to leave it in and let it soak. He's got a waiting list of five hundred, but we limit him to ninety of the very best a season. If he's going to make Leading Sire, we can't have him wasting his somewhat selective libido on any riff-raff.'

Rupert consulted his iPhone. 'He's not covering anything this evening,' he said.

'That'll please Mrs Wilkinson,' said Valent.

'Look behind you.' Rupert nudged Valent. Valent did and burst out laughing. Big, one-eared Safety Car had picked up the handle of a large brush with his teeth and was attempting to sweep the yard.

'He can't bear attention on any other horse. He'll play football for hours with Cuthbert and Gilchrist.'

'I ought to get back,' said Valent.

'Come and watch a covering. Thane of Fife's doing the honours.'

In a huge barn, with padded walls and a carpet of shredded black rubber – laughingly known as 'shagpile' – a lovely chestnut mare was being led in with a tiny grey foal trotting beside her.

'That's Cindy Bolton's mare, Wages of Cindy, known as Katie,' murmured Rupert. 'Amazingly, she's won a lot of races.' And there up in the viewing platform, giggling and waving, was Cindy Bolton herself, a very blonde, world-famous porn star, who lived in Valent's village of Willowwood. Accompanied by her dreadful, self-important, billionaire porn-merchant husband, Lester, she was now shrieking at the prospect of Rupert and sexual activity.

'Hello, Valent, hello, Rupert – come and join us up here. Surely Foalie oughtn't to see Mummy making babies,' she squealed. 'Someone ought to put their hands over his eyes.'

'Some mares get inordinately upset if they're separated from their foals,' Rupert called up to her, preferring to lean against the wall with Valent. 'And for Christ's sake, keep your voice down.'

'Isn't he macho?' sighed Cindy.

'What are those two doing here?' muttered Valent in horror.

'If breeders are forking out a hundred grand for a shag, or in Fifey's case twenty-five grand, they want to check it's happened – and with the right mare.'

Wages of Cindy was now having protective boots put on her feet by a girl stud hand dressed in a hard hat and protective clothing.

'Coverings can be very dangerous, and catastrophic for a stallion if a mare kicks out behind,' said Rupert, nipping out of the barn to take a call.

Another stud hand led the grey foal away from the action but to a place where he could still see his mother. The 'teaser', whose job it was to arouse the mare, was led in. A sweet little bay pony called Gloucester, the teaser was a smooth operator with a shaggy black mane and tail, who proceeded to sniff and lick Wages of Cindy, nipping her gently on the neck, then moving down her body, getting her ready until the mare lifted her tail, parted her back legs and let out a stream of urine. Whereupon the poor teaser was whipped away and a huge grey stallion thundered in, blond mane and tail tossing even more than Cindy Bolton's and giving great reverberating bellows.

Surely that's Love Rat, not Thane of Fife, thought Valent.

But an army of stud hands, all in safety helmets, were concentrating too hard to notice. One was hanging on grimly to the stallion's bridle, another was holding the mare's tail out of the way, another was poised to guide in the penis, another to hold the base of the shaft to see if ejaculation had taken place, and yet another to wind a twitch of rope round Wages of Cindy's nose and tighten it if she started playing up.

'Poor girlie,' wailed her mistress. 'Don't hurt her poor nosey. Goodness, what a winkle!' Her voice rose to a shriek again, as the stallion flashed the most enormous penis, nearly two foot long, grey, and circled halfway down by a smart pink band.

'Shut up,' hissed a returning Rupert. Some stallions could be distracted by a sparrow flying up into the roof. Then he gave a howl of rage. 'It's the wrong fucking stallion! It should be Fifey, not Love Rat.' Sprinting across the yard, hurling himself with huge courage at Love Rat's bridle, he tried to haul him away. But it was too late. Love Rat, feeling randy for once, had plunged his mighty Tower of Pisa into the excited mare – ten massive thrusts and it was all over.

The stud hands glanced at each other in trepidation.

'OK, he's ejaculated,' said one, feeling a shudder at the base of the shaft.

'Who the fuck is responsible for this?' said Rupert furiously. 'Where's Gavin?'

'Couldn't make it – wife trouble,' muttered the penis-guider.

'I don't want to snitch, but Gav definitely said Love Rat,' whispered the girl stud hand, releasing the twitch on the mare's nose.

Valent was distracted by a moan from the gallery. Glancing up, he saw Cindy Bolton slumped on the rail, a glazed expression on her flushed face. Behind her, Lester was smoothing his comb-over and zipping up his trousers.

As Love Rat was led back to his box, to be washed down with lukewarm water, Wages of Cindy was united with her foal and led off to the box where she would board for a week to see if she was pregnant.

By some superhuman effort, Rupert managed not to erupt in rage. As the error was on Penscombe's side, would he be able to sting Lester, as tight with money as Wages of Cindy's twitch, for a further £75,000 to make up Love Rat's fee? Would it be better, in fact, to abort the foal, who would only be the size of a fingernail, rather than have Love Rat's name on its passport – and try again later with Fifey? Bloody, bloody Gav.

Straightening her clothes, Cindy came down from the viewing platform to pat her departing mare.

'Good girlie, hope that didn't hurt you so soon after having Foalie. I've brought my latest for your dad.' She handed Rupert a DVD entitled *Spanky Panky*. 'I hope you'll have a little look.'

'Thanks,' said Rupert tersely as he pocketed it.

'Thanks,' echoed the girl stud hand, who'd taken off her hard hat, unleashing a cascade of shiny red hair, and who now accepted a leer and a £100 tip from Lester. 'You're welcome at Penscombe any time, Mr Bolton.'

'I do hope you'll train Foalie for us, Rupert,' simpered Cindy. 'And now I expect you're going to offer us a nice glass of bubbly.'

'I'm busy,' snapped Rupert, relieved for once to hear cries of, 'Cindy, Cindy,' as his dotty old father Eddie wandered into the stud with his flies undone, crying, 'Where's my lovely boy, Love Rat? Come and see him, Cindy.'

Old Eddie adored Love Rat and drove Rupert crackers, hanging around the boxes or the stallion paddocks, plying him with Polos and often leaving his gate or stable door undone.

Rather ashamed at how aroused he'd been by the whole covering, and sensing that Rupert was about to explode, Valent told him he'd better get back to Etta and that he'd firm things up over Mrs Wilkinson's foal in a few days.

4

As Valent drove to Willowwood, its thousands of willows swayed like pale-gold fountains in the setting sun. Reaching Badger's Court, he could hear strains of Bruckner's Seventh, and breathed in the heady mingling smells of his new wife's favourite scent, 24 Faubourg, of white philadelphus in a big emerald-green bowl on the kitchen table and garlic and parsley as Etta roasted a leg of lamb in happy memory of the first supper he had ever cooked for her.

Etta looked so adorable in a sky-blue dress he'd bought her in Paris and gave such a cry of joy as she ran to hug him, turning her face slightly away to hide the fact she'd just popped a piece of ripe Brie into her mouth.

'I missed you,' she said.

'And I missed you. How did Wilkie get on, opening her supermarket?'

'Brilliantly, loved every minute. Huge crowds and traffic at a standstill,' Etta said, squeaking with laughter. 'Chisolm ate the ribbon before anyone had time to cut it. Let me get you a drink.'

'I'll get you one.'

Both were still apprehensive of so much happiness. Both having been badly burned before, Valent couldn't believe Etta could be so loving and unpicky, unlike his previous trophy girlfriend, nor Etta that Valent was so kind and approving, unlike her powerful, bullying late husband.

Both were amazed the other was so easy to live with. At first, toothpaste consumption had rocketed and Etta had kept running upstairs to wash between her legs – such bliss to have a bidet – in case Valent wanted to make love to her. She also washed her ears every night instead of twice a week, and with five loos in the house, she was no longer embarrassed at leaving a smell in one of them.

As Priceless the black greyhound pattered downstairs, flashing his teeth in a smile and rubbed himself against Valent, and Gwenny appeared mewing at the window, it was so lovely that he loved her animals too. He didn't even mind Priceless taking over the spare room's bed and all the sofas, nor a thunderously purring Gwenny landing on his ribs in the middle of the night.

As he helped himself to another beer and poured Etta a glass of Sauvignon, he noticed she had been simultaneously reading a Bill Le Grice rose catalogue, *Country Life* and a book called *Equine Stud Management* by Melanie Bailey.

'It's awfully good the vet's coming to see Wilkie tomorrow. How was Rupert?'

'Obviously gutted about Billy Lloyd-Foxe, and he went ballistic because some drunken stud hand screwed up and Love Rat covered the wrong mare.'

'Golly, what did he say about Wilkie? I hope he doesn't think *she's* the wrong mare.'

'Not at all. Would you mind being in partnership with him, both share her foal and he'll train it for nothing?'

Etta took a great slug of Sauvignon and choked.

'D'you think he'd be kind to the foal? Wilkie loathed being at Penscombe before.'

'I think so.' Valent sat down on a big, dark-red button-back sofa which had come from Etta's house and made his kitchen much more cosy. 'He's obviously devoted to Love Rat and there was a grand horse called Safety Car wandering loose round the yard like a big dog. Evidently Love Rat's a sprinter with a fantastic turn of foot and Mrs Wilkinson is both fast and a stayer, so the combination should be dynamite.'

Valent shuffled forward, as Priceless the greyhound edged on to the sofa behind him.

'As Wilkie won't be racing any more, he wants us to ditch her syndicate. Thank God they only own ten per cent.'

'We can't,' gasped Etta, 'they so want to be part of Wilkie's foal. We can't ditch Dora or Painswick or Woody or the vicar or my own son-in-law, or darling Alban,' she added in distress.

'At least we can dump the Major, and Shagger and Phoebe and Seth Bainton,' said Valent craftily.

Etta shuddered. 'Yes! We definitely don't want Seth any more.'

Seth was the handsome, dissolute actor in his late forties who had impregnated Etta's teenage granddaughter Trixie, whose baby was due in September.

'Better to drop the lot of them,' urged Valent, who very much wanted Rupert's co-operation in pulling off a deal with China. 'Clean break's best – I'll give them £5,000 each. They wouldn't enjoy being lumbered with Love Rat's £100,000 stud fees. They can still come and see Wilkie and her foal.'

Having put the lamb in the Aga and leaving the potatoes to brown, Etta started vigorously chopping parsley for the broad beans. Noticing how her body wiggled, Valent couldn't resist coming up behind her, kissing her scented neck, feeling for her breasts which fitted so sweetly into his big, goalkeeper's hands.

'Oh Etta, d'you think dinner could wait half an hour?'

As they took their plates outside later, neither minded that the lamb was overcooked or that they had to cut the burnt bottoms off the roast potatoes.

They sat very close on a lichened bench looking down at a stream hurtling between banks of hostas and white and mauve irises, then reaching the fields between buttercups and green-ing cow parsley. Valent amused Etta with the antics of Cindy and Lester, then told her about the Stubbs, the spitting image of Rupert and just as 'stunning'.

'No one's more stunning than you,' she said loyally.

'Must lose ten pounds.' Valent patted his gut. 'I bumped into your son in the village shop, and the cheeky monkey told me I ought to join W.O.O.' This stood for War on Obesity, one of the charities for which Martin raised funds.

'How dare he?' stormed Etta. 'I love you all hunky.'

'Martin wants us to open the garden to raise money for W.O.O.'

'It's in no fit state,' said Etta crossly, then as Valent slid a warm hand between her thighs, 'I'm far too busy (oh, how lovely) opening my legs to open any garden.'

Meanwhile, back at Penscombe, Rupert had immediately gone on the warpath.

'Where's Gav, Celeste?' he asked the minxy red-head as she settled Wages of Cindy and her foal back in their box.

'He's been drinking all day. I don't want to drop him in it, but he caught his wife Bethany having it off with Brute Barraclough last night. They'd just parked up in the woods, a hundred yards from his house.'

Brute Barraclough was a rackety local racehorse trainer who enjoyed a lot of extra-marital sex. Rupert sighed. The trouble was that Gav was so bloody good. A beautiful rider with exquisite hands who could sort out and relax the most difficult horses, he knew exactly when they were ready for a race, and was a genius at spotting potential, advising Rupert which yearlings to keep. He was also invaluable where the sales were concerned, when Rupert needed help looking at some 3,000 horses a year.

Unlike most of his staff who either worked in the stud or the yard, resulting in great rivalry between the two, Gav was at ease in both. Even the trickiest stallions and most nervous foaling mares liked and trusted him. Terribly shy, he communicated with horses and was so abrupt with humans, he had been nick-named Mr Lean and Moody. Yet he had such a spare, hard body, such a beautiful, haunted face beneath a mop of thick black curls, there wasn't a single stable lass or visiting lady breeder who didn't long to replace the feckless, constantly unfaithful Bethany.

'A fellow damn'd in a fair wife,' reflected Rupert. He wished he could discuss the matter with Billy, who had had drink problems himself, and who had been a huge fan of Gav's.

Rupert found Gav passed out over his desk, where he'd been drawing up plans to send Rupert's stallions abroad to cover mares in the Southern Hemisphere. He didn't look beautiful now: pale skin threaded with red veins, bloodshot eyes puffy, reeking of drink, an empty bottle of Bell's in the wastepaper-basket.

Shaking him till he woke up, Rupert said: 'You've just lost us seventy-five grand, you little fucker. You've got two alternatives: you're fired or you go into rehab for three months.'

Still in the kitchen, Taggie wondered whether to ring Rupert. She'd loathed last night's row. She knew how bereft her husband was without Billy and wished she could comfort him. She'd ticked him off for chewing out Billy's wife Janey yesterday. But Janey, who had also inveigled Taggie into secretly paying a lot towards the funeral and doing most of the catering, had always demoralized her. She too dreaded Janey moving back into Lime Tree Cottage and dropping in all the time.

Taggie had just finished feeding the dogs, who were back panting in their kitchen baskets, except for Forester, a gorgeous brindle rescue greyhound, her first, very own dog since Gertrude the mongrel. Forester now lay upside down on the dilapidated olive-green kitchen sofa, stretching out a paw to draw attention to himself every time she passed.

It was the perceived wisdom that because she had never been able to give birth herself, Taggie's one delight was to look after other people's children. As an indication of this, Rupert's daughters Perdita and Tabitha and Taggie's sister Caitlin all seemed to be having blips in their marriages, which necessitated dumping their offspring, dogs, even nannies, 'to help you out', so they could slope off and spend 'us time' with respective husbands.

The house was very big but it seemed overcrowded with Young Eddie, Rupert's grandson, and his wild young friends, and Old Eddie and his carers, who invaded the kitchen stuffing their faces on Taggie's wonderful cooking, and going on about 'making a difference'. Taggie wished she were better at saying 'no'.

Outside in the dusk in the cool of the evening, she could see the foals, who'd been lying out in the heat earlier with only their bottle-brush tails twitching, now frenziedly romping round on long stick legs. Taggie adored the foals and loathed it when, all polished and plumped up, they were sent off to the sales. Rupert had never shed a tear over a horse, although he did dote on Love Rat and Safety Car, who was now sticking his great white face in at the kitchen window for an apple.

Hoping it would cheer Rupert up, Taggie had roasted the tenderest piece of beef, with Yorkshire pudding, roast potatoes, homemade horseradish sauce, runner beans, and apple charlotte for pudding.

'That smells good, I'm starving,' said a drooling Treasure, Old Eddie's current carer, who Rupert claimed had all to be over eighty and eighteen stone, to deter his aged father from jumping on them.

Young Eddie had already ransacked the Aga and, living on protein to keep to a racing weight, had hacked off great slices of beef. Thank goodness Taggie had already secreted a large plate of everything in a second oven for Rupert.

Having bawled out Gav, Rupert looked at his watch. He knew he ought to go in for supper and make it up with Taggie, but he got caught up in affairs in the yard. Having checked on his favourite brood mare, My Child Cordelia, who'd won The Oaks five years ago and who was also due to produce a foal by Love Rat, but in January, he went back to his office to watch another race at Woodbine.

Rupert had recently come across an utterly brilliant saying by Havelock Ellis, that 'What we call progress is the exchange of one nuisance for another nuisance.'

One nuisance recently had been the incessant wet weather, which had meant that horses, who prefer quick ground, hadn't run at their best, or not at all. Another nuisance was Young Eddie, his grandson. Having been a successful flat jockey in America, Eddie had grown too heavy and come over to England to try his luck over jumps. The fact had to be faced: he wasn't good enough, his forte being split-second timing and the ability to ride a finish needed on the flat – like driving a Ferrari rather than the four-wheel-drive of jump racing. The opposite of

Gavin Latton, who settled and relaxed whatever he was riding, Eddie over-egged horses and was screwing up too many of Rupert's. Irresistible to most girls, Eddie had, however, grounded himself by acquiring an extremely pretty girlfriend, Etta Bancroft's granddaughter, Trixie, who was about to have Seth Bainton's baby. Rupert very much doubted if Eddie was stepfather any more than jump-jockey potential. Teenaged Trixie, who planned to go to Oxford, also seemed far too intellectual for him.

Old Eddie, Rupert's father, was another nuisance. He was getting more and more senile, walking starkers into a stallion parade last year and cantering along beside his beloved Love Rat, whom he insisted on visiting every day, accompanied by one of his aggravating carers.

Having watched yet another race, Rupert then got caught up in the difficult birth of a very large, late foal. Finally, going back to the house to make it up with Taggie, he found curling roast beef in the oven, and Taggie fast asleep but still dressed on their bed. Even when he pulled off her clothes and admired her beautiful body, she didn't stir. Putting a duvet over her, vowing to pay more attention to his marriage, Rupert returned to the stud office and settled down to working out which horses to run at Royal Ascot in order to make the most prize money to bump up Love Rat and Peppy Koala's earnings.

Finding a bottle of water in Gavin's drawer he took a swig and, encountering neat vodka, spat it out. Gavin would have to be sorted.

5

Six months later, Gavin Latton celebrated (perhaps the wrong word) six months without a drink. Aware if he lapsed that Rupert, who'd paid for his three months in rehab, wouldn't let him back on a horse, which was where his genius lay, he had opted to work over Christmas and on New Year's Eve, when Team Campbell-Black were all getting hammered at the Dog and Trumpet down the road.

There should have been two of them on duty, but 'Woluptuous, woluble' Marketa from the Czech Republic, who couldn't say her 'vs', hadn't showed up. Gavin was relieved. Apart from a distant din of parties, the stud was quiet. No foals were expected. It was just a question of touring the boxes, filling up knocked-over water buckets, adjusting rugs and checking on one-eared Safety Car, who insisted on sleeping out in the fields, wrapped in his six sheep friends, with only a three-sided shed for cover. Safety Car whickered, nudged Gav in the belly and accepted a carrot, but the sleeping sheep didn't stir.

Gavin looked up at the winter stars, a glittering zoo overhead. There was Lepus the Hare lurking out of the way of Orion's Dogs, not to mention Taurus the Bull and Monoceros the Unicorn: constellations he'd taught himself during so many sleepless nights or when he had ridden out before the sun rose. He could see the russet glow of Rutminster and what, he wondered, would the New Year bring? He must accept that his marriage was over. Early on, Bethany had mocked him because desire had made him come too quickly. Later, drink, to blot out the pain of her infidelity, had rendered him impotent – mocked too by the plunging, potent stallions around him and the easy promiscuity of the stable lasses in the yard with their iron thighs and their thrusting movements.

'Why don't you go to a sex therapist?' Bethany taunted him. 'Or thera-pissed in your case.' She wasn't even satisfied when he stopped drinking. 'At least you were fun when you were drunk.'

Ironically, even if it didn't tempt Bethany, giving up the booze had given Gav back his looks. His thick dark hair was clean and glossy, his slate-grey eyes no longer puffy, though heavily shadowed, his eyeballs white, his olive skin clear, his stomach flat.

Now back in the stud office, he was surrounded by black leather head collars, grooming kits, first aid kits, Christmas cards and fridges full of colostrum: frozen mares' milk to build up a newborn foal's immunity. Reluctantly, because there was work to be done, he didn't pick up *Wilkie*, the story of Mrs Wilkinson, by Etta's son-in-law Alan Macbeth. The book was touching and very funny, especially the bits about the goat Chisolm, and had become a massive bestseller. Half the yard had given it to each other for Christmas.

Instead Gavin turned back to a pile of requests from breeders, avid – particularly if they were women – to bring their mares to Rupert's stallions. His job was to check if the mares were good enough. Here was a chestnut who'd won three Group Two races and the Irish Oaks. Love Rat loved chestnuts, so a tick for her.

Gavin knew that Rupert was looking forward to the imminent birth of two foals: the first Mrs Wilkinson's, the second to his favourite brood mare, My Child Cordelia, another chestnut who'd produced winner after winner. Both foals were likely to be future stars and boost Love Rat's earnings and his popularity.

'Coo-ee, coo-ee,' cried a voice. Fuck it, it was Celeste, the stud nympho, hardly covered by a gold tunic, showing off a ravine of cleavage, beech-leaf red mane snaking nearly below the groin-level skirt, green eyes slightly glazed, but avid for plunder.

Oh Christ, thought Gavin as, tottering on seven-inch heels, she fell deliberately into his arms.

'Marketa got hammered at lunchtime and carried on drinking. She's out of it, so I offered to take her slot. Sorry I'm late.'

As she gave him a long wet kiss on the mouth, her tongue probing and exploring, she tasted of drink. Gavin recoiled in horror.

'Stop being such a virgin,' she chided. 'I've brought some booze,' she produced a bottle of brandy out of her bag, 'to cheer you up.'

'You know I don't drink and I'm married,' Gav tried to joke.

'No point in being faithful when your slag of a wife had the gall to come into the pub with that vile Brute Barraclough. Don't get what she sees in him when you're so fit.'

'A bloody good fuck, probably. No, I *don't* want a drink. I'd better check the horses.'

'Kiss me first.' Celeste wound a hand round his neck. In those heels she was the same height as him. He felt her breasts squirming against him as she whispered, 'There's an empty box next door.'

She was very pretty. Gavin felt a flicker of lust but was not prepared to risk the humiliation of not getting it up. As he kissed her back, she was encouraged. If she couldn't manage to pull Rupert and only occasionally Young Eddie, whose girlfriend had just had someone else's baby, Mr Lean and Moody would do nicely, and it would give her a buzz to beat every other stable lass to getting him into his bed.

'Stop it,' he told her, removing a hand that was creeping inside his jeans. 'We're working.'

Setting out on his rounds of mares in foal, he was amazed to find Cordelia, who wasn't due for another month, sweating up, pacing her box, looking at her belly and scraping her bed of straw. Next moment there was a giant splash as her waters broke.

'Christ, she's foaling – come quickly!' Gavin shouted to Celeste.

'Shall I ring Rupert, or the Dog and Trumpet?' bleated Celeste in terror.

'Too late, got to pitch in.'

It must have been the quickest birth in history. Cordelia hardly had time to push with her powerful abdominal muscles before a very small foal, feet first, its hooves under its nose, emerged into the world. After a few minutes Cordelia struggled to her feet, whickering with joy, and a moment later, the after-birth followed. Gavin told Celeste to put it in a bucket and weigh it.

'I think that's everything out, beautiful little thing,' he added in delight, 'and, bloody marvellous, it's a colt.'

Cordelia bent her head to examine a foal much darker than herself with a white star on his forehead and one white sock.

'Oh how sweet,' sighed Celeste, despite having blood all over her gold silk tunic.

After they had washed down mare and foal, both were installed in a huge bed of straw piled up high round the side of the box. Whickering with love and pride, Cordelia was licking the foal, who was sticking out his tongue, making sucking noises, and trying to clamber to his feet.

Then, while Celeste gave the mare a drink of water and a warm wet mash and the foal an enema to get rid of any harmful substances, Gav in the office next door filled in the *Record of Foaling* form. This was admittedly much easier now he didn't drink, as he stated the time the waters had broken, the name of the sire, Love Rat, and the dam, My Child Cordelia, and the colour of the foal.

Any unusual behaviour in foaling? No. Presentation of foal? Normal. Time waters broke? 10.54. Time of foaling? 10.58. That was incredibly quick, reflected Gav. Time mare stood up? 11.10. Was mare quiet to foal and quiet with foal? 'Yes, yes, the little darling,' Gav wrote in joyfully.

As the foal struggled to his feet, found the nipple and began to suckle, dirty, bloodstained, triumphant, Gav and Celeste looked on and joyfully hugged each other.

'We deserve a drink too,' said Celeste, getting out her bottle of brandy as they returned to the office.

'There's probably some Coke in the fridge,' said Gav, taking the bottle to fill up a mug for her.

Then he nearly dropped the bottle, as rollicking over the midnight air came the bells of All Saints Church, Penscombe, ringing in the New Year. Looking out of the cobweb-strewn window, he could see fireworks exploding.

'Oh fuck, fuck, fuck,' groaned Gav. The worst had happened.

'What's the matter? It's midnight now, so you can kiss me properly. Happy New Year.'

'Don't you realize, that little colt's a year old now.'

'Happy New Yearling,' giggled Celeste.

'Don't be fucking stupid. Have you forgotten one of the silliest rules of racing? All horses have their birthday on January the first. This means that whatever day they are born on, the year before, they're officially one on Jan One. So even though that foal's hardly an hour old, as a racehorse he's now one. Next January the first, when he's only a yearling, he'll be officially regarded as a two-year-old, expected to go into training and run in two-year-old races. Then on the *next* January the first, he'll be not two, but officially three and expected to compete with three-year-olds in classics like the Guineas and the Derby. His career is fucked.'

'Happy New Yearling,' repeated Celeste, taking a slug of brandy out of the bottle. 'What are we going to do?'

'Chuck away that form.' Scrumpling it up, Gavin dropped it into the bin and hid it in a pile of bloodstained towels. 'We've got to fill in another form, to say it was born after midnight.' Then, when Celeste looked alarmed: 'I'll take the rap. You've just got to promise to keep your trap shut and no one will know.'

'What happens if you're found out?'

'Rupert would get a hefty fine, might even lose his licence. That's why he must never know, because any races the colt wins, posing as a two-year-old, would be disqualified.'

'Do you think it's safe?' Celeste took another slug.

They looked into the box next door, where Cordelia was gazing down so proudly at the little colt who'd collapsed back on the straw.

'Look at him, he deserves a future.'

Gav seized a new form, changing the date of birth to 1 January and recording that the waters broke at 12.16 and the foal was born at 12.20. By the time he'd finished filling it in, both he and Celeste were sweating more than the mare had done earlier.

'Are you sure we won't get into trouble? Rupert can't blame us if she was born too early.'

'We couldn't have prevented it,' Gav said. 'Rupert's been good to me, saved my career. I'm not going to fuck up the prospects of one of the best homebreds and his beloved Love Rat's foal. I'd better go and ring him.'

Glad of an excuse to leave his in-laws' party across the valley, Rupert came straight over. Even asleep in the straw with his coat ruffled and still a little damp, Rupert was ecstatic to recognize a ravishing colt. Taking the foaling record, however, and knowing how fatal would be the alternative, he raised an eyebrow.

'Sure it was January the first?'

'Quite sure – even Mrs Wilkinson's book couldn't keep me awake. I crashed out briefly, then suddenly, thank God, I was woken by the church bells, checked on the mares, saw Cordelia was sweating and pawing her belly. Then her waters broke, followed by the quickest birth ever.'

For a second, as he and Rupert looked at each other, Gav held his gaze.

'Sure?'

'Quite.'

'Good, I'll take your word for it.' Rupert looked at the two glasses.

'I was about to have a Coke. I wouldn't have been able to fill in that form with a steady hand in the old days.'

'Good, well done, well done, Celeste.'

'She was terrific,' said Gav. 'First foaling, kept her cool.'

'Good girl,' said Rupert. 'Sure it was January the first, not December?'

'Of course.' Celeste's knowing green eyes were the picture of honesty. 'I didn't know it mattered until Gav explained about

Jan first being their birthday. He came out so easily, we were so relieved everything went OK.'

'Better call him New Year's Dave,' said Rupert. He looked at his watch. 'The two o'clock shift'll be on in a minute. You'd better both come and have a drink – or a cup of coffee,' he added to Gav, who was reluctant to leave the colt.

Celeste, however, was dying to see inside Rupert's house. He looked so lush in that dinner suit, and he might even open a bottle of bubbly.

'We'd love to, just get my bag.' She scuttled back into the office.

Rupert was euphoric. Not least that Gav hadn't cracked under pressure and had a drink.

'Christmas must be hell for you,' he said. 'But well done.' He then added that Gav could start riding work, which meant exercising the horses, next week.

The evening had been such a strain, Gav clenched his jaw not to break down.

'Thanks, he's a lovely colt.'

'Jan One also marks the start of the new Leading Sire season for Europe and GB. I'm going to need you to rake in the winners.'

Rupert had been desperate to get Gav right, not just to train and ride the horses but also to see that no star slipped through the net at the sales. It also gave Rupert the added satisfaction of rescuing him and profiting from his genius, when Cosmo Rannaldini and Isa Lovell, for whom Gav had worked previously, had so brutally discarded and demoralized him.

Seeing them deep in conversation, Celeste plunged her hand into the bin, scrabbling round to retrieve the bloodstained scrumpled-up form headed: *Penscombe Stud, Record of Foaling*, and thrust it into her frilly gold bra.

She could hear voices outside; the relief watch had arrived and New Year's Dave was no doubt being shown off. With any luck Gavin might want to take her bra off later, reflected Celeste, and transferred the *Record of Foaling* instead to the inside pocket of her bag. One day it might come in useful.

6

An irritating, often bewildering aspect of Rupert's character was the way he tolerated people like porn star Cindy Bolton because she was so dreadful, she made him laugh. On the other hand, he didn't like Etta, who he thought was a drip – this because she had so disapproved of his training methods that when her now-husband Valent had transferred Mrs Wilkinson to Penscombe before the Grand National, she had boycotted the race.

Nor could he understand why Valent had dumped Bonny, his ravishingly pretty actress girlfriend, for such a dog as Etta; pity she couldn't be dumped like the rest of the Willowwood syndicate. However, love me, love my dog. Rupert realized that Valent was bats about Etta and if he wanted control of Mrs Wilkinson and her impending foal and any deal in China, he had better win her over and take her a present.

After New Year's Dave's unexpectedly early arrival, Rupert was determined to take no chances with Mrs Wilkinson's foal. But he got caught up with flying eight horses out to the Meydan carnival in Dubai in search of decent prize money. All the world's star jockeys were out there, and Rupert was delighted when his stable jockey, Lionel 'Lion' O'Connor, fought off many other overseas riders to win seven races.

Back in England, Rupert set out on the day after Valentine's Day, which marked the beginning of the covering season, to visit Etta in Willowwood.

Despite being paid £5,000 each by Valent for their individual shares, Mrs Wilkinson's syndicate had not been pleased to be discarded, particularly on learning that Rupert, who had the Midas touch, was involved. When she wasn't scuttling along with her granddaughter, Trixie's new baby, in his pram down Willowwood High Street to avoid them, Etta had been kept very busy making sure Valent's first birthday since their marriage, which fell on Valentine's Day, had been particularly special and excitedly getting ready for Mrs Wilkinson's foal.

For this she had ensured she had brought in suitable mineral and vegetable supplements. Plenty of colostrum to strengthen the foal's immunity was stored in the fridge. She had mugged up on the care of the udder. On the kitchen table she had amassed a basic kit of tail bandages and bin liners for the after-birth, disposable gloves, antiseptics for the navel dressing, enemas for the foal, two buckets in different shades of purple for water and for feed, and a set of bright-orange over-trousers and over-shirt topped by a matching baseball cap to keep her hair out of the way. These Etta couldn't resist trying on. As the mirror in Valent's kitchen had been hung for a man and he was a good eight inches taller than her, she clambered on to the dark-red sofa to have a look. The orange clashed hideously with her pink face, but everyone would be looking at the foal.

'Aren't they awful?' she sighed to Valent, who replied: 'I've never understood roober fetishes.' Etta was so pretty, but even she couldn't redeem those overalls.

He was watching Searston Rovers, his son Ryan's football team, putting up a great fight against Millwall. He and Ryan would talk after the game. One of the lovely things about Etta was that she'd embraced his family and they all adored her.

She'd also transformed his kitchen which, because his former girlfriend Bonny had hardly ever eaten, had been like a laboratory. Now there were bowls of hyacinths and narcissi everywhere, every ledge was covered with birthday cards, and on the walls were framed blow-ups of all their grandchildren, including one of Trixie's new baby, great footballing moments and of Valent, who was now wearing a new birthday shirt in pink and grey stripes from Harvie & Hudson.

All the windows were open on a wonderfully mild evening. Across the lawn spread a rainbow sweep of mauve crocuses, primroses, grape hyacinths, pink polyanthus and sky-blue scillas. A thrush was serenading them, shaking the pale-pink petals from an almond tree as it repeated its exquisite trill.

Etta was again poring over *Equine Stud Management*.

'Large studs have oxygen available, obstetrical rope, sedatives and antibiotics,' she read in a worried voice. 'Do you think we should get some? And oh Valent, it says unless veterinary attendance is guaranteed within fifteen minutes, such specialist equipment can save life.' Then she giggled. 'Within five minutes of the birth, the foal must have his first drink. Do you think he'd like a gin and tonic?'

'You need a first drink,' said Valent.

'Before that, I must get out of these hideous garments,' said Etta, then gasped in dismay for sauntering up the drive, tanned dark brown and white blond from the Dubai sun, came Rupert Campbell-Black.

It had been so mild, Wilkie and Chisolm were out in the orchard. Chisolm, always the opportunist, scampered bleating up to the fence to greet Rupert. Mrs Wilkinson, not a fan, bustled off to the far end of the orchard.

'Rupert's here!' cried Etta, tearing off the baseball cap in horror.

'Sorry, luv, I forgot to tell you,' said Valent.

And Etta was horned by dilemma. She longed to belt upstairs, tear off her awful orange overalls, tone down her flushed face, comb her ruffled hair and slap on some scent, but knowing dearest Valent was a bit uptight about Rupert, she didn't want to unnerve him. She had never actually spoken to Rupert before, and hadn't expected him to be quite so disconcertingly shy-making.

When she stammeringly asked him what he'd like to drink, Rupert said he'd like first to check on Mrs Wilkinson. Valent could take him, thought Etta hopefully, while she de-repulsived herself, but Valent was punching the air because Searston Rovers had just scored. So she had to squelch round the orchard after Wilkie, who, displaying aesthetic sensibility, didn't like the orange overalls either, and cantered about refusing to be caught.

'She had such a wonderful signing session at Waterstones, Cheltenham, this afternoon,' babbled Etta. 'Over five hundred copies of my son-in-law's book sold – it's probably gone to her head.'

'Shouldn't be jazzing around at this late stage,' said Rupert disapprovingly, as Mrs Wilkinson trundled past them again.

When Etta finally cornered her, she rolled her eyes and trembled ostentatiously as Rupert examined her.

'Her udders are swollen, I don't think it'll be long. They often want to be alone and retire to a quiet corner, like she's doing now.'

'That is because she doesn't like you,' Etta just managed to stop herself saying.

Back in the kitchen, Rupert rendered Etta speechless by presenting her with a beautiful pale blue, silver-threaded scarf from Dubai, which actually Taggie had bought in New Look. He then accepted a large mahogany whisky and a plateful of mushroom vol au vents straight from the Aga, which Etta had been warming up as a starter to her and Valent's supper.

'With you in a minute, game's nearly finished,' called out Valent, thinking it would be a treat for Etta to have Rupert to herself.

Rupert then dropped the bombshell that it was high time Mrs Wilkinson moved into a foaling box at Penscombe so she could settle in.

'She's due in another fortnight. She'll be surrounded by experts. CCTV'll tell us exactly when she's about to foal. With such a valuable foal, you don't want anything to go wrong. And your security's non-existent here – I walked straight in.'

Etta forbore to explain that Valent had abandoned his electric gates so Chisolm and Priceless the greyhound could push their way back in after escaping on jaunts.

'Any member of the public has access to her along the footpath.' Rupert's light, clipped voice was relentless.

'Wilkie loves that,' insisted Etta.

'Well, it's lunatic – easily get stolen. She'll be safe at Penscombe,

36

then eight days after the birth, Love Rat can cover her again.'

'No!' gasped a horrified Etta, who had cystitis from a surfeit of Valent; then wincing further, as she remembered how she'd been ripped apart giving birth to vast twins, Martin and Carrie, more than forty years ago, with Sampson reclaiming his marital rights three weeks later.

'She can't have sex so soon, she's too little. We must wait a few weeks so she's healed up.' She looked frantically across at Valent, but Ryan's match had gone into injury time.

'Coom on lads, coom on lads.'

'It's standard practice,' insisted Rupert. 'Mares come into season within eight days of foaling.' Then, at Etta's look of dismay, 'What you must realize is that successful sires like Love Rat or Peppy Koala can produce thousands of foals in their lifetime. But the greatest mare, even if she's fertile and robust, is unlikely to produce more than a dozen foals. Mrs Wilkinson mustn't waste any time – we're talking about a serious foal.' Rupert, who as usual hadn't eaten since breakfast, was hoovering up mushroom vol au vents. 'If Mrs Wilkinson went under the hammer at Tattersalls now, she could fetch several million.'

'We're not selling her.' Etta was aghast.

'Course we're not, I'm just pointing out how valuable she is.' Better humour the silly cow. 'I'll send the lorry over tomorrow. She'll see her father, just back from New Zealand and on top form, having covered 120 mares. How's that for a holiday romance? He's now rubbing his hooves at the prospect of another full book of mares at Penscombe.'

But Etta was not won over. Valent, meanwhile, gave a shout and punched the air as Searston Rovers scored in the closing seconds. 'Bluddy marvellous.'

'Oh Valent, Rupert wants Wilkie to foal at Penscombe.' Etta was near to tears.

'It's sensible, luv,' said Valent after Rupert explained the procedure. He sympathized with Etta, but the China blood-stock project was too important to risk falling out with Rupert. 'Joost for a couple of weeks, don't want to jeopardize anything.'

'What about Chisolm?' protested Etta, as on cue the little

white goat trotted in, helped herself to the last vol au vent and settled down on the sofa beside Valent to admire Ryan hugging his victorious team.

'Wilkie loathes being parted from her,' added Etta.

'Wilkie'll be far too interested in her own foal and should be left to bond with her. Chisolm had better go to kennels,' said Rupert.

'That's ridiculous.' Etta was losing her temper. 'I've bought all this stuff.'

'Any self-respecting foal seeing you in that kit would shoot straight back into the womb,' said Rupert acidly.

'Any thoughts of a name?' asked Valent, who'd missed this exchange but sensed tension. 'You like Shakespeare ones, don't you, Rupert? If she's a filly as fast as her mum, you could call her Mistress Quickly.'

'I like wives better than mistresses,' said Rupert, who was checking his iPhone. 'Must get back to Taggie. It's been madness since I got home from Dubai – I've hardly seen her. Thanks for the drink, I'll send the lorry over tomorrow morning.'

7

Mrs Wilkinson, however, who had always been a very good listener, had absolutely no intention of going back to Penscombe. Valent, who'd downed a bottle of red to celebrate Ryan's victory, fell asleep straight away that night. Etta didn't: fretting about Wilkie being hijacked and, if she were truthful, humiliated by disdainful Rupert, catching her looking so repulsive.

Light was beginning to filter through the curtains when she was roused by frantic bleating. Pulling on a pink silk negligée, yet another present from Valent, she ran barefoot into the garden, through the rainbow sweeps of flowers. Panting to the top of the orchard, she heard deep joyful whickering and there, under the bowed pale-green lichened branches of the oldest pear tree, stood the proudest mother in the world gazing down at a beautiful chestnut foal, with Chisolm bleating and supervising beside her.

Having read that mares must be left alone, Etta retreated, belting back and waking Valent.

'Quickly, quickly, Wilkie's had the most gorgeous foal all by herself with no one to help her, and boo sucks to bloody Rupert. Come and have a quick peep.'

As Valent charged downstairs in birthday blue and white striped pyjamas, Etta smiled to see her pile of pregnancy kit still on the kitchen table. She doubted if a charity shop would take the orange overalls.

Chisholm, meanwhile, was back bleating in the doorway.

'So clever of Wilkie to have a nanny in situ,' giggled Etta, who was feeling euphorically light-headed.

As she and Valent crept up the dew-drenched hill, they found Mrs Wilkinson licking and nudging the foal. Looking up, she gave another great whicker of joy, metaphorically putting her hoof to her lips, as she caught sight of them.

'Oh, you little beauty,' breathed Valent.

'I wonder what's happened to the afterbirth,' whispered Etta.

'Chisolm probably flogged it to the nearest fox. We had better leave them to bond. I wonder what sex it is? Do you think it should be lying on the wet grass?'

As if listening, the foal opened an eye, leapt to its feet, tottering off drunkenly on long giraffe legs, then scampering back again, butting under Wilkie's belly, finding the teat and starting to suckle.

'It's a colt,' crowed Valent.

Despite the approach of day and a deafening dawn chorus, a gold sickle moon and a bright silver star were still visible above the trees.

'The moon stayed out to welcome him. Oh Valent, isn't he adorable, isn't Wilkie clever?'

They turned to each other, tears streaming down their faces.

'Homebred ones are the best,' said Etta, then: 'Oh, I love you so much.'

'We're too old for babies,' said Valent, taking Etta's hand. 'But this is as good as it gets. I'm sorry I didn't stand up to Rupert.'

'I couldn't either. He's such a bully. We must stick together. Your first morning, little one,' called out Etta, as the foal collapsed on the grass again.

Valent wiped his eye with his sleeve. 'As he's a colt, let's call him Master Quickly.'

'Perfect. Do you think we should ring Rupert?' asked Etta as they reeled back to the house.

'No, let's keep it a secret for a bit.'

Fat chance. The moment the news reached Dora, texting and tweeting to rival any dawn chorus, the world knew.

IT'S A BOY! shouted the headlines. NEWLYWEDS VALENT AND ETTA EDWARDS ANNOUNCE THE BIRTH OF MRS WILKINSON'S SON, MASTER QUICKLY.

'My adorable foal arrived at 5 a.m. local time and weighed in at 120 lbs,' wrote Wilkie in her online diary. 'He is chestnut now but will probably go grey like myself and his sire, drop-dead gorgeous Love Rat Campbell-Black.'

'You'd think it was a royal birth,' remarked the syndicate sourly, as the world's press raced down to photograph dam and colt lying in a huge bed of straw with Priceless, Chisolm and Gwenny perched on Mrs Wilkinson's back, flanking them as godparents.

Rupert was not amused, particularly when the *Daily Mirror*, who published Chisolm's diary, printed a large unflattering picture of a yawning Love Rat with a caption 'Who's the Daddy?'

'You said you were desperate to raise Love Rat's profile,' protested Dora.

The first time Rupert visited him at Badger's Court, Master Quickly pretended to be fast asleep, then leaping to his feet, he snatched off Rupert's cap and scampered away up the orchard. From the moment he was born, he had attitude.

8

There was a tradition that every time a boy was born in Willowwood, as part of his christening ceremony, a weeping willow would be planted for him in the churchyard. As Mrs Wilkinson had been such a local heroine, this honour was being bestowed on her son, Master Quickly, by the Lady of the Manor, Ione Travis-Lock. Born Ione Framlingham, she and her sister were the only descendants of Sir Francis Framlingham, who had once owned the village and whose stone effigy lay in the church with a little whippet at his feet.

Ione's husband Alban, a charming ex-ambassador and reformed alcoholic like Gav Latton, had nobly driven the Willowwood syndicate minibus to the races. As he had been dumped along with other members of the syndicate, it was considered very magnanimous of his wife Ione to plant a willow for Quickly. In fact, the seriously green Ione had only agreed on condition Valent installed solar panelling at Badger's Court.

'Hurrah,' said Dora, who'd set the whole thing up. 'We can have a big christening party to celebrate.'

'Not too big,' pleaded Etta. 'People can handle not being asked to a small party, but not a great big one.'

She was already tearing her newly streaked hair out over the guest list. Because the Travis-Locks and Niall and Woody were invited, she would have to ask the rest of the disgruntled syndicate, which included Seth Bainton, the egregious, glamorous, middle-aged actor father of her granddaughter Trixie Macbeth's baby. Seth's mistress Corinna was such a famous actress and so self-obsessed, she hadn't twigged that Seth was the father. The party, if Dora had anything to do with it, would be swarming with press to promote Love Rat as Quickly's sire and Etta's son-in-law Alan Macbeth's biography of Mrs Wilkinson, which had just come out in paperback. And if a party were thrown to help Alan, Martin – Etta's fundraiser son – would push even harder for Badger's Court to be opened for one of his charity bashes. Etta hated her family imposing on Valent's generosity.

Many of the female members of the syndicate had threatened to boycott the party until, learning that Rupert Campbell-Black had been invited, they changed their minds and rushed off to buy new dresses, followed by new coats, in case one got frost or snow in mid-April.

To Gav's horror, Rupert had summoned him the evening before and ordered him to attend the christening in his place, virtuously claiming that he was taking Taggie away to France for a few days' break: 'She's been looking very tired.'

Then, when Gav looked mutinous: 'Need you to keep an eye on things. Quickly's an extremely valuable colt, might easily get loose. I don't trust that frightful syndicate not to sabotage things. And you'll get a bloody good lunch.' Seeing Gav looking even more sullen, he added, 'Do you good to get your nose out of a book or a horse for an hour and meet a few people. Can't live like a monk for ever.'

Bastard, thought Gav, behaving as though he was doing me a favour. Parties were torture. In the past, the only way he coped with his shyness and lack of small talk was to arrive three parts cut. Nor did a lovely evening with pink sky along the horizon, pale-green leaves blurring the trees or paths starry with primroses calm or cheer him, as he walked down to the Long Meadow by the lake, which was filled with foals and their mothers.

As he hung over the gate and whistled, his beloved New Year's Dave bounded out of the herd to talk to him, ready for any amount of patting.

43

The little colt was such a dream, Gav lived in dread that someone might find out he had been born on New Year's Eve. He'd managed to keep nympho Celeste at arm's length, saying he didn't want to provoke Bethany in the middle of a messy divorce, but he didn't trust Celeste not to sneak if he showed interest in anyone else.

Dave jerked his head up, bounding away as a voice shouted, 'Gav!' It was Rupert's grandson Young Eddie Alderton, deeply tanned from visiting his parents in Palm Beach. Even jet lag and nights of carousing didn't dim his golden beauty.

'What's up?' he asked, seeing Gav's face looking longer than usual.

'Gotta go to Master Quickly's christening.'

'I'll look after you.' Eddie pulled the invitation out of his jeans pocket. 'I've been asked to the same bash. I'll introduce you to Trixie. Are you up to Trix? She is so gorgeous. Etta's granddaughter, doing her A-levels. You can rabbit on to her about literature. If she wasn't only seventeen and a teenage mom, I'd be very serious about getting serious.'

'Helluva commitment.'

'Helluva. Don't want to hurt her. Father of the baby screwed her over, but she's special – and crazy about me.' Eddie grinned and rolled his cornflower-blue eyes.

Gav liked Eddie, who was arrogant, spoilt, opinionated, identical in looks and as wild and ragingly promiscuous as Rupert had been in his youth. They often fell out when Eddie was too rough on horses, but the boy was fun, and Gav felt warmed by his high spirits.

'I'm so pooped,' announced Eddie as they walked back to the yard, 'I'm going to bed alone for a change . . . or perhaps not,' he added as Marketa, the 'Woluptuous' Czech stable lass came out of the tack room. 'But I'll take you to that party tomorrow. Dora'll be there, you can drive the Ferrari and all the women'll think it's your car. Gramps is right, you need some fun.'

9

On the morning of the party Dora was in early, arranging a table with posters of Love Rat and Mrs Wilkinson, where Alan could sign copies of his book. Exciting the waiters who were lining up the Bollinger in the marquee, Trixie Macbeth, armed with a large vodka and tonic, strolled up to Dora's table. Brown cowboy boots enhanced her endless legs, a pale-brown suede dress with a fringed skirt fell to luscious mid-thigh. Shiny dark plaits were kept in place with a scarlet silk bandeau round her forehead.

'That kit would look ridiculous on anyone else,' sighed Dora. 'Red Indian above the knees, cowboy below.'

'Minnehaha, Laughing Vodka,' said Trixie, taking a slug. 'That bandeau's covering a zit.'

'The press are bound to mob you, looking so good. Promise to keep saying Quickly's the son of Love Rat,' begged Dora, as Trixie glanced idly at the guest list to see if her baby's father, Seth, was coming.

'Seth and Corinna never answer,' said Dora, reading her mind. 'But as soon as they suss the number of press rolling up, they'll be down here like a shot. Corinna can smell a photographer a hundred miles away. "I am recognized – therefore I am".'

'I'd just like Seth to see how cute Hereward is and how utterly I'm over *him*.'

'Hum,' said Dora.

'That's why I'd like Eddie Alderton to be here,' continued Trixie. 'Has he answered?'

Dora shook her head, then as an outraged Valent stormed up, she said to him, 'Doesn't Trixie look fabulous?'

'Taken enough bloody time on it,' snapped Valent. 'Hereward had Etta up twice in the night; she's just changed and fed him, and wants to know if she's dressed him in the right kit.' Seizing Trixie's arm, he frogmarched her back into the house. 'That's your job. Stop taking the piss. Etta's really stressed over this party and she needs to get ready.'

'I'm sorry.'

'Not nearly enuff. We're happy to give you a home, Trix, but not if you're going to constantly abuse your grandmother's hopelessly kind heart.'

Trixie found Etta with her dress over her head trying not to get make-up on it or dislodge her Carmen rollers.

'So sorry to desert you. Sorry, Granny.'

Hereward sat cooing in his chair, wearing little jeans, trainers and a T-shirt saying *Aren't you glad you backed me*. He smiled in delight to see his mother and waved a football rattle given him by Valent.

'He looks perfect, and that is a fuck-off dress,' noted Trixie, pulling down Etta's frock and zipping up the back.

But an alarmed Etta was looking in the mirror. The dress was a deep hyacinth blue, perfect with her big blue eyes and apple blossom complexion, but she'd only tried it on in a hurry, over tracksuit bottoms when she hadn't been wearing a bra, and hadn't realized how short or low-cut or tight it was.

'It's the age of the cleave,' said Trixie.

'Mine's too wrinkly.'

'No, it isn't. Dress it up with Valent's sapphires.' Trixie put the necklace on Etta and did up the clasp. 'I'd do anything to have a cleavage, I'd flaunt it all the time.'

Over at Penscombe, Eddie didn't show up and had switched off his mobile, so a reluctant Gav set off alone driving the twenty miles to Willowwood in his battered, filthy Golf – hardly a pussy magnet. Fractionally cheered up by the beauty of the day, with bluebells flecking the wild garlic and blackthorn foaming in white waves along the hedgerows, he was interested to drive past the yard of Marius Oakridge, who had trained Mrs Wilkinson.

Dropping down, he passed the heraldic gates of Badger's Court, a ravishing Georgian house surrounded by parkland, with the orchard in bloom, goal-posts on the lawn for grand-children, and people scurrying in and out of a huge marquee. Gav started to shake. 'Shyness is a lack of interest in people,' Bethany used to chide him. 'Look into people's eyes. Ask them where they live, what do they do, have they come far?' Methinks, it is no journey.

Willowwood was such a lovely village, with willows, their gold stems hidden by feathery green leaves and yellow catkins, hurt-ling down to the River Fleet. He passed the Wilkinson Arms sporting Mrs Wilkinson's sweet face on its inn sign and a statue of a handsome Cavalier, Sir Francis Framlingham, who'd planted the first willows. To the right was the church with its soaring spire and gold weathercock, and – oh God! – a church-yard swarming with people.

Everyone had agreed it was big-hearted of Ione Travis-Lock, fearsome termagent, who roared round Willowwood bellowing at people for not recycling or turning off lights, to plant a willow for Master Quickly.

They felt it was even more gracious of Niall Forbes, the ex-vicar of Willowwood and now a canon, who had blessed Mrs Wilkinson with such success before every race, to return and christen Master Quickly, when he and his boyfriend, tree surgeon Woody Adams, had also been dumped as syndicate members.

Pink-faced, boyish Niall could only feel relief that he no longer had to preach sermons under the beady eye of Ione Travis-Lock. He now felt free to amend the words of the prayer book for this sweet little foal and beamed at Etta as she led Master Quickly forward, to a flickering of cameras.

Niall then exhorted Quickly to renounce the devil and the sinful lusts of the flesh.

'Can't see that happening,' Trixie whispered to Dora.

'Not when he goes to stud,' whispered back Dora. 'Did you ever see so much press?'

'Grant that the old Adam in this colt may be buried and that the new horse be raised in him . . . ouch!' cried Niall, as Quickly deliberately trod on his toe. 'Grant that he may have power and strength to have victory.'

'I'll drink to that,' muttered Valent, thinking how gorgeous Etta looked.

'And to triumph against the world, the flesh and the devil.'

Quickly, however, was bored, and having tried to drink the holy water in which Niall was dowsing him, started to eat his gold embroidered scarf.

'That's enough, Horse,' ordered Ione Travis-Lock. Seizing the willow sapling by its slender trunk, she planted it in the large hole, dug and well watered for her by her gardener Mr Pocock, another dumped member of the syndicate. Then she picked up a spade to fill in the earth. Quickly, alas, had been taught by Chisolm to butt. Spying Ione's large tweed bottom, he gave it a sharp nip before shoving her into the hole.

'Quickly!' cried Etta in horror, as everyone else tried not to laugh. Click, click, click went the cameras.

'You little monster,' bellowed Ione. Struggling out, plastered in mud like a jump jockey, she brandished her spade at him, whereupon Quickly spooked and took off round the church-yard, narrowly missing screaming onlookers and tombstones, little feet hardly touching turf, soft and springy from being fertilized by the dead beneath.

'Christ, he's fast,' said Niall's tree surgeon, Woody, in wonder. 'Won't have any difficulty winning the Derby.'

'But not for us,' said the syndicate sourly.

'He's going to trip over his lead rope,' wailed Etta in anguish, as Quickly only just missed the rusty iron spiked fence surrounding a flat, mossy tombstone.

Next moment, Gav, who'd been lurking behind a plaguestone, dived forward and grabbed Quickly's lead rope, and after being dragged a few feet, tugged the foal to a halt, stroking his neck, talking to him quietly, circling him until he calmed down.

Then Mrs Wilkinson trundled up with an 'I've been search-ing for you all day' look on her face, whickering and nuzzling Quickly, who proceeded to have a good suck as Gav took hold of Mrs Wilkinson.

'Isn't he very small,' said Direct Debbie, the ultra-tactless wife of Major Cunliffe, the syndicate's bank manager treasurer.

'Rupert won't allow work riders to be more than ten stone,' said Dora.

'No, the foal,' said Debbie scornfully.

'First foals are often small,' Dora countered.

Seeing Quickly was safely moored by rather an attractive man, and that Ione had finished filling in earth round the willow tree, Niall addressed the embattled syndicate.

'I'd like to thank Mrs Travis-Lock so much for planting a willow for Master Quickly and to end with a special prayer, asking all of you to pray for your neighbours. Even those,' he added, 'you are fighting with, because like you, that neighbour is one of God's children.'

'Very debatable,' said Ione's gardener, glaring at Major Cunliffe, who'd failed to include breeding rights in the contract.

'Very,' agreed Alan Macbeth, Trixie's father and Etta's son-in-law. Then, as Quickly lashed out with both back legs at the Major, 'That colt's clearly a child of Satan.'

Quickly then turned back to his mother for another suck and Valent said, 'I think we all need a drink too.'

Wild garlic, warmed by the sun and trampled on by the crowds, gave off a heady smell, which made everyone hungry for lunch.

'I'll walk the horses and Chisolm back to Badger's Court,' said Gav. Anything to delay tackling that bunfight.

'Oh, would you?' said Etta. 'It was a bit of a hassle getting them into the bus, and you seem to have a magical effect on Quickly.'

'Lucky Quickly,' said Trixie in admiration. 'That guy's well fit.'

'Yeah, he is,' said Dora as Gav set off. 'Been screwed up by an awful marriage. Please look after him at lunch.'

'What's his name?'

'Gavin Latton.'

Trixie laughed. 'Small Latton and less Geek.'

10

By the time Gav reached Badger's Court, without incident except for Chisolm nicking a bunch of grapes from the village shop, a roaring party was under way.

Having tarted up in the portaloo in anticipation of Rupert, the ladies of Willowwood had joined their other halves on the lawn, and were getting stuck into the Bollinger.

'Well done, Gav,' said Dora, whisking Quickly and Mrs Wilkinson off to meet the press.

New blood, thought the ladies, eyeing up Gav. Tugging her skirt down and her top up, Etta rushed over to welcome him.

'Thank you so much for sorting out Quickly – such a show-off. You deserve an enormous drink.'

'I don't drink,' said Gav curtly.

'Oh poor you.' There was a long, long pause. Then Etta stammered: 'Quickly does love an audience, just like his mother.'

Seeing the sweetness in her face, Gav volunteered that Quickly was a beautiful colt.

'Soon get rid of that baby fur. Got a terrific walk like that greyhound,' he noted, as Priceless sauntered past and lifted his leg on the generator.

'I hope that won't fuse all the caterers' equipment,' giggled Etta. 'I do want Rupert to like Quickly. He is coming, isn't he?' she asked anxiously.

''Fraid not, can't make it, had to go abroad.' Gav paused, then added untruthfully, 'Sent his apologies.'

'Oh dear.' The delight faded from Etta's face. 'Everyone's so longing to meet him.' Then as a ravishingly pretty, slender girl with her dark hair in two long plaits, drifted over, Etta told her, 'Gavin works for Rupert, who sadly can't make it.'

So this is Eddie's girlfriend. She's heartbreaking, thought Gav – if I had any heart left to break.

'Don't tell anyone he's not coming,' advised Trixie. 'They'll soon be too hammered to mind.' And, turning to Gav, 'You're just as good-looking and much younger.'

A touch of colour stole into Gav's cheeks as she handed him a glass of champagne and, when he shook his head, drained it herself before summoning a waitress to bring a refill for herself and a glass of orange juice for Gav. As Etta rushed off to look after everyone Trixie asked him: 'What d'you do for Rupert?'

'Go to the sales, sort out tricky horses.'

'You'll have your work cut out with Quickly. He bites.'

'Like my husband Chippy Hackee,' said Gav idly.

'*Timmy Tiptoes!* I love that book,' cried Trixie. 'Singing in high squirrel voices, like all men out on the toot. But I don't like Rupert, even though I know he's your boss. I looked after a horse called Furious when he won the Gold Cup, but when he and Mrs Wilkinson were moved to Penscombe for the National, Rupert let Wilkie's stable lad move in and look after her, but he wouldn't let a stupid schoolgirl like me near the place.'

Gav said nothing; his silences made Trixie gabble. He was very handsome, she thought. If only his beautiful grey eyes with their thick black lashes would meet hers occasionally. Then he suddenly said, 'Rupert's been good to me. He looks after his own. His jockeys jump through fire for him.'

Trixie shrugged. 'Probably the preferable alternative.' Then, ultra-casual, 'Is Eddie coming?'

'Said he was. Promised to give me a lift, but didn't show. Probably jet-lagged.'

'Did he have a good time in America?' Trixie smiled at the press who were snapping away.

Gav, turning his back on them, said, 'He did, but he's decided to do another stint at Penscombe.'

'Oh really?' The tension seeped out of Trixie. 'Do you think he'll crack jump racing?'

'Not sure if he's got the patience or the discipline.'

'"Ride ten thousand days and nights, Till old age has snow white hairs on thee" – hmm, it's not quite Eddie.' Trixie grabbed another glass from a passing waitress then, taking a whole plate of canapés from another, she led Gavin to a bench under a cherry tree that was idly raining down pink blossom.

'Look at Wilkie,' she added fondly as Mrs Wilkinson wandered around, touchingly pleased to see her old syndicate friends. 'She's such a hostess, like Granny,' as Etta raced around, seeing glasses were full, offering food, gathering up anyone who looked lonely. As they watched, a tall, good-looking but self-important man bore down on her and, not seeing Gav and Trixie under the cherry tree, drew her in their direction.

'That's Granny's ghastly son Martin,' whispered Trixie. 'He's a fundraiser, always on the scrounge. No charity in his heart.'

'Now you've opened Badger's Court to the masses, Mother, we must earmark some dates for charity functions,' Martin began hectoring her. 'And make sure you introduce me to Rupert C-B the minute he arrives. I've got a proposal he'll find hard to resist.' Then, taking in Etta's cleavage: 'Not sure about that dress, Mother – it's much too short and low-cut. You're seventy now, try and act your age.'

'Bastard,' snapped Trixie as a crestfallen Etta, tugging down and pulling up simultaneously, rushed off to welcome some new arrivals.

'"The truth that's told with bad intent beats all the lies you can invent" – except it's not the truth. Granny looks gorgeous. "A robin redbreast in a cage puts all Heaven in a rage",' she went on.

'"A dog starved at his master's gate predicts the ruin of the state",' quoted back Gav.

'"A horse misused upon the road calls to Heaven for human blood",' ended Trixie in delight. 'That is such a good poem. I'm doing Blake for A-levels. He ought to be running the RSPCA

– wouldn't squander fortunes attacking hunting and the Grand National.'

'Blake probably wouldn't have been very keen on hunting. What other stuff are you doing?'

'*Kubla Khan, The Prelude, The Waste Land.*'

God, I adore this girl, thought Gavin in bewilderment. Everything turns upwards, her eyelashes, her little nose, her dark slanting eyes, her mouth when she smiles, her nipples lifting the soft brown suede. If she were lying in bed beside me, just talking and reading, holding hands, no pressure, I'm sure in time I'd be able to get it up. God, she was sweet. Look at the freckles on her nose and the little bitten nails.

'What happens after A-levels?' he asked.

'I'd like to go to Oxford, but I've got a baby of six months – called Hereward. I ought to go and check him,' she said reluctantly. 'Would you like to see him?' She flashed a white blob on her telephone.

'Sweet. Why didn't you have him christened today?'

'It's rather complicated. His father's an actor, who's known locally as Mr Bulging Crotchester.'

Unlike me, thought Gavin wearily.

'And I don't want to upstage Quickly.' As she reached out and brushed cherry blossom from Gav's hair, a 100 volts went through him. 'My father's a good writer, he's done really well with a book about Mrs Wilkinson.'

'It was very good, I enjoyed it.'

'And he's just shacked up with Tilda the village schoolmistress.'

Gavin shook his head. 'Just like *The Deserted Village.*'

'Oh, I love that poem too. "The bashful virgin's side-long looks of love, The matron's glance that would those looks reprove". That sums up Direct Debbie Cunliffe, that old bat over there, who rushes round Willowwood disapproving of everything.'

As a waitress came up with more food, Trixie picked out the paté and the smoked salmon and the vol au vents for Gav. 'You must be starving. I bet you got up at five. I didn't know that people who rode, also read. You're well-rode and well-read. Eddie doesn't read.'

'He reads the *Racing Post*.'

'Only when they write about him. He's divine but starry, and unlike the stars that appear to twinkle in the sky, the planets remain steady.' Just for a second Trixie betrayed the hurt she'd suffered. 'I want a planet. Was your wife nice?'

'Not a planet.' Gav was amazed he hadn't bitten her head off.

'How do you get over it?'

'Not sure.' Gavin had reached out for a vol au vent, when a blond child rushed up, scooping up canapés in both hands.

'Where are your manners?' snapped Trixie.

'Gone on holiday.' The child stuck a green tongue out at her and ran off.

'That little toerag is Drummond, Hereward's first cousin once removed – which is not nearly enough. That's his awful father Martin who was hassling Granny.'

Valent meanwhile had sought out his wife, who had covered herself in a pashmina, which he promptly pulled off, saying, 'Lunch is ready. You look so luvely, everyone's OK.'

People were flowing into the marquee, carrying their glasses, admiring posters of Love Rat and expressing wonder at the pastel miracle Etta had wrought in Valent's garden in only a year.

'Needs more colour,' said Direct Debbie sourly.

'I wondered if we were ever going to get any lunch – and where's Rupert?' said Phoebe, another ex-syndicate member. 'Shame when you think what fun we all had.'

'Rather selfish of Etta to close down the syndicate and forget her old friends,' grumbled Debbie. 'I suppose she's so rich now.'

Trixie, who was following them, had drunk a great deal of champagne on top of vodka.

'How dare you slag off Granny,' she shouted at Debbie. 'You're all bloody greedy. It was Granny who rescued Wilkie and nursed her back from the dead. You made a lot of money while she was racing. When Valent bought her for £600,000 we all cleaned up with £60,000 each. Valent flew up to the National, gave us a lovely day out and then gave us £5,000 for our shares when Wilkie retired.' Then, as a furiously mouthing Direct Debbie turned purple: 'You're an avaricious old bat.'

'I will not be talked to like that.'

'Why don't you spend some of that money getting another horse? But you're too bloody mean and lazy, you want everything done for you.'

'Hold your tongue, young lady,' cried Tilda, the schoolmistress, furiously. 'Apologize to Debbie at once.'

'You can't boss me about just because you're shagging my dad,' yelled Trixie.

The crowd, transfixed with interest, were buckling behind the squawking match. The press had moved in, snapping furiously, holding out tape recorders to catch the expletives, when suddenly everyone was distracted by a dark-green Ferrari storming up the drive. Parking at an insolent angle on the edge of the lawn, a tall, undeniably gorgeous man jumped out. He was wearing a baseball cap, jeans, and a blue fleece with *Rupert Campbell-Black Racing* in emerald-green letters on the back.

'Rupert!' cried the ladies, forgetting the squawking match and diving into the bushes, compacts aloft to de-shine noses or fluff up hair, scent rising like incense. 'He's come, after all.'

The media were going crazy. 'Isn't he awesome,' said the *Telegraph*.

'Absolutely awesome,' cried Trixie, racing over Etta's spring flowers. Hearing her call out, the man turned towards her, whipping off his baseball cap.

'Goodness, he's young-looking,' said *The Times* in amazement, as next moment, he gathered Trixie into a huge hug, kissing her on and on and on.

'Little tramp,' exploded Debbie. 'Disgraceful. I thought he was supposed to be faithful to his wife.'

'Hasn't got a grey hair,' said the *Daily Mail* in wonder.

'Hardly surprising,' giggled Dora. 'That's Eddie, Rupert's grandson.'

'Look who's here, Granny,' said Trixie, leading Eddie up to Etta.

'I'm so sorry I'm late, Mrs Edwards, I overslept,' apologized Eddie, wiping off lipstick.

'I'm going to take Eddie upstairs, to see if Hereward's awake,' said Trixie, whisking him into the house.

As she passed the bar she grabbed a bottle of champagne. In the doorway, she and Eddie could be seen locked in another embrace.

Gav felt overwhelmed by jealousy and disappointment. Somehow sensing this, Etta put an arm through his, and when he froze: 'Please come and have some lunch, you must be starving. I don't know what's become of Quickly.'

'Probably being interviewed by the *Observer*,' said Gav.

As people swarmed back towards the marquee, Etta thanked God she'd wildly overcatered. But as the waiters and waitresses had abandoned their posts to catch a glimpse of a suspected Rupert, Chisolm, Cadbury and Priceless the greyhound were having their own party, raiding the marquee, attacking the chicken Veronique, Chisolm particularly enjoying the grapes.

Quickly, meanwhile, after his earlier exertions had collapsed under a table laden with luscious puddings, then leaping to his feet, as the guests poured in, sent Pavlovas and chocolate roulades flying. Luckily, as he belted out of the tent in search of Mrs Wilkinson, who was talking to Sky, Gav managed again to catch his lead rope, walking him round and returning him to the orchard with his mother and Chisolm.

A couple of hours later, when tempers had calmed and everyone had drunk and eaten – except Etta, who'd been too busy scurrying – it was noticed that Eddie and Trixie had not reappeared, and a baby could be heard crying from an upstairs room.

Etta was about to belt upstairs when the crying stopped.

'Leave him,' ordered Valent. 'It's Trixie's baby, she's inside the house.' Then, when Etta looked worried, 'I'll go up and check.'

Tiptoeing along the landing, Valent found little Hereward, lying in his cot. Awake but content, he smiled and waved at Valent. In the spare room next door on the sea-blue counterpane of a double bed, their clothes in a jumbled pile on the floor, lay Trixie and Eddie, naked and asleep, in each other's arms. Trixie's body was as white as Eddie's was brown. Even their beauty didn't lessen Valent's rage.

'What the fuck are you doing?' he roared, then as Eddie opened an eye: 'Get up now and I hope you wore a sock, lad – and I don't mean on your foot.'

'Thank God Rupert never turned up. He'd have been horrified,' said Etta, as they closed the door on the last guest.

Next day, an ecstatic Dora rushed up to Gav, who was in a hut on wheels so it could be towed around, nicknamed the Love Tower, because staff often sloped off for a quick shag there. Gav, however, was watching the two-year-olds go up the gallops. Dora was brandishing a pile of press cuttings.

'Just look at these! The *Mail* and the *Sun* have both got hilarious pictures of Quickly and Ione Travis-Lock with mud all over her face, and a lovely picture in the *Telegraph* of you and Trixie and lots of plugs for Love Rat.'

'I'm busy,' said Gav.

'Trixie liked you very much.'

'Good.' Then, unable to contain his curiosity: 'What happened to the baby's father?'

'Seth? Serial philanderer, kept by a much older mistress, Corinna Waters. After he dumped her, Etta and Valent took Trixie in, but she still holds a large flicker of a torch for him and he for her. And then she started seeing Young Eddie, who's not ideal as a stepfather.'

At least ten two-year-olds had galloped past without Gav registering if they had wind problems or were ready to run.

'She loved talking to you,' persisted Dora. 'Why don't you ask her out?'

'Bugger off,' snapped Gav. 'I'm not into cradle-snatching.'

11

Quickly's behaviour did not improve, but his looks did as his patchy tufts of chestnut hair fell away to reveal a glossy iron-grey coat and a very fetching ash-blond tail and mane, which was beginning to turn over. Despite his small stature, his legs were long, his roving eyes large and lustrous and his long ears constantly pricked in curiosity. He possessed a terrible nosiness as he endlessly plotted how to get inside the house.

One early October evening, he achieved this by wriggling under the orchard gate, trotting up to the house, slipping in through another side door, over which one of Mrs Wilkinson's Grand National shoes had been nailed.

Stopping to sniff the row of gumboots and Barbours hanging from the walls, he nudged open the kitchen door. Here he found Etta and Valent enjoying an early dinner and watching *University Challenge*, during which they had gentle rivalry as to who could answer the most questions: Etta, being better on books and music, Valent on history and science. Trixie, better than both of them, had gone out to a party with Young Eddie, leaving her grandmother to babysit Hereward the Awake, as he was known, who had for once fallen asleep upstairs.

Etta and Valent burst out laughing as Quickly edged cautiously into the room towards the table, stretching out his neck to plunge his nose into and sample, first apple crumble and then the remains of sticky toffee pudding, then a tub of vanilla ice cream, curling his upper lip, then deciding he liked it, returning to the attack. Encouraged that Valent and Etta were now crying with laughter, he edged along the table, before trying a slab of cheddar.

'Not sure about that,' said Valent, wiping his eyes as Quickly's lip curled up again.

'Watch my glass,' squeaked Etta. Next moment, Quickly had knocked it over and was greedily licking up sweet Sauterne. He then wandered over to the television, utterly fascinated, nudging Jeremy Paxman with his nose.

Quickly's co-owner, Rupert, had not really forgiven Mrs Wilkinson for stealing a march or rather February on him. By giving birth in the orchard at Badger's Court, she had avoided getting covered again by Love Rat at Penscombe. Rupert had seen enough pictures of Quickly in the papers, but beyond despatching Gav, who'd returned with uncharacteristically enthusiastic reports that the colt was thriving, he hadn't bothered to visit Valent since.

He was soon off to the Far East for big race meetings in Hong Kong and Japan. As he was planning a detour into China, to investigate possible bloodstock deals, he needed Valent's advice and contacts. Valent had been avid for them to collaborate but seemed, since he married his soppy wife, to have gone off the boil and be taking the project less and less seriously.

Rupert's suspicions were confirmed, as he walked up Badger's Court drive, to hear roars of laughter issuing from the kitchen. Going in, he found Etta and Valent in hysterics, obviously plastered, and Quickly transfixed by David Attenborough, interviewing baboons.

'He found his way in,' explained Etta as Valent poured Rupert a large glass of red. 'Would you like some supper?' she added, getting the remains of a quiche out of the oven.

'Thanks, I've got dinner at home. I haven't come for long.'

To Etta's dismay, he had come to try and persuade Valent to join him on his trip to Hong Kong and then on to China.

'Coolmore, the Irish megaliths,' he announced, 'are evidently planning to send mares to China to start up a stud farm.

Godolphin, their great rivals, have already been sending stallions from Dubai. We mustn't miss the boat. France, New Zealand and Australia are all making overtures. Gav's got the horses in really good shape. Love Rat's colt Promiscuous has made a dazzling start at stud. Leading Sire for the year will be announced at the end of December. Both Peppy Koala and Love Rat have a great chance of knocking Valhalla's star stallion, Roberto's Revenge, out of contention and the smug smile off Cosmo's face.'

The steel and passion in Rupert's usually light, clipped voice betrayed how desperately he wanted the Leading Sire title.

'How thrilling,' cried Etta. 'I'm so pleased Gav's doing so well. Quickly adores him. We like him too, but he seems so sad and withdrawn.'

'Been going through a hellish divorce,' Rupert said, and glanced up at a lovely photograph of Gav and Quickly on the dresser. 'Bethany, his adulterous bitch of a wife, is taking him to the cleaners.'

Once the divorce was through, Rupert planned to promote Gav and give him a socking great rise, but he was damned if he'd let Bethany take half of it.

'Oh poor boy,' sighed Etta. 'We must ask him to supper. Why's he so good?'

'He knows exactly when a horse is ready, he's in the yard at five in the morning. If the horse kicks over a bucket, he'll wake and go and fill it. His hands are so gentle, horses must think he's guiding them with a silk thread.'

Etta so wished Rupert would say something nice about Quickly. And Rupert wished she'd push off so he could put the pressure on Valent to accompany him to China. Having as usual not bothered with lunch, he absentmindedly helped himself to a piece of quiche.

'He come here often?' He nodded at Quickly.

'No, it's the first time,' said Valent, as Quickly, bored with baboons and in need of another drink, returned to the table. Then, when Rupert refused to share his second piece of quiche with him, he plunged his teeth into Rupert's arm, whereupon Rupert punched him hard on the nose.

'Don't hurt him!' cried an appalled Etta.

'Got to stand up to them,' Rupert said sharply, as Quickly, rolling his watering eyes, attempted another dive at the quiche, 'or he'll get impossibly spoilt. No – bugger *off*!' Rupert punched Quickly again.

'Don't, please!' Etta jumped up and grabbed Quickly's head collar. 'There, poor little boy, I'll take him out.'

They were distracted by a wail, as Hereward, awake again, appeared in the doorway, then gave a scream of joy. Half tottering, half crawling, he crossed the room and pulled himself up on Quickly's leg, as turning his head, the colt nudged the child fondly.

'Who's this?' demanded Rupert.

'My great-grandson, Trixie's baby Herry.' Etta lifted him on to Quickly's back. 'They adore each other. Trixie's gone to some rave-up with your grandson, Eddie – such a lovely boy,' she added in an attempt to ease the situation.

She then kicked herself as an increasingly wintry-looking Rupert announced: 'That "lovely boy" should be sober and tucked up in bed. He's got two big races at Chepstow tomorrow.'

'Oh dear. Well, he's probably not drinking,' stammered Etta.

'Unlike Master Quickly,' said Rupert, as Quickly eyed up his glass of red. 'It's high time that colt was weaned and moved to Penscombe i.e. prep school.'

'Not yet,' pleaded Etta, removing Hereward and leading Quickly towards the door. 'Oh look,' she added, peering out of the kitchen window into the golden gloom. 'Wilkie and Chisolm have come to fetch him. We so love having him here, and he won't need to be broken in until the end of next year.'

'By which time,' said Rupert acidly, 'he'll be sleeping in your bed.'

Seeing his friends going back to the orchard, Hereward burst into escalating, inconsolable sobs, so to Rupert's relief, Etta took him off to bed. It would at least give her the chance to tone down her flushed face, she thought. Why must Rupert always catch her looking at her worst?

'I should be going,' said Rupert as Valent filled up his glass. 'Is Trixie going to live here for ever?'

Valent shrugged. 'You might have a word with your grandson – tell him not to hurt her, or get her up the duff. God help us.'

'Only if you don't indulge that colt too much.'

'I'll try, and I'll give you all my contacts in China. You'll find the Chinese polite but pretty arrogant and self-confident. "The future is ours" is implicit in everything. But they want us to accept their culture. Guard your phone with your life, or they'll hack into it.'

'What are the hotels like?'

'Very good, they've really improved. Twenty years ago I found a cockroach trap in my bedroom.'

'We could use one of those to catch Cosmo,' said Rupert, draining his glass. 'Christ, I hope we beat him. How are your Chinese lessons going?'

'Well, I discovered "Ma". Whichever way you pronounce it, it can mean "horse", "mother", "house" or "fuck off".'

'We'll have to be careful when we start selling horses there, although I wouldn't mind selling them my lazy cow of a mother-in-law.'

Coming downstairs, Etta found a laughing Rupert on the way out.

'Very, very best luck with Leading Trainer and Leading Sire,' she called after him.

12

But sadly it was not to be. Isa and Cosmo had a dazzling end to the season, winning every race on Champions Day at Ascot. This boosted Roberto's Revenge's progeny earnings so colossally, that neither Love Rat nor Peppy Koala were likely to catch him. As a result, Isa landed the Leading Trainer title in November and Roberto's Revenge was odds on to land second place to the great Irish colossus, Verdi's Requiem, in the Leading Sire contest at the end of the year.

Normally, Isa getting Leading Trainer and Roberto's Revenge's leap upwards would only appear in the racing press. But since Rupert and Cosmo were so inextricably linked – with Cosmo's father marrying Rupert's first wife, who had already eloped with Isa's father Jake during the Los Angeles Olympics, and Isa briefly marrying Rupert's daughter Tabitha, who was now married to Cosmo's elder brother, Wolfe – the whole thing went viral.

Cosmo, taking to Facebook, had a field day, dismissing Rupert as a has-been who'd totally lost his touch and saying that Love Rat's offspring were doing so badly, he should be taking Viagra, but he supposed Love Rats always left sinking shits like Rupert in the lurch.

Isa Lovell was more restrained but more hurtful when he tweeted that Rupert was failing because he no longer had Billy Lloyd-Foxe's wisdom and encyclopaedic knowledge to rely on.

Almost worse, Roberto's Revenge in his glossy dark-brown glory was featured on the cover of Weatherbys' latest, incredibly prestigious stallion book.

Rupert didn't react publicly, but privately went ballistic, particularly as he looked up at Rupert Black on Third Leopard. No one, however, could accuse him of a lack of courage. Such a humiliating defeat made him even more determined to crack Leading Sire next year.

So many things at home were annoying him. His father Eddie was driving him crackers. Last week, seeking out his beloved Love Rat, Eddie had left open the doors of three other stallions. And Eddie's carer, Marjorie, was even more irritating, calling him by his Christian name every second sentence as she took him on a disgusting verbal tour of his father's nether regions.

'I've just toileted your father, Rupert, he's had an excellent bowel motion, Rupert, enjoy the rest of your day, Rupert.'

Rupert was also fed up with Young Eddie, who was hellraising instead of learning to become a jump jockey. He and Old Eddie got into endless irritating silliness together, howling with laughter at porn on the internet. For Old Eddie's eighty-sixth birthday, Young Eddie had plundered the local sex shop and returned with a lifesize rubber sheep, equipped with a hole in the bottom, and horns to cling on to. A totally captivated Old Eddie insisted on the sheep, whom he'd called Mildred, sleeping on his bed.

Multi-married Old Eddie had always been a groper. The reason he'd had to give up his very successful television programme, *Buffers*, was because he wouldn't stop lunging at the female researchers and presenters. Unfortunately, on a golden autumn day towards the end of October, his daughter-in-law Taggie returned from shopping to find, to her horror, that Forester her greyhound, who suffered from separation anxiety, had shredded Old Eddie's rubber sheep Mildred all over the drawing-room carpet.

Knowing how upset Eddie would be, Taggie was frantically gathering up Mildred's remains when, wandering into the room, confronted by Taggie's long, still-coltish legs and delectable bottom, Eddie shoved his hand up her crimson skirt, pulling down her tights, as his fingers crept underneath her knickers.

Taggie's shriek of surprised horror, when she realized it wasn't Rupert, coincided with her husband coming in through the front door and catching his father crimson-handed. His bellow of rage had all the dogs, including Forester with his mouth full of shredded Mildred, rushing in from the kitchen, and Old Eddie scuttling upstairs.

'That is the final straw, the filthy letch,' roared Rupert.

'No, no,' pleaded Taggie, crimson as her skirt. 'It's OK, he's sweet and always a bit odd when the moon's full.'

'He's out of control. He's going into a home tomorrow.'

'He'd never get in – they've got a five-year waiting list.'

'I took the precaution of booking him a place at Ashbourne House a year ago,' said Rupert triumphantly.

'We can't, he'd hate it.'

Next moment there was another squawk, as Marjorie, Eddie's whiskery carer, bustled in.

'We're busy,' snapped Rupert.

'Ay'm sorry, Taggie, Eddie has just put one hand up my skirt and fondled my breast with the other.'

'Extraordinary how my father always goes for the same type,' drawled Rupert. For a second his eyes met those of Taggie, who was trying not to laugh.

'Ay'm afraid ay can't tolerate that kaind of behaviour.'

'You won't have to any more,' said Rupert. 'My father's going into a home.'

Marjorie's face fell. No more Taggie's cooking and a very pretty room, with Sky and her own microwave.

No more carers, thought Rupert ecstatically, and there was now no reason why Taggie, who had been looking desperately tired, couldn't abandon Penscombe for a month and join him on a round trip to Singapore, Japan, Hong Kong and China.

Taggie, to his fury, refused. There was far too much to do at home, she said, particularly in the run up to Christmas; filling up the deep freeze for the office party, finding turkeys for the tenants and presents for staff and family.

She and Rupert parted, not friends.

The moment Rupert, Cathal, his Irish travelling Head Lad, who was in charge of the horses once they left the yard, his stable jockey Lion O'Connor, and two stable girls – sweet, smiling Lark who loved Young Eddie and horses, and 'woluptuous, wolatile' Marketa from the Czech Republic who loved the opposite sex and Safety Car – flew off to the Far East with six horses, the family, as if by telepathy, knowing the coast was clear, moved in.

Tabitha Rannaldini, Rupert's daughter, and Caitlin, Taggie's sister, claiming the need for more quality time with their husbands, dumped their children, dogs and nannies on Taggie. Janey Lloyd-Foxe immediately invited herself for Christmas because she was so sad, exhausted and missing Billy.

Taggie was further demoralized, being dyslexic, by her step-grandchild, Timon Rannaldini, calling her 'a crap granny' because she couldn't read him a bedtime story. Even worse was Timon's sister Sapphire announcing: 'I think Daddy and Mummy are getting a devalse and Mummy says she, me and Timon will be coming back to live with you.'

Oh God, thought Taggie in terror, we've already got Young Eddie as a permanent fixture. At least with Marjorie gone, the chocolate biscuit consumption had plummeted.

Taggie's withers had also been wrung by putting Old Eddie in the care home. Sewing nametapes on all his clothes was like sending a little boy off to prep school, particularly when he sobbed and sobbed, clung on to the banisters, wept all the way on the journey and even louder when she left him. Taggie felt so dreadful that she insisted on visiting him every day, which took up even more of her time.

On her tenth visit on a dank, grey November afternoon, she was passed going the other way down the drive by Brute Barraclough. Brute, the foul trainer who was so unkind to his darling wife Rosaria, but had no intention of leaving her because she did all the work and kept owners and horses sweet. Brute, the on-off lover of both Gav's ex Bethany and Janey Lloyd-Foxe.

On arrival, Taggie was immediately summoned into the

office of Mrs Ramsey, the head of the home, who grumbled that she had just had to deal with Brute Barraclough who, discovering that someone's rich old mother, Mrs Ford-Winters, was a resident, had dropped in and managed to sell her a horse called Geoffrey.

'I'm not sure if she can afford it *and* our fees. You racing folk, Mrs Campbell-Black! And I'm afraid your father-in-law has been rather wayward.'

Old Eddie, it seemed, had been sliding his hand under too many tartan rugs.

'And I don't quite know how to say this, Mrs Campbell-Black, but in the afternoon your father-in-law's been wandering round, slipping his penis into our lady residents' mouths when they're asleep in front of the television. There have been complaints.'

Taggie fought hysterical laughter and was tempted to suggest the lady residents took their teeth out.

'I'm terribly sorry, Mrs Campbell-Black,' Mrs Ramsey concluded, 'but I'm afraid you'll have to take your father-in-law back home.'

'Oh please, can you keep him a day or two,' begged Taggie, 'while I sort something out?' Oh God! Rupert would go berserk to have the house full of Treasures again. Nor had she told him that Helen, his ex-wife, as well as Janey, were angling to stay for Christmas. She couldn't bother him when he was abroad concentrating on the horses and networking with rich Chinese.

For a second she thought how heavenly it would be if she could have gone with him or if their own children Bianca and Xav had been able to return from abroad for Christmas.

Quailing, she rang up Mrs Simmons at the carers' agency, who asked if Taggie wanted Marjorie back. 'She was very happy with you.'

'Not really, so embarrassing when my father-in-law made a pass at her. Might be better to have someone a little younger.'

By luck, said Mrs Simmons, they had a white Zimbabwean called Gala Milburn.

'She's a widow of thirty-four, had rather a rough time, not

been long in this country but she's a good cook and an excellent worker. We've had very good reports. She could be free in the run up to Christmas.'

13

In the year 2000, a land invasion had started in Zimbabwe when gangs of armed blacks, claiming to be veterans of Mugabe's Liberation Army, began seizing white-owned land, shooting farmers in the face, battering them to death, assaulting and torturing to death any black workers who remained loyal, ransacking houses, burning tobacco barns, butchering pets and livestock, and riding Land Rovers for fun into herds of giraffe. Everywhere, mud huts sprang up on raped and ruined land.

Gala and Ben Milburn had had a beautiful farm, but as their land was near a mine containing precious minerals, including emeralds worth £300,000 each, they were not likely to be left alone. During a prolonged court case to keep the farm, Ben and Gala were endlessly harassed by veterans.

The day after they won their case, their farm was burnt to the ground. Ben, who was a passionate conservationist and who doubled up as a game warden, was away from home. He had been trying to curb the excesses of a Chinese mafia warlord, a Zixin Wang who, not content with stripping mines of their emeralds and diamonds, was also targeting rhino horn and elephant tusk worth £60,000 each.

In SAS-style operations, Mr Wang's poacher gangs would load helicopters on to trucks so they needn't log a flight-path. Armed with machine guns, they would then mow down rhinos and elephants, hack off their horns and tusks, load these into the helicopters and fly them away.

Attempting to save a baby rhino whose mother had been gunned down, Ben was gunned down himself with fifty bullets in his body.

Gala, who'd been shopping, returned to discover at the smouldering farm that limbs had been hacked off their cows and horses, so they staggered around moaning on three legs, until she put them out of their misery by shooting them. Even more horrible, her adored Staffordshire Bull Terriers and Ben's black Labrador, Wilson, had had their throats cut and been hung up on posts. Only then did Gala learn that Ben had been murdered – but she had no means of fighting back. If you take on the Chinese mafia in Zimbabwe, you're dead in the (lack of) water.

All these horrors were so undeserved because Gala was a darling: big, brave, optimistic, intelligent with thick blonde curly hair, sleepy, kind dark eyes, a tawny complexion and an embracing smile. She also had a voluptuous body with big breasts, a big, uppity bottom and powerful thighs tapering down to slim ankles. Added to this was a frequent laugh and a lovely soft voice, like a warm breeze in the acacia trees.

Her once-happy life had now become unimaginably dreadful. She had lost all her money and, like many Zimbabwean women, found the only solution was to come to England and work as a carer, a job often satisfying but in Gala's case so demanding and even harrowing, it almost blotted out some of the previous horrors.

In the five months she had been in England, Gala had looked after a retired Colonel with dementia, who one moment would be ordering her to get out because he was going to call the police, the next moment asking her when they were going to bed.

The next client was in a wheelchair, but trapped Gala in her bedroom, leering and masturbating in the doorway. He also steered her hand towards his penis every time she washed him.

She then moved on to a husband and wife, who never stopped

complaining about her excellent cooking and were terrible snobs. The husband, who had multiple sclerosis, was also a multiple groper. But when they had people to lunch, Gala was mortified to hear the wife saying, 'Do you think *she* knows how to lay the table?' And when once Gala had remarked that Princess Diana had been very beautiful, had snapped: 'What do you know about our Royal Family?'

In fact, in Zimbabwe, Gala had had many of her own servants, and had taught African maids to cook, even delivering one of their babies single-handed.

In each new place, as a carer, it was a panic to locate the potato peeler, the tin opener, where to put everything as you unloaded the dishwasher and not to drive people crackers asking questions all the time.

One crotchety old lady kept looking for things for her to do, dispatching her to clean the car or weed the garden when she should have been taking a two-hour break, expecting her to make a pint of milk last a week and complaining that she was using too much lavatory paper – 'you only need two squares at a time.'

Unlike other carers, Gala couldn't storm out as she had nowhere to stay in England except where she was employed. Gala's parents were both dead, but she had an older sister Nicola, who was married with three children, lived in Cape Town and was often tapping Gala and Ben when he was alive for money. It was Nicola with whom Gala stayed when she was doing her week-long training to become a carer. This included how to use hoists to lift disabled clients, how to make them comfortable, give them their pills on time, and to ignore frequent abuse, because the old and, particularly those losing their minds, tend to lie or to forget, or say the first thing that comes into their heads.

The other problem was although the hours were punishing with only a two-hour break in the middle of the day, Gala had to spend long periods watching, with these clients, television programmes in which she had no interest. This left her too much time to mourn the devastating loss of her handsome, noble Ben, her beautiful farm, her lovely animals and Pinstripe her zebra, who had pulled a cart. *Why, this is hell, nor am I out of it.*

Somehow, she managed to hide her panic attacks, and smiled and smiled, repeating that she was 'fine, fine, fine'. Zimbabweans are a naturally kind and happy people, and if you were called out so often in the night, at least it cut short the terrible nightmares.

Gala was currently working for a mad old woman in the depths of Gloucestershire, filling in while their permanent carer was on holiday. By day, the old woman stood by the window, saying: 'When is Mummy coming to take me home?' By night, the big house creaked and groaned in the wind and the old woman laughed madly like the first Mrs Rochester.

Gala was therefore passionately relieved when the agency rang her about a possible next post.

'Could you pop in on your break?'

Gala borrowed the family car, then, after Zimbabwe's wide straight roads, terrified herself driving along narrow, winding, high-banked lanes and negotiating roundabouts and one-way streets through towns.

Mrs Summers at the agency, however, cheered her up with strong black coffee, chocolate biscuits and the words: 'You've been doing really well in some challenging jobs, so here's some-thing more exciting. The job is at Penscombe, home of Rupert Campbell-Black and his wife Taggie. She's an angel, the sweetest woman you could ever meet. Rupert's tricky, likes to call the shots, but he's pretty attractive.'

'Pretty?' Gala couldn't believe her ears.

'They've got masses of horses and dogs. You OK with animals?'

For a moment Gala couldn't speak, overwhelmed by visions of Dobson and Gregory, her Staffies, and Wilson, Ben's black Labrador, hanging from those poles gushing with blood. Could she bear animals again?

'No, I'll be fine.'

'There are cleaners, a PA and masses of staff in the yard and the stud, so you may end up cooking breakfast for the stable lads, but your main job will be caring for Rupert's father, whose dementia is advancing. He was quite a celebrity himself in a television programme called *Buffers*.'

'*Buggers?*'

'No, *Buffers*. Old generals and admirals arguing about military campaigns, so if you chat to him about the war, you'll be well away. Don't think you'll be called out much in the night. Frankly, Taggie needs a carer more than Eddie.'

When Taggie met Gala at Cotchester station, both were impressed by how attractive the other was.

Here's surely one Rupert won't object to, thought Taggie, praying on the other hand that Old Eddie wouldn't get carried away too soon. Taggie, in fact, looked shattered, her big silver-grey eyes reddened from seeing so many of her beloved foals setting out, all glossy, plump and unaware of their futures, to the sales. But she was still as beautiful and slim as the brindle greyhound, who rattled his tail and laid a comforting chin on Gala's shoulder as they drove back to Penscombe.

'Forester's rescued so he hates being left behind,' explained Taggie. 'I'm sure you'll like Eddie, he's very affectionate but a bit wayward, unless you grab each of his hands with one of yours. Nearly there,' she added, swinging into Rupert's chestnut avenue, passing a sign saying *Visiting Mares*, which to Gala sounded rather like Jane Austen.

She had Googled the house beforehand but never expected it to be quite so large or impressive. Her room looked south over a wooded valley, but with the leaves off the trees there seemed an almost African amount of cloudy sky reflected in Rupert's blue and white lake.

Braving the cold, leaning out of her window, she gasped at the extent of the operation. To the right was a huge yard for the horses in training and half a dozen distinctive royal-blue lorries, entitled *Rupert Campbell-Black Racing* and decorated with galloping emerald-green horses. Beyond, carved out of the wood, was the stud, where his stallions strutted their stuff. There were barns for the visiting mares and cottages for the staff, a tangle of flat and downhill gallops for every trip and surface imaginable, salt- and fresh-water swimming pools, and everywhere else lush fields full of glorious horses in royal-blue rugs.

'Oh wow, treble wow!' sighed Gala, shutting the window.

Her room enchanted her almost more with its palest pink walls, rose-red curtains, violet and pink checked counterpane, and paintings of flowers in different seasons. There was a dull red desk with Chinese carvings on the lid for her to write letters on, and to add to her comfort, a television, a little radio, and an electric blanket which she hoped she wouldn't fuse with her tears. On the bedside table were a tin of shortbread, a vase of pink geraniums and copies of *Tatler*, *Country Life*, *Dogs Today* and *The Lady* for her to read.

'Oh, quadruple wow!' Taking a piece of shortbread, Gala found it still warm from the oven.

The only downside was that the room was at the top of the house, which meant lots more steps for aching legs accustomed to Zimbabwean one-storey houses. Old Eddie's room was just below on the next floor. Taggie introduced him to Gala downstairs. He was wearing a tweed jacket with a badge on the lapel saying *Old Men make better lovers*, and acorn-brown cords with three fly-buttons undone. He was also sporting a green woolly hat, and carrying a brick on a plate, from which he attempted to cut her a slice.

'I'm fine, thank you,' said Gala. 'I've just had a delicious piece of Mrs Campbell-Black's shortbread.'

'This is Gala,' said Taggie. 'She's going to look after you from now on, instead of Marjorie.'

'Marjorie's gorn orf,' said Eddie, 'but we're not divorced. 'Spect she'll want half the house.' Then, seeing how young and luscious Gala was, his eyes gleamed. 'You can stay in my half if you like.'

But apart from the odd lunge and having to watch lots of military and sporting programmes, and locate occasional porn channels and then scarper, Eddie and Gala got on famously. Every day he liked her to read him *The Times*' Death Column, to see 'who's pushed orf and check I'm still alive'.

He then insisted she took him down to the stud to see Love Rat, who always trotted over and laid his great white face against Eddie's before accepting several Polos. She was soon taking Eddie on jaunts, including a first visit to Tesco's where, seeing a small boy and his sister riding in their mother's trolley, he exclaimed: 'Good God, do they sell children as well?'

That was one of the tragedies of being a widow, not being able to tell Ben things that had made her laugh. But at least James Benson, the Campbell-Blacks' smooth, still-handsome doctor, supplied Eddie with sleeping pills, which ensured that Gala's nights were usually uninterrupted, except by her own nightmares.

14

For Gala, the best part of the job was getting to know Taggie. Over a wonderful dinner of moussaka on her first night, Taggie confessed how she loathed the foals going off to the sales, and how, because she couldn't read or write very well, she dreaded coping with Christmas cards. She and Rupert got thousands and had had one printed this year with Love Rat, rearing up noble and unusually virile on the front.

The house seemed to swarm with impossibly spoilt children. Gala, used to Zimbabwean children, who didn't answer back and stood up when grown-ups came into the room, was shocked. Dogs were also everywhere: Rupert's black Labrador Banquo, two Jack Russells, Cuthbert and Gilchrist, nicknamed the Brothers Grin, and the ex-racing brindle greyhound Forester, who chased anything that moved and kept taking single shoes into the garden. One morning was spent searching for Eddie's teeth, until Banquo wandered downstairs clacking them. On another occasion, Forester dropped them in the drive and a horsebox ran over them.

Desperately missing her Staffies, and Wilson, also a black Labrador, Gala palled up with Banquo, who was missing Rupert and barked every time a door banged or a car drew up on the gravel.

'Your master's coming home soon,' she kept reassuring him.

Meanwhile Taggie had so much to do and Gala didn't think

Rupert's PA, Geraldine, who'd clearly like to be the next Mrs Campbell-Black, protected Taggie enough. Gala therefore took over the job, seeing off the vicar, for example, when he tried to persuade Taggie to read one of the Nine Lessons for a carol service. She was also soon helping Taggie out with Christmas cards – 'if only people would put in their surnames' – feeding and getting the children to bed, feeding and walking the dogs.

But reciprocally it was Gala's special kindness that touched Taggie. She would find her bed made, or wander wearily upstairs at night to find it turned down and a light on. Gala always left the kettle full up, and put back plugs if she'd pulled them out.

When Taggie staggered home from a punishing afternoon Christmas shopping in Cheltenham, during which she had bought Gala four thermal vests, several pairs of thick socks and some dark-brown Uggs, she found Gala had cooked her a wonderful Zimbabwean dinner.

'This is so gorgeous,' enthused Taggie, embarking on a second helping of chicken breasts cooked with mustard and honey. 'Did Eddie have some?'

'He did, he seemed to like it.'

'Must be in heaven. Marjorie never flavoured anything. To wind her up, Rupert once put a salt lick in Eddie's bedroom. I had to pretend it was for Mildred – that was Eddie's pet rubber sheep, which naughty Forester shredded. You must keep those Uggs away from him.'

'They're bliss,' Gala stretched a foot out, 'but I'll never take them off, so Forester won't get them. In Zimbabwe we lived on the edge of a conservation area where animals wandered in and out. You'd find elephants in the swimming pool, and monkeys were always pinching eggs. One day Ben came home and found a baboon sitting on a chair in the kitchen eating a banana.'

Rupert was always so busy, particularly since he'd become obsessed with nailing Leading Sire. Even when he was at home, he'd spend the evenings planning who would ride what horse and which races they'd run in, and watching re-runs of races at home or abroad so he could blast the jockeys next day. Taggie found it lovely to have another person to talk to, not a demoralizer like Janey, Helen or Geraldine or even her own mother, Maud.

Gala revealed very little about her terrible past, but showed Taggie a photograph on her mobile of the handsome, rugged Ben, displaying marvellous legs in khaki shorts and hugging a baby rhino.

'He was a Rhodi,' said Gala, 'which means very straight, macho, chauvinistic and conservative, but he was a total softie around animals.'

'He's absolutely gorgeous. Does it get any easier?'

'Not really, but it's not unrelenting, you do have sudden moments of happiness,' Gala smiled at Taggie, 'like now. I love being here.'

The cold, however, got colder and Gala put on even more jerseys, an overcoat with a hood, three pairs of socks tucked into her Uggs, and was passionately grateful for the electric blanket and assorted dogs who, with Rupert away, took every opportunity to get into bed with her.

One December afternoon, when Old Eddie was sleeping, Gala strayed out in her break to look at the horses. Chatting to her favourite, the little chestnut, New Year's Dave, who was certainly not going to any sales, she met up with Michael Meagan, known as Roving Mike – the foxy, lazy, engaging Irish work rider, who for a consideration sometimes helped out in the stud. He was now walking out Dardanius, the newest stallion, who would start covering for the first time on 15 February.

'He's beautiful too,' sighed Gala.

'Dardanius,' announced Mike, 'will be one of tree tings: he'll be popular and successful, or in Japan or in a can.'

'That's awful,' gasped Gala. 'They don't go for meat here, Taggie wouldn't allow it.'

'A stallion's useless if he isn't popular,' Mike told her.

Love Rat, recognizing Gala from her visits with Old Eddie, was whickering for Polos as they passed his box.

'He's fifteen tree, Love Rat, the perfect size,' volunteered Michael. 'Wonderful legs, always pricks his ears for photographers

– the perfect specimen, but he's lazy. Peppy Koala, on the other hand,' he pointed to a handsome chestnut, 'is our busiest stallion. He's covered 400 mares in three seasons.'

'Almost as many as you,' quipped Pat Inglis, the stud manager coming out of Love Rat's box. Then, as Gala moved down the row to stroke Titus Andronicus, who was gnawing away at his half door: 'Don't touch him, for God's sake. He'll have your hand off.'

'Who *was* Titus Andronicus?' asked Gala.

'Some general who killed an enemy Queen's sons, then served them up for her to eat in a pie. Hardly Nigella,' grinned Pat.

'Like to come out for a drink tonight?' asked Mike.

'I'd love to, but I've got to look after Eddie. Taggie's going over to her parents'.'

Taggie had her work cut out, but Gala found it hard sometimes not to be jealous of the beautiful house, the glorious pictures everywhere, the lovely mural of the hunt in the long gallery, all those fantastic horses and dogs; even the badly brought up children had their moments. If only she and Ben hadn't waited, she would have his child now – but how could she possibly have supported it?

And then there was Rupert, who was still away, now in Hong Kong. The place was evidently very relaxed without him. Impossibly handsome and arrogant, he seemed to challenge and mock her from every photograph.

On her break on a later afternoon, Gala had dropped in on another new friend, Louise Malone, a very pretty stable lass nicknamed Lou-easy because she was so free with her favours, particularly when vets and farriers treated her own horse Bennet for nothing. Louise was cleaning tack and reading *Hello!*. On the tack-room wall amidst a faded rainbow of rosettes from Rupert's showjumping past was a photograph of him hugging his favourite mare, Cordelia, after she'd won the Oaks.

'Lush, isn't he?' commented Louise.

'He's old, fifty-seven,' protested Gala.

'I dunno,' Louise put her head on one side, 'he has to fight off women breeders – and gay ones too for that matter. And as a boss he's the real deal. The lads grumble but they call him "Guv" and tip their hats to him. He wants everything done perfectly – and by yesterday. Luckily one's usually got a horse to sit on or cling on to when he's around, because he does make your knees give way. He doesn't seem old, just well fit, and it's such heaven when he praises you. And he can be kind. An owner gave me my horse, Bennet, when he retired from racing and Rupert lets me keep him here.'

It was the eve of the mighty Hong Kong Cup, a mile and two furlong, invitation-only race, which meant a horse had to be asked to enter.

'There's a two million dollar first prize,' explained Louise, 'plus a huge bonus on offer, if you win three races in three continents. Rupert's entered Love Rat's latest wonder colt, Libertine, who won the Coolmore stakes at Flemington and the Diamond Jubilee Stakes at Royal Ascot. If he nails this one tomorrow morning, it'll mean a gigantic dollop of prize money. Having been beaten by Isa Lovell as Leading Trainer this year, Rupert's hell bent on clinching it. We'll all have a happier Christmas if he comes home victorious.'

15

'It's the Hong Kong Cup tomorrow morning,' Taggie said to Gala as they loaded the dishwasher. 'I do hope I wake in time.'

'Can't we record it?'

'We can, but Rupert loves me to watch the big races, and since Billy died,' Taggie's voice faltered, 'he . . . well, he likes to ring me immediately afterwards. I wish you'd met Billy, he was so lovely.'

Having had a scalding bath to get warm, Gala found Old Eddie fast asleep and sucking his thumb in her bed, and managed to heave him out and back into his own. Once in her bed, she was so wracked by bad dreams, she gave up and finished her latest Ian Rankin.

At four o'clock, curious to see what Rupert looked like, she put on her Uggs and six jerseys over her pyjamas and, taking Eddie's baby alarm, crept downstairs into Rupert's office and turned on *At the Races*, where the team were already revving up for an earlier race, the Hong Kong Vase. Soon a crocodile of yawning dogs filed in and clambered on to the dilapidated sofa, to keep her warm.

Gala's eyes were soon distracted, noting a big oil painting of a black Labrador and a smaller, very attractive oil of Billy Lloyd-Foxe. Everywhere were framed photographs of Rupert and Taggie's adopted children Xav and Bianca, of Rupert's daughters Tabitha and Perdita, triumphing at eventing and polo, and of the pick of his 3,400 winners at the racetrack. There was also a gorgeous photograph of Rupert and Billy laughing together at the Olympics, back in the 1970s. Rupert was certainly breathtaking then.

Suddenly she caught sight of the Stubbs and wriggled out of a duvet of dogs to examine it in more detail. *Rupert Black on Third Leopard.* She was transfixed by the glossy splendour of the horse and the arrogant beauty of his rider, the white shirt showing off the perfect jawline, the curling-brimmed hat tipped over the long, narrowed blue eyes. How seldom sex appeal travelled down the centuries, Gala thought, although Charles II always looked as though he'd be pretty exciting in bed.

And there in the portrait was Penscombe Court itself, ghostly through the trees, with swans gliding on the lake. 'Pen' was the term for a female swan – perhaps that was where the house's name originated.

Then she heard a thump of tails, followed by a step, crossed herself and nearly fainted as the ghost of Rupert Black sauntered in. Clinging on to Rupert's desk, breath coming in great gasps, she slowly digested the fact that this identical twin of the man in the painting was wearing a dinner-jacket. He had taken off his black tie, and his blond curls were spilling over his forehead and the collar of his dress shirt. His blue eyes weren't quite focusing and he was carrying a bottle of champagne.

'Hell-lo, hell-*lo*.' He had a definite American accent. 'You must be Great-grandpa's new carer. Lucky Great-grandpa. I'm Young Eddie, and I have been texted by all the guys in the yard and stud about you.' And getting a glass out of Rupert's drinks cupboard, he filled it up and handed it to her.

'It's a bit early,' stammered Gala, noticing light sneaking under the curtains.

'Or a bit late, depending on your viewpoint. Admiring the Stubbs? Lovely, isn't it? Grandpa's got another one, of mares, in the living room.'

'This one's exactly like you.' Carers weren't supposed to drink. Gala took a guilty slug.

'Exactly,' said Eddie. 'A classic case of pre-potency. Happens in horses, so why not in humans? Grandpa's even more like

83

Rupert Black than I am. The picture was on show in the National Gallery last year, and when Grandpa sauntered into the press preview followed by Banquo, no one complained about dogs not being allowed, he has such force and charisma.'

Eddie then looked at the television. 'We'd better watch this race.' Taking her hand, he pulled her down on the sofa beside him, sitting disturbingly close, with only Cuthbert, the Jack Russell, between them.

'How you getting on with Great-grandpa?' he asked.

'Learning a lot about the First and Second World Wars. He's sweet. Even when he's in bed, he tries to leap up when I come into the room.'

'Not the only thing that leaps up.' Eddie examined her, and took another slug from the bottle. 'You are well fit, Mrs Milburn. Why were you called Gala?'

'It means "rejoicing" in Old French.'

'Nice name. Under all those layers I cannot tell what shape you are, but you are definitely a M.I.L.F.' As he leaned forward to kiss her, Gala jumped away on to Gilchrist, who squeaked.

'Sorry, darling,' she apologized. Then: 'What's a M.I.L.F.?'

'Mother I would like to fuck.' Eddie's grin was so unrepentantly engaging, Gala couldn't be cross.

'Actually I'm a widow, without any children.'

'Omigod, so young, what happened to your husband?'

'He was murdered,' said Gala tonelessly.

Eddie rolled his eyes. 'I'd have murdered him to get at you.'

'It's true.' Gala was about to storm out, when he caught her hand and, being very strong, pulled her back on to the sofa.

'What happened?'

'He was trying to protect a baby rhino from a gang of poachers who'd hacked off its mother's horn, so they gunned him down.'

'Omigod.' Eddie put an arm round her shoulders and buried his lips in her rigid cheek, his light blond curls mingling with her dark blonde ones. 'You poor, poor babe. How awful. God, I'm tactless.' There was a pause. 'But I'd still like to fuck you.'

Gala was ashamed how his words cheered her.

'Where have you been?' she asked.

'To the States to see my parents and tonight to a birthday party.' He took another slug and when he tried to fill up Gala's glass and she put her fingers over it, he lingeringly licked off the spilled champagne.

'I need a carer,' he told her. 'You could bath me all day, and keep me on the straight and narrow. I've got to ride two races at Plumpton tomorrow.'

'You'd better stop drinking then, or your grandfather won't be very pleased.'

'He won't know.' Eddie glanced at the television. 'Talk of the devil.'

In a stall off the pre-parade ring, Rupert, with his back to camera, could be seen calming down the young, dapple-grey Libertine, recently off the plane and about to face the biggest, loudest crowd of his life. Then he moved on to Safety Car, rubbing him down with a damp cloth, then drying him off with a dark-blue towel, soothing him as might a boxer's second. Marketa, the big and busty Czech with huge slanting dark eyes, a red, generous mouth and thick black hair drawn into a pony tail, was brushing Safety's mane and straggly, much less thick tail and chatting to him, so he was nearly asleep by the time they saddled him up.

Rupert, Gala noticed, had the broad shoulders and long lean body perfect for an off-white suit. Then as he turned round, she gasped, 'Oh wow!' He was gorgeous. He had a much harder, stronger, less vain and self-indulgent face than his ancestor Rupert Black, and it was shown off not by lustrous curls, but slicked-back blond hair to reveal a wonderful forehead and beautifully shaped head, which he now hid with a Panama that had been hanging on a nearby palm tree.

As he, with Lark leading Libertine and Marketa leading Safety Car, set off for the parade ring, a cluster of press in Day-Glo yellow waistcoats swooped like canaries, then fluttered off without a word as Rupert stalked straight through them.

'Grandpa loathes the press,' said Eddie. 'Look – he's wearing his lucky blue tie and his lucky blue and green striped shirt. He gets spooked without them. Taggie has to wash the shirt before every race day.'

The cameras were now concentrating on impossibly shiny and beautiful horses being led round the parade ring, and showing glimpses of the lovely racecourse surrounded by sea, emerald-green woods, and buildings soaring to a sky bluer than Rupert's tie.

'Who's riding Libertine?' asked Gala.

'Lion O'Connor, Grandpa's stable jockey. He's very conscientious, watches a video of every runner in every race, leaves footprints all over the track where he's walked the course a hundred times to see where the good ground is. Always does his homework, unlike me; lacks the killer instinct, also unlike me. Old Teddy Matthews, a geriatric living in Hong Kong and who used to work for Grandpa, is riding Safety Car, who's 100–1. It's probably Safety's last race. He's nearly eleven.'

The huge crowds were ever increasing, the women in pretty dresses but hatless, the men wearing baseball caps. Many spectators had bizarrely dressed up as horses, or mice topped with huge nodding heads, big teeth and staring eyes, enough to spook any horse. Gala herself was spooked to see so many affluent Chinese, conjuring up visions of Zixin Wang who would never come to trial for Ben's death. She began to tremble uncontrollably.

Unaware of the reason, drawing her towards him, Eddie kissed her lips, long and so lovingly that she found herself no longer worrying if she'd cleaned her teeth recently enough, and parting her lips and kissing him back.

Then she opened her eyes and found his were open and looking at the television. As she furiously wriggled away from him, Eddie laughed. 'Oh, Mrs M.I.L.F. Milburn, I'm taking a look at Grandpa's enemies.'

He pointed at a trio in the paddock: a short young man with oiled black curls, a pale demonic, dissipated face and large black rolling eyes, and a taller, thinner, older man – also very dark with a sallow, closed gypsy face. They were talking to a jockey wearing silks that were magenta and red as a drop of blood.

'That nasty threesome,' explained Eddie, 'is Cosmo Rannaldini, shit and slimeball whose father Roberto was a great conductor but so evil he was murdered. Must be catching, joke, joke, joke.' Eddie slid a sidelong glance at Gala, who commented on Cosmo's lack of inches.

'That's why he likes racing – people assume he's an ex-jockey. And that's his trainer, Isa Lovell, another shit, who worked with Grandpa, then stole all his ideas when he left to set up his own yard and stud. They both dissed Grandpa recently because their stallion Roberto's Revenge is higher up the Leading Sire list than Love Rat, saying Grandpa was a has-been and that you could see the rust. Then Cosmo made some fatuous joke about "Roberto's Revenge first, the Rust nowhere".

'That's Tarquin McGall, their stable jockey. He's bloody good but must be costing them a fortune. He fights dirty, sharpens his elbows, pushes you into the rails and uses his whip to hit other people's horses coming upsides, plus he's always pinching people's rides. He's the Go-to Jockey for the big occasion, big horses in big races. *He* wouldn't need to go to Plumpton on a freezing Monday morning.'

Gala could hear the longing and envy in Eddie's voice.

'Cosmo's spending zillions on horses, building up a huge arsenal to go to war with. Grandpa's trying to find out who's backing him.'

Then, as a beautiful middle-aged woman in a sea-green dress and turquoise hat, graciously waving her tail like Mother Jaguar from a *Just So* story, joined the trio: 'Now that's another M.I.L.F. – Mrs Walton, Cosmo's Squeeze. She's one of the mothers at the boarding school he only left four years ago. She fancies Grandpa, so does Cosmo's mother, some godawful opera singer.'

Next moment, Mrs Walton had broken away from the group to talk to Rupert and kiss him on both cheeks.

'If Grandpa lifted a finger,' said Eddie, 'she'd drop Cosmo like a mistakenly picked up adder. Look how furious he is. Grandpa's Book of Mares is longer than the Chinese phone book.'

Gala laughed and longed to ask if Rupert ever cheated on Taggie. Instead she said: 'Taggie's so sweet.'

'She's a saint, not a mean bone in her beautiful body. Everyone imposes on her, me included.'

'I hope I can make her life easier.'

'You have already, particularly if you tell her exactly what happens in this race, so she can pretend she has watched it when Rupert rings up. He hates her missing big races.'

They were interrupted by a voice quavering, 'Gala, Gala, where are you, darling?'

'It's the ghost of Rupert Black,' said Eddie in a sepulchral voice.

'Stop it.' Gala had been frozen with horror for a second. 'It's your great-grandfather on the monitor – I must go to him.'

But as Gala leapt up, Eddie pulled her back. 'Leave him, he'll go back to sleep. You've got to brief Taggie about the race.'

'I can hear heavy breathing.'

'That's Banquo, he often sleeps on Great-grandpa's bed.'

Next moment a snore rent the air.

'What did I tell you, M.I.L.F.?'

'Do you have a girlfriend?'

'Sort of. She has a baby of fifteen months – and no, it's not mine; it's always waking her up in the night so she gets tired, particularly as she's trying to get four starred A-levels to help her get into Oxford. She's only eighteen, very pretty but much too bright for me. I'd still like to fuck you. Which guys do you fancy in the yard?'

'I really don't know any of them. Michael Meagan's very friendly and Pat is really nice. What about the dark one, who never smiles or hardly speaks to anyone?'

'Gavin Latton. Mr Lean and Moody, destroyed by a nympho wife. He used to work for Isa, and found her in bed with Cosmo and two jockeys. Genius with horses. He sorted out Libertine; most women want to sort *him* out. He's madly intellectual for a horse guy, reads a lot, got on really well with Trixie, my girl-friend. But you'd have more fun with me.' Eddie filled up both their glasses.

'He started off working in the stud here, then Grandpa moved him over mostly to the yard; there's a terrific rivalry between stud and yard, a lot of backstabbing. Yard earn more in pool money, which is a percentage of any winnings. Stud only get £50 extra for every mare covered.'

Images of the great silver cup and the colours of the jockeys were imposed on the track as the runners went down to the start, led by Chinese riders in red coats, white breeches and black boots.

'Much cooler than those lumps on carthorses who ferry you down to post in the States,' said Eddie. 'Safety Car and Libertine will think they're out with the Cotswold.'

Lion's legs were hanging down out of the stirrups to calm a sweating, cavorting Libertine.

'That's Safety Car. Grandpa's pet.'

'Why does he love him so much?'

'He was off for seventeen months with tendon problems, practically lived in the house then won race after race. Titus was so jealous because everyone loves Safety that he bit his ear and most of his tail off, but it worked in the opposite direction; now racegoers all over the world recognize Safety because of his one ear and tail, and cheer him on. He's so kind. He's been flown out to calm Libertine and act as his pacemaker.

'Isa's using a very good horse, Nero Tolerance, as a pacemaker for Feud for Thought. Ironically, both Libertine and Feud for Thought have frightful draws in double figures but Safety Car's got the best draw, and he's 100–1. I've put £100 on him. He won't win, but look at the old moke still in his winter coat.'

'Like me,' said Gala.

The huge starting gates, with a tractor attached to lug them to different parts of the course, looked like a giant bus whose windows darkened as each horse was led into its stall. Libertine, way out in Stall 14, neighed anxiously to Safety Car in Stall 1.

'After Feud for Thought beating Dardanius in the Derby, it matters so much to Grandpa that Libertine beats the shit out of Feud for Thought today.' For once Eddie sounded serious.

'Why do you call him Grandpa?'

'To remind him of his age – mustn't let him get too cocky.'

A deafening roar, the gates crashed open and they were off. Isa's pacemaker Nero Tolerance set off at a cracking speed. Safety Car, despite his emerging winter coat, took advantage of his brilliant draw, hugging the rails, stripping off the paint, while both Libertine and Feud for Thought got stuck behind a cliff of horses, which soon included Nero Tolerance, who'd run out of puff.

Although Safety Car's wily old jockey could see the huge black shadows of rivals creeping up menacingly on the left as the rest of the field wrestled to overtake him, Safety, drawing away, battled on, refusing to give up. 'He's looking forward to the pint of beer in his feed when he gets back. Come on, Safety!' yelled Eddie.

And Safety, finding more and more, giving everything he was capable of, kept going, until he staggered first past a winning post, fantastically garlanded with flowers.

'Fucking marvellous, what a heart! Given himself enough time to choose one for his button-hole,' whooped Eddie.

Libertine, son of Love Rat, seeing Safety Car's straggly tail and reassuring dark-brown rump surging ahead, rallied and came second. Safety Car, however, was so exhausted, he crashed into the rails, and a sobbing, deliriously happy Marketa had, in between steadying hugs, to drench him with buckets of water until he recovered.

While Eddie and Gala had been yelling their heads off, so had the lads at Penscombe, who had been watching televisions in stud and tack room. Libertine, Love Rat's colt, had won $500,000, Safety Car more than $2,000,000, 5 per cent of which would be divided among them. Rupert, who'd put ten grand on Safety Car at 100–1 was ecstatically punching the air. Teddy Matthews could be seen crying with joy, both over a wonderful win and the fact that, as the jockey, he'd netted a 10 per cent $200,000.

'He and Safety can both retire,' said Eddie.

'And the *Racing Post*'s got the perfect headline: SAFETY FIRST,' giggled Gala.

Robert Cooper from *At the Races* had been trying to interview Rupert all day. Now grumbling: 'He's bound to push off to his hotel,' he was amazed when a euphoric Rupert almost hugged him, saying what a wonderful servant Safety Car had been to the yard, and how brilliantly Teddy had ridden him, and how Love Rat's son Libertine had come second.

He then delivered some withering put-downs about Valhalla's horses: 'Such a long way to come to get nowhere,' and happily posed for photographs with Safety Car, Libertine and their jockeys and stable lasses, Marketa and Lark.

God, he's handsome when he's happy, marvelled an unwillingly captivated Gala.

As a bell rang in the yard announcing a win, the telephone went: Rupert calling to compare joyous notes with Taggie. Eddie kept him talking while Gala rushed upstairs and, frantically apologizing for not waking her before, dragged Taggie out of the shower and gave her the glorious news. A dripping Taggie then rushed downstairs wrapped in a scarlet towel.

'Didn't they run brilliantly, darling Safety Car, darling Libertine, darling Teddy Matthews – give him my love,' she cried, crossing her fingers, then jabbering with apology because she and Rupert had rowed before he left, she was so sorry, she loved him so much, and Rupert was obviously saying how much he loved her. Taggie came off the telephone, tearful yet starry-eyed, like a moonbow at night.

'Some of the horses are going on to Singapore,' she told Gala and Eddie, 'and some are going on to Dubai. Libertine and Safety Car are coming home so we've got to greet them with a hero's welcome. Must go and give Love Rat a carrot, he'll probably be asleep. Rupert's whizzing up to China to follow up some of Valent's contacts. He'll be home around the twentieth – God, how blissful.'

Hearing the adoration in Taggie's voice, Gala was wiped out by longing for a lost Ben, who would never come home.

Seeing all those Chinese crowds only reinforced the fact that she'd never be able to prove Zixin Wang was behind the poachers' raid and bring him to justice. Tearing upstairs, her heart aching far more than her legs, she had just thrown herself sobbing on her bed, when Old Eddie's voice crackled on to the monitor.

'Gala, darling, I need a pee.'

So she laughed instead. At least someone needed her.

16

Young Eddie Alderton won neither of his jump races at Plumpton. Safety Car, Libertine, Marketa, Lark and Cathal returned to their hero's welcome. Gala buried herself in work and watched military programmes with Old Eddie, as she addressed hundreds more Christmas cards adorned with Love Rat's photograph and wrapped up endless presents she had helped Taggie buy on a trip to Cheltenham. Here she had nearly fainted over the variety and beauty of the clothes, but resisted buying anything. She mustn't waste money when her sister in South Africa needed it.

Christmas was the worst time to be missing Ben – with all the loving kindness of Christmas and the shops ringing with carols and songs.

'Last Christmas, I gave you my heart, and the very next day Wang took you away.'

She worked endless hours in the hope of being tired enough to sleep at night, and on her break she kept on wandering down to both the stud and the yard armed with Polos, so that all the horses were soon whickering in welcome. She also sneaked a glance at Gavin Latton, who was very attractive but still totally ignored her.

And she'd never been so cold. It gnawed into her soul, particularly when the temperature dropped and an icy wind howled up the valley from the Bristol Channel. She put on more jerseys, and with Rupert coming home soon, she'd have liked to have shed her spare tyres, but couldn't diet in such weather.

All the horses were inside except Safety Car, who kicked his box out when they tried to stable him, insisting on staying outside, heavily rugged-up with his six sheep friends. Rupert was due home on the twenty-first.

On 20 December it started snowing at lunchtime, and kept on snowing like a thief stealing the landscape, flakes pouring down like the plucked and swirling feathers of the doves that raided Taggie's bird-table. Gala, who had never seen snow before, was so excited she forgot the cold and raced round the garden trying to catch enough flakes to make a snowball.

The lads had checked if Safety Car was OK and, when he still refused to come in, they had gone off to a party in the next-door village and failed to get back through the blizzards and drifts. Nor could Taggie, who'd gone to cook her parents' supper across the valley.

Gala was so shattered that, having tucked up Old Eddie, she collapsed into bed, Ian Rankin almost immediately falling out of her hands. Her prayers that she'd be spared nightmares, however, seemed shot to pieces when she was aroused by a thundering on her door, which became more and more insistent. Groggily staggering to answer it, Gala found an enraged Rupert.

'Get up! Where the fuck is everyone? I need you outside – who the hell are you?'

He had arrived, not even bothering to log a flight-path, landing the helicopter suicidally dangerously in a raging blizzard and three feet of drifting snow.

'What's happened, what's the matter?' asked Gala.

'Get dressed and come down to the yard. Where's Taggie?'

'Gone to stay with her parents.'

'Where are the lads?'

'Gone to some party.'

'Well, hurry up for Christ's sake, and bring any duvet you can find.'

Gala grabbed every garment in her wardrobe, put them over her pyjamas and tugged Eddie's green woolly hat over her rumpled curls. Having not bothered to remove last night's mascara and eyeliner, her eyes were smudged like a panda. Oh, what did it matter!

Outside the front door she plunged into a wall of snow, flakes still hurtling down, a vicious east wind chucking crushed icicles in her face. Rupert's beechwoods soared like the Cliffs of Dover.

Slipping and sliding, the snow filling up her Uggs, she found Rupert and Gav in the yard breaking ice on water buckets with hammers and putting extra rugs on shivering horses. As Rupert snatched the duvets from her, there was an almighty crash followed by terrified bleating and neighing.

'Safety Car!' yelled Rupert. 'Christ, he's not still outside?'

Racing down to the paddock, he, Gav and Gala found that a huge sycamore branch, thick as a trunk, had collapsed, trapping Safety Car and his six sheep inside his three-sided field shelter with a buckling corrugated roof the only thing preventing the branch from crushing them all to death. One of the three sides had already caved in, scattering bricks over the sheep. Safety Car, pinned down on his side, gave a faint whicker and tried to scramble up as Rupert approached.

'No boy, stay still.' Rupert knelt down and stroked him. 'Get some ACP,' he hissed as he steadied the terrified animal, comforting him until Gavin rushed back with an injection to plunge into his veins. While this was kicking in, Rupert ordered Gala to slowly and delicately remove the fallen bricks, chucking them into the snow, enabling the sheep that weren't dead to wriggle free and bound off. Then he told Gala to take over from him.

Safety Car's big donkey ear was drooping. Feeling how cold it was, Gala hugged him, wiping snow out of his half-closed eyes. Despite being doped, he was growing more restless, particularly as another sheep wriggled free and bounded off.

'You'll be next. It's all right, good old boy,' Gala told him.

His shoulders were still trapped under the biggest branch, which Rupert and Gavin, their hands bleeding, were struggling to lift clear. Leaving Safety Car for a moment, Gala, proud of her strength, joined them in their struggles, but still none of them could shift the branch a centimetre.

Then, miraculously, Roving Mike, Cathal and Meerkat – all reeking of drink – rolled up, having waded across the fields. Meerkat was despatched to make Safety up a big bed, the other two roped in to help lift. Swearing, they all managed to raise the great branch a couple of inches.

'Hope to Christ he hasn't broken anything,' muttered Rupert.

But to prove he was OK, Safety Car grappled for a grip on the frozen snow with his unshod feet, plunged forward, ignoring cries of 'Steady, boy!', slipped then lurched upwards, swaying violently. Then everyone gave a cheer as he staggered to freedom.

'Everyone out!' bawled Rupert and glanced round to see they all were, as he and Gav let go of the biggest branch and both leapt forward to grab Safety Car's head collar on either side. 'You're coming inside for once, you old bugger,' said Rupert as, slipping and sliding, they guided the huge horse, swaying like a drunkard, to one of the foaling boxes, where straw had been spread over the floor and up the walls.

'Not deep enough,' Rupert said curtly, then to Gala: 'Go and rustle up more duvets from the house. Where are you going, Gav? Get Safety some mash and put a pint of beer in it.'

To Gala's amazement, Gav sharply told Rupert to ask one of the other lads. He was off to rescue any remaining sheep.

By the time Gala had staggered back with the duvets, Gavin had returned carrying the last survivor, a young ewe, too cold and tired to be frightened, and laid her bleating beside Safety Car, who nudged her and whickered sleepily.

'She'll comfort the old boy, Guv,' insisted Gav.

Having instructed another lad to make up Safety Car's mash with a pint of beer, he crouched down beside the old horse, reassuring him and raking his mane.

More lads had got through and were shovelling away the snow on pathways to the stable doors and chucking down rock salt to melt the ice. The horses were now whinnying and stamping impatiently.

'They need feeding,' ordered Rupert.

'They can wait ten minutes,' said Gav, getting up. 'Gala's frozen stiff.'

He knows my name, thought Gala in amazement. Her hands were so numb, she couldn't feel his fingers as he took hers and led her through the snow back to the kitchen up at the house, pushing her against the Aga, and putting on a kettle.

'Well done.' He was stammering again. 'Have you had horses?'

'Lots, but not in the snow. Easier in Africa.'

Gavin made two cups of black coffee, added a tablespoonful of sugar in each, and had just opened a bottle of brandy when Rupert stalked in and raised an eyebrow.

'Only in mine,' blurted out Gala through chattering teeth as Gavin poured a huge slug into her cup.

'What are you doing here anyway?' demanded Rupert. 'Are you a friend of Tab's?'

'I'm your father's carer.'

'Doesn't need one – whose idea was that?'

'Mrs Campbell-Black didn't want to worry you, but he was asked to leave the Home. He's so pleased to be back, like an escaped prisoner of war.'

Goodness, Rupert's glance could freeze far more than the weather. Gala scalded her mouth on a great gulp of coffee.

'Gala, Gala.' Eddie, clad only in a pyjama top, wandered into the kitchen. 'Are you coming back to bed, darling? It's very cold.'

'Oh fuck off, Dad. Take him back to bed, Gav,' said Rupert impatiently. Then, looking Gala up and down, 'Wonder if he'll propose to my mother on Christmas Day. He usually does, even though she's been dead for years.'

Gala glanced up at a new photograph on the dresser, of a jubilant Rupert with his arm round Safety Car after the Hong Kong Cup, and said, 'Thank God we saved him.'

'Did you see the race?'

'I watched it with Young Eddie.'

'Who's even worse behaved than my father.'

How unnerving he is, thought Gala. He must be twenty-odd years older than her. His face was seamed with tiredness yet he was the best-looking man she had ever seen, and quite the most high-handed, particularly when he brusquely ordered her to go upstairs, 'And sort out my father – and send Gav down at once. I need him in the yard.'

Ungrateful sod, stormed Gala, tempted to break off one of the icicles hanging from the gutter and ram it into him.

As she wearily climbed the stairs, she could see out of the landing window a huge red sun, firing the frozen lake, turning the white fields to rose, arrogant like Rupert, as if it were entirely responsible for such a beautiful day.

Upstairs, she discovered Gav putting a spare rug over Old Eddie, who had fallen asleep.

'Thank you,' he said. 'You did well.'

'More than your bloody boss thinks.' In the mirror, she caught a glimpse of herself: red-faced, woolly-hatted, mascara smudged. Then, ignoring Gav's finger to his lips: 'What a bastard! He's the most insufferably arrogant, ungrateful sod I've ever met, and he wants you back downstairs. Oh my God,' as Gav pointed towards Eddie's alarm. Rupert, if he was still in the kitchen, must have heard every word.

17

Alas, Simmy Halliday, the Estate Manager, had just joined Rupert in the kitchen and overheard Gala's outburst, details of which were instantly and gleefully texted round yard and stud.

The first Gala knew was when she was tipped off by a delighted Geraldine.

'Rather unwise of you to slag off the boss. He does call the shots and he's never been a fan of any of Eddie's carers.'

Gala started to shake. Oh God, would Rupert fire her? She had nowhere else to go and she'd been as happy as possible at Penscombe before he arrived.

A hellish day followed. After an interrupted night, Eddie was uncharacteristically difficult, rejecting his favourite shepherd's pie for lunch, constantly ringing his bell for the television to be changed, sulking because Gala thought the paths were too dangerously icy for him to visit Love Rat.

Matters weren't helped by Taggie ringing up full of apologies. She'd be home after giving her parents lunch. Meanwhile could Gala possibly feed the dogs and the birds, break the ice on the bird-bath and start Rupert's favourite, Beef Wellington, for supper.

'He likes the beef coated in pâté before you wrap it in pastry.'

Unlike his grandson Eddie, Rupert didn't surrender to jet lag nor snowdrift, and in a frenzy he swept through the yard, far fiercer than last night's killer gale from the west.

One of Simmy Halliday's tractor drivers had already cleared the yard and stud of snow; another, towing a gritter behind a farm buggy, was laying down grit. By ten, the snowplough attached to a tractor had cleared the gallops for first lot.

One could appreciate Rupert's ability to toughen up his horses as, in a 4 x 4 with the window open, he watched them storm up the all-weather; or later, as, clipboard in hand, he clocked them cantering round the covered ride, calling out differing instructions to the riders of apparently identical dark-brown or dark bay horses: even though he'd been away a month, knowing exactly what each one should do.

Despite the snow falling relentlessly, Rupert insisted each stallion was walked out several miles, getting fit for the covering season in February. Inspecting any foal bought at the sales, he in turn demanded why Cosmo Rannaldini had been allowed to snap up some brilliant filly.

Back in the office, he was delighted by the mares lined up for Love Rat and all the other stallions including Dardanius, who was about to start his first season. After Libertine's second in Hong Kong, Rupert ordered that Love Rat's stud fee should be raised by £10,000.

Hearing dire forecasts of full-scale blizzards bringing the country to a halt, staff members kept ringing to say they couldn't make it in. Whereupon Rupert dispatched Simmy Halliday in a four-wheel drive to gather them up. In the process, he found Celeste being pleasured by Brute Barraclough and Young Eddie similarly enjoying Marketa, then pleading, 'For God's sake, don't say anything to Trixie.'

In the afternoon, the snow stopped. A shaft of silver sunlight caressed the valley and Gala gave in to Old Eddie's pestering and, wrapping him up, she crackled with him across the frozen lawn. The snowplough, chugging along the top road, was putting up fountains of white. The lads on their break were making a snowman.

'Bugger!' cried Gala, as she stubbed her toe on a frozen molehill. She was just clinging on to Old Eddie for support when they went slap into Rupert, with Cuthbert, one of the

Jack Russells, perched like a parrot on his shoulder.

'Where the hell do you think you're going?'

'Your father wanted to see Love Rat.'

'Don't be so bloody silly. Broken hip is all he needs. Go back inside.'

Safety Car was equally fed up to be confined to his box, particularly when the mares were released, and, racing into the field, they rolled and rolled in the snow.

Desperate to see Taggie after so long a separation, Rupert had sent the gritter over to his in-laws' house across the valley to fetch her. Gala had stoked up the fire in the kitchen and was putting the finishing touches to the Beef Wellington when Taggie walked in looking lit up and utterly beautiful and, Gala realized, unusually wearing blusher and eye make-up. Her hair was still wet from the shower and she smelled of Eau D'Issey and toothpaste.

Next minute, Rupert came loping across the yard. They met in the hall.

'Oh, how heavenly to see you.'

'Christ, I've missed you.'

Followed by a long pause when they were obviously locked in a passionate embrace. Next moment they were racing upstairs, and the bedroom door banged, then opened again to let in a whining Forester, who'd been missing his mistress, and then the door slammed shut again.

God, it was cold. As she washed firelighter off her hands, Gala felt stabbed with envy. She took some chocolate cake and a cup of tea to Old Eddie, who was watching a porn film and gazing out of the window.

'I used to skate on that lake when I was a boy . . .'

Even Rupert and Taggie's bedroom was arctic. Forester crawled under the duvet as Rupert drew it up, reluctant to lose sight of his wife's adorable body.

'That was so lovely,' sighed Taggie. 'Until one has sex, one doesn't realize how much one has missed it.'

'I do,' said Rupert, pulling her head into the crook of his arm, his fingertips stroking her breast. 'So, what's Dad doing back home?'

'He got sacked from Ashbourne House.'

Rupert laughed when Taggie told him the reason.

'Why didn't you tell me?'

'I didn't want to worry you.'

'Where did you find that woman?'

'She's Zimbabwean, from the same agency. She's wonderful, Rupert, and absolutely sweet. We've done nearly all the staff and family Christmas presents, we've filled up the deep freeze for the office party and written nearly all the Christmas cards. She faked your signature so we could get the abroad ones off.'

'She'll be signing my cheques next – did you give her my pin number?'

'Everyone adores her, even Titus Andronicus. She's sweet.'

'You think everyone's sweet, but you're the sweet one. God, you're beautiful . . .' Feeling her nipple budding beneath his fingers, Rupert was tempted to make love to her again but it was dark outside and he still needed to check on Safety Car, ring Valent about China, and Evening Stables called.

'How was China? How did you manage not speaking Chinese?'

'I typed into my iPhone where I wanted to go, Google translated it into Chinese and I showed it to the taxi driver. Funny country – they all want to meet the Queen and play polo with William and Harry. I met a ridiculously rich aeroplane billionaire interested in buying horses, and another even richer one who only likes dealing with people born in the Year of the Monkey so I had to lie about my age.'

Taggie squinted up at him. 'You look wonderful, you don't need to lie about anything. I missed you so much.'

Kicked off the bed, Forester sighed. They were at it again, fat chance of him getting his supper for a bit.

In the kitchen, Gala made patterns in the Beef Wellington pastry and painted it up with beaten egg, ready to go in the oven. Then she cooked the rest of the egg, with smoked salmon for Eddie whose teeth weren't that good. As she took it upstairs, Forester was being let out of Rupert and Taggie's room.

She felt utterly exhausted. She didn't like Rupert but she must try and win him over, as she couldn't bear to go back to mad old ladies in draughty houses. Oh God, she'd forgotten to feed his dogs. Running downstairs, she gave a scream of horror.

Taking matters into his own paws, Forester had pulled the Beef Wellington on to the floor and, aided by Banquo and the other dogs, had wolfed the lot, except for the mushrooms, which Cuthbert was spitting out.

Oh help! Such a lovely piece of beef – Taggie would murder her. Fleeing to the pantry, Gala unearthed one of the lasagnes she'd made for the office party from the freezer and rammed it in the microwave.

She'd better check the fire and feed the badgers while the dogs were all safely inside. She was in the pantry clutching a bowl of leftovers when Rupert and Taggie, on hearing her shriek of horror, had dressed and come down into the kitchen.

Seeing three places laid for dinner, Gala heard Rupert say, 'Christ, she doesn't have to dine with us, does she? None of the other boots did.'

'She's not at all a boot,' protested Taggie. 'We've had supper together since she's been here.'

'She wouldn't want to have dinner with us, she thinks I'm an arrogant sod.'

Gala could hide no longer and emerged from the pantry.

'I'm desperately sorry,' she gabbled. 'I was late feeding the dogs and I'm afraid Forester got the Beef Wellington. I'm so sorry. I hope it's OK. I got one of the office party lasagnes out of the freezer and I've made a salad. I'll make another lasagne tomorrow.'

'Oh well done!' cried Taggie. 'Poor you, naughty Forester, it couldn't matter less. Have an enormous drink.'

Although she was gagging for one, steeling herself not to cry, Gala said: 'Actually I'm going to watch a bit of television with Eddie, if that's all right, then I'll put him to bed. I'm not hungry, honestly. You must have so much to catch up on, so I'll see you in the morning. Good night,' and she fled.

Appalled, Taggie turned to Rupert. 'She must've heard everything we said. Oh poor Gala and no supper.'

'Do her good to lose some weight.'

'She's not fat, she's just cold and wearing a thousand layers.

I'm sure she heard. Please, please, Rupert, go and get her. She lit the fire for us, she's a widow and lost everything and had such a terrible time.'

'I don't care.' Rupert poured a large whisky and opened a bottle of Sancerre for Taggie. 'I don't want to know.'

'Please, *please*, Rupert.'

Upstairs, Gala sat on her bed trying to cry quietly. 'Oh Ben, oh Ben.' If only she could feel his arms around her once more.

Next moment, the door opened and Banquo trotted in, jumping on to the bed beside her, licking away her tears as she flung her arms around his kind, solid body. His thick black tail slapped the bed as Rupert joined them, holding out a large vodka and tonic. Seeing Gala's eyes swollen with crying, he thought once again how plain she was.

'I'm sorry, I'm bloody short of sleep, I guess. Tag says you're doing a wonderful job and have been a real help to her. My father's fast asleep, even Cindy Bolton's latest DVD can't keep him awake. Please come down and have some supper. I can't have you seducing my dog.'

Gala half laughed. 'You wouldn't want to dine with a boot!'

'You're different,' said Rupert. 'You're the Beef Wellington Boot.'

18

Apart from the crucifying cold, Gala had been gradually mending and finding happiness at Penscombe. That all changed with Rupert's return.

After a brief rapprochement on his first evening, not only was she aware that her presence irked him, because he wanted Taggie to himself, but their obvious love and need to touch each other only made her own loss worse.

So Gala kept her distance, having meals in her room or with Old Eddie, not addressing any remarks to Rupert, edging past him with lowered eyes. It was hard to avoid him, however, when the staff speculated about him the whole time, pestering her with questions.

'Does he ever switch off? He was working in his office at four this morning. What does he talk about? It must be hard not being able to wander round his own house naked, or leave the loo door unlocked.'

Gala, having been overheard describing Rupert as 'an ungrateful sod', kept her trap shut, until one day a glamorous but rather raddled blonde dropped in when Rupert and Taggie were out. After greeting Old Eddie with affection, she introduced herself as Janey Lloyd-Foxe, a very old friend of the family, poured herself a large drink and began quizzing Gala, who was ironing in the kitchen.

'So you're Eddie's exciting new carer. Rupert was awful, he

referred to earlier ones as the boots and wished he could use the boot-rack in the hall to scrape them off. He must be thrilled with you.'

Gala said nothing, edging the iron down the blue and green striped sleeves into the cuffs.

'What's it like living in the house of the handsomest man in England? You must fancy him rotten.'

'He's miles too old for me,' retorted Gala

'Rochester was miles older than Jane Eyre,' teased Janey.

'Well, in this instance, frankly I much prefer Mrs Rochester.'

'Ah, the sainted Taggie.' There was an edge to Janey's voice. 'And you're about to burn that shirt.'

'Eddie wants the loo,' yelled Dora from the hall. So hastily Gala switched off the iron, snatched up any ironed shirts and fled. Grabbing her arm, Dora bustled her upstairs.

'Eddie doesn't,' she whispered. 'I was just rescuing you. Janey Lloyd-Foxe is an absolute bitch and the most dangerous journalist in the universe. She was married to Rupert's best friend, Billy, a saint, who died. She and Rupert don't get on and she is always trying to dish the dirt on him. Half my job as his press officer is spent seeing her off. She wanted to come for Christmas but he's banished her.'

'She was banging on about him being the handsomest man in England,' confided Gala, as they reached the landing.

'Well, he was to die for.' Dora pointed to a painting on the wall of a naked Rupert, slim and leggy as a yearling, lying asleep in a crimson four-poster. 'That four-poster boy portrait was painted by my father's first wife, a complete slag, a million years ago. She and Rupert had a terrific affair, long before he was even married to his first wife Helen. He's lush now but not as good-looking as my boyfriend Paris. You must come and have spag bol with us when he is back and you get a night off.'

As Christmas and the New Year passed, despite avoiding Rupert, who spent more time in the yard when he was at home, Gala found herself increasingly drawn to the stud. In her break, she was always sloping down to make friends with the stallions and gossiping with Pat Inglis, the Stallion Master. Broad-shouldered, stocky, red-haired, freckle-faced, with knowing, watchful yellow eyes, despite being happily married with three young children, Pat had an eye for the ladies and a slick line in repartee.

'That's the second biggest thing I've had in my hand today,' he told her as he washed down Love Rat's cock.

An excellent stock man, he also knew if animals were right. Although he adored his charges, he warned Gala: 'Never turn your back on a stallion, they're not to be trusted. In the old days, girls were never allowed to do colts.'

Gala hubristically persisted, however, with carrots and Polos, and was enchanted when even the psychopath Titus Andronicus whickered at her approach.

'How do you control him when you walk him out?' she asked Pat.

'With a chain through his mouth, which hurts like hell if you tug it.'

As well as Love Rat, Old Eddie loved going down to the stud to chat up Vanessa, known as Gee Gee which stood for Gentle Giantess because she was six foot, Junoesque and considered strong enough to look after the more biddable stallions. Meerkat, Rupert's second jockey, who was only five foot two, had a massive crush on her.

Once the covering season began, things became frantically busy with stallions expected to cover up to three times a day and mares who poured in from all over the world to board. An added problem was that they couldn't be put to their allotted stallion unless they were ovulating, which caused endless log-jams, and overcrowding of the car park.

'I'm fed up with being sworn at by French lorry drivers,' grumbled Roving Mike.

'I think they're lush,' simpered nympho Celeste. 'They can overnight in my room at the hostel any time.'

One slightly milder morning, instead of real snow, drifts of snowdrops spread across the lawn and the pale-blue sky reflected in the lake, beside which a group of Rupert's two-year-old fillies were ecstatically frolicking and guzzling their first grass in weeks.

Seeing Rupert by the covering barn, deep in conversation with Pat and Meerkat, Gala avoided the stud and wheeled Eddie back to the yard, where he loved to ogle the stable lasses. Here they found Fleance, one of Rupert's most exciting two-year-olds, a pure white, son of Love Rat and just back from the gallops. He had been tied up outside his box by Celeste.

Next minute Roving Mike, who had the hots for Celeste, rolled up and they both dived into Fleance's box, leaving the colt outside. It was not warm enough. Gala's lips pursed with disapproval. A second later, she was distracted by Titus Andronicus prowling by on his morning walk, towing along a very nervous stud hand. As keen for a shag as Michael and Celeste, Titus caught sight of the fillies by the lake. Bellowing with excitement, he went up on his hind legs, punching the air. Then, tugging the latch chain out of the lad's hands, he took off across the fields towards them.

Poor little fillies! Without thought, leaving Eddie in his wheelchair, Gala untied Fleance and, jumping on his back, with only a head collar to guide him, she hurtled out of the yard towards the lake, riding effortlessly in perfect harmony with the colt. She'd never been on anything so fast: joy overwhelmed her.

'Come on, Fleance! Come on!'

They were gaining on Titus who, endangering his manhood, cleared a fence into the field by the lake. At that moment, hearing her shouting, Rupert, Pat and Meerkat had come out of the covering barn (where for once Love Rat had performed quickly and effortlessly) and saw Gala thundering by.

'What the fuck?' yelled Rupert.

'My God,' said Pat. 'Titus has got loose.'

'Titus, Titus,' called a panting Gala.

Fortunately, as he reached the lake, Titus was pegged by rushes and she was able to catch up with him. Grabbing him, three tons of gleaming black muscle, just before he reached the fillies, Gala leapt off and set Fleance free. To her relief, Titus was then distracted by a swan flapping its wings on the bank and Gala's pockets were bulging with chopped carrots with which she just managed to mollify him until Pat, ashen beneath his freckles, pounded up.

'Thank Christ,' he panted, grabbing the latch chain, then as Titus reared up again: 'All right, laddie, calm down . . . Where in hell did you learn to ride like that?'

'I used to race a bit in Zim.'

'Bloody marvellous, well done. You OK?'

'Fine, I'll go and get Fleance,' who had wandered off to chat up the fillies and who was delighted with the rest of Gala's carrots.

'Well done!' cried Meerkat excitedly as Gala cantered Fleance back to them. 'You ride great, doesn't she, Rupert?'

But Rupert was looking at Fleance then at his stopwatch.

'That colt's trained on bloody well. He's just been twice up the gallops and now given a lot of weight and a beating to Titus, one of the fastest horses in the world. I know Titus is let down and not fit, but Fleance's definitely on for the Guineas.'

'Only if you put Gala up,' reproved Meerkat, who wasn't a bit frightened of Rupert. 'You ought to be more grateful. Gala's just saved you, your prized fillies and Fleance, and Titus' bollocks into the bargain.'

'She did,' acknowledged Rupert. 'If you lost a stone or two, you might be able to ride out.' Then, patting Fleance: 'This is a serious horse.'

'Roo-pert!' reproved Pat and Meerkat in unison, as a furious Gala swung round and cantered Fleance back to his box, outside of which she found Old Eddie ogling Celeste, who had just emerged zipping up her jeans, followed by Roving Mike, tucking in his shirt-tails.

'Oh, so *there's* Fleance,' said Celeste accusingly. 'What are you doing on him? You should have put on a rug.'

I hate Celeste, I loathe Rupert, thought Gala as she tackled another mountain of ironing that afternoon and miserably ate her way through a packet of chocolate biscuits. Hearing a step, she shoved the biscuit packet under the clothes she'd done and continued to iron one of Rupert's shirts.

'Where's Taggie?' asked Rupert, as he wandered in, followed by his pack of dogs who greeted Gala with noisy affection.

'Gone to Cheltenham.'

Rupert had been about to thank her for stopping Titus, but seeing she was ironing his blue and green striped lucky shirt, he snapped: 'For Christ's sake, don't burn it!'

'Iron it yourself then.' As she switched off the iron, gathering up the clothes, Banquo, with his Labrador nose, tugged out the three-quarter empty packet of chocolate biscuits which had melted all over Old Eddie's underpants and Rupert's dress shirt, which he was supposed to be wearing for a dinner that night.

'You won't ride out if you keep guzzling those.'

'Oh fuck off,' muttered Gala, stomping off upstairs.

Word, however, had got round about her courage and enterprise earlier.

An hour later, Taggie called up the stairs. 'Pat's outside – he wants a word, Gala.'

The 'words' were, in fact, a ravishing bunch of spring flowers. *Dear Gala, thank you from everyone at Penscombe Stud for saving Fleance and the fillies from Titus*, said the card.

As Gala started to cry, Pat put his arms around her and hugged her. 'Don't let Rupert get to you. We all think you're fantastic.'

Going back into the kitchen, Gala found that Taggie had bought her a pair of leopardskin wool pyjamas.

'Pat tells me you're the heroine of the yard.'

Tugging at a piece of kitchen roll with which to wipe her eyes, Gala noticed the label said *multi-purpose and super-absorbent*, which summed up Taggie.

'You are the nicest person I've ever met,' said Gala.

19

Gala, like most carers from Africa, particularly Zimbabwe, was terrified of the dark and went around bolting doors at night. She had been made especially twitchy by a spate of burglaries in the Gloucestershire area, where the thugs had broken in, emptied jewel boxes and particularly concentrated on gold and silver, which could then be melted down and sold abroad. A trainer in the next county had been stripped of every cup and trophy, many of them embarrassingly only lent for a year by the racecourses. Rupert, who in addition had pictures worth millions, had been warned by the police to watch out.

The house was empty one frosty late-February night except for a peacefully snoring Old Eddie. Taggie was staying yet again across the valley, doing a dinner party for her mother Maud. Young Eddie had gone to an all-night rave-up with Trixie. Rupert had been invited to some dinner and wasn't due back until tomorrow.

The house creaked and groaned, the wind whined down the chimney and rattled uncut-back creepers against the windows. A full moon was hidden by impenetrable ebony clouds. Gala had reached a black hole of despair. Tonight would have been her eighth wedding anniversary. Ben had given her a huge and beautiful emerald brooch for her seventh.

Oh Ben! At least no one would be woken by her bawling her head off. She had made the mistake of watching a film on saving the white rhino. Six hundred had already been slaughtered in Zim this year. Having taken out the dogs, she had locked up and had a boiling bath before putting on her new leopardskin pyjamas which were rather sexy and gave her back her shape. For what? she thought bitterly, but she pinned on the wedding anniversary emerald. Running downstairs to doublecheck she'd locked the front door, she found it open. She must be losing her mind. Bolting and locking it again, she put a big chair against it.

She was so tired, she fell asleep instantly, then – cruellest of all nightmares – dreamt about rhinos having their horns hacked off, leaving cavernous bloody wounds and terrified babies . . . and there was Ben, face dark and twisted beyond all recognition, trying to save them, then being lifted off the ground by machine-gun fire. Gala woke sobbing and screaming to hear a rattle of bullets outside, which became louder and more insistent. They were coming to get her. Petrified, heart pounding, she crept up to the window – nothing but dark, not a shaft of moonlight – then jumped in panic at another rattle of gunfire.

Why weren't the dogs barking? Was it burglars? She clutched her emerald brooch as she crept down the dark landing. Her mobile was back in her room, and anyway Pat Inglis' and Cathal's numbers could only be located on the board in the kitchen. She didn't dare switch on a light, in case the intruders clocked her.

Reaching a window looking out on to the front of the house, she jumped at another rattle, then died. As the moon parted the ebony clouds, lighting up a frost-sparkling lawn, there was the ghost of Rupert Black in the same white shirt, hair glittering white-blond. Then the clouds slid over the moon, followed by more gunfire. Locked and bolted doors don't keep out ghosts. Then the moon emerged again, and she gave a cry of relief as it lit up a plump black Labrador, and a brindle greyhound and two Jack Russells weaving round Rupert Black's feet as another volley of gravel hit the window.

'For fuck's sake, let me in!' howled a voice.

Oh God, it was Rupert. Hurtling down the stairs, Gala tripped and fell. Saving herself by grabbing the post at the bottom, encountering velvet, and switching on the light, she realized it was Rupert's dark-blue smoking jacket.

'What the hell's going on? I've been trying to get into my house for the past half hour!' he shouted as Gala's shaking hands struggled with bolts, keys and chains. 'Do you want me to freeze to death?'

'I didn't know you were coming back, I'm so sorry.'

Next moment, she was sent flying by a tsunami of dogs, barking excitedly, wagging, whining and weaving round her feet.

'I'm truly sorry. I didn't hear you come in.'

Seeing how pale and trembling she was, and on the verge of tears, Rupert said as he went into the kitchen: 'You'd better have a drink.'

'You honestly don't have to, I ought to go back to bed,' stammered Gala, thinking how utterly gorgeous he looked in that white shirt. In fact, compared with the long-legged yearling slenderness of him in the nude painting on the landing, he was now as powerful and solidly muscular as one of his stallions.

'Don't be silly,' he told her.

'Well, at least put something on.' Gala seized a thick dark-blue jersey drying on the Aga.

As Rupert shrugged into it, enjoying the warmth, he clocked the emerald on her pyjama top. 'Been robbing Cartiers?'

'Ben, my husband, gave it to me for our last wedding anniversary. Actually it would have been our eighth anniversary tonight.'

'Better celebrate then.'

Having switched on *At the Races*, Rupert got a bottle of champagne out of the fridge.

'Go on,' he nodded to the much-blanketed sofa, where she was instantly joined by Forester sliding behind her, and Banquo and Cuthbert taking up guard on either side of her and Gilchrist collapsing on her feet.

'You've certainly seduced my dogs. Where the hell did he get that emerald from?'

'Ben was diverting the river flowing through our land into a pond for the cattle. He found the stone on the river-bed. Thank you.' Gala accepted a large glass. 'And he took it to a local jeweller who turned it into a brooch. I've often wondered if the jeweller tipped off Wang, the local mafia warlord, that there were minerals on our land.'

'What did Ben do?'

'He was a farmer, but also a game warden, obsessed with saving the white rhino from the poachers. We were caught up in a court case to keep our farm. Finally, after five years of haggling, we won. Next day it was burnt to the ground. I'm boring you.'

'No,' said Rupert, who was watching a race on *At the Races Stateside* with half an eye.

'You told Taggie you didn't want to know.' Gala took a slug of champagne, the desire to unburden overwhelming. 'I'd been shopping in Harare to get some drink for a wedding anniversary party – seven years and no itch. I found,' she took a deep breath, 'that all the farmworkers who had been loyal to us had been murdered; they'd strung up our Staffies and our black Lab, then they'd cut and hacked the legs off our horses and cows.'

'Christ.' Rupert turned down the television. 'Where was Ben?'

'Saving a baby rhino. Poachers had killed its mother and sawed off her horn, but the baby had managed to survive for four days, crawling under her to suckle from her teats.' Gala gave a sob. 'Ben was trying to load the baby on to his truck. The poachers must've known he was there – they came back and fired fifty bullets into his body.'

'Christ, that is so fucking awful. What did the police do?'

'What police? They all work for the government, who are hand in velvet glove with Wang.'

'There must be some way of getting him.'

'You don't tangle with mafia warlords; they don't like being reminded of their transgressions,' said Gala bleakly. 'Wang's mining our land now.'

'I'm so sorry.' Rupert filled up her glass.

'I was having a nightmare about rhinos. I thought the rattle of gravel on the window was gunfire, then I looked out of the window and saw a blond man in a white shirt in the moonlight and nearly died. I thought it was the ghost of Rupert Black.'

Like a suddenly floodlit statue, Rupert's still face broke into a smile.

'Funny coincidence, I crossed swords this evening with a descendant of the guy Rupert Black's supposed to have taken out. A prat called Roddy Northfield. His elder brother Rufus, Lord Rutshire, owns Rutminster Racecourse. Roddy, who runs the racing side, wants to raise cash building horrid little houses everywhere.

'Rutshire's gay with no heir and not much into racing, so Roddy, who has a repulsive lumpen son, Alfred – who'll probably inherit – is already throwing his considerable weight around. He's got a new sponsor who wants to move their big July race from its midweek slot to Saturday, which will mean a logjam of about five races all worth £100,000 taking place within the same two hours. Bloody stupid. Roddy's the King of Waffle. The debate was entitled "Whither racing". "Going fucking nowhere with you at the helm", I told him.'

'Gosh, was he cross?'

'Bellowing like Titus. I was so bored I left before dinner.' He glanced up at the clock. 'I've got a runner at Saratoga in a minute, one of Love Rat's fillies.'

'You must be starving,' said Gala.

Going to the fridge, Rupert took out a dish of chicken paprika she'd made earlier, but before she had time to suggest she heated it up, he was spooning it up, nodding in approval.

'This is bloody good, nothing like the muck the boots used to serve up to my father.'

He offered the dish to Gala who, thinking what beautiful hands he had, shook her head.

'Not if I need to lose several stone.'

'In those pyjamas, you've actually got a body.'

'I usually wear ten layers, but it's getting warmer.'

'That is so awful, what happened to you.'

Don't be too nice, she thought, not wanting to cry. Kindness is the greatest aphrodisiac; she couldn't believe he was being so lovely.

114

'If someone did that to Tag or my dogs, I'd rip them apart.'

He put the empty dish in the washing up machine and took some chocolate tart out of the fridge.

'Did you have any children?'

'We were waiting for the court case to be settled.'

'What sort of bloke was he – Ben? Attractive?'

'Very. Honourable,' she hugged Banquo, 'like a Labrador but tougher, and very straight. I get panic attacks I'll never see him again. I want to Skype him in heaven to see if he's let the Staffies sleep on his cloud.' Her voice broke again. 'When we first got them he insisted they lived outside but within a month they were up on the sofa enjoying *The X-Factor*.'

But she had lost Rupert, who'd turned up the sound.

'Here's Love Rat's filly Flippity Gibbet being ponied down to the post, looks good, just three or four ribs showing. She's got his ears and wide eyes.'

He emptied the bottle into Gala's glass, never taking his eyes off the horses.

'Come on little girl, come on little girl . . . fucking marvellous!'

The dogs all wagged their tails as Flippity Gibbet scorched past the post, three lengths clear.

Gala was shocked at the joy she felt, as a euphoric Rupert opened another bottle. Next moment there was a bleep, Weatherbys' tracking system telling him any time of the day, anywhere in the world, that his horses had won or been placed in a race.

'Do you switch it off in bed?' Gala was appalled to find herself asking as he filled up her glass and quickly added: 'To Flippity Gibbet!'

'To Ben,' said Rupert, raising his glass to her. He sat down on a kitchen chair, looking at her. 'I cannot imagine a fraction of what you feel. But my great mate Billy Lloyd-Foxe died last year.'

'To Billy, then.' Gala raised her glass. 'He sounds so lovely.'

'He was. We go back such a long way, it's hard to kick the habit: even now if I have a win, or have a problem with a horse, I reach for my mobile. I've just bought a terrific South African stallion called Blood River to inject a bit of hybrid vigour into the stud. I wanted to share that with him . . . I keep texting him jokes.' Then, feeling he was displaying weakness: 'Are you being driven crackers by my father?'

'I love him. He's so appreciative and up for everything. When it's warmer, I'd like to take him to the races.'

'Not on Ladies Day in a high wind. We took him to Cheltenham last year, talk about Cleavage Hill – he practically fell out of the box, training his race glasses on all the boobs! So you're OK here?'

'I love it. I adore Taggie.' Gosh, she must be pissed.

'Mrs Rochester.' Rupert raised an eyebrow. 'Much preferred to Mr Rochester, who is far too old for you.' He glanced at himself in the kitchen mirror and then laughed.

'Oh God,' gasped Gala, going crimson. 'I'm sorry, someone called Janey was so pushy.'

'She's a cow, don't worry.'

'And I love Dora and Lark and Louise and Marketa and Meerkat and Gee Gee and Roving Mike and Gav – I wish one could cheer him up – and Pat is such a laugh.'

'Need to be tough to run a stud, although he cried his eyes out when a young stallion had to be shot last year. What did you think of Fleance?'

'Awesome. I've never ridden anything so fast, like a Ferrari. The more he quickened, the more he found. He could easily step up in trip and get one mile two furlongs.'

Drink had unlocked her tongue.

'You don't mind me going down to the yard? I don't want to get in anyone's way, particularly yours and Taggie's.'

'You won't. I mean it – get a couple of stone off and you can ride out. Dad can have a lie-in. I'll take you round the yard tomorrow.'

'I'd better go to bed. Thank you so much for the drink.'

Falling over Cuthbert, she steadied herself by clutching the kitchen table, and nearly stumbled again as she started up the stairs, giggling: 'Oh dear, I'm tripping up on step.'

20

Typical Rupert. He suddenly decided he liked Gala.

'Lovely woman,' he told Taggie the next morning. 'Had a ghastly time, don't know how she survived. Better marry Gav.'

Geraldine, his PA, was less amused. 'He's been slagging her off for months, now you'd think he invented her,' she said sourly.

Slightly regretting that he'd got pissed and so intimate with Gala, however, Rupert was cooler with her when he took her round the late-afternoon check, known as Evening Stables.

With 200 horses to look at, Rupert allotted a minute a horse, only pausing to feel its legs and sometimes fire off details of illustrious sires or dams, big races won and future prospects. Gala, who wanted to examine, marvel and ask questions, got hopelessly left behind.

'Come on, come on. Buck up, for God's sake,' called back Rupert, and Gala felt last night's intimacy slipping away.

'Like the American tourist in the Louvre,' she was amazed to hear a nearby Gavin murmur. '"If you keep stopping to look, we'll never get round".'

Gala laughed and again thought how nice he was when he added: 'The first boss I worked for used to blindfold the lads and expect them to recognize horses by their legs.'

'Could they do the same with women?'

'For Christ's sake,' yelled Rupert, who'd reached the end of the row. 'Why the hell did you bother to come?' And stalked back to his office.

From then on, as often as possible Gala did wander down to the stud to chat, especially to Gee Gee the gentle giantess, who as well as being the only girl considered strong enough to handle the odd stallion, was mostly in charge of the mares who came to give birth and be covered again.

One evening, Gala was comforting a homesick virgin mare, who'd won several races and who, the moment she ovulated, would be fitted into Peppy Koala's frantic schedule.

'Poor little duck,' said Gala, stroking her. 'After all those fists being shoved up your ass or thrust into your vagina, Peppy's prick will seem like a day in the country.'

She must get back to Eddie. Next minute, Gee Gee came out of Cordelia's box looking worried. A very special foal of Love Rat's was due any minute, but Rupert's favourite mare suddenly appeared in great distress.

'I've rung Rupert but he's not answering, nor is Pat and I can't get through to the vet.'

'Let me have a look.' Entering Cordelia's box, Gala stroked the sweating mare who was moving around, pawing her belly, then collapsing on to the straw.

'May I try? I think I might know what could be wrong.'

Sliding her long slim hand into Cordelia's vagina, Gala discovered, as she had suspected, that the foal's back legs were pointing upwards, threatening to puncture the mare's rectum.

'All right, little girl.' With infinite gentleness, she edged the legs round so they were pointing out of Cordelia's cervix, enabling the foal to slide very easily out into the world.

'Oh thank God!' cried Gee Gee, who had been lying down in the straw holding Cordelia's head collar.

Fortunately, Pat arrived just then so Gala beat a retreat back to the house, hoping Rupert would be pleased with her. Arriving covered in blood, however, she got bawled out by him for abandoning Taggie, who had people coming for supper and had had to feed and put Eddie to bed.

'Sorry, I've been helping out at the stud,' stammered Gala.

'A shade presumptuous,' said Rupert acidly. 'Your job first and foremost is to look after my father. Taggie's got quite enough to do.'

Gala just managed to bite her tongue, but as she fled upstairs, the telephone rang. It was Pat, ringing to say that Cordelia had had a colt and Rupert belted down to the stud where Gee Gee, always generous, told him how brilliantly quick-thinking Gala had been, saving both mare and foal.

Returning to the house, Rupert sought out Gala.

'I owe you an apology,' he told her. 'Cordelia's produced the most lovely colt, thanks to you. How do you know about these things? I thought you were a carer, not a midwife.'

'I had a farm in Africa, remember?' said Gala sardonically.

Next day, Rupert gave her a bottle of a lovely sweet scent called Elie Saab, which he'd whipped from Taggie's present drawer. On the label he'd written: *Dear Karen Blitzkrieg, Sorry and thank you. Love Cordelia and Rupert C-B.*

As the months passed, although Rupert and Gala sparred, to Taggie's relief they also spent much time discussing horses.

Gradually Gala thawed; the weather got better. She palled up with Young Eddie as they both struggled to lose weight, and with Gav, as he battled not to return to the booze. Both men liked her company, which irritated Celeste, who festered, unable to comprehend why they were attracted to this plump, almost middle-aged woman.

21

Come August and Rupert was enjoying a brilliant season, his horses notching up numerous Group One races both at home and abroad. Lion O'Connor, the dependable, was heading for Leading Jockey, and breeders were already excited by Blood River, the new South African stallion.

But looking ahead, Rupert wanted next season to be even better. New Year's Dave, and two potential stars called Touchy Filly and Blank Chekov were about to be broken; it was high time Master Quickly joined them, but silly bitch Etta Edwards was still stalling.

Valent on the other hand was utterly fed up with his delicious new wife being exhausted by caring for Hereward who, over two years old now, was into everything, and tidying up after Trixie and a frequently stopping-over Young Eddie. The situation looked unlikely to improve when Trixie, who had been partying a great deal, got too mediocre grades in her A-levels to ensure her a place at Oxford – so she was insisting on taking them again.

Valent, however, wanted Etta and his house to himself.

'I'm willing to pay for it,' he told Rupert, 'but could you find room for Eddie and Trix at your place?'

'Only if Master Quickly moves to Penscombe tout de suite.'

*

Meanwhile, Master Quickly was getting increasingly spoilt and colty. He was very bossy out in the field.

'Who do you think you are? What are you doing here?'

Anyone who stopped stroking him would get nudged then nipped.

Etta had taken to wearing long sleeves, not only to hide her wrinkling arms, but also the indigo bruises.

One boiling August evening when Quickly was seventeen months old, Etta was dead-heading roses and mourning the number of lilies flattened by Hereward's football. Glancing down at the footpath running through the lower paddock, she was alarmed to see Quickly with his nose rammed against the small of the very large back of a terrified lady rambler, propelling her along as fast as she could waddle.

Belting down to rescue her, Etta grabbed Quickly's head collar to lead him away, whereupon Quickly took off, tugging Etta so she tripped over a stray Cotswold stone, knocking out her two front teeth on the water-trough.

'Enoof is enoof!' exploded an enraged Valent.

Having flown Etta up to his smart dentist in London, he was determined to dispatch Quickly off to Penscombe to learn to behave. Easier said than done as Quickly had hitherto refused to load. Gav, who had often visited and made friends with him, was at the sales in Ireland or he would have been willing to walk him the twenty miles.

But Walter, Rupert's Head Lad, the yard NCO, as tough as Gav was gentle, and known as 'Walter Walter everywhere' because he stuck his nose into everything, turned up with two strong lads. Despite Quickly nearly kicking out the lorry, they delivered him within the hour.

'How did you manage that?' asked Dora, who'd hoped to wheel in the press.

'He was more frightened of me than the lorry,' said Walter. 'Although I was nearly gelded by that effing goat!'

'Isn't he small – but isn't he beautiful,' said everyone.

'If he grows a bit, we could enter him in the Greyhound Derby,' mocked Walter.

Etta, ringing from London, was desperately worried, not

just about Quickly but about the effect on Chisolm and Mrs Wilkinson.

'They're fine, luv,' insisted Valent. 'I think they heaved a sigh of relief to be shot of him and have immediately started planning bridge parties and shopping trips to Cheltenham.'

'Oh Valent,' half laughed and half sobbed Etta. 'You will make sure we can visit him as often as we like? I'm afraid he'll be terribly lonely.'

Quickly, in fact, missed Mrs Wilkinson dreadfully. Only now did he realize how much she had loved and protected him. Turned out on his first sweltering evening, he stood trembling, tired and hungry and too frightened of the other yearlings to graze or drink from the water-trough, crying himself hoarse, unable any longer to stand behind her to have the flies whisked off his face.

When she got home from London, poor Etta's face was so bruised and her mouth so swollen as she awaited her new set of teeth that, to her shame, she felt too embarrassed to visit Quickly and risk showing herself to Rupert in such an un-attractive light.

'You could always wear a burka,' said Dora.

To reassure Etta, Valent popped over to Penscombe next day.

'He's fine, honest,' he reassured her on his return, handing her a vodka and tonic with a straw. 'A lovely little lass called Lark is looking after him, and Taggie sends lots of love. Look what else she sent you.'

From a basket he unpacked a jar of Vichyssoise, a big cold omelette and a bowl of lemon sorbet.

'Oh, how sweet of her!'

'She adores Quickly – he'll be in the kitchen soon.'

'You're back, Granny! How lovely!' cried Trixie, rushing in with Hereward and a bunch of red roses. 'I won't kiss you as I might hurt your poor face. God, it looks painful.'

As Hereward raced forward to be picked up by his grand-mother, Valent grabbed the child.

'Granny's not well,' he told him, then turning to Trixie: 'She cannot babysit or do your washing or cook supper for you,' he told her firmly.

'Of course not,' said Trixie politely.

Two days later, however, Valent was working in the office he'd made out of the dovecote down the garden. Etta was so unused to inactivity, she found herself gathering up the washing littering the floor in Trixie's and Eddie's room. Putting away the laundry, she discovered a pair of Trixie's jeans terribly torn at the knees, and while listening to Glazunov's First Piano Concerto, carefully sewed them up.

Towards evening, Trixie breezed in, opening the fridge and cutting herself a huge chunk of Taggie's omelette.

'God, this is good.' She gave a slice to Hereward, who promptly spat it out.

'How are you, Granny, darling? How are you feeling?'

'Fine,' lied Etta.

'Sure?'

'Quite sure.'

'That's good. I honestly wouldn't ask if you were still feeling awful, but I'm running terribly late. Would you possibly mind bathing Herry and putting him to bed? Eddie's asked me to an amazing party with loads of celebs.'

Hereward, who was pulling all the cushions off the kitchen sofa, bellowed when his mother rushed upstairs then started taking all the saucepans out of the cupboards and smashed a pretty plate.

Etta sighed. She had been looking forward to listening to Beethoven's Ninth on The Proms outside with a gentle supper of cold omelette. She hoped Valent wouldn't be too livid.

Half an hour later, Trixie rushed in wearing only a scarlet bra and knickers, fully made up, newly washed hair flying, wafting Etta's 24 Faubourg.

'Help, help, I can't find my jeans anywhere.'

'They're here,' said Etta proudly. 'I've mended them for you.'

'You what?' shrieked Trixie, horror and incredulity spreading across her face. 'You stupid cow, they're meant to be ripped! How could you do something so bloody stupid? I've got nothing to wear now!' Her voice rose to a scream.

'That's enuff,' roared an incoming Valent, delighted to have a legitimate excuse to achieve what he wanted. 'How dare you speak to your grandmother like that, you spoilt brat. You'll move out tomorrow and take Hereward with you.'

'Oh Valent,' cried Etta. 'They can't.'

'Don't interroopt,' warned Valent. 'You've really pushed your luck, young lady!'

Appalled, never having seen Valent so furious, Trixie burst into tears.

'I'm so sorry I lost it, Granny. I wanted to impress all Eddie's friends – they're just so glamorous. Please forgive me.'

'It's OK.' Etta turned pleadingly to Valent, who shook his head.

'We've carried you long enough. Your parents can support you for a change.'

'I hate Dad's new woman and I hate Mum's new woman even more.'

'I don't care,' said Valent. 'Granny's not well.'

Next moment, as Young Eddie roared up in his dark-green Ferrari, Trixie raced out to him, wailing, 'Granny and Valent have thrown me out.'

'Well, that's OK, they need their own space.'

'Can I move in with you?' There was a long pause. 'Just till I get myself straight.'

She was looking so forlorn yet so sexy in those scarlet panties.

'Sure,' said Eddie.

22

Trixie was quite excited when she first saw the flat, which took up the top floor of a four-storey hostel, and which had central heating, Sky television, dishwasher and washing machine, a little extra bedroom for Hereward, and fine views on one side into the yard and on the other side over the paddocks and down the valley. As accommodation went, it was one of Rupert's best, coveted by most of his other stable staff – but anything to get Young Eddie and his din and friends out of our house, thought Rupert.

'This'll do for the moment,' said Trixie, who didn't want Eddie to feel trapped, 'but I'm sure Granny'll miss us and long to have Herry and me back in a week or two. I mean, they'll rattle around in that big house. What on earth will they do?'

'Each other most probably, they want the place to themselves,' said Eddie. As he switched on Radio One, he caught sight of Marketa sauntering across the yard and wondered if it were going to cramp his style living full-time with Trixie.

'Can't be having sex at their age,' mused Trixie, switching to Radio Three. 'Granny's led such a sheltered life, she thought Chlamydia was a lovely name for a horse the other day!'

'Don't teach your grandmother to suck cock,' quipped Eddie, as Berlioz' Corsaire galloped into the room.

*

One of the things that had brought Etta and Valent together was listening to music, particularly The Proms, and reading a new poem and then discussing it.

On his trip to Europe, Valent had just read some verses in which Ben Jonson bemoaned reaching the age of forty-seven (over twenty years younger than me, thought Valent) and complained about numerous grey hairs, a rocky face and a mountainous belly. The only way his mistress could fancy him, sighed Jonson, was if she shut her eyes and listened to his poetry.

Was he attractive enough for such a beautiful woman as Etta? worried Valent. Should he darken his hair and lose weight? As a result of his wife's lovely cooking he'd piled on twenty pounds, but his belly wasn't exactly mountainous.

Nor could he contain his excitement at having Etta and all of the house to themselves.

Although Etta was wracked with guilt for chucking out Trixie and Herry, she also couldn't contain her joy that at last she and Valent would be alone. Valent had just rung from Paris. He'd be home in a couple of hours, he said, and he wanted to make love to her under the stars, so she must wear something sexy for their first night alone.

They had first fallen in love whilst listening to a Prom of Mahler's First Symphony on the same kind of hot, still August evening. Tonight it was another favourite, Rachmaninov's Second Symphony, and Etta had put two bottles of Bollinger in the fridge and a bottle of red by the Aga. Valent's favourite Beef Stroganoff and a blackberry crumble just needed heating up – much later, thought Etta with a shiver of excitement.

Scented candles awaited them in the house. No scented candles were needed to scent the garden, where the sweet tobacco smell of buddleia mingled with peppery phlox and heady wafts of regalia lilies.

But Etta noticed reddening apples, yellowing wisteria leaves, pale-green conkers polka-dotting darker green horse chestnuts, ripe blackberries along the footpath: the first signs of autumn – and in me too, thought Etta. She and Valent mustn't waste time. What mattered in life, she told herself firmly, was putting this dear man first and making him happy.

'Wear something sexy.' Having washed her hair and herself, she smiled in the mirror: her beautiful new teeth had been worth the pain. Not being able to eat, she had lost ten pounds of her elderly spread and, resting in the sun, she had acquired a tan.

'Wear something sexy.'

She had a brainwave.

Cindy Bolton, Willowwood's porn star, had always had a soft spot for Etta who, as a syndicate member, had never patronized her, and Cindy had therefore given her and Valent a gift box from Ann Summers as a wedding present.

'To sparkle up your erotic life.'

The gift box had been briefly opened when they returned from their honeymoon. Objects entitled clit clips, vibrating nipple clamps and costumes for naughty nurses and teasing teachers had been giggled over and set aside for a fun weekend, but with Etta and Valent distracted by the arrival of Hereward, a romping deterrent, the box had been shoved in the wardrobe and forgotten about.

Valent, as a great goalkeeper, had developed arthritis in both hands and had difficulty opening champagne bottles so Etta saved him the bother by opening one of the Bolly bottles in advance. Then, pouring herself a large glass, she dropped a silver spoon in the neck of the bottle.

Unearthing Cindy's box from the wardrobe, she discovered raspberry and banana-flavoured lubricant 'to make licking a delight' and what could one do with Bubblegum Slide N Ride? It would get stuck in one's bush. She took a slug of champagne, then as Gwenny the cat rolled up and started weaving round Etta's legs, 'Oh look – here's some Cock and Pussy Rub for you, darling.'

Taking another slug, Etta delved deep into the red satin bag and discovered underwear.

'Gosh, gosh, gosh!' She tried on a black Quarter Cup bra called Edie, over which her breasts rose like a soufflé, and a 'show-stopper' crotchless thong in black and scarlet, held up by four narrow ribbons over the bottom.

She was just dickering between a peephole bra called Fiona

and another crotchless thong called Arabella, such grand names, but felt the way her breasts flowed over the quarter bra was more sexy.

At the bottom she could see whips, paddles and a 'sex and mischief' leather flogger. Gwenny jumped into the box and started playing with a 'spank me silly' paddle.

'I'm quite silly enough,' giggled Etta. Topping up her glass, settling finally for Fiona and Arabella, she pulled on a pair of black fishnet hold-ups and slipped into some never worn before four-inch heels.

Ann Summers' lease hath all too short a date, she sighed.

She really should put on a lot of black eye-liner and scarlet lippy; instead she drenched herself with 24 Faubourg.

As she pressed a button, the Allegro Moderato of Rachmaninov's Second Symphony flooded the house. There was going to be nothing moderate about their lovemaking tonight. Etta examined herself in the long mirror in their bedroom and felt pretty pleased with herself. Her nipples protruded like bullets out of Fiona and parting Arabella, she could see a glisten of pink.

'I am a member of the Labia Party, Gwenny,' she announced, then jumped as she heard a crackle of tyres on the gravel outside. She took another gulp of champagne and, seizing the banisters, waggling her hips, she danced down as the Second Movement of Rachmaninov drew to a close.

Valent had arrived just in time for the heartbreakingly beautiful Adagio.

'Darling, darling Valent, welcome home,' she cried, as clutching her glass with the other hand, she reached the bottom of the stairs.

'Granny,' called a voice. 'Where are you?'

'Gaggie,' cried Hereward. Next moment, the front door flew open and Etta was flooded with sunlight.

'We've brought you some flowers,' began Trixie. 'Herry missed you so much I thought you might like to spend a few hours . . .' Her words slithered to a halt. 'Oh my God, Granny, oh my God. Are you going to a fancy-dress party?'

'I thought you were Valent,' stammered Etta, seizing a stuffed duck-billed platypus on the hall table and holding it over her bush as Priceless came bounding down the stairs to greet Trixie.

'We came to pick up the pushchair, Herry's trike and a couple of Eddie's shirts. Oh my God!'

Stymied by her unfamiliar high heels, Etta's only recourse was to swing round the banister and totter towards the kitchen, on her way grabbing an ankle-length Barbour that Trixie's mother Carrie had given her when she moved to Willowwood and had never worn. She then went slap into Eddie, who'd come in the other door through the kitchen, having retrieved Hereward's tricycle and the pushchair. He immediately wolf-whistled and burst out laughing.

'Oh God!' squeaked Etta, desperately trying to find the arm-holes in the Barbour. 'I was expecting Valent.'

'Lucky Valent, you look sensational!'

'So sorry, so sorry,' moaned Etta.

Hereward was still crying because he'd wanted to see his great-grandmother and Eddie was still crying with laughter as he drove them back to Penscombe.

'I cannot bee*leeve* it,' stormed Trixie.

'She looked terrific,' protested Eddie. 'She's in great shape for a geri. You ought to get some of that kit. With her boobs falling out and "a thong in her parts",' he sang.

'Oh shut up – and shut up, Herry, for God's sake,' Trixie screamed at her bawling child. 'What on earth will Valent think? They can't be having sex at their age.'

'Oh grow up, everyone has sex, given the chance.'

'Oh yuk, oh yuk, talk about a Yuk Fuck.'

'Yuk Fuck – oh, that's very good.' Eddie wiped his eyes. 'With a thong in my parts . . .'

Arriving ten minutes later, Valent was greeted by Priceless wagging his tail and flashing his teeth even more than Etta. Inside he was greeted by Etta in a Barbour, battling tears and laughter.

'You going out?'

'Oh Valent,' she wailed, 'oh darling, something so terrible

and embarrassing has happened. I wanted to make it up to you for all the times we haven't been alone together. I wanted to look sexy for you, but I heard a car, thought it was you and ran down in these clothes, or lack of clothes, and I think I've utterly traumatized Herry and Trixie and made a complete fool of myself.'

'Hush, hush.'

'No, don't look, you'll hate it.' Thank God she hadn't worn black eye-liner as the tears spilled over.

'Shoot oop.' Valent pulled open the Barbour and gave a gasp of delight. 'Oh God, Etta, you look so goddam sexy, you lovely, lovely woman. Look at your breasts.' As he covered them with his huge hands, he could feel his cock soaring like Concorde, particularly as he parted the crotchless Arabella, finding soft slippery flesh. 'Oh Etta, let's go upstairs, I'll lock up.'

Turning, he locked the front door and carried her upstairs, where he undressed in a trice, untangling his boxer shorts from Concorde.

'Get off, Priceless and Gwenny!' He shoved them out of the door. 'Let me have another look. Oh Etta, leave everything on.'

Then, as she lay back on the bed, he confessed, 'I won't last a moment. I never went to prep school.'

And now he was on top of her. No longer Concorde but the QE2 sliding inside her crotchless thong, kissing her breasts, burying his face in her cleavage and then exploding a glorious burst water-main inside her.

'So sorry,' he muttered. 'I told you, I didn't go to the kind of school where you learned to recite Latin verbs to stop yourself coming.'

'It's wonderful, I wanted to excite you,' whispered Etta. 'You are the most heavenly man in the world, and all mine.'

'Now I'll make you come,' promised Valent, rolling off her.

'Do you want some banana gel or toffee apple or raspberry ripple lube to make licking a pleasure?' giggled Etta. 'I opened Cindy's wedding present. It's like a sweet shop.'

'You taste lovely enough as it is.' Valent's arthritis in no way hampered a most delicate touch as his fingers slid between her legs. His tongue was even better. Moaning with delight, Etta was driven to shuddering ecstasy.

After she'd come, he wanted to come again, so Etta tried some toffee apple lube which made it even better. Then he fetched the second bottle of champagne.

'You look so gorgeous,' he sighed.

'I hope I haven't put Trixie off for life.'

'Was she trying to drop Herry off again?' asked Valent.

'I don't think so,' lied Etta.

'With any luck she might consider you utterly unsuitable to look after him any more.'

'But I love him, in small doses. She wants a pussy rub,' added Etta, as a thunderously purring Gwenny joined them on the bed, then confessed, 'Eddie couldn't stop laughing. He did say I looked great.'

'He's right. Good boy. The most erotic thing of all,' Valent ran his hand over her belly, 'was that you wanted me enough to do this.'

'You'll never guess what else there is in the box – a feather tickler whip and a leather flogger. If you give me more than eight whacks, we'd have to have a stewards' enquiry.'

Long after midnight, ravenous, they heated up the Stroganoff, drank the bottle of red as they sat in the scented garden under the moon and blew out the scented candle after moths flew into it. They then took Priceless out for a run and went to see Mrs Wilkinson and Chisolm.

'Do you think they are missing poor Quickly?' sighed Etta.

'Not at all,' said Valent. 'And now Quickly's gone I am going to install new electric gates again. I'm not having droppers-in interrupting my nights of passion!'

23

Quickly soon cheered up at Penscombe, taking chunks out of sweaters, upsetting all the other colts on the horse walker by cantering round, pushing it faster and faster, and whenever possible, creeping into the house to inveigle treats out of Taggie, who already adored him.

'Quickly's in the kitchen again,' went up the cry.

The question arose, which stable lad was going to look after him? Tough Walter Walter, the Head Lad, tried to persuade Rupert that the colt would fare better with a disciplinarian, who would stand no nonsense. Rupert, however, listened to Gav, who recommended Lark, one of the youngest stable lasses, a slim fair-haired Essex girl who laughed and sang all day, was always cheerful and already worked so hard looking after New Year's Dave and other two-year-olds. Lark, who didn't put out, and who, as well as going to Penscombe church on Sundays, came in to do her horses rather than let anyone else look after them.

Mocked by Celeste and some of the tougher, older stable lasses, Lark also had a massive crush on Eddie Alderton and tried to hide her sadness when he and Trixie moved into the hostel top flat together. Gav felt she needed the distraction of taming an equally wayward Master Quickly.

Gav himself took on the immediate task of breaking Quickly, which he reckoned would take at least three months.

Quickly, hating the constriction of anything on his back or in his mouth, kicked out wing mirrors all the way down Penscombe High Street when he was first ridden out.

'He'll break me before I break him,' sighed Gav, who fortunately had endless patience. He was, however, amused by a misprint in Dora's column for Rupert in the *Racing Post*, describing Quickly as 'half bother to New Year's Dave'.

More a whole bother, reflected Gav.

One of Quickly's problems was that he was rendered conspicuous by his unique beauty. His coat was the silver-grey of the night sky when the full moon was out, his tail and mane the luminous silver-blond of the moon itself. Like his mother, he was proud of his little feet which, like a ghost's, even when he galloped, hardly left a mark on the turf.

Also like his mother, who went berserk if anyone picked up a whip – but unlike Love Rat, who lay on his back waving his hooves in the air – Quickly had to be doped before he let the farrier fit any plates. Pills had to be given inside a Polo. A liability when turned out, if denied his own way he would lash out at the other colts.

'Are you sure Titus isn't his sire?' queried Roving Mike.

'Dora should know, she arranged the covering,' said Gav.

Quickly was therefore turned out with Safety Car, the kindest horse in the yard. Retired from racing after his great victory in Hong Kong, he was kept busy leading the two-year-olds on the gallops, nipping them if they overtook, helping them get used to the starting stalls.

Safety Car was also desolate that his last sheep friend had died; he needed a new mate. Quickly gave him a hard time, nagging and bossing him, but called out piteously if ever Safety Car went out without him.

Quickly, who pondered a lot, noticing people loving Safety Car and laughing at his antics, was found by Gavin holding a yard brush between his little teeth, trying to sweep up the golden leaves cascading down. One of Safety's party tricks was playing football with Gilchrist and Cuthbert, the Jack Russells, kicking the ball so they could keep tearing after it and retrieving it. Spoilsport Quickly kept muscling in, trying to pinch the ball.

Quickly's second friend was feline. Lark had rescued a long-haired black cat she'd found wandering in the woods and, calling him Purrpuss, had installed him in her room in the hostel.

'When he's had his supper, you can call him Purrpussfull,' said Dora. Celeste, who lived in the next-door room, was incensed and complained to Walter that cats were dirty animals who gave her asthma. Walter said with so many dogs around, the cat's days were numbered anyway.

'Oh please let him stay, he'll keep the mice down,' pleaded Lark.

Ignoring her, Celeste seized Purrpuss next morning and chucked him out into the yard. Instantly the pack, led by Forester, gave chase, whereupon a terrified Purrpuss took refuge on the silver back of Quickly, who was tied up outside his box.

As the ravening horde closed in, Quickly squealed, bared his teeth at them and lashed out with all fours until the dogs retreated, whimpering, and even Rupert applauded.

'That is an encouragingly brave horse.'

From then on, the pair were inseparable. Whenever Quickly was inside, Purrpuss took up residence on his back, even lapping saucers of milk or eating cat food up there, standing up in the manger to wash Quickly's face and ears, curling up against his belly like a hot water bottle at night.

Dora sent a photograph to *Owner & Breeder* with the caption: 'Son of Love Rat and Catch a Rat'.

Turned out, Quickly would race round his paddock with his tail in the air, charging up and spooking any passing horse. Confined to his box with Purrpuss on his back, he would hang over the door, thinking about fillies. When one little two-year-old, Nerissa, of whom Rupert thought very highly, started getting fatter, Rupert berated Gav and Walter for not getting her fit. Like Quickly and Dave, she was due on the racetrack in a few months but still looked like a lard barrel. No amount of roadwork or galloping made any difference – until it was realized that the poor creature was in foal, impregnated by Quickly, the son of a Grand National winner. Despite being thought too young by Gav, he must have hopped over the fence into Nerissa's paddock one day.

'A teenage pregnancy,' cried a delighted Dora. 'Will she qualify for a free loose box?'

'Better if the randy little sod was gelded,' said Walter, who'd been bitten too often by Quickly, and wasn't a fan.

Better if Quickly and both Eddies were gelded, thought Rupert, who was furious at having lost a brilliant filly before she'd had time to race.

He wasn't any happier with Young Eddie, who was still not cutting it as a jump jockey, and not pulling his weight in the yard, either. Eddie was mortified repeatedly, appearing in the *Racing Post*'s Cold Jockeys list, which stated the increasing number of days since he'd had a winner.

Even though the jump season had started full on in October, Eddie was not getting rides from other trainers, and Rupert's obsession with nailing Leading Flat Sire meant he now only kept a couple of jump horses. Eddie was missing the buzz of being a poster boy, chased by all the girls.

In addition, he and Trixie were not getting on. Trixie was taking her A-levels again and got fed up with Eddie coming in late with cronies, and waking Hereward, who was teething and cried a lot. This disturbed the lads in the flats below, who had to get up at five in the morning.

Eddie was desperately trying to lose weight to ride on the flat, and Trixie's junk food – supermarket lasagne heated up in the microwave – was a far cry from Taggie's Dover soles and fillet steaks. Trixie, realizing how much Etta had done for her, was horrified that she was expected to cook Eddie's dinner, make his bed, wash and iron his shirts, and do all his other laundry as well as Herry's and her own.

Trixie felt desperately hard done by, particularly when Eddie got mad when she shrank a purple cashmere jersey, which Taggie had given him for his birthday, down to Action Man size.

'Be an incentive to lose more weight and get back into it again,' she snapped back at him.

No longer was there endless access to babysitters. Rupert had made it quite clear that he didn't want them using Taggie or Gala, 'my father's enough trouble,' nor dropping in, raiding the fridge at all hours.

'Bloody martinet,' Trixie had stormed.

'Martin ate what?' Eddie had asked, not looking up from his laptop.

'Martinet means disciplinarian, or control freak,' screamed Trixie, just stopping herself from adding, 'Dumdum! Retard!'

That was another thing; Eddie was a philistine, who never read a book.

In fact, Gav was the only person round here with any intellectual pretensions, except Dora, who had told Trixie that Gav had liked her a lot after they talked at Quickly's christening, but he hadn't made any moves, and nor had any of the other lads.

One October afternoon, Trixie was trying not to think about Seth, Hereward's handsome, dissolute, middle-aged father, who Eddie always referred to as 'Mr Grecian Too Tousled', who had rung yesterday on the pretext of meeting his son sometime. Trixie had seen from the papers that Seth had just dyed his hair dark red because he had landed a huge part as Renny, the charismatic hero of Mazo de la Roche's Jalna books. She mustn't think of Seth, she didn't when she and Eddie were getting on well.

'We're out of bog paper,' called Eddie from the bathroom.

'There's a box of tissues beside the basin,' called back Trixie.

Would she ever get to Oxford, she wondered, retaking her A-levels in Greek and Latin as well as History and English. Would they admit her if she had a baby? She was writing an essay on *The Iliad* and had never realized that, like Seth now, Menelaus had red hair. No wonder Helen had run off with Paris. She couldn't share such reflections with Eddie. On the other hand, she was irritated by Lark's thumping great crush on him.

Hearing cries of: 'No, Quickly, no,' through the open window, she glanced out to see a flat-eared Quickly, like an angry gander, chasing Lark around the paddock.

'No, Quickly!' Her voice rose as he caught up, poised to take a bite out of her shoulder, when a voice yelled, 'Starp that!' and Eddie vaulted over the fence. Sprinting across, he seized Quickly's head collar, shaking him until his eyes watered, but still he snapped at Eddie.

'Little fucker!' shouted Eddie, raising his fist.

'Don't hurt him,' pleaded Lark.

'I'm only not beating the daylights out of you, little fucker,' Eddie shook Quickly's head collar again, 'because your kind minder begged me not to, but you don't deserve anyone so sweet or pretty looking after you, Quickers. Imagine if it was that lazy cow Celeste – she'd never brush your mane.'

Lark, blushing crimson at being described as pretty, stammered that Quickly was usually as good as gold; he was probably just feeling colty.

Eddie looked more closely at Lark. In that olive-green T-shirt, which matched her eyes and clung to her breasts, she had a very fetching little figure.

He couldn't resist saying: 'Don't blame him. I wish you'd look after me and put quarter marks on my ass. We must have a drink sometime.'

They were interrupted by Mrs Mitchell, the bossy vicar's wife, nicknamed Constance Sprightly because of her obsession with flower arranging. She had come to pester Taggie.

'Nice to see you in church, Lark. Your brass-rubbing is quite excellent – I hope you are coming to Harvest Supper? Hello,' she looked at Quickly, 'what a pretty pony, what's his name?'

'Little fucker,' said Eddie.

'Eddie!' gasped Lark.

'I beg your pardon?'

'Mucker,' said Lark. 'As in, "he's my mucker"; his real name is Master Quickly.'

'Mucker . . . I must remember that,' said Constance. 'I'm on my way to find Taggie – hope she'll do some desserts for Harvest Supper.'

'She's out,' lied Eddie.

'I'll just check,' said Mrs Mitchell firmly, setting off towards the house.

'What's brass-rubbing?' mocked Eddie. 'I'd rather rub you without a bra.'

Couldn't be that funny, thought Trixie, as she noticed Lark going scarlet and then them both laughing. If Lark had such a crush on Eddie, then she could jolly well babysit.

Living with Trixie did cramp his style, reflected Eddie. He'd regularly enjoyed Marketa and Lou-easy. He'd got a long-distance plan for Gala, and noticing close up how cute Lark was, he'd also like a crack at her.

Now he lived with Trixie, he found he had to account for his every move. How could he possibly lose weight? Sex took your mind off food; he'd been used to pulling girls every time he went to a party. Peppy Koala shagged three times a day, so why couldn't he?

Why then had he been furious to see Trixie had torn out a piece in the *Guardian* about Seth playing Renny, and made a bitchy remark about it 'being a change, hearing about him landing a large part, rather than having them.'

'Nice for Herry to know something about his father one day,' snapped back Trixie.

24

The flat season was drawing to a close. Rupert looked to have won the Leading Trainer title back from Isa, and Love Rat looked all set to edge up to second place behind Verdi's Requiem.

'Why are you such a great trainer?' asked Clare Balding.

'Because I breed great racehorses,' replied a curt Rupert.

Alas, with the endless changing fortunes of racing, Ivan the Terrorist had a huge win at Ascot on Champions Day, pushing his sire, Roberto's Revenge, into second place below Verdi's Requiem and knocking Rupert off the Leading Trainers spot.

Isa and Cosmo had been hugely aided by the rivalry of their two stable jockeys, Scottish Ashley McIntyre and Irish Tarqui McGall, who Rupert always referred to as 'Sodom and Begorrah' because Ash was gay and Tarqui went every which way.

Both jockeys were determined to end the season as Champion Jockey. Machiavellian Isa had now introduced his son Roman Lovell, who'd been cleaning up in Australia, into the equation – which made Ash and Tarqui even more competitive.

Cosmo, interviewed about nudging Verdi's Requiem in the Leading Sire title, smiled evilly.

'Rupert Campbell-Black is a has-been who couldn't train ivy up a wall and Lion O'Connor, his stable jockey, must be fed up with seeing the asses of our jockeys getting smaller and smaller.'

Again, Rupert didn't react but his determination hardened, and, once again, he agonized over who was backing Cosmo and Isa. They must be getting shedloads of money to outbid all the major players at the sales and to entirely rebuild the stud and yard at Valhalla.

The last straw was Lion O'Connor breaking and shattering his pelvis after a fall on Fleance in Japan, which meant he would be off for at least six months.

Rupert, outwardly remaining upbeat, only betrayed his despair to Valent after a third bottle of Mouton Cadet one evening.

'I've fucked up. I've been too reliant on Lion. I hoped Young Eddie would come back to the flat and step in as second jockey with Meerkat not far behind, followed by young Jemmy as an apprentice. I like to grow my own jockeys, but this time I'll have to poach one.'

Valent was touched by Rupert's despondency.

'May seem a stupid parallel, but Rachmaninov.'

'Who?'

'A great composer, he was hugely successful, but his First Symphony was a massive flop, crucified by the critics, took him two years to get his nerve back.'

'I can't wait that long.'

'Then along comes his Second Symphony – a towering masterpiece, best thing he ever wrote. You're going to have a brilliant year, next year. You've got great horses like Quickly, Dave and Touchy Filly coming up.'

'I better have a cracking Christmas party then, to rally the troops,' said Rupert.

The Christmas party was wild, held in the emptied helicopter hangar with champagne flowing and amazing food, including Gala's Beef Wellington, served throughout.

Because Rupert was second in the Leading Trainer charts, there was plenty of pool money to divide between the yard staff, and to encourage those who worked in the stud, Rupert was offering them a half per cent of the price of each foal or yearling they sold – which, when many were making six figures, was a tidy sum. So the party was brightened by optimism.

Lots of bad behaviour occurred, with people vanishing into loose boxes and feed barns. Opening a tack-room door, Rupert discovered Roving Mike going down on a mostly naked Celeste, and without missing a beat, called out: 'Good lad, that's the spirit,' before slamming the door.

'He never recognizes any of his staff with their clothes off,' giggled Dora.

Lou-easy, gorgeous in plunging midnight-blue velvet, who paid the vet and the farrier with services rendered, was slightly stretched when they both rolled up at the party. Fortunately, Marketa was only too happy to help her out.

'Please God,' prayed Lark, 'but only if You think it right, God, make Eddie dance with me.'

'I didn't know Lark had tattoos all over her arms,' observed Jemmy Carter, the apprentice, as he bopped with Clover, the youngest stable lass.

'No, they're bruises from Quickly,' said Clover.

Trixie, looking stunning in backless black, drank far too much and was just about to ask Gav to dance when Roving Mike, returning from Celeste and the tack room, swept her on to the floor. Here she watched beadily as Gala, who'd definitely won the turn-out in a beautiful red silk dress that Old Eddie had given her the money to buy for Christmas, had a long sexy dance with Young Eddie, who then pulled her behind a pile of hay-bales for a kiss.

'I have the hots for you, Mrs Milburn. You've got to promise to sleep with me when I get down to 122 pounds.'

Meerkat longed to dance with Gee Gee, he told Eddie, but was too embarrassed to ask because he only came up as high as her boobs.

'Worse things to talk to,' quipped Eddie, 'and lying down, it doesn't matter.'

Gav, ordered by Rupert to be present, had lurked in the shadows until sought out by a ravishing but plastered Trixie, whereupon he'd fled to the stables where he talked to Quickly, who'd turned on the light outside his box and was furious not to be allowed to join the party.

'It's going to be your year, boy,' said Gav, scratching Quickly's

141

neck as Purrpuss tightroped down his mane, 'and you've got your own black cat to bring you luck.'

Soon Quickly, Touchy Filly, whose sire was Titus Andronicus and whose nickname was PMT, and New Year's Dave would go into training as two-year-olds. New Year's Dave had turned into the most adorable colt, as gentle and loving as Quickly and Touchy Filly were tricky. His dear chestnut face with the big white star adorned Rupert and Taggie's Christmas card this year.

But there remained the smouldering gun of Celeste, La Prima Donna on her mobile, wildly jealous of Lark and Gala, who were always discussing horses with Gav, nor did she feel appreciated enough by Rupert or Cathal Gogan, who was also happy to shag her but not prepared to take her on trips abroad.

From time to time, Celeste looked at the bloodstained crumpled record of Dave being foaled on 31 December which was hidden under the lining paper of her bedroom drawer. She knew the disgrace it would bring on Penscombe if the truth came out.

Now she left the office party and joined Gav and Quickly in the yard.

'We must remember to send Dave a Happy Third Birthday card on New Year's Eve.'

'Shut up!' hissed Gav, going ashen.

'I think you owe me a nice New Year's Eve dinner after Christmas,' cooed Celeste.

Loathing himself, Gav agreed. Never had he been more tempted to go back to the party and drink himself insensible. Seeing them both set off on New Year's Eve, with Celeste looking fabulous, Gala was surprised how very sad she felt.

25

Rupert had never trained his horses on communal gallops, like those at Lambourn or Newmarket, where everyone could roll up and assess what everyone else was up to. He preferred privacy, disliking the press and never making any attempt to ingratiate himself with them, which in turn added to the mystique.

Horses had always thrived at Penscombe because there were masses of steeply sloped turn-out areas, full of wonderful grass so they could build up bone and muscle, which was further strengthened by working on equally steeply-sloping gallops.

And because these gallops were not overlooked by other yards, security had always been tight, producing an element of surprise when one of Rupert's new horses burst on to the public.

None could be more unpredictable than Quickly. If a pheasant went up on the gallops, you'd end up in Cotchester. 'Cough-and-you're-off' joined 'Little Fucker' as his nickname. Quickly's favourite game was 'dump the lad' but slowly, slowly and with infinite patience, Gav was bringing him on, settling him, relaxing him, taking him endlessly back and forth through starting stalls, which Rupert deliberately built narrow, so horses would feel a freedom when they entered stalls at an actual racetrack.

But now Lion was out of action, who was going to ride Quickly and other star two-year-olds in their first races? Cathal, Walter, Gav and Rupert, when he was at home, spent hours pondering over the possibilities.

A very promising apprentice was Jemmy Carter. He had been put into care at five because his drug addict Welsh mother couldn't cope, and then moved from foster family to foster family until, just before his fourteenth birthday, he'd been settled in with a Gloucester family, whom he loved. Having got a part-time job as a stable lad at Penscombe, Jemmy was devastated when the foster family chucked him out the moment he was sixteen, because they would no longer be remunerated for his upkeep.

Too proud to tell the other lads he was homeless, Jemmy had shacked up in one of the barns, sleeping rough and turning up for work. Then one day, after he had fainted and crashed to the ground on the gallops, he was followed back to the barn and rumbled by Gav and Gee Gee. Happily, everyone loved Jemmy, who was such a natural rider and had huge potential as a jockey. Rupert, who'd reached the bit in *King Lear* about 'poor naked wretches' being pelted by the 'pitiless storm', and urged by Taggie and Gav, had taken him in as an apprentice.

He now lived in one of the staff hostels, next to Lou-easy and Marketa, who adored and fussed over him. Despite his skill as a rider he had little ambition and spent his wages on betting or in the Dog and Trumpet at the weekends.

Jemmy's best friend was Rupert's second jockey, Stevie O'Dell. He was known as 'Meerkat' because he was very short with huge hazel eyes, and when someone announced that a pretty girl had come into the pub, Meerkat would bob up and down, calling, 'Where, where?' Meerkat supplemented his income by modelling sofas in television commercials. He was so little, he made the sofas look huge. Brave as a lion despite his size, unlike Eddie he had no weight problems.

Celeste, meanwhile, was livid when Rupert stopped her riding out because her lousy seat was giving the horses sore backs and because she was constantly defying him by talking on her mobile. If it hadn't been for Gavin reluctantly defending her, she would have been fired long ago. She was so lazy and bitchy, still reserving her venom for Gala who, despite being much larger than Celeste, was allowed to ride out – when she could be freed up from taking care of Old Eddie.

Gala, despite Celeste's constant jibes about 'barrels of lard', had, in fact, shed most of her spare tyres. Eddie, nearly down to the required 120 lbs to ride on the flat, looked so infinitely touching with his blond curls and bright-blue eyes dominating his thin face, that everyone, especially Lark and Gala, wanted to mother him.

Lark didn't think Trixie, who had been taking her A-levels again, cherished Eddie nearly enough, and every week in Penscombe church she prayed: 'If You think it's right, Lord, please let Eddie ride Master Quickly.'

Then she would dream of leading them in after Quickly won the 2000 Guineas, because after big races, they included the names of stable lasses and lads in the *Racing Post*, so hers, Lark Tolland, would lie beneath the jockey, Eddie Alderton.

Rupert was still away a lot, but put everyone on the jump when he came home, invariably on fault-finding missions. He was not a great one for early-morning chat, but out on the gallops, riding Safety Car, his narrowed eyes missed nothing.

On one lovely June morning, Second Lot, which included Quickly and Dave, had just reached the start of the two-mile grass gallop when Eddie erupted out of the house, whooping with joy, leaping over fences and running towards them wearing nothing but jeans to show off his emaciated six-pack and his new beautiful body.

'I'm down to 122 pounds, for Christ's sake!'

'Oh my goodness,' breathed Lark.

Meerkat and Jemmy were already up on Touchy Filly and Dave. Gav was about to mount Quickly, but Eddie was too fast for him, vaulting into the saddle and giving Quickly's flanks a whack with his hand.

Despite Lark trying to hang on to him, Quickly took off, with Eddie encouraging him, whooping louder and louder, faster and faster, off the end of the gallop and into rough grass and the buttercups, nearly over the horizon, but still near enough to show how dazzlingly he could ride at speed. He only managed to pull Quickly up when they were blocked by a barn, crammed full of hay in black plastic bags.

Quickly's inflamed nostrils were as big as side-plates, his heaving flanks a snaking mass of veins, but he was still leaping around as, bare-chested and bare-footed, Eddie rode him back into the yard.

'This is the fastest horse I have ever ridden. He cannot be beat,' he ecstatically told Rupert and Gav. 'He is the fastest horse anyone has *ever* ridden. Can I have him for my birthday?'

A for-once speechless Rupert was poised to yell at him when the normally quiet Gavin, who'd devoted nine months to settling Quickly, asked Eddie if he really wanted to fuck up a great horse? And, pulling him to the ground, hit him across the yard.

'And you've just lost the chance to ride Quickly in his first race,' roared Rupert. 'I'm bloody putting up Meerkat.'

'That's cool,' piped up Meerkat. 'Quickly's so little he'll make me look huge.'

Despite spats, everyone was looking forward to Quickly's first race. He still had a tendency to plant himself on the gallops or refuse to go into the starting stalls, but once off, he let no one overtake him and was effortlessly beating even the best three- and four-year-olds on the gallops with New Year's Dave not far behind.

Dora Belvedon, thrilled with a new star to promote, had great plans.

'Just think, if Mrs Wilkinson could accompany Quickly to all his races, it would give her adoring public a chance to see her again. She could become a cult – or, ha ha, colt – figure, like Andy Murray's mother.'

'Don't be fatuous,' snarled Rupert, who wanted Quickly out of the limelight. Nothing was more alarming for a young colt in his first race than screaming crowds and cameras flashing. He refused even to let Ed Whitaker, the *Racing Post*'s star photographer, take any pictures of Quickly.

The press, however, revved up by Dora and remembering Mrs Wilkinson's Grand National and Love Rat's sprinting glories, were already flagging up Quickly's date with destiny, and training their long lenses on the gallops.

26

Quickly's first race, so he wouldn't be stressed by a long journey, was a six-furlong sprint at nearby Rutminster, where back in the eighteenth century Rupert Black had triumphed on Sweet Azure.

Since then, relations between the Campbell-Blacks and the Northfields had never been cordial. Lord Rutshire, who owned Rutminster Racecourse, was, for example, continually outraged that any attempt to cover parts of the land in houses had been blocked by action groups, their websites invariably adorned by words of support accompanied by a photograph of an arrogantly handsome Rupert Campbell-Black.

This particularly infuriated Lord Rutshire's younger brother Roddy Northfield, reminding him that forty years ago, his fiancée, now wife, Enid, had been seduced by Rupert at a hunt ball in a blue and green William Morris-curtained four-poster.

Enid, although thoroughly taken in both senses, had been wise enough to appreciate no future lay with rackety Rupert, but her eyes softened at the mention of his name and she still dressed up more and attended meetings when Rupert's horses were known to be running.

Rupert had always pushed every rule to the limit, whether it was running a half-fit horse to keep its handicap down or apply-ing team tactics to rein in an opponent, or even secretly persuading a clerk of the course to water it, if one of his horses needed less quick ground.

Roddy, a keen horseman, had started life as a steward before rising to the position of Stipendiary Steward. These were paid professionals who moved around different enquiries, advising the resident stewards what to do.

This invariably involved giving Rupert Campbell-Black and his jockeys a hard time. Recently Roddy had been appointed to the board of the British Racing Association, laughingly known as BRA, the governing body who attempted the almost impossible task of keeping a vast multi-faceted sport clean and in order, a sport that was, in addition, chronically underfunded and resistant to change.

Neither Rupert nor Roddy missed an opportunity to take a swipe at one another. Rupert, taking delight in winning at Rutminster, felt it would be the ideal spot for Quickly to make a not too public debut.

Having been abroad chasing winners, what he'd forgotten was that during an awards ceremony at Rutminster Racecourse three years ago, Quickly's mother Mrs Wilkinson, nominated for Sports Personality of the Year, had been believed to have been killed when a bomb went off in the stable block. In fact, Mrs Wilkinson had been whisked away to a safe haven just beforehand, returning in glory to dry the tears on the faces of thousands of mourners at her memorial service in Rutminster Cathedral.

The publicity team at Rutminster, aided by Dora, felt it would really pull in the crowds if Quickly's first race coincided with his mother's return to the racecourse to open the rebuilt stable block. Dora then wrote glowing press releases about the Debut of the Decade and Quickly combining Love Rat's sprinting glory with Mrs Wilkinson's stamina.

Returning from America and discovering in addition that Cosmo's star two-year-old I Will Repay had been entered in the same race, a furious Rupert ordered that Quickly be scratched.

'Far too public, it'll freak him out – and Touchy Filly,' who was making her debut in an earlier race. Gav, however, talked him round.

'He's ready, Rupert. He really needs the race and Roddy Northfield will accuse you of being chicken.'

'If you pull out,' begged Dora, 'think of the disappointment of people who've come miles to see him and Mrs Wilkinson, and how reassuring for Quickly to have a family member present.'

'Don't use that ghastly expression,' snapped back Rupert.

It was on an intensely cold June day, grey, foggy, with torrential rain and a vicious wind turning Rutminster's lowering woods inside out, that Cosmo's helicopter, bringing Tarqui McGall from Ireland to ride I Will Repay, was nearly blown off-course.

Stalking the course with Gavin, and a furiously striding Rupert, poor little Meerkat had to run to keep up, and was further humiliated when Roddy Northfield ordered him out of the weighing room because: 'Children aren't allowed in here.'

Lark, who hadn't slept, had spent yesterday's break praying for Quickly to win. Her heart beat faster as the horseboxes of the great trainers, Isa Lovell, Tommy Westerham, Charles Norville and horrible Brute Barraclough, rolled into the lorry park. Quickly looked wonderful; a few new dapples had enabled her to get a shine on his silver coat. But to avoid stress, she'd forborne to plait his mane or stencil patterns on his quarters.

Despite the vile weather, the crowds had turned out to see Mrs Wilkinson open the stable block and cheered tumultuously when she did a lap of honour with Chisolm at her heels. People were also fascinated to see how Quickly would respond to meeting his long-lost family again – with rapture like that programme about humans on television? But predictably when led out, Quickly flattened his ears and took a bite out of Mrs Wilkinson and lashed out with both barrels at Chisolm. So Lark and Dora hastily whisked them apart.

Valent and Etta, in a stylish periwinkle-blue coat, had been asked to lunch in the Northfield Suite, which lay at the end of the stands.

Roddy Northfield, despite a port-wine face and the bulging eyes and pouting lips of a predatory turbot, fancied himself with the ladies. He also regarded himself as a bit of a character, encouraging privileged acquaintances to call him 'Rodders' and celebrating his penchant for wearing too-tight red trousers.

'So clever to match them to his face,' bitched Rupert.

Having heard rumours that Rupert and Etta were not bosom friends (and what a pretty bosom she had), 'Rodders' set out to charm her and Valent, who would make the ideal sponsor.

'We're thinking of naming a new race the Mrs Wilkinson Cup next year over our jumps course – wondered if you'd be interested in sponsoring it?'

'Oh Valent, wouldn't that be lovely?' said Etta who, despite being sick with nerves about Quickly's debut, was being cheered by several glasses of champagne.

Looking out of the window, she could see Mrs Wilkinson, with Chisolm and Dora, going walkabout in the crowd and shaking hooves with her fans.

'She does love these outings,' she said thoughtfully. 'I wonder if she ought to race again?'

'Why not let her have another foal,' suggested Roddy, 'and send her to Roberto's Revenge. He loves greys.'

'Rupert would have a coronary,' muttered Valent.

'Rupert not here?' said a disappointed Enid Northfield, who was wearing a lot of scent and a willow-green wool dress with a label saying £350 still attached.

'I think he's walking the course,' said Etta.

Enid, who had put on weight and would have taken up most of the William Morris-curtained four-poster, if she and Rupert had re-enacted any romping, was also nicknamed 'Damsire' because she was always rabbiting on about horses' pedigrees.

In the same race as Quickly, she and Roddy had a two-year-old called Red Trousers, and she went into a long preamble tracing his genealogy back to the Ark.

'He's out of Scarlet Woman and by Happy Hipsters,' she told Etta, 'and has an excellent page.'

'Like Good King Wenceslas,' giggled Etta.

'I actually think I Will Repay will walk it,' said Roddy. 'Isa Lovell is such a good trainer, much more thorough than Rupert

C-B.' That should please Etta if she weren't too keen on Rupert.

Pretty woman, he couldn't resist whisking her next door to the Royal Box where, amidst the portraits of famous horses was an oil painting of a man with dark red hair, fox-brown eyes slightly too close together, and a thin clever face. He was seated at a desk holding a book on painting. At his feet lay a white mastiff.

'Who was he?' asked Etta. 'Lovely face, sweet dog.'

'An elder son, James Northfield,' said Roddy, 'who was killed in a race back in the eighteenth century. The title passed to my great-great-great-great-great-great-grandfather, Rufus Northfield, who became Lord Rutshire; the title has now been handed down to my elder brother, Rufus. That's his portrait over there.'

On the opposite wall, four times as large, was a splendid new oil of the Hon. Roddy in a white tie and a red hunting tail-coat. The artist had tactfully toned down the port-wine complexion, slightly narrowed the bulging cheeks, added shape to the turbot mouth and blended grey into the dark red hair, giving the face a distinction it didn't possess.

'Who painted that?' asked Etta.

'A conservationist,' drawled a voice, as Rupert drifted in, wet from walking the course. 'Make the perfect poster for *Save the Hippopotamus*.'

Whereupon Roddy turned magenta and Enid went into gales of laughter.

'Naughty Rupert,' she said, then, holding her scented cheek up to be kissed, 'we're so looking forward to seeing Master Quickly. Who was his damsire?'

'Peppy Koala,' said Rupert. 'Bloody cold out, I need a drink.'

So did Master Quickly, who was livid at being deprived of food and water before his race, and when Lark tried to compensate by sponging his mouth, tried to eat the sponge. Lark, on the other hand, hadn't touched the sandwich Gav had bought her, insisting she eat something. Not to appear ungrateful, she'd shoved it in her jacket pocket. She mustn't transmit her nerves to Quickly.

In his jockey's bag, Meerkat stole a look at the Good Luck card from Gee Gee. If he came in the first three, he'd ask her out.

Back at Penscombe, Gala watched the race with Old Eddie and Young Eddie.

'God, those woods are sinister. Were they the ones through which Rupert Black and James Northfield raced?' asked Gala. 'You wouldn't be able to see a thing.'

'Can't see much today,' said Eddie, who was eating his way through Old Eddie's huge box of chocolates.

The runners were circling the paddock, some horses controlled by a stable lad on either side. Quickly was led only by Lark. Gav felt he'd fret less and feel freer with just one person.

'Pretty girl that,' said Old Eddie.

'Very,' said Young Eddie. 'I Will Repay looks bloody good too – he's twice the size of Quickly.'

And here was Meerkat walking out with the other jockeys, a rainbow of colours on such a dark day.

It should've been me, thought Eddie bitterly, scooping up a couple more chocolates. Without rides he had lost his incentive to lose weight.

Nice to see Etta and Valent, such an attractive man, holding hands, thought Gala, as the couple joined Gav, who was chewing gum, and Rupert to brief Meerkat. The draw wasn't brilliant, with Quickly furthest away from the rail.

'Stay on the outside – he hates being hemmed in,' Rupert told Meerkat. 'Keep him as balanced as possible, and let him loose at the furlong pole.'

As Gav legged up Meerkat, Quickly took the opportunity to tug Gav's cheese sandwich out of Lark's pocket and wolf it down before she could grab it back. Lark went crimson, but catching Gav's eye, they couldn't stop laughing.

'I'll try and get a word with Rupert Campbell-Black,' said Sean Boyce from *At the Races*, adding, 'Well, perhaps not,' when Rupert told him to 'beat it'.

*

Down at the start, it was even colder, the woods beetle-browed, glowering down on the water meadows. The spire of Rutminster Cathedral waved an admonitory finger.

Quickly had been led away from the other horses, as one by one they were loaded. Perhaps the ghost of James Northfield's horse Spartan was putting a hex on him as, shivering ostentatiously, he lashed out at the loaders in their dark-green jackets, lifted his tail and crapped lengthily into the television camera, then refused to budge.

'Come on, Quickly,' begged Meerkat.

To fox him, the loaders unearthed an orange and black hood to put over his eyes, and circled him to kid him he wasn't going into the stalls. But Quickly was not to be fooled.

'For fuck's sake, move it, Meerkat,' yelled Tarqui McGall. He was trying to calm I Will Repay who, like the other horses, was stamping and plunging to get out of his stall.

Outraged at Meerkat tugging at his tail, having been lifted off his feet by the entire six-strong loader team into a stall, which turned out to be much wider than those at home, Quickly pondered, then calmly lay down, stretching out on his belly, until Meerkat's feet were resting on the ground.

There was an aghast pause.

'At last you've got a horse the right size for you,' mocked Tarqui.

'Get up, Quickly!' screamed Meerkat.

Jockeys and loaders were crying with laughter as Quickly took a pick of grass, decided it was muddy and, closing his eyes, pretended to go to sleep. The only answer was to open the gates and let the other runners go.

The dark-brown I Will Repay bounded away to finish four lengths in front of Roddy Northfield's Red Trousers, and notching up yet another win for Roberto's Revenge. Valent was livid. Etta, who'd had several glasses of champagne, got the giggles.

'Quickly reminds me of a lovely children's book by Beverly Nichols called *The Tree That Sat Down*,' she said, and got a murderous look from Rupert. Turning on Gavin, he snarled: 'I thought you said that horse needed the run.'

Roddy Northfield was in heaven.

'Pity Campbell-Black let the day down. He shouldn't spend so much time abroad – loses track of things.'

Everyone else thought it hilarious. The press had a field day.

'Great White Hype,' said the *Sunday Times*.

'Belly Flop,' said the *Racing Post*, adding that 'Master Quickly enhanced neither the reputation of his sire nor his dam when he refused to start at Rutminster.'

Lark was in despair; Gav, hiding his bitter disappointment, resisted having a drink and went back to the drawing board.

27

In his second race at nearby Bath, in front of a much smaller crowd, and having bitten several loaders, Quickly decided to run. Meerkat had been told to stay at the back and move up slowly, using Quickly's turn of foot to pick off the leaders.

This time, an over-excited Quickly, battling for his head, fighting an impotently hauling Meerkat, set off like a rocket, until the rocket ran out of fuel at the furlong pole and Quickly out of puff. Stopping dead, shooting Meerkat over his head and on to the rails, he started to graze as all the other runners overtook him.

'Don't you ever feed him?' tweeted Cosmo.

With poor Meerkat sidelined with a cracked wrist, and constant pleading from Gala and Taggie, Rupert agreed to let Eddie ride Quickly at an evening meeting on the All-Weather track at Wolverhampton.

The journey was worthwhile because in later races were entered Touchy Filly, who was no longer a maiden, and a two-year-old called Dick the Second, whose chestnut coat had a roan tinge like King Richard II's horse Barbary. Rupert would miss the race because he was in America.

Lark was thrilled. At last she would lead up Prince Charming on his white charger. Frogmarched into Cheltenham by Marketa, she had been persuaded into the skinniest jeans and a clinging turquoise T-shirt.

After a sleepless night, she rose at four to wash her hair. In the lorry, Dora, Marketa, Lark and Eddie, who'd had a row with Trixie because she'd forgotten it was his big day and asked him to pick up Hereward from nursery, sat behind Gav, who was reading *War and Peace*, and the yard driver, Bobby Walker.

Lark dropped off the moment the lorry left Penscombe, falling across Eddie, and only waking as they approached Wolverhampton to find him laughing down at her and stroking her face.

'If I win, will you sleep with me?' he murmured.

'Shut up, Eddie!' snapped Gav, Dora and Bob in unison as a horribly embarrassed Lark shot bolt upright.

A glorious day cheered them all up. Wolverhampton is a much prettier course than it looks on television. The leaves of the cherry trees, lining the course, danced in the June sunshine. At the top of the course was a large pale-blue factory which evidently cleaned trains.

'Pity it can't clean trainers,' said Dora, glaring at dodgy Brute Barraclough, who was running a very ugly liver chestnut colt called Geoffrey, which Brute had managed to flog to some dotty old lady, Mrs Ford-Winters, when he'd visited her at the same care home that had kicked out Old Eddie for pouncing on residents. Brute's sweet-faced wife, Rosaria, who did all the work at the yard, was devoted to Geoffrey and believed he had great potential. Brute, who bullied Rosaria and cheated on her the whole time, was a lover both of Janey Lloyd-Foxe and Bethany Latton.

Will I ever go to the races and find someone who's not slept with Bethany? Gav thought wearily.

The entrance to Wolverhampton Racecourse lay through the foyer of a big hotel, and in the lift to the various racecourse boxes, restaurants and trainer and owners stands, one passed floors full of bedrooms. These were often occupied by professional punters, but it was also where Brute Barraclough was alleged to have pleasured Celeste several times. Tonight he was planning a romp with his Head Lad, Alison.

Valent had also booked a room for himself and Etta, so they

157

could either celebrate or drown their sorrows, depending on the result of the race.

On the way in, Gav saw a loader from Quickly's second race who turned pale at the thought of loading him again. Lark, who had groomed Quickly earlier, had only to give him a brief body brush and rub him over with a wet tea-towel to make his coat gleam like glass.

'He looks wery well,' cried Marketa. 'Go and get changed, I'll look after Quickly.'

Celeste had been known to spend over an hour to tart herself up before leading up horses but Lark took only a few minutes to brush her teeth and wriggle into her new jeans and turquoise T-shirt, which clung excitingly over her new Wonderbra.

'You look stunning, wery woluptuous,' said Marketa as she powdered Lark's nose and applied a dab of green eyeshadow and mascara to her pale lashes.

Etta and Valent stood in the centre of the parade ring. Both too nervous to have any lunch, they were planning dinner in the reputedly wonderful restaurant upstairs. A bottle of Bollinger was already on ice so they could watch later races on a television set at the end of their table.

With Rupert away, Dora had marshalled the press to witness Eddie's first ride back on the flat. Towering above the other jockeys, he looked much more glamorous, Rupert's sapphire and emerald colours bringing out the brilliant blue of his eyes and, despite the dramatic weight loss, he still had long legs and broad shoulders.

Brute's colt Geoffrey, with his huge flopping donkey ears and half-closed eyes, was certainly the plainest in the parade ring.

'That 'orse ain't a two-year-old,' shouted a wag in the crowd. ''E's an old age pensioner!'

Wincing at the guffaws, Rosaria, who was leading him up, patted Geoffrey protectively.

Gav, standing with Etta and Valent, was briefing Eddie.

'Ride him positively, try and sit behind and move up near the end. He can get through any gap.'

But he'd lost Eddie, who was looking at Lark as she led up a jig-jogging Quickly.

'Wow,' said Eddie. 'You should've won the best-turned-out prize. You've definitely got to promise to sleep with me if I win.'

'Shut up, Eddie,' snapped Valent and Gav as the latter legged him up.

Lark waited near the finish, clutching Marketa's hand, glued to the big screen. 'Oh please, please dear God.'

Gavin had gone down to the start with Quickly, walking him round quietly, away from the other horses. Quickly rolled his eyes but decided to behave. Having gone straight into the stalls, even though not jumping out as fast as some, he clearly hadn't listened to Gav's instructions and went straight to the front to avoid having grey grit, known as kickback, in his pretty face.

As they hurtled round the course, it could be seen how brilliantly Eddie rode and how his body seemed to melt into Quickly's. Although Quickly hung right and interfered with several horses, including Geoffrey, he didn't run out of puff and scorching past the post an amazing ten lengths clear, he ran halfway round the course again before Eddie could pull him up.

Back at Penscombe, as the bell rang out for a win, yard and stud were yelling their heads off, particularly Jemmy who had put all his wages on Quickly.

'Thank God we persuaded Rupert.' Taggie and Gala were hugging one another. 'Let's go and take carrots to Love Rat.'

Even though it was only £1,000 prize money and only 10 per cent for Eddie, it was his first win on the flat in England.

Camera crews and journalists centred on Quickly's overjoyed stable lass racing up the course, particularly when Eddie bent down and kissed her, on and on until Quickly bit her to break them up.

'Nice one,' observed Trixie, who was awaiting the results of her A-level retakes and who'd been so engrossed in a piece she was writing for the *Guardian* that she'd only just remembered to switch on the television.

Touching his hat in the same nonchalant way that a snoozing Forester flicked his tail an inch upwards when Taggie entered the room, a grinning Eddie acknowledged the applause as he rode into the winner's enclosure. Noticing the tears pouring down Lark's cheeks and the heaving prettiness of her breasts in that T-shirt, he slid off, shook hands with an ecstatic Valent and Etta, unsaddled Quickly, weighed in and after returning for a joyful photograph, took Quickly's reins and threw them at Marketa. Then, ignoring a battalion of press, he whisked a besotted Lark out of the winner's enclosure and into the hotel.

'Where are we going?' she gasped.

'For a victory shag. Stupid Brute dropped his key card – I overheard him telling Alison which room he was in.'

'We can't,' cried Lark. 'Trixie! Quickly!'

But Eddie shut her up, kissing her all the way up in the lift. Brute's card slid easily into the door. Inside was a huge double bed and a lovely view on to the course.

'Eddie, we can't – you've got to collect your prize.'

'You're my prize. Etta and Valent will collect it.'

'I've got to hose Quickly down and walk him round till he stops blowing. He needs me.'

'Not nearly as much as I do.'

'What about Dick the Second? He's in the next race.'

'It's the one after next, we've still got time.'

He was so handsome, so hot, so happy and so certain as with amazing speed he pulled her T-shirt over her head.

'Lovely,' he unhooked her bra, 'even lovelier,' and still kissing her, unzipped her jeans and despite their tightness managed to tug them off.

'Look at you, look at you.'

'What happens if Brute comes back?'

'He's got a horse in the next race.'

'Eddie, I haven't done it before.'

Eddie only stopped for a second. 'You haven't? You're a virgin?'

Lark nodded. 'I'm so sorry.'

Eddie drew down her pink pants and slid a hand between her legs.

'Not that one would know it.' And he lifted her up, laid her on the bed and was out of his silks, boots and breeches in a second.

'Eddie, I love you but I don't know how to do it.'

'Leave that to me.'

'I don't know if I've got a hymen.'

'Probably lost it, riding so much. Hi! Man,' grinned Eddie. Next moment he was on top of her. 'Oh you beauty, you've brought me luck.'

'Ow, ow, ow!' Lark gave a scream, as he thrust a considerable cock inside her. 'I love you. Ow, ow! I've always loved you.'

It was all over in a minute.

'Next time I'll make you come,' promised Eddie, kissing her.

There was blood all over the sheets, but it didn't show up on her black jeans.

Outside they ran into a hen party, a dozen drunk women wearing 'Kiss Me Quick' hats and blowing squeakers.

'Love you for supper!' they shouted at Eddie as he took Lark's hand and raced her down the landing, past maids with trolleys, piled high with towels and little bottles.

Only when they emerged outside to a baying pack of press did Eddie realize.

'You've missed a stewards' enquiry,' howled Gav.

Brute had evidently complained that Quickly, hanging right and careering round like a drunkard, had cost Geoffrey, who'd come second, the race – clearly absurd when Quickly had won by such a vast margin. But Eddie hadn't been there to fight his corner. The stewards, having watched the race several times, gave it to Geoffrey and a ten-day ban to Eddie for contempt of court.

The fall-out was hideous. Cathal would have won a vast accumulator. Jemmy had blown all his wages. Valent, who'd bet £5,000, yelled at Eddie. He and Etta had been so looking forward to hanging a silver plate on the wall, empty since Mrs Wilkinson's National Cup went back.

In the middle of Valent's dressing down, Rupert rang from America, sacked Lark until talked round by Gav, and told Eddie he'd never get a ride for the yard again.

Eddie got home to find Trixie had walked out, taking Herry and all her belongings back to Seth Bainton who, having landed this huge part, wanted to up his macho image by leaking the fact he was Herry's father.

'Seth, who is even more unsuitable than Eddie,' cried a distraught Etta.

Eddie was utterly devastated. Poor Lark, poor Trixie. How could he have behaved so appallingly? Across the valley, up in the sky, he could see the pale moon, two days short of the half-way mark, so it resembled a jockey's sad, emaciated face, his hair hidden by his helmet, turned-down hollowed eyes and nose just smudges, the mouth a blur above a pointed chin.

That's me, he thought despairingly.

Even Taggie was furious with him, having pushed his cause with Rupert. He'd let down Gav and Quickly, who'd run like an angel, not to mention poor, poor Lark.

The press had a field day with endless jokes about Eddie putting himself rather than the race to bed and pictures of him and Lark everywhere.

'What a good thing we bought you those smart jeans and that cool T-shirt,' crowed Marketa. 'You look really good.'

Matters weren't helped by Valent bollocking a returning Rupert for spending so much time away.

'To hell with Love Rat, you should be here to keep an eye on things.'

Whereupon an irate Rupert chewed Gav out for not keeping *his* eye on Eddie, whereupon an irate Gala flared up: 'That's not fair! Gav's been sorting Quickly out ever since he came here. He's done an amazing job on him and Eddie.'

'Has he now?' said Rupert in his 'whatever gave you the right' voice. 'That horse will end up as a supermarket burger if he doesn't get his act together.'

'Oh burger off!' yelled Gala.

With Eddie and Trixie gone, the much-coveted top flat of the hostel, formerly known as 'The Shaggery', was available again. Not that it was a very attractive proposition, neither Eddie nor Trixie having done any housework since they moved in. Hundreds of unwashed socks festered under the bed, scrumpled-up tissues lay like snow, washing-up in the sink hit the ceiling, alongside discarded green-with-mould yoghurt tubs. Jokes were flying around about Quickly's friend Purrpuss being offered a spot of moonlighting to get rid of the mice or Safety Car being recruited to sweep the floor.

Celeste was pressuring Gav to suggest to Rupert that she and he moved in, but for once Gav stood firm. He was needed to keep an eye on the yard in his rooms over the tack room.

So Rupert offered the flat to Louise, Marketa and Lark, who herself proceeded to do most of the blitzing. She also had to fight off endless pressure from her parents to leave such a den of iniquity and return home to a safe secretarial job in Essex. She tried to forget Eddie, who'd fled back home to Palm Beach, and buried herself in work, comforted that both Dave and Touchy Filly were cleaning up and Quickly must win a race soon.

Happily, a solution was at hand. Quickly, albeit only two, was as over-sexed as Eddie. In the paddock before his next race over six furlongs at Windsor, he caught sight of a dear little dark-brown filly with neat white socks on her hind legs like a schoolgirl, called Trans Jennifer. Quickly proceeded to get all colty, arching his neck, lifting his back, snorting and trying to mount her.

'Naughty,' said Lark, shaking his bridle, embarrassed that the press were still taking her picture.

'How's the Wolverhampton Wanderer?' shouted a wag in the crowd.

Windsor is the most lovely racecourse with a white clubhouse, willows everywhere, through which can be seen boats gliding up a River Thames flickering in the evening sun. Etta and Valent arrived in one of these boats.

Rupert was away again, so Gav gave instructions to Meerkat, who was apprehensive of riding with a wrist still tender and weak.

'The course as you know is in the shape of a figure of eight, which means many bends, so for a change try and get Quickly, who has an outside draw, far ahead so you are not overtaken on the bends by horses on the inside.'

163

Quickly, however, had ideas of his own. When the bell told the jockeys to mount, he mounted Trans Jennifer.

'Oh Gawd, not again,' said a loader as Quickly bounded down to the start and tried to follow Jennifer into her stall, and when her door slammed in his face, shot into his stall next door and was so busy whispering sweet everythings into her ear, he missed the kick when the doors swung open.

Having shown phenomenal acceleration by the speed with which he made up ground forfeited in the stalls, he then proceeded to show off by hurtling down the course beside Jennifer, whisking in and out of the figure-of-eight bends, surging ahead of her to win by a very turned head and jumping on her again in the winner's enclosure.

'Randy little sod, like his trainer,' tweeted Cosmo.

Etta, Valent and Gav were overjoyed, so was Meerkat whose wrist had held out.

'First ride back, he really looked after me,' he told Robert Cooper from *At the Races*. 'He's the real deal, nothing gets near him at home.'

'And at least Quickly's no longer a maiden,' crowed Dora.

28

The great Ebor Festival takes place at York at the end of August. Four days of fantastic racing, to which Rupert always took a stack of horses, and which included two huge races where two-year-olds could compete. Rupert proceeded to enter New Year's Dave, already unbeaten in five starts, in the Gimcrack – an extremely famous race for two-year-old colts and a Group Two, which is the equivalent of the Championship Division in football and which offered splendid prize money of £200,000. Dave was second favourite with Cosmo Rannaldini's dazzling colt I Will Repay as favourite.

Even more audaciously, Rupert had entered Master Quickly for the Nunthorpe Stakes, one of the few Group Ones (the equivalent of football's Premier League) which allows two-year-olds to race against their mighty elders. This fastest race in Europe is a five-furlong hurtle for a vast £250,000. Quickly, being only two, would get a massive weight concession to compete with older, stronger horses including several previous winners and Cosmo's four-year-old, Ivan the Terrorist, a dark-brown belter with a raking stride.

Rupert was taking a terrific risk with Quickly. The only way to win the Nunthorpe was to explode out of the stalls and scorch down the straight York track. To prepare a horse, you must put him on a high-energy diet twelve days before, allowing him as little exercise as possible, and then only on a tight rein and at a hand canter . . . not yet, not yet . . . till on race day, he's right on the edge, ready to explode, coiled like a spring – yet somehow you have to stop him fizzing over. The problem was how to get anything as volatile and hyped-up as Quickly down to the start, in front of a vast clamorous crowd and a mass of press.

The calming process began when Quickly travelled up to Yorkshire with Purrpuss in a cat basket. Purring loudly, and ignoring the swallows swooping around, he instantly settled on Quickly's back in the beautiful and tranquil stables. Quickly was in Box 73, which was once home to the great Sea the Stars and which Assistant Clerk of the Course Anthea Morshead had recommended because it was quiet, and would mean Quickly couldn't see people coming and going into the yard. Rupert had also applied to bring Safety Car to 'pony' Quickly down to the start. Quite a euphemism for a seventeen-hands-high, one-eared horse with a straggly tail.

Next door to Quickly and Safety Car was stabled New Year's Dave, on whose chances the *Racing Post* were very keen.

DAVE THE RAVE said the headline above a lovely cover picture of him sticking out his tongue for a Polo. They were less enthusiastic about Quickly's chances.

'So far Mrs Wilkinson's foal has shown little beyond an ability to make a nuisance of himself.'

All the stable staff were thrilled to be going to York, which had a marvellous canteen and fantastic accommodation, with travelling Head Lads given rooms to themselves.

Marketa and Louise made no secret of their excitement at going, getting their hair streaked and tactlessly going on about how, with the overnight stay, they'd get the chance to pull Gav. Celeste was furious to be left behind, particularly as Lark would be up there as well, the little goody goody.

'I'll have to stay at home with Celeste,' said Jemmy Carter gloomily.

I'll have to stay at home with Old Eddie, thought Gala, who once again wished she was working in the yard.

Lark, who had to share a room at York, was reduced to

holding a pillow over her head to avoid hearing Marketa noisily enjoying A. N. Other, who turned out to be one of Isa Lovell's lads.

'Did you learn anything useful about Isa's horses?' asked Gav, the next day.

'No, he was much too good in bed.'

'My roommate,' grumbled Roving Mike, 'stinks the room out with curry and keeps me awake praying. I got up in the night to have a pee and fell over him.'

York is the most beautiful racecourse, set in lush parkland known as the Knavesmire, where public executions were once staged. Lovely houses peep out of huge dark-green trees in their full summer glory. Near the stands soar massive pillars, covered in posters of last year's winners and unashamedly announcing, *Welcome to Yorkshire! England's biggest and most magnificent county.*

A vast copper beech shaded the parade ring, the bands played, and the glamorous First Day crowd, dressed up to the nines, were out to enjoy themselves. It had rained heavily in the night, but Rupert and Gav weren't too worried. Dave loved the mud as much as hearing the *rat tat tat* of his feet on a quick surface.

'The greatest horses go on any ground,' said Rupert as he, Gav, a yawning, hungover Cathal and Meerkat, running to keep up, splashed the course.

Valent was overjoyed at a chance to show his beloved county off to Etta. Driving instead of flying to York so they could appreciate the scenery, they passed houses of faded roan brick and ploughed fields the warm red-brown of bay horses. In other fields, giant gold cotton reels were being harvested. Bright pink willowherb and scarlet mountain ash berries brightened the verges.

A signpost pointing one way directed them *To the North* and *To the South.*

'Just like I feel,' sighed Etta. 'Oh please God let him run well.'

'He's brilliant.' Valent put a hand on her thigh. 'Master Quickly's only rival is himself.'

What enchanted Etta were the flowers all over the racecourse; even the stables were brightened by hanging baskets of crimson petunias. Quickly seemed very chilled when they visited him. Purrpuss, stretched out on his quarters, was washing behind his black ears.

'Oh dear, that means more rain,' noted Etta.

As the course was half a mile away from the stables, horses had to leave about fifty minutes before the race. This calmed down some horses because they enjoyed the long walk across the Knavesmire; others became over-excited by the wide-open space and upset by a different routine, particularly if an earlier race was still in progress. Taking no chances, Isa Lovell had opted to box any horses over.

'I do hope the going won't be too testing,' (a new word she had learnt) said Etta.

She and Valent had been invited by the Chairman, Lord Grimthorpe, to lunch in the Ebor Stand. Etta, who was wearing a new daffodil-yellow suit, was far too nervous to do more than toy with a first course of goats' cheese and asparagus, followed by lobster, crab and prawn salad. She was, however, encouraged to knock back several glasses of magical white wine by the charming trainer on her right, who was called Tommy Westerham. Tommy said he tended to read wine lists rather than books, and was puffing away on an electronic cigarette to help him give up smoking.

'Training horses,' he added, 'is such a stressful profession.'

'Does that cigarette have any side-effects?' asked Etta.

'It's made me impotent.' Tommy roared with laughter. 'No bad thing with four children at boarding school.'

Tommy, who had a big white-faced bay in the Nunthorpe, called Mobile Charger, knew all about Love Rat, Mrs Wilkinson and Quickly.

'Seems a tricky bugger.' He also asked lots of questions about Rupert – 'an even trickier bugger.'

Etta felt comforted but changed the subject to the thrill of having Mrs Wilkinson's foal running.

168

'Having a homebred win,' agreed Tommy, 'is the most exciting and satisfying thing in the world. Breeders are a different species, in it for the long haul. They care far more deeply for their horses; they get a sense of dynasty. Colts and fillies you've bred are like grandchildren.'

'Much less of a worry,' mused Etta, thinking of Trixie back with Seth.

'I'm not very good with little people,' confessed Tommy, 'and not very good with little adults either. Jockeys drive me round the twist, cocky little bastards – particularly the successful ones.'

Across the room, Etta noticed Lord Grimthorpe leaping up to kiss a drenched but pretty dark girl who'd just arrived and was overflowing with apologies and 'please don't bothers' as he found her a chair and whistled up a large drink.

'Who's that?' asked Etta.

'Darling Rosaria Barraclough, married to the unspeakably vile Brute. She does all the work and he takes all the credit and any money she makes, and sells on any horse that looks like being any good. Today, for instance, she's had to do all the driving, mucking out and leading up herself because Brute's taken any remaining lads off to Goodwood. Normally she'd be in the stables roughing it and Brute would be in Hospitality. She's got an unbelievably plain horse called Geoffrey running in the Gimcrack.'

'I know Geoffrey,' said Etta. 'Quickly beat him at Wolverhampton. Rosaria looks so sweet.'

'She is. Hi, darling.' Tommy waved at Rosaria, who went crimson and waved back. 'Someone ought to rescue her. Do you mind if I eat your lobster?'

'Oh please, such a waste to leave it.'

Another charming trainer called Chas Norville had sat down in the empty place on Etta's left, apologizing for being late. Having agreed with her that he was far too nervous to eat, he then wolfed four cream buns, washed down with three large glasses of champagne.

Chas had a three-year-old in the Nunthorpe Stakes, a filly called Trans Jennifer, who turned out to be Quickly's girlfriend.

169

'She's gorgeous. Perhaps he'll come out of his gates to keep up with her,' said Etta hopefully.

'Did Valent really give you Mrs Wilkinson as a wedding present?' asked Chas. When Etta nodded, both men said she and Valent *must* come to their Open Days in Newmarket. Etta was sure they were only being sweet to her because she had a very rich husband who might buy their horses, but she was having fun.

'Horses are no problem, it's the owners,' Chas said. 'Rupert's so lucky he's only got you, who's clearly adorable, so only himself to please. Imagine the horror when you have two owners in the same race.'

Then, as Cosmo strolled in with Mrs Walton: 'God knows who's bankrolling him. I've just sold him Trans Jennifer's half-sister, a beautiful filly, for an absolute fortune. She's brilliant, bound to win lots of races.'

'How can you bear to part with her?'

'Can't afford to fall in love with horses. I've got a hundred people working for me who need to feel secure in their jobs. So I had to sell her.'

'Oh goodness,' murmured Etta. 'There's Roddy Northfield,' who was pressing his turbot lips against Rosaria's hollow cheeks.

'He's my owner,' Tommy told her, 'and easily the worst. Pompous ass, always shouting if his horses lose.'

'How on earth,' Roddy was bellowing to Lord Grimthorpe, 'did Campbell-Black get that delinquent Quickly into the Nunthorpe?'

'He's won two races,' said Lord Grimthorpe reasonably.

'Wolverhampton and Windsor, they were flukes. He only beat mediocre horses.'

'One of which was mine,' called out Chas.

Roddy looked round. 'Etta, Etta.' He changed red-trousered legs briskly. 'How good to see you. Is Valent here?'

'He's over there.'

Glancing across the room, Etta saw that Valent was also having fun with glamorous blondes, one of them Lady Grimthorpe, on either side of him. Looking up, he blew a kiss to her. It was so heavenly not to worry, as she always had with Sampson, her late husband, that Valent might surreptitiously be making assignments.

'Nice people,' said Valent, taking her hand afterwards. 'You look lovely.'

Big racecourses often have wonderful art. On the way out, Etta was enchanted to pass a portrait on the wall of a legendary horse called Voltigeur, whose favourite companion had been a cat, who'd sit for hours on his back. Just like Purrpuss. What a great omen!

Back at Penscombe, the excitement was mounting with all the staff in the stud and the yard gathering round television sets. Leaving Old Eddie having an afternoon sleep, Gala had just slipped out to join them when she felt hands round her breasts and a lingering kiss on the back of her neck. Swinging round, she found a laughing suntanned Young Eddie back from America.

'What are you doing here?' shrieked everyone.

'I knew Grandpa was at York.'

'Don't think he's quite ready to serve up the fatted calf,' said Gala.

'It's not fatted calves I'm interested in.' Eddie ran his hands up her legs. 'You're looking stunning – we must sleep together soon.'

'Only if Quickly wins tomorrow.'

When Jemmy had put all his wages on Quickly that morning, word had flashed around the bookmaking world. Stable lads usually knew something. As a result, Quickly's odds shortened dramatically.

Up at York, the two-year-olds were coming into the paddock for the six-furlong Gimcrack watched by Taggie, Rupert and Gav, the two men very tired from racing at Deauville and gruelling sales in America.

Led up by Lark, New Year's Dave looked an absolute picture as, with ears pricked, he sauntered round the paddock, full of confidence, taking everything in. His dazzling white star set off his gleaming chestnut coat, and on his quarters Lark had stencilled a leopard in recognition of Rupert Black's legendary sire.

'She's marvellous, that girl,' Rupert murmured to Taggie.

'That's Rupert's Dave,' said the crowd approvingly.

New Year's Dave was followed by Geoffrey, shambling, eyelids drooping like a lizard, led up by Rosaria.

'Give him some Botox,' yelled another wag in the crowd.

Rosaria blushed and put a protective arm round Geoffrey. Then, as the jockeys came out and her jockey, Dermie O'Driscoll, came over awaiting instructions, she stammered, 'Thank you so much for riding Geoffrey. He's a good old boy and much faster than he looks.'

'He's fine,' said Dermie, determined to win for Rosaria because she was so sweet.

The other discomforted person in the parade ring was Gav, who couldn't stop shaking, and not just from nerves. Nearby, admiring I Will Repay in his radiant dark-brown glory, were Isa Lovell, Cosmo, in a Panama and a very sharp pale-beige suit, and his mistress Mrs Walton. Cosmo, whom Gav had once dis-covered enjoying a foursome with his ex-wife Bethany and jockeys Ash and Tarqui, who themselves had just strutted up in Cosmo's scarlet and magenta colours.

'Poor old Gav,' Cosmo had sneered at the time. 'Can't get it hup, hup, hup,' and Gav had staggered out into the night and drunk himself insensible, keeping on drinking until Isa had fired him.

'Still not getting it hup, poor Floppy Dick?' Cosmo now murmured to Gav as everyone drifted out of the paddock to watch the race.

'Leave this to me,' murmured Rupert who'd overheard the exchange, and proceeded to call out: 'Ruth, darling, how are you?' Then as Cosmo's ravishing mistress turned back, delighted to see him, Rupert kissed her lovingly. 'When are we going to have lunch? You're not still with that poisoned dwarf surely?' he added loudly, whereupon Cosmo's face blackened with rage.

It was an even greater satisfaction to Gav when New Year's Dave gave Meerkat a flawless ride, weaving through gaps, never breaking his stride, stealing up the inner and mugging I Will Repay, and Tarqui, who was admiring himself in the big screen, on the line. Geoffrey, his spindly legs whirring, was only a nose behind them.

Racing down the course, Lark flung her arms round Dave's hardly sweating neck. 'Oh well done, Meerkat! Well done, Dave!'

Hot on her heels was Rosaria. 'Oh thank you, Dermie, thank you, Geoffrey.'

'He ran great. He's bloody fast.'

'Thank you so much. He did wonderfully.' Rosaria was reeling with relief. Geoffrey's third would enable her to pay the wages and feed the horses for another month.

The crowd was ecstatic as Rupert's royal-blue and emerald colours were superimposed on the course once more. The King was back.

Amid the joyful celebrations at Penscombe, Gala broke off dancing with Young Eddie to give Love Rat a large carrot to celebrate a great win by one of his offspring.

29

Rupert's ritual at York, which had brought him luck in the past, was to watch his runners, standing by the winner's podium and smoking a cigar. He wondered how this would work for Quickly, whose turn it was the following day.

Quickly had enjoyed walking across the Knavesmire with Safety Car. So excited were the crowd to see the old warrior with his one ear and straggly tail, that they cheered him to the rooftops; cheers that Quickly assumed were for him. The worry was how he would behave in the parade ring – into which Safety wasn't allowed. Apart from spooking at Peppa Pig, and walking around on his hind legs, however, Quickly decided to behave himself, not even showing any interest in a disappointed Trans Jennifer.

'That colt suffers from commitment phobia,' sighed Louise.

The Nunthorpe was such an important Group One race that the twenty jockeys had to line up in front of their own wooden posters which flagged up their colours, their names and that of their horses. Meerkat, the smallest jockey in the race, was so proud. All this and another good luck card from Gee Gee.

'Nice ass,' said Ash, pinching his bottom.

'Fuck off!' squealed Meerkat.

'When are we going to bed again?' called Rupert across the paddock, deliberately to wind up Cosmo.

'Naughty,' giggled Mrs Walton.

Rupert turned back to Valent. 'Have you backed Quickly?' he asked quietly.

'I have.'

'Well, back him again.'

Rupert was equally economic in his instructions as he looked down at Meerkat's green and blue quartered cap.

'Miss the kick and you're dead. Let him dominate the race – you just steer.'

'I didn't know you were breeding centipedes, Rupert,' mocked Cosmo, because Quickly, still greyhoundy, was about half the size of Ivan the Terrorist, Cosmo's hunk of a four-year-old, whose coat, being dark brown, gleamed far more glossily. Ivan was being led up by a ravishing brunette in pink hot pants, which was perhaps why Mrs Walton was flirting so pointedly with Rupert.

'Rupert, Rupert!' cried an excited Dame Hermione, Cosmo's diva mother, resplendent in white, with a huge hat, as though a turquoise flying saucer had landed on the side of her head.

Safety Car waited patiently for Quickly outside the parade ring, and such was his reassuring presence, as he ponied him down to the start, that Quickly went straight into his stalls without any fuss.

Ahead was a great green Mississippi of grass. Two minutes to the off, Cosmo and Isa, applying gamesmanship, ensured that both Violetta's Vengeance and Ivan the Terrorist went down as late as possible, knowing that young Quickly would act up if he had to wait too long.

'Why can't they fucking hurry?' asked Meerkat between chattering teeth, raking Quickly's mane to calm him as other fretting horses starting bounding and jogging.

'Fifty-eight seconds and it'll all be over,' comforted Dermie O'Driscoll, who was in the next-door stall.

The crowd were boiling over, willing Rupert, still their favourite, to get a double. Ivan the Terrorist was last in . . . and then they were off – twenty of the fastest horses in training. Exploding out of the starting stalls, Quickly set off at a furious pace, with all the fancied runners – Ivan, Mobile Charger and Trans Jennifer – struggling to keep up, past the red houses and the woods with a deafening thunder of hooves. Flabbergasted, the crowd waited for Quickly to run out of petrol but, like Dave, he ran absolutely straight, finding more and more.

Glancing between his legs, Meerkat would have needed a telescope to see the other runners. Nor was Quickly daunted by the tumult. He galloped even faster, determined to give the yelling hordes on left and right a thrill.

The race, in fact, was eerily reminiscent of Rupert Black's win more than 200 years ago: Quickly winning by so many lengths that the television screen was empty for an eternity before Ivan the Terrorist and any of the other runners passed the post. Whereupon a stunned silence was followed by the kind of roar that greets a great pianist finishing the Grieg Piano Concerto at the Proms. Quickly had smashed the course record by five seconds.

Many cameras were on Rupert's face, completely deadpan then suddenly blazing with triumph as he turned and kissed a screaming and ecstatic Taggie. Then he chucked away his cigar, so it landed in the cleavage of Enid Northfield.

'Rupert, Rupert, Rupert!' Next moment, he was engulfed by press.

'What a horse,' he told a waving flotilla of mikes. 'No one's ever seen speed like it.'

Once again, Lark pounded up the course, throwing herself on a red-nostrilled, red-eyed Quickly. Meerkat, riding in to deafening applause, could hardly speak to Channel 4 for the excitement of his first Group One win.

'He's absolutely fearless,' he gabbled.

Then, as a fanfare of trumpets welcomed him into the winners enclosure, he fingered Quickly's shoulders which were black with sweat. 'Look where his wings have sprouted – and we should all thank Lark for looking after him – she does Dave proud too.'

'Don't forget to touch your hat,' cried Lark, delighted the next moment to be embraced by an overjoyed Gav.

Quickly had fulfilled his date with destiny.

'Only beaten mediocre horses,' repeated Roddy Northfield, fishing Rupert's cigar butt out of his wife's cleavage.

'That's mine,' said Enid, snatching it back, 'and you can hardly call Ivan a mediocre horse, his damsire was Terrible Twin.'

Isa and Cosmo, who'd gone parsnip-yellow with rage, were being debriefed by Isa's son, Roman Lovell, back from Australia, who'd ridden Ivan the Terrorist.

'That Quickly's a freak, no one could beat him.'

'BF stands for Bloody Fool, not Beaten Favourite. How could you get so far behind?' raged Cosmo, getting a sharp look of reproof from Isa, who agreed with Roman that Ivan had run well.

Quickly, preening in a beautiful soft white winner's rug, perfect for Purrpuss to curl up on, decided he liked crowds. Showing a reluctance to leave the winners enclosure, he tugged off Dame Hermione's turquoise flying saucer when she tried to shove Mrs Walton aside and give Rupert a congratulatory hug.

Back at Penscombe, a large group from the yard had gathered in the Easy Lay, the bookies in Penscombe village, to watch during their break. They included Jemmy, who'd put all his £3,000 winnings on Dave back on Quickly, who was now 2–1 for the Guineas, which was a classic race for three-year-olds the following year.

Throughout the race, Banquo the Labrador, whom Gala had brought along because he was missing Rupert, kept barking and barking and being told to shut up. It was only after everyone had exploded in excitement and stopped hugging each other over new riches that they glanced round and found Banquo still barking, the bookmaker tied up and a thief who'd emptied the till legging it down Penscombe High Street. Fortunately Eddie, who had been jogging to keep his weight down, accompanied by Banquo, was able to catch up with him and retrieve the takings.

'Quickly won,' Gala told Old Eddie when she got back. 'He just raced away.'

'Who came second?' asked Old Eddie.

'Daylight,' said Gala.

And back at York, Etta, equally ecstatic as breeder of the winning horse to receive a prize of £6,000, came reeling out of the winners room half an hour later, having consumed several more glasses of champagne and brandishing both a memory stick and a framed photograph of the race which was given to winning connections.

'So brilliant,' she cried, tucking her arm through Taggie's. 'When heavenly things happen like Quickly winning today, or Valent and my wedding, you don't remember a thing afterwards unless you have a record.'

Next moment, they'd bumped into Cosmo on the way to the parade ring for the next race. Cosmo who'd always had a yen for Taggie, now raised his Panama to her, saying smoothly, 'Congratulations are in order.'

'Not from you, you horrible man,' gasped Taggie. 'Don't you ever call my husband a has-been again.'

After Quickly had been hosed down and dried off and Edward Whitaker had taken a flash photograph of him in his Nunthorpe winner's rug with Purrpuss on his back, a still-giggling, shell-shocked Lark and Marketa started packing up, preparing to load the horses into the lorry, which Gav was driving back to Penscombe.

Gav was unbelievably touched that Rupert had told the press that he, Gav, was entirely responsible for Quickly's victory. Gav had even managed to stumble a few words out himself. He was touched too that Rupert had invited him to join them for a celebratory dinner, but had refused because he couldn't get pissed like everyone else. He didn't mind because he wanted to get Quickly, Dave and Safety Car safely home, so the lorry could turn round and bring back Rupert's other horses, particularly Fleance, who were racing tomorrow. He was so happy with the way things had turned out. Both the Gimcrack and the Nunthorpe had unearthed future champions and the Gimcrack in particular had been won by Mill Reef and Rock of Gibraltar.

The celebrations would probably be over by the time he got home, but later he could watch the races over and over again.

At Penscombe, Eddie was surprised how jealous he felt, seeing Gav hugging Lark, and how nice and understanding it would have been to fall into bed with her that evening.

'Lark's got further than any of us,' sighed Gee Gee. 'Isn't Gav heaven when he smiles? I wonder if she's pulled him.'

'Don't be ridiculous,' spat Celeste.

Everyone in the world seemed to be having a ball except her. She had noticed, however, how furious Cosmo and Isa had been that New Year's Dave had beaten I Will Repay. Later, she texted Gav: 'Good thing Isa and Cosmo don't know Dave's a three-year-old,' and, as Gav swung off the motorway, taking the exit for Cheltenham, all the euphoria drained out of him.

30

The festival ended gloriously for Penscombe, with three-year-old snow-white Fleance defeating mighty older horses including Cosmo's Herb Roberto by winning the 1 mile 6 furlong Ebor Stakes, which clocked up another £200,000 for the yard and confirmed Rupert as Leading Trainer of the meeting and Love Rat its Leading Sire.

Knowing he wouldn't approve of her treating with the enemy, Dora waited until the dark-blue helicopter carrying a euphoric Rupert and Taggie had taken off for Penscombe before having an early-evening drink with her old friend Cosmo Rannaldini at his hotel.

Downing a bottle of Krug, they sat in a bar watching happy home-going racegoers, the men tieless, their shirts no longer tucked into waistbands, the women carrying hats and high heels, limping past in bare tattooed feet.

Cosmo and Dora had been friends from school, where Dora had been aware of Cosmo's iniquities, but secretly flattered to be singled out by a boy, three years her senior, who bullied everyone but herself. They laughed at each other's jokes, shared secrets and Dora had made a considerable sum selling Cosmo's and other pupils' more outrageous exploits to the press. Cosmo had won her eternal gratitude when he gave her illegal immigrant chocolate Labrador, Cadbury, sanctuary in his study and was even more amused when Cadbury devoured his entire stash of cannabis. Cosmo's aim in life was to make as much money and mischief as possible.

As he topped up Dora's glass, Cosmo appeared most interested in the goings-on at Penscombe. Not only was he incensed that Rupert had emerged as Leading Trainer and Love Rat as Leading Sire of the meeting, but even angrier that Rupert had been hitting on Mrs Walton.

'Bloody Campbell-Black, thinks he's got a divine right to all women. A light to lighten the genitals. He's nearly sixty, for Christ's sake.'

'He's only winding you up,' said Dora, hoovering up peanuts. 'He does the same to pikestaff-plain Enid Northfield just to bug Rodders. It's your fault for being horrible to him, saying he couldn't train ivy up a wall and Love Rat's a yak.'

'He's nearly sixty,' Cosmo repeated, and smiled evilly.

'But still beautiful,' mused Dora. 'The best-dressed woman on Ladies' Day asked if she could have him instead of a car.' Then, seeing Cosmo's face darken, she added hastily: 'I expect Rupert's a bit jealous. You make such a glamorous couple, and Mrs Walton is *soooo* beautiful. What's it like, living with Helen of Toyboy?' Then seeing Cosmo looking even blacker: 'Is it difficult having someone so much older?'

'I've always been old for my age.' Cosmo was checking his messages.

'You're doing so well at the moment,' continued Dora, knowing Rupert would be delighted if she could find out who was bankrolling Cosmo. 'You're got such amazing horses. Hiring Tarqui and Ash must cost a fortune – and did you really spend nearly two million for that yearling at Deauville?'

Cosmo raised an eyebrow. 'Sure Rupert didn't ask you to pump me?'

'No, no, they've gone home.'

Cosmo admired the blonde curls, the tiny nose, the large but speculative blue eyes, the sweet pink mouth. Dora was really pretty.

'How are you and Paris?' he asked.

'Sounds an awful touch-wood thing to say, but we trust each other, so Paris can get on with acting and getting a First at

Cambridge, and I with my PR and journalism, without worrying about each other.'

Did she catch a flicker of envy in Cosmo's face?

'Why don't you make it up with Rupert – send him a card congratulating him on being Leading Trainer.'

'Don't be fatuous, he'd light his cigars with it. Tell me about the adorable Taggie.'

'She is, isn't she? She's less stressed these days because Old Eddie's carer, Gala Milburn, takes a lot of work off her.'

'What's she like?'

'She's very voluptuous, with lovely sleepy brown eyes. Everyone wants to cheer her up – Young Eddie, little Jemmy, Mike, Pat and Gav.'

'Gav won't be much good to her.'

'I love Gav,' protested Dora. 'He's worked marvels with the horses, all the stable lasses are crazy about him.'

'Fat lot of good it'll do them. He can't get it up – erectile dysfunction.'

'Don't be horrible,' said Dora, then she giggled. 'Rupert's got tile dysfunction. Taggie feeds such lush food to the birds, they hang about on the roof with their beaks watering all day, dislodging tiles.'

She shot a sideways glance at Cosmo, who told her not to be so silly then asked: 'Does Rupert fancy this Gala?'

'Not obviously. She and Rupert spar a lot because she sticks up for people he bawls out. But he doesn't mind her bringing Old Eddie down most days to see Love Rat and he'd never let Eddie's other carers near the place. Plus he lets her ride out sometimes.'

'Hmm . . .' said Cosmo. 'What about the Wolverhampton Wanderer? The one he banished for shagging the stable lass after that win.'

'Oh, Young Eddie. Gone back to Palm Beach. He's a brilliant jockey but he lacks the work ethic. Taggie'll plead for him, so I expect he'll be allowed back soon.' Dora looked at her watch. 'They should be home now.'

*

'All things bright and beautiful, all horses great and small,' sang Lark all the way home. She was so proud of Quickly, Dave and Fleance: Love Rat's Three Musketeers. People kept texting her and leaving messages. Back home, having settled the horses, she went into the tack room to find the *Racing Post* open at reports on the races, her name Lark Tolland listed as the groom, and a joyful picture of her flinging her arms around Quickly after the Nunthorpe.

'Reading all about yourself?' observed Celeste nastily. 'You missed a wild party last night. Everyone got tiddly and off with everyone. Eddie Alderton . . .'

Lark jumped like a startled hare. Eddie was in Palm Beach, surely?

'How w-w-was he?'

'Much the same. Got hammered and ended up finally shagging Gala.'

'Gala? Are you sure?'

'He's always had the hots for her – not that he's choosy; any porthole in a storm.'

Sadness overwhelmed Lark, but what right had she to mind? Stumbling out of the tack room she went slap into Dora who'd just flown down with Etta and Valent, and who asked why she was crying.

'I don't know, I'm just tired, I guess.' Then when pressed, confessed that she'd just learnt that Eddie had gone to bed with Gala.

'I'm sure he didn't. He sees her as a mum – they're friends.'

'Celeste said.'

'She is such a bitch. Her only aim is to prick people's bubbles.'

A furious Dora later sought out Celeste, who was holding court in the Dog and Trumpet.

'Pretty name, Celeste,' Shaheed, a new Pakistani stable lad, was telling her.

'My mother loved an actress in *High Society* called Celeste Holm, and named me after her,' simpered Celeste.

'Celeste was the Elephant Queen in the Babar books,'

announced Dora. 'She was a lovely character so you can't be named after her,' at which everyone laughed.

'What is that supposed to mean?' snapped Celeste.

'There's nothing lovely about your character,' snapped back Dora. '"Mean" is the operative word, telling poor Lark, who's crazy about Eddie, that he shagged Gala last night. Can't wait to check that out with Gala.'

'Don't you dare,' hissed Celeste.

31

Quickly emerged from his trip to York in fighting form, bucking and squealing and definitely grander. He knew that he'd won and, turned out in the fields, he bossed the other horses more than ever. He even took to leaning over the fence and pulling off Dave's fly-sheet, leaving his gentle half-brother exposed to all the summer bugs.

By winning the Nunthorpe, Quickly had qualified at the end of October for the Breeders' Cup, America's most illustrious race meeting, and would receive free entry, a guaranteed start gate and $40,000 in travel expenses.

Geoffrey, who came third in the Gimcrack, only beaten by Dave and I Will Repay, had also qualified but not for travel expenses, and as vile Brute had already blued all Geoffrey's prize money, a heartbroken Rosaria could no longer afford to send him; the gallops had to be maintained, the horses fed and wages paid.

Quickly would be racing in the Breeders' Cup Juvenile Sprint for two-year-old colts and geldings, with a tempting £348,387 for the winner. Gavin spent hours walking Quickly in and out of planes, getting him used to flying.

'He'd like a window seat,' said Dora.

But when the day came and he, Lark and Safety Car, the comfort blanket, left in huge excitement for the airport, Quickly set about the wholesale demolition of the plane, even before it took off. Just like his mother, Mrs Wilkinson, who had also refused to fly, nothing would calm him. Back home in total disgrace, Purrpuss the cat was the only thing prepared to miaow to him.

To add insult to injury, I Will Repay came second in the Juvenile Sprint.

As the flat season was drawing to a close, to keep his hoof in, Quickly was entered for an all-weather race at Kempton. Sulking because Rupert had put him in a tougher bit so Meerkat could stop him bolting, despite the patience of the loaders patting and petting him, Quickly proceeded to lie down again in the starting stalls.

As a result of such appalling behaviour, he was asked to take a stalls test. This involved arriving a week later, half an hour before racing began at Rutminster. A steward would be present, seeking evidence that Quickly was capable of loading quietly, standing in the stalls for three minutes and, when the gate opened, galloping down the track. Alas, the steward turned out to be Roddy Northfield. Naughty Quickly, who didn't like Roddy's bellowed instructions, promptly lay down again, idly picking at the grass before rolling over on his side and pretending to go to sleep, once again reducing the loaders to fits of laughter.

Consequently, Rupert was fined heavily and Quickly banned from racing for six months, the only redeeming feature being that the ban lasted over the winter, which would give Gav a chance to sort Quickly out before the 2000 Guineas at the beginning of May.

On the good side, Love Rat's progeny, particularly New Year's Dave, had had such a brilliant year that the stallion had leapt six places in the Leading Sire charts, to just behind Roberto's Revenge – so things were looking promising for when the results would be announced at the end of December.

32

The time in December had now arrived for Rupert to return to York and, as the winning owner of the Gimcrack Stakes, to deliver a key speech on the state of racing at the incredibly prestigious white-tie Gimcrack dinner.

For many owners this had been a terrifying ordeal in which they'd only stumbled out a few sentences. Other speeches had been highly contentious, sparking off rows ending up in the High Court or with powerful sheikhs threatening to take their horses away from Britain altogether.

'Not sure if we ought to let Campbell-Black loose,' blustered Roddy Northfield, a long-term Gimcrack stalwart. 'Always driven down bus lanes, bound to cause havoc and say a host of inflammatory things. Etta Edwards, the co-owner, is the most delightful woman – why don't we ask her? I could brief her, or her husband Valent Edwards – bit of a rough diamond but sound ideas.'

Etta, however, who had no desire to fall at the first fence, insisted the task was left to Rupert. This year, as well as one hundred and twenty men, august members of the racing world, six women had been invited, including Taggie.

As she and Rupert walked out to the helipad at Penscombe, Rupert noticed Celeste, yakking on her mobile, riding past on Dorothy the grey practice mare, and crossed himself. A red-head on a white horse always foretold disaster.

'What the hell are you doing on Dorothy?' he yelled.

'Just popping into the village for a birthday card.'

'Well, get off her and bloody well walk.'

Worried that some terrible accident might befall them, Gav felt passionate relief when Rupert, with a host of instructions, rang to say they'd landed at York.

'Good luck,' said Gav.

The Gimcrack dinner was held in York's Old County stand, a lovely Victorian domed dining room with red and green curtains, a green carpet and big gold chandeliers.

At the bottom of the room hung a huge portrait of James Melrose, Chairman of York Racecourse Committee for over fifty years; he had a sweet face and a white rose in his button-hole. At the top end hung Stubbs' lovely portrait of Gimcrack, the gallant little grey colt after whom the club had been named, who had won twenty-seven out of thirty-six races back in the eighteenth century. Held by a groom in a black hat and a stylish long beige coat, the equally stylish Gimcrack had very slim legs, blue eyes and a flowing white tail held at a jaunty angle.

'He reminds me of Quickly,' cried a delighted Taggie.

'Let's hope Quickly leaves the same footprints on racing's landscape,' said Rupert.

The great and the good, many of them in hunting tail-coats, sat around and up the insides of a table shaped like a horse-shoe. Rupert at the top with Gimcrack's portrait behind him was between his friend Lord Grimthorpe, the Chairman of the racecourse, and a local stud-owner, Lord Halifax.

Five seats away, his tail-coat straining to contain his hulking shoulders, Roddy Northfield, representing the British Racing Association and Rutminster Racecourse, looked on in outrage, anticipating trouble. Enid hadn't made the cut and Roddy for-bore to hand on her message, 'to give special luck and love to Rupert'.

In the old days, winning owners were expected to provide six dozen bottles of champagne, but today only the fireworks. Taggie, down the table between the charming Nick Luck of Channel 4 and her favourite trainer, Tommy Westerham, was having a lovely time. She was really pleased with her new dress, silver-grey silk to match her eyes, and it was heaven to eat something she hadn't cooked herself. She couldn't read the menu so every delicious mouthful had been a surprise: warm duck and orange ravioli; halibut, crab and scallops in a wonderful pink shellfish bisque; chocolate brioche with ice cream; and Welsh rarebit, all accompanied by unbelievable wine. She had therefore really stuffed her face and drank every drop of offered Pouilly Fumé, Fleurie, champagne and brandy, and was now as giggly as a teenager at her first party. The men round the table were having a lovely time looking at Taggie.

'What are you going to talk about, Rupert?' asked Lord Grimthorpe. 'Rachel Hood was awfully good last year.'

'Hood was good, Hood was good,' murmured Rupert as he got up to speak.

Taggie in turn thought he had never looked handsomer or happier because of the brilliant year he had had. The white tie and tails set off a magnificent Far Eastern tan.

'Remember there are ladies present,' warned Roddy Northfield.

'Gimcrack, winner of twenty-seven races, was admired by the public for his fighting spirit. Only fourteen hands, he once ran twenty-two and a half miles in an hour, with twelve and a half stone on his back. He was also a great star at stud,' began Rupert idly, 'and was probably a rival of my great-great-great-great-great-great-grandfather's stallion Third Leopard, who won the St Leger and was Leading Sire for five years towards the end of the eighteenth century.

'The Gimcrack has a proud history of great winners, like Mill Reef, Caspar Netscher, Showcasing – and none potentially greater than my own New Year's Dave. As a result of his and Master Quickly's sensational victories, Love Rat's foals and yearlings have been setting the sale rings alight this autumn. Love Rat is the sire whose name you want on your passport.'

'Oh, cut out the commercial, Rupert,' shouted Tommy Westerham, pelting him with petits fours.

'None of that,' barked Roddy, turning pucer than his fifth glass of wine.

Rupert took a hefty slug of brandy then launched into an attack on every aspect of racing: the greed of the bookies, the lack of government support, lousy prize money, avaricious racecourses resulting in far too many races and too many meetings on the same day, the massive over-breeding of horses, a prohibitive handicap system, so that good horses went abroad because they had nowhere to race, amateur stewards often so terrified of the bookies they'd do anything to let a horse keep a race, and bookies going offshore and not paying anything back into racing.

'I used to train horses for other people, but gave up because I found them even more selfish and tiresome than myself,' he told his startled audience. 'And because they all tried to pull my wife.'

'Oh Rupert,' protested Taggie, wishing the green carpet would swallow her up.

'On the other hand, owners have a lousy deal. Go to any meeting and after a race you will find nineteen out of twenty disappointed connections being lied to: "it's the draw, it's the rain, it's the start, it's traffic, it's interference, it's the trip, it's too firm, it's too testing, it was a messy race," and so on. I hated telling lies – another reason I gave up training other people's horses.'

Then, like a small boy with a brick on the end of a rope, he attacked all the ruling bodies of racing for incompetence, pusillanimity and the inability to stick together.

'How can hounds catch a fox, if they all rush off giving tongue in different directions. The British Racing Association, BRA, as it's known, is a misnomer.'

'Rubbish,' thundered Roddy.

'Because they often provide *no* support. They'll accuse a trainer or jockey of something then spend months gathering evidence, by which time his owners or his rides have drifted away. If you asked me to sum up the state of British Racing today, I'd say it's got too big, it's destroyed the ground at too many tracks, the breed has been weakened, there are far too many horses bred, many often bad or unsound horses. I would cut the fixture list by twenty-five per cent, but the managing directors at the racecourse have different aims. Stable staff too should be paid properly and should be given decent time off.

'And, if you want decent crowds, build up the horses like Frankel, Black Caviar, Kauto Star and Master Quickly's dam Mrs Wilkinson and my own Safety Car, who make people flock to the races. Owners should also have the guts to keep these great horses in training as four- and five-year-olds and not whisk them off to stud, so the public has a chance to fall in love with them, like little Gimcrack.'

The audience were looking stunned, so Rupert switched tack, making them laugh with a few jokes, bluer than his wickedly sparkling eyes.

'I repeat, there are ladies present,' boomed Roddy, turning even pucer.

'Gimcrack,' went on Rupert, ignoring him, 'had a sire called Cripple and an uncle called Bloody Buttocks, neither of which would have got through Weatherbys today.'

He then gave an impersonation of the ladies of Weatherbys trying out horses' names on each other, to check if there were any double entendres, repeating in a prim voice words like 'Forced King' and 'Far Canal' over and over again until the audience were crying with laughter.

'Finally,' Rupert took another slug, 'I'd like to thank York Racecourse Committee and the Gimcrack for an absolutely marvellous dinner, and congratulate them for being an equally marvellous racecourse where nothing is too much trouble.'

Then, remembering how Roddy had banned Quickly, 'So unlike our local Rutminster Racecourse, which has potholes all over the track, rotten food and spends fortunes on portraits of today's committee. It's hardly surprising Rufus Rutshire wants to build houses all over it.'

'Rupert,' murmured Lord Grimthorpe, 'Rodders is about to have a coronary.'

'To end,' concluded Rupert, 'I'd like to propose a toast to the health of British racing and to this year's Gimcrack winner, New Year's Dave, who is as sweet-natured as he is brilliant.'

As he sat down to moderate cheers, Taggie mouthed down the table: 'You are so clever.'

'God knows how he got away with it.' Nick Luck was shaking his head. 'He'd better not do anything to prompt a stewards' enquiry for a year or two.'

Roddy was hopping like a maddened bullfrog.

While more speeches followed, Rupert carried on drinking then reluctantly got up to go, having an early flight to Singapore in the morning.

Aware that most of the audience would like to throttle him, he hustled Taggie down the steps and out into the weighing room, where they were accosted by a reporter from the *Scorpion* sidling up, to break the very sad news that Jake Lovell, the great showjumper and silver medallist of Rupert's era, had just died at the tragically early age of fifty-nine.

'Really,' drawled Rupert.

'How do you feel, Rupert?'

'Profound gratitude. Particularly,' continued Rupert, 'for his ridding me of my first wife, Helen. Jake did me a huge service by running off with her in the middle of the Los Angeles Olympics, leaving a depleted but utterly determined British team to take the Gold.'

'Rupert, no!' gasped Taggie in horror.

The reporter gasped too, reeling from a mixture of shock and scoop.

'What is running through your mind, Rupert?'

'I repeat, profound gratitude for ridding me of my pseudo-intellectual, pretentious and totally unsuitable first wife, and freeing me up to marry the angel who is my wife today,' said Rupert as he stalked out of the building.

'I'm really, really sorry for Tory and Isa and all the family,' Taggie stammered to the reporter before she fled after Rupert. 'How could you?' she panted when she caught up with him. 'Poor Tory and poor Isa, he'll be devastated.'

'Payback time indeed. I have absolutely no sympathy for that weasel who pinched all my ideas. Talk about Leading Sore.'

33

Rupert arrived at Penscombe to find the paparazzi outside the drive and all the way down Penscombe High Street – and that a colossal row had broken out.

Isa, who adored his father, was insane with rage at Rupert's universally reported comments, particularly on behalf of his mother, who had been nursing a desperately ill Jake for months. Rupert's diatribe had been the only negative in a fountain of eulogy. The press were already regurgitating all the old stories about Rupert bullying Jake, both at school and on the show-jumping circuit, and how the feud had continued because of the annexing of Helen – right down to the acrimonious departure of Isa, as Rupert's stable jockey and assistant.

Turning on her laptop first thing to check how Rupert's speech had gone, Celeste smiled in triumph. Gav deserved to be punished for resisting her advances, Rupert for jocking her off.

She was not going to be demoted to shovelling shit unless it was over those two. Joyfully she drew out the bloodstained foaling certificate from under the lining paper of her bedroom drawer. It was still readable: 'chestnut colt – 31 December'. Picking up her mobile, she dialled Cosmo Rannaldini's number.

'I've got some interesting information on Rupert Campbell-Black, Gavin Latton and New Year's Dave,' she said.

'Come right over,' purred Cosmo. 'Get yourself to Aston Down and I'll send the chopper. *Gotcha!*' he shouted as he put down the telephone.

'This is how I should always travel,' reflected Celeste as Cosmo's scarlet and magenta helicopter flew over the rustic cathedral town of Rutminster, with its olive-green sweep of racecourse. There was the long drive, winding up to Rutminster Hall, the Georgian mansion belonging to Roddy Northfield's brother, Lord Rutshire.

Roddy always gave her a lovely smile on the rare occasions beastly Rupert had allowed her to go to the races, and there, as the helicopter began its descent, was Valhalla, the great grey abbey guarded by its dark army of trees. Rooks fluttered out of a white shroud of mist as they landed.

A chauffeur in a Chelsea tractor met her and whisked her through rusty gates, bearing the inscription *Amor Vincit Omnia*. A stunning girl with an amazing willowy body and long shining dark hair was waiting at the door. She introduced herself as Sauvignon, Cosmo's PA – which stood for phenomenally attractive, thought Celeste, feeling upstaged. Having led her along endless dark passages to Cosmo's office, Sauvignon announced that he would be with her in a few minutes.

When Rupert gave her a hard time, Celeste had always fancied a job at Valhalla, and studied the place on its website. But looking out of the window, she was taken aback by the splendour of the stud and the yard, which had been carved out of seemingly impenetrable woodland. Below lay a spaghetti of racetracks and gallops, runways for jet and helicopter, an equine swimming pool, indoor gym, massive indoor schools, lovingly tended gardens, endless stables and racehorses in rugs, out in stallion pens and fields, sweeping down to the River Fleet.

There, on the right, was the famous Valhalla maze, where Cosmo held wild parties. Soon she'd be one of the guests. There, deep in the woods, was the watchtower where Cosmo's sinister father, Sir Roberto, had composed, edited, ravished and near which, Celeste gave a shiver, he had been murdered.

No doubt billions had been spent on the place. Cosmo's study included a grand piano, two sofas draped in fur rugs, shelves filled as much with orchestral scores as racing files. Apple logs crackling in the fireplace scented and warmed the room. On the mantelpiece was a gilt and ormolu clock of *Apollo Driving the Chariot of the Sun*; the horses would be non-runners on such a dark day.

On the walls were a Picasso Clown, portraits of Cosmo's heroes – Byron, Wagner, the Marquis de Sade, his father, Roberto Rannaldini – and Roberto's Revenge in his gleaming dark-brown glory, rearing up, towering over his handler. Celeste was giggling over a naughty painting of Don Juan, humping some lady of the manor in the orchard while casting an eye over her pretty maid, who was hanging out her mistress's washing, when Cosmo swept in, still in indigo silk pyjamas, wafting very strong, musky aftershave.

'Celeste.' He took both her hands, then in his deep, caressingly beautiful voice, 'So sorry to have kept you. Welcome to Valhalla.'

'I've been admiring your office, and this amazing view. It reminds me of Penscombe.'

Just for a second, Cosmo's face hardened into the steely glare with which his father had petrified entire orchestras, then he relented. 'But vastly superior. Let me get you a cup of coffee. We'll save the champagne for later.'

'Lovely property,' gushed Celeste. 'Is it very old?'

'Very. During the Civil War, it was a Royalist stronghold.' Pouring into a blue cup coffee even darker than his eyes, Cosmo pointed to one of the mullions on which was carved the head of a cavalier. 'Alleged to be Prince Rupert of the Rhine.'

Another Rupert's head might soon be on the block, Cosmo thought happily as he handed her a plate of pink sugar biscuits, and directed her to the end of the sofa near the fire, plumping a cushion on which was embroidered *I may be here, but my heart is on the racecourse.*

'Well, well,' Cosmo said gently, sitting down beside her. 'Ah, here's Isa.'

Celeste had always fancied Isa – taller than most jockeys, the black cobra with his wild black hair and closed gypsy face.

Today, with reddened eyes and extremely pale, he seemed more vulnerable. Before leaving, Celeste had tarted herself up in the briefest, cutest little black leather mini-skirt and jacket. Fortunately, she'd washed her hair last night so it floated long, lush and gleaming red. She had drenched herself in the last of Lark's scent.

'I'm so sorry for your loss, Isa.'

'Thanks.' Isa handed two black armbands to Sauvignon, to give to Tarqui and Roman Lovell, who were about to set off with four horses for the All-Weather at Southwell. Even death didn't stop the show going on. 'Tell Roman not to talk to the press.'

Getting up to put her coffee cup on the table, Celeste could see from the big gilt mirror how lush she was looking. All this was wasted on Isa and Cosmo, however, who were only interested in Dave's original foaling certificate.

Pretending to search for a tissue, Celeste switched on her tape recorder. Before she handed anything over, she wanted big money. Cosmo took a snort of coke and switched on his own tape recorder as he examined a Christmas card from Roddy Northfield, showing Rutminster Manor in the snow.

'Well.' He smiled at Celeste.

'I hate to be commercial but my career's on the line, so I'd like something up front.'

'Of course.' Cosmo opened his desk drawer and handed over a couple of grand of laundered money in fifty-pound notes.

'For starters?'

'Of course, we promise.'

'And a job and protection, once the story breaks? I can't return to Penscombe, Rupert would rip me apart.'

'Of course,' Cosmo said, reflecting that she was a tough little thing. A smile like eastern light spread across his face as he and Isa pored over the faded bloodstained document.

'"Chestnut colt – thirty-first December",' muttered Isa. 'Whose writing is this?'

'Gavin Latton.'

'Oh, Floppy Dick in person.' Cosmo was jubilant.

'He swore me to secrecy,' sighed Celeste. 'Got pretty nasty. He's powerful at Penscombe. I'd lose my job if I snitched.'

'Rupert knew,' snapped Isa.

'Must have done. He and Gavin are as thick.'

'As thieves,' added Cosmo. 'This will bring them both down. Corrupt and fraudulent behaviour. Rupert could lose his licence for ten years, and Gavin'll probably never work again.'

The Horses of the Sun tolled one o'clock.

Out of the window, mighty, magnificent, bounding, white L-shaped blaze identifying him, Roberto's Revenge could be seen dragging a nervous stud hand along a grass track, getting fit for the next covering season.

'Leading Sire-in-waiting,' Cosmo gloated. 'Oh boy, this will help him.'

'Is that I Will Repay?' asked Celeste.

Isa got out a calculator.

'New Year's Dave must have won nearly a million running illegally as a two-year-old. He'll be disqualified from all those races, which will push Rupert right down the Leading Sire list. Dave beat and prevented I Will Repay from winning the richest Group Two for two-year-olds, and I as the owner would have made an infinitely better Gimcrack speech,' sighed Cosmo. 'Poor Rupert will never be forgiven for last night's tirade. The timing is perfect, he's offended everyone. There isn't a stake-holder in racing who won't want to ram a stake into his heart. And what about the poor punters?' Cosmo started to play an imaginary violin.

'And what about compensation for poor Rosaria and her repellent husband,' said Isa. 'If Geoffrey had come second in the Gimcrack, they might have scraped enough money together to have taken him to the Breeders' Cup.'

'Oh Rupert.' Cosmo had another snort of coke. 'You really are up shit creek.'

'What happens now?' asked Isa.

'I'll telephone the British Racing Association Integrity Department,' said Cosmo, looking at his watch, 'who will probably be at lunch.'

'And I'm ready for that glass of bubbly,' piped up Celeste.

'Sure,' said Cosmo. Then, as Sauvignon walked in, 'Can you take Celeste to the canteen and give her some lunch.'

When Celeste looked outraged, Cosmo added, 'We'll sort things out later. We really appreciate you telling us, I've just got to put the wheels into motion.'

'But I still need to get my stuff from Rupert's before you break the story!'

'Sure, sure.'

When a reluctant Celeste had finally left, Isa said: 'We can't give *her* a job. She didn't even recognize Roberto's Revenge.'

'Course not,' said Cosmo soothingly, 'but we've got to keep her sweet till after the enquiry. She's a key witness.'

Isa, however, had collapsed on the sofa with his head in his hands.

'I've got to sort out Dad's funeral. Mum wants it tiny, but the press'll never leave us alone.'

Cosmo put a hand on Isa's shoulder. 'It's horrible, I'm sorry. We couldn't bury my father for months after his death. When they've been as ill as your father, you think it would be a relief, but once they're dead, you start remembering their old selves, and you miss them appallingly. My father was a monster, but he made me laugh. At least you had a father you were proud of. *Console-toi.*' Cosmo poured Isa a brandy.

'I've got to get hold of the death certificate, and there's so bloody much to do for the funeral.'

'I'll help you with the readings and the music, and I'll get the New Year's Dave thing started,' said Cosmo. 'This'll be a death certificate for Rupert, and to cheer yourself up, Dave's now favourite for the Guineas and the Derby, but on January first, he'll be a four-year-old, which rules him out of both of them. And even if Rupert denies everything and hangs Gav out to dry, it means Gav won't be here any more to nurture Quickly and Touchy Filly. Oh, gotcha, gotcha!'

'Celeste's frantic to get her stuff out of Penscombe,' Sauvignon told Cosmo after she returned from lunch. 'I pumped her about Rupert's horses, but she didn't seem to know much about them. She's a nympho, eyeing up all the lads in the canteen. When she went to the Ladies, I found a tape recorder in her bag.'

'Perhaps she should come and work for us.'

'I took out the tape,' said Sauvignon.

An ex-model just turned thirty, Sauvignon was spectacularly glamorous. She had a smallish straight nose, perfect for photographs, and a mouth made bigger with carefully applied scarlet lipstick, which lifted a hard, cold face when she smiled. The wine which she had renamed herself after was the same amber as her hypnotic yellow eyes. She had also had elocution lessons to iron out her Cockney accent.

Cosmo employed her to lead up his horses to draw maximum attention to them in the paddock. She also instilled fear into his staff, who nicknamed her the Nazicist. This was because as well as being spiteful, she was also utterly self-obsessed. When she was talking about herself to someone, her eyes swivelled constantly to find someone more important to talk about herself to. Very spoilt because of her looks, she was accustomed to getting her own way.

Cosmo found Sauvignon useful for manipulating people. Mrs Walton, his mistress, detested her. Used to drawing the glance of every passing man, how mortifying when they instead all looked at Sauvignon.

Sauvignon Smithson's mission in life was to marry a vast amount of money.

34

Rupert's hangover after his Gimcrack speech was further punished by furious telephone calls.

From his first wife, Helen: 'How dare you say those outrageous things about the mother of your children?'

From Tory Lovell's sister, Fen, about to fly over from America: 'How dare you slag off Jake like that and resurrect his affair with Helen, the one thing that crucifies Tory? She's in pieces. How come you're such a bitch, Rupert?'

From his gentle son, Marcus, in Moscow and his volatile daughter, Tabitha, in Germany: 'How can you be so vile about Mum?'

Rupert was wondering if he could keep down a cup of black coffee when he was cheered by an email confirming that Quickly and Dave were entered for next year's Derby, and Dave was favourite.

Wandering into the kitchen in search of Alka Seltzer, he winced at the smell of a bowl of Whiskas that Taggie had put on the kitchen table, so Purrpuss could eat in peace away from the dogs.

'You OK?' she asked.

'Ish. Everyone's incandescent that I slagged off Helen. I must have been pissed.'

'Can I tell you something utterly shaming?' Taggie put her arms around him, hanging her head so he couldn't see her face beneath her dark cloud of hair. 'I absolutely adored you slagging off Helen. Everyone always goes on about how beautiful and clever she is, and she's always been so patronizing and made me feel so thick. It was such heaven, hearing you say how up herself she is, and then such blissful things about me.' Her gruff voice trembled. 'Is that awful of me?'

'No, because it's absolutely true.' As he forced her chin upwards, her eyes were still smudged by last night's make-up. 'I think my hangover might improve dramatically if we went back to bed.'

Cosmo and Isa moved fast. As Rupert had said in his speech, the BRA often took some time to carry out an enquiry, keeping unfortunate trainers and jockeys, unable to earn, their reputations dwindling, in a vacuum for months. But the following morning, Rupert returned home on Safety Car, from watching a river of matchless two-year-olds flow up the all-weather gallops, to be greeted by a troupe of BRA investigators armed with tape recorders.

Back in Rupert's office, refusing a cup of coffee, their leader, a Mr Wilde, who had a round pink face, spiked hair combed forward to hide any bald patches, and a flat North Country accent, announced: 'We have evidence that your colt, New Year's Dave, is being passed off as a two-year-old, born on January the first, when he is, in fact, a three-year-old, born on the thirty-first of December, who has won nearly a million pounds under false pretences.'

'Do you honestly think,' Rupert didn't miss a beat, 'I'd call a horse New Year's Dave, drawing attention to the fact that he'd been born on New Year's Eve?'

'Can we look at your records, sir?'

Soon they were going through passports, telephone bills, medical records, scrumpled love letters, records of foaling. Finding Dave's, they then compared it with a photocopy of the original record, passed on by Celeste, and showed it to Rupert.

'One doesn't need to be a graphologist to recognize the writing is identical. At the top, it says "attended by Gavin Latton". The only difference is the dates.'

'Someone must have copied Gav's handwriting to frame him. How did you get hold of this?'

'I'm afraid we're not at liberty to say. What were your movements that night, sir?'

'I was seeing the New Year in with my in-laws across the valley. I can't remember the exact time, about two in the morning, Gav rang in great excitement, saying Cordelia had dropped a foal in record time. She's one of our best mares, but quite old. The sire was our leading stallion, Love Rat, the foal was a colt: all cause for celebration, so I belted back here – probably shouldn't have been driving – saw a beautiful foal, mother fine, so we went up to the house and had a bottle of champagne, at least Celeste and I did. Gav doesn't drink.'

Mr Wilde looked at his notes. 'We'd like to interview Pat Inglis, Marketa Bolokova and Celeste.'

But Celeste had flown. Her room was empty, cupboards bare of her clothes and shoes.

'She's left. Said she was going away for the weekend,' said Louise.

'That's our whistleblower,' said Rupert grimly. Glancing out of the window, he saw Gav riding into the yard on Quickly. 'There's Gav now – I'll go and get him.'

Sprinting across the yard, Rupert reached Gav before any of the investigators. 'BRA's here, claiming Dave's a three-year-old,' he hissed. Then, as the colour drained from Gav's face: 'Don't admit anything.'

Dramatically accelerating its customary procedure, the BRA convened a disciplinary hearing three weeks later in the middle of January, and summoned Rupert and Gav to their headquarters in Holborn Lane.

They had acted like lightning because Rupert was such a big fish in racing. Although he had many high-powered enemies, the public adored him, and whenever his horses ran, they put thousands on the gate.

Dora, as Penscombe's self-appointed press officer, back from a blissful Christmas with Paris, was on full throttle.

'You've got to look as young as possible,' she told Gav, 'a raw young stud hand, who had no idea of the implications. You must cut your hair and wax it upwards, or wear a beanie and perhaps an earring. Or perhaps you could pretend you had a New Year's Eve lapse, went back on the booze and got the date wrong.'

'Shut up, Dora,' ordered Rupert, who was reading an online report in the *Scorpion*, headed: NEW YEAR'S EVIL.

'The crucial thing for you and Gav,' Dora turned to Rupert, 'is to well up. It takes a real man to cry – the panel will think you're sincere and contrite. It's no good being arrogant and flip, you'll only antagonize them. You must think of something really sad to make you cry. Didn't you have a stepmother who died last month?'

'I had four stepmothers and I loathed them all.'

'Well, someone that really chokes you. What about Billy Lloyd-Foxe?'

'Get out!' howled Rupert, hurling Weatherbys *Stallion Book* across the room at her, sending Geraldine's vase of daffodils flying. 'Just get out.'

But as Dora scuttled out of the office, Rupert reflected that never had he needed Billy's jokes, wise counsel and reassuring presence more. But he must keep resolutely upbeat for the troops and not even countenance the fact that he could lose his licence.

There were even more Good Luck cards on the shelves than Christmas cards with, ironically, this year's Christmas card flaunting a lovely photograph of Dave winning the Gimcrack, which the *Scorpion* had reproduced with a headline: THE YOUNG PRETENDER.

Gav insisted on taking the blame.

'What's the point in your admitting anything, Rupert? You didn't know. I lied to you. You'll lose your licence and bring this whole place down. Everyone loves working here.'

'Except Celeste,' said Rupert.

'She's been blackmailing me for months, that's why I kept sticking up for her, begging you not to sack her, taking her out to dinner – she was always threatening to tell the world that Dave was a December foal. She must have retrieved my first scrumpled-up certificate from the bin. I should have made sure it was destroyed, but Cordelia foaled in such a hurry, I was too preoccupied with that.'

'Easily done,' said Rupert. 'We were all in a state of euphoria.'

Gavin couldn't believe Rupert was being so nice. All the same, he was feeling utterly suicidal. Never more desperately had he wanted a drink to drown his sorrows. He knew Rupert had a loaded gun in his office. How easy for everyone if he ended it all, leaving a full confession. Bethany wouldn't care, no one would really mind. Alive, he would lose his job and the horse he loved most and, far worse, his actions could bring down Rupert and the yard.

Cosmo had leaked the story of Rupert's suspected cheating to the press, who had written about nothing else for days. Both yard and stud were in a complete panic; if Rupert lost his licence for ten years, they would all lose their jobs. In anticipation of massive pool money from all Dave's winnings, they had also spent fortunes on Christmas presents, new cars and down payments on houses. Meerkat, too well known as Dave's jockey to get sofa commercials any more, had splashed out on a Cartier watch for Gee Gee. There was endless speculation that Rupert and Gav must have been in cahoots or Rupert would have hung Gav out to dry.

Rupert and Gavin had a meeting before the enquiry with Marti Gluckstein, Rupert's lawyer, who had got him out of endless scrapes over the years, and who looked like an old eagle, poised to swoop down on any weakness in the opposition's argument.

Marti was in complete agreement with Dora. 'Don't get arsy or they'll bury you. Act contrite, no jokes, take the whole thing seriously.'

He was also relieved that Gav was prepared to take the blame. 'You didn't know, Rupert. Being abroad so much, you trust your staff implicitly, it's the essential part of the deal.'

Worried he wasn't eating, on the night before, Taggie had brought Gavin out a cheese omelette. Not wanting to hurt her by putting it in the bin, he gave it to a delighted Forester.

'Comfort ye, comfort ye,' sang the tenor in *The Messiah*, which Gala had given him for Christmas. Not to hurt her either, Gav had hidden his two existing sets.

'Comfort ye, comfort ye.' Unable to find any, he stole downstairs and crept into Dave's box, where he discovered a sobbing Lark: 'I can't bear him to be taken away.'

Dave, getting quite portly from so many commiserating Polos and apples, rubbed his pink nose against Gav, then held out his off fore hoof to be shaken.

'I'm sure things will turn out OK tomorrow,' wept Lark, kindly but unconvincingly.

Rupert, who couldn't sleep either, wandered out on to the lawn. Amazing how a tiny gold sickle moon could light up the valley. The winter stars gleamed in the lake. His equine stars slept in their stables, their futures blighted if he lost his licence.

Banquo and Forester snuffled ahead as he went to talk to Safety Car, who whickered with delight. The east wind was rattling the bare trees. Safety Car quivered.

'All right, old boy, they're not going to fall on you.' As he hugged Safety, Rupert wondered who was comforting whom. Oh Christ, he didn't want to lose his licence.

Both he and Safety jumped as his mobile rang; it was his daughter, Bianca, Dora's great friend, now living in Perth with her boyfriend Feral Jackson, who was playing football for a top Australian side.

'Please don't worry about money, Daddy,' she said. 'You work so hard, it's time you put your feet up. Feral's earning so much a week now, he can always help out. He wants to wish you good luck too.'

And Dora wanted something to make him well up, Rupert thought.

As he returned, propped against the back door was a parcel. Inside was a shocking pink tie covered in black cats, and a card saying: *Good luck, Guv, from Lark.*

35

The enquiry, held on a bitterly cold day, coincided with the January sales. Holborn Lane had never seen anything like it as shoppers, revved up by the media, abandoned any thought of bargain hunting for little tops in Oxford and Regent Street or Tottenham Court Road, and poured in to catch a glimpse of their idol, Rupert, joining a ravening pack of journalists from all over the world, desperate for a story. Broadcast trucks, parked at all angles, had brought traffic on pavement and road to a standstill. Punch-ups were already breaking out as camera-men battled for better positions.

Both William Hill and the Red Lion, near the BRA entrance, were doing a roaring trade at ten in the morning. 'Here he is,' went up a shout. Camera flashes, flickering like a forest fire, set off a stampede.

'Rupert, Rupert, Rupert, Gav, Gav, Rupert, Gav, Rupert – to me!' yelled the media and fans.

But such was Rupert's height and man-eating tiger menace that the rugger scrum parted, and no one ripped off his dark suit as he dragged Gav, as reluctant as Quickly to enter any starting stalls, through the howling mob.

'Rupert, Rupert!' screamed the shoppers, holding up little cameras. 'Isn't he gorgeous? He's wearing his lucky shirt, but not his pale-blue tie. This one's pink wiv black cats on. Good luck, Rupert, good luck. Isn't Gav good-looking too?'

'Lupert, Lupert,' cried a group of adoring Japanese schoolgirls.

'Cheat!' shouted a man with a ginger beard, in a woolly hat, as they passed and was immediately John Lewis and Heals carrier-bagged by enraged shoppers, hissing, 'Don't you dare!'

'Hello, darling.' Rupert unfroze a fraction of a second to kiss Kay Burley of Sky and to wave up at Ed Whitaker who'd climbed a lamp-post to get a better shot for the *Racing Post*.

'Good luck.' An adoring and adorable Indian girl thrust three red roses into Rupert's hand, and a bunch of carrots for Dave.

'Thanks, darling. Come *on*, Gav.' Glancing round, he saw that Gav had been hijacked by Alice Plunkett of Channel 4, and, reaching back, he dragged him into the BRA, down three flights of stairs to the basement – meant for base people, Orpheus into the Underworld, thought Gav numbly.

Remembering he was supposed to act serious, Rupert forbore to grin up at all the BRA female staff who were falling over the banisters to catch a glimpse. Passing a lovely blow-up of Fleance winning at Ascot, the two men were ushered into a breakout room, entitled *Red Rum*, by two pretty girls called Fiona and Danielle. Marti Gluckstein, the eagle, had already landed and was drinking black coffee with lots of sugar. Fiona then plied Rupert and Gav with coffee, found a vase for Rupert's red roses and, seeing his hands were bleeding from clutching the thorns, rushed off to get a sticking plaster.

The room could not have been more anonymous and functional, with black office chairs, a shiny, modern brown table, pictureless white walls, and a grey and beige striped carpet. Any colour or fireworks would be provided by the participants.

'I can tell you who the panel are,' said Marti. 'Sam Bridlington QC, mad about racing, handles lots of racing cases. Member of the Pegasus Club.'

'I know.' The Pegasus Club was so exclusive and stuffy, Rupert had recently referred to them as a lot of 'fossilized wankers'.

'And Sally Stonehouse, a steward from a Lancashire racecourse – nice lady, firm but courteous – and finally, Roddy Northfield.'

'Oh bugger,' sighed Rupert. 'He hates my guts.'

'Any reason?'

'Pompous prat, lots of ancient history, I slept with his wife during a hunt ball, years ago.'

'Did you sleep with Sam Bridlington's wife?'

'Not that I remember, so if I did, he probably wouldn't remember either.'

Marti shook his head. 'Cuckolds have longer memories than elephants.'

You can say that again, thought Gav wearily.

Rupert was flipping through the *Racing Post*, who'd led with a headline: DAVE OF RECKONING. He had two runners at Lingfield this afternoon. If he lost his licence, would they still run? He must have a bet.

'Cheer up.' He smiled at a trembling Gav. 'You're going to have to bat your eyelashes at Sam Bridlington and Sally Stonehouse. We've got to have a majority vote.'

Marti handed Rupert and Gav some typed sheets. 'Here are transcripts of your interviews with the BRA officers down at Penscombe. See if you agree with them.'

Down the passage, the Enquiry Room, equally neutral and functional, contained the same black office chairs, arranged around a square made up of tables. Sitting at the top, facing a clock and two television screens, the Panel conferred. The Chairman, Sam Bridlington QC, looking young for his years with twinkling grey-blue eyes, was an excellent after-dinner speaker and a very popular member of the Bar. He had frequently battled with Marti, respecting him, but disliking Marti's ability to gloat when he won.

Sally Stonehouse, well known for lowering the tempo at post-race enquiries, was popular with jockeys and trainers alike. Attractive, in her early fifties, she had a high-complexioned face from riding in all weathers, kept in check by beige foundation, grey hairs concealed by expert highlighting, hazel eyes, and a good figure enhanced by a yellow cashmere dress, bought for a wedding but chosen for today when she had heard she'd be judging Rupert Campbell-Black.

Many years ago, Rupert had turned his back on her at dinner

to chat up Diney Clarkson, who was reputed to water the course at Rutminster if one of Rupert's star horses needed less quick ground. Sally Stonehouse thought Rupert was spoilt and arrogant, and despite constantly racing his horses at York and Doncaster, he'd never bothered to run them at her course in Lancashire, of which she was extremely proud. Flipping through the interviews, the case seemed pretty straightforward and could be over by lunchtime, allowing her time to buy a new winter coat in the sales, to match her yellow dress. She was irritated that the press seemed to be swinging in Rupert's favour.

'If he loses his licence, they won't have anything to write about,' grunted Sam Bridlington.

Roddy Northfield, who'd abandoned his red trousers for a dark suit, was fired up at the prospect of nailing the bastard. 'This is the darkest day in racing,' he boomed, taking a third chocolate biscuit. 'Campbell-Black has cheated; we have a responsibility to the integrity of the sport to end this corruption.'

Sally Stonehouse nodded in agreement.

'I think we should hear the evidence first,' said Sam Bridlington.

'After the things he said at the Gimcrack,' boomed on Roddy, 'it's clear in what contempt he holds racing and all its stake-holders. He had the gall to boast how brilliantly he had done this year, and how he'd almost topped the Leading Sire table with Love Rat, when all the time he'd been cheating other trainers out of fortunes – not to mention the punters.'

Sam Bridlington looked up from his brief. 'Classic case of hubris.'

'Hugh who?' queried Roddy.

Sally Stonehouse exchanged a quick smile with Sam Bridlington, deciding he was rather attractive. Racing was full of attractive men. Gosh, it was hot – she wished she hadn't put a thermal vest under her dress, but it had been arctic when she'd left Lancashire.

'Christ, it's hot in here. Talk about Red Hot Rum,' grumbled Marti. 'BRA heating bills must be astronomical.'

'If you don't win today,' drawled Rupert, 'my cheating bill is going to be even more astronomical.'

'Don't be flip,' snapped Marti. 'This is going to be bloody.'

'If Roddy's wearing his red trousers, the blood won't show up.'

All jumped at the knock on the door.

'We're ready for you, Mr Campbell-Black, if you're ready for us,' said Danielle, so they followed her.

'Hi, Clare,' called out Rupert, as Clare Balding appeared at another door, deeply irritated the enquiry was to be held *in camera* with the proceedings taped. The press would only learn the outcome at a conference at the end. Allowed to wait upstairs, or outside, most of them repaired to the Red Lion.

In the Enquiry Room, Rupert, Marti and Gav were ushered to the right of the Panel, with Marti making sure Rupert was next to Sally.

Opposite them sat the prosecuting BRA lawyer, Norman Thomas, a pink-faced blond young man, with very clean ears. Any witnesses called would sit opposite, under the screens. There were no windows. Tape recorders whirred, picking up Gav's tummy rumbling like Vesuvius.

Seeing a maroon leather-bound volume of *The Merchant of Venice* in Rupert's hand, Roddy assumed it must be a Bible. Bastard's going to need it, he thought happily, and didn't pass on Enid's message of good luck. How ridiculous was that shocking-pink tie, swarming with black cats!

Norman Thomas then outlined the evidence against owner/ trainer/breeder Rupert Campbell-Black in that New Year's Dave had been running under false pretences for a year. He then showed films on the black screens, to gasps of admiration, of all the races Dave had won and of Rupert accepting vast trophies on his behalf, scooping up large sums of money illegally, and cheating other owners and punters out of their winnings.

Gav Latton in particular had allowed the foal's registration to be submitted with 1 January as the date of foaling in the full knowledge that the actual date was 31 December, and by thus falsifying the date, ensured the colt would not be classified as a yearling until the first of January the following year.

'You filled in this form with intentions that your employer Rupert Campbell-Black would obtain some unjust advantage which he would not otherwise have obtained,' Norman told Gav. 'This is a fraudulent, rather than corrupt, practice. I'd like to confirm you didn't inform Mr Campbell-Black that you had incorrectly registered the foal until December the twelfth, nearly three years later.'

As a quivering, deathly-white Gavin rose swaying to his feet, Rupert put a steadying hand on his arm.

'Take your time, Mr Latton,' said Sam Bridlington kindly.

Gav pulled himself together. 'Only when I heard Penscombe church bells ringing in the New Year,' he told the judges without a trace of a stammer, 'did I appreciate the full tragedy that I had just delivered a December the thirty-first foal. It hadn't sunk in when I filled in the first form. I knew how much this particular colt meant to Rupert. His dam and his sire were both especial favourites. It was an unbelievably quick birth – four minutes from the waters breaking to the time of foaling. Rupert,' Gav's voice broke slightly, colour creeping into his ashen cheeks, 'has been incredibly good to me. He picked me up from the gutter when my wife left me and I'd been sacked by Cosmo Rannaldini, got me off the drink and was allowing me to ride his best horses. Most importantly, he trusted me enough to leave me in charge of the stud, on a New Year's night when I might easily have gone back on the booze.

'In a moment of insanity, I wrote out a new certificate and lied blind that the foal was born on January the first. I know it was breaking the rules, but I still feel it's a wicked rule and criminally unfair, all because a foal is born an hour too early, sabotaging his entire career. Far unluckier than a child born at the end of August who has to go through school a year early, penalized through accident of birth; as unlucky as a younger son, who has to relinquish everything – title, grand house, family fortune – to an elder son.'

His passion was undeniable. Good boy, thought Rupert. As a younger son, Roddy nodded his head in unwilling agreement.

'You never felt the need to come clean and tell?' he asked.

'It became far harder. Dave was not just the most brilliant

colt from the start, but also the most lovable. We all adored him. I couldn't bring myself to kill the dream.' His voice broke, and he paused for a second. 'But I swear Rupert didn't know, and I also ordered Celeste not to say anything. It's entirely my responsibility. I'm so very sorry, but I'll pay all the money back somehow.'

'Nearly a million, rather a tall order,' said Norman Thomas acidly.

'Very nice boy,' murmured Bridlington to Sally.

'Very,' agreed Sally. Turning, she met Rupert's eye and he smiled at her. Blushing, she found herself smiling back. He really was absolutely gorgeous.

The Chairman then announced they would call a Miss Celeste Frithwood, as a witness. It would therefore be fitting for Rupert and Gavin to retire. Marti would stay, so he could relay to them what Celeste had said.

'Little Miss Whistleblow-job,' muttered Rupert to Gav, as they caught a glimpse of Celeste, dressed by Cosmo and Sauvignon in a grey midi-dress with a white collar. She wore only a touch of make-up, had tied back her red locks with a ribbon, and smiled very sweetly at Roddy, who winked back at her.

Throughout her interview, Marti harrumphed and sneered, and rattled papers noisily as he wrote down notes, until Sam Bridlington told him to cool it. Norman, the BRA lawyer, charmed by Celeste, took her through the events of the evening.

'Marketa got quite a bit tiddly at the pub, so I offered to stand in for her. I was very new to the job but was worried about Gavin with his drinking problem, being on his own.'

Now it was Marti's turn.

'When you whistleblew to another trainer, why did you pick Rupert's deadliest rival?'

'I've always admired Isa Lovell as a caring trainer, and following Rupert's cruel remarks about my mum's hero, Jake Lovell, after the Gimcrack dinner, I couldn't stay silent.' Celeste noticed Roddy nodding in approval. 'Gav and Rupert are so close, I cannot believe Rupert didn't know which day Dave was born. Gav rang Rupert on the night and let him know, and Rupert left a party and came straight home to see the foal. Rupert and Gav had plenty of time to talk while I straightened up the office. We then had a glass or two of bubbly up at the house.'

'If you were so new to the job,' asked Marti silkily, 'why unearth the original foaling certificate from the bin?'

'Although I didn't realize the full implications,' Celeste didn't like Marti, 'nothing added up. Gav filling in one form in ecstasy, then swearing as the New Year bells rang out – such a lovely sound – then scrumpling up the form in panic and filling in another one.'

'Why didn't you take the first certificate to Rupert, then and there?'

'Gav,' Celeste's eyes filled with tears, after all, she wasn't wearing mascara, 'threatened me that if I snitched, I'd lose a job I adored. I was so thrilled to work at Penscombe, it's so hard to get into racing. I was very frightened of Mr Campbell-Black.'

'I suggest you knew the implications all along, and have been blackmailing Gavin Latton that you'd spill the beans, if he didn't persuade Rupert not to give you the sack.'

'No, no!' Celeste started to cry.

Sam Bridlington, who was dying for a pee, and Sally, who wanted to take off her thermal vest, asked for a ten-minute break.

As he entered the Gents, Sam heard a familiar soft clipped voice and found Rupert on his mobile: 'Is that Ladbrokes? Account RC-B1. Hi Joel, I'd like five grand to win on number four, Foxymoron, in the 1.40 at Lingfield, and five grand each way in the 2.30, on number 5, Petruchio. Thanks, Joel.'

Switching off his mobile, Rupert grinned ironically at Sam. 'May be my last bet on my own horses, and I'll need a winner to pay that massive fine you're no doubt about to impose on me.'

'We're having a ten-minute break,' said Sam. 'You're next.'

I like this man, he thought, waiting for Rupert to leave, then getting out his mobile, rang his bookmaker, putting five hundred pounds on Foxymoron and one hundred each way on Petruchio.

A BRA executive, at a nearby urinal, beetled off to tell the staff.

36

A deadpan Rupert faced the Panel. Not by a flicker did he betray the fear inside him.

We'll nail him, thought Roddy gleefully.

Isn't he heaven, thought Sally, putting a nose bag on the horse she was doodling. I'd water the course for him any time.

'Act contrite,' murmured Marti.

'I didn't know,' idly, Rupert examined a green biro which said *Larchmere Dental Practice* – where the hell had that come from? – 'because I didn't want to know. I raised the odd eyebrow the day/night Dave was born, but didn't push it. I suppose you could say I held my binoculars to both blind eyes.

'Gav, on the other hand, was only a junior stud hand. He delivered a prize colt under amazing pressure, at phenomenal speed – as he said, four minutes from the waters breaking to the birth – and, probably in a state of shock, filled in the form, not appreciating the consequences until later, by which time, the whole of Penscombe had fallen in love with Dave.' He smiled at Sally.

'I have to say I agree with Gav that it's the most stupid, destructive rule in racing, that a wonderhorse, born an hour too early, the best I've ever trained, is utterly damned, denied any career as a two-year-old, denied a crack at the Triple Crown, even though he's favourite for the Guineas and the Derby.

'We need hero horses to pull in the crowds. With this rule,

racing is rejecting potential heroes. I'm sorry other owners have been deprived of their winnings and I realize Dave must be disqualified from all his races. Naturally I will pay back all the money and compensate Geoffrey, in particular, for missing the Breeders' Cup, but I would like to reiterate that Gav only acted out of intense loyalty to me. There is no way I would ever fire him.'

Shoulders hunched, Gav sat with his head in his hands.

'Is that because, if you had done, it would have drawn attention to his culpability?' asked Norman Thomas.

'No, because he's so bloody good at his job.'

'What about the loss to the punters? How will they be paid back?'

'What about all the lucky people who backed Geoffrey to lose?'

'Don't be impertinent!' roared Roddy.

Norman Thomas couldn't dent Rupert, so another break was called so the Panel could deliberate before making a decision. Sally Stonehouse, who had nipped to the Ladies to whip off her thermal vest in the earlier break, returned to do her face.

Two secretaries came in. 'Never seen crowds like it,' said the first. 'Chantelle tried to get to the sales, and she was mobbed by press and public, dying from the cold, desperate for any news. I think they'll lynch this Panel if he loses his licence. Ooh, he is gorgeous, that Gav's lush too. Oh, sorry, Mrs Stonehouse,' as Sally came out of the loo.

Rupert, Marti and Gav returned to *Red Rum*.

'You did very well,' Marti told Gav, as Danielle and Fiona entered, carrying plates of sandwiches.

'We've got cheese, or egg and cress, or chicken, or ham, with some green pepper and cauliflower to dip in hummus. Tea or coffee, still or sparkling?'

Rupert would have preferred a quadruple whisky in the Red Lion, but felt it unfair to Gav. *Ping* came a text from Taggie: 'Thinking of you, hop its gowing okay. Luv to Gav.' He showed it to Gav. *Ping* came a text from Weatherbys. Foxymoron had sauntered up in the 1.40. Did he hear cheering outside?

*

215

Over in the Enquiry Room, deliberations were less harmonious. Roddy, his mouth full of chicken sandwich, brooded over the fact that Rupert had never missed an opportunity to flout his authority or take the piss. 'Now that we've heard all the evidence, Campbell-Black is clearly culpable. I suggest he loses his licence for ten years. We cannot condone cheating.'

Roddy, however, had irritated both Sally and Sam so much, and Sam had just won a grand on Foxymoron. Switching off his mobile, he cleared his throat. 'I am reluctant to prosecute Campbell-Black. I know it is our duty to uphold the rules of racing, but this is a prohibitive one, and it is also our duty to popularize it, and Campbell-Black certainly does that. Racing, as he pointed out, does need heroes.'

'You've changed your tune!' exploded Roddy. 'I thought we agreed to ensure integrity in the sport. Sally?'

'I agree with Sam,' said Sally dreamily. 'We must encourage Rupert to stay in racing, which would be fatally weakened if he pulled out. I've just talked to a couple of girls upstairs, and they say the crowds are growing by the minute despite the bitter cold. No name carries more weight than Campbell-Black.'

'But he cheated, and the BRA must not flinch in bringing justice to bear. We cannot have this black cloud hanging over British racing. We have an example to set other countries.' Roddy comfort-ate the last chicken sandwich which Sally had had her eye on.

Sam dipped a piece of green pepper in the bowl of hummus then thought better of it.

'The man's a bounder,' Roddy snarled, 'not nearly as valuable to the sport as the Arabs or Qataris, or the Irish at Coolmore.'

In *Red Rum*, Rupert was running through the latest list of Love Rat's nominations. Several breeders wanted to pull out or pay less.

'Tough tits,' Rupert emailed back to Pat. 'Their contracts stand.'

Danielle was back: 'The Panel are ready for you, Mr Campbell-Black.'

As they filed in, Rupert was encouraged to see that Roddy

had turned magenta. 'Looks absolutely hopping,' he murmured.

'Too fat to hop,' murmured back Gav, and thought, The only way I can ever pay Rupert back is to turn Quickly into a world-beater.

'The Panel,' said Sam Bridlington, putting on his spectacles, 'have appreciated Mr Campbell-Black's agreement to refund all the prize money won by the colt, following his disqualification. The Panel also bears in mind,' went on Sam, 'that after his initial refusal to admit the truth, Mr Latton showed open and honest co-operation. His actions have never been motivated by personal gain, only by loyalty and devotion to the yard and his employer; he takes full responsibility, and has expressed his sincere regret before the Panel for his actions. The entry point for this breach of the rules would be £3,000, and three years. However, the Panel recognize significant facts in mitigation. We therefore disqualify you, Mr Latton, for five months, written reasons to follow. You are not to associate, during this period, with anyone from a racing yard – and anyone in a racing yard who associates with you will endanger their careers. You must leave Penscombe within the next two days.'

Rupert looked at Marti incredulously.

Oh Christ, thought Gav numbly. I won't be here to make sure Quickly has first crack at the Triple Crown.

'Thank you very much,' said a highly gratified Marti.

'Thank you.' Rupert kissed Sally. 'I'll come and race all my horses at your racecourse.'

'It's a majority vote, Roddy,' warned Sam Bridlington, as they went downstairs for the press conference. 'I know you're disappointed at the result but I hope you're not going to reveal how deeply we were divided.'

'Fucking hell,' muttered Rupert.

'Why aren't you more grateful?' said Marti in outrage. 'You nearly lost your licence for ten years.'

'Instead, I've lost the best work rider I've ever had.'

'You can have him back in June.'

*

As they returned to *Red Rum*, Danielle and Fiona were full of congratulations, and said to Gav: 'The time will pass very quickly.'

'Here are your roses, Rupert.' Fiona had wrapped them in silver foil and soaked tissue paper.

'You keep them, sweetheart.'

'No, no, we both put twenty quid on Foxymoron, and Petruchio.'

Despite the bitter cold, the crowds were still outside awaiting a result, and they cheered to the top of the Post Office Tower when they heard Rupert had kept his licence.

37

Sam Bridlington smiled at Sally Stonehouse. 'I think we made the right decision.'

'I'm sure we did. Racing would have been a lot drabber.'

'Since the Hon. Rod wolfed all the sandwiches, shall we go and have tea, or something stronger, at the Dorchester?'

'Oh, do let's. I feel rather emotional.' Sally discovered she was blowing her nose on her thermal vest.

Roddy was less amused to receive a call from Enid. 'Well done, well done, how splendid you all listened to the voice of commonsense and let Rupert keep his licence.'

His next call came from a fuming Cosmo. 'You assured me it was in the bag!'

'It was. Mrs Stonehouse and Sam Bridlington changed sides. Campbell-Black smarmed them round, bloody disgrace.'

'It's disastrous. Changed the whole financial picture,' said Cosmo evilly, adding that he wasn't sure now how he could give that two million to Rutminster Racecourse to support Roddy's development plans.

The moment Cosmo rang off, he got a call from Celeste. She'd been hung out to dry, she said. She'd fought the battle against Rupert without any support. Now it was her turn.

'I can't stay with my sister for ever, Cosmo. Have you decided where I'm going to live, and when can I start work at Valhalla?'

'The moment you provide me with a reference from your previous employer,' purred Cosmo.

'That's ridiculous,' squawked Celeste. 'Rupert'd never give me a reference. He wants to kill me!'

'Exactly.'

'But you promised.'

'Nothing,' said Cosmo, and hung up.

Rupert and Gav, both jolted to the core, didn't talk much on the way home in the helicopter. Rupert spent the time on his mobile, Gav wondering what the hell to do next. He must somehow pay back the money. He couldn't endure going home, and his parents ranting on and on about how his divorce, drunkenness, and now cheating, had brought shame on the family. A loner, he didn't want to impose on anyone. He'd have to find a bed and breakfast, terrified of going back on the booze.

Night had fallen. Through the darkness, they could see a lit-up Penscombe.

'You OK?' asked Rupert. 'Must be shattered. What do you think I should do about Quickly?'

'I think you should employ Gala. She's a bloody good rider, and Quickly adores her, and respects her.' Worried that Gala might be gone by the time he was allowed back, Gav took a deep breath and voiced a fear that had haunted him for months. 'She's getting restless.' Then, when Rupert glanced up: 'Your father's getting much more demanding, not taking her mind off things. She misses Ben and she hates the English weather.'

'She's not going to like it any more at six o'clock on the gallops.'

'She loves horses. It's her birthday next week – I was thinking of getting her a rescue Staffie puppy. Enough of them in the dogs' homes.'

'Might do better with a working Cocker – more biddable.'

I'd settle for a working cock, thought Gav wistfully.

'Anyway, we've got enough dogs. Christ, look at that.'

Both were amazed by the triumphal welcome that greeted them. Balloons, flags and banners all down the drive. Most of Penscombe village had rolled up for a party, bringing bottles.

The village band was playing, somewhat discordantly, 'Here's to the Heroes'. A great cheer and several rockets went up as the dark-blue helicopter landed. They'd all seen the telly and knew that their jobs, of which they were so proud, were secure. They had also been the recipients of appalling bitching from other yards.

Gav, the new poster boy, had got off with a slapped wrist and would be back in a few months. The dogs swarmed out, barking, weaving and whining round Rupert's feet, followed by an ecstatic Taggie, who hugged Gav and then kissed Rupert passionately, to more cheers. How lucky they are, thought Gala and Lark, from the shadows.

Rupert then called for quiet. 'We're OK. We're safe. Thank you for all your support over the last few months. Sorry I've been so utterly bloody. You probably wouldn't have minded if I *had* lost my licence, but I was trying to hide the fact I was shit-scared.'

Everyone noticed how tired he looked.

'But once again, we've routed the Northfields, as my ancestor, Rupert Black, did back in the eighteenth century. Gav was brilliant, by the way. His evidence saved us.'

Tumultuous cheers!

'Gav's been the fall guy, but he'll be back in five months and from tomorrow, we'll get back on track. Thank you for my lucky tie, Lark – I think it did the trick. If you want to push off to the Dog and Trumpet, the drinks are on me, but I want you up at the same time tomorrow. We've got to start the fight back.'

Walking back to the house, Rupert beckoned Gala to follow him. Like the rest of his staff, she looked lit up with joy that he'd survived, and in addition, absolutely gorgeous in her clinging crimson Christmas party dress, showing several inches of lush cleavage.

'You'd certainly win the turnout,' he said approvingly. 'Look, I need your help. Gav's been through hell – bloody easy for him to go back on the booze. Can you keep an eye on him?'

Everyone wanted to commiserate with Gav, but he'd sloped off to his rooms. On the way, he clocked Venus, glowing mockingly in the dusk. Orion the Hunter was on the march.

Poignantly, he passed Dave, looking adorable in a new red Christmas rug which extended like a polo neck up to his ears, and whickering over his half door, which was covered on either side by plaques, recording his seven wins. Would they now all be ripped down?

'I'm sorry, boy.' Gav hugged him.

Up in his flat, he looked round at the security which he must now relinquish. He ought to pack, but he had to write notes on all the horses. He jumped at a thundering on the door. At least it wouldn't be Celeste any more. Instead it was Gala, wafting Coco Chanel, ravishing in her crimson dress, and clearly three parts cut.

'Just come to check you're OK.' She swayed towards him. 'Must have been hell.'

'I'm fine – lovely dress.'

'I'm a scarlet woman. Let me give you a hug.'

Gav froze as she put her arms around him, feeling the bounciness of her breasts, her scented curls, the bump of her groin. God, he wanted her. Gala herself felt liberated. Rupert had trusted her to look after Gav. His mouth was level with hers, so she kissed it, caressing his tongue with hers, murmuring, 'I've always wanted you.' One hand undoing his shirt buttons, the other creeping between his legs. 'Let's go to bed.'

But Gav panicked. There was no way he'd ever get it up.

'Sorry,' he muttered, tugging away the hand that was stroking his chest, wrenching the other from his groin. 'Sorry,' he repeated, then, groping for a joke, 'No one in racing is allowed to associate with me. You wouldn't be allowed to ride out any more.'

'Do I revolt you?' asked Gala furiously.

'No, no, of course not.' He longed to level with her, but only managed: 'It's been a long day. Look, as I said, I'm sorry.'

'Well, I'm not. You've made it quite clear that you find me repulsive, a drunken old cow. Sorry I bothered you.' Grabbing her coat, she stumbled, sobbing, down the stairs. She'd be scarlet all over from humiliation and embarrassment for the rest of her life. How could she have thrown herself at him?

She'd thought he liked her. How could she have misread the signals? She must get another job at once.

Quickly, bored and leaning out of his box, whickered as she passed. 'You're the only thing that loves me,' she wept into his shoulder, 'and you too,' as Purrpuss slid down Quickly's neck and butted her wet face.

'You OK?' said a voice. It was Cathal, the yard's Orion, who'd also liked the red dress.

'I'm fine – missing Ben,' sobbed Gala, fleeing back to the house.

After a quick catch-up and supper with Taggie, Rupert retreated to his office to think. Outside it had started to snow. What was to be done about Dave? Now officially a four-year-old, if he raced against three-year-olds, he'd be clobbered by huge extra weight, punishing for a little horse.

The problem was sorted by a telephone call in the middle of the night from one of his most charming former owners, Australian tenor Baby Spinosissimo, the ex-lover of Isa Lovell and current boyfriend of Rupert's brother, Adrian, who had been so livid that gay Uncle Cyprian had left the Stubbs to Rupert. Baby was presently in Sydney, where he was singing the Duke in *Rigoletto* and Rodolfo in *La Bohème* at the Opera House.

'Thank God you won, Rupert, thank God you saw off that two-timing bastard, Isa Lovell, and Cosmo Rannaldini. Who would have expected such a fiendish kid to have grown into an even more fiendish adult? Poor darling Dave, such a sweet little horse. Listen, I've been thinking.'

'So have I,' said Rupert. 'What if I were to send Dave over to you?'

'I'll buy him,' said Baby.

'Well, at least he can have a few months off, enjoying the sunshine. He's had a tough year. Then, because your seasons are six months ahead of ours, from July first he can run against other three-year-olds, and if he keeps on improving, have a crack at the Melbourne Cup in November, without having to lose form in quarantine.'

'Great, he can live at my yard. Peppy Koala loved it here, shagged himself insensible. I'm not having Titus Andronicus back, mind. Tricky bastard – none of my lads have any fingers left.'

'It's a deal, Baby. I'll send him into quarantine next week. He's a sweet horse, deserves the chance.'

Thus empowered, Rupert rang up his favourite son-in-law, Luke Alderton, in Palm Beach. An ex-international polo-player, Luke was now chef d'equipe of the American team. Somehow staying married to Rupert's tricky daughter Perdita, Luke was a sort of male Taggie – tougher, but with the same stamina needed to cope with a Campbell-Black.

'Hi, Luke.'

'Ah've been meaning to ring you.' How soothing was that warm Texan drawl. 'So good you kept your licence – bloody stupid rule.'

'Very close-run thing. We were lucky. How's Perdita?'

'She's good. And Eddie won a couple of races last week.'

'I noticed. Bloody cold here, snowing outside. I've got a favour to ask you.'

'And I you. You go first.'

'Gavin Latton's gone through hell. He's a loner, ex-alki, carried the can for New Year's Dave, not allowed to stay in any racing premises here, needs a complete break. Wonder if you could use him in Palm Beach for a few months? He's bloody good, anything that needs breaking or sorting out. Could do with some sun and a change of scenery. You're the kind of bloke who could settle him.'

'Sounds good. I'll put him to work on the young US team horses.'

'And in return?'

'Can Ed come back? He's gutted he screwed up. He's learned his lesson. He's riding beautifully but he's fighting with Perdita, and although you may not realize it, he thinks the world of you and Taggie.'

'Probably Taggie. I need him actually. I'll send Gav out at once, if Eddie could just stay a few days to settle him in. He's very shy, and he can wise Eddie up about the horses. I've got a brilliant colt called Master Quickly.'

Luke laughed. 'Oh yeah, I've heard all about him.'
'Thanks, Luke.'

Gav agreed to go, because he couldn't think what else to do, and because he was so bitterly ashamed of blowing out Gala. How could he have humiliated such a sweet, vulnerable woman like that? If only he could have levelled with her, and they'd just lain in each other's arms, reciprocally comforting.

38

Next morning, the papers were full of Rupert, by the skin of his excellent teeth, not losing his licence. Pat Inglis and his staff were already flat out reminding nervous breeders that they had signed a watertight contract to send mares to Love Rat, and his invincibility as a sire was in no way diminished.

None of this was helped by the *Racing Post* leading on Dave being stripped of his glory. 'How is the mighty fallen,' they wrote, and about Love Rat dropping to eighth place in the Leading Sire chart because of the loss of Dave's prize money. There was also a beautiful photograph of Roberto's Revenge, Valhalla's Colossus, moving up to second place, with progeny earnings of six million.

Meanwhile, rumours were now confirmed that Roberto's Revenge would be the first husband of Darkness Visible, the mighty American mare, named Eclipse Horse of the Year. Rupert threw the *Racing Post* across the room.

So, it rested on the twitching shoulders of Quickly to redeem the yard. In two days, Rupert would be setting off to Dubai with eight horses, in search of prize money to pay his three million wage bill.

Word had already flashed round the yard that New Year's Dave was off to Australia. Lark was distraught. She doted on Touchy Filly, Quickly and her fourth horse, a dark-brown delinquent called Blank Chekov, but sweet, loving Dave had compensated a little for missing Young Eddie so much. She had tried to forget Eddie. She had been crucified, learning that he and Gala had got it together. She'd been fond of Gala, but seeing her last night stealing across the yard to Gav's flat, Coco Chanel following her like a witch's trail, looking so gorgeous in her crimson dress, reinforced Lark's shame at her presumption that anyone as plump, round-faced and ordinary-looking as herself could ever compete.

Having ridden her horses round the indoor school, and groomed and fed them, she screwed up courage and knocked on Rupert's office door, setting off a massive thwacking of tails with Cuthbert's wriggling rump nearly sending Rupert's iPad flying.

'Yes?' Rupert looked up. He was very fond of Lark and was surprised to see woebegone eyes and no beaming smile. 'You OK, angel?'

'Could I have a brief word?' she said shyly. 'I love Dave so much, could I possibly go to Australia and get a job looking after him? I don't want him to be lonely.'

'Oh Lark,' sighed Rupert. 'I can't lose you. Touchy Filly and Quickly will go into a decline. Dave's going to Baby Spinosissimo's yard where he'll be spoilt absolutely rotten. He'll be going into quarantine in Newmarket in a couple of days.'

'Can I go with him? He's always tried so hard, it's so sad he's lost everything.'

'I know, it's awful. But he's so good, he might have a crack at the Melbourne Cup.'

'That would be very exciting,' said Lark flatly.

'Quickly needs you. Without Dave, he'll have no one to bully.'

'I know I'll miss him, I can only give Dave a Polo if Quickly isn't looking. I'm sorry, I'm just, I'm just . . .'

Hopelessly hooked on my wayward grandson, thought Rupert.

'OK, you can go. And if Dave comes back to England, you can come with him. Your job will always be open. I'll ring Baby. He's fun, you'll like him.'

'Thank you,' stammered Lark. 'I won't let you down.'

Outside, the snow was covering the landscape. It was bitterly cold. Reluctant stallions were being led around, getting fit for the covering season, starting on the day after St Valentine's next week. An even more reluctant stud hand was lunging Titus in the indoor school, wondering how soon Titus would lunge at him.

Rupert called a meeting of his senior staff, including Cathal, Bobby Walker the lorry driver, Simmy Halliday the Estate Manager, Roving Mike and Walter. All poleaxed with hangovers from last night's celebration, they staggered in, clutching bottled water and cups of black coffee, trying to find chairs or sofas that weren't taken by dogs.

Rupert was back to his usual form. 'Two sheep have strayed on to the gallops,' he said sharply. In addition, he'd noticed a filly on the horse walker without a rug. 'No horse must travel without a bridle, and must be checked hourly.

'Now, OK, this is the state of play. Dave, as I'm sure you know by now, is off to Australia, so he can race as a three-year-old from July one. So, we've lost our best horse. Gavin, on the other hand, has always claimed Quickly is the better horse – if we can sort out his head. Unfortunately, the rider who could sort him out, Gav, is off to Palm Beach for five months to work in my son-in-law's polo yard.'

'Lucky sod,' said Roving Mike, 'escaping this bloody winter.'

'Which is a disaster for Quickly.' Rupert glared at Mike. 'Another setback is Lark, who has just been in here, begging to go into quarantine and to Australia with Dave. So in several words, Quickly, Touchy Filly and Blank Chekov will be without Dave to bully, without their stable girl, Lark, and without Gav to prep them for next April. Quickly, also outlawed for failing his stalls test, will miss all the Guineas trials, and the Guineas is less than four months away.'

The television was turned to *At the Races* at Southwell, where the snow was pouring down, and jockeys, bulked out against the cold, could be seen going down to the start for the first race.

'I also heard this morning that Lion's doctors have advised

him not to ride again for six months, if at all. Agents have been jamming the telephone with offers all morning. I know some of you aren't fans, but my grandson, Eddie Alderton, will be back in a couple of weeks. He's been winning races in America, and has promised to mend his ways.'

'For starters, he owes £1,500 in fines for coming in late,' snorted Walter. 'If he can't settle bills, how can he settle a horse?'

'Who's going to do Lark's horses, and ride them?' asked Roving Mike.

'The person Gav was keen on joining the yard was Gala,' replied Rupert, then, looking at the sceptical faces, 'She's a beautiful rider and knows how to settle horses, but won't stand for any nonsense.'

'Gav's keen on Gala, full stop. She's an amateur and too fat,' grumbled Walter, who'd been turned down too often by Gala, as had Cathal, who agreed.

Simmy Halliday, however, looked up from the *Daily Mail* crossword. 'I agree with you, Guv. She's a great rider.'

'She's getting restless here,' said Roving Mike. 'Louise heard her ringing up her carer agency this morning.'

'Get another carer who can do mornings,' suggested Pat Inglis. 'Free Gala up to ride out. It'd be worth it. Quickly's such a monkey, he could go to pieces without Gav.'

'And my father'll go to pieces without Gala. You'll never keep him out of the yard. OK. I'll talk to Taggie.'

Back in the kitchen, shoving a couple of slices of smoked salmon between two pieces of brown bread, Rupert asked Taggie: 'Can we get another carer to free up Gala to work in the yard?'

'More than she is already?' Taggie nearly snapped back, but instead she said, 'I don't know what happened last night, but her face is really tear-stained this morning, although she wouldn't talk about it. It's her birthday tomorrow. I've found her a lovely bottle-green polo neck from us, which might cheer her up, and I must ice her cake.'

Next day, it turned blissfully mild, with a blinding low sun returning and melting the snow. Word had got around it was

Gala's birthday. When she went down to the yard on her break, to thank everyone for signing her card and giving her a beautiful brown scarf decorated with horses, Roving Mike, Cathal and Simmy Halliday gathered her up and chucked her into the icy cold water-trough.

Whereupon Gala flipped, screaming expletives: 'Fucking bastards! How dare you, you fucking juveniles,' slapping Cathal and Simmy's grinning faces, before leaping into her car and storming off. Sobbing her heart out, she drove down to the churchyard. No one was inside the church, the flower arrangers had gone. Shivering violently, Gala slumped over the back of a pew, kneeling on a cross-stitched owl.

'Oh Ben, oh Ben.' If he was up there, would he ever forgive her? Was she being punished for her attempted infidelity, by being rejected by Gav whom she'd tried to get off with, so conceitedly imagining he fancied her? Old mare syndrome, mutton dressed as lamb.

'Oh God, please help me, help me,' she howled.

Suddenly she felt a warm hand on her neck, which, as she jumped in terror, held her down.

'Don't cry.' It was Rupert.

'What are you doing here?'

'Came to put flowers on Billy's grave. What's the matter? You're soaking!'

'They threw me in the water-trough, shouting Happy Birthday. I lost it. I'd just washed my hair. I screamed back at them, behaved like a fishwife.'

'Fishwives gotta swim.' Idly Rupert stroked her drenched hair as if she were Cuthbert. 'It's a sort of compliment if they do it on birthdays – means they regard you as part of the yard and want you to transfer. I've brought you a present. Happy Birthday, Gala.'

As he led her back into the churchyard, she noticed a big bunch of daffodils in a jam jar on Billy's grave. And when he opened his boot, wriggling frantically on a red carpet rug was a brindle Staffordshire Bull Terrier puppy.

'Oh, oh, oh, oh,' gasped Gala. 'How sweet!' As she gathered

up the puppy, he melted into her arms, frantically licking away her tears. 'He's the most adorable thing I've ever seen.'

'For you,' Rupert told her. 'Look at his disc.'

Glinting in the sunlight, it said: *Milburn, Penscombe Court, Gloucestershire*, with the telephone number.

'It should also say, *please stay here.*'

'Oh, I love him . . .' Then Gala thrust the puppy back at Rupert. 'But I wouldn't be able to take him to my next job.'

'You're not going anywhere. I need you, you're going to work in the yard.'

'I can't, I'm too fat – and what about your dad?'

'Well, for starters, we'll get in a part-time carer so you can work mornings in the yard, and do ride work on Quickly and Touchy Filly. Eddie's coming back from Palm Beach and you can work together.'

'Are you sure?' The tears were starting again.

Handing her his blue silk handkerchief, Rupert put down the puppy, who charged around the churchyard, knocking over Billy's daffodils then wriggling back to Gala, wagging and giving little whimpers to be picked up again.

'He loves you already. I remember you telling me how broken-hearted you were to lose your Staffies,' said Rupert smugly. 'And no more talk about getting another job. Quickly needs you.'

Before he left for Palm Beach, Gav left Gala a note: *Sorry about last night. One day I'll explain.* Gala emailed back:

Don't give it another thought. I'm going to work mornings in the yard. All Rupert's idea. To persuade me to stay, knowing I adored Staffies, he went out and especially bought me a puppy, called Gropius. He's so adorable – not just the puppy, Rupert. You're quite right, people do misjudge him.

Fuck Rupert, thought Gav.

Meanwhile, Marketa and Lou-easy were distraught about Lark leaving The Shaggery which they had all shared, and going off to Australia. Who would clean the place, and cook them supper now?

Lark had finished packing, and was putting labels on her luggage, when Dora came in to say goodbye.

'I can't bear it that you're going. You're easily the best stable girl in the yard, and the nicest. It's so sad I won't have you to gossip to any more. I'll send you lots of emails. You know Gav's gone to Palm Beach to stay with Young Eddie's parents? Once Eddie's settled Gav in, he's coming back to Penscombe, so fun and games are here again.'

'What?' whispered Lark. 'Rupert's letting him back?'

'I imagine Rupert did a trade-off for Luke and Perdita taking Gav. Gav'll probably get hooked on polo and stay there – he's such a brilliant rider.'

Oh my God, thought Lark. I'm going to the end of the world, and Eddie's coming back. It was too late to ask Rupert if she could stay; the labels were on her suitcase and poor Dave needed her.

'And have you heard,' went on Dora, 'Gala's going to transfer to the yard. It's a compliment to you. Rupert doesn't want Quickers and your other horses to go into a decline without you, so she's coming in mornings to do them, and ride out. Rupert will leave no stonewall unturned, until he's cracked Leading Sire and annihilated Cosmo.'

Over at Valhalla, as night fell, an unidentified guest was ushered into Cosmo's study, and shook hands with him and Isa.

'No one must know we have spoken,' said Cosmo. 'But if the BRA are incapable of annihilating Campbell-Black, we'll have to do it ourselves.'

'I have more reason to bring him down than either of you,' said the stranger, jumping at the gunshot pop of a cork.

'Granted,' agreed Cosmo, pouring champagne into three glasses. 'We're going to bring him down, destroy his business and break up his marriage.'

'No marriage is rock solid,' said Isa. 'My father took Rupert's first wife off him.'

'So it can't be too difficult to take the second,' said the stranger.

'What a divine prospect,' sighed Cosmo, raising his glass. 'Vengeance is ours. We will repay.'

39

Taggie had never been a grumbler. But listening to Gala going on and on about Gropius, the Staffie puppy, that Rupert had given her, and how flattered she was that he wanted her to transfer to the yard, and how she'd misjudged him, and how, underneath, he was a really sweet man . . . wistfully Taggie was reminded of the time before she was married. Her family had all forgotten her birthday and an enraged Rupert had rolled up and presented her with a Springer Spaniel puppy. This, her father Declan O'Hara had named Claudius, after the King in *Hamlet* whose Queen was called Gertrude, the name of Taggie's adored little mongrel. Gertrude, who'd died when Cosmo's evil father Rannaldini had hurled her against a filing cabinet because she'd attempted to defend Rupert's daughter Tabitha, when Rannaldini tried to rape her.

Learning Rupert was briefly back from Dubai, having notched up a £100,000 victory there, Declan dropped in at Penscombe. Once the BBC's hottest property, Declan's interviews of the great and very famous had gone out in prime time and been avidly discussed by the entire nation. Declan, however, had never got above himself because his beautiful, feckless wife Maud had taken no interest in his career, and constantly put him down.

To the huge regret of his millions of fans, Declan had given up television and, having finally completed a brilliant, glowingly reviewed biography of Yeats, was now wrestling with a big book on Irish literature, which he very much regretted taking on.

The roaring boy was seventy now; his thick black hair had turned completely grey. Worry, work and heavy drinking had dug deeper lines on each side of his mouth and round eyes as dark and sombre as a starless night. Two pairs of spectacles clattered from his neck, and his famous gap-toothed schoolboy grin, because of a dread of dentists, more resembled a Halloween pumpkin – but, tall and huge-shouldered, he was still heroic.

In the stud, the covering season was about to start. The lorry park was once again jammed with swearing foreign drivers trying to unload whinnying mares to be mated with stallions revved up to a height of fitness. Taggie was no doubt putting flowers in their boxes, reflected Declan, stopping to chat to Pat Inglis and admire Blood River, the gleaming new dark-brown stallion from South Africa, who'd fallen in love with Charlie Radcliffe, the vet, and very expensively liked to have him in attendance during every cover. Pat was also sorting out the dark grey Dardanius, a first season sire who, despite numerous goes on Dorothy, the practice mare, kept mounting her from the side.

'Oh, Lord O'Hara.' Clover, the youngest stable girl, sidled up. 'I've ordered your book on Yeats for my dad's birthday. He's mad about racing and Yeats is his favourite horse – fancy winning four Gold Cups! When it arrives, can I bring it over for you to sign?'

'I hadn't the heart to tell her it was the wrong Yeats,' sighed Declan in his world-famous, husky smoker's voice. 'I'd probably have done better if I had written about horses.'

He'd have to work to the day he dropped to support his extravagant wife and children, and to stop them tapping Taggie, who hated squandering Rupert's money.

Now in Rupert's office, his vast hand curled round a dark glass of whisky, studying his son-in-law's bleak, handsome face as he scoured the monitors for worldwide wins by Love Rat's progeny, Declan was reminded of Yeats' poem to Maud Gonne:

> With beauty like a tightened bow, a kind
> That is not natural in an age like this
> Being high and solitary and most stern,
> Why, what could she have done, being what she is?
> Was there another Troy for her to burn?

Cracking Leading Sire was Rupert's Troy. But would being abroad so much destroy his marriage?

Declan then chided Rupert that Taggie was looking desperately tired, that the family descended the moment Rupert went away and that Gala seemed to be spending more and more time in the yard. Despite a part-time carer coming in every morning from the village, an increasingly dotty Old Eddie hadn't taken to her, and poor Taggie was having to look after him. Yesterday she'd lost him in Waitrose, and tracked him down at the checkout, asking the girl there to cut his nails. Only that very morning, Old Eddie had driven the whole household demented by vanishing for two hours and being found sleeping peacefully in his beloved Love Rat's box.

'If he'd chosen Titus Andronicus, that might have sorted all our problems,' growled Declan. 'You need a proper full-time carer.'

Oh God, not another 'treasure', jerking off about making a difference, thought Rupert. But hearing how well Gala was doing with Quickly and Touchy Filly, and what an asset she was already proving in the yard, he was very reluctant to order her to spend more time with Eddie. He therefore rang Mrs Simmons at the carers agency.

'I don't know how you'd feel about a male carer?' she said.

'Well, at least my father wouldn't goose or rather geese him. He's jumped on so many.'

'Oh Mr Campbell-Black! A very nice South African called Jan, pronounced Yan, Van Deventer recently arrived in England and has just joined our agency. He's an ex-army officer, so he can talk to your father about army things, and he's an experienced carer.'

Thinking of Charlie in *Casualty*, Rupert said: 'Send him over.'

40

Valentine's Day dawned. Out of a pale-green sky flecked with sooty black clouds shone a silvery Venus.

The Planet of Love is on high, thought Gala.

She hadn't felt so happy since Ben died as, oblivious to an icy cold wind, she cantered Master Quickly, his blond mane caressing her face, marvelling at the power of his acceleration, amazed by the speed with which he made up ground. Too fast for any of Rupert's other horses, he had to be sent up the gallops on his own. There was talk of trying to steady him by using his beloved Safety Car as a pacemaker.

The rest of the yard were not fans, having been nipped by Quickly too often, but he'd been sweet to Gala, not biting her at all. Missing Lark, Dave and Gav, he'd transferred his affection to her, crying like a baby when she returned to the house to look after Old Eddie at lunchtime. He and Purrpuss were also devoted to one another. The moment Quickly returned from the gallops, Purrpuss would be waiting in the manger to wash Quickly's face and thoroughly clean his ears before settling on his back. At night when Quickly lay down to sleep, Purrpuss curled up, a hot water bottle against his belly.

Last night too, Gala had been cheered by such a long chat with Rupert about the horses, particularly the next lot he'd be taking to Dubai for the World Cup in March.

It was a beautiful day. The birds were singing their heads off.

Rupert's lawn was edged with yellow aconites, with their little green ruffs of leaves, and drifts of snowdrops. Daffodil buds were turning downwards as the red postman's van staggered up the drive, weighed down by everyone's Valentines. Returning to the yard office, Gala was thrilled to have one from Palm Beach: *Hi, sexy, missing you, not long now*, which meant Gav hadn't taken offence at her last letter. She also got a Valentine from Gropius – must be from Rupert. The Planet of Love was on high, but she must stop her thoughts straying in his direction, particularly as he'd got hundreds and hundreds of Valentines.

'Won't even bother to open them,' grumbled Geraldine, gathering them up.

If Rupert got hundreds, Taggie got ten. The one in a pale-blue envelope without a stamp, bought at the airport, containing the words: *To my only darling*, was from Rupert. The rest, she immediately shoved under the blue and white striped lining paper in a kitchen drawer, in case Rupert saw them and had a tantrum. It was a comfort, she told herself, that he minded so much, particularly when Geraldine that very morning had remarked what a nice change it must be for Rupert, having someone in the house with whom to talk horses.

'Pity someone can't put a cross noseband on that poisonous bitch to keep her mouth shut,' observed a passing Dora.

After that, Valentine's Day went even more downhill for Taggie. A man coming to service the burglar alarm was even more alarmed to find a naked Old Eddie masturbating on the stairs. Then the part-time carer rang in with a migraine and Taggie managed to say, 'Poor you,' before slamming down the telephone, and saying: 'Oh fuck.'

By the time she had led Eddie upstairs, washed and dressed him and given him his breakfast, new puppy Gropius had chewed up one of Rupert's loafers and Forester had gone awol. Oh, how she missed darling Lark, who had so often walked the dogs in her break, and kept an eye on them in the yard. With all those lorries delivering mares and leaving gates open, Taggie was terrified Forester might have sloped off hunting.

Next moment the telephone rang. It was an hysterical Constance Sprightly from the vicarage. Forester had chased her tabby cat up a tree and was furiously barking at the foot. Not stopping to put on a coat, Taggie rushed out, ignoring the wolf whistles of traffic-jammed lorry drivers as she hurtled across the fields. However, by the time she reached the vicarage, Forester had moved on without mishap and disappeared at a brisk trot towards the village.

Another of Forester's maddening habits was that the louder you called him, the faster he tended to run away. Only when he couldn't see Taggie did he get curious and deign to come back and look for her. The hedges on each side of the road had been hacked back. Taggie was feeling so sorry for the young shoots and buds that would never realize their promise, when she also realized that in her haste, she'd left Forester's lead behind. Taking cover, she removed her white bra. Unable to see her, Forester, pink tongue lolling, totally without contrition, decided to return.

Taggie's now heaving, famously beautiful breasts which had never dropped with feeding children, were enhanced by a pale-grey T-shirt. Her pale cheeks were flushed from running. Walking home leading Forester by her bra, she was overtaken by a car. Inside was a suntanned, incredibly good-looking man with close-cropped hair the rich red-brown of the rain-soaked beech leaves carpeting Rupert's woods. Laughing brown eyes and a wonderfully smiling mouth with a jutting pillow of lower lip were enhanced by very white teeth and dark designer stubble.

Taggie was five foot ten and looked down on most men, particularly jockeys, but the man who jumped out of his car was broad-shouldered and at least three inches taller than her.

Could she tell him the way to Penscombe Court?

'Just up the road and turn left – no, I mean right,' she stammered in her deep, growling voice. 'I'm Taggie Campbell-Black. See you up there.'

'I'm Jan Van Deventer, mam, and I love your lead.'

On arrival, clocked by a gawping Marketa, Louise and Clover, who were just riding in from fifth lot, Jan was taken by a thoroughly over-excited Geraldine to meet Rupert. If taken aback by such an Adonis, Rupert was too proud to show it, even when Jan picked up Taggie's photograph on a nearby table and congratulated Rupert on having such a beautiful daughter.

Less cool than he makes out, thought Rupert, noticing with satisfaction how Jan's hand shook as he smoothed his hair.

'Wonderful picture,' observed Jan, looking up at the Stubbs. 'Not meaning to be personal, sir, but that handsome guy looks just like you.'

'He was an ancestor; the horse was Leading Sire of his day.'

'Gather Blood River's standing here – magnificent animal, saw him win the Cape Derby.'

As Geraldine shimmered in with a latte from their new machine for Jan, a very black espresso for Rupert and a plate of chocolate biscuits, Rupert noticed that she'd put on lipstick, done her eyes and was wafting J'Adore.

Jan proceeded to tell Rupert he was thirty-nine, and had spent ten years in the army – 'mostly to stop blacks killing blacks, they're so tribal' – before becoming a golf pro at which he was a great success, particularly, he didn't tell Rupert, with the ladies, who wriggled back against him when he put his arms round them to demonstrate a golf shot.

'Feeling there was more to life,' he went on, 'I decided to become a carer, and found the job immensely satisfying. My parents are Afrikaners of Dutch Huguenot origin.'

Getting up with a surge of energy to glance out of the window – 'Beautiful place, sir' – he caught sight of photos of Xavier, Bianca and Feral, and raised an eyebrow.

'My children,' explained Rupert, interested in how Jan would react, 'both adopted from Colombia. They always fought like cat and dog, so you would have been useful in the old days, stopping black killing black. The boy with Bianca is a footballer called Feral Jackson, bloody good, plays for a top team in Perth. You like football?'

'I prefer rugby, sir.'

Gazing round Rupert's office, and seeing so many paintings and photographs of great horses, Jan commented bitterly that 326,073 gallant horses had died in the Boer War.

'I know,' said Rupert.

Jan, who had a loud voice with a strong Afrikaans accent, then told Rupert that he came from Port Elizabeth which, because of the number of horse casualties, boasted the first great memorial to animals in war.

'A kneeling soldier,' he explained, 'holds up a bucket of water to a horse, with the inscription: "The greatness of a nation consists not so much in the number of its people or the extent of its territory as in the extent and justice of its compassion".'

'Right,' said Rupert, suppressing a yawn and irritated by a picture in the *Racing Post* of the great mare, Darkness Visible, arriving at Valhalla. He was desperate to get on with his day.

'You married?' he asked.

'Divorced, but amicably, sir. I've two kids in South Africa, Boetie and Beulah. I Skype them every day.'

Rupert was just wondering how wise it would be to let a stud like this loose in Penscombe, when as if reading his thoughts, Jan said: 'I'm gay, sir. But not broadcasting the fact. Not a great idea to come out in South Africa. Afrikaners are particularly homophobic, and my parents couldn't cope.'

'How many caring jobs have you had?'

'About eight, sir.'

'Think you'll be able to cope with my father? He's pretty eccentric.'

'I like feisty old people. Looked after a splendid old lady who cut her head after a fall. When she had to go to hospital she refused to let them give her any blood, insisting: "I've got my own blood and it's blue".'

'You should get on with my father, who's mad about the Army.' And with that voice, reflected Rupert, at least an increasingly deaf Eddie would be able to hear what Jan was saying.

'When can you start?'

'Straight away, sir.'

'You'd better come and meet my wife and my father and our present carer.'

'She won't be upset?'

'Not at all. She wants to work in the yard. Loves horses. All hers were butchered in Zimbabwe, farm burned to the ground. Husband and dogs all slaughtered at the same time.'

'Omigod, poor lady. Lots of that going on in South Africa.'

Gala had returned to the kitchen, unable to resist telling Taggie she'd had a Valentine from Gav.

'How lovely.' Taggie was delighted. 'I hope he's OK there, he's so shy. Young Eddie's coming back next week, I've missed him so much. Oh hell.' She took a plate out of the washing up machine and examined it. 'It hasn't washed it at all.'

'I never had a dishwasher in Zim,' said Gala sanctimoniously.

'Oh gosh, we're so spoilt in England.'

Gala laughed. 'I had a maid instead. What am I going to give Eddie for lunch?'

'There's plenty of smoked salmon and the remains of a fish pie. I wonder what that incredibly good-looking man was coming to see Rupert about? I know a tan helps, but he was gorgeous.' Taggie peered out of the window. 'Look at the stable girls sweeping a perfectly clean yard to catch a glimpse of him. Oh gosh, Rupert's bringing him over here. Am I very shiny?' She peered in the kitchen mirror.

Gala proceeded to peel off all her layers, to reveal a clinging orange T-shirt bearing the words: *I know I'm perfect, I'm also Zimbabwean.*

'I must look like nothing on earth after riding out,' she wailed, fluffing up curls, flattened by her hat.

'This is Jan Van Deventer,' announced Rupert, leading Jan into the kitchen.

Jan, who Taggie now noticed was wearing a thick grey gilet over a brown and white check shirt, brown cords and a seriously large Cartier watch on his big tanned wrist, smiled in amusement at Taggie and Gala, admiring them both as he said: 'What a terrific kitchen.'

'Great news,' said Rupert briskly. 'Jan's starting tomorrow as Eddie's full-time carer.'

'He what?' cried Taggie and Gala in horror.

'Gala wants to work full-time in the yard,' continued Rupert. 'Jan is free and Eddie could do with a slightly firmer hand, having spent the morning in Love Rat's box.'

Taggie looked from Gala to Jan in dismay.

'But it's so sudden! I'm sure you'll be marvellous,' she added, blushing, to Jan, 'but do you really want to go, Gala?'

'Not just like that. I thought I could do both jobs.'

'Well, you can't. Taggie's exhausting herself looking after Dad. I got a bollocking from your father yesterday.'

'I'm not,' stammered Taggie, 'and what will poor Eddie say? He's devoted to Gala.'

'Well, he'll still see her about the place. Gotta go.' Rupert turned to a mutinous Gala. 'Perhaps you'd show Jan where he'll be sleeping, introduce him to Dad and give him a run-down on routine. The good thing, Jan, is that Gala'll be close by, so any questions you need to ask . . .'

'And where am I going to sleep?' demanded a furious Gala.

'You must move into one of the other spare rooms,' said Taggie quickly.

'That'll confuse Dad,' said Rupert. 'She could take Lark's place in The Shaggery, but as it's warm and comfortable and unoccupied, I suggest she starts off in Gav's rooms over the tack room, until he gets back.'

Gala was suddenly terrified of losing her safe haven in the house. As Rupert set off for the yard, she raced after him.

'It's a disgrace, I've been railroaded.'

'You have not. You said it would be a dream come true sorting out Quickly, now you can do Touchy Filly as well.'

Fascinated to find out what was going on, Geraldine came through the door, brandishing a huge scented bunch of spring flowers. Grabbing them, Rupert returned to the kitchen where he found Jan smiling down at a distraught Taggie.

'Don't worry, mam, Mr Campbell-Black knows what he's doing. We'll sort it out together. I'll take care of things.'

'Ahem,' interrupted Rupert, handing the flowers to Taggie. 'For my daughter,' he said acidly to Jan.

41

Nothing was too difficult for Jan. He was a huge success from the start. Old people love jaunts and Jan was wonderful with Old Eddie, taking him to see Love Rat between shags every day, and to watch other stallions covering, taking him fishing, and to cricket as soon as summer began, and frequently to the races at Rutminster. Almost more importantly, Jan proceeded to transform Taggie's life. Hating badly-behaved children, he kept the visiting hordes in order, organizing barbecues and wild South African games all over the garden and the beechwoods.

Nothing was too much trouble, carrying the Dyson upstairs for besotted daily women, watering the plants, protecting Taggie from Helen and Janey, whose calls Geraldine always let through, keeping the dog-pack in order so that even naughty Forester followed in his footsteps.

Taggie had always felt guilty that Eddie's carers, even Gala, got exhausted from such long hours, but Jan never seemed too tired. When she asked him how he was, he'd just reply: 'I'm just fine, mam,' and she found it a comfort that he stayed up much later than her, watching sport or the *US X-Factor*. In addition, he had such wonderful manners, always opening car doors, pulling out and slotting in her seat belt, just gliding his hand across her breasts in a comforting, not threatening way, or legging her up into four-wheel-drives.

'I do hope the worst of the winter is over for you,' Taggie told him.

'I'd love to take you to South Africa, mam,' replied Jan. 'You'd love the beaches and the special African smell of diesel, woodsmoke and ripe fruit.'

All this was watched with grudging fascination by staff at both the stud and the yard. As Dora, who whizzed over to case the joint, observed: 'Rupert must be obsessed with nailing Leading Sire, if he's prepared to leave Taggie in the house with such a drop-dead gorgeous hunk without Gala to chaperone them. Hasn't even put an electric fence around her.'

Both loved cooking, and without any loss of masculinity, Jan was happy to discuss and try out recipes with Taggie all day.

'Watch this spice,' giggled Dora.

Gala meanwhile felt hopelessly unsettled. She'd never dreamt stable staff worked so hard. Twelve hours a day with only one weekend off in two.

Before, when she'd ridden out on Rupert's horses, someone else had done them first; similarly if she'd got on horses in Zimbabwe her stable staff had done all the donkey work. She was now expected to feed, groom and skip out Quickly and Touchy Filly and ride them out on dark, freezing mornings, when the rest of the world was asleep.

She also detected less friendliness in the stable staff, no longer hanging on her every word, avid for gossip about Rupert and Taggie and goings-on in the house. Fit young girls and boys in their early twenties, they made her feel an outsider as they scanned their iPhones and discussed their sex lives in the crudest terms. Were they resentful because she'd been handed two-star horses, not that they seemed very starry when Quickly carted her or moody Touchy Filly lashed out with both hind legs.

The weather was so cold, Gala couldn't diet and lost her nerve rather than any weight.

In the past, if she wanted to escape, she could whisk Old Eddie off on jaunts, but she could hardly take Touchy Filly shopping in Cheltenham or Quickly to the cinema. In the past too, it had been fun to flirt with the stable lads, even the yard letches, knowing she could retreat into the safety of Rupert's house. But in Gav's bedsit she was open to the world. Walter Walter, after getting tanked up at the Dog and Trumpet on her first Saturday, had tried it on so forcibly Gala had kneed him in the groin. Hell knows no fury like a Head Lad scorned. Next morning, Walter ordered her up on to the trickiest horse in the yard, the dark-brown delinquent Blank Chekov, known as Chuckoff, who had her on the floor three times. In future, said Walter, she would be doing Chekov as well as Quickly and Touchy Filly. He then ordered her to tidy up the muck-heap and brush the yard.

There was also the problem of little Gropius, who missed Rupert's dogs dreadfully and kept escaping back to the house, or howling if he were left in the bedsit over the tack room. Finally, there was the shock of her first pay-packet, dropping from £550 a week with all expenses paid, to a mere £300, so she wouldn't be helping out her sister Nicola any more. Rupert was in Dubai, going on to China, so she couldn't tackle him. Nor had she appreciated how shielded from the loneliness and sadness of widowhood she had been, living at home with Taggie.

Gavin's spartan bedsit had been furnished only with classical CDs and books. Sweet Taggie had done her best to feminize the place with a velvet patchwork quilt, a fluffy bedside rug, an electric blanket, half a dozen soft towels, a properly placed magnifying mirror, rose-scented shower gel and bowls of narcissi and pink hyacinths.

'I'm so sorry you had to move out so fast,' she had stammered on the day of eviction, 'and so sorry we can't have a farewell dinner tonight, but Valentine's Day is Valent Edwards' birthday and we've sort of committed to go out with him and Etta. Promise to drop in any time. I'm going to miss you so much.'

42

Gala had gone for supper a week later, and felt very de trop. Taggie, she noticed, was looking particularly pretty. Gala had taken Gropius with her who, pixillated to be among friends again, hurled himself round the ground floor, sending tables and ornaments flying.

'Stop that,' snapped Jan. Amazingly, Gropius did.

Jan had insisted on cooking: poached salmon in white wine with asparagus, new potatoes tossed in butter and parsley and Hollandaise sauce. 'Which he actually made,' confided Taggie. Followed by a lovely pudding of passion fruit and cream.

Taggie was too tactful to praise Jan's cooking too much and kept saying what a marvellous cook Gala had been. 'It must be an African thing,' and adding, 'you must go and see Old Eddie, Gala. I'm sure he's missing you.'

Eddie, who was watching a film called *For Your Flies Only*, kissed her in delight but couldn't remember which of his five ex-wives she was. 'Which year were we married, darling?'

Noticing she looked crestfallen on her return, Jan patted the sofa and sat down beside her, expressing real sorrow that Ben had died, and all the animals, and how terrible it must have been when the house had burnt down. Gala, who'd been looking up at a group photograph of Rupert in the cricket team at Harrow, said the worst thing had been losing all the past.

'The only photographs I've got of Ben are on my phone.'

'Where did he go to school?' asked Jan.

'Prince Edward's.'

'Very posh.'

'I don't want to talk about him any more.'

And when Jan asked lots of questions about Quickly and the yard, she found herself answering in monosyllables. As Jan put more logs on the fire, she felt miserable because it was so cosy and familiar here; Gropius looked so happy lying on top of Forester and next to Cuthbert, Taggie and Jan getting on so comfortably.

Jan wouldn't let Taggie feed the badgers in case she slipped on the icy path and said he and Gala would have to organize special barbecues, known as 'braais', for her in the summer.

'We work weekends in the yard,' snapped Gala. What had got into her?

'What do you miss most about Africa, Gala?' asked Taggie.

'I miss Ben.' Gala's voice broke. 'I must go – have to be up at five. I'm fine,' and gathering up Gropius, she fled home and cried herself to sleep.

Ten days further into the job, she reached an all-time low.

It was so cold, she found it impossible to diet; if she got any heavier, she wouldn't be allowed to ride Quickly. She had just dined on a baked potato packed with Philadelphia, and was now trying to resist a chunk of cheddar and a packet of chocolate biscuits, misery-eating after a vile morning.

Quickly had been gooder than gold, trotting round the covered ride, but the moment he put his foot on the grass of the gallops, a pheasant went up, and he was off, carting her all the way until he reached Penscombe High Street, narrowly missing an oncoming bus. On her return, leading Quickly, she was bawled out by Walter, particularly ratty because he'd given up drink for Lent, telling her she wasn't up to the job.

'You're too fat and too weak and that horse needs a firm hand.'

Gala was tempted to ask Taggie for her job back. But through the kitchen window she saw Taggie and Jan laughing together, and Geraldine wasted no opportunity to tell her what a huge success Jan was.

'I don't know why they never thought of getting a male carer before,' she had remarked only that morning. Then, as Gropius crashed into her legs: 'Go away, you dreadful beast. It's not just the horses that have got sore shins round here. Why on earth don't you take him to dog-training classes.'

'You could start off by going to bitch-training classes,' retorted Gala and stormed off.

Now in her leopardskin pyjamas, she could hear the stamping and neighing of a horse, kicking his stable door, banging his feed bowl against the manger, pawing the ground, pacing his box. It was Quickly, outraged because Purrpuss had gone off on a mousing spree.

Gav's bedsit gave her claustrophobia. There was no lovely view of the valley, no sun rising and setting, no stars, even if they were out. There was nothing on television so she helped herself to a chunk of cheddar and took an anthology of poems down from the bookshelves. It fell open at Shelley, marked by a photograph of a beautiful dark woman, a tigress with devouring eyes and an amazing body.

Gav had underlined the words: 'Out of the day and night, a joy has taken flight.'

Oh poor Gav. Gala scooped up a couple of chocolates – no wonder he wasn't drawn to overweight Zimbabweans. At least he'd sent her that Valentine from Palm Beach.

She flipped the pages. 'Two loves I have of comfort and despair,' was also underlined. Sitting down on the bed, Gala stroked her own 'love of comfort', little Gropius. His tummy tight with a much larger supper than hers, he slept fitfully, whimpering and thumping his tail in dreams. Was he playing with Forester? She kissed his striped forehead. Rupert had given Gropius to her and had been utterly determined she should look after Quickly: Rupert, who could get her over anyone. 'I must not think of thee,' she read, 'and tired yet strong, I shun the love that lurks in all delight.' Summed it up really.

Out of the window, she could see Purrpuss padding across the yard, leaping in through the half door, butting Quickly's face, greeted by an arpeggio of whickering. Lucky them. Next moment, Gala jumped at a hammering on the door.

'Go away!' she screamed, triggering off furious barking from Gropius.

'It's me, Eddie, let me in.'

As she opened the door, he smelt of drink and aftershave. His beauty was from a different world of sun and laughter. Shorter blond hair no longer flopped in his cornflower-blue eyes. A tan emphasized a smile disturbingly like Rupert's. He was leaner, more honed, and, putting down two bottles, he folded her in a bear hug.

'How yer doin', babe?'

'Bloody awful, but so pleased to see you.'

'How come they imprisoned you in this badger sett?' Eddie looked round in disapproval.

'Your grandfather wanted me to integrate – with the yard. How was Palm Beach?'

'OK. Beginning to fight with Mom. Glad to be back, sorry I missed your birthday.' He handed her a bottle of Coco Chanel and proceeded to open the second, of Bollinger.

'That's heavenly,' cried Gala in ecstasy. 'Thank you, you are kind.'

There was a pop, and Gropius rushed over and caught the flying cork.

'Good boy, should be fielding for England. Must get you some glasses,' said Eddie, emptying champagne into a cup and a tooth mug. 'Gav was probably avoiding them.'

'How is Gav?'

'Pretty well, mortified at nearly bringing down the yard but pleased to be sorting half a dozen screwed-up polo ponies for Dad, who thinks the world of him. He's beginning to relax.'

'Wish he'd come and sort out Quickly, who's not beginning to relax. Everyone here thinks Gav's the only person who can deal with him.'

Buoyed up by a second glass of champagne, Gala poured out her heart at her failure with the horses, particularly Quickly, and the sneering of Walter and Cathal.

'They're jealous,' said Eddie dismissively. 'I had the same problem – they resent outsiders succeeding. Gav said the secret with Quickly was to coax, not to coerce. He's so strong-willed

251

and got such a temper, he'll only do something if he thinks it's his idea.'

'Walter put him in a cross noseband and he went berserk, nearly stopped breathing.'

'Bloody stupid. He's got learning difficulties, but we've got three months to teach him to rocket out of the stalls and on the right leg – they're so much faster in the States – and then settle to preserve his energy, capitalizing on his acceleration for the last furlong.'

Eddie emptied the remains of the champagne into their mugs.

'This is the last drink before the Guineas. We'll start tomorrow. I'm getting up at six every day to prove fucking Walter and Cathal were wrong. Where's Lark, by the way?'

'Gone to Australia with Dave.'

Eddie looked appalled. 'That is a hammer blow. Who's going to iron my shirts and look after me? Without Lark I've got yearning difficulties.'

'Where are you sleeping?' asked Gala.

'In the house to chaperone Taggie. What gives with this new cad on the block?'

'Jan. He's been a huge success. Taggie adores him, so does Old Eddie. Rather galling for everyone else.'

Eddie shook his head. 'So bloody good-looking, can't imagine why Grandpa's allowed a stud like that alone in the house with Taggie.'

'He claims to be gay,' said Gala. 'He got married, then came out. Everyone's got a yen for Jan. Like those women who were bats about Rock Hudson in the old days. He and Taggie were in hysterics the other evening because they'd both fed the badgers.'

'Brock Hudson,' grinned Eddie.

'I heard you've won seven races – that is so amazing. Rupert pretended not to be pleased, but he was blown away.'

Eddie looked gratified. 'Do you think he'll put me up full-time this season?'

'If you behave yourself.'

'Oh good,' said Eddie, 'you've still got my Valentine up.'

'*Your* Valentine?' Gala just stopped herself saying in horror.

But Eddie had been distracted by the photograph that had fallen out of the poetry book.

'That bitch,' he said, picking it up.

'Who's that?'

'Bethany. Gav's ex, crucified poor old Floppy Dick.'

'What are you talking about?'

'Gav. She called him Floppy Dick because he couldn't get it up.'

'That's atrocious.'

'Horrible, and the booze didn't help. Women all over him in Palm Beach. Still too scared to risk it.'

And I tried to force him into bed, thought Gala, appalled yet comforted. At least it wasn't just her lack of attractiveness.

Eddie drained his glass.

'You sure?' He took her in his arms. 'I've always fancied you.'

'And I you.' Gala kissed his cheek. 'Let's have each other as a treat after the Guineas. Bloody Cathal said it would be better to by-pass the Guineas and wait till Gav gets back and go for the Derby.'

'You and I are going to prove him wrong.'

43

Gallingly for Gala, Young Eddie was soon as captivated by Jan as everyone else. Not only did Jan jog daily with him and, as the days grew warmer, played violent games of tennis, but he also supervised Eddie's diet so he grew stronger and fitter.

The yard were still transfixed with interest. So Dora was dispatched to quiz Young Eddie.

'Has Jan made a pass at you yet?'

'Not lifted a finger, why should he?'

'Geraldine was listening at the keyhole. Evidently he told Rupert he was gay and had a wife and children, but that could be just to lull Rupert.'

'He's a nice guy,' said Eddie. 'He and Taggie get on really well.'

'Why don't you take him down the pub, and pump him.'

'I'm off the drink,' sighed Eddie.

'Have a spritzer.'

It was getting milder at the end of March. The Dog and Trumpet inn sign swayed in a gentle west wind. Louise, Roving Mike and Walter were sitting at an outside table, and nudged and winked as Eddie and Jan, who still wasn't used to English winters, went inside. Around the walls were pictures of dogs and fewer of trumpeters. Eddie, accustomed to girls staring at him, noticed the barmaid and any women around the bar looking excitedly at Jan as he returned with a bottle of red.

'You're allowed a drink today. You must be nearly down to nine stone.'

'Thanks.' Eddie yawned. 'I was up all the night sorting out my tax problems. The tax man's just got wise that I've been earning in two countries. Thank God it wasn't much.'

'I by-pass the tax man,' said Jan. 'Pay most of my wages into a German bank. A mate at home gives the equivalent in rands to my ex to support the kids.'

Eddie took a long gulp of red. God, it tasted great.

'You must miss them.'

'Yes, but I Skype them most days. I'll go home for a week later this year.'

'Do your parents see a lot of them?'

'My mother does. She gets on with my ex.'

'And your dad?'

'Afrikaans men tend to be very macho and rigid. My dad was rough on me when I was a kid. I went into the army to get away and impress him. While I was in the army,' for once Jan's loud harsh voice was soft and confiding, 'I realized I was gay. Afrikaans men are very homophobic. They don't do gays, so to please my mum and dad, I married a childhood sweetheart. We split up after a couple of years. I decided to come to England and came out.'

'Hard on your wife.'

'Very, that's why I feel I must support her.'

'You got a boyfriend?'

'Not yet – I want to get my head straight.'

'Rather than your body,' grinned Eddie, topping up their glasses.

Dora would be pleased with him. Appropriately, as background music, Eddie Calvert, a past and very famous trumpeter, was playing his greatest hit, 'Oh Mein Papa'.

'I'm very close to Mum,' said Jan. 'Dad was hard on her, went through the housekeeping bills, hated her spending too much on clothes. I used to hear her crying. That made me determined to always be nice to women.'

At that moment Roving Mike came in from outside to top up

their drinks and behind Jan's back, held up his hand and camply dropped his fingers. Eddie tried not to laugh, he was feeling quite pissed. Wistfully, he breathed in the smell of shepherd's pie as plates were carried past. At least his jeans were loose.

'Rupert's very homophobic, isn't he?' asked Jan.

'Actually he's not. Marcus, his son, is gay. Perhaps prepotent fathers produce gay sons. Marcus, lovely bloke, was terrified of Rupert finding out. It all blew up at some piano competition. The *Scorpion* outed him, then, despite some massive asthma attack, Marcus won the competition. He now lives with some Russian ballet dancer. Rupert adores them both. Winning helped.' Eddie smiled. 'Rupert regards failure as a far worse crime than sodomy.'

'How do you think I should play him?'

'Don't get too close to Taggie.'

Taking out Gropius last thing, Gala heard Jan and Eddie returning from the pub roaring with laughter. Gala felt ashamed of feeling miserable that again she was losing out. First Taggie, now Eddie.

Rupert returned in April. Fleance had won a huge race on World Cup day. Hell Bent Hal and Petruchio had also been placed in earlier races. Rupert had gone on to China and chatted up more billionaires.

He was surprised and delighted with the progress of Quickly, who, ten days after the Dubai horses returned and were rested, was tested on the gallops against them. It was a dank, foggy morning. Setting off eight lengths behind them, Quickly's white face emerged from the mist ten lengths ahead. Eddie pulled him up, equally white-faced.

'Omigod, Quickly's giving Fleance fifteen pounds' (which confusingly in racing parlance meant, Quickly was carrying 15 lbs more than Fleance), 'and he still beat him in a canter. This horse is faster than light.'

Conversely, Rupert was totally undelighted by Jan's ubiquity and endless Panglossian enthusiasm, referring to him as the 'horse-bellower' because of his loud raucous voice.

'Doesn't your dad look great in his new red cords?'

'Only if he keeps them on,' replied Rupert dismissively.

Jan was always popping in and out of the office without knocking, charming an infatuated Geraldine.

'He's changed Taggie's life and he's marvellous with computers,' she told Rupert. 'The house is running so smoothly. Realizing I didn't have a moment to eat yesterday, with you just back, he brought me some delicious lentil soup.'

'Wish he'd bring me some earplugs,' said Rupert.

Rupert was annoyed by the way Jan spent any break taking photographs of everything and everyone. He was fed up with his discussing recipes with Taggie, 'bit more chilli here, a bit more ginger there.'

'He's such a help,' protested Taggie, 'and having been in the army, he loves watching your father's Old Buffer pro-grammes.'

'An officer and a lentilman,' drawled Rupert, irritated that Taggie didn't laugh.

Rupert was further irritated that when he came into the kitchen, Jan tried to win him over by talking about racing. 'You should put some horses in training in South Africa, sir. It only costs £80 a week.' He then expressed delight that the South African stallion Blood River was proving a smooth operator, with a full book of mares.

'At least he's not gay,' said Rupert, not looking up from his iPhone.

'Don't be mean, Rupert,' murmured Taggie.

Next morning, Jan took Old Eddie down to the gallops to watch second lot, greeting everyone at the top of his voice. Spying Gala, trying to remember which wife she was, Old Eddie lurched out of his wheelchair, falling flat on his face in the mud and spooking Touchy Filly, who took off.

At which point, Rupert flipped, yelling: 'Get him off the gallops, take him fucking home. I don't want outsiders down here or in the yard or the stud. You've got the whole of fucking Gloucestershire to choose from, so take him there.'

*

Gala still fought jealousy, particularly when she glanced in at the kitchen window and saw Young Eddie, Taggie and Jan chatting together. Then after one taxing March morning at the yard she returned to her rooms in the lunch-break to find Jan waiting with a big brown envelope in his hand. 'For you.'

'Must be my notice,' observed Gala sourly. Then she gasped as she drew out a dozen different photographs of Ben: adorable and flaxen-haired at primary school, purposeful, clear-eyed in cricket and rugby teams at Prince Edward's, clutching a baby rhino on his appointment as game warden, surrounded by dogs and Pinstripe the zebra, and at his happiest and most handsome in a wedding photograph with Gala.

'Oh my God, oh my God.' The tears spilled over, which she kept wiping away to stop them falling on the pictures. 'Oh my God, these are fabulous, how d'you get hold of them?'

'I emailed Prince Edward's – they were so happy to hear from me. They'd been trying to trace you; they were so sorry. Atty Graham, the headmaster, a great bloke, said he'd taught Ben geography and what a fine young man he was. He gave me the email address of friends of Ben's and his primary school, and they all came up with the goods.'

He put a hand on Gala's heaving shoulders.

'I can see why you loved such a good-looking bloke.'

At last Gala managed to stammer out a few words.

'I cannot believe this. You went to all that trouble. You are so unbelievably kind. I'm so sorry I misjudged you,' she mumbled into his dark-blue fleece. 'I was so jealous of you. Rupert didn't give me time to adjust to the change. Penscombe had become my home, living with Taggie.'

'I know. She's marvellous. Please drop by more often. She misses you.'

'And you really wrote to all those people. I'm so, so touched.'

'They were all delighted to know you were doing so well in England and hope to see you again.'

'I didn't have time to say goodbye. When the Chinese mafia commit a crime they want to bury any witnesses. I knew my days were numbered, so I fled.'

Gala started leafing through the photographs again. 'These

are miraculous. I'll never be able to thank you. Sorry I've been such a bitch. This has really brought back Ben to me. I somehow don't feel I've lost him any more.'

Looking up, she saw in return how genuinely thrilled Jan was.

44

The 2000 Guineas, the first classic of the season, approached. With £400,000 prize money and £178,000 for the winner, Young Eddie in anticipation had really pulled himself together, cutting out drink, rising at six every morning to ride, winning half a dozen lesser races and poring over the videos of the other runners.

Despite being nearly six foot, he now clocked the scales at eight stone eight, helped by a tiny saddle more suited to Sapphire's rocking horse, which only weighed half a pound and required immaculate balance.

'Probably fall to pieces if Quickers starts playing up.'

Eddie had been hugely helped also by Gala. Quickly had usually jumped straight out of the starting gates and exhausted himself battling for his head. Now he settled into a steady rhythm, had stopped weaving from right to left like a drunkard, and ran in a straight line. He was also much stronger, and had filled out in the right places.

'You've worked wonders, both of you,' said Rupert, and put Eddie up on Quickly in the 2000 Guineas, and on Touchy Filly in the 1000 Guineas.

There were snide remarks within the yard, particularly from Walter Walter, which hardened Eddie and Gala's resolve to prove they would triumph without Gav.

Dora moved in to improve Eddie's image.

'You never pat your horses after you've won,' she told him sternly, 'and you should rake their manes, pull their ears, and kiss them when you get off.'

'Whatever for? Formula One drivers don't pat their cars.'

'They probably thank their mechanics. The public love jockeys who love their horses and reward them. You must also praise the horse and the team when you talk to the television, and always flatter the interviewer by using their Christian name – and thank Rupert for putting you up. And try and well up after a win to show you care, or at least run your fingers along your cheekbones after a victory. The public love tears.'

Then when Eddie put his fingers down his throat: 'You're already the handsomest jockey in England, this will make you the most lovable and a poster boy. The more visible you are, the more other trainers will want to put you up, which will galvanize Rupert into giving you more rides.'

In the days before the Guineas, however, strange things started happening. Despite the grass being religiously harrowed several times a day, on Quickly's last workout big stones were discovered scattered over the track. Eddie only just yanked Quickly out of the way in time. Men with binoculars were discovered spying in the hedgerow and driven packing by Rupert's dogs. A lone magpie for sorrow was also haunting the yard. Louise, wildly superstitious, rushed round looking for its mate.

'Probably on her nest,' mocked Cathal.

Many of the runners, in both first Classics, live in Newmarket and just walk through the town to the racecourse on Guineas morning. Coming two hundred-odd miles from Gloucestershire to avoid rush-hour traffic, Rupert decided to take his horses up the day before, leaving at midday. As Purrpuss and Quickly had grown increasingly devoted, Rupert had arranged with his friend Amy Starkey, the Managing Director of Newmarket, not only for Purrpuss to sleep in Quickly's box, but also for Quickly to avoid the 2000 Guineas parade in front of vast excited crowds, and be ponied down to the start by Safety Car, who like Purrpuss had always calmed him.

Gala in anticipation had packed several tins of Whiskas and tuna fish for Purrpuss, and washed the fluffy blue rug to line his cat-basket, only to discover half an hour before they were due to leave that he'd gone missing. Normally he never left Quickly's box except on the occasional ratting jaunt.

Soon the whole stud and yard were searching for him, calling out, banging tin plates, looking in every field, shed, stable or cottage – nothing. Quickly meanwhile had got himself into a lather, pacing his box and endlessly checking the manger, looking out of the door, yelling his head off. Gala was demented. Frightened of Forester, Purrpuss never went into the house, but Gala still searched every room.

'We've got to leave,' ordered Cathal, 'or we'll hit the rush hour. Safety has to leave his sheep behind.'

Gala also hated leaving Gropius who, seeing her suitcase, looked the picture of desolation.

'I'll look after him,' promised Taggie. 'Rupert and I aren't flying up till tomorrow. And we'll all keep searching for Purrpuss. Cats often go walkabout, we'll bring him with us.'

Jan was sympathetic too, and carried Gala's suitcase to the lorry, where she joined Cathal, driver Bobby, Marketa, Louise and Eddie.

A distraught Quickly proceeded to drive everyone crackers, squealing, whinnying, stamping all the way to Newmarket. Trying to deafen him with Radio 2 was to no avail.

As they trundled along, Dora amused them with anecdotes from a book on Newmarket.

'Did you know that Gala's hero, Charles II, was one of the few kings that ever rode a winner at Newmarket, and that the Rowley Mile, the demanding, undulating course over which both Two Thousand and One Thousand Guineas are run, was named after him, or rather after "Old Rowley", Charles II's favourite hack who later became a prepotent sire like himself?'

'Like Rupert Black,' said Eddie, chewing gum to stop himself eating the chocolate Louise was handing round.

'The Rowley Mile,' went on Dora, 'is the finest, toughest test of thoroughbreds in the world. Please note, Quickly,' as another agonized whinny echoed through the lorry.

'Oh listen.' Dora started to laugh. 'William III also adored Newmarket, and won a match race there on a horse called Stiff Dick. Can you imagine the commentary? "And now Stiff Dick is coming up the inner".'

'Better than Floppy Dick,' bitched Cathal.

'Hush, he'll be back next week,' chided Louise.

They were nearing Newmarket, travelling down a green lane called Six Mile Bottom.

'Good name for I Will Repay's groom Harmony – she's got a vast arse,' said Cathal.

'Oh shut up, Quickly. Should I go and check?' wailed Gala.

'No, we don't want him escaping.'

Back at Penscombe, despite yard and stud being interrupted by increasingly desperate telephone calls from Gala, 'Quickly's doing his nut,' there was still no sign of Purrpuss.

Taggie, wondering what to pack, which she always did at the last moment not to upset the dogs, took out a powder-blue suit, which was not really warm enough. The forecast was wet and very cold. She'd laid out Rupert's lucky blue and green striped shirt, but couldn't decide on a lucky tie – the lucky shocking-pink one covered in black cats would hardly match.

Sapphire, of the blonde curls and huge blue eyes, was staying the night while her mother Tabitha went to her husband Wolfie's première in Paris. She was playing with Eamonn, Taggie's big childhood teddy bear that lived at the end of the double bed.

'Can I come to Nudemarket with you, Granny?' she asked Taggie, who laughed.

'That's a good name for it, darling.'

'And I know how babies come out, but how do they go into the mummy?'

Taggie was saved from answering by Gropius who rushed in, yapping furiously, wriggling his little body, grinning and beckoning her to follow him, yap, yap, along the passage, up the stairs, yap, yap, yap, to a distant unused box room. Suddenly, over the yaps, Taggie heard a faint mew.

Tugging open the warped door, choking on the dust as she stepped over old *Racing Posts* and *Horse & Hounds* festooned with cobwebs, the mewing increased. How could he be shut in here? Pulling open the middle drawer of an old chest of drawers, she found an outraged Purrpuss, leaving black hair over ancient tablecloths.

'Oh poor old boy, how long have you been here?'

As Purrpuss jumped out, Gropius bounded forward to welcome him and gave a shriek, as the ungrateful cat delivered a punishing right hook. Taggie carried Purrpuss back to the kitchen and immediately left messages on Rupert's and Gala's mobiles. Two minutes later, Rupert called back.

'How the hell did that cat get shut in there? Must have been deliberate. We'll take him down to Newmarket, or Quickly'll exhaust himself. I'll be home in twenty minutes, we'll leave at one.'

'I can't. I've got filthy hair and Sapphire for the night and I haven't packed. Can I go tomorrow?'

'No, come now. Tell Geraldine to organize the flight, and ring Noel at the Bedford Lodge – tell him we need a room for tonight.'

'I haven't got time,' wailed Taggie.

Thank God for Jan.

'Don't worry, mam, I'll look after Timon and Sapphire.'

'But I haven't fed the dogs and Gropius likes different dog biscuits and . . .'

'I'll feed the dogs and the birds in the morning and the badgers. I'm going to start a zoo.' He smiled and Taggie began to relax.

'I must get Purrpuss's cat-basket.'

'It's in the hall. Go and have a shower, mam. I'll pack for you.'

'The forecast is frightful. I need my dark-brown boots.' But she'd never looked very good in the sludge colours and khakis favoured by the racing fraternity.

Jan got a white trench-coat and a red trilby out of her wardrobe. 'That'll look great.' He plonked it on her head. 'Stunning, mam.'

'I mustn't forget Rupert's lucky shirt.'

'Don't worry.' Jan was shovelling underwear into the side

pocket of her suitcase. 'That was the bra you used for Forester's lead.'

'I want to go to Nudemarket,' cried Sapphire.

Somehow Jan got her packed.

'You're a miracle,' gasped Taggie, hugging him.

'Come back soon, mam,' said Jan, holding her a little longer than necessary, listening to the pounding of her heart then, looking down at her, he planted a kiss on her forehead.

'The house'll be horribly empty without you.' Holding a beaming Sapphire by the hand he waved them off.

'Thank God Sapphy adores him,' sighed Taggie.

'There's not a bird he hasn't charmed off the trees,' said Rupert, as he revved up the helicopter. 'Expect he's stolen Louise's magpie. And how the fuck did that cat get shut in the drawer?'

Livid at having to exchange one prison for another, Purrpuss yowled all the way to Newmarket. It was then quite a rigmarole getting him into the racecourse stables. Any doubts security might have had, however, were dispelled by the warmth of the reunion. As Quickly went into a thunder of whickering, which was augmented by Fleance, Chuck-off and even sourpuss Touchy Filly leaning out of next-door boxes, Purrpuss jumped on to Quickly's neck, purring even louder before settling down to wash his ears. Having eaten a huge supper of tuna and Whiskas, Purrpuss-full snuggled up under the warmth of Quickly's rug and, clearly exhausted, went to sleep. Only then would Quickly agree to wolf down feed and hay, pausing every so often to give Purrpuss a gentle nudge.

'Aah!' said everyone, as Dora took a lot of pictures to post on to Quickly's Facebook page.

'Take some of Gala and Quickly,' said Rupert, putting a hand on Gala's shoulders. 'You OK?'

'I am now. Thank you so much for bringing him.'

Having checked all the horses, Rupert said, 'Well done, every-one. Go and have a large drink on me, but only one, and I want you all in bed early and alone.' And he went off to join Taggie for dinner.

45

Gala was so nervous for Quickly and Eddie, she couldn't sleep a wink or eat any breakfast in the stable lads' canteen. There were three big races before the Guineas, so she had time with Jemmy, Marketa and Louise to wander round and take photographs of each other in front of the statue of the great Eclipse, the founder of the English thoroughbred, unbeaten in eighteen starts.

The papers were really dissing Quickly. '"Under the shadow of nearly losing his licence last year",' read Dora gloomily, '"and a poor start to the season, Rupert Campbell-Black is unlikely to redeem his reputation when his only classic contender today is the temperamental Master Quickly, off the track for seven months for lying down in the stalls at Rutminster. One wonders at the wisdom of running him without the benefit of a prep race or even a racecourse gallop, and putting up a jockey whose main claim to fame is being Rupert's grandson. Master Quickly is 33–1, will he start? With a vast crowd, unlikely".

'Good thing Quickly can't read,' Dora sighed.

By contrast, the well-behaved I Will Repay, winner of the Craven Stakes and two Derby Trials, was a massive favourite at 1–2. Dark brown, with his sire's upside-down L-shaped white blaze between his big, kind brown eyes, he adorned the cover of *Racing Post* with a headline 'REPAY BACK TIME'.

'Everything has gone to plan,' said his normally taciturn

266

trainer Isa Lovell. 'He is simply the best horse I have ever trained.'

Never missing an opportunity to gloat, Cosmo had taken a page in the race card, showing Roberto's Revenge – 'The most exciting stallion in the world' – then devoting a second page to his latest and classiest foals.

'Sleep well, Quickly,' tweeted I Will Repay.

Flaunting a Dubai suntan, wafting Bleu aftershave, Isa's jockey Tarqui McGall drifted into the weighing room to find valets polishing boots and hanging up silks, and jockeys in various states of undress. Chucking down Louis Vuitton bags, with a clatter of deodorant and diet pills, Tarqui got out gel to coax up dark hair flattened by a helmet, and proceeded to tell a Channel 4 interviewer there was no way I Will Repay could be beat. Glancing at the television screen, which listed the runners in the next race, accompanied by little photographs of their jockeys, he grumbled: 'That's a shit picture. I need a better one.'

Then, catching sight of Eddie in his underpants, 'Hello, pretty boy. Grandpa's put you up, has he? Only way you'll get a ride in a Classic. Not that you will, because Quickly won't go, particularly in front of this crowd. Hope you've given him lots of black coffee.'

'Don't rise,' murmured Geoffrey's jockey, Dermie O'Driscoll. 'He's deliberately winding you up, knowing it will stress Quickly.'

Once dressed, Tarqui's clothes were weighed down by sponsors' names. Above his coccyx were painted the words *American Bravo*, which was Cosmo's father's record company.

'Ought to say *Tradesman's Entrance*, with an arrow pointing downwards, the goddam faggot,' spat Eddie.

The goddam faggot proceeded to get a double in the next two races.

Rupert, as has been said, had got permission from his friend Amy Starkey, Newmarket's Managing Director, for Quickly to miss the Guineas parade where, led by I Will Repay, whose odds had shortened to 1–3, the fifteen runners would walk in numerical order past the stand and then go straight down to the start.

The course was well named Nudemarket. On a bitterly cold day, the flat landscape stretched to infinity, punctuated by pylons, a few brave trees and a sense of history. A vicious cross-wind fretted flags, ruffled manes and thrashed the yellow gorse flowers. It had started to rain an hour before the big race, silvering the grass, driving off the punters, red, yellow and blue umbrellas shooting up like magic mushrooms. Clare Balding was diving under brollies to interview luminaries.

'How's Master Quickly?' she asked Etta and Valent.

'Working well at home. He's more furnished and mentally mature.' Using her latest phrases, Etta crossed her fingers.

Having polished Quickly to a pitch of silver perfection, Gala nipped into the Ladies to do her face, putting concealer on the dark circles under her eyes. Even though the rain would wash it away, she wanted to look good for Rupert. She was wearing the regulation Campbell-Black waterproof navy-blue jacket and trousers, and a blue bandeau to hold down her shaggy, tawny curls. Her hands were shaking so much she was just repairing the damage caused by a deviant mascara wand when she heard sobbing and Harmony, I Will Repay's bulky stable lass, stumbled out, blowing her nose on loo paper.

'What's the matter?' asked Gala.

'I've fed, groomed, mucked out and cared for Repay since he was a yearling. I've taken him to every race, got him up lovely today, and now he's going to be led up by that bitch Sauvignon,' Harmony's tears doubled, 'because Cosmo doesn't like fat, ugly girls.'

'You're not ugly,' stormed Gala. And, although she knew Rupert forbade his staff to consort with the enemy, she put her arm round Harmony's huge, heaving shoulders. 'You're not ugly at all, you've got lovely eyes, and Repay will hate someone else leading him up.'

'Gala, come on!' yelled Marketa in horror. 'The runners are already in the parade ring.' Seizing Gala's arm, she dragged her outside. 'Rupert'll get really windictive if he catches you talking to her.'

Lads formally dressed in suits and ties were walking their charges round a parade ring, crowded out with press, owners and trainers. Geoffrey shuffled along, sleepwalking, led by Rosaria Barraclough, while her husband chatted up owners.

Among the other runners were Tommy Westerham's Mobile Charger, Chas Norville's Unsocial Worker, and Cosmo's second horses, Boris Badenough and Bone to Pick. A great deal of money had gone on the French colt Leconte de Lisle, ridden by the French ace, Manu de la Tour, known as 'Menu' because he was always complaining about racecourse food.

Gala was walking Quickly around in his mother's green brow band, limping where he'd trodden on her toe. Hating the rain, he was lashing his tail. Quickly's coat would never shine like I Will Repay's. Nor could she ever compete with the divine Sauvignon, her undulating body and endless legs encased in a black PVC jump-suit, her dark-brown pony tail flowing out of a purple Breeders' Cup baseball cap to remind everyone of Repay's former glories.

None of the photographers could take their cameras off her, particularly when I Will Repay won the £200 turnout, and Sauvignon smilingly accepted it.

'Harmony should have won that,' said Gala in a loud voice.

'Not if you're sixteen stone, most of it spots,' sneered Sauvignon.

Taggie shivered in her white trench-coat, trilby and horribly uncomfortable new boots, which she'd rushed out and bought that morning, having packed two right ones.

No one looking at Rupert's still face could guess the fury churning inside him. He felt an absolute prat in this hastily bought olive-green gingham shirt. He had already bitten Taggie's head off for not packing his blue and green striped one – although she swore she'd put it in – the lack of which was entirely responsible for Tarqui McGall's double and second in the first three races, and Penscombe's horses not troubling the judges.

He could throttle little Cosmo, who was exuding complacency and triumph in the parade ring as he shared with Ruth Walton a rose-red umbrella which cast a glow over her lovely features and his normally sallow ones.

Out surged the jockeys to join their connections. Cosmo's

red and magenta silks suited Tarqui's suntan and lean, power-ful body. He was followed by Eddie, teeth chattering, blue with cold as Rupert's colours.

'That's my goal for tonight,' leered Cathal, nodding at Sauvignon.

'Christ, look at that girl.' Noticing her too, Eddie forgot his terrors for a second.

'Concentrate,' snapped Rupert, who was trying to brief him. 'Don't make your run too early – Quickly thinks he's won the race if he's in front too long – but don't leave it too late. Tarqui specializes in the flying finish.'

'Where's your lucky shirt, Rupert? You're going to need it,' shouted a punter.

'Good luck, Eddie,' chorused Taggie, Etta and Valent as Rupert legged him up.

'Pretty mediocre race,' Roddy Northfield was telling Channel 4. 'When Frankel and Sea the Stars won their Guineas, they blew the other runners away like a dandelion clock.'

46

Dizzy from nerves and lack of food, Gala clutched on to the rail in front of the stands, where she joined Marketa, Harmony and the grooms of the other runners, so they could duck under and retrieve their charges once they'd passed the post.

On the big screen, down at the start awaiting the other runners she could see Eddie looking curiously vulnerable, limbs folded like a daddy-long-legs over the tiny saddle. Beneath him, Quickly was having a mega-strop, tail lashing, head shaking to avoid the icy wind and rain. Next moment he boiled over and took off, back round the course, covering two furlongs before a hauling, bawling Eddie could pull him up and canter back, as the last runner was being loaded.

'Oh Quickly,' wailed Gala, winded with disappointment.

'Thank Christ I didn't back him. He's exhausted himself, hasn't a chance now,' grumbled Walter Walter as yard and stud back at Penscombe gathered round the television.

'Gala and Eddie,' said Geraldine smugly, 'have clearly been wasting their time.'

As a stall handler in brown and blue grabbed Quickly, he took a nip at him, then pulled away, then bounded forward, then stuck in his toes, as half a dozen handlers weighed in, practically lifting him into his stall. Just nine inches more, and they could slam the gate behind him and get on with the race.

'Move it, you bugger.' A flustered Eddie booted Quickly in the ribs.

Tarqui, on the beautifully behaved I Will Repay in the next stall, reached out a black-gloved hand, stroked Quickly's cheek, ruffled his blond mane and taking his rein coaxed him gently forward.

'Don't touch my horse,' spat Eddie as the gate slammed behind them.

'Don't be ungracious, pretty boy, one can do anything with kindness,' mocked Tarqui. Nearby jockeys grinned.

As Quickly reared up dangerously, the other runners pawed the wet ground, the last handler scuttled to safety, the gates flew open and they were off. First Classic of the season, £178,000 to the winner. Quickly, frantic to escape, shot out ahead of the field. Down the straight course, Gala could see the runners approaching like tiny scrabbling ants.

Slotted in on the rail, behind Boris Badenough, Quickly was not amused to have mud kicked in his face. Eddie was pondering whether to swing out of the line of fire, when Isa's son Roman Lovell, riding Bone to Pick, moved up on his right, hemming him in, galloping along beside him so he could neither overtake nor accelerate without ramming Bat Out of Hell up the backside.

'Lemme out, you bastard!' yelled Eddie.

'That's team tactics,' shouted a furious Gala.

'Perfectly legitimate,' said Sauvignon, who was putting on lipstick.

Next moment, the field had plunged into the famous Rowley Mile dip which is like an extra step at the bottom of the stairs – unless a horse is perfectly balanced, which Quickly was not, particularly as the track then shot steeply upwards. Losing momentum, he dropped swiftly back into twelfth place.

At the very same moment, Repay roared past with an astonishing burst of speed.

'This is how to do it, little tosser,' yelled Tarqui insolently, looking back through his heavily sponsored thighs for non-existent rivals as he went six lengths clear to thunderous cheers, scarlet and magenta colours vanishing like a setting sun.

'Wait, Quickers, wait,' begged Eddie, reluctant to commit too soon. There were nearly two furlongs to go. The other jockeys were going crazy with their whips; the bookies were slitting their throats.

'Get your ass into gear,' howled Rupert, his race glasses misting over.

'Too late for wictory,' moaned Marketa as she and Gala inconsolably watched Repay streaking up the near side.

Then Eddie squeezed Quickly: 'Go for it, Buddy.'

And swifter than an arrow from an Amazon's bow, or a cheetah after an eland, faster than light, Quickly took off from the back. Dark legs a blur, with Eddie's jubilation growing, body thrusting suicidally forwards, hands touching Quickly's Purrpuss cleaned ears, belting up the far side, passing runner after runner, joyously yelling: 'I've got you, I've got you,' wiping the smug victory smile off Tarqui's face.

Immediately Repay rallied and fought back, but Quickly, having none of that, found another gear and hurled himself past the post a half-length in front.

Total silence, a bewildered moment of disbelief – and the crowd erupted. Even if they hadn't backed Quickly, the punters recognized class and were overjoyed Rupert had won. They liked the way he had stood up for Gav and been saddened by his poor season. The King was back. Overwhelming their love of money was their love of racing.

Instantly the camera tracked the euphoria stealing across Rupert's aloof, deadpan face, as he turned to kiss Taggie. 'Sorry I've been a bastard.'

Jockeys were gathering round Eddie shaking his hand. Gala, on the rail, was screaming her head off, crying unashamedly, being hugged by Marketa and even Harmony, picked up and swung around by Bobby and Cathal. All around her, people were thumping her on the back and shaking her hand. She couldn't speak as, panting and gasping for breath, she ran down the course.

Thank God there was a long pull-up area and Eddie was able to swing round Quickly now, as brown with mud as I Will Repay, cantering him back to hug a sobbing, ecstatic Gala. 'Don't forget we're going to bed later,' he said. His wide white smile, splitting his beautiful mud-spattered face, reminded everyone of Rupert.

Emma Spencer, of Channel 4, in short white mac and high-heeled boots, had to run to catch up with him.

'Well done, well done, Eddie. What a victory – he'd already run halfway before the race began.'

'Quickly's only small but he's got the heart of a lion,' said Eddie, remembering to pat him, 'and he's been brilliantly trained by my grandfather Rupert Campbell-Black and looked after by Gala Milburn.'

'You've just won your first Classic; tell us, what is going through your head, Eddie?'

'Well, I'll probably be able to pay my tax bill and,' Eddie grinned down at her pretty face, 'I'd love to shag the ass off you, but Mick Fitzgerald was right – winning's better than sex.'

'Eddie,' gasped Gala, appalled.

Did he really say that? The Channel 4 talking heads looked at each other in amazement. 'He's as outrageous as Rupert was. Terrific ride though.'

The wildly cheering crowds roared even louder; there was a flourish of trumpets, as Gala and a tearful but thrilled Etta, flanked by a beaming Valent, led Quickly into the winners enclosure.

'We've had vintage years with Sea the Stars and Frankel,' called out Clare Balding on the loudspeaker, 'but please show your appreciation of an extraordinary racehorse. Master Quickly is up with the greatest, particularly as he's just smashed the course record created by Mister Baileys, trained by Mark Johnston way back in 1994, winning the race in one minute thirty-five seconds.'

'Three cheers for Rupert Campbell-Black,' bellowed a voice, and the applause rang out.

Quickly, hardly blowing and now wearing a joke rug thrown over his winner's rug, saying, *Ha, ha, I won*, was suddenly enjoying himself, pricking his ears, arching his neck, posing for the photographers.

Nothing meant more to Eddie than the smile on Rupert's face.

'Fucking marvellous, well done, timed it perfectly, quickened twice, mugged them on the line.'

Then Taggie was hugging him. 'Your parents and Gav have just rung, and they are so, so excited. Darling, clever Quickly.'

Rupert had turned to Gala, holding out his arms, which tightened round her protecting her as the crowds shoved them together. For a second their eyes met, for a second he was about to kiss her, she melted . . . then in one panicky moment of self-preservation, the road not taken, lost for ever, she ducked her head away, so his lips landed on her cheek. Still he held her, murmuring into her drenched hair, 'Well done, we did it,' until Valent tapped him on the shoulder.

'Channel Four want a word.'

Rupert, with his arm round Quickly, then faced an army of press.

'This is the greatest comeback since Lazarus,' he told them. 'My grandson Eddie knows how to ride horses. Look at his pedigree, look at Quickly's. Love Rat, his sire, is the most exciting stallion in the world. His dam, Mrs Wilkinson, won the Grand National; his damsire Peppy Koala the Derby. Gala Milburn,' he drew her forward, 'has been working on him for months. She's a total star – she and Eddie have made the horse together. Frankly, he can be a little bugger, but he came good today.'

'Derby next?' asked Marcus Townsend of the *Mail*.

'Have to see how he comes out of today.'

'He's happy,' murmured Cathal to Marketa. 'He had twenty grand on Quickly at 35–1.'

Tarqui was not faring so well.

'What happened to the greatest finisher in racing?' hissed Cosmo. '*You're* finished. You blew it, started your run too bloody early. You got mugged.'

Sauvignon, still attracting the photographers, was walking I Will Repay round.

'Well done, Eddie,' she called out, as she passed.

'Thanks. How about a drink later?'

'Don't treat with the enemy,' snarled Rupert.

'Well done, Rupert,' called out Sauvignon.

Rupert glanced round, then laughed. 'You're right, she is pretty.'

Taggie was ringing home to see if everyone was all right. Jan had found her boot, said Geraldine. 'Forester had taken it into the flowerbed, and evidently Sapphire had wandered off with Rupert's lucky shirt.'

'I don't expect he'll take off the green gingham one he wore today,' laughed Taggie. 'Wasn't Quickly wonderful?' In the background, she could hear the lads cheering.

It had started raining again, and I Will Repay had had enough. On his way back to the stables, he caught sight of his beloved Harmony. Giving a whicker of joy, he charged towards her, pulling Sauvignon in her high-heeled boots flat on her face in a puddle.

'You did that deliberately,' screamed Sauvignon, as two lads leapt forward to pick her up. 'I've twisted my ankle.'

'Repay did it,' said Harmony happily.

'Such a well-mannered horse,' mocked a passing Gala.

Her Robin ringtones were chirping like a summer morning, with messages from people she hardly knew – Walter, Dennis the landlord of the Dog and Trumpet, Pat, Gee Gee, Geraldine. Jan texted: 'Always knew you could do it.'

Gav also texted her: 'Marvellous, well done.' He'd watched it with Eddie's parents, Perdita and Luke, who sent equally over-joyed messages. They'd be coming over for the Derby.

Back in his box, the mud washed off, Quickly, who'd been hol-lering for his tea, was snatching mouthfuls of feed and then hay as Gala dried him down. Purrpuss was looking for a dry spot on which to curl up.

'Wonder where Sauvignon's staying,' said Cathal.

'Cosmo can't be sleeping with both her and Mrs Walton,' said Eddie.

'Wanna bet?' said Cathal. 'Let's go out and get legless.'

'Not too legless,' said Rupert. 'You've got the One Thousand Guineas tomorrow.' He drew a wad of notes from his wallet. 'Go and get yourselves a decent dinner – see you all when I get back from Hong Kong.'

Gala felt really low. Why had she jerked her head away, sure in that moment that he wanted to kiss her? But she loved Taggie too. Depression is supposed to be 80 per cent tiredness, she recalled, and she hadn't had much sleep recently.

She was woken next morning with her clothes still on, and Marketa chucking the *Racing Post* on her bed.

MASTERLY QUICKLY, shouted the cover. 'The King is back and a cat can look at him,' was the caption beneath an adorable picture of Purrpuss on Quickly's back, gazing up at a jubilant Rupert.

47

'I know it's a bit OTT,' confessed Valent as his private jet took off from Heathrow, 'but, chasing deals, I never saw enuff of my first wife Pauline. I'm determined not to make the same mistake this time.' Proudly he patted the butterscotch-coloured upholstery. 'Means I can spend as little time in the air and get back to Etta as quick as possible.'

Opening another can of beer, he waved at a hovering steward to pour Rupert more whisky. A wonderful smell of beef, wine and garlic wafted from the kitchen.

Their euphoria at Quickly's victory doubled with the news that Valent's son Ryan's football team had triumphed at Wigan.

'Etta's such a sweet woman,' sighed Valent. 'All my kids love her. Ryan even sent her a Mother's Day card. Etta burst into tears, bless her.'

'Nice,' said Rupert, who was looking at his iPhone. 'Tag's a marvellous stepmother too. Bloody hell, Ladbrokes have got Quickly evens for the Derby, and 5–1 for the Triple Crown. Nothing could have beaten him today.'

'That Gala's done a good job.' Valent glanced out of the window as London gave way to fields, emerald green from summer rain. 'Attractive woman.'

'Very,' agreed Rupert.

'She got anyone else?'

'Not that I know of,' said Rupert, surprised how little he liked the idea. 'She obviously thought it was sexist of us to bugger off to Hong Kong and miss Touchy Filly in the Guineas.'

But the possibility of Fleance notching up £600,000, if he won the Hong Kong Queen Elizabeth Cup, and meeting up with Genghis Tong had seemed more important.

'I've got a couple of cracking bottles of red to go with the beef,' said Valent, 'but we mustn't get too hammered. Genghis Tong, despite his foony ways, is shit-hot businesswise.'

Mr Tong was a very powerful aeroplane billionaire who had capitalized on the ever-increasing disposable income of the Chinese middle classes. As wealth increases, so does travel.

In the hope racing would finally take off in China, Mr Tong wanted to get in at the start and was planning a yard and a stud farm with a hundred racehorses, fifty brood mares and a couple of stallions. One of Mr Tong's latest inventions was a little green plane with a powerful engine called the Green Galloper, into which you could load one horse and three or four humans, and which Rupert and Gav, who had pilot's licences, could fly.

'Tong wants to sell it worldwide. We can help with the publicity,' said Valent.

This, Rupert believed, might be the answer for taking Quickly overseas.

'Christ, I'm hungry,' he went on, as two plates of chips and large steaks swimming in dark-red sauce arrived.

'You taste the wine,' said Valent. 'I'm no good at that sort of thing.'

'Bloody marvellous,' said Rupert. 'We are going to get hammered, we're going to be hongover with Genghis Tong in Hong Kong. Wasn't Quickly marvellous?'

'I've never seen the poison dwarf more outraged,' said Valent, smothering his chips in tomato ketchup. 'Tong is very status conscious. He's got eyewatering sums of money, but he wants to strut his stuff at Royal Ascot and meet the Queen and Prince William.'

'Better stop butchering white rhino then,' said Rupert.

'Don't think he does,' said Valent. 'I had dinner at his place in Beijing. To impress guests, you pass the white Ferrari, the blue Rolls-Royce and the Galloper in its hangar on the way to the house.'

At the Races had just established a link screening online into China. Rupert was planning to flog Mr Tong a horse in Hong Kong tomorrow which would enable him to wow his guests even more. By switching on the television in Beijing, he could then watch his horse racing in his own colours in England.

'It would blow him away,' said Valent.

'I can't sell him a complete goat,' said Rupert. 'He might come over and expect it to win at Royal Ascot.'

Valent had been doing business with Genghis Tong for several years. To ease negotiations, Rupert had invited Tong's twenty-one-year-old son Bao over to Penscombe to work in the stud and the yard this summer.

The following morning, which was Queen Elizabeth Cup day, Rupert and Valent went down to the racecourse stables at Sha Tin to meet up with Roving Mike, Louise and sweet Fleance who had travelled, eaten up well, and was looking sleek and ready to race.

They were soon joined by Genghis Tong, looking small, rotund, and rather incongruously dressed in a loud check suit and a large flat tweed cap. Exuding amiability, he liked dealing with congenial star signs and was delighted Rupert, like him, had been born in the Year of the Snake, that most energetic, ambitious of signs and Valent in the Year of the Strong Willed Dragon.

'Although I'll be breathing drink fumes, rather than fire, over him this morning,' groaned Valent, his face glowing redder than a Dutch cheese. 'Christ, I feel rough.' Irritating that Rupert, who had put away even more than him, still looked marvellous, towering above the gathering crowd, who all took pictures of him. Valent only gained the ascendancy by being able to converse with Tong in Chinese, albeit in a broad Yorkshire accent.

If Mr Tong was anxious to buy a flashy horse to race in England, the limiting factor was that he only liked large horses who talked back to him, and who were born in the Year of the Ox, who got on with Snakes.

Other dealers were also anxious to sell to Mr Tong. Louise and Roving Mike were wetting themselves as one hopeful horse after another was led up to him, only replying to his cries of 'Hello, Horsey,' with the odd snort.

Mr Tong looked wistfully at Fleance the trier, only to be told he was taken. Happily out of the next-door box hung a white-faced bay called Beijing Bertie, who had been found for Rupert by his friend and ex-jockey Teddy Matthews. As Mr Tong moved down the row, Louise, primed by Rupert, appeared behind him brandishing a bowl of nuts, whereupon Beijing Bertie launched into a concerto of joyful whickering, nearly nudging off Mr Tong's cap.

'Hello, hello, Horsey' – and the deal was sealed. Vocal Beijing Bertie would fly back to Penscombe with Fleance, and Quickly could jet around the world in the Green Galloper.

The cake was then iced by Meerkat and Fleance resisting all challenges in order to take the £663,000 Cup: only to be topped by the 1000 Guineas back at Newmarket. The favourite, Cosmo's Violetta's Vengeance, was coming into season and played up at the start. Tarqui, who had had enough tongue-lashing from Cosmo, clouted her with his whip. Whereupon Violetta's Vengeance sulked and refused to get out of a canter for her bully of a rider. The equally moody Touchy Filly, given a dream ride by Eddie, won by a length. This meant three Group One wins for Love Rat's progeny, pushing his earnings so early in the year past the three-million mark for the first time.

'Can it get any better?' whooped Rupert. 'You and I are going to have another hangover tomorrow morning.'

They dined with Mr Tong in his beautiful apartment looking over skyscrapers and a rippling green ocean of trees. Here they met his pretty, much younger second wife, Aiguo, who didn't seem very interested in her stepson Bao coming to spend the summer at Penscombe.

Mr Tong, clad in a salmon-pink smock, took Rupert on to the balcony to discuss logistics.

'You must make Bao work very hard, Rupert. When I start my racing yard here I want him to run it. He is good boy. He miss his mother, who has married again. New, very powerful husband doesn't make things easy. He will enjoy family perhaps with you. He is very good pilot and will fly your planes for you. You take Beijing Bertie back to England to run at Loyal Ascot, and fly him there in Green Galloper.'

'Of course,' agreed Rupert, reflecting he'd probably have to carry Bertie over the line.

Back in the drawing room, Aiguo Tong was reading Valent's palm, and Valent, with his wrecked goalkeeper's knees, was wondering how he'd ever get up from the very low yellow sofa.

'Is that Bao?' he asked, pointing to a photograph on the red carved desk. 'Good-looking boy.'

'No, it's my brother,' snapped Aiguo, who later preferred holding Rupert's hand and foretelling the future of those born in the Year of the Snake.

'Expect an exciting year, not necessarily for the faint of heart. You must have the courage to face emotional truths and still be true to what your heart tells you.'

'The snake's fate is mine *and* your husband's,' said Rupert. Looking at her cold, beautiful face, he found his thoughts drifting to Gala and how nearly he'd lost it and kissed her after the Guineas.

CAMPBELL-BACK trumpeted the *Racing Post* next day, above pictures of Quickly, Touchy Filly and Fleance all winning.

While Rupert's and Valent's fortunes were being told by Aiguo, Taggie and Etta were flown back to Penscombe in Rupert's helicopter. The moment they landed, the dogs came racing down the grass to meet them: Forester flashing his teeth in a silly grin, whining with delight and batting his head against Taggie's thighs. Little Gropius, the slowest and last to arrive, slunk back in disappointment to find no Gala.

'She'll be back in a few hours, darling,' Taggie comforted him.

They found the yard *en fête*, as they awaited the return of Gala, Marketa and Cathal with the horses. Balloons and streamers adorned the stables, particularly the boxes of Quickly and Touchy Filly. They had just seen Fleance's triumph in Sha Tin and a great party was in train, as Pat and Gee Gee tearfully recalled a sleepless night waiting for Fleance to be born.

'Little pet came out with his ears pricked,' sighed Gee Gee.

Having popped in with Etta to congratulate everyone, Taggie said she had better get home to relieve Jan who'd been holding the fort for so long. As Rupert, not Etta's greatest fan, was away, Taggie wondered whether to ask her to supper. She felt guilty that, without realizing it, she'd done her face and slapped on some Issey Florale in anticipation of seeing Jan. And there he was, in a new speedwell-blue denim shirt, a huge happy smile spreading across his face as he took both her hands.

'It's so great to see you, mam, we've all missed you so much.'

Taggie blushed and stammered it was lovely to be back and removed one hand because Etta was behind her.

'Congratulations, Mrs Edwards. You must have heard our cheers in Newmarket when Quickly won.'

'I was wondering, if it's not too much trouble, if Mrs Edwards could stay for supper?'

'Nothing's too much trouble. I've taken your bags upstairs. I'll get Mrs Edwards a drink.'

'Granny, Granny,' Sapphire hurtled in. 'Did you bring me a present?'

'I did.' Taggie got a red parcel out of her bag.

'What do you say?' demanded Jan.

'Open it,' ordered Sapphire.

Then as Etta and Taggie smiled, Jan snapped, 'Don't be so rude. Where are your manners, young lady? Say sorry and thank you. At once!'

For a second Sapphire looked mutinous, then mumbled, 'Sorry and thank you,' and fled.

'Bedtime,' Jan shouted after her, 'and your own bed tonight. She was missing you, mam, and a bit lonely and she loves your old bear, so I let her sleep in your bed last night, but I've changed the sheets.' *That's where I'd like to sleep*, said his eyes.

'You are wonderful.' Taggie tried to ignore the message. 'I must get out of these boots.'

Going into her bedroom, Taggie gave a cry of delight, for propped up in a blue and white striped armchair was a beautifully framed photograph of Love Rat, with his huge dark eyes peering out of a gleaming blond mane, noble head raised like a creature of fable. Forester, lying on the bed, eyeing up Taggie's bear, thwacked his tail.

Kicking off her boots, Taggie ran down the passage and found Jan reading Sapphire a story: '"And Good Dog Tray is happy now, he has no time to say Bow Wow!"'

'Oh Jan, it's genius. How did you get Love Rat to pose like that?'

'It took a bit of time, mam, getting him out in the sun with his hair tidy. You can't get horses to say "cheese", I suppose they say "feed". But I think he looks every inch a Leading Sire.'

'It's beyond beautiful. Rupert'll be knocked out.'

For a moment Jan looked vulnerable. 'I'd like him to like it, mam. I know he finds me a nuisance round the place.'

'Of course he doesn't,' blustered Taggie. 'He's been under a lot of pressure recently, everything getting on his nerves, but this weekend's changed all that. Funny how it all happened when he wasn't wearing his lucky shirt. He'll probably never take off that green gingham he was forced to buy. Honestly, he doesn't think you're a nuisance. Goodness, that picture of Love Rat is beautiful, thank you so much.'

As she went downstairs, she thought how tidy the place looked after an invasion of grandchildren laying waste to it. No half-eaten apples in all the chairs or half-drunk glasses of Ribena or all the televisions locked into some game or strange DVD.

She found Etta on the terrace rhapsodizing over the beauty of the Cotswold spring with wild garlic flowers starring the woodland floor, white cherry blossom, greening cow parsley, and the soapy smell of hawthorn sweeping down the valley.

'Aren't we lucky to live here?' said Etta.

'Look what Jan's done.' Taggie held out the photograph of Love Rat.

'Oh,' gasped Etta, 'that is amazing! How could Mrs Wilkinson not have fallen in love with him?'

Down at the yard, however, they were not such fans of Jan.

'He was a bloody nuisance spending hours taking Love Rat's

picture,' grumbled Pat to a returning Cathal. 'Used it as an excuse to hang around photographing everything.'

'And he was evidently in and out of Geraldine's office and Rupert and Taggie's bedroom all weekend,' added Walter Walter. 'Claims to know all about nature, but he's not so good on birds.'

'That figures. The guy's supposed to be gay,' said Cathal.

'No, *bird* birds. "Hello, Robin Redbreast", he said, pointing his camera at a bloody bullfinch.'

48

Rupert returned euphoric from Hong Kong and, blown away by Love Rat's picture, insisted Dora use it for a full-page ad in *Owner & Breeder*, with the copy: 'The most beautiful stallion in the world.'

He then set Purrpuss among the pigeons, announcing that Bao Tong would be arriving from Beijing in ten days' time to work in stud and yard with a view to starting up a similar organization in China. To begin with, Bao would be staying in the house. Everyone must make him very welcome.

After the slaughter of Ben and everything she loved, however, Gala was absolutely appalled.

'If any Chinese move in here, I'm off,' she stormed to Young Eddie.

Nor was she the only person to be horrified.

'It's madness,' raged Etta, who'd just read a piece in the *Mail* about China enslaving the world. 'The symbol of China is a circle with one dot inside it on the right and one word saying *When?* i.e. when they take over the world. They own more than eight per cent in Thames Water and are taking major stakes in the English nuclear power industry.'

'So they can nuke us,' agreed Dora furiously. 'There's only one equine hospital in the whole of China. And they eat dogs and ram them in cages and they skin rabbits alive – you can hear them screaming – and rich Chinese offer powdered rhino horn at parties.'

'They're planning to start racing over there,' said Taggie. 'Valent and Rupert have been investigating.'

'Hundreds of thoroughbreds from the West went to Beijing when the government appeared to be going to OK racing. And when they didn't,' Dora said grimly, 'all the horses were slaughtered. Charming.'

'How awful,' cried Taggie.

'And they recently burnt one thousand dogs alive just to feed people at some festival.'

'They'll be eating people soon,' said an aghast Taggie.

'Well, as long as they eat the North Koreans,' said Dora.

As a result, when Bao landed on a beautiful mild May evening, Dora, Gala, Etta and a hovering Taggie picketed the helipad with anti-dog-eating placards and posters condemning brutality to rabbits, rhinos and horses. Bao, after a very long flight, didn't realize the significance of the protest, as Dora waved a *Don't Dine on Dogs* banner in his face.

'Get up on Quickly, then cough loudly,' she harangued him, 'and you'll be back in Beijing in a flash.'

'Hands off our horses!' cried Etta, waving a poster of a sobbing elephant.

'You're not welcome, murderer,' shouted Gala.

Valent and Rupert were absolutely furious and, jumping from the helicopter, grabbed placards and posters.

'Bloody childish behaviour! What in hell are you playing at, scuppering a deal we've been working on for months?' roared Rupert.

Valent meanwhile was busy explaining to Bao in broken Chinese that it was a tradition in England for the women of the house to wave banners of welcome, then turned on Etta, bawling her out in language she'd never heard from him before.

'Don't you realize,' Rupert hissed at Gala and Dora, 'as part of the bargain, Genghis Tong, Bao's father, is giving us a small plane so we can get Quickly used to flying.'

'Quickly's got wings already,' protested Dora.

'Don't be fatuous, and you should bloody well know better,'

he yelled at Taggie. 'Go and be a fucking hostess and welcome him.'

This task, however, was taken over by a beaming Jan, driving a quad bike down to the helipad for Bao's very expensive luggage. He then took the bewildered visitor's hands.

'Welcome to Penscombe, Bao. I know you'll be as happy here as I am.'

'Thank Christ someone knows how to behave,' observed Rupert, as Bao bowed and smiled. 'Go back and show him to his room,' he ordered Taggie.

Dora, Taggie, Etta, even Gala felt rather foolish when Bao turned out to be the most delightful boy with wonderful manners. He was also very good-looking, arriving in a beautifully cut navy-blue suit and white silk shirt, hardly creased from the journey. His kind eyes and excellent teeth were emphasized by a mouth that never stopped smiling.

The dogs had been held back from running on to the helipad, 'in case Bao's feeling peckish,' Gala observed sourly. But as they greeted him in the house, he crouched down to pat them in delight.

'Here is Labrador black and hound grey, Russells Jack, Bull Staffordshire, what wonderful dogs. My mother has Poodle Standard. We love him,' he told Taggie.

'For dinner,' hissed Dora.

'Shurrup,' hissed back Rupert, as Taggie took Bao up to his room. 'If you can't learn to behave, get out.'

Dora and Gala were about to, when Jan whisked out of the kitchen with a bottle of Bollinger and glasses, so everyone flocked into the drawing room.

When Bao came down, expressing pleasure over the Stubbs mares and foals and the Turner sunrise opposite the fireplace, he produced a pile of presents beautifully wrapped: Longines watches for Rupert and Valent, Hermes silk scarves for Taggie and Etta, and two extra unwrapped bottles of scent for Dora and Gala. He then produced a picture of his mother's Poodle on his smartphone.

'We love him,' repeated Bao, patting Banquo.

Glancing warningly at Dora, Rupert raised his glass. 'Welcome to Penscombe, Bao.'

'What does Bao mean?' asked a thawing Etta.

'It mean leopard.'

'Then you are our fourth leopard,' teased Taggie, who'd already put her shocking-pink scarf round her neck. 'This is so lovely.'

'Perhaps you'll win the St Leger for Rupert,' suggested Dora, melting slightly.

'Dinner will be ready in a minute,' said Taggie, 'if you're not too tired.'

'No, I am hungry very, but could I first say hello to Bertie Beijing?'

'Gala will take you,' said Rupert, adding softly, 'unless you want to be fired.'

Furious, ostentatiously leaving her bottle of scent behind, Gala took Bao out to a field by the lake. She then had to listen to his rapture, both at Penscombe's greenness, gilded by the setting sun, and at seeing Beijing Bertie again. The white-faced bay, who was already benefiting from the lush grass, was in turn delighted with a whole packet of Polos.

Bao bowed and shook hands with Gala when she returned him to the house, where he was hugely appreciative of roast lamb and potatoes, celeriac purée and the first asparagus from the garden, but clearly trying to keep awake over raspberries and cream. A completely won-over Taggie escorted him to his room where again he bowed and shook her hand.

'I am happy very to be here.'

When she came back ten minutes later to check he was OK, he had fallen asleep, with an English phrasebook in his hand and the light left on. He looked so sweet, she was tempted to tuck him in and drop a kiss on his forehead.

Over the next week while Jan was out with Old Eddie, Taggie talked a lot to Bao.

He was an only child, he confided, because China had a one-child policy and it was his great regret that his parents had given his younger sister up for adoption in England. It had broken his mother's heart, and probably, he felt, his parents' marriage. He would like to try and find his sister.

'I promise you she'll be loved.' Taggie showed him photographs of Xav and Bianca. 'We went halfway across the world to adopt them.'

Bao was also pleased that British and Chinese racing were getting together.

'It is my father's dream that Beijing Bertie win at Loyal Ascot. It is Year of the Snake, so Campbell-Black Rupert and my father both ambitious snakes should have successful year.'

'What sign am I?' asked Taggie.

'You are good-hearted Pig.'

As an only child, Bao had been very strictly brought up and was a very hard worker, constantly asking stable staff what he could do to help. He didn't mind mucking out, or being bucked off, and laughed when the forklift truck which threw bedding into each stable covered him in straw. Consequently, he fitted in perfectly, particularly as he was extremely generous and always buying rounds for everyone at the Dog and Trumpet. He also listened, whenever possible, to classical music, was a wizard technologically, and could sort out anyone's computer problems.

Above all, he loved the Gloucestershire countryside. 'It is so clear here. In Beijing you look up weather on App. She say, "wear mask". And we have no birds left.'

His favourite pastime was to sit on the terrace in the evening listening to the nightingales and blackbirds and trying to identify stars he couldn't see in Beijing.

It was interesting, observed the yard, that while Taggie's fondness for Jan irritated the tits off Rupert, he didn't appear to mind her doting on Bao.

One morning Dora and Gala came into the house on their break to take the dogs out and found a wagging Gropius chewing up Taggie's blue teddy bear, Eamonn, all over the hall carpet.

'Oh my God,' screamed Gala.

As Bao came running downstairs, Jan came out of the kitchen and flipped, kicking Gropius really hard in the ribs then hitting him back and forth across the head before grabbing his jaws to ease his Bull Terrier grip on the bear.

'Don't hurt him,' screamed Gala, as Gropius howled and yelped.

'Leave him alone,' yelled Dora, 'you horrible great brute. He's a puppy, it's only a bear.'

'It's Taggie's bear,' yelled back Jan, aiming another kick at Gropius. 'Taggie's special bear.'

'Look, here's its eye,' cried Dora.

'Give it to me,' snarled Jan.

But Bao, too quick for him, had picked it up. 'This isn't an eye.'

'Course it is.' Jan snatched it away from him. 'I'll get the whole thing mended – Taggie would be heartbroken,' and he bore bear and remains off upstairs.

That's not an eye, it's a bug or a camera, reflected Bao, whose English was a great deal better than he made out.

Gathering up Gropius and Cadbury, Dora and Gala retreated to the garden.

'Are you thinking what I'm thinking?' asked Dora. 'Must be bats about Taggie to overreact like that.'

'D'you think he's pretending to be gay with all that Mary Berry chat to fool Rupert, or rather to appease him?'

'Not much appeasement,' said Gala. 'Rupert can't stand him; it was as much as he could do to be nice about Love Rat's photo, which is stunning, admittedly.'

'If he's gay, perhaps he's after Rupert.'

'No more Mr Nice Gay, I'll never forgive him for beating up Gropius.'

'I wonder if Jan's a journalist,' mused Dora. 'He's always taking pictures. He never gives pens back and is looking at newspapers online, even when he's cooking.'

The following week, screaming was heard from upstairs. Taggie, who was petrified of snakes, had discovered one writhing around in Rupert's dressing room. She was very impressed when Jan picked it up and deposited it in the long grass by the lake.

'I love snakes,' he admitted on his return. 'That was only a little adder. I kept snakes as pets when I was a child. I used to feed them on live mice which I bred myself.'

'That is gross,' said Dora in horror.

'But good omen for Campbell-Black Rupert, born in Year of Snake,' said Bao.

'And even better news for him: Gav'll be back soon,' said Dora.

49

The King was back; his horses were flying, winning races all over the world. Quickly had left the rest of the field for dead in the most challenging of Derby trials, the Dante. As the Derby itself approached, the gurus of racing dissected the colt's pedigree. Would he have the stamina, the temperament, to cope with the one mile four furlongs? And, watching endless replays of the Guineas and the Dante, wondered if he could possibly be beaten.

Eddie, as his jockey, was extensively interviewed and, emerging as James Blond, the new poster boy, was attracting fanmail and hordes of young to the racetrack. Jan had taken a stunning photograph of him, wearing Etta's Master Quickly baseball cap on one side. Wasted down to nine stone, he was too thin to strip to the waist, but Jan's borrowed denim shirt brought out the blue of his wicked, laughing eyes.

'Gerry's been sending out hundreds to fans,' said Jan proudly.

'She's called Geraldine, and next time get him to put that cap on straight,' snapped Rupert, who was fed up with Jan invading his office.

As the Derby approached, Rupert grew increasingly uptight. So much was at stake, not just the second rung of the Triple Crown, but the million-pound prize money would put the Leading Sire title within Love Rat's reach. As a result, he was biting everyone's heads off, including Taggie's.

By contrast Jan was sweetness itself, finding a lovely purple silk rose to jazz up Taggie's last year's hat, delving into her wardrobe to discover and press a pale-pink blazer, in case the weather went cold. He had also polished Rupert's black top hat with a handkerchief dipped in Guinness to give it a special shine. This tip he'd learned from Old Eddie, who'd always loved going to the Derby in the White's Club bus.

On Derby Day, Taggie stole down the back stairs into the kitchen in her purple dress, lilac hat and pink blazer, so Jan could see how good she looked.

'Oh wow, mam, you are a knockout,' gasped Jan.

'I wanted to creep out of the house without poor Old Eddie seeing me.'

'Don't worry, he and I'll watch it on TV. We'll look out for the most beautiful woman, and he'll think he's there.'

Young Eddie was panicking. He hadn't slept all week, watching endless replays of the Guineas and the Dante. He had thrown up last night's fillet steak and half bottle of red wine drunk to steady his nerves, followed by this morning's bowl of cornflakes. He hadn't been to the gym sufficiently often. Would he be strong enough to hold up Quickly?

Hoping sex might send him to sleep last night, he'd hardly had the energy to yell: 'Groom service!' outside The Shaggery or give much joy to Lou-easy when she obliged.

The rest of the night was spent thinking longingly of Sauvignon, smiling at him and calling out, 'Well done, Eddie,' after the Guineas. He knew that Rupert and Valent had had vast ante-post bets, and that the yard and particularly the stud, who were coming to the end of a knackering four-month covering and foaling season, had put their bonuses and pool money on Quickly.

Finally, he'd been half-longing, half-dreading (in case he screwed up) his parents, Luke and Perdita, coming over, only to learn yesterday that his father had broken his leg in a fall from a polo pony, and that Gav, also due back, was staying on in Palm Beach to help Perdita run the yard. Last night, Eddie had

Skyped his father, who was clearly in a lot of pain. Gav had sent him an email.

Nor was Valent Edwards at all happy when he learnt that Sheikh Abdul Baddi from Qatar, who was snapping up horses like a little boy in a sweet shop, had wanted a Derby winner and through Rupert's bloodstock agent friend, Bas Baddingham, had offered twenty million for a majority share in Master Quickly. Alas, Etta, who hadn't even been very happy sharing Quickly with Rupert, wouldn't dream of it.

'He's only a horse, Etta,' begged Valent, 'and a very tricky one at that. He kicked your teeth out and bit his mother and Chisolm, and everyone else. Might not win the Derby, might be a disaster at stud. Do you really want to pass up twenty million?'

'Yes.'

Typical, thought Rupert furiously. Oil's well that doesn't end up well, the stupid bitch.

At least Etta and Valent had got a fine tan for the Derby, having just spent ten days in Mauritius.

'Have I got to wear a topper?' grumbled Valent. 'I feel such a prat.'

'It really suits you, as long as you wear it tipped forward,' said Etta. 'The dress code says I've got to wear a substantial fascinator.'

'You're substantially fascinating in that frock,' quipped Valent, admiring his wife rising out of her pink spotted silk dress.

'Bit too substantial.' Etta patted her tummy. 'Shouldn't have stuffed my face on holiday.'

Rupert's dark-blue lorry, driven by Bobby, carrying Cathal, Marketa, Meerkat, Jemmy, Gala, Quickly, Safety Car, Hell Bent Hal, Mrs Wilkinson and Chisolm had nearly reached Epsom. Most of the journey had been spent bitching about Rupert's short fuse. Gala, with Purrpuss in his collar and lead, purring on her knees, was feeling the most fed up.

Rupert was still so pissed off with her for joining the protest and shouting back at him when Bao arrived that he'd deliberately punished her by assigning her Bao, to learn about prepping a horse before a big race. How could she concentrate on getting Quickly calm and to a pitch of fitness and beauty with some little Tiananmen Squire hanging around, pestering her with questions and asking what he could do to help? Bao had cheerfully put up with being nipped and even kicked when Quickly had to be tranked before being shod on Tuesday, so he could work his new plates in before Saturday and the drugs would be out of his system in time.

As the lorry rumbled through the pretty town of Epsom with its village green like a cathedral close, crowds were streaming along the pavement, including a surprisingly large number of young people.

'Perhaps Poster Boy Eddie really is pulling them in,' sneered Cathal, admiring the bare shoulders, plunging cleavages and vast expanses of plump white leg on show.

'My God, can those skirts go any higher?' said Bobby, nearly ramming a lamp-post.

'Christ, look at all those people,' gasped Jemmy as they reached the racecourse. 'No wonder the Guv's uptight.'

The biggest crowd in years had come out on a lovely day in expectation of a Campbell-Black victory. Quickly was a massively short 2–1. No one was more excited than Jemmy, who was going to lead up Fleance and pony Quickly down to the start on Safety Car. One day perhaps he'd be riding in the race instead.

Taggie and Rupert were lunching in the Ladbrokes box. Liking to take presents, Taggie had asked Jan to get her a big box of chocolates. Instead he produced a tin. Inside was a huge iced cake decorated with the words *Lovely Ladbrokes* and a galloping grey horse.

Taggie's eyes filled with tears. 'Oh thank you, that is so beautiful. What,' she hugged Jan, 'would I do without you?'

'You'll never have to do without me,' whispered Jan, his arms closing round her. 'I'm here for the long haul.'

Taggie melted, then jumped out of her Issey-scented skin as Rupert yelled: 'Taggie, for God's sake hurry up! Eddie and I've got to walk the course.'

As Quickly had flatly refused to fly in the Green Galloper, Fleance had been loaded instead. Fleance, born whickering with his ears pricked, had inherited all Love Rat's sweetness. His fellow passengers in the Green Galloper were Etta, Valent, Taggie and Young Eddie. Rupert flew the plane so he didn't have to talk to Etta, who spent the flight stroking Fleance's white face.

Bao, on the other hand, had been shopping and bought a dark-blue Lamborghini which he was longing to try out, so he gave his new friend Dora a lift to Epsom. He was wearing a really sharp pale-grey suit, a white shirt, and pink tie.

'Lovely suit,' said Dora.

'Of the pig – you think she's OK?'

'Stunning,' giggled Dora. Tweeting, emailing, Facebooking, checking messages, she also proceeded to give Bao a racing lesson.

'The Derby is the most demanding race in the world, the one everyone wants to win. One fascinating aspect of the race is that, although the great Aidan O'Brien and his son Joseph have been the only trainer and jockey father and son combination to win the Derby, Rupert and Young Eddie could be the first grandfather and grandson combination. Rupert's not very keen on that angle, although Cosmo adores it, and the *Racing Post* have a picture of him and Eddie on the front page, headed: GRANDFATHER'S DAY?

'Nor is Rupert utterly delighted that Eddie's getting more fanmail than him – not that Rupert ever opens his. But Eddie's Facebook crashed this morning, with so many women wanting to be his friend and more.'

'Campbell-Black Rupert is handsome man.'

'He is. What he minds about is Eddie's screaming fans unnerving Quickly. Sometimes I wonder if Rupert understands the value of publicity. He isn't remotely pleased that Quickly's darling mother, Mrs Wilkinson, Chisolm her goat companion and Amber Lloyd-Foxe, who won the Grand National on her, will be parading this afternoon before the Derby. Just grumbles that the din will upset Quickly even more.

'And he was really rude about my idea of painting black

stripes on Mrs Wilkinson's white coat, like the Investec zebra. It would have blown Investec's minds. Life is very hard.' Dora sighed. 'All Rupert cares about is that Quickly's got a lousy draw out in the car park. Nearly there. This is Surrey,' she added as they passed large, handsome modern houses with electric gates. 'Footballers' houses. Rupert's daughter Bianca lives in Australia with a footballer called Feral Jackson. One of these houses would suit them perfectly.'

The gardens blazed with azaleas, rhododendrons, bright-pink hawthorn, laburnum and lilac, like jockeys' colours mingling at the start. Driving on, they passed hedges strewn with wild roses, Pony Club paddocks, low-slung woods full of oaks and bracken.

'Bracken means adders,' shuddered Dora.

'Good for the Year of the Snake,' said Bao, overtaking a hurtling Ferrari.

'Are you enjoying it at Penscombe?' asked Dora.

'I am happy at stud. Pat Inglis is very kind. Love Rat speak to me and I love Blood River, he look out on loading bay and think every mare arriving for him.'

'Like Young Eddie,' said Dora, getting out her make-up bag.

'My father wants me to be hands in, but Milburn Gala, she doesn't like me.'

'Well, she had a bad time,' said Dora, applying blue eye-liner. 'The Chinese mafia killed her husband and all her animals in Zimbabwe and burnt her house down. She is very sad and thinks Chinese people are cruel to animals. I don't, of course,' added Dora, conveniently forgetting her placard-waving at Bao's arrival.

'I will be very kind to Purrpuss and Quickry,' said Bao. 'What do cats like? There is pet shop.' The Lamborghini screamed to a halt.

50

Cosmo continued his sledging. He and Isa had three horses in the Derby: the perfect gentleman, I Will Repay, black Eumenides, who'd won one of the Derby trials, and Boris Badenough, the dark-brown pacemaker. They were no doubt planning team tactics to hem in Quickly.

Rupert had refused to retaliate or talk to the press except to say that Quickly was very well. As he stalked the course with Eddie, and Meerkat panting to keep up, Eddie grew paler as he appreciated why Epsom's slopes and cambers made the Derby so demanding.

'You probably don't realize it,' announced Rupert, 'but during the race, the track rises by a height of nine double-decker buses on top of each other, and then slopes downwards the height of seven more double-decker buses.'

'Wow!' said Meerkat.

'As Quickly's drawn in the car park, you'll probably spend most of the race trapped on the rail.'

'Rupert!' They'd been ambushed by a hot-eyed, very done-up journalist from the *Scorpion* called Rhiannon Tate, who was wafting scent and entrapment.

'Morning, Rupert. You worried Cosmo Rannaldini has three horses running?'

'Not at all,' snapped Rupert. 'If they want to avoid humiliation, I'd advise all three to stay home in their boxes.'

'Wow!' Rhiannon was wearing so much mascara, it was hard for her eyes to widen. 'You so certain Quickly's going to win?'

'Of course. Now piss off.'

'Cluck, cluck, cluck, cluck,' sighed Eddie.

'What's that supposed to mean?' snarled Rupert.

'Counting chickens before they're hatched.'

'Couldn't cluck if they hadn't hatched. Not if you ride that horse as you've been told. This is the highest point. Quickly will only cope here if he's well balanced as you race downwards. And keep the whip in your left hand to stop him running down the cambers or you'll be done for interference.'

'Eddie, Eddie!' Two ravishing blondes had kicked off their stilettos and dived under the rails towards him. 'Can we have your autograph?'

As he signed their race cards, the first blonde caught sight of Rupert's steely face. Pretty lush for an older man, she thought. Her forehead wrinkling – he looked familiar. Confident in her beauty, she asked: 'Can I have yours too? I can't quite place you.'

'No, you can't,' said Rupert, striding off towards the finishing post.

'You idiot,' said the second girl. 'That's the King.'

Many, many trainers have been kept going because of betting. Rupert had always bet with Ladbrokes and over the years both sides had made a great deal of money out of the other. Today he had accepted an invitation to lunch in the Ladbrokes box, although with Hell Bent Hal in the Woodcote Stakes and Fleance in the Coronation Cup for four-year-olds and upwards, and Quickly in the Derby, he wouldn't have time to do more than pop in for a drink from time to time. But it would be nice for Taggie, Etta, Valent and Bao, the latter both potentially powerful customers, and Dora to have a base and enjoy a nice lunch.

Taggie was so relieved. Rupert always wanted her to watch the big races with him and be there to accept any cups, but he was always so busy with the horses, she was often left on her own, and being very shy, she found it hard to talk to random horsey strangers.

But even if she'd turned up without Etta and co, Ladbrokes staff and customers were so warm and friendly, and when she took Bao out on to the packed balcony, the crowd immediately beckoned her through to the rail to appreciate the full splendour of Derby Day.

And Bao just gasped. Shaggy dark-green woods stretching to the horizon formed the perfect backdrop on the far side of the track to a glorious funfair of coloured merry-go-rounds and roller-coasters, couples screaming on Walls of Death or in the giant beaks of vast birdlike cranes. Below them, spilling over like Young Eddie's chest of drawers, were rows and rows of open-topped buses crammed with eating and drinking revellers, which was where Old Eddie would have been with his chums from White's.

On both sides of the track more picnickers, men and women in bright colours, spread over the grass enjoying the glorious sunshine. But to the left, crammed together on a little lawn fenced off to keep the riff-raff at bay, were men in top hats and morning coats, and women in pretty dresses and hats in more subtle colours: the Investec Set.

'And that's the winners enclosure – not big enough for a Shetland pony,' pointed out Dora.

There were Investec zebras everywhere, and overhead floated a huge zebra balloon.

'Oh poor Gala, I've never seen such crowds – and all these zebras to remind her of Pinstripe,' sighed Taggie.

There was a deafening roar as the Red Devils parachuted down on to the course.

Then the band started up and the crowd became a sea of waving Union Jacks, as the limo carrying the Queen in royal-blue and the Duke of Edinburgh came slowly past.

'Hope my horse goes faster than that,' said a jolly man in a shiny pinstripe suit, filling up Taggie's glass.

Bao was ecstatic. 'Your Queen is so beautiful and Edinburgh Duke too,' he cried, frantically snapping with the camera on his smartphone.

Dame Hermione, in strapless gold to match her highlighted

hair, then welcomed Her Majesty with the National Anthem, accompanied by the Band of the Royal Marines.

'Probably had them all, the old tart – that's Cosmo's mother,' said Dora dismissively.

'What is old tart? Harefield Hermione, wonderful singer,' cried Bao, taking even more pictures. 'I have plenty of his CDs.'

Going inside, the box had filled up with Ladbrokes high-rollers, many of them professional gamblers, wearing lots of gold and striped shirts with white collars. Vast wodges of notes were being paid in and out of the mobile betting till at the entrance. Taggie and Etta were seated next to the jolly man in the pinstriped suit, who was called Barney.

'Your husband and Quickly are going to bankrupt us today,' sighed Rupert's handsome friend, David Williams, who was Ladbrokes' Media Director.

The first race had started, the jockeys' breeches like tiny white bugs bobbing along the rail in front of the dark trees lining the track.

The din in the box was incredible. 'Come on, come on 'Eavy Duty, come on 'Ollygofaster, get to work, get your arse into gear,' yelled the high-rollers.

'He looks nice,' said Etta as a man went up to accept a large cup after the first race.

'Should be,' said Barney, 'he's werf five hundred million.'

Ladbrokes were thrilled with Jan's cake. 'We'll have it for dessert. We need some comfort,' they told Taggie. 'Your Quickly's one to three now.'

'He's never seen a crowd like this before,' fretted Taggie.

'Is it true one isn't allowed to bet in China?' asked Barney as Bao extracted his own wodge of notes and set out for the mobile till.

'I think so,' said Taggie, 'but he's making up for it now.'

'What are you on?' Barney asked a returning Bao.

'Hell Bent Hal and then Fleance in the Coronation Cup. I like Fleance, he talk to me.'

'Would you like to join Ladbrokes?' asked David Williams.

Having eaten the most delicious pâté, they moved on to rack

of lamb. With his napkin tucked into his shirt collar, Barney was gnawing away like a starved dingo.

Hell Bent Hal and Meerkat hacked up in the Woodcote Stakes.

'I lumped on that one,' said Barney as Bao came back to the table with a fistful of notes. 'Should have listened to you, Bao.'

A great cheer went up as Taggie accepted Hal's Cup.

'What a lovely lady,' said everyone.

Fleance and Meerkat won the Coronation Cup – a mighty race worth £170,000 to add to Love Rat's figures and a double for Rupert. As Taggie took Bao down to accept the Cup, she just managed to prevent him asking for a selfie with the Queen. Still giggling, fuelled by champagne, she escaped to a corner of the Ladbrokes box to ring Jan.

'Everything's wonderful, clever Hal and Fleance, and Ladbrokes adore your cake, such a success. Is everything OK?'

'Fine, all the dogs are fine – I'll go and give Love Rat a carrot.' His voice softened. 'I miss you so much, mam; you looked so lovely accepting the Cup.'

'And I . . . I mean we – are missing you.' Taggie jumped out of her skin, as on the television screen appeared Janey Lloyd-Foxe, most dangerous of journalists, always looking for cracks in Rupert and Taggie's marriage.

'It was the proudest moment of my life,' Janey was saying as she mopped her eyes carefully, 'my daughter Amber winning the Grand National on Mrs Wilkinson. But it was a bittersweet moment, because just afterwards my beloved husband Billy Lloyd-Foxe, great showjumper and broadcaster, died in hospital. I'm sure he's looking down from heaven, so proud that Amber and Mrs Wilkinson, Master Quickly's dam, are parading before the Derby this afternoon.'

'Pissed,' said Dora as she joined Taggie. 'She's had a hell of a lot of work. Botoxic bitch.'

'What are you working on at the moment?' Mick Fitzgerald asked Janey.

'A sort of autobiography about my life with Billy, who was of course Rupert Campbell-Black's best friend so it'll be all about Rupert too. It's going to be called *Billy and Me*.'

'Look forward to it,' said Mick.

Oh God, thought Taggie, what will she dig up?

The vast crowd, in expectation of a Campbell-Black treble, cheered themselves hoarse as Quickly's mother, with beautiful Amber on her back and Chisolm trotting behind, came grandstanding, showboating and parading up the course. Mrs Wilkinson, always a frightful show-off, loved every moment, graciously acknowledging the applause, approaching the rail from time to time to press a white nose against a patting hand, posing for every photographer.

Taggie, Dora, Etta and Bao hung over the balcony to watch her.

'She'll be off to shake hooves with the Queen,' said Dora. 'Amazing she produced a thug like Quickly.'

'I'll always be grateful to that little mare,' said Barney. 'I was on her in the National, paid for a house in Malibu; you must come and stay, Etta.'

'And you must come and meet Mrs Wilkinson. She'll sulk terribly when she realizes she's not racing.'

'Let her have another foal,' said Barney. 'Breeders should breed.'

'It's the Thoroughbred Breeders Awards next week,' said Dora. 'If Quickly wins the Derby, Mrs Edwards will certainly win Small Flat Breeder of the Year.'

'Nuffing flat about Mrs Edwards,' guffawed Barney, admiring Etta's cleavage.

'Let's go down to the parade ring,' said Dora. 'Quickly'll be in soon.'

'Must go and help Milburn Gala,' said Bao.

51

A terrific tension was building up. Half an hour to post time, the weighing room was unnaturally quiet; no one was joking. Most of the jockeys were dressed in their Derby silks. Some watched the television to see the odds and what was being said about themselves and their horses, others were doing crosswords, playing cards, checking their mobiles or psyching themselves up for the race ahead.

Handsome Manu de la Tour, the French jockey whose father Guy had been Rupert's showjumping rival back in the 1970s and who was riding the third favourite, Leconte de Lisle, was playing poker on his phone. Tarqui, who was riding the black Eumenides, was talking to Dermie O'Driscoll, who was riding Geoffrey.

The *Racing Post* fluttered like a captured seagull in Eddie's hands as he read a piece headed: CAN QUICKLY BE BEATEN? suggesting the colt was a monkey and it was loyal of Rupert to keep it in the family, but surely he needed a more experienced rider. Eddie jumped as Ash wandered out of the bog, naked except for a large tattoo of David Beckham on his chest and a soft white towel which he dropped in front of Eddie, turning and thrusting high, taut buttocks in his face.

'Look at my arse,' he told the startled company as he reached for his tights. 'That's all you're going to see in the next race.'

Two minutes later, his valet helped Ash into purple and gold silks.

Christ, thought Eddie, those are Sheikh Abdul Baddi's colours. Cosmo must have sold him a huge share in I Will Repay.

Down at the grey brick stables, Gala was even more nervous. She shut the green half door to keep out the din and activity outside. At least Quickly looked wonderful. He carried no excess weight. Running her hand over his silken silver coat, she rejoiced in the hard slab of muscle beneath. Haydn's Trumpet Concerto on the radio prepared him for the trumpeters ahead. Irritably he delved in her pockets in search of the food he had been denied for several hours, and kicked his bucket for he had also been denied water. Purrpuss was lying in the manger. Finding nothing there, Quickly nipped Purrpuss's shoulder. Mewing furiously, Purrpuss retaliated with a punishing left hook which only just missed Quickly's eye.

'Pack it in, both of you,' yelled Gala. Oh God, she must keep calm.

The other Penscombe staff were still off celebrating Fleance's magnificent victory. Rupert was poised for a treble – Quickly mustn't let them down. She needed a pee so badly she'd be reduced to going in the corner of the box.

For once she was pleased with her appearance: dark-blue stretch jeans and a gorgeous shirt patterned with pink, white and yellow frangipani, her favourite flower. The only thing missing was the heavenly scent.

A perfect fit, she'd found it in her holdall wrapped in gold paper with a label saying: *You have been very kind to me, Gala, and answer my questions. This is from Bao.*

Gala had wanted to weep. How did Bao know about frangipani? And she'd been so vile to him. And now here he was knocking tentatively on the door.

'I am not nuisance?'

'No, no, come in, shut the door, thank you for my wonderful, wonderful shirt. You are so kind.' She hugged him really hard and Quickly gave a surprising whicker.

'See? Even Quickly loved it.'

'You look very beautiful,' said Bao, 'and so does Quickry.' He patted him several times, then out of his pocket produced a box of Temptations. 'I have something for you, Purrpuss.'

Asking Bao to keep an eye on Quickly, Gala fled to the Ladies. She was horrified to find a long queue.

'Let me through, I'm leading up the Derby favourite,' she pleaded and sportingly they did.

Washing her hands afterwards, she saw a really pretty woman in the mirror and gasped because it was herself. The shirt was so divine. Eat your heart out, Sauvignon.

Then she heard sobbing, and huge Harmony had collapsed on her shoulder.

'Gala, it's not fair. I'm still not allowed to lead up Repay. Cosmo promised I could to stop me leaving and now he's broken his promise, just said there wouldn't be room for me in the winners enclosure, and Sauvignon's leading him up instead.'

'Sorry, sorry.' Gala wriggled away from Harmony. 'I can't leave Quickly any longer – so, so sorry, we're going down any minute, talk to you later,' she cried and fled. Oh help, she'd be punished for lack of compassion.

She found Purrpuss, turbojet-purring in Bao's arms.

'I like him, Gala, he likes cat sweets.'

Cathal banged on the door. 'They're going down, Gala.'

Fighting through the crowds, Bao joined Dora and Barney on the parade-ring rail. Beside a clump of silver birches, Etta, Valent and Taggie were ignoring Cosmo, Mrs Walton and Isa Lovell, and there was Bao's heroine Dame Hermione. Standing proudly near them was Repay's new co-owner, Sheikh Abdul Baddi, surrounded by dark men in dark glasses and morning coats: his Qatari retinue.

Bao had never seen such beautiful horses, a gleaming cavalcade of wonder – Irish, Japanese, German, French as well as English. The tone was, as usual, slightly let down by Geoffrey, ears flopping like an old donkey, led up by a blushing Rosaria.

'Lamborghini pedigree,' said Barney sardonically.

'His stable girl's a darling,' protested Dora. 'Actually she's the trainer's wife. That's Brute, her foul, lecherous husband, talking to the owner's son.'

Both men were leering at Sauvignon, who was leading up I Will Repay in bright-pink hot pants.

Dora then dragged Bao over to look at Quickly, still in the saddling boxes. Like a make-up artist calming an actor before he went on set, Rupert, having handed his top hat to Gala, was checking girths and every bridle strap, soothing Quickly with a damp cloth, dipping a brush in water to tidy his mane, putting a wet sponge in his mouth.

'Why he do that?' asked Bao.

'Horses aren't allowed any water for several hours before a race,' explained Dora. 'They get terribly thirsty, but water makes them sluggish so they can't run properly. Also, it can give them colic, so it's very dangerous.'

Out spilled the jockeys, strutting in their rainbow colours.

'Shit,' said Rupert, clocking Ash preening in Sheikh Baddi's purple and gold colours. 'That was twenty million down the drain that could have bought into Quickly.'

Eddie came out last. He had superstitiously put his left foot first in his breeches, carried his whip in his left hand, left the weighing room last and was determined as he entered the parade ring to put his left foot on the grass. But he was clobbered by screaming girls wanting autographs whose biros wouldn't work on race cards, and he discovered he'd put down his right foot. Oh Christ, there was Sauvignon who'd monopolized his dreams, looking breathtaking in those shorts. He tried to take in Rupert's instructions.

'He's a little horse, so try not to get him bumped at the start. Get him into a good rhythm on the outside as soon as possible. Don't hit the front too soon. Then rely on his turn of foot at the furlong pole.' Rupert might have been talking Swahili for all Eddie was taking in.

Jockeys were being legged up for the parade. Rupert ordered Eddie to get Quickly down to the start as fast as possible. Being ponied down by Jemmy on Safety Car, however, was a mixed blessing. Spectators, yelling good luck to Eddie, were almost more thrilled to see their old friend Safety Car, who had, in the past, won them so much money.

Waiting to reassure Quickly down at the start, Gala and Cathal were appalled to discover he'd shed one of his very light off-fore plates.

'It was there in the parade ring,' cried Gala. 'Oh Jesus, get the farrier.'

Even with Cathal, Gala and four loaders hanging on to his sweat-drenched body, Quickly fought against being shod and lashed out with hooves and teeth, as the other runners arrived from the parade. The minutes ticked by, the expletives flew bluer than the sky, as half the jockeys dismounted and led their horses round.

'We'll have to go without him,' said the starter, as Quickly lashed out again. Two loaders then held up his hind leg so he couldn't kick out without falling over.

'Nearly there,' called out Marti Farrell, the farrier. 'Stay still, you bugger.' As the last nail went in, Quickly squealed and plunged.

Immediately the orange blindfold went over his eyes, and more loaders joined forces, yanking one foot in front of the other, and another and another, forcing him into his padded cell – the dreaded No. 1. The moment Eddie, distraught at holding up furious jockeys, crawled into the stalls, to mount from the side, Quickly reared and plunged, threatening to bash Eddie's head on the steel roof.

'Don't hit the front too soon,' Eddie told himself.

Fat chance. As the gates flew open, he whipped off the orange blindfold and Quickly lurched forward. Badly bumped at the start by Eumenides, anything to escape the claustrophobia of being trapped on the rail, Quickly hurtled ahead, battling desperately for his head, pulling and pulling.

'Get him balanced, for fuck's sake,' yelled Rupert.

Quickly was soon so far ahead, he must win. The great excited roar of the crowd lifted him up, rising and rising, to the height of nine buses. Reaching Tattenham Corner he was eight lengths ahead, then there was a collective groan as he suddenly ran out of fuel and seemed to go backwards. Boris Badenough, Repay's pacemaker, meanwhile had set a sluggish pace for the rest of the field, but began to accelerate. Trapped behind a wall of horses, I Will Repay swung right and then straightened up, the purple and gold colours of Sheikh Abdul Baddi coming down like a wolf on the fold, as Ash overtook jockey after jockey. Realizing Quickly had nothing left, Eddie put down his whip, as Ash's beautiful arse flashed by to win by three lengths, with Eumenides second, Geoffrey an amazing third and Boris Badenough fourth. Total victory for Cosmo and Isa.

All the jockeys gathered round Ash, patting his shoulders, shaking his hand, even though they detested him, in order to appear on television as magnanimously good blokes. Eddie was fighting back the tears as Quickly hobbled home last, and radiant Sauvignon raced up to lead in I Will Repay.

The cheers ringing round Epsom were muted and only came from bookies. Few top hats were hurled in the air. Having so much money on Quickly, many of the punters booed and jeered Eddie, shouting that a monkey could have won on that horse.

And that was nothing to the vitriol poured over him by Rupert.

'Did you listen to a fucking thing I said?'

'Go easy on him, Rupert, it's only a race,' pleaded a tearful Etta.

'You're one to talk.' Rupert turned on her. 'Quickly's now totally fucked as a stallion prospect and we'd be twenty million better off if you'd let us sell him.'

Across the parade ring, he could see Sheikh Baddi and his retinue dancing round in ecstasy that their horse had won.

'Don't you insult my wife,' shouted Valent.

'It's not Eddie's fault,' stormed a panting Gala, having raced over from the start. 'Quickly's crippled lame.'

'Don't be so bloody silly, how the hell did you not realize he'd lost a plate?' Having reduced her to tears, Rupert picked up Quickly's hoof. 'For Christ's sake, the nail's gone into the sole. I'm going to sue that farrier.'

'Not that straightforward,' observed Cathal. 'Quickly was leaping around like a lunatic – it's a miracle that Marti Farrell got him plated at all.'

'He must have been in agony, poor boy,' said Dora, as a fascinated media gathered round for a comment. 'We must tell the press how bravely he galloped through his pain barrier.'

'I've nothing to say,' snapped Rupert. 'Quickly shed a plate and he's lame.'

'Let's go and have a drink with Ladbrokes.' Taggie took his rigid arm. 'They're so longing to see you.'

Rupert looked at his watch. He and Meerkat had a plane to catch for an evening race in Chantilly.

'Just for half an hour then.'

As he went into the Ladbrokes box, he was greeted with loud ironic cheers.

'Thanks, mate. Shame for you, but Quickly saved our bacon.' David Williams thrust a large glass of champagne into Rupert's hand.

Next moment, an exuberant Barney rushed up and shook Rupert's other hand.

'Fanks, Rupe. Saw Quickly dripping perspiration in the paddock, backed 'im to lose instead, made fifty grand. But he's a great horse, he'll come back.'

'I hope to God you're right.'

52

Nowhere is no prizes for coming second more emphasized than in the Derby, where I Will Repay was led into the tiny jampacked winners enclosure, and the runners-up tied to second and third posts down the course outside.

Isolated from his stablemates and his beloved Harmony, I Will Repay in his blue and white winner's ring whinnied plaintively. From above he looked like a mere slit in a charity tin, the massed top hats like caviar, as their owners took the opportunity to brush up against sinuous Sauvignon in her pink hot pants.

Cosmo was delighted to receive the Derby Cup from the Queen, who was near enough him in height for him to whip off his dark glasses and smoulder at her. Sauvignon drove the photographers even crazier as she accepted a silver photograph frame and a little Investec zebra. As I Will Repay's and Ash's names went up on the Roll of Honour, a euphoric Cosmo was asked about his plans for the future.

'I'm going to have a large drink and raise a toast to about-to-be Leading Sire Roberto's Revenge,' he said, then added maliciously: 'All the King's horses and all the King's men couldn't put Rupert together again.'

Rupert gritted his teeth, but the show had to go on so he popped into the stables to check his horses before they set off for home. As he arrived, a white and shaking Bao sidled up to him.

'Mr Black-Campbell, I must speak to you.'

'Not now, Bao, I'm off to France.'

'It's important,' protested Bao. 'I know you are angry with Milburn Gala and Eddie, but it is not their fault. You will want to send me home and never forgive me. I lose Quickry the race.'

'No, you didn't.' Rupert drew Bao back into Fleance's box.

'I know English think Chinese very cruel to animals,' stammered Bao, 'and I know Milburn Gala didn't like me because Chinese man kill animals and husband and burnt her house. But she has been very kind to me. I wanted to show I love animals. She ask me to watch Quickry while she went to Womens. Quickry seem very thirsty, he kick his bucket, so I give him bucket of water, and he drank her all so I gave him another bucket and he drank her all too. Then Dora tell me it is bad for horse to drink water before race. I realize you lost millions of pounds. I am so, so sorry. I will try and pay you back. I have had good day betting on Fleance and Hal.'

Looking up, he was amazed to see Rupert was almost laughing.

'It's OK. Water didn't stop Quickly. It may not have helped, but the fact that he ran so far with that nail through his hoof means he's a very brave horse. I'm going to email your father and tell him you're doing great. Got to go. I'll be home later tonight and we'll catch up tomorrow.'

As the lorry rumbled out of the racecourse, a man with a black bag was sweeping up *Racing Posts*, race cards, betting slips and Union Jacks. Women had kicked off their stilettos to walk in flip-flops.

'I wish poor Quickly could wear flip-flops,' said Gala.

'More flop than flip in Quickly's case,' said Cathal.

'Where's Eddie?' asked Marketa.

'Couldn't face us,' said Cathal. 'He's driving himself home.'

'Poor boy,' said Gala.

Eddie was in total despair. Thank God his mom and dad hadn't come over. He'd screwed up yet again and let everyone down. The yard wouldn't get their 7 per cent of a million-pound prize money; they'd all lost fortunes betting on Quickly. And he'd made Rupert, who told the press he was certain of victory, look an idiot.

As he approached Gloucestershire, the jockey moon was on high, sailing in and out of sinister grey and brown clouds. And to think he'd had the presumption to take his own car in the hope of whisking Sauvignon off for a drink. She'd never look at him now with I Will Repay already 1–2 on in the St Leger.

Around midnight, Gala went out to check on Quickly, and found Eddie in his box sobbing his heart out.

'Oh Gala, I'm so, so sorry.'

Gala pulled him into her arms. 'You poor, poor boy, it wasn't your fault. After you'd gone, Rupert picked up Quickly's hoof. The farrier had rammed the nail slap into the flesh.'

'Omigod, he must have been in agony.'

'With adrenalin coursing through his veins he probably didn't feel it at first, but that's why he died on you.'

Quickly nudged Eddie in agreement. Purrpuss, after a long day, didn't stir.

'Oh thank God. Is that true?' Eddie looked so sweet with tears rolling down his wasted cheeks.

'Absolutely. Come on, another day, another race. Gav will be back soon to sort things out. Come with me.'

Upstairs, she drew him towards the bedroom.

'You sure? I haven't eaten all day, I must taste horrible – can I use your toothbrush?'

When he returned, he said, 'I'm all sweaty.'

'I don't care.'

Feeling her warm breath on his face, Eddie kissed her tentatively, and gradually they caught fire, tongues caressing each other's. His hands were on her lovely soft body, unhooking her bra so her breasts tumbled out.

'Omigod, I have dreamed of this.'

Next minute they were tearing off their clothes.

'I haven't shaved down there for months, I'm like a forest,' confessed Gala. 'I haven't been to bed with anyone since Ben died.' There, she'd said it.

'Fuck off, Gropius,' said Eddie as they fell into bed.

'You ought to go to sleep,' said Gala as she stroked his blond curls.

'I don't want to.'

Sliding his hand between her legs he found a clitoris budding: 'Down in the forest something stirred.'

Then, as they both shook with laughter, 'You're so wet it's a rainforest. And a tiger's entering it.'

As he slid inside her, she gasped in ecstasy.

'Oh, that is the best feeling. I'd forgotten how wonderful sex was,' said Gala as he finally rolled off her.

Petruchio hacked up in Chantilly and Rupert and Meerkat flew straight back to Penscombe, landing after midnight.

Having been shouted at by Valent for being rude to Etta, feeling much guiltier that he'd reduced Gala to tears, Rupert went into the yard. Here Louise, the nightwatchman, informed him that Quickly could hardly put his foot down when he was unloaded. Walter had called Charlie Radcliffe, who found that the nail had also gone through an abscess. He'd poulticed Quickly and given him antibiotics and painkillers.

'Why didn't anyone ring me?'

'Vet said it wasn't life-threatening.'

'Where's Gala?'

'Gone to bed about an hour ago. She was shattered,' said Louise accusingly. 'Done everything she could.'

Going into Quickly's box, Rupert found him asleep. Purrpuss, tucked up between his legs, mewed warningly: 'Don't wake him, poor boy's had a rough day.'

Going out into the moonlit night, Rupert saw a light on in Gala's flat.

'She was upset,' chided Louise.

'I was vile to her – better go and apologize.'

'Sure she'd appreciate it,' said Louise gleefully.

The flat door was ajar. Gropius, for once on the sofa, banished from Gala's bed, wagged sleepily. He liked Rupert, who always made a fuss of him.

No one else was in the sitting room. Gala must have fallen asleep with the light on, thought Rupert. He'd leave her a note to cheer her up in the morning. Searching for a pen, he glanced through the open door into the bedroom and froze. Utterly sated, entangled on the rumpled old spare-room duvet covered in red roses, lay Gala and Eddie. Eddie had his head cushioned by her splendid breasts, his hand between her thighs, down the inside of which gleamed silver evidence of recent pleasure. A smile softened Gala's strong, sexy features; a hand still wearing Ben's wedding ring rested protectively on Eddie's golden curls. His clothes, evidence of rapid removal, lay tangled with hers on the floor. Eddie's sticking-out ribs showed the cruel amount of weight he'd lost, but his smile was angelic.

Rupert was blasted with fury. How dare Eddie take advantage of Gala, how dare Gala cradle-snatch Eddie! He somehow managed not to yell at them, or to drag Eddie off the bed and hit him across the room. They both ought to be shot.

He jumped as a solid object hit his calf. But it was only Gropius, always hopeful of a snack.

'They're setting you a bloody bad example,' hissed Rupert.

They both looked so bloody beautiful. He was appalled by the intensity of his rage.

Out in the yard, the moon had shrugged off a shawl of black cloud, and lit up Rupert's set, murderous face. Louise laughed in delight as he stalked past her. What a marvellous piece of gossip.

Back in the house, Taggie was waiting anxiously in bed.

'Are you OK? I heard the plane land.'

'I dropped in to check on Quickly and found Gala in bed with Eddie.'

'Gosh,' giggled Taggie. 'I'm so pleased, that should cheer them both up.'

'Not funny, he's got two rides at Goodwood tomorrow.'

'You must be shattered. But oh, Rupert, Janey clobbered me as I was leaving Ladbrokes' box. She's got wind of the fact that Lime Tree Cottage is going to be empty and she wants to rent it for the summer to relive memories of the time she lived here with Billy.'

'Bloody not,' said Rupert, wriggling out of his green gingham shirt and dropping it in the bin for the luck it hadn't brought him. 'We're not having that shit-stirring bitch within a hundred miles of the place. Gala had better move in then when Gav comes back.'

As it was a fourth Sunday, it was Gala's turn to lie in. She was woken by a telephone call from Eddie.

'Never, never guess what.'

'What?'

'Grandpa popped in to apologize to you last night and caught us fast asleep after that utterly sublime fuck.'

'Omigod. How did he react?'

'Furious, incandescent. "How dare you take advantage of a vulnerable widow?"'

'"Only too easily," I said. "Have you got the hots for her too? She's sensational in bed."'

'Oh Eddie, you didn't.'

'He roared at me not to be impertinent. And Louise saw him coming and going last night, so it's all round the yard and stud.'

'Omigod, he saw us in bed with no clothes on!'

'In flagwaving delicto, America and Zimbabwe's finest. I told him it wasn't your fault – that I'd been trying to get you into bed for yonks. When can we do it again? Funny, he wasn't at all upset when he caught Mike going down on Celeste at the Christmas party. Just said: "Atta boy." And when Gav returns, you can come back to the house and live down the passage from me.'

Before Gav returned, however, Gala had instead moved into Lime Tree Cottage, the sweet seventeenth-century house so coveted by Janey Lloyd-Foxe. Originally inhabited by game-keepers, it stood in the heart of Rupert's woods to the west. But since his empire had expanded down the valley, it lay only a hundred yards into the trees.

'See how you get on,' said Rupert. 'If you find it's too isolated, we'll find you a room in one of the hostels.'

'I love it,' said Gala, joyfully breathing in the sweet scent of lime blossom, happy that from her bathroom she could see foals romping in the fields behind the stud.

53

Gav was dreading coming home. He could imagine the press: CHEAT TAKEN BACK – and how would the staff react? His confidence had been much boosted by working with Luke. They had talked a lot, particularly after Luke broke his leg, mostly about horses and books, which they both loved.

Luke had introduced him to an ex of his, a beautiful divorce lawyer called Margie.

'How did it go?' asked Luke after their third date.

'Not great, she suggested I go to a therapist. I said I'd have to be pissed to do that, and I can't go back on the booze. Only booze kills shyness.'

'Sure, I understand.'

'Only an ex-alki has any idea of the grey wasteland of sobriety. Sorry, that sounds nauseatingly self-pitying.'

'I guess all you need,' Luke said, 'is a woman who really loves you.'

'If it doesn't work out with Rupert, and he's tricky,' Luke had insisted on Gav's last night, 'come back and work for me any time. And look after Eddie. He's more vulnerable than one thinks.'

He had given Gav a copy of Robert Frost's poems as a leaving present. Gav immediately went to his favourite, 'Stopping by Woods', in which the poet wants to explore the snowy woods, but knows he should go straight home because he has 'promises to keep'.

Gav's promises were to get Quickly right and Rupert to the top of the Leading Sire list.

When he returned on the second Monday after the Derby, however, he was overwhelmed by the warmth of his reception. Penscombe was in need of a celebration after Quickly's Derby debacle. So the balloons and *Welcome Back Gav* signs went all the way down the drive. Almost more cards awaited him than for Rupert on Valentine's Day. Best of all, when he went into the yard, Quickly put his head out and gave a great whicker of welcome and tried to scrape down his door. Every horse in the yard then looked out and joined in until the whickering and scraping became a thunderstorm. Whereupon Safety Car rushed in, dropped his broom and trotted up to Gav, laying his head on his shoulder in ecstasy, following Gav from box to box as he greeted old friends, staying with him when he toured the stud and the adjoining fields. Walter and Pat accompanying them were amazed: Gav seemed to know the name and pedigree of every horse, even able to recognize recently born foals, and identify their sires and dams.

'That's a Dardanius, that's a Titus.'

As the mares gathered jealously around him, nudging and nuzzling, Walter sneered: 'Pity he's not as successful with women.'

'Shut up,' snapped Pat. 'Not through want of their trying.'

Next, Gav had a session with Rupert at his office. Here he noticed again a framed Breeders' Cup race card, the year Love Rat won.

'How is he?' he asked.

'Getting lazier. Thank God the season's over. He just goes to sleep on the mares: "Hang on, I'm just having a fag". I'm not sure he's up to another season.'

Gav grinned to see a new clock of a stallion mounting a mare, waggling his near hind leg in time to the ticking.

'Eddie bought it for me to make up for the Derby,' explained Rupert. 'We'd better talk about that . . .' but the telephone rang. It was the *Racing Post*.

319

'I gather Gavin Latton's back,' said Lee Mottershead. 'What are your plans for him?'

'Well, I don't know anyone more conscientious than Gav, so he's going to be my Assistant Trainer.' And, at Gav's look of amazement, Rupert added: 'Of course, I have every confidence and more,' and rang off.

Then he was back to the Old Rupert, noticing on his laptop that one of Cordelia's foals, which Gav had dismissed as a dud, had just won a huge race in France. 'Why the hell did you let that filly slip through the net?'

'Do you mean it about Assistant Trainer?' stammered Gav.

'Yup.'

'I'm not great with people. I want to work with horses.'

'What's your take on the Derby?'

'Eddie needs to be got as fit as Quickly. I think he's bingeing and flipping and taking too many laxatives and it's fucked up his digestion. And he's spending too much time in the sauna. He needs to jog, go to the gym and build up muscle so he can hold up horses when he needs to. He's got to stay off drink and women.'

Particularly Gala, Rupert found himself thinking.

Next he heard Gav saying: 'He must go back to protein, chicken, steaks, salmon.'

'Yansy Pansy can sort that,' said Rupert.

'Quickly also needs a pacemaker to calm him down. Safety Car isn't quick enough. We've got to make sure Quickly doesn't pull and exhaust himself. I have found exactly the right horse – a bay three-year-old called Bitsy, or See You in a Bit, who could be ridden by Meerkat or even Jemmy.'

'Well, go and buy him.'

Leaving Rupert's office, Gav met Gala riding the dark-brown delinquent Blank Chekov back from fourth lot and thought how gorgeous she looked. Embarrassed at having blown her out, he was too shy to meet her eyes. Gala, thinking in turn how divine he looked, his pallor replaced by a Palm Beach tan, but still mortified how she'd drunkenly jumped on him, finally broke the ice.

'Awfully sorry about last time, you could do me for sexual harassment.'

Gav smiled slightly. 'You could equally ban me as a non-trier.'

As they both laughed with relief, Gav thanked her for leaving his rooms above the tack room so tidy and in such good nick.

'I've probably left the odd book and things.'

'Are you OK in Lime Tree Cottage?'

'I love it.' Gala was on the brink of asking him to come and have a drink, when Taggie came running out and kissed Gav.

'Oh, it's good to have you back; everyone's missed you so much. Rupert, in particular, has been tearing his hair out,' and she drew him back into the kitchen. 'You will come and have supper with us tonight? We've got lovely goulash.'

But Gav was still too ashamed of nearly bringing the yard down.

'Honestly,' he stammered, 'I ought to unpack and things.'

'Oh please. We can eat outside and you can tell Bao what the stars are. He's such a dear boy.'

At that moment, a hunk came out of the kitchen and took Gav's hand in both of his.

'Gavin, welcome home, so good to see you here. I've heard a ridiculous amount about you – all great, I promise you. Please stay to supper. Taggie made a Pavlova with our first strawberries – you won't be able to resist that.'

Glancing up into Jan's film-star face, marvellously strong features lifted by a huge smile, dark red hair visible in the V of an open-neck check shirt, Gav suddenly felt raped.

'Please stay,' urged Jan in his loud harsh voice. 'It would delight Taggie so much.'

What right has he to presume? thought Gav.

'Sorry, got to settle back in. Lot to catch up on.'

'Understood. How about tomorrow or the next day?'

'Up to Rupert or Taggie,' said Gav tersely. 'Need time on their own, without half the world butting in.' Grabbing a handful of the carrots Jan had been chopping for the goulash, he returned to the yard, where he met Safety Car, who dropped the yard brush and wolfed the carrots before they were offered to anyone else.

'I suppose I owe you,' muttered Gav, scratching Safety in the ribs, where normally the older horse would exchange mutual nibbling with Quickly. 'See You in a Bit's going to take over your job as pacemaker from now on.'

Pacemakers are the great unsung heroes of racing. Always the bridesmaids, they are ridden by the trainer's second jockey and will set exactly the right pace to settle the star horse ridden by the first jockey, who will scorch past and take the race at the last moment.

Blessed are the pacemakers, sighed Gav, for they inherit fuck all.

See You in a Bit, or Bitsy, arrived a week later from America, to act as Quickly's pacemaker. Quickly both adored him and bullied him unmercifully when they were turned out together, not letting Bitsy anywhere near any proffered carrots or apples, and livid when Purrpuss sat on Bitsy and washed his ears. But when Gala took Bitsy out for a bit of light relief – a ride on his own round the village – Quickly grew even crosser and called out for him continually.

Bitsy was a bright bay, with long white socks on all four legs.

'You are the dearest horse in the world,' sighed Gala.

'I bet you say that to all the bays,' quipped Eddie.

Eddie and Gala noticed wryly that when Quickly, ridden by Gav, set out after Jemmy and Bitsy, Quickly looked a completely different horse.

Things in fact improved dramatically after Gav's return; he noticed details others didn't. He was impressed by Jemmy, who as an apprentice had an invaluable 7 lb claim, which meant he was allowed to ride 7 lbs lighter, and should be used more. He got to work on Beijing Bertie who, as a four-year-old, he felt was capable of winning a few races. In addition, he encouraged Bao to ride him and soon had them both cantering up the gallops, which would please Mr Tong when he and Mrs Tong arrived for Royal Ascot, the most glorious week in the Racing Calendar and which was fast approaching.

Bookies were already offering 10–1 on what coloured hats the Queen and then Taggie Campbell-Black would be wearing on Ladies Day. Jan had bought Taggie a silver-grey picture hat with a pink ribbon as an early birthday present and with such inside information planned to have a huge bet.

Among numerous horses entered for Royal Ascot, Rupert had great hopes for Quickly ridden by Eddie in the mighty St James's Palace Stakes. Dave meanwhile had won his fourth Group One in Australia and looked a serious candidate for the Melbourne Cup.

A few days before Ascot kicked off, however, Gala, returning for Evening Stables, discovered Old Eddie coming out of Quickly's box.

'Careful you don't get bitten,' she warned.

'Too interested in carrots. He's so greedy he nearly took off Eddie's signet ring,' said Jan, who'd been chatting to Louise in the tack room.

'You look well,' said Old Eddie, admiring Gala's sunburned legs.

'I'm getting a bit more sleep now I've moved into Lime Tree Cottage out in the woods,' admitted Gala. 'Living over the yard one never gets a lie-in, because from five-thirty onwards Quickly starts hollering for his breakfast.'

Next morning when she came into work, however, Gala was surprised not to be greeted by a noisy Quickly. Entering the box she found him standing in the corner, head drooping, last night's hay and feed untouched, Nurse Purrpuss weaving round his fetlocks.

'Poor old boy,' cried Gala. 'What's up?'

In answer, Quickly started coughing. His nose was running and as he sneezed he scattered droplets all over Purrpuss, who spat and jumped away. Found to have a high temperature, Quickly was placed in isolation, and was so depressed he didn't even attempt to kick the place down. Unable to put his hoof over his mouth, Quickly must have sneezed over the other horses yesterday because by the evening Touchy Filly, Bitsy, Hell Bent Hal, Blank Chekov, Fleance and Beijing Bertie were all hacking away, struck down by a mystery virus which completely ruled out Royal Ascot.

Taggie couldn't wear her silver-grey hat. All this was also particularly disappointing for Mr Tong, who had been planning to wear white tie and tails, while his wife Aiguo, who had been watching *My Fair Lady*, had purchased a red hat too huge to get through the gates of the Royal Enclosure and been practising shouting '*Not Bruddy Likely*'.

As a result, the meeting was a riot for Cosmo, with Ash as his first jockey winning seven races including the great St James's Stakes with I Will Repay, which qualified him for the Breeders' Cup Turf in October.

Royal Ashcot shouted the headlines. Tarqui, still being punished for not winning the Guineas, and given horses with 50–1 odds to ride, was about to walk out.

54

No one, as Roberto's Revenge edged up the Leading Sire list, was more in despair than Rupert. But change was afoot.

The Leading Sire charts had hitherto been divided into different localities. Rupert and Cosmo, for example, were competing to amass the most prize money just in races in Europe, with the title being awarded on 31 December. Other Leading Sire titles were awarded at different times in the Far East, Australia and South and North America.

For the first time, however, a massive new category had been introduced for a Global Leading Sire, whose progeny had stacked up the most prize money worldwide. The title would be awarded at the end of March, after the World Cup in Dubai.

In this, Rupert would be competing against stallions from Japan, the Americas and Australia and New Zealand, as well as Europe and Great Britain. Verdi's Requiem had just announced his retirement, so Roberto's Revenge was a favourite to win this mighty new overall title. Rupert, as a result, became even more obsessed with taking his horses overseas in search of the biggest prizes. So obsessed that at the end of June, whilst he was in the Far East, he forgot Taggie's birthday. His PA Geraldine who, as had been said, would have liked to be the next Mrs Campbell-Black, should have reminded him.

Jan, however, remembered and alerted the children. At 6.30 in the morning Taggie was woken by Timon, spilling milk over the carpet, bringing her Cheerios in bed.

'Happy birthday, Granny.'

'It's a bit early, darling,' mumbled Taggie.

'Can I eat them instead?' asked Timon.

'Please.' Taggie tried to burrow back into sleep, particularly when she was roused five minutes later by Timon in her bathroom.

'Gran-ee, can you come and hold my willy so I don't have to wash my hands.' And when Taggie staggered in, he went on: 'It's easy for girls. You just sit down, you've got a hole.'

Taggie giggled. So beautiful, so blond, Timon had his father Wolfie's dark eyes.

'How did you know it was my birthday?'

'Jan told us. You've got to come downstairs. My birthday's next month. I want an Aston Martin and a tattoo on my willy like David Beckham.'

'I don't think he's got one there.'

'Come on, Granny, Happy Birthday!' shouted Sapphire up the stairs.

Taggie gasped as she went into the kitchen. There were red *Happy Birthday Taggie* balloons bobbing from every chair, crisps and sweets all over the kitchen table and Jan thrust a glass of fresh orange juice into her hand.

'Many, many happy returns, mam.'

'You are so unbelievably kind,' gulped Taggie, as she opened scent and bath salts from the children and then a huge pink fluffy rabbit, to join the blue teddy bear, now mended, at the bottom of her bed.

The telephone went. It was Rupert, jubilant that Fleance had won a big race in Singapore.

'That's wonderful.' Taggie retreated into the larder, glimpsing a huge birthday cake.

'Everything OK? How's Banquo?'

'Missing you – we all are.'

'So am I,' said Rupert. 'One day we'll organize our lives so we're never apart.'

Through the glass Taggie could see a layer of green mould on a pot of raspberry jam.

'OK, love you, see you Wednesday.' Rupert was clearly in a hurry.

'Love you, darling.' Taggie scraped the mould off the raspberry jam: quite OK underneath, like her marriage.

Back in the kitchen Young Eddie, who'd brought her a huge bunch of red roses, gave her a hug.

'Grandpa remembered, after all.'

Taggie shook her head.

'I hope you told him. He'll be mortified.'

'I didn't want to ruin his day. Fleance won the cup.'

'You're too bloody saintly,' said Eddie. 'He'll be much crosser when he finds out and that Jan Pan has taken over.'

Everyone else remembered. Bianca and Feral, Xav and Aysha, Marcus her stepson from Moscow, Declan and Maud, her brother Patrick, Caitlin her sister who sent a pretty vase accompanied with a request to drop her children off for a week in July. Taggie also received a charity card from Rupert's first wife Helen: *Probably be in your neck of the woods next month.*

Among the presents she most adored were a ravishing silver-tinted leopardskin dress from Bao, and a blown-up photograph of Forester on the front of a cushion, from Gala.

In the evening, Jan organized a birthday bash. Among the guests were Sapphire and Timon's mother Tabitha, who'd been riding in some local three-day event, and who was bored by her husband Wolfie's obsessively filming in France. Arrogant, blonde and beautiful, Gala found Tab disturbingly like Rupert, but, if that were possible, even more high-handed. Rupert's star horse Promiscuous, who'd gone to stud but been found infertile after two seasons, had just been gelded. Tab wanted to retrain him for eventing. Gav, however, felt that small, nippy, lightning-fast Promiscuous might do better as a polo pony and should be steered Luke and Perdita's way. This didn't endear him to Tab.

Other guests besides Gav and Gala included Bao, Dora and Young Eddie.

The only condition was, Taggie was to do nothing. Jan, who

was determined to serve up a feast, had a sweating Bao racing round, helping him.

Despatched to change, wanting to look her lushest, Taggie couldn't find her new leopardskin dress anywhere, so had to settle for her old cream lace. Everyone raised their glasses as she came out on to the terrace.

'You are still the most impossibly glamorous grandmother,' sighed Dora.

'Hear, hear,' said Jan, as he turned steak on the barbecue.

It was a magic evening, the setting sun caressing the utterly still trees. The birds had given up singing, overtaken by the buzzing of insects. Dora was making a daisy chain.

'Gosh, I'm starved,' said Eddie.

Going up to change, Tab had taken with her a vast Bloody Mary. Everyone gasped as she came out, silver-tinged leopard-skin showing off a wonderful body and legs.

'That's Taggie's dress,' said Eddie in surprise.

'Yeah, but I didn't know there was going to be a party so I didn't bring anything special.' Tab beamed at Taggie. 'I know you're never heavy about clothes.'

'Bao had the dress specially made for Taggie,' said Jan icily.

'Really? I thought it was pretty big in the bust.'

'Take it off.'

'Wowee, macho man.'

'Naughty Mummy,' said Sapphire gleefully. 'Go and sit on the naughty step.'

'She is Taggie's naughty step,' said Dora, as Tab filled up her empty glass with champagne.

'Take it off,' insisted Jan. 'Go and change into something else. And that's her scent you're wearing.'

'You should know,' taunted Tabitha, flouncing out. She returned in borrowed black five minutes later.

Taggie somehow managed to hide the fact that she was livid; she'd so longed to look gorgeous in the dress for Jan.

Everyone except Gav proceeded to drink a lot, particularly Tab who was difficult from the start.

'I want Promiscuous,' she kept saying to Gav. 'You've got to persuade Daddy.'

The food was wonderful, Master Chef had excelled himself. 'How d'you get this beef so tender?' asked Gala.

'I've marinated it.'

'Ought to marinate Grandpa. Might make him a bit more tender towards Taggie,' said Eddie, 'and remember her birthday.'

'Oh stop it,' blushed Taggie.

After sunset and the blowing out of candles on a cake, decorated with sugar greyhounds, Safety Car arrived, lapping up a bowl of wine, and being petted by everyone.

'We ought to give him bread dipped in salt like The Maltese Cat,' said Gav. Safety Car then retreated to play football with Gilchrist and Cuthbert, booting their ball down the lawn, so they hurtled off fighting to be the one to retrieve it, and drop it at his feet to roars of applause from the terrace.

Jan kept ordering Bao to pour drinks and take plates away. 'Sit!' he ordered Taggie, whenever she leapt up to help him.

While Dora, Gav and Gala talked Penscombe horses, Tab targeted Jan, telling him about her eventing career and finally dragging him off to Rupert's office to look at a framed picture of her Olympic horse, The Engineer.

'And what's so awful,' she told him, stumbling over a step, 'is Furious, the horse Eddie screwed up on in the National, who had to be put down, and was only in the yard two weeks, is buried in the graveyard next to Taggie's mongrel Gertrude and Rock Star, Daddy's great horse, and soon there won't be room for The Engineer. You must have seen the Stubbs,' she went on. 'I hope Daddy leaves it to me – Marcus gets asthma from horses. I must tell you the story of our ancestor, wicked Rupert Black.'

Jan was close to her now, dwarfing her, his white shirt showing off his beautiful suntanned brown chest. God, he was heaven.

'Rupert Black's our skeleton in the cupboard. During a match race, James Northfield and his horse Spartan were killed falling down a ravine.' Tab took another gulp of champagne. 'But did Rupert Black's mare Sweet Azure hang right and push them over? The Northfields couldn't give a stuff because James Northfield had got some kitchenmaid up the duff and even worse, married her. She was Dutch evidently, and was packed off back to Holland.'

'What happened to the baby?' Jan's voice for once had sunk to a whisper.

'History doesn't relate.' Tab was suddenly aware of him rigid and trembling violently beside her.

'I want you too,' she murmured, sliding her hands inside his shirt which was damp with sweat. 'How about it? Daddy has another door leading upstairs – no one would miss us.'

Reaching up, she drew his head down and joyfully kissed him. Next moment Jan had thrust her away, muttering that there were too many people around.

'Another time.' He kissed her cheek.

Tabitha sauntered back to the kitchen where Taggie was loading up the dishwasher.

'Jan has just made a pass at me,' she said nonchalantly. 'I think he pretends to be gay to keep the ravening hordes away. That's a poem. I'm definitely going to use him for stud purposes.' And she strolled off to the drawing room for another drink.

Why am I crying? thought Taggie furiously, breaking a precious glass engraved with a picture of My Child Cordelia as she rammed it into the dishwasher, and cutting herself picking up the fragments.

Then Jan walked in looking elated, so perhaps it was true.

'What have you done?' he shouted, seeing her hand gushing blood. 'Why are you crying?' He grabbed some kitchen roll, one piece to dry her eyes, the other to staunch the blood. 'What's the matter, mam?'

'Nothing, just a bit tired, and such a pretty glass.'

Even when he applied plaster, blood immediately seeped through.

'Can't staunch love.' For once the harsh Afrikaans voice was soft. 'You're the one I want, mam, not spoilt little Rupert Black's kids. You must know I adore you and how hard I am trying to be good.'

'We must, we must,' gasped Taggie, terrified how much happier she felt.

Meanwhile out on the terrace, Gav was pointing out emerging constellations to Bao – Virgo, Leo the Lion, Boötes the Shepherd – and conversation moved on to Rupert's obsession with landing Global Leading Sire.

'My father's hang-up,' Tab filled her glass again, 'is he can't be Leading Sire himself. Some of us have done well enough – I got an Olympic Gold, Perdita's played polo for England – but I'm a girl, so I can't inherit and so's Perdita, but she's illegitimate and a girl so she can't carry on the line either any more than you can, Eddie; and Bianca and Xav can't because they're adopted and not blood relations.'

'Unlike you, who's a bloody awful relation,' snapped Dora.

'Tabitha,' warned Taggie, coming in with a tray of coffee cups.

'Marcus, my brother,' went on Tabitha, ignoring her, 'is the most brilliant pianist, but he's gay so he's not going to produce an heir.'

'Elton John did,' protested Dora.

'Lots of gays amongst the Campbell-Blacks,' said Tabitha bitchily. 'Uncle Cyprian, who left Daddy the Stubbs, was as gay as a daffodil, so is Daddy's brother Adrian who runs an art gallery. I wonder if you can breed gays.'

'Your father certainly isn't,' said Dora.

'Oh, I don't know. People often implied Daddy and Billy Lloyd-Foxe were a bit that way. It's taken Daddy long enough to get over him.'

'Will you shut up, Tab!' screamed Taggie. 'If you're going to be so foul about everyone, I'm not having you here any more. You can get out in the morning.' She was amazed by the round of applause that greeted this.

A big black cloud had moved over the moon. Calling the dogs, grabbing her torch, fighting back the tears, Taggie stumbled into the garden, down to the lake. Then she gave a moan of horror as the torch gave out; she had only put a new battery in that morning. It was dark around her; a row of trees blocked the light from the house. There was a bridge over the ha-ha, below which flowed a deep stream, which had to be negotiated before she got back to the house. The dogs, all weaving around her, were no help; she couldn't see a thing.

Then she gave a sob of relief as, like an unleashed shooting star, a torchbeam came bobbing towards her.

'Oh thank God,' she called out.

It was Bao, who shyly took her hand and guided her back towards the house.

'Thank you,' she breathed. 'You are wonderful.'

'You are very kind to me, Mrs Campbell-Black. I was told English food very bad, but everything, even your lice is wonderful.'

'Are you happy here?'

'Velly, velly happy.' Then, as Taggie kissed him on the cheek, 'Tabitha is velly lucky to have a stepmother like you. My step-father is not kind nor my stepmother, and Tabitha is velly lucky to have brothers and sisters. We only children in China, so that is another reason I am happy here.'

Mumbling more thanks, unable to face the din still going on out on the terrace, Taggie fled upstairs. She was just turning out the light when there was a bang on the door.

Jan, she thought, half thrilled, half terrified, but it was a sobbing Tabitha.

'Oh Taggie darling, I'm so, so sorry. I don't know what's getting into me – not Wolfie any more; he's having an affair with Sarah Western.'

Bao meanwhile went and dialled a number. It took a minute or two to pick up.

'Yeah,' snapped a half asleep, but still curt voice.

'Mr Campbell-Black, it's Bao.'

'What d'you want? Is everything OK? Is Mrs Campbell-Black OK?'

Bao took a deep breath. 'Forgive me for bothering you. Mrs Campbell-Black is OK, but she is very sad.'

'Why, for fuck's sake?'

'Because it's her birthday today.'

Rupert went ballistic. Bao's arms weren't long enough to hold the telephone sufficiently far away.

Why the fuck hadn't anyone told him? He'd rung that morning!

'It's probably wrong, but she love you so much, I have never seen woman love man more, and he is not quite twelve o'clock.'

'I'll ring her. Thank you, Bao, you did the right thing.'

Taggie was trying to comfort Tab, saying she was sure Wolfie wasn't having an affair. He wasn't the type and he adored her.

'She had carpet burns on her back so they couldn't film her,' wailed Tab. 'She's a nympho – Dora sent Paris out there in a chastity belt. My problem is, I'm insanely possessive like Daddy.'

They were interrupted by Bao. Mr Campbell-Black was on the telephone.

Rupert was devastated. 'Darling, I'm so sorry. Christ, I'm sorry. Why the hell didn't you tell me? I love you so much – I'm so bloody self-obsessed. I'll be home the day after tomorrow. We'll go out to dinner, I'll bring you the best present in the world. And now, thank God, I've got a legitimate excuse to fire Geraldine.'

'How did you find out?'

'Bao rang me. He's a sweet boy.'

'He's given me a beautiful dress. Will you bring him a nice present?'

'I'll bring him a gun.'

Jan, next day, was absolutely furious with Bao. 'How *dare* you interfere?'

55

Gav was uneasy. Rupert had been such a beast, it was not surprising Taggie was drawn to Jan, and his being foul to both had obviously triggered off a comfort fuck between Eddie and Gala.

There were also odd things happening – gates and stable doors being left open. Could Safety or Old Eddie be letting out their friends? How had Quickly picked up a flu bug, or Purrpuss got locked in that chest of drawers? And why was there no petrol in the small lorry, always kept filled for emergencies, like rushing a horse with colic to the equine hospital? About to pay for a horse at a sale, Gav found his credit card missing, only to find it later back in his flat over the tack room. Even worse, a terrified Cuthbert had been discovered shut in a turned-up rotating horse walker, nearly trampled to death by Chekov.

Gav didn't think Jan was kosher. On the other hand, Rupert's newest lucky shirt had been found in the back of Bao's shirt drawer before a big race. Was the smiling teenager a snake in the grass?

Rupert's rage that no one except Bao had reminded him about Taggie's birthday was tempered when he saw how Gav on his return was transforming the horses, particularly Quickly, who was now flowing up the gallops in such perfect rhythm behind See You in a Bit, ridden by young Jemmy, that the older generation were making jokes about Jemmy and the Pacemaker.

Meanwhile Eddie, who when he wasn't off winning races, rode Quickly 'work', which meant exercising him at home instead of Gav. He was also eating sensibly, had given up the booze again, and was spending time in the gym dreaming about Sauvignon, who was only interested in human winners.

Gav also noticed wistfully how Gala had blossomed. Sunbathing during her break down at her new home, Lime Tree Cottage a little way into the woods, she had acquired a lovely golden tan. Weight loss had made her curves even more voluptuous. She seldom appeared without a pale coral lipstick on her full luscious mouth, which was no longer bitten and pursed with unhappiness over Ben or the tension of making good in the yard. She was glowing. If only he hadn't pushed her away. He must seek help from a doctor.

Fleance, looking an increasingly likely stallion prospect, had left the opposition for dead in the mighty July Cup at Newmarket. Rupert was so delighted with Quickly that he took the bold step of supplementing him and Bitsy at a substantial £75,000 each in the even mightier King George and Queen Elizabeth Stakes at Ascot at the end of July. Similar to the Nunthorpe but at one mile four furlongs, much longer, it accepted horses of all ages. Thus you had the greatest four-year-olds in the world with massive quarters and shoulders, overseas riders in their about-to-be stallion glory, toughing it out in the best middle-distance race in the world, for prize money of over a million pounds.

Gav thought Rupert was insane and said so. 'Quickly's too little, too young and not ready; you'll ruin all we've achieved. It's crazy to overface him.'

'Quickly likes right-handed tracks,' said Rupert. 'And as Eddie's flying, he can ride Touchy Filly and Blank Chekov in earlier races.'

The racing press agreed with Gav, and wrote of suicide missions and Quickly having as much hope as a one-legged ostrich.

After the King George and Queen Elizabeth, Rupert, who had persuaded star artist, Katie O'Sullivan, to rustle up a ravishing portrait of Forester for a late birthday present, was also intending to fly Taggie off there and then to a romantic surprise location to make up for forgetting. He was therefore outraged when she stammeringly protested she couldn't get away because she was manning the cake stall at the Penscombe Fete.

'Don't be ridiculous, your woofter boyfriend can do that.'

'Please don't call him that. I promised, Rupert, and a pack of grandchildren who adore the fete are all entered in the Dog Show, and Helen as well.'

'She's such a bitch, she'll probably win first prize,' raged Rupert. 'Why in hell did you ask her?'

'She sort of caught me on the hop, said she never saw her grandchildren.'

'That's because they can't stand her.'

'I'm so sorry, I didn't know about the King George.' Taggie didn't dare add that one of the fete auction prizes, bullied out of her by the vicar's wife, Constance Sprightly, offered dinner cooked by herself to the highest bidder.

Picking up the cake-stall details, Rupert read: '"Anything will be greatly appreciated: cakes, biscuits or tarts." If you want tarts, why not take Bethany, Janey Lloyd-Foxe and Dame Hermione? Utterly ridiculous, putting a fete before the King George.' And he stormed off.

'Serves him right for all your favourite foals he's selling,' said Dora.

'He'll calm down, mam,' Jan comforted her.

But Taggie, looking over the valley, where her parents' house in summer was hidden by the trees, remembered how longingly she used to gaze across to catch a glimpse of Rupert before they finally got together. She stared up at the lovely portrait of Forester. She must pay more attention to her marriage.

Four days before the King George, it started to rain and kept on raining.

'It was soft when Quickly won the Guineas,' said Gala, trying not to be pleased that Taggie wasn't coming. 'Great horses can run on any ground.'

Gav shook his head. 'But this is going to be a bog – although it's to his advantage that so many of the overseas riders, Japs, Australian, French, much prefer quick ground.'

On Saturday, the skies lightened and the rain eased. Ascot looked sensational, with its huge pillars on each side of the entrance draped with Union Jacks, and Union Jacks like nodding horses' heads all the way down the High Street. The parade ring and the winners enclosure were a mass of scarlet geraniums. A huge crowd had braved the drizzle to witness the clash of the Titans, particularly the mighty dark-brown Simone de Beauvoir, winner of the Arc de Triomphe and, at 570 kilos, the largest horse in the race. Notoriously cross-grained and given to lashing out with both barrels, she was forgiven because of her brilliance and the good looks of her jockey Manu de la Tour, whose breeches and silks were cut better than anyone else's.

Both Manu and Guy, his father, who trained the mare, were eyeing up Sauvignon who, in a white linen shirt, crimson hot pants and a little black top hat, was sauntering up I Will Repay. Every man in the paddock had an umbrella at the ready to protect her if the rain started. Repay's new co-owner Sheikh Abdul Baddi and his swaggering retinue, all in morning coats and black toppers, looked as though they'd like to slap a burka over her.

Other stars included Sydney Opera House, who'd won the Melbourne Cup, and a huge Japanese star, Noonday Silence, belonging to a syndicate who'd all paid four million yen a share, so the parade ring swarmed with interpreters. Noonday Silence's star jockey Hiroshi, having paddled the course in bare feet, had told the press he'd come to win. Finally, a top American jockey, Hammond Johnson, a little smiling bald man with colossal strength, was riding a big Chestnut Breeders' Cup winner called Dependable Guy.

'Classic case of oxymoron,' giggled Dora.

Penscombe's day had started magically with Young Eddie getting a double on Touchy Filly and then on Chekov, wearing blinkers for the first time.

'Stopped him being distracted by seagulls,' quipped Dora.

Bao had huge bets on both of them.

'I wonder if Ladbrokes are regretting giving him an account,' said Dora as she, Etta and Bao gathered in the paddock for the King George. The runners' numbers were on the outside, so the magnificent animals, mostly bay and brown, were almost indistinguishable.

'That must be Simone de Beauvoir,' squeaked Etta as a vast liver chestnut with a white blaze prowled by.

'She ought to give her 15 lb mare's allowance to the boys,' said Dora. 'She's massive.'

'I wonder how she'll run on bottomless' (her latest word) 'ground,' mused Etta.

'She's certainly not bottomless,' said Dora. 'That great arse powers her forward.'

Then, catching sight of the liver chestnut's tackle, they decided it couldn't be Simone de Beauvoir. Sydney Opera House from Australia was wearing a rug to keep himself warm. Noonday Silence, the Japanese horse, looked very girly in a red and white bridle, his mane done up in bell-shaped plaits and red and white bows.

Then along came Bitsy led by Jemmy and Quickly led by Gala.

'Doesn't he look beautiful, but absolutely tiny,' sighed Etta.

Quickly, in colty mood, had no difficulty identifying the sex of the real Simone, edging up, mounting her and nearly getting kicked in the face.

The rain was sluicing down now, straight hair going curly, curly hair going straight. In the weighing room the jockeys were putting on long white trousers to stop the rain falling into their boots. Rain was jumping off the tarmac, appearing like frogspawn on the television screen, blurring out entire faces like victims of abuse.

'Do we risk it? It's softer than guacamole,' Rupert asked Gav.

'Yup. We've got this far. We can trust Eddie to pull him up if things get hairy.'

'Nice for him to get a treble.'

*

Eddie was disappointed no one in the weighing room had congratulated him on his double.

'They don't like too much success in the young, particularly on big race days,' warned Gav. 'Don't get cocky, wait for them to praise you.'

To celebrate Touchy Filly's and Blank Chekov's wins, Rupert, still fed up with Taggie, took Gala into the box belonging to Weatherbys, with whom he banked. Filled with flowers, it had a lovely picture of the Queen on the wall. As people joked that after two wins, his account must be looking pretty healthy, Gala sipped iced coffee and noticed, piled on a shelf, everyone's Panama hats including Rupert's, which had the red and blue ribbon of the Household Cavalry. Gala remembered him wearing it tipped over his Greek nose with the same off-white suit when she'd first seen him on television in Hong Kong. Had she really fallen in love with him that early? What was going to happen to her?

Back at Penscombe, the fete was well underway. Taggie had been invited into the vicarage to watch the King George, which would probably kick off bang in the middle of the auction. Husbands kept sidling up to her, saying they were going to bid for dinner with her. Thank God for Jan, who was everywhere looking after everyone, keeping Helen plied with cups of tea and, later, Pimms.

The runners were lining up for the King George. Quickly, led by Gav and Gala, and accompanied by his new friend Bitsy with Jemmy up, was behaving very well. Connections were so terrified of Simone de Beauvoir getting kicked or sexually harassed at the start, they'd insisted on an empty stall on each side of her. Quickly decided not to bother.

Up in the stands, Etta was feeling old: too deaf to understand the commentary, her eyes not good enough to distinguish the colours. Despite the ravishing view, everyone's binoculars were trained on the big screen. Beside her, one of Noonday Silence's Japanese owners was very quietly saying, 'Yew, yew, yew.'

Little figures miles away . . . and they were off. Like a Wimbledon ace, Quickly exploded out of the stalls on to the right leg, staying on the outside, led by Bitsy at exactly the correct speed to settle him in the early stages, so no mud was kicked in his face. Eddie, meanwhile, showed what a beautiful rider he'd become, his body low over Quickly in perfect rhythm, shoving, pushing, hands in Quickly's ears.

Ahead of him, having travelled all that way with all that prize money and reputation at stake, the Goliaths battled, barging, realigning, swearing in different languages as they fought for supremacy.

Whips cracking, they swung round the bend for home. At the three-furlong pole, Bitsy quietly moved out and Quickly slid past him, fresh as a daisy, past I Will Repay, and Eumenides, past Sydney Opera House, Simone and Dependable Guy, past Noonday Silence in his red and white bridle, Quickly's little muddy legs going faster and faster, showing he could not only trounce his elders but win at any distance.

'Come on, you geriatrics,' yelled Eddie. 'Get out your Zimmers!' And as if in answer, both Simone and Noonday Silence rallied, and drew level again, making the crowd bellow in anguish.

But a second later, Quickly detached himself, and it could be seen that the clever little scamp had merely been giving himself a breather as he bolted away to win by five lengths . . . and the audience broke into an ecstatic roar.

Simone de Beauvoir came second, Noonday third, I Will Repay fourth and Dependable Guy fifth. For once, Eddie had no difficulty pulling up, as Quickly swung straight round and cantered back, looking for Bitsy.

Trumpets could hardly be heard for the deafening applause following Eddie into the winners enclosure. Led by an overjoyed Etta and giggling, tearful Gala, Quickly still called plaintively for Bitsy. Jumping off, Eddie was greeted by a jubilant Rupert.

'Bloody marvellous, well done.'

Having hugged Eddie and patted Quickly, Rupert turned to Gala. 'We won, we did it!' they both cried simultaneously, gazing at each other for a moment. She looked so adorable; before Rupert could stop himself, he was kissing her on and on, oblivious of the cameras and an utterly transfixed crowd, lips devouring, pulses drumming, knees giving way. Gala could only stay upright by clinging on to him. Heaven in her arms.

'Half time, half time,' reproved Valent, tapping Rupert on the shoulder. 'We need a photograph, and Eddie needs to weigh in.'

'Red card, red card,' grinned Eddie.

An outraged Gav, who'd been tipping the bucket away from Quickly so water wouldn't get up his nostrils, was about to chuck the rest over Rupert and Gala, who were still smiling as they broke apart.

'So sweet, the way he always kisses his wife,' said an old trout.

'Not sure it is his wife,' said her friend.

Nor were the photographers. They had abandoned Sauvignon, who was looking livid, as was Mrs Walton.

'Who is she? Who is she?' rippled the crowd as a half-moon of journalists gathered round Rupert.

'Quickly's shown he can win at any distance,' he told them. 'He's a little horse, with a huge heart and a massive engine, and he's extremely resourceful.'

Quickly, who'd snatched a mouthful of red geraniums, agreed.

'I've been abroad,' added Rupert. 'Gav, Eddie, Jemmy and Gala have been working on Quickly and Bitsy – they're all total stars.'

'Who were you kissing, Rupert?' asked Matt Chapman from *At the Races*.

'Quickly's stable lass, we were celebrating.'

Taggie had insisted on going into the vicarage to watch the race. She had wanted to take just Jan, but Helen insisted on coming too, bringing Sapphire. Taggie was yelling her head off, clutching Jan as Eddie romped past the post, then with tears of joy, watching Eddie and Quickly come into the winners enclosure, being particularly delighted that Rupert was hugging and praising Eddie. Then he was kissing Gala on and on and on and on and on.

'Oh God.' Taggie fell silent.

'Bastard, don't look,' snarled Jan, his arm closing round her, murmuring, 'don't worry, mam. This is one of the biggest races in the world, incredible victory for Quickly, just euphoria, darling mam, don't be sad. Look, everyone's kissing everyone. Etta's hugging Gala. Look at that beautiful girl Sauvignon kissing Eddie – he looks pleased, but that won't please Cosmo. Don't be sad.'

'Why was Grandpa kissing Gala?' demanded Sapphire.

Helen turned to Constance Sprightly, saying, 'Could you take the little people outside for a moment?' Then, putting a hand on Taggie's arm: 'I'm so sorry, Taggie. I'm afraid Rupert's just reverting to type. Bound to happen sooner or later. I should know.'

'Don't talk rubbish.' Jan turned on her furiously. 'Rupert adores Taggie, he was just carried away. If you'd seen how upset he was when she loyally came to the fete instead of going to the King George with him . . .'

Helen had gone scarlet with rage – Jan was *her* ally – when Constance Sprightly popped her head round the door:

'Time for the auction, everyone. And South Africa are 280 for no wicket.'

Meanwhile, back at Penscombe the yells of excitement when Quickly flashed past the post, and the winners bell rang out, were followed by howls of '*Ker-rist!*' as Rupert kept on kissing Gala.

'She's got to first base,' squealed Lou-easy. 'That was more than a peck on the cheek.'

'Throw that bucket of water over them, Gav.'

'Lucky thing.'

'God, I wonder if Taggie saw it.'

'He was livid when he caught Gala with Eddie.'

Now Eddie was talking to the press: 'Wonderful horse, Quickly, he's manned up, and I was determined not to come too soon.'

'Makes a change,' said Pat to howls of laughter.

'What a wictory – Gropius won the Dog with the Waggiest Tail,' announced Marketa, who'd just returned from the fete with him.

'I should think his mistress has the even more waggiest tail after that clinch,' said Roving Mike. 'Jesus!'

Jan orchestrated the auction out in the vicarage garden, talking up and getting good bids for magnums of champagne, pictures by local artists, free wedding flowers, days out at Longleat.

Taggie was too fazed by the goings-on at Ascot to take in much, until she heard Jan saying: 'And now the most exciting lot of the afternoon, dinner, cooked by the best chef and the prettiest woman in Gloucestershire, Taggie Campbell-Black,' followed by loud cheers.

'Oh help!' But before she could get too embarrassed, the bids came storming in, pushed by Jan, up and up to £700. This came from incredibly lecherous Brigadier Littleton and was then finally topped by Jan himself with £750 – a huge amount when he was sending so much home to his family. The vicar was beaming. The stalls had been counting their takings: Jan's bid should push the total to over £5,000.

'You are a darling,' said a deeply embarrassed Taggie. 'It's far too much.'

'And you're not doing any cooking,' said Jan. 'We're going to Calcot Manor, next week.'

Taggie was so grateful to him, particularly for telling Helen to shut up. She was just wondering why Rupert hadn't rung when she realized her mobile was switched off. Immediately, he called.

'Where have you been? We won, we fucking won. Did you see it?'

'I did, it was wonderful, so proud of you – everyone said he hadn't a hope. Do congratulate Eddie.'

'I will.' There was a pause. 'Sorry about Gala and me. We were all so excited, got carried away, so used to kissing you. How's the fete going?'

'Fine. I'm . . . so thrilled you won. See you later.'

Eddie was in heaven. He loved being congratulated by the Queen and being presented with a little glass horse.

He was even more elated when Sauvignon took him aside.

'Well done, Eddie. Why don't you join us for a drink this evening?'

Gala might have felt jealous. She didn't trust Sauvignon with her baby boy, but next minute, as Quickly's stable lass, she was called up to collect a silver photograph frame, and Rupert's hand had brushed hers as they lined up for the photographers.

'We shouldn't have done that,' he murmured, 'but it was incredibly nice.'

'Incredibly.'

'Sauvignon's asked me for a drink,' crowed Eddie to both of them.

'Which pub are you going to?' asked Gala.

'All of them,' grinned Eddie.

But fame and tranquillity are seldom good bedfellows, fame being a spur which often sticks in the side. While Gala and Jemmy went home with the horses, Eddie stayed in Ascot and, having been off the booze for a month, got drunk very quickly.

'What have you done to yourself?' asked a horrified Gala when he finally made it back to Penscombe the following afternoon, with two black eyes and a badly swollen wrist.

'I fell out of a helicopter.'

'Good God.'

'I was hammered – it was on the ground.'

'Whatever happened?'

'I don't remember. There were lots of jockeys there, Manu, and Ash and Hammond Johnson. I went outside for a piss. Someone must have beaten me up.'

'That someone must have been jealous – you'd done much too well. Trebles mean trouble. Did you get off with Sauvignon?'

'I think I'd remember if I had. The saddest thing was, my glass horse got smashed.'

There were, however, compensations. Eddie was touched to receive a congratulatory text from Lark in Australia: 'Well done you and Quickly.'

Darling Lark, how unutterably sweeter was she than Sauvignon?

There were also pictures of him in every paper as 'Rupert the Second' with Alastair Down in the *Racing Post* describing his win as a masterpiece, reminiscent of the time Rupert, the greatest rider of his generation, had won an Olympic Gold medal with a trapped nerve.

Even better, Quickly's victory had pushed Love Rat above Roberto's Revenge in the Leading Sire charts.

Rupert also apologized again to Taggie.

'I'm sorry, darling, I was missing you. Gala'd done a fantastic job and I got carried away. I'd have kissed the vicar if he'd been there.'

56

After the King George, Declan O'Hara turned up to see his daughter Taggie. He was desperately broke and had just had a gruelling session with his bank manager, who chided him.

'Do you realize, Mr O'Hara, your overdraft is larger than my annual salary?'

After a long pause, Declan had growled: 'Then I suggest you get a better job.'

Feeling he had scored a cheap point, Declan, a sweet man, had sought comfort by dropping in on Taggie, to find her out for dinner. Rupert was at Windsor, so Declan had several drinks with Gala, who was dogsitting.

It was another exquisite evening out on the terrace. The air was heavy with meadowsweet, Traveller's Joy rioted primrose-yellow over the hedgerows, green fields turning gold formed little triangles between gaps in the darkening treetops. Except for cooing pigeons the birds had fallen silent. The dogs sought shade and panted. Declan liked Gala very much, but suspected, having seen the clinch on Saturday, she was dangerously drawn to Rupert.

'No grandchildren?' he asked.

'No, for once. Everyone uses Taggie as a hotel, although her food's much better. She's so kind she never says no to anyone. How's your book going?'

'Backwards,' sighed Declan. 'It's on Irish literature. It's a terrible confession, but I'm so bored with it.'

Then, unable to resist talking about Rupert, Gala asked: 'Were you pleased when Rupert and Taggie got married?'

'Yes. When we battled for and won the Venturer contract together I got to know him really well.'

'Must be difficult,' Gala was fishing, 'for such a ravishingly attractive man to stay faithful when he's away so much. So many beautiful women hang around the racing circuit and descend on him in droves.'

Declan laughed. 'He's always been lethally attractive. I'm amazed the entire Pony Club hasn't come out of the woodwork and sued him for *not* sexually abusing them. My wife Maud was bats about him. He fucked for England,' Declan refilled their glasses, 'before and during his first marriage. Helen's a pain in the arse, but he did give her a hard time.'

'She's convinced he's still in love with her,' said Gala, 'and that explains his animosity.'

'I've never subscribed to that "who never loves, that hated not at first sight" theory,' reflected Declan. 'Then he met Taggie, who was desperately insecure, dyslexic, never been able to read well, brother and sister both very clever and beautiful. But Taggie was like a gentle giraffe – she touched his heart. She was eighteen years younger than him but so vulnerable; he fell madly in love with her. For months he fought it, then, although he knew Taggie adored him, in one of the few sacrifices,' Declan smiled, 'of a pretty selfish life, refusing, as he said, "to foist his utterly bloody promiscuous nature on her", he fled to America, but after a week was unable to stay away.

'On his return, Taggie surprised him at the airport, declaring her love, and the rest is very happily married history. In *The Faerie Queene*, Una tames the fierce lion by sheer goodness. I think Rupert feels with Taggie as he did with Billy Lloyd-Foxe, that her loving him is a kind of reference that he can't be that much of a shit. His very, very disguised insecurity,' Declan bent to stroke Forester, 'I think stems from multiple married parents and a succession of indifferent and antagonistic stepfathers and stepmothers. Old Eddie's not particularly fond of Rupert. Just take, take, take. Never says thank you. Born in Scorpio, that most jealous passionate sign, Rupert is terrified of losing Taggie and going back to the anarchy of his old life, like Othello's chaos coming again.

'He is insanely jealous. Never got over Malise Gordon preferring Jake Lovell to him. He also had a perfectly frightful owner called Shade Murchieson, who had twenty horses and made a pass at Taggie. Roving Mike sneaked to Rupert, who told Shade to fuck off on the gallops, then loaded up all Shade's horses and dumped them outside Shade's office in St James's Square. Never, ever underestimate his jealousy.'

'Gosh,' sighed Gala. 'You are warning me off, aren't you?'

'Yes,' said Declan. 'The marriage is proof of a marriage working and gives security to so many people, staff, family, friends and each other.'

Declan's gorgeous voice, deep, husky and Irish, softened everything he said.

'I wish you were twenty years younger,' said Gala.

'Where's Taggie?' asked Declan.

'Gone out to dinner with Jan.' Gala burst out laughing. 'He caused lots of talk bidding £750 for dinner with her at the village fete. And he picked the night Rupert's away at Windsor. Are you going to warn Jan to back off as well?' She'd had too many glasses of red.

Then, as Declan looked at her: 'If Rupert's jealous like Othello, Jan's Iago,' she said. 'He's much keener on Taggie than he is on Rupert.'

'You don't like him?'

Gala shrugged. 'He tries to be all things to all men, but not dogs – he beat up Gropius once. He can be very kind. He tracked down lots of pictures of my husband Ben, because I lost them all in the fire in Zimbabwe. And he's very good at his job and a huge help to Taggie – for her, it must be suddenly like having wheels to help you pull along a huge suitcase – but he acts as though he owns the place. Rupert can't stand him.'

Seeing the bottle was empty, Bao brought them out another one and some pâté on toast.

'Thanks, Bao, I need that to stop me getting completely

indiscreet. He is such a sweet boy,' confided Gala when he'd gone, then taking a deep breath: 'Because some Chinese mafia warlord in Zimbabwe took out my husband and destroyed everything I loved, I was vile to Bao when he arrived, but he's so good-hearted. He was even brave enough to ring up Rupert in Singapore and tell him he'd forgotten Taggie's birthday.'

'What was the name of the mafia warlord?' asked Declan.

'Wang. Zixin is his Christian name. He's got houses in Beijing and Zimbabwe.'

'I'll check him out,' said Declan, noticing how much she was suddenly trembling, then wondered if Wang was actually the cause, as Rupert's helicopter came chugging through wisps of clouds turned salmon-pink in the sunset.

'Goodness, he's back early. He's not expected till tomorrow.'

Believing Rupert was spending the night in London, Taggie had guiltily put on Bao's leopardskin dress, fluffed up her shining clean hair, taken great care with her make-up, drenched herself in Eau de Mandarine, her new birthday scent, and looked so gorgeous, all the diners at Calcot Manor clocked that Mrs Campbell-Black was dining out with a man much younger than, and almost as good-looking as, her husband.

Realizing how shy and nervous she was, Jan immediately ordered a bottle of Sancerre.

'You'll have to drink most of it, mam, as I'm driving, and I'm going to sit opposite you, so I can really gaze for a change. You look so beautiful.'

They were dining in the conservatory with lilies everywhere and a lovely view of the garden. Knowing she'd have trouble reading the menu, which was full of delicious refinements like truffle-mashed potato, quails' egg and fig dressing and seared turbot with bacon, Jan chose her a starter of crab mayonnaise.

'Then why don't we share salmon en croute with a champagne and caviar sauce?'

The only problem was that carers, worried about abandoning their clients, eat very fast, and Jan had wolfed two thirds of the salmon en croute, before Taggie confessed she was full up after a couple of spoonfuls.

'I'm so sorry, such a waste.'

'I'll finish it up, mam, and we're going to share a sweet.'

Only halfway through a mouth-watering passion fruit and banana soufflé with mango sorbet did Taggie realize they were using the same spoon, and he was feeding her.

'Do you miss South Africa?' she asked.

'Not when I'm with you, and I don't miss the danger. There've been three murders in our area this week. And people broke in to my father's barn and smashed all the windows. The police won't do anything about it. My father knows who the thieves are. They'll even hail him in the street.'

'How awful.'

'They only attack during a full moon because car lights turned on would give them away. I worry about my kids. It's a strange country. Black police tend to be lenient with blacks but when I applied for a new passport before coming to England, black queues were going twice round the building, but the white passport lady gave me a stamped one straight away.'

'You must miss your children so much.'

Jan shrugged. 'I married to please my parents, and give them grandchildren to boast about at the golf club and bridge parties.' He felt guilty, he added, about his wife, Matilda.

'Did she marry again?'

Jan shook his head. 'That's why I've got to support her.'

Taggie felt bad that he'd blued so much on the auction and now on dinner. She'd also had three glasses of Sancerre.

'Marcus, Rupert's son, has got a lovely boyfriend. Do you think . . .' then went crimson as Jan took her hand, caressing the inside of her wrist with his fingers.

'I'm feeling less gay by the day, mam.'

The other diners, many of whom had seen pictures of Rupert and Gala's clinch after the King George, were utterly riveted.

'You must bring your children over for a long visit,' said Taggie.

'I don't think Mr Campbell-Black would like that very much.'

Any more than Rupert liked getting home from Windsor to find his wife out to dinner with Jan. Particularly when he then picked up a call from Helen to thank Taggie for the weekend; predictably, she told him about Jan's massive bid for dinner with Taggie.

'The vicar was so delighted. It's so nice too, for Taggie to have someone her own age who can talk about something other than horses.'

If his father-in-law hadn't been there, Rupert would have been tempted to sweep Gala out to dinner. Instead he worked himself up into a fury with Taggie, who had refused to come to the King George for the most important race of Quickly's life, but could find time to go out on the toot with Jan. But when she came home, she looked so bloody gorgeous, he couldn't resist taking her to bed instead.

As a result, he liked Jan even less, and clocking that Jan didn't like Bao, deliberately cultivated the boy, taking him shooting on August the twelfth, where Bao shot everything out of the sky.

Meanwhile, Cupid continued to fire arrows at Penscombe. Taggie couldn't sleep the night following the dinner at Calcot Manor. Rupert was away again and she couldn't stop wondering if Jan would have kissed her on the way home, if he hadn't seen the Green Galloper parked in the field. Suddenly she heard Old Eddie's bell, and leaping out of bed in her short pink night-gown, met Jan on the landing just in pyjama bottoms. As they rushed to attend to Eddie, Taggie noticed Jan's sleek brown shoulders only flawed by a scar from a crocodile bite.

Eddie then grumbled that he'd been looking everywhere for a VD called *Horny Housewives*.

You've got one here, thought appalled yet amused Taggie.

As she and Jan tucked Eddie back in bed, their hands brushed, and as Jan's crept upwards to stroke her face, Taggie couldn't stop herself kissing his fingers.

'When am I going home?' asked Eddie, putting a hand on Taggie's breast.

'You are home, sir,' said Jan, removing it.

'Lovely girl, give me a kiss.'

Pecking him on the forehead, Taggie stumbled back to bed, past the nude of Rupert on the landing. A moment later, Jan knocked on the door.

'I know you're married, but I want to tell you you're the sweetest, most beautiful woman I've ever met.'

'Oh gosh, thank you, but we truly mustn't,' stammered Taggie, not knowing whether to be relieved or disappointed when Jan smiled regretfully, said OK and went back to his room. Out of the window she could see a fox, silver in the moonlight, wolfing the badgers' food.

A week later, getting out of the bath, she discovered a peacock butterfly fluttering dangerously near a light bulb and managed to cup it in her hands. Unable to dress or cover herself up, she ran downstairs to release it out of the front door. 'There, darling.'

Returning, she went slap into a laughing Jan, holding out her white dressing gown.

'I w-w-was just setting it free.'

'If I were a butterfly, mam,' Jan whispered, 'I'd rather stay in your room than be turfed out into the cold.'

57

September approached. The willows were already streaked with yellow. The sun shone golden instead of silver, particularly in the early mornings, and the moon grew larger. Rupert's ailing chestnut avenue was turning a warm brown, his beechwoods tinged with orange. The constellation Pegasus reared out of the east as Quickly, coached by Gav, was rearing out of the starting stalls. All Rupert's horses in fact were flying.

Ahead lay the gilded highway of the richest races: the St Leger, the Arc, the Champion Stakes at Ascot, the Melbourne Cup, Breeders' Cup in America, on to Japan and Hong Kong, leading to Dubai and the World Cup in March – opportunity knocking for Love Rat's children, chasing each other down the corridors of the world with a real chance at last to topple Roberto's Revenge.

The St Leger, oldest and longest of the classics, held at Doncaster, drew near. Although the Triple Crown had eluded Quickly, Rupert was hell bent on emulating Rupert Black and Third Leopard and nailing the race.

Dora, back from a summer in France, where Paris was still filming *Le Rouge et Le Noir*, was intoxicated by a wonderful PR opportunity. She promptly concocted a press release, reproducing Stubbs' portrait of the divinely handsome Rupert Black alongside equally glamorous photographs of Rupert and Young Eddie. She then pointed out that 230 years ago, Rupert's ancestor had triumphed in the Leger with mighty Third Leopard, who became Leading Sire for years afterwards. Now it was Master Quickly's chance to repeat history, and carry Rupert Black's descendants to victory.

'What a story,' she crowed to Taggie who was making moussaka in the kitchen for another descending horde of grandchildren. 'And Channel Four are interested in making a feature film. Paris can play both Ruperts *and* Young Eddie; he's the only actor handsome enough.'

'Have you run this past Rupert?' asked Taggie in alarm.

'He'll love it – you know how privately knocked out he was when Alastair Down described him as one of the greatest riders of all time. Now he can prove he's as good a trainer as Rupert Black.'

'Fuck!' exploded Jan, who never swore, but had cut himself chopping aubergines.

'I hope the Stubbs doesn't get stolen,' sighed Taggie.

Publicity opportunities grew even better for Dora. On the first day of the Leger's meeting, a Legends charity race was held in which stars of the past would compete not only to win but to see who could raise the most money for charity. The competitors were chiefly ex-flat and jump jockeys, but Rupert was such a crowd puller, the organizers begged him to take part.

Learning Isa Lovell was entered, Rupert's competitive streak was aroused. In a weak moment – after all, Billy had died of cancer – he agreed to take part. Instantly he regretted it, as the fundraisers weighed in, led by Etta's perfectly dreadful son Martin who, unannounced, barged into his office.

'Congrats on riding in the Legends race, Rupe! What charity are you supporting?' shouted Martin over the furiously barking dogs.

'Cancer,' snarled Rupert. 'What the hell are you doing here?'

'Cancer's excellent, perfect for your image. Just give me the names of all the wealthy folk you know. I'll message them for sponsorship, and they can follow you on your dedicated website, which'll be even better for your image.'

'Get out,' howled Rupert. '*Out!*'

Next moment, Weatherbys *Stallion Book* flew through the air, far faster than any of the stallions it featured, missing Martin's left ear by inches.

'The other jockeys will be raising hundreds of thousands.' Martin stood his ground.

'I'll write a cheque then. GET OUT.'

'Ouch,' screamed Martin, as Cuthbert bit his ankle.

Rupert turned on a giggling Dora. 'It's not funny. If I'm approached by another crone waving a bucket I'll kick her teeth in.'

'Kick the bucket, kick the bucket.' Dora was reading Clover's notes. 'The money raised will go to Jack Berry House, which is run by the Injured Jockeys Fund and – lovely typo – the Northern Raving College. Didn't know they did much raving. Jemmy said the girl students were very much kept from the boys.'

A worse problem for Rupert was that a hard finish needs a very fit man. By jogging and giving up alcohol and not snacking on cheese or chocolate, he managed to lose ten pounds, making him leaner and meaner. But with travelling to sales and race meetings all over the world, it was difficult to exercise on a plane.

One baking evening in late August, he flew back to Penscombe in time for evening stables. Having caught a glimpse of Taggie and Jan in the kitchen, he whisked off round the yard and stud checking every horse, then dropped into the office to see the latest emails.

'God, you look tired,' said Geraldine. 'Have a drink.'

'Fresh drinking whisky should always be available,' sighed Rupert. 'I must stay off it until after this bloody race. Where are the dogs?'

'Gala waited for it to get cooler, then she walked them.'

In the kitchen he found Young Eddie, who was not riding tomorrow, tucking into a bottle of red and talking to Taggie and Jan, who was marinating steak for a barbecue.

'I'm going for a jog before dinner,' Rupert told them.

'Why don't you play tennis with Jan?' asked Eddie. 'In this

heat, you'd burn off much more fat than pounding round the valley.'

Rupert, whose brilliant eye and timing had made him a great showjumper and crack shot, had also been an effortless tennis player. It would be quite nice to annihilate the smug bastard.

'I thought he was cooking my father's dinner.'

'We've got time,' said Jan. 'Your dad's happy enjoying Fiona Bruce for the next hour.'

'Please rest, darling,' said Taggie in alarm. 'You must be so jet-lagged, and far too tired to play tennis.'

'Meaning I'm not up to it.'

'No, no.'

'I'm game if you are,' said Jan. 'I've started up the barbecue. The steak'll only take a few minutes.'

'OK, just a couple of sets.'

'I'll come and umpire,' said Eddie, gathering up his bottle of red.

'Watch it, he's bloody good,' warned Gav as Rupert set out.

The tennis court lay to the left of the house, reached by a gravel path bordered by white buddleia, covered in peacock butterflies enjoying the last of the sun. After evening stables, the lads usually played rounders or football before drifting down to the Dog and Trumpet. This evening, however, word had gone around of more fascinating diversions, and a crowd bringing glasses was gathering on the grassy bank above the court.

Eddie, three drinks up on an empty stomach, perched glass in hand on a high chair, was regaling them with Wimbledon chatter. Rupert rolled up in a dark-blue polo shirt and an old pair of denim shorts, which he had to belt because of his ten-pound weight loss, and threw a net of green balls down on the court. Next moment, Jan ran down the path, flexing his shoulders, brandishing four rackets and a big fluffy towel to a chorus of wolf whistles. Very Wimbledon in very short white shorts showing off long tanned legs, a white Federer bandeau holding down his conker-brown hair, he was in superb shape and twenty years younger than Rupert.

As Jan picked up a green ball and unleashed an Exocet down

the court, it was plain he was good enough to play for Port Elizabeth if not South Africa.

The sun had retreated behind the beeches and was gilding the fields across the valley; the bank was covered in gaping stable staff. By the time Jan, five games up, had floored Rupert with ace after ace and sizzling returns of serve that sent Rupert racing all over the court, it was hard in the half-light to see the ball.

'Fifteen love,' giggled Eddie, as Rupert's ball shot into the bushes.

Jan to serve, irritatingly bouncing the ball over and over again, chucking it miles in the air, and as he reached up to hit it, pulling his white T-shirt out of his shorts to show even more bronzed flesh.

'Wow,' cried Lou-easy. 'Come to Federer, leave him for deaderer.'

'Thirty love,' said Eddie, taking another slug of wine.

Deliverance was at hand as Gala returned from walking the dogs, and the entire pack surged over the court, throwing themselves on their master in noisy ecstasy.

'Dogs stopped play,' shouted Eddie. Everyone roared with laughter, except Jan.

'Get them off the court,' said Gav, scenting trouble.

Gala had hardly complied before Jan unleashed another scorcher, whereupon Banquo rushed in and seized the ball before Rupert got to it.

'Ball-ee,' cheered the audience. 'You could get a job as a ball boy any day.'

Next moment, Cuthbert had found the ball Rupert had hit into the bushes and rushed back, dropping it at Rupert's feet. Whereupon Jan lost it and fired an ace straight at Cuthbert, who squealed with pain as its force knocked him sideways.

'What the fuck did you do that for?' yelled Rupert. Dropping his racket, he gathered up Cuthbert. 'There, poor little boy, come to Daddy.'

'I thought we were playing singles, not doubles,' snapped Jan, who had totally abandoned his deferential manner.

357

'Come on, Cuthbert. I'll take him,' cried Gala, grabbing him from Rupert.

Returning to the baseline, Jan unleashed another rocket, then moved to the right-hand side and, after unleashing yet another, went towards Eddie's chair to change ends. Rupert, however, didn't shift. 'That was out.'

'I don't think so.' Jan had picked up a towel to wipe off non-existent sweat unlike the dripping Rupert.

'It was out.'

For a second the two men glared at each other.

'I think it was on the line,' giggled Eddie. 'You should have gone to Specsavers, Grandpa. First set and macho to Jan.'

The second set was turning into just as embarrassing a rout when Safety Car, who'd been plied with red wine by spectators, catching sight of his beloved master, trotted on the court to more screams of laughter, nudging Rupert in delight before having a long pee on the service line.

'Piss stopped play,' shouted Eddie, nearly falling off his chair.

Another service, hit into the trees by Rupert, was retrieved by Banquo who, returning it in the middle of a rally, dropped it at Rupert's feet.

Jan lost it. 'Are we playing tennis?' he yelled.

'Jan, Jan,' cried a voice.

It was Old Eddie, pushed in a wheelchair by Taggie, who'd been to see the foals. Now, taking a look at Jan and Rupert's furiously set faces, picking up the tension, she called with rare firmness, 'Eddie wants his supper, Jan.'

Old Eddie, catching sight of lots of female legs usually hidden by breeches, decided he didn't, and he'd rather watch some tennis.

'He's hungry,' insisted Taggie. 'I've lit the barbecue, and Valent rang from Beijing. He wants you to ring him soonest, Rupert.'

Rupert looked at Jan. 'We'd better call it a day.'

'Another time,' said Jan, balancing his rackets across the handles of Eddie's wheelchair, and stalking off.

Safety Car, having enjoyed another bowl of red wine, invaded the court again and kicked a few tennis balls before laying his head on Rupert's shoulder.

'You still have me.'

Rupert shook his head, and grinned at Taggie. 'You didn't tell me he was better than Federer.'

'I tried to warn you,' said Gav.

'I didn't,' said Eddie unrepentantly. 'He beats me every time. Just wait till the Legends race, then you can show him what an awesome rider you are.'

Rupert dropped a kiss on Safety Car's forehead. At that moment he decided to ride him. Gav had already been getting him fit in case Rupert wanted to hunt him. And it would be so nice for the old horse, who so loved crowds, to race again.

'I'm going to ride Safety,' he called out to Gav, then to the horse, 'but you'll have to give up the booze, old boy.'

'You sure that's wise?' said Gav. 'Owners are already lending other Legends some pretty serious horses. Isa's bound to ride something spectacular.'

'Safety can out-fox anyone.'

Once again the yard seethed with gossip.

'Wasn't Jan rude to Rupert.'

'Serving balls at Cuthbert,' agreed Dora. 'Showed his true colours. Remember how he beat up Gropius?'

Back at the house, Rupert told Taggie he was tempted to fire Jan. 'Bloody insubordinate. Could have killed Cuthbert.'

'Oh please not, he's so brilliant with your father and all the grandchildren. I'm sure normally you'd beat him. He was match fit while you'd just got off the plane. The light was awful.'

Rupert went out on the terrace. His staff were setting out for the Dog and Trumpet. God, he could kill for a drink. Cuthbert, who was sitting on his knee, growled as a voice said: 'I want to apologize, sir.'

It was Jan, back in cords and a dark-brown T-shirt. 'I'm afraid nerves got to me. Eddie said you were a great player. I got carried away, all those dogs invading the place. I didn't mean to be so rude. I'm sorry. Just lost my sense of humour.'

'Didn't know you had one,' said Rupert coldly.

Jan proved he had by laughing heartily. Then, as Rupert returned to his messages: 'Supper's ready.'

'I'm not hungry,' lied Rupert. He was damned if he'd accept anything from Jan.

'Just steak and salad – keep up your strength for the big race, sir, and you ought to put on a sweater. Enjoy your meal,' he urged Rupert, as he put a big plate of beef in front of him on the table.

'Is this your way of apologizing to my dogs?' Rupert peeled off a slice for Cuthbert. 'All right, apologies accepted, but don't ever touch them again.'

58

Gav helped Rupert by explaining that flat racing was exhausting.

'Jump racing's different; you can take a breather at fences. This will be flat literally out. You've got to be as still as possible to settle the horse, you need balance and calves of iron. When you move, squeeze with your legs and push with your arms and your whole body. You use your reins more; flat horses have much harder mouths and like to take up the bit.'

'I know all that.'

'I know, but you've never ridden in a flat race before.'

Rupert was far more preoccupied with a little chestnut two-year-old whom he'd recently bought in France. Appropriately called Delectable, she was as sweet and affectionate as Touchy Filly was snappy and permanently pre-menstrual. Rupert had entered her in a fillies race before the Legends race, about which he refused to give any interviews.

He was not unpleased, on arriving at Doncaster, however, to learn that he'd put an estimated 20,000 on the gate.

In the programme, John Sexton, the compère and a racing journalist, had described the Legends taking part as united by: 'a ravenous will to win, a competitive streak, a pride, a passion and a burning desire to succeed'.

'Not a million miles from Rupert,' observed Cathal.

Stars with a thousand winners under their belts, the Legends were euphoric to be back in the weighing room, experiencing the camaraderie and the banter, howling with laughter as cock-ups and triumphs of the past were recalled.

'D'you remember how Charlie held up the favourite by hanging on to its tail until we nearly fell off our horses laughing?'

The Doncaster valets, delighted to see old friends again, were busy sewing on buttons. No matter if the old kit was too tight or it took endless tugging and talcum powder to pull on old boots. The Legends were rightly proud of raising more than £100,000 for charity and having a chance to shine again.

''Tis not too late to seek a newer world.'

They were polite to Rupert when he came in to hang up his kit, but slightly irked by an outsider stealing their thunder. Rupert himself felt equally out of it, isolated from the ragging. He was very tired and just off another plane from the Keeneland sales. Never needing a bucketful of whisky more, he felt he had strayed into someone else's school reunion, particularly when he had to line up before the race for a group photograph and towered head and shoulders above the other Legends, a Great Dane among Jack Russells.

After weeks of sunshine, the rains had come with a suggestion of thunder, but nothing could dampen the spirits of the crowds on Legends Day. Doncaster was a beautiful course, a huge oval of fields and woods within the town.

Before the race, the Legends and their guests had been invited to a splendid lunch party in the hospitality block, whose roofs rose like whipped meringue. Sartorially the occasion was a challenge. Many of the ladies, excited that the Princess Royal would be present, despite the rain, had dolled up in high heels, hats and pretty dresses, only to find the sensible Princess had arrived hatless in flat boots and a warm woollen coat.

Apart from the race itself, the greatest challenge for the Legends was this party. Having wasted for weeks, desperate to psych themselves into a mood to annihilate their rivals, they were expected to sit down to a delectable fine-wine-fuelled lunch of seafood pâté, chicken poached in Madeira and frangipane tart, and then be charming to a myriad of admirers around them, giving the sponsors the chance to meet their idols.

Taggie, who'd donated her unworn Ascot hat to the auction, found herself at a table with Etta and awful Roddy and Enid Northfield, who was soon rabbiting on about 'damsires'.

On each table were envelopes for donations and iPads with which to bid.

'I can't work those things,' confessed Etta. 'I'll probably end up bidding millions of pounds by mistake.'

'I'll show you, Etta,' said Roddy, bolder because Valent was in China, taking her hands and placing them on the iPad.

'I'd like to bid for Fred Archer's whip,' said Dame Hermione, who was sitting at the next table with Cosmo, Mrs Walton, and Isa's boyish wife Marti, who looked at Taggie without warmth. And, oh help, there was Janey Lloyd-Foxe, at the same table as vile Brute Barraclough, who had been a very mediocre jump jockey to achieve Legends status.

'It's a very emotional day for me,' Janey was telling everyone. 'My darling husband Billy died of cancer.'

Brute kept dropping his race card or the programme as an excuse, when retrieving it, to bury his face in Janey's crotch. Meanwhile, down at the stables, poor Rosaria was getting his horse ready.

'Do you have horses?' Taggie asked the sponsor on her right.

'No, I have daughters.'

'Delicious chicken,' said Etta, amused to see Legends all round picking at their food, while their spuds were forked up by their larger wives.

'Where's Rupert?' demanded Dame Hermione, irritated by his empty place as was every other woman who wasn't hanging around the pre-parade ring for a first glimpse.

Rupert, in fact, had glanced inside the hospitality block, seen Cosmo, Dame Hermione and Janey at adjoining tables, and Roddy and Damsire at his own, and gone sharply into reverse, as had Isa.

'Typical bad manners,' thundered Roddy. 'All the sponsors have forked out to meet the Legends.'

Tommy Westerham, who'd notched up two Derbys and a St Leger as a jockey, having discovered that the sponsors to his right and left had no interest in buying horses, was reading about his exploits in the programme.

As people bid for next year's Cup Final tickets, visits to smart yards, lunch at Weatherbys boxes at Ascot and Taggie's big grey hat, every table was also being exhorted to put £20 notes into waiting envelopes as they tucked into frangipane tart. Rain was lashing down the windows. On the monitor, Rupert and Isa could be seen respectively saddling up their latest stars, Delectable and Jezebella, for the fillies' race.

Damsire, bored of Roddy doing a number on Etta, had swung round her chair to talk to Cosmo.

'Jezebella's definitely the standout in this race. She's a Roberto's Revenge, of course. I can't think of a stallion I'd rather put a mare to than Roberto.'

'I'd rather have a Joomper than a flat horse,' said a fat sponsor.

'The only joomper you're going to have,' said his even larger wife, 'is one round your neck.'

There were huge cheers as little chestnut Delectable, wearing blinkers for the first time, at Rupert's suggestion, hacked up in the fillies' race. Threading her way through a dozen other runners, she was ridden with great panache by Eddie, whose overjoyed blue eyes could be witnessed as, once the race was over, he shoved his goggles above the peak of his hat. Rupert was hugely pleased, particularly as Jezebella had come last.

'You must get changed,' Gav urged him. 'You've got to weigh out. Safety Car and Marketa are already in the pre-parade ring.'

But Rupert had been distracted by a row in the unsaddling enclosure.

Jezebella, Sheikh Baddi's latest extremely expensive purchase, had been running for the first time in his colours. The Sheikh, in a suit which glittered like a pale-grey moonlit sky, had assumed he'd go into the winners enclosure to welcome her home.

Jezebella had been ridden by Tarqui McGall, the go-to jockey, who because of his contumely had been jocked off by Isa and Cosmo, but who had been given a chance of a comeback in this race. On form, Tarqui ignited horses – but despite every effort, he couldn't galvanize Jezebella.

Leaping off her, turning to Isa, Cosmo, the Sheikh and his entourage, he yelled: 'This horse is focking useless! Isa, why are you wasting my time on such a focking awful yak?' which even Sheikh Baddi and his retinue, who included his second wife and daughters, understood.

'Not all Qatari on the Western Front,' grinned Rupert. As he sprinted towards the weighing room, he noticed how white were Isa's knuckles as he gripped Tarqui's muscular arm.

'That's the last horse,' Isa was telling him, 'you'll ride for me till you learn to behave.'

'What about the Leger?'

'Roman can have your ride, and you can bloody well apologize to Sheikh Baddi.'

'For not shifting a yak? Not bloddy likely.'

And Tarqui stalked off into the weighing room.

Rupert had only seconds to pull on breeches, boots and body protector.

'You need a body protector down to your ankles to guard you from those ravening women, dearie,' quipped his valet.

As he helped Rupert on with his blue and emerald silks and tied his hat ribbons, he reflected that Rupert had the perfect lean features for a helmet.

Pleased to weigh out at eleven stone, Rupert handed his saddle to Gav. Huge cheers greeted him as he sprinted down to join Gala, Bao and Marketa, who'd been leading up Safety Car, who was revelling in almost more applause than Rupert.

'I can't give myself instructions,' Rupert told them, 'so I'll leave it to Safety.'

Isa, having finished roasting Tarqui, was being legged up on to the magnificent dark brown Eumenides.

Only when Rupert mounted did he realize that the breast girth was missing. This was a second strap attached to the saddle and running round the horse's chest above his front legs to stop the saddle slipping back.

'Christ, where is it?' Rupert asked Marketa.

'I put it in the spares bag. I saw it there,' said Gala.

'So did I,' said Bao.

'Where the hell is it now? Someone must have stolen it.'

'Come on, Rupert,' said a steward, 'you're holding everyone up. We're running five minutes late.'

The other Legends had in fact got down to post earlier than usual because their calmly parading horses had leapt out of their skins when Dame Hermione launched into 'Here's to the Heroes'.

'Use her instead of starting stalls,' growled Tommy Westerham, desperately trying to stop his mare, Auntie Depressant, carting him. 'Put that horse whisperer Gary Witheford out of business.'

To watch the race, Gav and Gala decided to go down to the rail near the finish. From here they could see it on the big screen. To not lose her as he led her through the huge excited crowd, Gav took her hand. It felt nice, thought Gala, and a good way to make a first move. She was so nervous for Rupert, and Gav was such a calming influence on everyone.

Without the breast girth, feet out of the stirrups, Rupert hunted Safety down to the start. Irritated to be kept waiting, the other Legends were circling.

'Come on, Rupert,' yelled Tommy Westerham. 'You in the next race?'

'That's why they call him the "bank robber", because he holds everyone up,' sneered Brute.

Nerves had finally got to Rupert: mouth dry, legs trembling. As they lined up he could feel Safety also trembling, his heart pounding through his ribs.

'It's OK, boy, I'll take care of you,' and they were off.

Rupert kept as motionless as possible, but found it hard to balance on the little racing saddle at high speed. Safety Car's dinner-plate feet were soon raking up the divots. Like Quickly, not liking mud in his face, he surged forward, enjoying powering through other horses, overtaking first Tommy and then Brute, and Gay Kelleway, Mick Kinane, and Kevin Darley.

Isa and Eumenides were still ahead. Rupert gave Safety a pause as they turned the corner so the horse could take a big gulp of oxygen, and as they surged into the long home straight he could hear an explosion of cheering. The sun was in their faces but they were gaining on Isa's black shadow.

Rupert picked up his whip.

'Come on, Safety, we can do it, mustn't make our run too late.' Down came the whip again and again. As he drew level with Isa, he leaned forward, hissing in Safety's donkey ear. He must push harder and harder, helping Safety with the thrusts of his body. Whack, whack, thrust, thrust . . . they had left Isa behind.

The post loomed. 'Go for it, Safety. Bugger!' He'd lost an iron and with no breast girth to secure it, the tiny racing saddle lurched backwards and sideways. Safety's body seemed to give way beneath him like an earthquake, then as he tried to cling on, the girth itself appeared to snap. As the ground came up like a knock-out punch, he could hear the horrified screams of the crowd. Winded, utterly exhausted, he lay motionless, only aware, as the field came thundering past, of the smirk on a leading Isa's face.

'No, no,' screamed Gala, about to scramble over the spiky little hedge and rail and run to Rupert, when Gav grabbed her arm and slapped a hand over her mouth. When she tried to bite him, crying 'Lemme go!' he said in her ear, 'Shut up, just shut up. The press are everywhere. He's a married man, he's not free,' and clamped her against his body.

Then, as she wriggled to get away, kicking backwards, she was pre-empted by Safety Car who, having skidded to a halt, leaving great tracks of mud on the course, trotted back to nudge his master, gently breathing in his face, his white face splattered with mud. 'Please be OK.'

The crowd's screaming stopped instantly. 'Ah, ah, ah, how adorable.' There was a collective sigh of relief, as Rupert put his arms round Safety's neck and struggled groggily to his feet, clinging on as his knees gave way. The ambulance roaring up was followed by Taggie racing down the course.

'Darling, are you OK? You poor thing.'

'No, I'm bloody not. Someone stole my breast girth and must have cut the girth – this was a new saddle. I'm going to object. I'm perfectly OK,' he snapped as ambulancemen took both his arms.

Refusing any help, deathly pale, he insisted on walking a nudging Safety Car back to the parade ring, receiving ten times the applause of Isa the winner.

Applause which nearly drowned the ding, dong airport sound indicating a stewards' enquiry, orchestrated, horror of horrors, by his old enemy Roddy Northfield.

The race replayed in slow motion at the enquiry was like some danse macabre. As Rupert overtook Isa, his saddle unravelled and he crashed to the ground.

Roddy then had colossal pleasure in chucking any objection out of court.

'It's not the racecourse's fault you forgot your breast girth, and there's no indication the main girth's been cut. It just snapped.'

Then, as Rupert was about to argue his corner: 'I'm afraid we'll have to suspend you anyway, because you hit that poor old horse ten times. That's two over the limit. Such a pity, when he's been such a good servant to your yard.'

'I hardly tapped him,' said Rupert furiously. 'He didn't look very upset when he trotted back to me, did he?'

'There's nothing more to be said,' Roddy took a long drink of water, 'except at your age you ought to be a better loser.'

'I hardly tapped him,' repeated Rupert, adding, as he went towards the door, 'you must be fucking blind.'

'What's that, Campbell-Black?' called out Roddy.

'Fucking deaf too,' added Rupert.

Meanwhile a triumphant Cosmo bore Bao off to meet Dame Hermione, who was reading *Fifty Shades of Grey* for the third time.

'I have many fans in China,' she said, scribbling on Bao's race card, before dwarfing him in a selfie.

Having urged Cosmo to bid for Lester Piggott's whip, she was thrilled to hear that Rupert had got a whip ban.

'Has Rupert got any exciting new horses in his yard?' she asked.

'Only a Trojan one,' purred Cosmo. 'The enemy is within the gates.'

59

The only other casualty in the Legends race was Brute Barraclough, who was stretchered off with a broken finger.

'Must be the one he puts in the till,' observed Cathal.

Unaccountably, the envelope of £20 notes had disappeared from Brute and Janey's table.

Despite Taggie's pleas for him to come home and take it easy, Rupert insisted on flying straight off to the foal sales in America, saying he'd be back to watch Quickly in the St Leger.

Returning to Doncaster's Robin Hood airport on Saturday morning, he found a crowd hanging round a communal television watching a clip of himself on *The Morning Line*. This clip was followed by one of the Stubbs of Rupert Black – what in hell was that doing there? – followed by a clip of new poster boy, go-to jockey Eddie Alderton, winning on Delectable. The programme was being transmitted from Doncaster Racecourse, now empty but which would be filled to bursting in a few hours.

By the time Rupert had sprinted into earshot, the camera had switched to Young Eddie in a sky-blue shirt lounging on a purple sofa. He was giving a history lesson to Nick Luck, Mick Fitzgerald and David Williams, Media Director of Ladbrokes, who sponsored the Leger and – good God! – Sauvignon in the shortest orange shift. She'd been placed at the end of the sofa, so her glorious Saluki legs were not hidden by that console at which presenters kept jabbing away to pick out individual horses.

Anyone would be consoled by Sauvignon's legs. But Rupert was singularly unamused that Young Eddie hadn't shaved and was wearing a Master Quickly baseball cap on the side of his head. Perhaps he was trying to look like a teacher as he carried on his history lesson.

'My Great-great-great-quadrupled-grandpop and great trainer Rupert Black won the St Leger with a fantastic horse, Third Leopard, back in the Dark Ages. Today I'm gonna try and win the same race for his descendant, my grandfather, and an even greater trainer, Rupert Campbell-Black, with an even more fantastic horse, Master Quickly,' followed by a clip of Quickly looking goofy with a mouthful of geraniums.

There was a pause, as Nick Luck was momentarily distracted by Sauvignon's slo-mo uncrossing of her legs. Then he asked: 'You fancy Quickly's chances?'

'You bet. If Quickers gets out of bed the right side nothing'll beat him.'

Mick Fitzgerald, also dragging his eyes away from Sauvignon's legs, was jabbing at the console. Up came a clip of I Will Repay, surging out of a pack of horses.

'Quickly saw off Repay in the Guineas and the King George,' went on Eddie, 'quite different trips. He likes Yorkshire. One of his owners, Valent Edwards, is very well known here. Quickly's beautifully bred. His mother won the Grand National.'

Nick Luck turned to Sauvignon.

'I'm sure no one knows I Will Repay better than Sauvignon Smithson, who looks after him.'

'Lucky I Will Repay,' sighed Eddie.

The Panel tried not to laugh.

'How is he?' asked Nick Luck.

'He's well,' drawled Sauvignon, who'd obviously been coached, 'a pleasure to look after – a real gentleman; he looks great in his skin.'

'So do you,' said Eddie.

'Hush,' smiled Nick Luck.

Such were the impeccable manners of the *Morning Line* team, they didn't pull Sauvignon up when she then produced one howler after another, saying I Will Repay was 'six hands', the height of a Shetland pony and that he might run in the National next year.

'My governor, Isa Lovell,' she continued, 'who beat Eddie's Guv in the Legends race . . .'

'Because his saddle slipped,' snapped Eddie, then relented. 'The only reason Repay might beat Quickers is because he can't bear to be parted from Sauvignon, and will race like mad to get back to her.'

Sauvignon smiled slightly. God, she was sexy. With her dark shiny hair drawn back in a pony tail, you could appreciate the mesmeric heavy-lidded yellow eyes, and the full sensual lips. Eddie suddenly realized Nick Luck was speaking to him.

'That was a nasty fall. Is Rupert OK?'

'I guess. He flew straight off to the States. He is so tough.'

'Must be pleased – you're having a great season.'

'Who do you think are the greatest challenges to I Will Repay?' asked Mick Fitzgerald.

Sauvignon hadn't a clue, so Eddie came to her rescue. 'Quickly, of course. Geoffrey, Mobile Charger, Nuit de Josephine – that filly's tougher than Grandpa. But you don't tell mares what to do, you ask them.' He smiled at Sauvignon, who at the end of the programme turned to him and said there was a party after the Leger, and would he like to come?

Eddie hardly had time to be excited to be invited, particularly because Rupert, after the drubbing he'd got after the Legends race – 'Rupert Tumble-Black' – was refusing to talk to the press. Eddie therefore was interviewed all morning and found it hard to concentrate on the race ahead.

Quickly, Bitsy and Purrpuss had travelled up to Doncaster in the morning, so Quickly wouldn't have the stress of sleeping in a strange box. The lorry left at 6.30 a.m. and arrived at 9.45 a.m. so it was like any other day.

The trees, less advanced and greener as they drove north, seemed to bend over the road and kiss each other. Willowherb feathered, bracken browned, docks reddened on the verges.

Bao and Marketa slept, Cathal and Bobby, who was driving, raved on about Sauvignon, Gala thought about Gav and how he'd stopped her racing out to a fallen Rupert. Dora regaled everyone with snippets.

'Did you know there was a horse that ran in the Leger called Sweet But Naked? Never get that past Weatherbys today.' Then as they drove through a town called Coleshill she went into fits of laughter. 'This is the origin of my favourite limerick:

> There was a young lady of Coleshill,
> Who sat herself down on a molehill.
> An inquisitive mole put his nose up her hole,
> Miss Coleshill's all right, but the mole's ill.'

Everyone laughed, but Gala found she couldn't stop – and then she started to cry.

'Oh God,' she said as Gav put an arm round her. 'I'm sorry, I'm just so desperate for Quickly to win. Rupert needs a boost after the Legends and Valent's so keen to succeed in his own county.'

She wanted to look good when she led Quickly up, but how, after a sleepless fretting night, could she ever compete with Sauvignon?

A vast crowd of 50,000 had gathered for the St Leger. They know how to party in Yorkshire. Sitting round gold tables which glittered in the sunshine, the women dressed up, showing off a glorious amount of tanned flesh.

'Sweet When Half-Naked,' observed Dora.

Red oblong Ladbrokes flags fluttered in the breeze, and as race followed race, the cheering grew more raucous, with huge heartening applause for each winner. In the weighing room, sixteen jockeys were getting ready for the oldest and final classic. Jealous perhaps of his starring with Sauvignon on *The Morning Line*, the other jockeys except Meerkat, who was riding Bitsy, ignored Eddie.

Etta and Valent had a quick drink in the bar before the race.

'The horse that comes last in the St Leger has frost on its tail,' quoted Valent, 'because it signifies the beginning of winter.'

'How romantic,' sighed Etta. 'I wonder if I should have brought the geraniums in. Oh dear, we're into Christmas already,' she added as Santa Claus rode by on an ostrich.

'He's got more chance than Quickly,' sneered a passing Cosmo.

In the parade ring, the band played as lads in suits and ties led up the runners. I Will Repay and Sauvignon in the tightest black jeans and a cream silk shirt were followed by a chorus of wolf whistles. Geoffrey, slopping along beside Rosaria, looked half asleep, unlike Quickly who was leaping all over the place, snatching Valent's carnation, flashing his cock as he again tried to mount the French filly Nuit de Josephine.

'Why don't you give her your card, Quickers, and say you'll meet her next year in the covering barn,' chided Gala, as the crowd admired the white rose of Yorkshire she had brushed on his quarters.

'That's a nice touch – thank you, Gala,' said Valent.

The crowd, having enjoyed Eddie on *The Morning Line*, were disappointed when he missed the parade and to stop Quickly getting more het-up, took him down early to the start.

Here it was very quiet and rural. Only after a furlong or two could you glimpse a house. A lot of spectators, however, had gathered there – including a man with a Collie.

'Nice dog,' observed Eddie, as he walked Quickly round.

'Concen-fucking-trate,' snapped Gav. 'If you don't beat I Will Repay, you'll have to walk home. Win it – and Love Rat'll take over Leading Sire.'

And once again Eddie realized the magnitude of his task, how much it meant to Gav and Gala, Rupert and all the yard who'd backed him. If he won, Sauvignon might even come out with him. He mustn't screw up.

The St Leger takes no prisoners. It is played out on a big open galloping track with a long, long straight. By 3.40 the ground had been cut up by earlier runners, and the crowds were getting rowdier. Soon Meerkat and Bitsy, whickering with joy to see Quickly, had joined them.

'If Quickly's on his own at the end,' Gav told Meerkat, 'try and keep up with him, so he's got something to race.'

Now in the stalls, Eddie was raking Quickly's lustrous mane; Geoffrey next door was so relaxed he was nodding off. Eddie caught a whiff of aftershave from Manu de la Tour, riding Josephine on the other side . . . and then they were off to a massive roar, gallant Bitsy setting a cracking pace as Quickly streaked after him. They were soon leading the field by six lengths, scorching past the row of conifers, past the rain-darkened woods, down Rose Hill – quite a steep slope – swinging round the corner. Eddie knew they were on a roll. Quickly had never felt better. Ahead lay the long, long straight.

'C'mon, Quickers.' Eddie didn't even need to pick up a whip as they overtook Bitsy. Glancing round, he saw Repay was challenging but couldn't get near him. Eddie gave a Tarzan whoop: ahead lay the line and a multitude bellowing him home.

'Oh my God!' screamed Gala, hi-fiving Marketa. 'He's going to do it!'

Eddie was so overjoyed he stood up in his stirrups 100 yards from the post, punching the air with one hand, the other brandishing his whip. Next moment, something so scared Quickly, he leapt to the left in panic, as though he'd seen a ghost or been bitten by a snake, and Eddie, losing his balance, crashed to the ground. The deafening roar stopped like a power failure in utter silence, followed by screams of horror as a terrified Quickly hurtled round the track again, past the conifers, and a sobbing Gala chased after him.

I Will Repay and Ash six lengths behind took the race. Geoffrey was second, Josephine third.

Cosmo turned to Mrs Walton in triumph.

'This is the way the Campbell-Blacks ride,' he sang, 'gallopy, gallopy, gallopy and *down* into the mud.'

Ash, riding back in Sheikh Baddi's purple and gold colours, was in heaven.

'It does make it easier for the rest of us,' he told Emma Spencer, 'when Penscombe jockeys can't stay on their horses. I guess both Rupert and Eddie should take some riding lessons.'

Rupert, never one to worry about living in glass houses, bawled Eddie out.

'You stupid little fucker, you little rat, how many times have I told you to get over the line! You've utterly fucked Love Rat's chances, and Gav and Gala who've put so much work into Quickly, and Valent and Etta, and Quickly himself as a stallion prospect.'

'I'm sorry, Rupert, I'm sorry,' Eddie stammered, 'but something in the crowd spooked Quickly.'

Valent was even angrier. 'You've wrecked the stud career of a great horse, you've broken Etta's heart, you'll bloody well sell that puke-green Ferrari and pay back the staff.'

'OK, OK, I'm sorry, but Quickly was got at.'

'Only by you.'

'Please, Rupert,' implored Taggie. 'Something must have frightened Quickly.'

But in the play-back, nothing could be seen except Quickly shying violently, which could have been caused by Eddie leaping up and waving his whip.

For a devastated Eddie, who got booed all the way back to the weighing room, the only solution would have been to get legless with Sauvignon, but he received a very pointed text from her instead.

'Sorry can't make it, we're off to celebrate.'

Ash was over the moon. In gratitude, Sheikh Baddi had given him a new BMW.

Immediately after the St Leger, Rupert flew back to Keeneland and to the sales. On the way to the airport, along one of Doncaster's most prosperous roads, he passed numerous retirement homes, and felt tempted to dispatch Young Eddie to one. Instead he called Tarqui McGall.

'Not a great Doncaster for either of us. How would you like to come and work for me?'

'It's a deal, let's nail the fockers.'

'When can you start?'

'As soon as possible.'

'I'll need you to take horses abroad. You got a contract?'

'Cosmo doesn't do contracts. He owes me last month's salary. What about young Alderton?'

'You'll be stable jockey.'

'And Gav's not my greatest fan.'

'I'll sort Gav.'

'I've got a girlfriend and a baby on the way.'

'That's OK. Should reassure Gav.'

'If I were you, I'd approach Harmony at the same time. She's bloody good and absolutely gutted with Sauvignon taking all the credit.'

'She's too fat.'

'She's lost a lot of weight, and Repay'd go into a decline if she left. Tanks, Rupert.'

Someone, however, had hacked into Rupert's mobile. Within an hour, it was all over the internet that Tarqui was moving to Penscombe.

POACHED EGO shouted the *Post*, predicting Titanic clashes between Rupert and Tarqui.

Isa was absolutely furious. As Tarqui's long-term lover, he had tolerated the girlfriend and baby on the way. Nobody galvanized horses like Tarqui, and Isa needed to play him off against Ash.

Young Eddie was devastated. He was utterly mortified. He'd screwed up the Leger, enabling Roberto's Revenge to gallop further and further out of reach of Love Rat, and he'd been blown out by Sauvignon. However, he bit the bullet and didn't walk out, because the thing he wanted most in the world was Rupert's approval.

Back home, Gav and Gala watched the Leger again and again. Something *had* terrified Quickly, but beyond a slight bruise on his neck on the stands side, nothing could be detected.

60

Morale was rock bottom at Penscombe after the Leger. Matters weren't helped by Tarqui's arrival.

Lover of Isa and some time of Bethany, a relentless seducer of both sexes, Tarqui the go-to jockey who never rode work or went to Wolverhampton on a cold Monday morning, had recently settled more or less down with his girlfriend Tresa and was quite chuffed she was expecting his baby. Capricious, dissolute, histrionic, Tarqui was also very expensive.

He was furious that Rupert, before flying off to Canada, had issued instructions that he should rise early and ride several lots a day to familiarize himself with the horses. Tarqui proceeded to gee them all up, wielding his whip on the gallops, reducing little Delectable, who'd never been hit, to a jelly, insisting Quickly wore a painful new noseband to stop him bolting, even demoralizing the sweet, phlegmatic Fleance, who always tried his hardest and more.

Tarqui was particularly insensitive towards Gav, ostensibly now his boss.

'Is his divorce through yet?' he demanded from the back of a sweating, eye-rolling, plunging Quickly. 'Who's the tramp shacked up with now?'

'Shut up, Gav'll hear you,' hissed Gala. 'And unless you want to end up on the moon, don't smack Quickly any more.'

'This horse is totally feral,' snapped Tarqui, as he slid to the

377

ground. 'Old Floppy Dick's as useless at training horses as he was in bed.'

'Don't be so foul.' To her horror Gala found she had slapped Tarqui's face really hard. With her fingermarks crimsoning his sallow cheeks, Tarqui spat that it was not just the horses who were feral round here. A shouting match escalated, with Tarqui complaining to Rupert the moment he returned from Keeneland and Rupert promptly summoning Gala to his office.

'What the hell are you playing at?'

'How could you bring in that arrogant, insensitive, vicious little twat?' stormed Gala. 'He's undoing all Gav's brilliant work with the horses. Delectable's gone to pieces, he hit Touchy Filly round the head because she bit him, Fleance doesn't need hitting and Quickly nearly choked to death trying to breathe in that cross noseband. And he's bloody tactless, making no secret he's an on-off lover of Bethany.'

'Everyone's an on-off lover of Bethany.'

'Gav's so stoic, he doesn't need his nose rubbed in it. You'll lose him or drive him to drink.'

Since when had Gala got so protective about Gav?

'This place needs stirring up,' said Rupert angrily.

'It wouldn't if you spent more time here.'

'Since when did you start calling the shots? If you're not happy, get out.'

Gala gave a sob and fled from the room.

'Shall I draft an email giving her notice?' said a delighted Geraldine.

'No, wait till I get back from France. Hell,' he added, looking up at the stallion leg-waving clock. He'd have to leave in half an hour. 'Must go and see Tag.'

In the old days he'd have whisked her upstairs for a quick fuck, and he loathed leaving the dogs, who couldn't believe he was off again.

'You have upset the boss,' gloated Geraldine to Gala. 'He's asked me to draft an email giving you notice. How long have you worked in the yard?'

The only person lower than Gala was Eddie, who should have been on the helicopter to ride Petruchio, and Chekov in

Deauville. Nor would he ride Quickly in the Champion Stakes. And Fleance was off with Marketa to Newmarket, to go into quarantine before the Melbourne Cup, with Tarqui riding him. Suddenly, Eddie realized how much he'd been looking forward to seeing Lark again in Australia.

'Why the hell am I lusting after that bitch Sauvignon?' he asked Gala, as during a sweltering hot lunch-break at Lime Tree Cottage, some days later, they pondered what to do with the rest of their lives.

Next moment, Dora rolled up looking very fetching in a pale-grey denim shirt and shorts.

'How are you both?'

'About to be fired.'

'Well, you'd better come to a party tonight.'

'Where is it?' asked Eddie listlessly.

'Valhalla.' Dora rolled her eyes. 'Cosmo's giving an Indian Summer fancy dress party, which is bound to deteriorate. His father's orgies were legendary. The police once turned up to complain about the noise and were soon shagging everything in sight. Lady Chiselden, a local JP, got off with a man dressed as a pantomime donkey, only to discover after a two-hour session in the broom cupboard that her seducer was Rannaldini's gardener. Here's the invite.'

Dora waved a card on which were printed the words: *Cosmo Rannaldini requests the pleasuring. Please dress for chess.*

'So everyone's going as chess pieces: kings, queens, castles, bishops, pawns and things. I'm sure most people will dress up as porn stars or pawnbrokers. Oh, come on, it'll be a laugh.'

'I hate fancy dress,' said Gala.

'Well, come as you are. I know Isa won't bother with it.'

'Isa! God, Rupert would kill us.'

'He won't know as he's not back from Tattersalls Ireland till tomorrow. You'll die laughing when you see what I'm wearing.'

'I would like to see Valhalla,' said Gala. 'It's medieval.'

'It's very fuck-off,' said Dora, adding slyly, 'Sauvignon's going as a bishop, so you can unfrock her, Eddie, and get to meet Roberto's Revenge. They're sure to parade him.'

'That would be something. OK, let's go,' said Gala.

Eddie shrugged. 'I guess one might as well get drunk at some-one else's expense.'

'Shall we try and take Gav?' suggested Gala.

'Not a hope,' said Eddie. 'Doesn't drink, hates parties. Cosmo and Isa fired him and Bethany might be there.'

Bao, still anxious to convince Gala that China was an animal-loving nation, offered to dogsit Gropius.

As Gala was leaving Lime Tree Cottage, Gav rang.

'Please don't go, they're evil.'

'As opposed to medi-eval. I want to case the joint.'

'You'll get plenty of those. Evil things happen there. If you have any problems, ring and I'll come and get you.'

As he'd sold his beloved green Ferrari, Eddie drove to the orgy in Dora's Golf. Even on a beautiful, very hot September evening, the great abbey, lurking behind its conspirator's cloak of woodland, looked sinister.

'Are there any ghosts?'

'A former Lord of the Manor evidently surprised his young wife in bed with the local blacksmith,' confided Dora. 'Fleeing on his horse, the blacksmith was strangled by some overhanging cables of Old Man's Beard. Villagers often hear the clattering of ghost hooves, and horses spook and refuse to go down that lane.'

'Horrible,' shivered Gala.

'Staff in the house catch glimpses of the heartbroken young wife and hear her weeping, but women are always weeping at Valhalla, and particularly when Cosmo's father was alive. It's a pretty spooky house, full of priest-holes and secret passages.'

'Now you tell us,' grumbled Gala, giving a shriek as, turning the corner, they found the main gates swarming with photographers. 'Hurry, Eddie, please. Rupert will kill us if he finds out.' She pulled a copy of *Racing Post* over her head as long lenses closed in on the windows.

'Slow down, or they won't get any decent pics. These are the big time,' pleaded Dora, waving happily. 'Hi, guys. There's Richard Young and George Selwyn . . . I'm fine, how are you? And Dan Abraham. Hello, Dan. That's why I'm not changing into my fancy dress till we get there, or they'd never recognize me.'

Valhalla, in fact, was looking wonderful, the sun slanting in just the right direction on the park and its shaggy woods, the flowerbeds full of roses with no weeds, unlike Penscombe. Below, like a huge python waiting to swallow you up, coiled the yew hedges of the maze. A full orchestra was belting out *The Rite of Spring*. Carrying on the theme of 'Dress for Chess', Cosmo had laid out a 30-yard by 30-yard chessboard on the lawn. Guests armed with large glasses of champagne were already playing against each other. Kings and Queens proliferated. Ash had dressed up in full drag as the young Queen Victoria. Cosmo, his curls brushed off his forehead and down the sides of his face, had come as an old queen: Oscar Wilde. Bishops, castles, knights and pawns and predictably porn stars abounded. Tommy Westerham, who couldn't stop laughing, had come as a pawnbroker, his testicles plus a third one attached, painted gold. Chas Norville had donned a horse's head, and was telling everyone between neighs: 'I'm Sir Roger de Covering Yard.'

Mrs Walton, who in anticipation had spent a week at Champneys, was showing off red ribbons round each sun-tanned thigh.

'I'm the Knight of the Garters.'

Young Eddie had boldly rolled up as a porn star in just a leopardskin thong, brandishing a whip, which frightfully excited Dame Hermione.

'You are so like your grandfather, Eddie,' she told him. 'I do hope you'll test that whip on me later.'

Dressed as the Queen of the Night, she then launched into an ear-splitting flood of Mozart.

Dora, meanwhile, caused complete hysterics by emerging from the Ladies as Lester Bolton, Willowwood's dreadful porn millionaire, in a too tight shiny suit and orange comb-over draped across a rubber skull.

'That should deter any letches until Paris arrives later,' she told Gala. 'They made a film of *Don Carlos*, the opera, here, and based the big drawing room on the Throne Room at Buckingham Palace.' This had entailed cherry-red walls, and gilded mirrors down to the ground.

Huge amounts of drink and drugs were being consumed, but

there was no sign of supper yet, although in the Great Hall next door, coloured cushions were scattered round low tables. People were openly snogging and beginning to undress each other. Drunken games on the chessboard were being accompanied by cries of 'Checkmate!' as people charged off into the bushes.

'You look so like Lester Bolton, Dora,' a passing beauty giggled. 'I can't believe you're not going to grope me.'

Up in the minstrels' gallery above the ballroom a small orchestra was playing Ravel's *Bolero*, minus the flautist who, armed with binoculars, was gazing out of the window behind him on to a lawn below, where a blond youth was snorting up a long line of coke from the flat belly of a comely brunette.

'Good thing Gav didn't come,' Dora whispered to Gala. 'That's his ex, Bethany.'

The place was awash with beautiful young people, Cosmo's friends.

'Mrs Walton must feel as if she's giving a children's party,' added Dora.

61

Gala felt completely outclassed. If only she'd washed her hair and bothered with something more appealing than a black shift which, since she'd been up since five, matched the shadows under her eyes. Was she being paranoid, or did she note several female guests clocking with satisfaction that the woman seen kissing Rupert so ecstatically after the King George was nothing to text home about? Dora and Eddie had vanished. One man she talked to slid away the moment another man joined them, and after two minutes, the second man slid away too: 'Must go and check on my wife.'

If no one had talked to her at parties when she was married, she could always join Ben. She realized once again how sheltered she was at Penscombe, with people always around to combat her loneliness, and Gav and Eddie looking after her, and Rupert to dream about. Oh God, she hoped he wasn't going to find out she was here.

'Hel-aire, hel-aire.'

There was a din at the front door as Famous Grouse and Damsire swept in.

But Roddy was going to find nothing to grouse about this evening. He was wearing a check suit, check tie and check shirt, with Damsire in a check patterned dress.

'We're checkmates, ha, ha, ha.'

Both were also clad in an air of self-congratulation, aware

they were the oldest people there, but invited because, 'We get on so well with the young.'

'Don't think I've ever seen you without your red trousers, Roddy,' said Mrs Walton.

'Roddy, Roddy, great to see you.' Cosmo glided up and led them into the morning room, thrusting huge glasses of champagne into their hands, showing off the beautiful silver and gold St Leger Plate won by I Will Repay, which was now filled with giant prawns and oysters.

'Pity we can't drink Krug out of it,' quipped Cosmo. 'Not a good Doncaster for the Campbell-Blacks or Love Rat.' He raised his glass to Roddy. 'Thank you for seeing off the King in the Legends race.'

'Terrible loser,' boomed Roddy, scooping up a handful of prawns.

'He's a loser,' purred Cosmo. 'Revenge is so far ahead, Love Rat will never catch him.'

The orchestra was playing *Prince Igor*.

'Hold my gland,' sang Cosmo, 'I'm a stranger in Paradise. I hope you're both going to behave very badly, Enid.'

Gala looked at her watch. If only she could go home. She escaped into the big drawing room. There was Sauvignon wearing a dog collar and a black cassock, shiny dark hair drawn back, yellow eyes matching her gold chasuble, black lashes falling on flawless cheekbones. Surrounded by a group, she had positioned herself in front of one of the long gilt mirrors so she could admire her own reflection while checking if anyone more interesting was behind her.

Gala went to the window to watch the game on the huge chessboard.

'Hi, Gala.' Casting aside her entourage, Sauvignon joined her. 'Do you play chess?'

'Not very well.'

'Chess,' said Sauvignon, 'is a war game between two armies who line up and face each other. The aim is to take out your opponent's King.'

'I know that.'

'Look at that little pawn, Ruth's daughter Milly, surreptitiously creeping up the chessboard to the opposite end. If she gets there, she becomes a second white Queen, a rival to the Queen *in situ*.'

'I'd forgotten that rule.'

'You surprise me,' mocked Sauvignon. 'Wouldn't you love to become Queen of Penscombe?'

'Don't be ridiculous.' Gala was blushing furiously.

'We all saw you enjoying a terrific snog with Rupert after the King George.'

'That was euphoria, a victory hug.'

'Much more than that, surely. Wouldn't you like to take Taggie's place and run things better?'

Hypnotized by the knowing yellow eyes, by the tongue snaking lasciviously over Sauvignon's lower lip, Gala stammered, 'Of course not. Taggie's a darling who runs the place brilliantly. She holds everything together.'

'That figures.' Sauvignon smiled evilly. 'The Queen is the most powerful piece on the board; she can move in any direction to threaten or capture. Unlike the King, who appears all-powerful, but is actually the weakest character, the most vulnerable; he can only move one square at a time. But if he's not successfully defended, all is lost – like King Rupert.'

'That's bollocks, you could hardly call Rupert weak. You seem to know a lot more about chess than you did about I Will Repay on *The Morning Line*.'

For a second an expression of hatred spread across Sauvignon's face. Her eyes were the colour of amber traffic-lights, warning: *caution, don't go there*. At the same moment the cassock fell open, showing large bare breasts.

'Hel-aire, hel-aire.' It was Damsire and Mrs Walton.

'We were talking about Rupert,' said Sauvignon silkily.

'How is the dear chap?' asked Mrs Walton, her oiled shoulders gleaming in the fading light. 'He's always pestering me to dine with him and bring an overnight bag.'

'That's just to wind up Cosmo,' said Gala rudely.

'Unkind.' Mrs Walton raised a plucked eyebrow.

'Rupert was an ex of mine,' countered Damsire. 'Roddy's madly jealous. I don't know how Taggie puts up with him.'

'They're fine, they adore each other. I see them all the time. Oh look,' Gala paused in mid-rant, 'here comes Roberto's Revenge. Isn't he beautiful!'

'Just like Rupert,' murmured Mrs Walton, as they all surged out on to the terrace.

As Harmony led Roberto's Revenge up the gravel path between the big lawn and the house, chess players stopped fooling around, couples uncoupled, castles glided up, bishops slid diagonally, knights jumped and emerged from bushes, dancers left the floor and their drinks.

All were marvelling over the stallion's priapic splendour, every dark-brown muscle rippling, barrel-chested, powerful-quartered, noble head with the same upside-down L-shaped blaze as I Will Repay, gold nameplate on his head collar glittering in the setting sun, which was just hanging round to bid a fellow superstar goodnight. Harmony only kept him in check by a savage chain bit. As he reared up, punching the air, screaming and whinnying, his audience broke into applause.

'Ladies and gentlemen,' Cosmo had seized a microphone, 'meet the Leading Sire, Roberto's Revenge.'

'What a magnificent beast,' boomed Roddy. 'How can he not keep the title for years to come?'

'Slightly up behind,' observed Damsire, and received an icy look from Cosmo, who pointed out that this year, Revenge had covered a phenomenally strong book of mares, and had turned away thousands.

'One of his head collars sold at auction for £30,000 this week. Ode to Awesome, one of his mares in foal, went for four million dollars.'

'Is he going to the southern hemisphere?' called out Damsire.

'Far too valuable for that, particularly as one of his progeny, I Will Repay, has just won the Derby and the St Leger,' followed by more applause.

'All right, on with the party,' Cosmo laughed. 'Let the sun go down like everyone else.'

Gala wanted to scream out that Quickly would have left Repay for dead, if Eddie hadn't screwed up. Then glancing round, she saw Eddie's stricken face as he watched Revenge clip, clop back to the stud. Seeing Gala was talking to Sauvignon, he nearly came over then retreated into the house.

'Pity about Roberto's handler,' said Sauvignon, pulling a naked waiter towards her by his cock, so he could fill up her glass. 'That fat frump lowers the tone. She ought to wear a burka to lead him up, although she'd need a marquee.'

It irritated the hell out of Sauvignon that Cosmo refused to sack Harmony in case Repay and Revenge went into decline.

'Evidently she's brilliant at massaging bad backs,' said Mrs Walton.

'At least in that way, one wouldn't have to look at her face,' mocked Sauvignon.

'If I don't eat soon,' said Roddy, twanging one of Mrs Walton's garters, 'I'll fall over. Oh good.' His turbot mouth watered, as great platters of lobster, crab and stuffed sea bass were borne by the nude waiters towards the Great Hall.

There was a further kerfuffle as Janey Lloyd-Foxe, looking really good in a gold dress and little diamond tiara, walked in.

'Janey,' said Cosmo, kissing her. 'You look marvellous – who are you meant to be?'

'Queen Astrid of the Nether Regions,' giggled Janey. 'I'm not wearing any pants.'

'So you aren't.' Cosmo's hand disappeared under her skirt.

Janey was followed by a large man in a gorilla onesie.

'This is Colin Chalford, he's come as King Kong. We could have come as Elephant and Castle, but I couldn't think how to dress up as a castle. Colin, this is your host, Cosmo Rannaldini.' The gorilla pushed back his head and a great red, roaring-with-laughter face emerged.

Gala leapt behind a curtain. If Janey saw her, she'd be bound to sneak to Rupert and Taggie.

'Pleased to meet you, Cosmo, thank you for asking me,' said Colin, who was gazing amazed at the cavorting couples, and the naked waiter who shimmied up with the St Leger Plate groaning now with slices of foie gras.

'Colin has led a very sheltered life,' giggled Janey.

'I must say I'm very hot in this kit,' panted Colin.

'You can take it off and have a dip later,' said Cosmo.

'Great you won the Leger and the Legends,' said Janey. 'Rupert must be incandescent, losing them both.'

'Descent is the operative word.'

'And Geoffrey was second, so Brute's very happy,' added Janey.

As Brute Barraclough walked in, very much in character as King Lear and already salivating at the talent on show, he was followed by Rosaria who looked even more washed-out than usual.

As Janey introduced them both to the gorilla, Dora drew Gala aside, whispering, 'That Janey Lloyd-Foxe is a worse bitch than Sauvignon. The poor guy dressed as a gorilla met her on the internet. He's looking for love and thinks she's legit, and doesn't realize she's doing a piece for the *Scorpion* on meeting different men online.'

'That's awful,' exploded Gala, 'he looks sweet,' then, as Colin bellowed with laughter, 'and determined like Jan to prove his G.S.O.H.'

'Evidently he's very rich, so I expect vile Brute will try and persuade him to buy some horses.'

As he looked round, Brute Barraclough, muttering how he must try and track down Sheikh Baddi about some deal, disappeared into the throng. A minute later, having furnished Colin and Rosaria with large drinks, and pecked Colin on his red sweating cheek, Janey murmured, 'Must go and network for a bit. I'll leave you two lovely people together,' and followed Brute into the throng.

62

Escaping through a side door, passing copulating couples and threesomes, Gala ran past the yard down to the stud.

Overhead, a very white moon looked wistfully from a still blue sky. 'Why don't you join the party?' Gala called up to her. She found Harmony settling Roberto's Revenge for the night. If she could get Harmony to show her around, she could report on the latest equipment to Rupert.

'Isn't he beautiful?' Gala put out a hand, but the stallion flattened his ears.

'Don't touch him,' cried Harmony. 'I'm the only person Vengie likes.'

'I'm the same with Titus,' countered Gala. 'I'm the only person he doesn't bite.'

Feeling guilty because she'd run off and not comforted Harmony when she was crying because she'd been ousted by Sauvignon before the Derby, Gala had brought Harmony a present.

'This is for you.'

She handed Harmony a box containing a brooch of a galloping silver horse with a jockey on its back.

'Oh thank you,' said Harmony, looking as though she'd been kissed under the mistletoe for the first time. 'It's absolutely lovely. No, you can't have it,' she added to a nudging Vengie. 'You don't know if it's a filly,' and with shaking hands she pinned

389

the brooch on her green T-shirt, so it looked as though it was galloping across a vast fertile plain.

'It's so lovely, very like Quickly – thank you, Gala. I'm so sorry about the Leger. Poor Eddie must have been devastated.'

'He wanted to make history,' said Gala.

'Hum.' Harmony opened her big pale mouth, then shut it, then glanced out over the half door. 'Have you watched the video?'

'A million times, but the camera's not on the crowd. Something must have spooked him.'

'I shouldn't be telling you this, but were there any marks on Quickly's neck?' Then, when Gala nodded: 'See if you can get a clip of the crowd.'

'We were so distraught at the time, we didn't notice anything.'

'Well, watch out. Cosmo and Isa have it in for Rupert, particularly since Tarqui was poached.'

The music and the yells of, 'Checkmate!' were getting louder.

'It's like the Ritz here,' said Gala, looking round the stud. 'Who's bankrolling Cosmo?'

But Harmony felt she had already said too much. 'I'd better feed Vengie.'

As Gala returned to the party, the moon had turned yellow in a paler blue sky and the orchestra were alternating pop music with a pulsatingly sexual beat, with jazzed-up classical music, which Gav would have recognized. Gala so wished he were here.

Meanwhile, Cosmo was talking to Dora.

'Isa's missing Tarqui, how's he getting on?'

'Upsetting everyone, winding up the horses, set back Quickly a thousand years.'

Cosmo laughed. 'Still working for us then.'

'It seems so, and he's so bloody to poor Gav. He said, in his hearing, that he was as lousy at training horses as he was in bed. Gala was so furious, she slapped Tarqui's face.'

'Really?' Cosmo's eyes gleamed. 'So she's got the hots for Floppy Dick as well as Rupert.'

'Stop stirring it – Gav's her friend. I must go and see if she's OK.'

'She was fratting just now with Harmony, down at the stud.'

On her way back from the stud, in order not to make herself too conspicuous, Gala climbed through a ground-floor window, into an office with a picture of Byron on the walls. On the shelves were catalogues, files, yellow and green passports and on the desk a framed photograph of a very beautiful Chinese woman with her arm round I Will Repay. What was that about? The woman looked vaguely familiar. Gala was tempted to have a good snoop. Hearing footsteps, however, she dived for the door, turning and fleeing down endless dark and twisting passages, catching glimpses of heaving couples through half open doors, until she heard music and the party roar and emerged into the Great Hall, slap into Cosmo.

'Gala, how are you?'

'Fine.' Gala was reluctantly flattered he knew who she was.

'How did you like my beautiful Vengie?'

'Utterly awesome. How did you know I saw him?'

'I know everything.' Cosmo had a deep, very beautiful voice. 'We haven't really met. Do you think the party's going all right?'

'Like wildfire. Oscar Wilde Fire.'

Cosmo smirked and opened a nearby door, where a couple were copulating so vigorously, they took no notice.

'That's rather affecting.' He shut the door again. 'Tommy Westerham making love to his own wife. I don't expect they get much time in the school holidays. I can never understand people sitting married couples next to each other at dinner parties. The sleeping plan this evening has been such a headache.'

'Why didn't you put up a board telling people who to get off with?'

'My father gave wonderful orgies. One mustn't let the side down.'

There was nothing youthful about Cosmo. Although only twenty-three, he seemed born years ago. Incredibly self-assured, his night-dark eyes never left her face.

'I've only had four people complaining about the noise tonight and they're simply neighbours livid not to be invited. And some charity asking for £50 a week and my bank details. I bet Rupert gets sackloads of those.'

'I don't want to talk about Rupert.' Then as Cosmo beckoned a waiter to bring them more drink, 'I must have something to eat. I'm getting hammered.'

'I'm glad you're leading up Rupert's horses. It's good for Sauvignon to have some competition in the parade ring.'

'Hardly,' said Gala acidly.

'Are you good at chess?'

'No.'

'The aim is to take out one's opponent's King.'

'I know.'

'How is your King?'

'Why the hell do you call him that? Why can't you stop bitching him up?'

'Because he's so arrogant. And has the kind of sex appeal that transcends gender. I'm convinced that if, for one moment, he'd been nice to my father, asked him for a drink or for his advice, my dad would have rolled over and worshipped him.'

'Your father married Rupert's ex-wife, tried to rape Rupert's teenage daughter, killed Taggie's beloved dog – hardly ingratiating behaviour.'

'I know,' sighed Cosmo, refusing to take it seriously. 'Come and dance.' Taking her hand, he led her into the Great Hall, where the cherry-red walls, gold ceiling and floor-length gilt mirrors were lit by a thousand candles.

'How lovely,' cried Gala.

'A room fit for a Queen,' murmured Cosmo, kissing her hand, then flicking his fingers at the group in the corner, who launched into Irving Berlin's 'Cheek to Cheek'. And Cosmo turned out to be a most wonderful dancer, singing along in her ear with his beautiful husky voice.

Ben had been very straight and mainline on the dance floor. Cosmo was able to gaze into her eyes, guide her, touch her firmly, holding her against his taut, surprisingly lithe body, or sway seductively in front of her.

'Why did you choose Oscar Wilde?'

'I admire him inordinately. Like him, I can resist anything but temptation. I was tempted to come as Lady Windermere's fanny.'

'Nice aftershave,' said Gala, as he drew her closer.

'Maestro – my father always wore it. It was created for him.'

'Do you work out?'

'Only how to get women like you into bed. You're very attractive – no wonder the King's got the hots for you.'

'Stop it,' snapped Gala, angrier with herself for feeling comforted by his compliments.

'What about young Eddie Alderton?'

'We're just friends, for God's sake.' Cosmo must have spies everywhere. 'How come you and Mrs Walton . . . I mean, she's stunning, but old enough.'

'To be my mother. I need a mother. My own's rather eccentric.'

Cosmo led her through a side door into another passageway, and revealed through a two-way mirror Dame Hermione spread-eagled over a cherry-red sofa, her vast reddening bottom being whacked by Young Eddie, who was drinking a pint mug of champagne and reading *Horse & Hound* at the same time.

'Harder, harder, it really doesn't hurt.'

Gala burst out laughing. 'Any moment, Damsire's going to roll up and say "with quarters like that, your mother would make a better jump horse".'

Cosmo paused in front of another two-way mirror where Sheikh Baddi could be seen playing with himself as he watched Gav's wife Bethany and a well-stacked blonde pleasuring one another.

'Good heavens!' and then on to another mirror.

'Oh my God, that is shocking,' raged Gala. 'Revolting Brute Barraclough and Janey Lloyd-Foxe. He said he was just disappearing for a second to track down Sheikh Baddi, while Janey disappeared for a sec to network. That was an hour ago, and they've left poor Rosaria with that huge gorilla. God, I hate, hate, hate people cheating.'

Cosmo grinned evilly.

'The good Taggie must be reassured you're not wife-threatening.' Then at Gala's look of outrage, Cosmo ran a hand over her unwashed hair.

'I'm sorry about your husband,' he said softly. 'You must miss him. Will you have dinner with me one evening, away from here?'

'Of course I can't,' exploded Gala.

63

The moment Janey and Brute left Rosaria and Colin Chalford on their own, Rosaria tried to be polite and hide her terror that Brute, overspending as usual, was determined to sell Geoffrey. Some Chinese buyer and Sheikh Baddi were already interested, and with Geoffrey in the Champion Stakes and qualified for the Breeders' Cup, he was a very attractive proposition.

If he sold Geoffrey, Brute would pretend to the horse's owner, old Mrs Ford-Winters at Ashbourne Care Home, that her horse had gone for peanuts and pocket the rest of the millions to pay his own debts, and there would be no income left to save the yard. Rosaria loved Geoffrey so much. He had been the ugliest, most adorable foal and hadn't a mean bone in his body. She must pull herself together.

Colin Chalford, pouring with sweat in his gorilla onesie, was looking furtively round for Janey. If only he weren't too ashamed of his plump body to strip off for a dip in the pool.

'Janey's such a pro,' said Rosaria, to comfort him. 'She can't miss an opportunity to look for stories. She's always working.' Rosaria drained her glass of white wine and longed for another, but she couldn't afford to lose her licence.

'How did you and Janey meet?'

'Online actually. I'm a bit of a workaholic, and don't meet many women. Mother died recently.' He went even redder. 'I'd like to find someone to love, so I decided to try my luck.'

'Weren't you terrified?' asked Rosaria.

'Petrified. You submit a photograph of yourself. I cheated and only handed in a head shot and I wore a hat, so you couldn't see how bald I am, and I lied about my age and my weight.' He hung his head.

Rosaria started to laugh. 'What did you wear for the first date?'

'Running shoes – so I could escape. But Janey is so sweet. She didn't mind about my weight at all, said the more of me the merrier. She was also looking for friendship leading to an ever-lasting relationship. She's so caring.' Averting his eyes, he beckoned to a naked waiter to fill up their glasses.

'I've got to drive, and we're racing tomorrow . . . oh well, per-haps just a half.'

'Can't believe anyone as beautiful as her could bother with someone like me. But we've had three dates,' went on Colin. 'It's her birthday next week; I want to get her something lovely. Have you had any pudding?' he added, looking down at Rosaria, thinking what a sweet face she had when she smiled. 'I'm going to get you some.'

When he returned with two big platefuls of chocolate tart, saying, 'I know I'm supposed to be losing weight,' Rosaria found herself telling him all about Geoffrey and showing him a photograph on her telephone.

'I'd like to meet Geoffrey,' said Colin.

'You must get Janey to bring you down. I'm talking far too much about me,' she went on. 'What d'you do?'

'I'm a banker actually, bit of a dirty word these days. I started work as a bank clerk. Our manager used to dance around the office whenever we had a slack period. He said, "the most important asset, Colin, as a banker is to learn to dance. If you impress the wives on the dance floor, they'll praise you to their husbands, and you get their accounts." It seemed to work.'

The music was now booming like surf. Colin sang along to Cole Porter's 'So in Love'. 'Come and dance,' he said, holding out furry arms.

And he was right. Despite his huge bulk, he was as nifty a dancer as Cosmo and was soon whisking her round the floor.

Looking down as a thousand candles lit her face, he thought how pretty Rosaria was, and wished he could do something to make her less tired.

Eddie was loathing the party. However hard he whacked Dame Hermione, he couldn't work off his fury with himself. He hated seeing foie gras handed round in what should have been Quickly's St Leger Plate. When he'd edged up to Sauvignon, she'd made it quite clear there were other people more important than him to talk to.

'Fancy a fuck?' he asked Dora, even though she looked grotesque as Lester Bolton.

'Sweet of you,' replied Dora, 'but Paris is due any minute. It'll be like the first day of the sales when he arrives.'

In one of the gilt mirrors, Eddie could see Sauvignon nose to nose with Cosmo, and was amazed when, glancing in his direction, she smiled and beckoned him.

'Are you going to unfrock me, Eddie?' she murmured.

Bishops are diva-ish and attack diagonally, thought Gala. Castles approach head on like Gav. God, she wanted to go home. Hell! With all that dancing and climbing in through windows, she had lost the taxi number. So she rang Gav, who snatched up the telephone immediately.

'You OK?'

When she said she'd lost the minicab number, he said he'd ring them for her.

'When d'you want it?'

'As soon as possible. You are kind.'

As Eddie followed Sauvignon upstairs, he passed the open door of an office. Inside, Isa, 'the black cobra', capable of any evil off and on the course, was watching races overseas, and making lists of people riding work tomorrow. Despite the heat, he was wearing a black polo neck. His lowering black eyebrows and slanting black eyes dominated a pale, expressionless face. Showing several days of stubble, his tousled hair uncombed, inwardly he was missing both Jake – his father – and Tarqui. Looking up, he glanced at Eddie.

'Pity about the Leger. Quickly ran a great race.'

'More than I did.'

'Tarqui taking all your rides?'

'I guess so.' Eddie was so flabbergasted Isa was being friendly, he forgot Sauvignon for a second.

'If it all gets too much, come and ride for us,' said Isa.

'Come *on*, Eddie,' called back Sauvignon.

Waving a tape recorder, to pretend she'd been working, Janey, on her way back to Colin Chalford, was intercepted by Cosmo. 'I'm going to have the biggest scoop for you in a few weeks, darling,' he told her.

'Enjoy your male,' he murmured to Sauvignon, as she passed him on her way to the bedrooms, then added mockingly to Eddie, 'Mind you put covering boots on her or she'll geld you.'

Cosmo went into his office, which used to be his father's, with paintings of Byron and the Marquis de Sade on the walls. Having snorted a line of coke, he turned on a switch to reveal a wall of monitors showing different couples. There was a tangle of bodies round Sheikh Baddi, and there was Tommy Westerham, still fast asleep beside his own wife.

'Trainers get tired,' explained Cosmo, as he was joined by Ash who, having not pulled as Queen Victoria, had changed into just the jacket and trousers of a pale-blue silk suit, with the tattoos of David Beckham peering out between the lapels. Ash was immediately riveted by a third monitor where Eddie was stroking Sauvignon's face and kissing her with such love, before plunging into her and bringing her to apparent ecstasy with the same powerful thrusts with which he drove winners past the post.

'Wow, he's cute,' sighed Ash.

'So is she,' drawled Cosmo. 'That boob enlargement cost her almost a year's salary.'

'She'd have done better with a heart enlargement. Such a bitch.'

'But positively glowing,' noted Cosmo. 'Women are so much more radiant when they're ovulating.'

'Ovulating?' It took a minute to sink in.

'And much more likely to conceive,' gloated Cosmo.

Even Ash was shocked. 'That's a stitch-up, utterly appalling.'

'I know – I'll give you a copy of the tape.'

Gala was in despair. How could she have flirted with Cosmo? She felt horribly disloyal to Rupert and guilty that she was missing him more than Ben. Eddie was her great friend too and she felt depressed he'd finally got off with Sauvignon. Seeing Lester Bolton hurtling joyfully into the arms of a most beautiful youth with white-blond hair made her feel even lower.

Everyone was much too drunk and occupied to notice that she'd slipped away. A pinky-orange moon was sinking into the trees. Oh God, she hoped Gav had got through to the car-hire firm, but she couldn't see a taxi anywhere. Then a car drew up, a door opened and out of it erupted a squeaking animated rubber cannon ball, projected by a frantically wagging tail. 'Gropius darling, what are you doing here?'

Then as a man got out of the car: 'Gav,' she gasped. 'Oh Gav.' Bursting into tears, tripping over Gropius, she fell into his arms. 'Oh thank you, you are the dearest man in the world. You were right – it was the most hideous party. I'm not making a pass at you, I'm just so grateful to escape.' She took his face in her hands, gazed into his hollowed eyes, and kissed him on the cheek. 'Please take me home.'

'I see Rodders is here.'

'And Damsire commenting on the confirmation of every shagging couple.'

'Lots of drugs?'

'Lots.' Gala just stopped herself telling him about the cocaine on Bethany's belly, then anxious to get off the subject, 'I saw Roberto's Revenge – he's awesome and the stud's like the Ritz – but Harmony's frightened. I'm sure if it weren't for Vengie and Repay, she'd walk. But she did imply that something had nobbled Quickly in the Leger. I couldn't press her but she asked if he had got any bruises on his neck. She also said Rupert had better watch out.'

As Gropius curled up blissfully on her feet, Gala glanced at Gav's lean, inscrutable profile and wished he would curl up in bed beside her at Lime Tree Cottage. If only she could have

Gav, she was sure she would stop lusting after Rupert. They always said the best way to get over someone was to get under someone else.

64

Having switched on her computer the following morning, Geraldine gave a sigh of happiness. 'Oh dear, Rupert is *not* going to like this.'

Eddie was on to Dora instantly.

'Christ, have you seen the *Mail*? Those security guys must have been paps in fancy dress. They've got pix of you, me and Gala, even one of Gala smooching with Cosmo on the dance floor. Talk about sleeping with the enemy. Even worse, poor Gav must have picked Gala up because there's a picture of them in a clinch in the car park.'

'Omigod, omigod, I am so sorry.'

'Wasn't you who sold the story, was it . . .?'

'No, it bloody wasn't. Must have been Janey Lloyd-Foxe. Could have been Sauvignon, although she was otherwise engaged.'

'Shurrup. What do we do? Rupert's bound to fire us now.'

Gala, who was rubbing down Delectable, also went ballistic. The entire awful evening had totally convinced her how happy she was at Penscombe, and of the horror of never seeing Rupert again; but equally she'd been overwhelmed by Gav's kindness and now he'd been totally compromised. She steeled herself to ring Geraldine. 'You've got to tell Rupert, Gav wasn't at the party. Out of the kindness of his heart, he drove over and picked me up, and I was hugging him out of gratitude.'

Back from Deauville where Tarqui got a double, and finding

Taggie out with the dogs, Rupert stalked into his office. 'Bloody traitors, I'm going to fire the lot of them.'

Fortunately, Geraldine had gone to gloat in the tack room, so he caught sight of an email from Dora before Geraldine binned it.

Dear Rupert, it is entirely my fault. Gala and Eddie were low because you were cross with them. I persuaded them to come to Cosmo's party, and it's particularly not Gav's fault, Gala couldn't get a taxi home so he heroically drove over and collected her. He tried to persuade us not to go. So please forgive us all. We all love working at Penscombe.

Dora had then photostatted:

> The quality of mercy is not strained,
> It droppeth as the gentle rain from heaven
> Upon the place beneath. It is twice blest;
> It blesseth him that gives and him that takes:
> 'Tis mightiest in the mightiest; it becomes
> The throned monarch better than his crown;

Before he read any further, ecstatic squealing dogs poured into the office to welcome him. Taggie must be back, so he stalked into the kitchen.

'How lovely you're home,' she cried, hugging him, then having been briefed by Jan, 'and how brilliant to get that double in Deauville. You must be thrilled you've taken on Tarqui.'

'About the only thing I am pleased about. Half the yard went to Cosmo's orgy.'

'Not Gav,' said Taggie quickly.

'I don't want any excuses. Gala really got into the party spirit, wrapping herself round Gav and Cosmo – she's a whore.'

A muscle was going in Rupert's jaw; he was much angrier than he should have been.

'You were going to fire her anyway,' said Taggie, 'now you've got even more of an excuse.' She took a deep breath. 'Honestly, you've been so beastly to all the staff, particularly Gala and

Eddie recently, I don't blame them for going. Think of the fun that will go out of the yard if Dora and Eddie leave, and Gala is such a darling and Gav's miraculous with the horses.'

Rupert glared at her but carried on reading Dora's email:

Copy for *Racing Post* due today. How about you start off with being in Deauville 'notching up a spectacular double with my newly acquired jockey Tarquin McGall', then go on:

'As security is extremely tight in the top yards, I am proud that several of my staff wangled invitations for Cosmo Rannaldini's *Dress for Chess* orgy on Sunday night which enabled them to case the latest developments in stud and yard, including an underground water treadmill. Participating owners included Sheikhs Baddi and Rehab without their wives, Enid and Roddy Northfield, who were seen enjoying a jerk – anyone we know?' (Do you think *Racing Post* will allow that joke?) 'Other excitements included naked waiters, Sauvignon Smithson, half dressed as a bishop, and foie gras served on the St Leger Plate.'

A grinning Rupert pulled Taggie into his arms, looking down at her sweet, worried face. 'Thank God for you,' he said, then, groping for a suitable quote: 'Thou art my true and honourable wife, as dear to me, as are the bloody drops that visit my sad heart.' Then he grinned again. 'At least you needn't waste time making all those lasagnes for the staff party this year – Cosmo's already done the honours.'

65

Rupert was very cool with his defecting staff, but he forgave Gav first because he had tracked down an exciting red chestnut filly who was coming up for sale at Tattersalls on 15 October. No one else seemed to have sussed her because she was coming under the hammer on Book Three of the sales, which is when the less good horses are on offer.

Gav and Rupert proceeded to concoct a plan that Rupert would stay away on the day, because if he showed interest in such an ostensibly insignificant horse, rivals or their reps from all over the world would flock in.

Gav would roll up, therefore, because he was known to recce everything and Gala would arrive separately and bid for the filly so as not to arouse anyone's suspicions.

Gala was honoured and passionately relieved to be forgiven.

'You are lucky,' sighed Dora. 'Tattersalls is intensely theatrical and cosmopolitan, and with all the young bloodstock agents, trainers, breeders and owners, you'll see the most glamorous men in the world, and horses going for the same price as houses in Chelsea. Although you might not on Book Three Day, but it'll be very exciting.'

Gala was also pleased at the prospect of a day out with Gav; she was so grateful to him for rescuing her from Cosmo's party, and for defending her to Rupert, saying Cosmo was a manipulative snake.

'What's so special about this filly?' she asked, as they set off for Newmarket with Radio 3 playing Brahms' First Symphony.

'I got a tip-off. A yearling of no pedigree, sire some obscure Turkish stallion, escaped from her paddock in the National Stud at the crack of dawn and got loose on the gallops. Two serious four-year-olds and several three-year-olds were over-taken by her. OK, she wasn't carrying any weight, but she left them for dead. No one was about, so fingers crossed.'

'Like Eclipse,' said Gala. 'No horse could catch him if they ran to the world's end. How exciting. You are clever, Gav.'

Gala had lost more weight and was wearing new jeans and a tight peat-brown jersey which showed off her sleepy dark eyes.

She's gorgeous, thought Gav, and being with her was like get-ting into a hot bath on a freezing day and easing one's aching bones. Both Chuck-Off and Quickly had had him on the dry, firm ground this week.

The whole yard were revving up for Champions Day, the culmination of the flat-racing season at Ascot on Saturday, when the leading trainer almost certainly would be revealed.

'Where's Rupert?' asked Gala.

'Gone to the Proms. Marcus is playing Prokofiev's First. Rupert's bound to nod off and Helen will wake him with one of her very sharp elbows.'

'Poor Eddie's still desperately low about the Leger,' said Gala.

'Poor boy,' agreed Gav, 'although the surest way to imprint your name indelibly on the turf is a spectacular failure – think about Devon Loch.'

'I do hope Sauvignon's not going to hurt him,' mused Gala. 'She was taking him to some party last night, and he re-did his hair with product three different ways, then she cancelled. He did say her enlarged boobs felt as hard and rubbery as wine gums.'

'When we get to Tattersalls, we'll split up,' said Gav, 'so people won't associate you with Rupert. I'll go and look at the filly, hopefully the only person who's asked her to come out. In the big sales,' he went on, 'the stand-out foals get so exhausted, dragged out of their boxes a hundred times to be looked at, they can hardly walk when they get to the sale ring, although it didn't stop a Roberto's Revenge yearling going for over a million last week.'

When they arrived, Gala, who'd disguised herself in dark glasses, baseball hat and high-necked leather jacket, went and admired the famous fox statue, surrounded by flowers in his domed pillared home, the symbol of Tattersalls. Hopefully she'd be as crafty as him in her bidding. She then hung over the rail watching horses parading before they were sold, and taking a good look at the men, who were certainly gorgeous. Inside, the sales ring was surrounded by tiers of seats going up to a high ceiling, except where a rostrum of suave and witty auctioneers were expertly revving up buyers and setting rivals against each other. The auctioneers were flanked by pretty girls, well-bred fillies armed with clipboards, keeping an eagle eye out for bidders. Above the rostrum was the money machine where the amount wagered flashed up and was immediately translated into guineas, yuans, dollars, euros, dirhams and roubles. The machine had been known to explode when a bidder went astronomically high.

The yearling being sold was led round the ring anti-clockwise with a sticker containing a number on each quarter like an apple. In the centre was a thick circle of straw like shredded wheat, on which a minion deposited the droppings of nervous horses.

Once a foal was in the ring, crowds filled up the exit and the entrance, particularly when a fancied lot was up for sale. Gavin posted himself in the entrance beside a pillar topped by an acorn. Gala took up her position near the exit, through which horses that had been sold went to their destiny and where stairs led up to the gallery.

On the left of the entrance, a sign said *Bidders Only*. Here, on Book One and Two Days, gathered the big guns: famous blood-stock agents and buyers from all over the world, often the bitterest of enemies, getting a sexual charge from outbidding each other, holding catalogues groaning with yellow stickers.

'Do you think I can do it?' Gala was suddenly terrified and rang Gav. 'I don't want to screw up. Rupert's cross enough with me. Hadn't you better do the bidding?'

'You'll be great. People'll associate me with Rupert.'

Sliding in separately four lots before theirs, Gala watched a pretty blonde with a clipboard come up to a man who'd just bought a bay colt, then when he signed the receipt, she urged him: 'Enjoy your purchase.' Gala giggled.

Gav, on the other hand, was outraged to see Isa in the Bidders Only gallery. Who the fuck had tipped him off? Rupert and he had only spoken about the red chestnut filly once on the telephone. Someone must have hacked into their call.

In the end, Gav had not even viewed her, to avoid suspicion. She was absolutely beautiful, with ears pricked and a huge stride for her little frame, looking around, neighing imperiously, taking everything in. Learning that a big player like Isa had rolled up to bid, the auction house quickly filled up. The bidding started at a negligible 3,000 guineas, then rocketed upwards. Every time Gavin put an idle finger on the acorn, and Gala raised her hand to bid, a ripple of interest went round. Who was this beautiful, vaguely familiar buyer, going so high? And who was she bidding for? Isa, whose nod was imperceptible, was bidding against her, pushing her up to a mighty 250,000 guineas. Gradually, the handsome bloodstock agents, the Irish, the Arabs, Russians and French fell away. The girl from the National Stud leading up the filly couldn't believe it. It would give her such kudos.

Isa had gone to 400,000 guineas.

Gala paused.

'She's a lovely filly, don't stop now, madam,' cajoled the auctioneer. 'Can you afford to let her go? Think of the joy of seeing this filly every day. Think of the rewards she'll bring you.'

Shaking with nerves, Gala glanced across the sale room. Gavin's finger was on the acorn. Taking a deep breath, she raised her hand.

'Four hundred and fifty thousand guineas. It's with you now, sir.' The auctioneer turned to Isa. The room was crackling with excitement.

'Look at the way she walks.'

Isa nodded again. He had gone to 550,000. The press were

hovering to interview Gala. The auctioneer, who deserved an Oscar for histrionics, turned towards her. Knowing how much Rupert wanted the filly, Gav fingered the acorn and glanced across the sale room. Silence. Total silence. No bid came. The filly let out a whinny.

'She wants to come and live with you, madam.'

Everyone laughed. A second later, Gala had crashed to the ground.

Knowing he should have taken over the bidding, but unable to stop himself, Gav fought his way through the crowd to the tier near the exit where he found Gala in a dead faint. Gathering her up, stumbling down the steps, he carried her outside, laying her on the grass, grabbing the bottled water from her bag and dashing it in her face.

'What's the matter, Gala? What happened?'

By the time she came round they had lost the sale. The hammer fell at 550,000. 'Enjoy your purchase, Mr Lovell.'

Gavin had never seen anyone so grey or more terrified than Gala. She was shuddering worse than Forester in a thunderstorm. Then as reality reasserted itself, she was mortified she'd lost the lovely filly, led off out of the sale ring by her euphoric ex-stable lass.

'Rupert will never forgive us. I'm so sorry, I'm so sorry,' she whispered through white lips and frantically chattering teeth.

Putting his arms round her, Gav tried to steady and comfort her. 'It's all right. She probably isn't any good.'

Then Gala started in terror, as a Tattersalls nurse rolled up, all kindness and sympathy.

'So sorry about losing the sale. Would you like to come to the office for a cup of tea and a lie down?'

'No, no, I'm fine.' Gala's eyes swivelled everywhere in panic; her only desire was to escape.

'Could you get us out of here, without alerting the press?' asked Gav.

66

Only when Gav was driving out of Newmarket past the vast rearing stallion sculpture did Gala break down, and between frantic sobs reveal that just as she was about to bid again: 'I glanced round, and emerging from behind a pillar was that monster Wang.'

'Who?' asked Gav.

'Zixin Wang, the Chinese warlord whose mafia thugs gunned down Ben in Zim, then burnt our house to the ground and butchered all our animals. He hung the dogs on the gate-posts . . . Oh my god.' Her sobs doubled. 'Bastard, bastard, what the hell's he doing here? He murdered my Ben. But no one questioned it, he's so in with the government. I ought to kill him, before he kills me.'

'It's OK, this is England.' Gavin pulled up on the verge of the hamlet called Six Mile Bottom, and took her in his arms. 'It's OK, sweetheart, it's OK. Did he see you?'

'I d-don't know. I don't know if he saw me or if he recognized me. He kills lots of people. He murdered his first wife and replaced her with some beauty. "Fucking Great Willy of China", Ben used to call him.'

Gav had never seen anyone so terrified. He longed to kiss her better, but tried to keep the conversation matter-of-fact.

What would induce Wang to come down to a minor sale to buy a totally unknown filly? Someone must have tipped him and Isa off. Gavin wondered if it was Bao. Chinese buyers were hardly ever seen at British auction houses, particularly as they didn't like to do their own bidding. They felt they had lost face if they didn't win. Suddenly Gav wondered whether Mr Wang was Cosmo and Isa's big backer.

'I can't bear the thought of him getting anywhere near that darling filly,' sobbed Gala.

They both started violently as the telephone rang. It was Rupert. Had they got the filly?

'Nope.'

'Christ, who did?'

'Cosmo.'

'What the fuck? How much for?'

'Five hundred and fifty thousand. I thought we'd gone high enough.'

'That's peanuts.'

Gala, able to hear Rupert's stream of abuse, grabbed Gavin's mobile and said: 'It wasn't Gav's fault. It was entirely mine.'

Waving his palm from side to side, Gav grabbed back the mobile.

'I'll explain when I get back,' he said, then he switched it off.

All the way home, stumblingly between apologies for screwing up the deal, Gala told Gav about Wang and how he'd destroyed her, sketchy details of which he'd already learnt from Rupert.

Every time a car overtook them, which was rare because Gav was a very swift and good driver, she cast a terrified glance to see who was inside it.

Back at Penscombe, evening stables were over, the horses being settled down for the night. Gala fled upstairs and attempted to repair her ravaged, tear-blotched face. She cleaned her teeth to get rid of the sour taste in her mouth, and splashed on the last of her Elie Saab. Then, saying sorry, she wouldn't be long, to an appalled Gropius, she went in search of Rupert, desperate to explain why Gav wasn't to blame.

Rupert wasn't in his office or the yard, so she ran down to the stud. Here, to her horror she found the place deserted, the door of the diabolical Titus Andronicus' stallion box open, and the bird flown. What the hell was going on? Titus, however, was her friend, who whickered when she passed, and always accepted her Polos and her petting. So she tore off in pursuit then froze, appalled. Someone had left the gate open to the field where Safety Car was living with new sheep friends acquired since Quickly moved in with Bitsy. Titus, who loathed Safety Car, was prowling round in search of booty. If he got one of Safety's sheep, it would be a fight to the death.

Calling out to Titus, Gala raced into the field. Recognizing her, he trotted back whickering and she was able to grab his collar.

'Come on, boy, back to bed.'

For a second he put his black nose against her neck, breathing in her scent, then with squeal upon lusty squeal, he attacked her, ripping apart her brown cashmere jersey with his teeth, catching her flesh beneath. As Gala screamed, Titus proceeded to pin her against the fence, then knocking her to the ground, reared up, poised to kneel on her and rip her to pieces or crush her underfoot.

'No, Titus, it's me!' she yelled.

Then Titus gave a bellow of frustrated rage as someone turned a fire hose on him, grabbing Gala by her arm and yanking her under the lowest bar of the fence, before leaving her in the dust and racing to shut the gate.

'You stupid, stupid bitch,' howled Rupert. 'What the fuck are you playing at?'

'Someone had left Titus' door open and he got into Safety Car's field,' wept Gala. 'I was terrified he'd kill Safety.'

'Safety's in Frogsmore Meadow – there's nothing in that field.' Rupert pulled her to her feet.

'I was just taking Titus back to his box. He's always been so friendly, then he went for me.'

'You stupid bitch,' repeated Rupert softly, 'coming down here reeking of scent. Don't you know that turns stallions on? He could have raped you or killed you, and I'd have had to shoot a twenty-million-pound stallion.'

Gala burst into tears.

'Why not shoot me instead? I've just lost you a lovely 550,000 guineas filly and it wasn't Gav's fault.' And she stumbled off into the stud office, crumpling up, about to faint again when Rupert caught her.

'You OK?'

'Of course I am, he only ripped my sweater.'

For a second he looked down at her. 'I'll buy you another. I was worried. I'm sorry.'

Gala had straw in her hair, and her face was smudged. For a moment they gazed at each other; his eyes were as blue as the distant hills. Then to lighten a highly charged situation, he said idly, 'Someone must have wised up your dancing-partner boy-friend Cosmo that Gav and I were after that filly. Wasn't you, was it?'

'Bastard,' exploded Gala. As her hand shot out to slap his face, Rupert caught it. Next moment, feelings they'd both been trying to suppress for months exploded and he was kissing the life out of her, and she was kissing him back. They were just about to collapse on a big bed of straw in the empty stallion box, when they heard a footstep and leapt apart.

Smoothing his hair, Rupert looked out of the tack-room door. Whoever it was, the night-watch, or Jan or Bao, had retreated into the shadows.

67

Everyone was talking about Rupert's sixtieth birthday at the end of October, with the press frantic for interviews. Janey Lloyd-Foxe was planning to celebrate the event with a big piece. Helen, having seen Aidan O'Brien, the great Irish trainer, in a woolly hat, suggested Rupert should wear one instead of a trilby to keep him in the loop. Rupert's reply was unprintable. He also kept insisting he didn't want any kind of party, particularly a surprise one.

Taggie, however, aware that Rupert was so furious about lost fillies and Legers and still not nailing Leading Sire, decided to defy him and cheer him up with a tiny surprise party – and promptly regretted it.

The main problem was that Rupert's birthday fell around the date of the Breeders' Cup in Santa Anita and the Melbourne Cup, which would have meant Taggie flying the family: Perdita and Luke, Tab and Wolfie in Germany, Bianca in Perth, Xav in South America, Marcus and Alexei in Moscow, Rupert's brother Adrian in New York, either to Australia or Los Angeles. Kind Bao asked Taggie if she'd like to borrow one of his father's jets. The only answer, decided Taggie, was to give the party at Penscombe on the day after the Melbourne Cup. Australia was nine hours ahead and although this would barely give Rupert the time to get home, at least he'd have the chance of a good sleep on the twenty-four-hour flight.

413

But once the word got round, how could she possibly hold back the gatecrashers? The weather was so unpredictable at the end of October. Rupert would go ballistic if guests poured into the house clocking his pictures, which meant a marquee – which everyone who hadn't been invited would see from the top road. If only one could acquire a marquee to put over a marquee, sighed Taggie.

Another problem was that Taggie's father Declan still hadn't finished his book on Irish literature, and with his prodigal wife Maud running up fearful debts, he wanted to borrow £60,000 from Taggie who, determined to pay for the party herself, was reduced to selling a lot of jewellery and doing all the cooking at home.

Rupert, who was still reading *Othello*, was therefore not amused by Taggie disappearing into other rooms to answer secret telephone calls, or whispering in corners with Jan, as they shoved canapés and puddings into freezers. Scorpios, Rupert's star sign, according to Dora, 'are brooding, intensively competitive, wildly jealous, very highly sexed and ruled by the privates'.

Valent comforted Rupert that sixty was nothing; even seventy was not so bad, particularly if one was lucky enough to win the love of such a lovely woman. Rupert, still not a fan of Etta's, made no comment.

'You will ask Mummy, won't you?' begged Tab.

Oh God, Rupert detested his first wife. 'It's not fair to ask people Rupert doesn't like,' wailed Taggie.

'There seem to be an awful lot of them,' observed Jan, who was being simply wonderful. He was so brilliant at finding television programmes that totally absorbed Old Eddie, that it left him lots of free time to help Taggie, and he had marvellous ideas of exciting South African dishes to liven up the menu.

Thank goodness Rupert was away so much when people started ringing up for birthday present ideas.

'Give him some product to coax his hair into little tendrils,' suggested Dora.

'What *do* you give a man who has everything?' asked Etta.

'Except the Leading Sire title,' said Valent drily.

In fact, Rupert was now so utterly obsessed with cracking the new Global title, he seemed to be the only person unaware that a party was being arranged.

There were also endless sales all over the world that needed to be policed, in case superstars of the future slipped through his fingers. All the stallions were being photographed with their hair carefully ruffled to make them look more virile for Weatherbys *Stallion Book,* and nominations sought so each of these stallions had a full book of mares for next year.

Having risen at five to watch New Year's Dave win another big race in Australia, a delighted Rupert took his dogs out for a walk in the woods. It had rained all night, but the sun was now idling through the clouds and a warm breeze bringing down showers of gold and orange leaves. As he approached Gala's cottage, he noticed that the lime tree in front of her bathroom window had shed its lemon-yellow curtain, and he could see her soaping her boobs. God, he wanted her. He was so tempted to drop in, particularly when his dogs she'd walked so often surged snuffling towards her door, but 'chaos would come again'. Regretfully he called off the pack.

In a couple of hours, he'd have to leave for Ascot, and the culmination of the season; Champions Day with a massive £4,000,000 prize money. Despite the virus the horses had caught earlier in the year, he'd just notched up over 200 winners. Sadly, Eddie, who'd been allowed back into the fold, was so desperate to ride winners, he'd been banned for barging and over-use of the whip, and Meerkat had flu, so only Tarqui was free to ride.

Dressed for Ascot, Taggie looked so adorable in her violet suit and hat, Rupert chided himself for lusting after Gala. He was rewarded for his abstinence by a miraculous afternoon. Despite ground like a quicksand of toffee, Tarqui, who'd finally got his act together, won four races on Touchy Filly, Delectable and Blank Chekov, finally romping home on Quickly in the 1 mile 2 furlongs Champion Stakes by so many lengths the other horses seemed to have fallen out of the television.

Tarqui, undemonstrative towards animals, actually patted Quickly and used his blond mane to wipe away a tear. Taggie and Rupert watching on the rail felt the thunder of hooves in counterpoint to the roar of 'Quickly, Quickly, Quickly!' Taggie, with tears of joy streaking her mascara and all her make-up kissed off, still looked enchanting.

Gala tried not to let jealousy spoil her euphoria as she and Quickly lined up for the photographers. Still terrified in crowds of spotting Wang again, she noticed that Harmony, who was looking much thinner, not Sauvignon, was leading up Ivan the Terrorist, who'd come second. I Will Repay was obviously being saved for the Breeders' Cup. What was surprising, Cosmo didn't look remotely upset by Rupert's clean sweep.

'We must have a drink later, Mrs Milburn,' he smiled at Gala, which was immediately clocked by Rupert.

'She's got better things to do,' he said icily, sharply ordering Gala to walk Quickly round to cool him down and then get the horses on the lorry as soon as possible so they'd miss the worst of the traffic.

'And don't go fraternizing with that toxic midget,' he added, not even bothering to lower his voice.

Rupert then, for a fourth time, bore Valent, Etta, Taggie and Gav back to celebrate in the Winning Connections Room, which had a photograph of the great Frankel over the fireplace and a picture of the Queen being presented with the Ascot Gold Cup by her son the Duke of York. Here they drank more champagne, and watched several re-runs of the Champion Stakes.

68

'That Quickly's a marvellous horse,' said Chris Stickels, Ascot's Clerk of the Course. 'But before you move in here for good, Rupert, you'd better drink up. The entire world's press is outside wanting to talk to you.'

To cap a glorious day, Geoffrey won the last race for Rosaria, so to avoid Brute stealing all her thunder as he invaded the Winning Connections Room, Rupert was finally persuaded to shoot off to meet the media, who gave him a round of applause. After a great deal of champagne, his deadpan face was lifted by a broad grin; the man-eating tiger was actually purring. This was the best day's racing of his life. Tarqui had ridden like an angel. Gala and Gav had worked their socks off getting the horses spot on, the yard was flying.

'What's your secret?' asked Clare Balding.

'The horses having something to beat at home. They're all running so well, they stretch and challenge each other.'

'Do you feel guilty at pinching Valhalla's stable jockey?'

'Not remotely. Cosmo and Isa should have put him up on their best horses.'

He then announced that he would be supplementing Quickly for the Breeders' Cup.

Outside, he could hear the crowds still cheering.

After deflecting a few more questions about Fleance in the

Melbourne Cup, he said: 'OK, guys, that's enough. I need another drink.'

Next moment, a hard-eyed red-head had pushed her way to the front. 'How much are you looking forward to your sixtieth birthday?'

'Not particularly.'

'You having a big party?' asked Marcus Armytage.

'No party at all. Definitely not.'

'I'd have thought you wanted to celebrate,' taunted the red-head. 'Becoming a great-grandfather – isn't that the greatest sixtieth birthday present?'

'What are you talking about?' snarled a returning man-eating tiger.

The room fell silent. As every tape recorder was switched back on and thrust forward, accompanied by a firework display of flash-bulbs, Rupert realized it was the same red-head he'd told to piss off at the Derby.

'Did you know Sauvignon Smithson has posted a picture of you on Facebook, with a caption: "Hello, Great-grandfather Rupert"?'

'Don't be utterly ridiculous.'

'Is this true?' asked Matt Chapman, over the rumble of excited speculation.

'Course it isn't.'

'Sauvignon Smithson has just tweeted that she's over the moon, she's expecting Eddie Alderton's baby. And she hopes you'll be equally thrilled with such a wonderful sixtieth birthday present.' Smiling lasciviously, Rhiannon turned to Taggie. 'And congratulations to you, Mrs Campbell-Black. You're so young to be a great-grandmother.'

'I don't know what you're talking about,' stammered Taggie.

'Is that why Eddie Alderton's no longer riding for you, Rupert?'

'He's got a whip ban, for Christ's sake.'

Next moment, Rupert had grabbed Taggie's arm and made a run for it, racing to the middle of the course where helicopters and planes were parked, giving the Green Galloper the best publicity of its career.

By early evening the news had gone viral: RUPERT CAMPBELL-BLACK TO BE A GREAT-GRANDFATHER, with pictures of Rupert, Eddie and Sauvignon: 'Is this the handsomest woman in England?' And jokes flying back and forth about Eddie not firing blancs at Sauvignon.

Gav, the only sober member of the party, flew the plane. Fuelling the media frenzy was a truly bitchy piece by Janey Lloyd-Foxe, already posted online, which, thank God, Taggie couldn't read.

What with becoming a great-grandfather and reaching sixty, wrote Janey, Rupert was going to need a lot of counselling. The piece was accompanied by a for-once unflattering photograph of Rupert, who hadn't put back on any weight since the Legends race, looking gaunt and shadowed.

'No longer the handsomest man in England,' crowed Janey. 'No longer the cure for loss of female libido.'

'I'm sure it's not true,' soothed Taggie, as Rupert chucked his laptop on the floor in fury.

'Cosmo will have set the whole thing up to get at you,' said Gav, 'and Sauvignon's incapable of telling the truth. It would suit Cosmo to link Eddie and Sauvignon, who Mrs Walton is extremely beady about.'

Rupert tried to ring Eddie, but his mobile was permanently engaged.

Back at Penscombe, the lights were all on, as yard and stud became a hive of gossip and celebration. Four winners and an heir on one afternoon. Cheers lifted the valley as re-runs of the races were watched over and over again. The press were already camped outside the gates, offering large sums to all the staff to dish the dirt. The pool money from the four-million-pound prize money would be enormous.

Eddie, who'd been texted by Dora, was on to Sauvignon in a trice.

'What the fuck is all this about? Are you really pregnant?'

'Of course, I took a test yesterday.'

'Why didn't you tell me? How the hell do you know it's mine?'

'That's rather ungallant. You're the only guy I've slept with. Cosmo's got some lovely footage of us at the chess party. Talk about Ride of the Month. You certainly provide a stiff finish, you should be flattered.'

'Don't be fucking stupid: you're not going to keep it.'

'Of course I am, I'm nearly thirty.'

'Well, I'm only twenty-three, not old enough to start a family. Kids need a mom and dad.'

'This baby'll have both.'

'Sauvignon, for Christ's sake. Rupert'll go ballistic. He's uptight enough about being sixty, he'll throw me out. Why the fuck didn't you tell me instead of the whole fucking world, then I could have broken it gently to him and Taggie? And what about my mom and dad?' Oh Christ, his mother Perdita had been conceived at an orgy.

As they approached Penscombe, Rupert spied the towering red blaze of his beechwoods, and the tawny-yellow brick road of the horse chestnuts along his drive. As the Galloper landed, a great fountain of gold leaves rose upwards, and they could see the dogs running across the lawn, Forester leading the pack.

As Gav opened the door, a roaring party din and cheers could be heard. Rupert, not stopping to congratulate anyone, went straight to his office and poured himself a treble whisky. Rupert Black, astride Third Leopard, so like him and Eddie, waved his whip jauntily: 'Good on you, lad, pre-potent sire carrying on the line.'

It wasn't that Rupert minded being sixty or even being a great-grandfather that much. It was the accusation of cradle-snatching Taggie, depriving her of her youth, that he detested. He went into the drawing room where Forester, sulky at being left, had chucked all the cushions on to the floor.

Taggie, who'd changed out of her violet suit into a dark-blue jersey and jeans, was trying to comfort Rupert when Eddie wandered in, pale and trembling. Like a Bacchante, he had two fallen leaves in his blond hair.

'I'm really sorry, Grandpa, I didn't know anything about it.'

'You presumably slept with her?'

'Well, I certainly didn't stay awake.'

'Don't be fucking lippy.'

'But only once at Cosmo's party. The only time she wanted to.' Eddie had turned his mobile off, but could feel it vibrating and jumping in his pocket.

'You're a fucking disaster. Can't you keep your dick in your trousers?'

It was as though he was under Vesuvius being stoned with molten lava. As Rupert ranted on, Eddie edged towards the drinks table. Any moment all the silver horses, won as trophies, would bolt in terror. One by one the dogs slunk out of the room except Forester, who lay on his back with his legs apart, aping Sauvignon. Taggie opened her mouth and shut it.

'It's your own bloody fault for going to Cosmo's orgy in the first place and getting pissed. You were bound to get stitched up,' snarled Rupert.

Suddenly Eddie lost it.

'It must be in the genes then. You're always banging on about pre-potent sires. You're a goddam hypocrite – my mom was conceived at an orgy. Everyone had Grandma Daisy that night, including you. Mom didn't know you were her father until she was twenty. At least it was just me and Sauvignon. You accuse me of being promiscuous when you were shagging half of Gloucestershire.'

'Eddie, stop it!' screamed Taggie. 'Both of you stop it, we're talking about a baby.'

'I guess Grandpa's got great-grandkids littered all over the West Country.'

Hideous, hideous silence followed. Forester let out a sulphuric fart.

'Get out,' howled Rupert. 'You can pack your bags, get out and don't come back.'

'Oh, please Rupert.' Taggie burst into tears. 'We must discuss it, there's going to be a baby. You can't turn Eddie out.'

'And you can shut up too.' Rupert turned on her. 'It's fuck-all to do with you,' and stalked off to his office.

'I'm so sorry, Taggie.' Eddie's voice broke, and he fled. Outside, he bumped into a hovering Jan, who was wearing a striped blue apron and waving a wooden spoon. A delicious smell of roasting lamb and garlic followed him from the kitchen.

'You in for supper?'

'I guess not – I've been fired.'

Fighting back the tears, he wandered across the lawn, rustling through kite-shaped chestnut leaves, conkers crunching beneath his feet. He longed for Gala. She'd understand. But she'd be still driving back from Ascot. He jumped as a conker landed on his head and his mobile vibrated again. Numbly he answered it.

'Hi, baby boy.' It was Cosmo. 'Congratulations.'

'Whatever for?' Eddie's voice broke again. 'Rupert's just fired me.'

'How ill-judged of him. Come and join us immediately. Sauvignon's just told me the great news about the baby – she's so excited. You can move in here and ride all our horses, and together we'll shaft geriatric Rupert. Go and get packed. Have you been drinking?'

'Not at all.'

'Then drive over at once.'

Eddie felt there was no alternative. How had Cosmo got his mobile number, he wondered, and got on to him so fast? Perhaps Sauvignon did love him a bit and had persuaded Cosmo to hire him.

Mindlessly he wandered towards the lake, jumping as a mewing Purrpuss rubbed against his legs. To get Quickly used to travelling catless to the Breeders' Cup, he had not been taken to Ascot.

As Eddie gathered him up, the cat turned into an ecstatic rumbling bundle. They were joined by Safety Car, who'd been drinking red wine at the celebrations; he gave a whicker of pleasure, hiccuped, nudged Eddie in the chest and got bopped with a sheathed claw by Purrpuss.

Pulverized by misery, Eddie realized how much he'd miss Penscombe: the animals as much as the people. It had become his home, and he'd blown it, never taking the job seriously enough.

Going back to the house, Eddie bumped into an overjoyed

Tarqui, dressed in a sharp suit and new red shirt to go out on the pull. He was already several drinks up, but sobered instantly, utterly appalled by Eddie's news.

'Don't go, for Christ's sake.' His mocking swarthy face was for once serious. 'I don't want to disillusion you, but Cosmo's only employing you to get his revenge on Rupert for poaching me and tings working out so spectacularly. He's evil. Rupert wants Leading Sire, Cosmo wants to bury Rupert. He took on a young Italian jockey earlier this year, persuaded him to move house and bring his wife and three children, then sacked him last week without a qualm. Please, Eddie, I beg you. Isa hates Rupert almost more than Cosmo does. And Ash is a focking sex maniac – he adores blue-eyed little poster boys. Take a chastity belt, put a wardrobe against your door.'

'For Christ's sake, Purrpuss,' swore Eddie, as a clutched-too-tightly cat clawed his way free.

'And don't trost Sauvignon, she's evil. You don't want her as mother of your children.'

'Full Hammer House of Horror then?'

'No – Harmony's nice. Go to her if you need help. But honestly, I beg you, don't go. Rupert will never forgive you.'

'That's enough, Tarqui.' It was Jan.

'I don't know what to do,' said Eddie.

'I'll come and help you pack,' said Jan. 'Let Rupert cool down.'

'Where's Taggie?'

'Just had a blazing row with Rupert.'

Eddie still wondered who had tipped Cosmo off.

As he was leaving, Bao, who had just given Timon and Sophie a Mandarin lesson, sidled up.

'I will miss you very much, Mr Eddie Young. I'd like you to accept good luck charm.'

It was a rabbit, exquisitely carved from ivory.

69

Uncheered by orgy din, pounding music and bright lights, Valhalla seemed the creepiest place. Although faint from lack of food, and wearing only a polo-shirt and jeans, Eddie had fortified himself with a stiff gin and tonic at the nearby Pearly Gates, to find the great abbey almost in darkness, an icy east wind stripping the leaves from the trees. As the huge oak door opened, he was almost asphyxiated by wafts of scent and after-shave. Cosmo, in a dinner-jacket, and Mrs Walton, glittering diamonds and smothered in mink, were on their way out.

'Hail and farewell,' purred Cosmo. 'I'm so sorry to desert you on your first night, but Ruth and I have a previous engagement. We will talk through everything in the morning. Isa will be over shortly.' He waved to a lurking manservant, who looked more like an undertaker. 'Logan will bring in your bags and see that your car's parked, and he will show you your room and find you something to eat.'

'I need to talk to Sauvignon,' stammered Eddie, clinging to the door-handle for support.

'Of course you do,' smiled Mrs Walton. 'And do put on a jersey – you look frozen.'

'Sauvignon!' Cosmo yelled up the stairs. 'Eddie's here. Go into the drawing room,' he told Eddie. 'She'll be down soon.'

Sauvignon kept him waiting ten minutes. With her newly washed hair straightened and gleaming, her flawless skin slightly flushed, wearing a red polo neck and the tightest of black leather trousers, she looked all set for a night on the tiles.

'This is very dramatic,' she said, draping a black leather jacket over a chair and offering just a cheek for Eddie to kiss, 'moving to Valhalla. You should have warned me.'

'So should you. Why the hell didn't you?'

'I wanted to be sure.'

'I need a drink.'

'Help yourself.'

Eddie sloshed more gin and a breath of tonic into a glass. 'What do you want?'

'Nothing, thanks. I've got to drive.'

'You're going out, for Christ's sake?'

'It is Saturday night.'

'I'll come with you.'

'Alas, you can't really. I'm meeting a girlfriend, whose partner just left her.'

'Surely you and I are more important.'

Logan the lugubrious manservant appeared in the doorway with Eddie's suitcases.

'Mr Alderton's in the Gold Room,' Sauvignon told him.

'I am fucking not, I'm sleeping with you.'

'We can't. The doctor said no intercourse for the next three months in case I miscarry.'

'Probably the best solution.'

'Don't be obnoxious.'

'We could have gentle sex and talk.'

'No.' Sauvignon shook her head, her sleek dark mane swirling like I Will Repay's. 'You're far too attractive; if we slept in the same bed I couldn't trust myself.'

You're a lousy actress, thought Eddie. As she ran a finger along his lip, he captured her hand and drew her towards him, but when he tried to kiss her she ducked her head and wiggled away.

'Why did you post Rupert's picture on Facebook?' he asked.

'Because he's so up himself and not at all nice to you. How's he taken it?'

425

'I doubt if he'll ever speak to me again.'

'You're better off here – Isa'll give you some decent rides.'

'Sauvignon, for God's sake, my life's in smithereens.'

'Not for long. Ah, here's Isa to sort it.' She kissed Eddie's cheek. 'See you in the morning, babe,' and she was gone.

Eddie drained his glass and was just refilling it when Isa grabbed the bottle. Not in carnival mood either, unamused by Champions Day without wins, Isa weighed in immediately.

'The average jockey has the body weight of a thirteen-year-old girl. You're much too fat. From now on, you're going to run twice a day and not go to the gym – that puts on heavy muscle. You're to stop drinking and get in the sauna. No diuretics, no laxatives, no flipping, you need to be fit. Go to bed now. I want you out on the gallops at 6.30 tomorrow. The Breeders' Cup's in only a fortnight.'

Too weak to argue, Eddie followed Logan along endless twisting, dark passages, past suits of armour, nude sculptures and tapestries to a room with just a chest of drawers, a wardrobe into which his clothes had been unpacked, a large chair, a bookcase full of Felix Francis novels and a big four-poster with frayed gold curtains.

Fighting utter desolation, Eddie opened the window, which had creepers as curtains, jumped as a raped vixen let out a shriek, then again as his mobile rang.

'This is Harmony Bates,' said a breathy voice. 'Gala called me, asked me to look after you. I thought I'd bring you a bowl of soup.'

Eddie was never so grateful to see anyone, as he inhaled wafts of tomato and basil, picked up a spoon kept upright by lentils, and took a bite of hot white bread and butter.

'You are kind, thank you so much – this is better than Claridge's.' Then when Harmony retreated, 'Please sit down and talk to me.'

'You must ask me if you need anything.'

In her dark-green pyjamas, Eddie thought, she looked much thinner, and less plain than he remembered her. As she couldn't comfort him about Sauvignon, whom she loathed anyway, she asked him how he'd got on with Isa.

Eddie laughed for the first time that day.

'Like S and M without the sex.'

Out on the gallops beneath a silver sky next morning, the grass was drenched with dew, owls hooted, foxes barked, a tiny sickle moon lit the east. Only he and Isa went out through the deer-haunted parkland. Isa was riding Eumenides. Eddie realized he'd been put up on I Will Repay, who was being kept fresh for the Breeders' Cup.

'OK, let him go, fast as you can.'

And Eddie's terror turned to ecstasy as he felt the power of the horse beneath him, the long, raking stride – then, as the deer fled at their approach – the lightning acceleration. The further they went, the better Repay travelled.

Eumenides was a class animal, but I Will Repay beat him by nine lengths. Eddie was laughing with joy as he pulled up.

'What a beautiful, beautiful horse – I've never ridden anything like him. He makes Quickly with his little stride seem like a Shetland pony.'

Isa glanced at his stopwatch. 'Five furlongs in one minute ten, that's not bad, although you ought to lie lower over him.'

Isa was not stupid; he knew that success in jockeys was a lot about confidence.

'I can't teach you anything,' he went on. 'You're a bloody good rider, and you're an American so you understand how they ride over there – exploding out of the gates, ballbreaking rough and tumble, and because they don't push forward as much as British jockeys do, they hit their horses far harder.'

For a moment, Eddie was speechless, close to tears; it had been a hellish twenty-four hours.

'D'you really mean that?'

'Yup, and you're coming to the Breeders'. You can ride in the Junior Turf and show your effing grandfather how good you are.'

Without their realizing it, the sun was rising, turning the silver valley to rose and the trees a singing flame-red. When they got back to the yard, Ash had rolled up, furious to see Eddie riding his horse.

'I don't want Repay picking up any bad habits.'

The yard was off to the Breeders' Cup at the end of the week, taking Herb Roberto for Eddie to ride in the Juvenile Turf. The rest were for Ash, who kept up his bitching as Eddie stuck to his fitness regime, and rode as many horses as he could.

He was comforted when Dora rang him.

'We're all worried stiff about you. Life's not the same here. How's it going?'

'The clocks go back this weekend,' sighed Eddie, 'but not cocks. Sauvignon won't let me near her, not even to talk. I don't know what game she's playing.'

'Bitch – we all miss you. Old Eddie's inconsolable – he's got no one to watch porn with.'

'Have the horses gone to Santa Anita?'

'Going next Tuesday.'

'When's Rupert off?'

'He's at the Horses in Training sales in Arqana, but he's off to the Breeders' on Thursday. Taggie's not going, although she hasn't told him yet. They had such a frightful row because he was so foul to you, and Taggie's going to say that she's got too many grandchildren coming for half-term. Really, she wants to get the surprise party organized. You're coming, aren't you?'

'Not fucking invited.'

'Course you are. Gala also had a row with Rupert over firing you, so she's had a couple of days off, and Quickly had colic and may not go to the Breeders' Cup and certainly not with Gala, Rupert's so cross with her. So it's all up in the air.'

The press were still utterly obsessed with the drama. Rupert had poached Tarqui; Cosmo and Isa had poached Eddie. The *Scorpion* ran a story that Eddie had moved to Valhalla to be with the mother of his forthcoming child, and how hypocritical of Rupert with his promiscuous track-record to chuck Eddie out.

Eddie found comfort in talking to Harmony, who said how fond she was of Gala and wasn't Taggie lovely.

'Doesn't she get lonely with Rupert away all the time?'

'Well, she's got Old Eddie, my grandfather, and Jan, Eddie's carer, a handsome South African who looks after her – too well for Rupert's liking – and a sweet Chinese boy called Bao Tong.'

'Where have I heard that name . . .?' Harmony's forehead wrinkled.

'Everyone's called Tong in China. Bao gave me this rabbit for luck, when Rupert chucked me out. It's made of ivory. Gala would do her nut – poachers killed her husband.'

Eddie was amazed how nice Isa was being to him. 'What the hell am I going to do about Sauvignon?' he asked him, as they rode back from the gallops one morning.

'I don't know,' said Isa. 'I had to get married – Tab was pregnant. I fancied her rotten but I didn't love her. Then she lost the baby, and we were stymied.'

'Tab's awful,' volunteered Eddie.

'Not nearly as awful as her mother Helen, who nearly destroyed my parents' marriage.'

Ash was wildly jealous of Isa and Eddie's friendship, never missing an opportunity to bitch, and when Eddie was in the sauna, hovering outside so Eddie couldn't escape and the pages of Felix Francis got very wrinkled.

Valhalla was a terrifying house after dark, with rooms on all levels, enabling people to peer out of mullioned windows through creepers into other rooms.

'Any ghosts here?' asked Eddie.

'I'm more frightened of the living,' shivered Harmony.

Aching for Sauvignon, Eddie was sleeping appallingly. If only they could have sex to ease his tension, he might have dropped off. He'd never read so much in his life.

Two days before they left for Santa Anita, the house was creaking in a high wind like a rheumaticky old man. It was after midnight when Eddie heard a step, then another step. As he shoved the big armchair against the door, and switched off the light, he heard the screech of another raped vixen, and leapt back into bed. Next moment there was a crash, the door was forced open, then slammed and the light switched on. It was Ash, reeking of aftershave and wearing a purple paisley silk dressing gown, which fell open to reveal the huge tattoo of David Beckham.

'Get out, you slimy toad,' yelled Eddie.

'That's not very friendly, poster boy. You know you want it. You won't get it from Sauvignon, and once you've tried it with a guy, you'll never want to go back.'

'I bloody won't.' Eddie jumped out of bed, wearing only a long T-shirt bearing the words: *single but straight.*

Next moment, Ash had grabbed him. Incredibly strong from driving horses across the finishing line, he pulled Eddie close, his medallion scraping Eddie's chest. His breath tasted sour from making himself sick so often as he rammed his tongue between Eddie's lips. His left hand reached round to caress Eddie's buttocks, parting them, fingering and probing. As Eddie struggled frantically to escape, he could feel a ramrod-hard cock jabbing his belly button. Then, as Ash rolled him over on his front on the bed: 'There you go, poster boy.'

'Get off,' screamed Eddie. 'Just fuck off, you revolting faggot.' Fury fuelling his strength, swinging round, he hit Ash across the room – and as Ash landed on the wooden arms of the big chair, pushed aside from blocking the door, there was a fearsome crack of bone. A minute later, Cosmo, who'd been watching the whole thing through a two-way mirror, came storming in.

'What the hell have you done to him? He's got the Classic on Saturday.'

'He's fucked me,' screamed Ash.

'Au contraire,' drawled Cosmo, 'you were about to fuck him.'

Cotchester Hospital confirmed Ash had broken his arm and three ribs. Dawn was breaking, a tiny flicker of flame beneath glowering dark-grey clouds, as Ash got home. Immediately, he and Eddie were summoned to Cosmo's office.

'When will you learn to control yourself, you stupid goat?' Cosmo's voice was so venomous, Eddie nearly crossed himself and could hardly take it in, when Cosmo turned to him, saying, 'You're going to ride Repay in Santa Anita.'

'Omigod, I'll be riding against Quickly.'

'And you know exactly how to beat him.'

70

The Breeders' Cup, America's richest, glitziest race meeting, was this year being held in Santa Anita in California. A place Rupert was always edgy returning to because it had once witnessed his greatest humiliation: his wife Helen running off with his teammate Jake Lovell, in the middle of the Los Angeles Olympics.

Ascendancy had been regained by Rupert then clinching the Team Gold with an epic clear round, when he'd jumped using only one arm, the other having been rendered useless by an excruciatingly painful trapped nerve.

Helen's departure in such a conflagration of publicity, however, still rankled, which was why Rupert felt it imperative on any return to Santa Anita to be accompanied by an adoring, much younger and infinitely more beautiful second wife – particularly this year when there'd be so much guff in the paper about his sixtieth birthday and approaching great-grand-fatherhood.

Despite the ongoing froideur over the firing of Young Eddie and Taggie's irritating but perennial sadness at beloved foals going off to the sales, Rupert automatically assumed she would be accompanying him to Santa Anita, and then on to the Melbourne Cup. From there, to avoid any fuss and festivities, he aimed to return late on the Wednesday of his birthday.

After several days away at the sales, he came home to find

Taggie in the kitchen baking a cake. Having pecked her on the cheek and removed several pumpkins from the sofa, he sat down, opened the *Racing Post* app and to placate her announced that they'd be staying at the Langham, one of her favourite hotels, only three and a half miles from Santa Anita Racecourse.

Whereupon Taggie went as scarlet as the poppy pinned to her luscious grey cashmere bosom and stammered that she wasn't coming.

'But it's all booked.'

'I told Geraldine a week ago.'

'Rather than me.'

'You weren't here to tell.'

'Don't be bloody silly, of course you're coming.'

At the tone of his voice, the dogs, who'd been swarming around him, slunk back to their boxes.

'I can't get away, I've got too much to do.' Taggie was furiously creaming butter and sugar together.

'Like what? Last time it was the cake stall at the fete.'

'Both Sapphire and Timon are coming – it's half-term and Tab's still mending her marriage.'

'Why doesn't she get a bloody sewing-machine? What else?'

It was Sapphire's birthday, stumbled on Taggie, and Caitlin's two sons were coming.

'They've got parents, for God's sake.'

'And I've promised them a Halloween party this Saturday: we're going off trick or treating round the village.'

'Am I hearing this right?' said Rupert softly. 'Quickly is running in one of the greatest races in the world and you're hawking yourself round Penscombe, touting for confectionery?'

Taggie wanted to hurl a pumpkin at him and yell, 'No, I'm trying to organize a surprise party for you, which is ballooning by the second,' but she only said, 'I'm truly sorry, I can't.'

'Yansy Pansy's so brilliant with children, why can't he organize this bash?'

'Because,' snapped back Taggie, 'since you fired Eddie, your father's got no one to watch porn with and keeps wandering into the stable lasses' bedrooms looking for him.'

At that moment, anxious to create their own porn, Cuthbert chose to mount Rupert's leg so vigorously that Gilchrist decided to mount Cuthbert – behaviour which would normally have sent Rupert and Taggie into fits of laughter, had not Jan barged in with a broomstick between his legs and sporting a witch's hat.

'Just the thing for you to wear at Royal Ascot, mam,' and he grinned, showing red plastic Dracula fangs.

Whereupon an outraged Rupert gave a goal kick, sending both Jack Russells flying through the air, and stalked off to bollock Geraldine, who was also in a foul mood. She and the rest of the office were run off their feet, unravelling Breeders' Cup red tape, with Quickly, Delectable and Touchy Filly flying out tomorrow, several days early, to adjust to a much hotter climate and get over the journey.

'I can't believe you and Taggie hadn't discussed it,' said Geraldine bitchily.

And Rupert thought for the millionth time how much he'd love to sack her, if only she hadn't been so efficient. Being away so much, he needed her to cover things.

'Rupert's furious I'm not going,' a distraught Taggie told Jan.

'Don't worry, mam, he'll understand once he appreciates what a great party you've organized for him. We could never have got it together if he'd been around. That's neat.' He picked up a sugar bat Taggie had made, and swooped it around the room. 'Don't cry, mam.'

Glancing back as he stalked towards the yard, Rupert saw the fucking poofter's arm around Taggie.

Gala, who'd also rowed with Rupert, had taken her one weekend off in four to stay in London with an aunt visiting from Zimbabwe.

Yet knowing Rupert was due back this morning, she had washed her hair and splashed Bluebell, a lovely new scent she'd treated herself to, behind her ears. Her heart somersaulted with excitement as she and Quickly reached the bottom of the gallops on his last workout before flying to America. There was

Rupert's Land Rover parked outside the Love Tower, whose windows he'd opened so he could tell if any passing horse had breathing problems. As third lot thundered by, Rupert was delighted. Hardly moving out of a canter, Quickly beat the yard's best by ten lengths. Gala rode beautifully, reminding him of Fenella Maxwell, his showjumping teammate in Santa Anita.

As she rode back, Rupert came out of the Love Tower and beckoned her over. Quickly, hardly blowing, took a bite out of his dark-blue jersey. Despite the freezing day, Rupert had been so cross with Taggie and Jan, he'd stormed out without a coat.

'Quickly's really well,' said Gala.

'I hope so.' Looking up, Rupert noticed the cold just gave a glow to her golden skin, whereas English girls tended to turn red or purple. Telling Louise, who was riding back on Touchy Filly, to take Quickly home and put two rugs on him, he took Gala back into the Love Tower. Worrying how Quickly would cope with a long flight, the heat of California, and with the incredible whooping din of an American crowd, he felt the colt needed people he loved around him.

'I don't know if I'm crazy,' he told Gala, 'but I've entered Quickly in the Classic,' which was the biggest race.

'But that's on dirt. Quickly's never run on dirt and he detests having mud in his face.'

'Exactly. He hates it so much, he'll bolt to the front.'

While she had been away, explained Rupert, Cathal and Gav had taken Quickly with half a dozen others for a racecourse gallop on the all-weather at Southwell, where the Fibresand surface was very similar to dirt.

'Quickly loathed the kickback so much, nothing could catch him.'

'Dirt's even worse, particularly if it rains.'

'Exactly, so he'll run even faster.'

'Why can't he run on the Turf as planned?'

Rupert glanced out of the window across the valley, where a once grey, now white stallion in a dark-blue rug was hanging over the fence in search of someone to chat to.

'Because the Classic has a larger five-million-dollar purse. If

Repay wins the Turf, he'll be almost too far ahead in the Global Sire charts for Love Rat to catch him.'

'Poor Quickly,' sighed Gala.

'He's tough, he's the fastest horse on the planet and at least Gav and Bao have got him used to loading on to a plane, but he needs people around who he trusts and loves. I want you to come to Santa Anita.'

Gala glanced up, amazed. Yet Rupert seemed completely serious. 'I'd love to. But aren't Cathal, Louise and Clover already going?'

'Marketa's gone to Melbourne with Fleance, and Gav'll be pushing off to the sales, so he won't be around to disapprove.'

'Disapprove?' Had she heard Rupert right? 'Are you sure?'

'Very.'

'Then I'd absolutely adore to.'

'Good.' Then, closing the Love Tower window, 'We don't want fourth lot to overhear any heavy breathing.'

As Gala laughed, he took her face in ice-cold hands, studying it for a second, then kissing her. The cleanness of his mouth, the lazily exploring tongue felt so right. As fourth lot thundered by, she opened her eyes for a second, to find his eyes tight shut.

'We mustn't,' she mumbled, pulling away. 'I love Taggie.'

'So do I. But she's refusing to come to Santa Anita, some fatuous Halloween party. So you're coming instead.'

Gala felt dreadfully guilty, not levelling with him about the surprise party, but she had been sworn to secrecy.

'What about Gropius?'

'He can stay with our dogs. We'll have to watch it. Helen left me, thank God, in the middle of LA Olympics. If I return without Taggie, the paps will be everywhere, so I'll put you in the hotel where Gav and the jockeys are staying.'

'Is it too risky?' Gala glanced out as Tarqui and Chekov hurtled past.

'No, it's worth it.'

Drawing her towards him, feeling for her breasts, kissing her neck, breathing in Bluebell with all its promise of spring, he murmured, 'Etta and Valent will chaperone us.'

Valent Edwards loved coming home, creeping up to the window and finding his wife waltzing around the room to Classic FM with Gwenny the cat in her arms. Even to watch Quickly in the Breeders' Cup, he knew she loathed leaving Mrs Wilkinson, Chisolm, Gwenny, Priceless and her garden.

Etta was relieved they'd be back for Guy Fawkes Day. Priceless was terrified of fireworks – so, for that matter, was she, still nervous of pyrotechnic Rupert and glad Taggie would be with them to smooth things over. Dora and Paris, who were pet-sitting, had promised to let Wilkie, such a proud mother, and Chisolm watch Quickly's race.

Back in the office at Penscombe, they were wrestling with endless Breeders' Cup documents, and insurance forms to be filled in, providing photographs and fingerprints for racecourse passes, wading through endless regulations about drug abuse and not using growth hormones or animal venoms, aware that a horse, even after a 3,000-mile flight, would be scratched if anything weren't adhered to.

'And when you think how they pump their horses full of stuff,' exploded Geraldine.

Dora was giggling over the handbook: '"*All runners must meet the starter to make him aware of any special needs*". Sex and Polos in Quickly's case. Oh, and listen to this. "Geldings are allowed twenty nanograms of testosterone".'

'Gav could do with that,' sighed Louise.

'Oh look.' Dora turned the page. '"If you win the Breeders' Cup Classic, you receive a high-performance cooler." What's that supposed to be?'

'Those two could do with some cooling down,' muttered Louise, as Rupert drove Gala back to the yard.

'Do you think they're having it off?' asked Dora.

'Not yet, but he drank from her bottle of water at a meeting the other day without wiping the top.'

'Hum. I'm going to pinch Old Eddie's badge, saying *Old Men Make Better Lovers*, and give it to Rupert for his birthday.'

*

There was feverish excitement in the yard when it was revealed that Gala was going to Santa Anita and not Taggie.

'You must keep an eye out and tell me what's going on,' Dora begged Louise, who would be setting out with Gala, Clover and Cathal the following day. This was a week before the Breeders' Cup kicked off, so the horses could get used to the climate and time changes. The Classic was run at 12.55 a.m., English time, when Quickly would normally be tucked up in bed. Also, because it was intended that Quickly should make-all in the Classic, which meant shooting to the front and staying there, he wouldn't need a pacemaker, so Rupert had decided to leave Bitsy at home.

'I do hope he doesn't miss Bitsy and Purrpuss too much, particularly on the plane,' said a worried Gala.

'He'll have Delectable – and get him *Seabiscuit* as an in-flight movie,' suggested Dora.

71

It turned out to be boiling hot in Santa Anita, but the stables were beautifully air-conditioned. In the first forty-eight hours in quarantine, Team Penscombe had to wear white space suits and shower when they went in and out. The horses also were only allowed Breeders' Cup food and water. Gala was worried how Quickly would adjust to the American custom of runners being led down to the post by a rider on a pony who wasn't Safety Car. Out of quarantine and cantering on the Wednesday, he met his 'pony person', a jolly old cowboy called Paul with a skewbald mare called Minnie, whom Quickly promptly fell in love with, so he didn't mind being ponied at all.

Louise, Clover and Gala meanwhile were having a lovely time; Lou-easy at the prospect of thirty-one veterinarians tending the foreign horses, Gala at the thought of Rupert arriving. They'd also been to Hollywood and Disneyland where they'd swum with dolphins and Clover had danced with Mickey Mouse.

Most of all they were enraptured by Santa Anita, which must be the most beautiful racecourse in the world. Eighteen miles from Hollywood, stands for 80,000 racegoers look across an oval track with phenomenally sharp bends. Within the cinnamon-brown dirt track lies the acid-green turf track, and inside that, rhubarb-pink buildings, so from the air the whole thing resembles an avocado and salmon roulade. Beyond the tracks lie green barns, housing the horses, against the theatrical backdrop of the San Gabriel Mountains, rearing up as purple as the ubiquitous Breeders' Cup jackets. Everywhere could be seen the lovely Breeders' Cup symbol of a horse's head with his mane coaxed forward to echo his pricked ears.

Rupert was flying out on Thursday. Taggie couldn't bear him going off without their making it up. If she weren't so dyslexic she could have written a proper letter telling him how much she was going to miss him. She had found him an early birthday present of some cufflinks, made specially by Theo Fennell, of a tiny Love Rat looking out of his stable.

She was just finishing ironing his latest lucky shirt, which was peacock blue. Out of the window she could see the leaves fluttering down. Each one caught meant a happy day. Rupert had always claimed he fell in love with her when he watched her scampering round a wood with his children catching leaves to bring him happiness.

If she dashed out now, she could perhaps catch seven for each day he was away in Los Angeles and Melbourne running up to his birthday, so he would understand the coded message. Returning pink and panting a quarter of an hour later, just shoving yellow and scarlet cherry leaves into a Jiffy bag, she was horrified to see a Majestic lorry coming up the drive to deliver the drink. If Rupert came back from the gallops, he'd be bound to rumble the party. Yelling out to Jan, asking him to hide the little parcel and the Jiffy bag of leaves under the shirts in Rupert's case, she rushed out to head off Majestic.

Having not made it up with his wife, Rupert's mood didn't improve when, on arriving in Santa Anita, he found that horses from overseas were not allowed out on the turf tracks for exercise, in case they gave diseases to the local horses, until later in the morning. This was far too hot for Delectable, who just needed a gentle workout before running her race later in the day.

Not that the late start upset Quickly. Having been up all night hollering and kicking his box for apples, he liked to lie in in the morning, and bit Gala on the ankle when she tried to wake him. Being fair-skinned, however, he had been driven crackers by mosquitoes.

'Why the hell haven't you put something on them?' demanded Rupert.

'Because insect repellent's a banned substance,' snapped back Gala.

She'd been thinking of hardly anything else but Rupert since she arrived in Santa Anita and was devastated when he greeted her with apparent indifference. He was so offhand it was as though the clinch in the Love Tower had never happened. Not that he was being nicer to anyone else, snarling at the ubiquitous press in their Day-Glo green waistcoats whenever they approached him.

Massive crowds were already pouring in for the Friday of the two-day meeting. There seemed to be no dress code. Hats, mostly Stetsons and baseball caps, were worn much more by the men, who also wore shorts rather than suits.

Saddling up was a nightmare. In England you retreated into a little stall, where onlookers could only peer in from a distance. Here, when Gala joined Louise trying to calm little Delectable, the boxes were open to the public, frantic to see their equine heroes. Only divided by three-foot-high partitions, topped by wire netting, these boxes allowed any trainer to see what their rivals were up to. Penscombe and Valhalla, who had entered a filly called La Tempesta, totally ignored each other.

Santa Anita being close to Hollywood, the glamorous crowds swarmed with celebrities, who all gazed at Rupert, still dazzling despite crossness and lack of sleep.

'What have I seen him in?' pondered a passing beauty.

'A foul mood recently,' said Gala sourly.

In the parade ring, however, a pretty blonde pop star was belting out a song called 'The Best is Yet to Come'.

'I promise it is,' murmured Rupert to Gala as adjusting Delectable's bridle, his signet ring touched her fingers on the lead rope.

Happiness rolled over her, and even more so when Delectable and Tarqui beat La Tempesta, ridden by Roman Lovell, by a head, earning a cool two million dollars. As the cheers rang round the purple mountains, Delectable immediately became favourite for the 1000 Guineas, and she was draped in a garland, almost bigger than herself, of bright-yellow asters, edged with purple and topped with purple and white orchids, grown specially for the Breeders' Cup.

Louise was crying with joy, so was Tarqui, and an exultant Rupert had an excuse to kiss Gala and mutter he'd come to her room sometime before midnight, but wouldn't ring for fear of hackers.

Next minute, a blonde in a burgundy jacket and blue jodhpurs, wearing a black hat with wires rising out of the top came cantering up to a returning Tarqui, screeching: 'How special is it to be the rider of a Breeders' Cup winner?' expecting him to take her through every special yard of the race and thank every special person from the trainer to the stable cat.

Gala had never heard anything like the joyous din greeting a winner, connections hugging each other, whooping, hollering, hi-fiving in orgasmic ecstasy. As race followed race, the celebrations grew more raucous. Touchy Filly was in the last one – the Longine Distaff for mares and fillies – and didn't like the US custom of a large loader standing up in the starting stalls and hanging on to her bridle until the gates opened, so she bit him and shot out to escape reprisals. Although she was competing against older horses, she didn't stop running until she was only just beaten into third place.

More ecstasy for Penscombe, as they celebrated Delectable and Touchy Filly's triumphs. Rupert, however, warned them not to get too plastered. 'We've got to do Quickly justice tomorrow,' he told them. Then: 'Slope off early, tell Etta and Valent you've got a headache,' he murmured to Gala.

'I thought women claimed to have headaches when they didn't want sex,' Gala murmured back. 'You'd better be careful, Tarqui and Louise are two doors down.' She glanced across to where the two were laughing uproariously, Tarqui saying, 'A first and a tird – you can't do better than that.'

'Although,' added Gala, 'they'll probably be too busy having a victory shag to bother about us.'

441

72

Gala's pretty room in a hotel near the racecourse had on its primrose-yellow walls framed photographs of Judy Garland, Hedy Lamarr, Tyrone Power, Rock Hudson and equally famous equine stars: Seabiscuit, Secretariat and Zenyatta. Quickly might be up there soon, prayed Gala.

Collapsing on to the largish single bed, she wondered if it would be big enough to contain their passion. She couldn't stop trembling, hollow with longing, yet terrified as a virgin bride on her wedding night. Was it really going to happen?

Presumptuously, before she left England, she'd splurged a month's wages on a white silk nightgown from Cavendish House. This beautifully set off her all-over fake-tan. Waiting for Rupert she'd downed three quarters of a bottle of wine, showered three times – be careful who you wash for – cleaned her teeth every ten minutes. Make-up was another dilemma, without it her tired eyes looked tiny, but she didn't want mascara and eye-liner all over the pillows. She also drenched herself, and particularly her hands, in Bluebell body lotion, to combat the allegedly Brillo-pad paws of stable lasses.

Oh help, help! She leapt at a thunderous banging on the door, but, opening it, found only a man with long blond hair wearing dark glasses and a Stetson.

'Go away,' she screamed, slamming the door.

There was another rat-a-tat.

'Let me in, for fuck's sake.' It was a grinning Rupert. Removing the dark glasses and Stetson, he patted his blond locks. 'I pinched Dame Hermione's wig.'

'How did you get hold of it?'

'She'd shoved it into her bag like a Cocker Spaniel puppy so I rescued it.' Then he tore it off, singing 'Here's to the Heroes' in a high falsetto, making Gala laugh, dispelling her nerves.

'It's pissing with rain outside,' grumbled Rupert. 'Be like a quagmire tomorrow – Quickly had better learn to swim.'

'Do you want a drink?'

'Yes, down here.' He slid a hand between her legs until she writhed away in ecstasy, then, putting her hands round his neck, she kissed him, only breaking off so he could pull her white nightgown over her head. 'My God, you are so beautiful,' he sighed. How could breasts be so soft and nipples as jutting as biro tops?

He was wearing a navy-blue shirt. As she undid the buttons, she asked: 'Is this your latest lucky one?'

'It is now.'

As her hand crept down to unzip his trousers, she gasped. 'Oh wow, talk about a cock star.'

'Don't take the piss.' He led her over to the bed. 'Christ, I hope we don't fall out.'

'We're always falling out.' She had to joke not to betray the force of her passion. 'Promise not to fire me for at least a week.'

'I only want to fire you with enthusiasm.'

He tried to take it slowly, but desire swept them away.

'Christ,' he said, as he slid his hand inside her. 'They ought to issue a flood warning in here as well as outside.'

And after a few moments of stroking, he couldn't resist plunging his cock into her . . . oh, the rapture! 'Buttercunt,' he murmured, 'oh, you lovely buttercunt,' because she was so warm, slippery and welcoming, and gripped him so tightly as he moved in and out in perfect rhythm.

Rupert tried to stop himself coming by studying the differing confirmations of Seabiscuit and Secretariat, but it was no good. Next moment they both stiffened and shuddered in ecstasy, then he slumped on top of her, mumbling, 'Oh you darling child.'

'I can't help it,' gasped Gala. 'I love you, I love you.'

Rupert smiled down at her, pushing her hair back. 'And I too,' and he kissed her damp forehead.

Coming back to earth, she rolled him on his back, crouching between his legs and getting to work on him, licking him everywhere. He'd never been given head like this, and in no time, shot into her once more.

'Now it's my turn,' he said, a moment later. 'The foreplay's the thing.'

Gala woke at five; it was still dark. Rupert was dressed and looking at the weather on his app.

'I don't know what'll happen later in the day, but that was definitely the Classic,' he said, kissing her.

Security was tight down at the racecourse, with a guard parked outside every stable. Having fed Quickly nuts and a little hay, Gala took him out, to discover that last night's rain had turned the dirt track into a sodden pudding, which had been subsequently closed for training purposes.

Reeling with happiness, Gala didn't care and instead cantered Quickly on the turf. Mid-morning, she joined Etta, Valent and Rupert for a typically stylish Breeders' Cup breakfast of scrambled eggs, caviar blinis and Bloody Marys. Etta vowed she was only going to have one of the latter.

'Wasn't yesterday thrilling? I've put Delectable's yellow garland in water. How's your headache, Gala? I nearly popped into your hotel to give you some Neurofen.'

'That's so kind. I had a wonderful night actually.'

Gala caught Rupert's eye and nearly laughed, even more so, when he said, 'That's the stupidest of the Three Wise Men going past,' as Dame Hermione strode by in a large crimson turban.

Rupert and Gala were going through the entries in the Classic, which included the greatest horses in the world. Simone de Beauvoir, the French battleaxe, had an all-powerful rival in To Die For, America's favourite mare, who'd won the Triple Crown, ridden by America's top jockey, Hammond Johnson.

Hammond's photo could be seen on the wall: a little man with tiny legs and muscular brown arms bulging out of a white sleeveless polo neck, and strong enough to hold up an army of horses. Also in contention again was the Japanese Hiroshi on Noonday Silence, Hernandez, a Mexican on a wonder bay called Special Angel, and Finger Prince, ridden by America's leading woman jockey, a beauty called Sharon Peters.

'Oh Quickers, you've got a lot to beat,' sighed Gala.

'All change, all change,' said the irrepressible Matt Chapman from *At the Races*, sitting down at their table. 'I Will Repay's switched to the Classic – and guess who's riding him?'

'Who?'

'Your grandson, Eddie Alderton.'

'Don't be ridiculous.'

'He flew in last night.'

'Don't be ridiculous.'

'Ash evidently doesn't go. Has a broken arm and three broken ribs – that's how Eddie got the ride. Rumour has it, Ash hit on Eddie and Eddie hit him back even harder.'

Rupert was silenced.

'Not a bad idea,' went on Matt. 'The boy's used to American tracks, he's ridden on dirt before.'

With some amusement Matt waited for fireworks but the cool bugger didn't miss a beat.

'Surprised they're fielding such a Second Eleven jockey,' drawled Rupert. 'Thought they could have found a decent local. Good, that gives us even more chance.'

73

Racing in America is much more of a battleground. Tracks don't have the undulations and ups and downs of England, but the turns are sharper, and horses explode out of the starting stalls, hurtling towards the first bend, with a huge amount of jostling, swearing and barging – a terrifying stampede.

Eddie had been throwing up all night from nerves. Huddled in the corner of the weighing room, he was aware that in three quarters of an hour, he'd be racing against his gods. He was so pleased that his parents Perdita and Luke awaited him in the parade ring. When they met him at the airport yesterday, they seemed chilled about his and Sauvignon's baby, but furious with Rupert for firing him, as was Uncle Adrian, Rupert's gay brother, who had flown in from his New York gallery to cheer on Eddie, his godson. Adrian, a paler version of Rupert with light-brown hair and hazel eyes, unlike Rupert, always remembered Eddie's birthday.

Eddie, hurt that Sauvignon hadn't even sent him a good luck text, was surprised how fond he'd got of I Will Repay, who'd never been spoilt rotten like Quickly and adored attention from the public, growing a foot every time he saw a camera, pricking his ears and pulling faces to order.

'The only time he bites me is when I brush his tummy,' confided Harmony, of whom Eddie had also grown very fond. She reminded him of a plain Lark and gave him lots of confidence.

'You've improved so much from Isa's crash course,' she'd told him last night. 'And for Repay, it must be like dancing with Anton on *Strictly*. Ash hits his horses so hard and saws on their mouths.' Now, noticing how Eddie's pallor was emphasized by wearing Sheikh Baddi's purple and gold silks, she added: 'It's going to be OK, I promise.'

The razzmatazz had increased tenfold on the second day of the meeting. Twenty minutes before they left their stables, the runners in the Classic had to have two more vials of blood taken, which made Quickly even edgier. The crowd were really intrusive, hanging round screaming for their heroes, following the runners down the chutes. Gala was terrified Quickly would kick someone.

More and more discarded betting slips littered the ground like autumn leaves as the climax of the afternoon – the Classic – approached. The parade ring was so crowded, the only way jockeys and connections could find each other was by a number written on the grass.

So many of the mega-rich American owners seemed to know and admire Valent and were delighted to meet his new-ish wife, pretty in pink and wearing a blue baseball cap bearing Master Quickly's name, in which Rupert thought she looked ridiculous.

Etta had just called Dora, who said all the animals were fine and had eaten up. Mrs Wilkinson and Chisolm were coming into the kitchen to watch the big race.

'Every time they flag up Quickly's name,' said Dora, 'they add that Etta Edwards is the breeder. That is so cool.'

'Isn't it,' squeaked Etta.

'How's Rupert?' asked Dora. 'He looks cross. He really should take a media-friendly course.'

Each jockey was televised as he came into the paddock to huge cheers, and had to announce his own and his horse's name. 'Just like *University Challenge*,' giggled Etta.

'Not quite,' said Valent as Tarqui and Manu de la Tour puckered their lips and kissed the camera lens.

Quickly looked magnificent, his silver coat set off by a red saddlecloth with his name on. Nor was he having any truck with Penscombe not fraternizing with Valhalla. Catching sight of Eddie, receiving last instructions from Isa and Cosmo, he gave a great whicker and towed a giggling, swearing Gala across the paddock to nudge Eddie in his concave stomach.

'Good luck, Eddie,' said Gala defiantly. 'We all miss you, please come back.'

'Fuck off,' hissed Cosmo.

'Rupert's come without Taggie,' drawled Ruth Walton, 'so I'm in with a chance,' which annoyed Cosmo even more.

The runners were parading down to the start, so sleek with their slim jockeys, compared with the ponies, often buckling under the fat pony persons in their purple jackets, leading them. The crowd, not wanting any overseas rider to take the big one, were yelling for To Die For and Hammond Johnson, now wearing a little red bow-tie at the neck of his red and white silks, and also for Finger Prince ridden by the lovely blonde Sharon Peters. Hernandez, the Mexican on Special Angel, couldn't stop crossing himself; Hiroshi from Japan had got his bare feet very dirty walking the course. Tarqui knew and was joking with all of them.

'Godspeed, Tarqui,' cried Gala as she handed him and Quickly over to Paul the cowboy, their pony person, who said he wanted to be 'part of the Quickly experience'. Quickly agreed, and stopped jig-jogging for a second to mount Minnie.

The press were everywhere in their Day-Glo green smocks. A rock star sang 'The Star-Spangled Banner', the trumpeters blew a tantivy and a huge American flag was laid over the course. God Bless America.

A curious biblical light had bathed the racecourse in brilliant sunshine. Dark clouds with dazzling white undersides gathered on top of the San Gabriel Mountains, which had turned a deep purple.

'Oh Angel Gabriel,' prayed Harmony, as she took up her position on the rail opposite the big screen, 'lend Repay your wings for a few minutes.'

Down at the start, weeping willows reminded Eddie of Valent and Etta's house, Badger's Court. He wished yet again he were riding Quickly for them and Grandpa.

The kind loaders, all in purple, patted each horse as they led them into their stalls. Quickly didn't like sharing his with one of them, who stood up on the ledge and hung on to his bridle, so like Touchy Filly, he bit him, then was distracted by Simone de Beauvoir and wafts of Manu's aftershave on the left.

Rupert, Gala, Etta and Valent were on the rail, opposite the big screen, so they could see the bobbing hats of the jockeys above, revving up horses. Rupert's hand slid into Gala's for a second. Quickly, still gazing at Simone, spooked, as the roar of 'They're off!' reverberated round the purple mountains, and missed the kick. Not that it mattered. Outraged to have so much dirt in his face, Quickly hurtled to the front on the inside rail and stayed there. The horses' legs couldn't be seen for the flurry of cinnamon-brown mud. Every time anyone tried to catch up with Quickly, he eyeballed them and accelerated away.

'Oh well done, Quickly,' screamed Etta and Gala, but were totally drowned by the Americans bellowing on dark-brown To Die For as she gradually edged closer. Playing hard to get, however, Quickly changed legs, scorched round the bend and shot away again. Tarqui, the swooping king, used to finding daylight between the most closely packed horses, was for once making all.

'Look at that acceleration. Too fast, he'll run out of petrol.' Rupert glanced at his iPhone for a second. Then: 'Christ, he's breaking the record.'

Eddie, however, had Bao's good luck rabbit in his pocket. Despite being badly bumped at the start by both Finger Prince and Special Angel, and getting a face full of sand, I Will Repay had a huge heart and battled on bravely, as Eddie got him on a lovely rhythm at the back.

Eddie also knew Quickly backwards – that the colt was indelibly competitive and would exert every atom of energy not to be overtaken. With To Die For lurking on the inside rail and Hernandez and Special Angel hovering on his offside, Eddie knew that as either of them challenged, Quickly would accelerate . . . so he and Repay waited on the far right.

As they thundered past the three-furlong-pole, he started cranking Repay up, swooping from last to the front but letting

Quickly keep ahead, ahead, ahead. He must only swoop at the very last moment, not giving Quickly time to retaliate.

Quickly was also a brave horse, but with To Die For and Special Angel snapping at his heels from the left and right and escalating thunder from the crowd, the tiring colt lost concentration for a second and missed, on his off-side, a horse and rider scorching past in a tornado of mud; silks and L-shaped white blaze unrecognizable. The pair's identity was only revealed as victory was snatched in the shadow of the post, and the rider's mud-coated face was transformed by an ecstatic, white grin.

Eddie, however, had learnt his lesson, and didn't punch the air, nor take his hands off the reins until, glancing up at the big screen, he saw the results. I Will Repay had got up by a nose, from Quickly, with To Die For third and Finger Prince fourth.

Next minute, Eddie's gods – Hammond, Hernandez, Hiroshi, Tarqui and Manu – were gathering round, pumping his hand, clapping him on the back. Cosmo and Isa and Mrs Walton were in raptures, Dame Hermione yelling her red-turbanned head off.

'Oh, well done, Eddie, and well done, Quickly. He was second – clever boy, the smallest horse in the race,' screamed Etta, hugging Valent and Gala. But turning to hi-five Rupert, her hand met air and her face felt scorched by the white-hot fury on his face.

'W-what's the matter?'

'That must have scuppered Love Rat's Leading Sire chances.'

Next minute, the presenter with wire shooting out of her hat charged up on a lovely pale chestnut, rising at the trot worthy of the Pony Club. 'Congratulations on winning the Breeders' Cup Classic, Eddie,' she screeched. 'How special is this very special moment to you?'

'I'm sitting on a very special horse,' laughed Eddie, 'who's in love with his very special stable girl Harmony, and he ran so fast because he wanted to get back to her.' He must stop saying that every time he had a winner.

'Take us through this very special race.'

'I knew Quickly would never let me pass him, so I mugged

him on the line. I'm very grateful to Cosmo Rannaldini for giving me the ride, and Isa Lovell for coaching me, and as an American I'm very proud to win America's greatest race.'

'And your daddy played polo for America, and a little bird told me the very special news that you're going to be a daddy too.'

But Eddie didn't want to talk about babies. As happy as a sand boy, he hurled his whip into the yelling tumult, and the whole crowd seemed to leap to seize it. Then he turned to Harmony, galumphing up like Nellie the Elephant, sobbing her eyes out, hugging Repay, sponge ready to wipe the dirt out of his eyes, before the lovely garland was thrown over his withers.

'We did it, we did it!' she cried. 'Isn't yellow Repay's colour?'

Returning through the whooping, screaming crowd, seeing a forest of cameras, Repay became a yard taller as Cosmo and Sheikh Abdul Baddi took his reins on each side to lead him in.

On the way to weigh in, Tarqui passed his ex-lover Isa, who held out a hand. 'You did well.'

'Tanks,' said Tarqui. 'You did better.'

For a moment, they exchanged a brief bittersweet hug then moved on. Cosmo, Mrs Walton, Sheikh Baddi, Isa and Harmony were now blissfully flanking a head-tossing I Will Repay for the photographers. Eddie, returning from weighing in to join them, saw Rupert approaching and put out his hand.

'Quickly ran super, Grandpa.'

Totally ignoring him, Rupert walked straight past.

'For Christ's sake, Rupert, don't be so fooking unsporting,' exploded Valent. Then, turning to a stunned Eddie, 'Well done, lad, fantastic ride,' and he hugged him, as did Etta.

Gala was horrified. 'Poor Eddie, he was utterly brilliant.'

Perdita was equally appalled. 'How can you be such an ungenerous bastard, Dad?'

'Have you ever known him to be anything else?' observed Rupert's brother Adrian.

The lack of exchange had also been clocked by the world's

media and transmitted worldwide. For Eddie, any joy of winning evaporated. Cosmo, however, was in heaven.

'Stupid, stupid Rupert,' he told the vast throng of press. 'Eddie rode a dream of a race because since he joined our yard, he's worked with Isa Lovell, a far better trainer. I was annoyed with Rupert for poaching Tarqui, my stable jockey, so when Rupert sacked Eddie Alderton, his grandson, I asked Eddie to join us. We got the better bargain, Eddie got the better horse, and this win confirms our stallion Roberto's Revenge as Leading Sire.'

Isa loathed the press, but was happy to put the boot in.

'My late father Jake Lovell got a silver medal here, beating Rupert Campbell-Black back in the seventies. Today I Will Repay, trained by another Lovell, beat Rupert's horse again.'

'That's very special. Imagine your father cheering in heaven.'

For a second Isa couldn't speak. 'That's a good thought.'

Repay's connections were then swept off to the presentation where a very camp celebrity, who clearly didn't know one end of a horse or a whore from another, handed over the lovely Breeders' Cup trophy of a horse, with an equally camply-raised foreleg. Having congratulated them on a very special win, he then quipped that it was odd to have Eddie the jockey so much taller than Cosmo the co-owner, which didn't please Cosmo one bit – even though he did later get to kiss Bo Derek.

Eddie, meanwhile, was in pieces.

'I wanted a place in history but not on a horse that robbed Grandpa of Leading Sire.'

The Classic was clearly the race that mattered. Eddie had never had so many emails and texts – but still not a word from Sauvignon. And up in the sky, platinum blonde with a flickering gold halo, hung the jockey moon. Despite massive worldwide praise, Eddie cried his eyes out all the way home on the plane.

By English time, Taggie and Jan watched the Classic after midnight. Taggie had been icing Rupert's cake, topped with a big picture of Love Rat. Watching Rupert adjusting Quickly's bridle in the parade ring, she noticed he wasn't wearing any Love Rat cufflinks. She was so sad he hadn't acknowledged them or the fallen leaves, and had been terse and offhand on the telephone.

She felt ashamed that she and particularly Jan cheered their heads off for Eddie, and when she tried to call Rupert and congratulate him for Quickly coming second, he didn't pick up.

'Oh heavens,' she cried, catching sight of Rupert in the winners enclosure, 'he's just blanked Eddie.'

'That's a disgrace,' said Jan. 'I suppose it's because Repay's win added two million dollars to Roberto's earnings and Quickly's second only nine hundred thousand to Love Rat's.'

'So, no carrot for Love Rat,' sighed Taggie. 'Oh poor old boy – and poor Rupert.'

Bursts of cheering for Quickly were still coming from the yard, where the consensus of opinion was that Rupert had behaved like an absolute shit.

'*Plus ça change,*' said Pat.

No prizes for coming second, thought Gav, as he watched the race in Keeneland, but he was still so proud of Quickly. On the other hand, a knife twisted in his heart to notice the body language between Gala and Rupert, before and during the race. They'd clearly enjoyed a great night. Lucky to come at all, he thought wearily.

74

Valent was furious when Rupert refused to stay for any post-race celebrations.

'The little horse did bluddy well, why can't you wait till tomorrow?'

'I've got business to do in Melbourne.'

'Roobish. No one does any business in Melbourne in the run up to the Cup, and even less afterwards. It costs the nation over 540 million dollars in lost productivity.'

Ignoring him, Rupert took a Saturday-night flight, arriving in Melbourne the following afternoon. It was the middle of the night in England, which he felt was hardly the time to wake Taggie and make it up.

Churning with fury over Cosmo's gloating, aware that he'd been vile to everyone, particularly sweet Gala, whom he'd left with hardly a word, Rupert didn't sleep on the flight. Checking into his hotel, he was about to ring his daughter Bianca in Perth, hoping they could hook up at the Melbourne Cup, when he was pre-empted by a call from his old friend, Baby Spinosissimo, summoning him to supper.

'I'm bushed, Baby.'

'Of course, you've lost a day on the flight. You'll sleep far better if you stay awake till tonight.'

Baby, a hugely successful tenor who'd just had a big hit, singing the Duke in *Rigoletto,* was the on (occasionally off) boyfriend of Rupert's brother Adrian. Baby lived in a ravishing beach house overlooking the ocean. He had always kept racehorses and had bought New Year's Dave from Rupert after the 31 December scandal. He was also putting up Fleance, who'd come out with Meerkat and Marketa and was hopefully going to be 'wictorious in Wictoria', in the Melbourne Cup.

Going straight to the stables, Rupert was delighted to find both Dave and Fleance in great nick and gratifyingly pleased to see him.

'We've been working Fleance on the sands and in the sea,' said Marketa, who was wearing a leopardskin cap back to front, and who seemed to be enjoying the plethora of bronzed Australian stable lads drifting about.

Rupert was even more delighted when a gorgeous suntanned blonde raced up, flung her arms round his neck and kissed him, and he realized it was Lark.

'How lovely to see you,' she gabbled. 'I'm so sorry about Quickers in the Classic, he ran brilliant, he'd never have got beat if Eddie had been riding him. So awful, threatening Love Rat's chance of Global Sire, and revolting Cosmo gloating. But there's still time, and Dave,' she stroked New Year's Dave's satin shoulder, 'is going to do his best to boost his dad's earnings, and Fleance too, he's grown into such a lovely horse – they call him Fiancé round here.'

She paused, blushing and gasping for breath.

'Oh Lark,' Rupert hugged her, 'you always say the right things, and you've grown so beautiful. Everyone misses you at Penscombe.'

Lark blushed even more. She was dying to ask about Young Eddie and Sauvignon's baby but instead said, 'How's Taggie?'

'Fine,' lied Rupert. Seeing Lark's sweet, sympathetic face, he suddenly wanted to pour his heart out about being a great-grandfather. Also that Taggie had not forgiven him, resulting in no love notes in his suitcase, horribly stilted telephone conversations or being told Taggie was shopping in Cheltenham with Jan.

'Come and see Peppy,' said Lark, leading him down to the stallion boxes. Peppy Koala, who was staying for the Australian covering season, gave a throaty whicker when he saw his master.

'Look how pleased he is to see you. Beastly Cosmo, dissing him and saying Roberto's Revenge was far too valuable to shuttle to Australia, when Peppy Koala came from here in the first place.'

Reflecting that Lark kept up with everything, Rupert gave Peppy a Polo and said, 'Peppy's coming home in January – why don't you come back with him? Your job's open at any time.'

'I couldn't leave Dave.' Then Lark glanced furtively over the half door, her face darkening. 'I shouldn't tell you this, but I think if Dave wins the Cup tomorrow, Baby might retire him or sell him on.'

'Surely not?'

'Baby always seems to need money,' whispered Lark, 'and some beastly Chinese man's been hanging around. Dave's been lapped in love all his life.' Her voice trembled. 'I'm not sure how he'd get on at stud in China.'

'He's not going, I'll talk to Baby.'

It was an exquisitely gentle evening. Looking out on the peacock-blue sea flecked with seagulls, watching dogs chasing sticks along the beach, Rupert and Baby dined on a veranda with grey-gold light flickering down through a ceiling of gum trees.

Missing his dogs, Rupert was charmed by Baby's yellow Labrador, Siegfried, who kept snatching napkins off the table.

'He used to carry my cheques to the bank,' said Baby. 'Even when they blew me out recently, he still went on taking them back to them.'

With his blond locks, cute turned-up nose and long eyelashes, Baby still looked like the most fancied choirboy, but had added a second chin and several inches round the waist. He had always loved his food, and now tucked into pâté de campagne, followed by tagliatelle with green pesto sauce and avocado and bacon salad. More beautiful youths, taking the opportunity to gaze at Rupert, kept topping up their glasses with miraculous red wine.

Baby was pleased Rupert thought his horses looked well, but complained that he'd recently been such a success, both as the Duke, and Rodolfo in *La Bohème* at Sydney Opera House, he was being pressured to join the production on tour.

'But I'm too old for that sort of caper, acting madly in love with tiresome divas. I want to stay home with my horses and Siegfried. If Dave does well on Tuesday, I'm gonna retire him.'

'That's crazy,' exploded Rupert. But suddenly – it must be tiredness – he wondered if he still had the appetite for pursuing the Global Leading Sire title all over again next year, particularly without Dave's help.

'I want to retire,' said Baby. 'I'm fed up with worrying about money.'

'Can't help it, if you go on drinking wine as good as this.'

'I've been offered thirty million for Dave.'

'By the Chinese.'

'Yes, actually. They've bought a stud farm north of Melbourne.'

'If he wins the Cup tomorrow, you'll have stallion masters ringing from all over the world offering twice as much. Let him have another year, bring him to Royal Ascot and the Arc.'

'I'm sick of working my butt off, and your brother wants us to get married.' Baby spooned chocolate roulade into bowls for himself and Rupert.

'What?' exploded Rupert for a second time.

'I admit he's too old for me.'

'Adrian's three years younger than me.'

'But you're much more attractive – you ought to be playing the Duke.'

'I know.' They grinned at each other.

'He wants to retire too. He's fed up with flogging Old Masters and me singing my head off: my tiny assets are frozen. He wants us to be together and solvent.'

'He bitterly resents Uncle Cyprian leaving me the Stubbs.'

'He does – and he really wants us to get married.'

'Where, for God's sake?'

'He's set his heart on Cotchester Cathedral.'

'That's where Taggie and I got married,' said Rupert in outrage.

'They won't have us. Church don't do gay marriages so it'll have to be some smart golf club. It's terribly complicated,' sighed Baby. 'Do we come up the aisle together? And which is the bride? Does one of us get given away? Do we have bridesmaids?'

'And what about a best man?'

'I said I wanted Dancer Maitland as my best man and Adrian threw a hissy fit, said *he* was my best man.' Baby giggled and helped himself to another chunk of chocolate roulade.

'Dancer sang at our wedding,' said Rupert. 'He was madly in love with Ricky France-Lynch.'

Then he remembered Taggie coming up the aisle and how he'd so desperately wanted to be alone with her that he'd whisked her away from the reception even before the cake was cut. He must ring her.

'I was hopelessly in love with Isa Lovell,' Baby said. 'And he's so in with Cosmo now. You ought to get that pretty grandson out of that den of vipers. No good will come of it.'

He waved to the minion to give Rupert some more pudding wine.

'I had better buy Dave back myself,' said Rupert. 'Don't sell him to the Chinese. And I'm not sure you should marry my brother. He's very dull.'

'But you'll be my sister-in-law,' grinned Baby. 'This wine is spectacular. Let's hope we'll be drinking it out of the Melbourne Cup on Tuesday night.'

75

Meanwhile, back at Penscombe, Taggie was going spare. The issuing of the invitations had been so cloak and dagger, and people had been so wary of ringing in to accept in case they got Rupert, that a huge number hadn't answered at all. How could she possibly make a seating plan?

Presents, however, were beginning to pour in and Taggie was finding it impossible to keep track of them. Rupert's friends, Basil Baddingham, Drew Benedict and Hengist Brett-Taylor, had sent him a rather good grey yearling called Jerry Hatrick.

At midnight Taggie was trying to find room for sixty candles on his cake, when Jan came into the kitchen.

'Darling,' he said, 'you look shattered, go to bed.'

'I've got too much to do and the Melbourne Cup'll be on in a minute.'

'Not until our five in the morning. I'll wake you in plenty of time.'

Upstairs in her bed she found a hot-water bottle. No sooner had her head hit the pillow, than she was asleep.

Good as his word, Jan banged on her door half an hour before the race. Having cleaned her teeth, washed her face, put on some base, she splashed herself with Issey Florale, then washed it off again. She must behave. But Jan had called her 'darling' and lit a fire in the kitchen. Yawning dogs thumped their tails: what was going on? Jan then gave her a bowl of hot stock from the venison he'd been marinating for days and insisted she sat down on the sofa. He then reported progress.

At least 300 filo pastry baskets, contained in muffin tins, had only to be filled with lemon and garlic prawns that had been tossed in melted butter. Goats'-cheese tartlets, mini-kebabs, sausage rolls and cheese puffs only needed heating up, so if Rupert were delayed, there would be enough canapés to keep everyone going.

As the choice of main course there was Beef Wellington, lamb shank encrusted with rosemary, venison and endless veg already prepared.

'Then finally for dessert,' said Jan, 'we've got lemon meringue pie, cheesecake, sticky toffee pudding, fruit salad steeped in sloe gin, and,' he added triumphantly, 'because your husband went to school there, we're having Harrow, rather than Eton Mess. We only need to add the cream and we are on course, or rather, three course.'

'That is so brilliant.' Taggie's voice broke. 'I used to try and learn a new word every day, but I could never find one good enough to thank you properly.'

For now, Jan had also made some toasties: fried cheese and tomato sandwiches tied up with string and served with some delicious mulled wine, which Rupert loathed. Taggie found she was really hungry.

As Jan turned on the television they could see musicians clad in red sitting in red armchairs, accompanying Baby Spinosissimo, Australia's darling, singing 'Here's to the Heroes' to thunderous applause and not a dry eye in the vast exuberant crowd of beautiful suntanned people.

'I love this tune.' Taggie sang along gruffly.

Then the camera showed the lovely racecourse in the middle of a town full of parks and wide straight roads, with the Prussian-blue sea idling in the distance, then panned in on the explosion of yellow roses swarming round the parade ring and over an archway through which the runners were being led.

'Look at those crowds,' sighed Taggie. 'I hope Fleance won't get too het-up.'

Fleance was 30–1: the Australian press had been pretty dismissive of his and Meerkat's chances.

'Not so Timon,' said Jan, sitting down beside her and topping up their glasses, 'who I found tugging out a front tooth, because he needed tooth-fairy money to bet on Fleance.'

Smelling toasted cheese, Forester wandered over and clambered on to the sofa between them with his head on Taggie's lap, his quarters on Jan's.

'Forester the chaperone,' grinned Jan. As they both stroked his silken body, their hands touched and retreated.

'I've given Eddie a sleeping pill,' he added.

'That venison soup was heaven. You are a dear.'

'No, the deer were dear.'

In Melbourne, the runners were coming into the paddock.

'Oh look – there's Lark leading up Dave. He is so like his mum, Cordelia,' cried Taggie, 'and Lark's got so pretty. She was hopelessly in love with Young Eddie and led up Quickly after his first win with Eddie riding him. Eddie was so excited he whisked her upstairs to bed, missed a stewards' enquiry and lost the race. Rupert was livid.'

'Is he ever anything else?'

'Rupert says she's the best stable girl he's ever had – adores her horses, working all hours.'

Jan ran his hand down her cheek. 'No one works harder than you.'

Taggie tried to move her face away, but found she couldn't. Then she jumped in guilt, as she saw Rupert in the paddock. Noticing all the women gazing at him and everyone holding up cameras, she wondered how could she possibly be married to so glamorous a man?

'He's not wearing his white suit,' she said in surprise.

'Probably doesn't want drink spilt all over it.'

'Probably doesn't want to upstage Fleance.' As a dazzlingly white Fleance sauntered into the paddock.

Leading him, falling out of a strapless flowered dress, was Marketa, who was promptly ordered by an official to cover her-self up with the regulation red tunic.

A huge cheer went up as Baby, trailing an entourage of beautiful young men, arrived.

'That's Dave's owner,' explained Taggie. 'He's the boyfriend of Rupert's brother Adrian. They haven't answered the invitation to Rupert's party. Baby's an ex-lover of Isa Lovell, who was also a boyfriend of Tarqui.' If Jan were really gay, she wondered, did he fancy any of them?

As Marketa led Fleance up to Rupert, who adjusted his bridle, Taggie noticed sadly yet again that he wasn't wearing the Love Rat cufflinks on his latest lucky shirt. He must be really cross with her.

Dave was being ridden by Clay Roberts, Australia's champion jockey, who was very good-looking. It was alleged that women's legs opened as automatically for him as did gaps on the racecourse.

Down at the start, Meerkat was trying not to transmit his nerves to Fleance. Three minutes away, he could see sky-scrapers stabbing the bright-blue sky and the Promised Land of the stands and the winning post.

'Look, there's your friend Fleance,' said Taggie, turning Forester's brindle muzzle towards the screen.

Twenty-five rivals: French, German, American, Irish, Chinese, British, French and Australian, the best against the best hoping for the best – and they were off. Rupert had told Meerkat to track Clay Roberts and Dave, and follow them through their gaps. But Clay had changed tactics, lurking at the back, so it was hard to follow him, particularly as Fleance, upset by the ear-splitting roar of the crowd, tore off after the leaders, tiring himself, as Meerkat battled to restrain him.

Slowly, slowly Clay Roberts edged through a solid wall of horses, patiently waiting for the gap which Dave the brave now took him through, and surged away, with Meerkat and Fleance belting after them.

Hurtling side by side, Dave and Fleance drew away from the pack. Revved up by the multitudes yelling him home, Clay Roberts went berserk with his whip. But as Dave inched ahead, Meerkat knew Fleance the trier would be giving his all. During the final desperate stampede, few jockeys could have resisted beating the hell out of his horse, but Meerkat didn't touch Fleance, aware his gallant colt had done everything of which he was capable.

'Come on, Fleance, come on, Dave!' screamed Taggie.

There was such a jumble of colours, such a bellow from the crowd, they were not sure who'd won.

'It's Dave,' yelled Jan, but so close, it was a photo – and a whole minute before they flagged up the placed horses. Taggie and Jan clutched each other. 'Fleance's second,' shouted Jan. Taggie gave a cry of delight. Next moment, their eyes met and their clutching had blossomed into a blissful not-at-all-gay kiss, their hearts pounding louder than hooves thundering. Only a protesting groan from Forester finally parted them, as they turned back to find Meerkat and Clay Roberts shaking congratulatory hands.

Then the cameras picked up Baby, the crowd's favourite owner, and his entourage erupting into a dance of ecstasy, hi-fiving, punching the air, all the glamorous gays taking the opportunity to hug Rupert, who'd bred first and second. Coming from first to last, Dave had won by half a length, pushing up Love Rat's global earnings by several million.

Clay was enchanted. 'Dave had to fight,' he told the interviewer. 'The pace was suicidal, exhausted a lot of horses. I'd like to say thank you to Baby, a wonderful owner, for letting me ride this wonderful horse.'

'No wonder he gets a lot of rides,' said Jan.

In democratic Australia, the cameras also concentrated on a joyfully sobbing Lark, racing up to Dave, hugging and kissing him, and pumping Clay's hand until he broke off a yellow rose and handed it to her with a kiss. The crowd erupted.

'Starp that,' yelled Young Eddie, who had stayed up to watch the race at Valhalla.

During the endless speeches afterwards, special tributes were paid to Lark, whose birthday it was and who'd come all the way from England to work because she couldn't bear to be parted from her beloved Dave. Lark's radiant smile was not entirely due to being presented with a little gold horse. She'd just been sent to heaven by a text: 'Well done Dave and Lark, look homeward angel, all love, Eddie.'

Baby, surrounded by press, was holding up the trophy, a beautiful golden, long-stemmed, three-handled loving cup, patting his yellow curls and admiring his reflection. Then he made everyone laugh by saying he'd always admired himself, but this was the nicest mirror he'd ever had.

'Plans for the future, Baby?' asked the Melbourne *Age*.

'I believe in stopping when you're going good.'

'Shut up,' snarled Rupert.

Back at Penscombe, Taggie and Jan stared at the screen, trying to absorb what had happened to them. Had that magical kiss changed the world?

'I guess I ought to walk you round for half an hour to cool you down,' said Jan.

As hand in hand they took the dogs outside and presented a carrot to Love Rat, Leo was rising in the east to join brilliant Jupiter, Taurus lay on his side, the Pleiades shimmered. Orion was also taking his dogs for a walk above the Penscombe Road, yet no star blazed brighter than the one on Dave's forehead.

But back home, Rupert hadn't rung.

'He wouldn't want to wake me,' said Taggie, then as Jan took her arm to lead her upstairs, she gazed up at him, overwhelmed with longing. Then, remembering that Rupert would be sixty now, and she had a vast party to orchestrate, she must try and be good. So she stammered, 'I can't spell the word "congratulations", will you text him for me? "Darling Rupert. Well done, so proud of Fleance and Dave. See you later."' Adding firmly: '"Masses of love, Taggie."' And she reluctantly bolted upstairs.

Returning, not remotely sober, to his hotel to pack before the flight home, Rupert picked up a text from Taggie: 'Dear Rupert, well done, Fleance and Dave, from Taggie.'

So he texted Gala: 'Sorry I had to push off, keep yourself on ice till I get home.'

76

One of the joys of travelling first class with Emirates was you could have a shower on the plane, washing away jet lag and hangover before landing. Sluicing his body, Rupert reflected that even if he were sixty, he hadn't run to fat, and there was no grey in his thick blond hair as he slicked it back from a smooth, suntanned forehead. The ebony half circles beneath bloodshot eyes, however, indicated a sleepless, churning night.

Packing his cases to fly home, he'd discovered, tucked far away in an inside pocket, two parcels: one containing seven dead leaves to give him happy days and the other, Theo Fennell's cufflinks. Taggie must have gone to so much trouble to get the horse so like Love Rat. *Darling Rupert, I luv yoo from the bottom of my hart*, she had written on the card. He nearly wept. Extraordinary that in twenty-two years, he, the biggest ram in the world, had never been unfaithful to her until Friday night with Gala, which had been equally extraordinary. They had come and come and come until Gala had threatened to call the fire brigade. As he reached for a towel, he realized he had an enormous hard-on.

'Get back to your box,' he told it sternly.

Taggie's lovemaking had always been so touchingly gentle and tender and utterly satisfactory. But Gala was in a different league. She had been hurt enough by Ben's death, but equally he couldn't bear to hurt Taggie. Would Gala rock the boat, or would she back off? But he didn't want her to back off.

God, he was tired. Thank goodness there was nothing happening at home. He just wanted to get back to Taggie and his dogs, check the office for the latest stallion bookings and on Gav's progress in Keeneland, watch Beijing Bertie running at Nottingham, whizz round the yard and stud followed by a leisurely birthday lunch: roast beef and a bottle of Mouton Cadet, just him and Taggie. Billy being with them would have made it perfect, followed by the afternoon in bed and probably not waking up until next morning.

Putting on a pale-blue shirt which sadly didn't need cufflinks, and jeans, which he wondered if he was too old to wear at sixty, he returned to his seat.

Here he was gratified to see the admiration in the brown eyes of the beautiful, smiling hostess, waiting with a glass of champagne. 'Happy Birthday, Mr Campbell-Black.'

Sitting down, Rupert picked up *Julius Caesar.*

Wherefore rejoice? What conquest brings he home?

Not good enough. Fleance second and Quickly second. He must stop Baby retiring Dave. Then, flicking over the pages: *Thou art my true and honourable wife* . . . He had said that to Taggie; he must try and behave himself.

Gala was also in turmoil, appalled how crazy she was about Rupert. That was the most glorious fuck she had ever had. He had melted every part of her body, she wanted to devour him. But was it just a flash in the pan? She had only one text to go on:

'Sorry I had to push off, keep yourself on ice till I get home.' She had read it a thousand times, wryly reflecting it was hard to keep yourself on anything else but ice with the approach of the English winter.

She hadn't slept all night, tossing and turning so violently that Gropius, who liked uninterrupted sleep, had retired to the sofa. On her return to Penscombe with Quickly, Touchy Filly and Delectable on Monday, she had demanded Tuesday off.

'I've been on for nine days.'

'Sunning yourself in LA,' sneered Walter Walter. 'You can come in for second lot.'

'I will not.'

Instead, she had taken herself to Cheltenham and, for Rupert's party, had bought an amazing leopardskin dress with a snarling leopard on the front, his huge eyes on a level with her boobs. She had lost weight, but mostly on the waist, which made her body even more voluptuous. She hoped it would be warm enough outside – she didn't want to diminish the dress's impact with cardigan or shawl.

Switching on the light to look again at Rupert's text, she caught sight of Ben's photographs all round the room, which Jan had tracked down for her. Ben had disapproved strongly of adultery, particularly if one adored one's other half. On her return, Gala had found a little moussaka, a lettuce and some chopped chicken for Gropius in the fridge.

Was it already dawn filtering through the curtains? Getting up to check, she discovered it was moonlight. Picking up a poetry book she'd borrowed from Gav, the pages fell open at James Joyce, writing of 'the deep, unending ache of love'. Oh, how she ached for Rupert!

The big marquee with windows overlooking the lake and the valley had taken two days of great clanging and banging to put up like some giant steel Lego because the lean and handsome marquee men had been so distracted by comely stable girls. The stable girls had been even more distracted by the sight of Tristan de Montigny, the great French film director whose Oscar-winning film of the opera *Don Carlos* had been part-financed by Rupert and starred Baby Spinosissimo and Dame Hermione.

Tristan was now transforming the marquee walls with videos and blow-ups of Rupert's achievements. Huge vases of dark-blue delphiniums with green leaves echoed Rupert's colours. Each of the twelve tables was named after Rupert's greatest horses and adorned by their photographs. A loudspeaker was belting out 'The Galloping Major', the 'Post Horn Gallop' and Mozart's Horn Concerto, and the showjumping theme tune, which was also by Mozart.

'Isn't Tristan the fittest man you've ever seen?' sighed Gee Gee. 'And he's taller than me.'

Louise and Gee Gee had spent hours on Tuesday writing out place-names tidily, as Taggie struggled to work out a seating plan, which should have been easier without Rupert around, saying, 'I'm not sitting next to that ugly cow.'

Sapphire and Timon, who came over for tea, were full of advice. 'Put Gala next to Grandpa – she's always gazing at him – and Granny next to Jan – she always smells nice when he's around.'

After which Jan decided to dispense with a seating plan as too difficult for Taggie.

'Bloody man,' stormed Louise. 'Who's running this joint? We wasted all this time writing names.'

Jan, in fact, had made himself very unpopular. Gardener Colin Caper was aggrieved that his conservatory had been stripped of flowers to decorate the tables, and being ordered to cut back more undergrowth which was masking all the animal sculptures, so Clover and Jemmy could tie blue and emerald ribbons round their necks.

Already fed up by their female staff being distracted by marquee men and Tristan de Montigny, Walter Walter and Pat Inglis were even less amused when Jan ordered both stable lasses and lads to do their work in the stables earlier, so they could be available to lay tables and blow up balloons.

'What about the horses?' said Walter furiously.

'Let them eat cheesecake,' giggled Louise – not that she minded if all the men were as lush as Tristan. Pity he had a wife, Lucy, who was going to do Taggie's make-up.

Jan was constantly reassuring Taggie that the party was going to be a huge success. Even more wonderful, as well as running up giant beetroot tarts for each table and rubbing a paste of olive oil, coarse salt, black pepper, herbs and garlic into great haunches of venison, he had commandeered the telephone for the last twenty-four hours.

'Terribly sorry, Dame Hermione. Numbers are very tight. Even if you are very good friends with Mr Campbell-Black, the answer is No.' And the same to Damsire and Janey Lloyd-Foxe. He even kept the family at bay. 'Sorry, Tab, but Taggie's exhausted. I appreciate it's your home but she needs an early night, not your kids breaking up the place, so we'll see you midday tomorrow.'

Then despatching Perdita, Taggie's sister Caitlin, and Helen, who claimed they wanted to help, in the same way.

'Isn't he marvellous?' sighed Taggie.

'And absolutely mad about you,' reflected everyone.

Party day dawned. After finishing her horses, and leaving a furious, gleaming Quickly in his box because he was going to parade later, Gala was ordered into the kitchen to peel more potatoes. As Jan braised red cabbage and put the finishing touches to filo pastry baskets and asparagus and sweetcorn, she realized the enormity of the operation. The dogs were acting up because Jan had moved all their baskets out of the kitchen so they kept stealing back and getting under his feet.

'You'd better feed them,' he ordered Gala.

'*You* feed them. It's eleven o'clock – I've got to go and change.'

'You look fine as you are. All you need put on is a *Happy Birthday Rupert* sweatshirt. They're in the utility room.'

After she'd filled up the dog bowls, Gala said, 'I'm amazed you haven't asked me to feed the badgers as well,' and flounced out.

Jan had got so bossy. God, she missed Gav and Eddie with whom to bitch about him.

One person Jan couldn't shift was Geraldine, who shimmied in wearing a neat little emerald-green dress with a Rupert's colours blue scarf.

'Go and make a list of the presents coming in and who sent them,' Jan ordered her.

To which she replied: 'I'm here as Rupert's PA. I know every-one – it's essential I mingle and circulate.'

77

Simmy Halliday, Rupert's Estate Manager, had tuned into the Flight Radar App charting Rupert's progress across Europe. Cheers greeted the news on the loudspeaker that he and his plane were over Italy.

Tears filled Gala's eyes. 'But, please God, not over me.'

A reluctant Cathal and Jemmy had set off for Nottingham with Beijing Bertie.

'Cheer up,' said Louise. 'The party'll still be going when you come back.'

Certainly the loveliest autumn in years had come out to welcome Rupert. His chestnut avenue had thinned, its leaves wrinkled rust and olive, but his beeches retained enough red to raise a towering inferno to the cloudy skies. Berries soft pink and orange shone on the spindles, glowing ruby on guelder rose bushes. The gutters ran with crimson crab apples.

Bao had departed to Heathrow to await Rupert at the VIP terminal. Having had a lunatically large bet on Beijing Bertie and having been beseeched by Taggie not to give the game away about the party, he couldn't stop shaking. He had deliberately not taken the *Racing Post*, which on the cover had a large picture of Cosmo gloating over Eddie, his new stable jockey, who, on returning from the Breeders' Cup, had had a double at Southwell yesterday.

Back at Penscombe, the turned-out horses were lining up at

the fence, to admire 'Happy Sixtieth Birthday Rupert' super-imposed on the lawn, and bobbing six-zero balloons waiting to be released by the staff in their blue *Happy Birthday* sweatshirts.

'Hoohoo, yoohoo.' It was Helen, an hour early, in a lovely gold silk suit, perfect with her red hair. 'I know there's something I can do – I *am* family. Let me arrange those flowers. I can't think why Rupert's being so uptight about being a great-grandfather when our Queen's a great-grandmother and he so admires her.'

Even though guests were being discouraged to go into the house, Taggie was panicking around making sure photographs of every child, stepchild or grandchild were equally on show.

Jan, however, discovered Tabitha taking down Perdita's photograph in Rupert and Taggie's bedroom.

'What the hell are you doing? Where are your kids?'

'Watching television.'

'Well, get out of here at once.'

'Why, have you moved in?'

'Don't be obnoxious – and put that dress back.'

'You're not my father, although I know you'd like to steal his job.'

'Don't be fatuous.' Jan grabbed her arm. For a moment she thought he was going to hit her, then hearing a shriek, he let go and racing downstairs found a distraught Taggie and a glisten-ing dark-grey Forester, who'd rolled from top to toe in badger crap. 'I must bath him.'

'I'll do it, mam. Bloody dog,' roared Jan, grabbing Forester's collar.

'He only does it to make himself more attractive,' pleaded Taggie, 'like Issey Florale.'

'Go and get changed, mam.'

Upstairs, Tristan de Montigny's wife Lucy had arrived to do Taggie's make-up; she said her lurcher James had always rolled at the wrong moments.

'Rupert's over Paris,' said the loudspeaker.

Dragging Forester to an upstairs bathroom, Jan compromised by getting in the shower with the dog. Having washed and dried them both, he retreated to change. On his bed he found a large wrapped parcel.

471

Dear yan, thank you for awl yor help, luv Taggie, said the message on the label. Inside was a big dark-brown cashmere jersey and a honey-coloured corduroy jacket.

Taggie herself got a round of applause when she came down in clinging rose-red silk which had given colour to her ashen cheeks. Lucy had emphasized her huge eyes, hidden the dark circles beneath them and painted her lovely mouth rose-red to match her dress.

How could I ever compete with that? thought Gala wistfully. She's prettier than anyone in the world.

Jan clearly thought so.

'You are quite breathtaking, mam – wow,' he murmured in her ear. 'Thank you for the marvellous gear, mam. I don't know what I've done to deserve them. Helping you in any way is my pleasure. God, you look lovely.'

'So do you.' Jan was wearing the cashmere jersey the same rich brown as his eyes. The cord jacket showed off his magnificent shoulders.

'Look at those two,' muttered Louise. 'Those must be the clothes she bought in Cheltenham last week. God, he scrubs up well.'

'Wery wirile,' agreed Marketa. 'Someone ought to chuck a bucket of water over them.'

'High time Super Bastard came home to claim his rights.'

Taggie looked out of the window as the clouds darkened. 'Oh gosh, I hope it's not going to rain.'

Instead guests poured in and she was soon going spare, welcoming, introducing, stumbling over names, assuring everyone over the deafening party roar that Rupert would be here soon. Jan was in the kitchen carving venison, but emerging every few minutes to put a reassuring hand on her shoulder and murmur that everything was going brilliantly.

Soon, despite her worries, she was overwhelmed with joy to see Bianca, ravishing in mid-thigh-length flamingo pink and her handsome boyfriend Feral Jackson, the star striker, who was soon playing football on the lawn with all the children.

'So funny, Mum,' giggled Bianca. 'Dad rang up and tried to

persuade Feral and me to fly down for the Melbourne Cup. I had to pretend Feral had a match.'

Bianca was soon joined by her brother Xavier and his Indian girlfriend Aysha, who were in turn enchanted to see Janna and Emlyn Hughes, the headmistress and history master who'd got them through GCSEs and who now showed them photographs of their sweet children. Screams of delight greeted Dora and Paris, who'd been at Bagley Hall taking GCSEs at the same time, and their headmaster Hengist Brett-Taylor and his wife Sally.

Another noisy, ecstatic group was the England polo team whom Rupert had galvanized, back in the 1990s, to annihilate America in the mighty Westchester Cup. They included Ricky France-Lynch the captain, married to Perdita's mother Daisy. As Young Eddie's grandmother, Daisy had been commissioned by her grandson, before he'd been fired, to paint a portrait of Love Rat for Rupert's birthday. She had brought the portrait with her, and later would be screwing up courage to beg Rupert to reinstate Eddie. Perdita and Luke, who'd looked after Gav in America, were soon nose-to-nose with Rupert's other polo-playing chums, Bas Baddingham, roué and bloodstock agent who owned the Bar Sinister, and Drew Benedict, whose son had been killed in Afghanistan, and whose wife Sukey had put on weight. Howls of delight greeted the Carlisle twins: Seb and Dommie, also part of the team, who used to pretend to be each other to seduce the other's girlfriends. They now announced they had brought Rupert a Zimmer and a ton of Viagra.

The noise level was rising; everyone was wolfing Jan's canapés.

'Gav not here?' Luke asked Taggie.

'He's in Kentucky, he hates parties.'

'Nice guy, attractive too – how's his love-life going?'

'Hi, Luke!' shouted Fenella Maxwell, and Dino Ferranti, Rupert's old showjumping cronies. 'Eddie did great in the Breeders' Cup.'

Flora Maguire, daughter of pop megastar George Maguire, who herself had starred in *Don Carlos*, and her husband George Hungerford, who'd bankrolled the Rutminster Orchestra, were

473

now swapping music gossip and baby photographs with star vio-linist Abby Rosen and her husband, horn-player Viking O'Neill. They were soon joined by Tristan and Lucy de Montigny, all speculating whether Baby Spinosissimo and Rupert's brother Adrian would make the party or were still celebrating Dave winning the Melbourne Cup.

More shrieks of joy followed as Rupert and Helen's son Marcus, the pianist, and his boyfriend Alexei, the great ballet dancer, arrived from Moscow.

'Marcus, Marcus, you came.' Helen rushed forward. 'How wonderful you look.'

'She always liked him better than me,' said Tabitha sourly. 'So does Daddy – went all the way to London to Marcus' Prom. Only time he gets a few decent hours' sleep.'

'Amber,' cried the GCSE gang, as Billy and Janey Lloyd-Foxe's daughter, looking ridiculously beautiful and happy, wandered in with her husband, champion jump jockey Rogue Rogers.

Having four years ago ridden Master Quickly's mother to victory in the National, Amber said she must go and con-gratulate Quickly on his second in the Breeders' Cup.

'You'll need earplugs. He's been confined to box and yelling his head off because he's got to parade later,' Dora told her.

'Didn't he do well?' said Etta, who'd just rolled up with Valent.

On her way, Amber had popped into Penscombe churchyard to put flowers on Billy's grave. Later she managed to murmur to Taggie how dreadfully sorry she was that her mother kept writing ghastly things about Rupert.

'She's got a man called Colin Chalford, met him online and refers to him as Mr Fat and Happy. He's sweet, much too nice for her.'

Tabitha was determinedly chatting up her ex-boyfriend, Tristan de Montigny, and ignoring her producer husband Wolfie, Cosmo's stepbrother, who'd turned up with Sarah Western, his nymphomaniac leading lady, who was playing opposite Paris in *Le Rouge et Le Noir*.

'Good thing Jan's over-catered, she'd devour the lot,' sniped Tab. 'Who did you eat for breakfast?'

474

'Worse than Sauvignon,' murmured Dora.

'Sauvignon's more interested in power than sex.'

Gossip was seething, everyone surreptitiously asking what was going on with Sauvignon and Eddie – had Rupert really kicked him out for good? – and hoping he'd turn up at the party.

People were spilling out on to the lawn, high heels pegged by the soft going.

Bas Baddingham, the bloodstock agent, was looking at the horses in the field, wondering which might be worth buying for someone else.

'Where's Rupert?' he asked his harassed hostess on his return. 'God, you look pretty. Do you remember I took you to that hunt ball in another red dress, and we danced to "Lady in Red", and I think it dawned on Rupert that night that he was absolutely mad about you. You're even more gorgeous now, I should have hung on to you.'

'Don't be silly,' reproved Taggie. 'Are you getting enough to drink?'

Less surreptitious was Helen, her lovely silk suit matching the gold of a nearby gingko, as she loudly asked: 'Where's Eddie? I must congratulate him on that brilliant win on I Will Repay, and I'm really looking forward to meeting Sauvignon – she looks quite lovely. Do introduce me, Taggie.'

'She's not actually coming,' stammered Taggie.

'Not exactly persona grata, Mum,' hissed Tab.

Helen shivered. 'It's quite chilly. Lend me your jacket, Jan.'

'I'll get you a wrap,' Jan told her firmly.

The roar increased, more helicopters landed, champagne flowed, canapés were devoured, as 1.45 p.m. approached.

'Have you ever seen fitter men?' Marketa sighed to Louise. 'Who's that?'

'Lysander Hawkley. He's lovely – used to be Rupert's Head Lad, now set up on his own. He married Rannaldini's second wife Kitty, a friend of Taggie's. She's marvellous, copes with all the admin, leaving Lysander to sort out the horses. They're doing very well.'

'Wish he'd come back instead of Walter Walter.'

Valent Edwards was nose-to-nose with George Hungerford, discussing trading with China and trying not to eat too many canapés. Etta was talking to George's wife Flora, one of her favourite singers, when Flora cried: 'Look, our Don Carlos has arrived, Baby, Baby – over here. How the hell did you get back from Melbourne quicker than Rupert?'

'We took a private plane,' whispered Baby, hugging her. 'God, you look great. Oh, there's Tristan,' he rushed off to kiss his ex-director, 'and Lucy darling,' hugging her, 'just the person I need: can you whizz upstairs and give me a bit of base and put in a few Carmens? It's such a hell of a long journey.'

'Where's Adrian?' asked Fiona.

'Coveting the Stubbs,' grinned Baby.

'Oh look, here's Mum.' Flora flew across the lawn to hug a beautiful older woman, whose red hair and fake-fur red collar were being ruffled by the wind.

'That's Georgie Maguire,' squeaked Etta to Valent and George Hungerford.

'My mother-in-law,' said George proudly.

'I love her records,' babbled Etta, 'and goodness, there's Dancer Maitland. I love his records too. Isn't he gorgeous?'

'He sponsors Ricky France-Lynch's polo team,' explained George Hungerford, as yells of 'Dancer, Dancer,' greeted him from the polo contingent.

In the same way that their hands shoved forward their horses to encourage them on the gallops, Marketa, Louise, Roving Mike, Shaheed and Clover were brilliant at pushing bottles at guests and taking the odd swig themselves.

'Taggie,' Geraldine tugged her sleeve, demanding that Taggie rescue her boyfriend Denzil, 'he's been stuck with that rather dull woman for ages.'

'That's Kitty Rannaldini,' exploded Dora. 'She's a darling, and unlike you, looks as though she's enjoying herself.'

78

Gala had retreated to Lime Tree Cottage, psyching herself up to join the party. Putting on her leopardskin dress, she noticed how her nipples stuck out directly behind the leopard's eyes. As she reached the lawn, Rupert's randy friends Drew and Bas wolf-whistled. 'That is an incredibly sexy dress,' said Drew.

'And the eyes are perfectly positioned,' grinned Bas.

Next moment, Geraldine had grabbed Gala's arm.

'That dress is completely OTT – you're supposed to be working. Go and put on a *Happy Birthday Rupert* sweatshirt at once, or people will think you're a guest.'

'She looks stunning,' snapped Louise, handing Gala a huge glass of champagne.

'I wonder how Rupert will react,' muttered Bas to Drew. 'Poor sod, after a twenty-four-hour flight, probably been celebrating all the way back, he'll be hopelessly hungover and jet-lagged.'

'He did bloody well,' said Drew.

'Sure, but he didn't get a winner. Rupert thinks second sucks.'

'Oh God, here comes the cabaret.'

It was Old Eddie, in a morning coat with his *Old Men Make Better Lovers* badge on the lapel, and striped trousers held up by an Old Harrovian tie. He was getting away with much goosing and bottom-pinching because many of the beautiful women he attacked assumed he was one of Rupert's dogs.

'Eddie's on the loose,' Taggie beseeched Jan.

'I'll sort it. That carer's not fit for purpose.'

He found Local Janet on her fourth glass of champagne in the kitchen.

'You're supposed to be looking after Eddie,' he said, removing it and handing her Cindy Bolton's latest porn DVD, *Cardinal Cindy*. 'Give him this to watch.'

'My great-grandfather's got Alka Seltzer,' Timon was informing Etta and Helen, ten minutes later. 'He's watching porn in the sitting room. I'm going to join him. We're having sex education at school – it's gross, all those hairy fannies. Porn's much nicer.'

Helen choked on her drink.

'Rupert's over Lambourn,' said the loudspeaker, and a great roar went up.

Safety Car had also joined the party, thrilled to see Lysander, nudging old friends and socializing.

'He's a much better host than Taggie,' observed Tabitha. 'Who's that divine man who's just walked in?'

'My brother Jonathan,' said Dora, who was rushing round photographing everyone. 'He's a brilliant painter, he's done a gorgeous portrait of Taggie for Rupert, and his wife Emerald (she's a piece of work but they adore each other), has done Rupert a lovely bronze of Banquo.'

Cries of 'Do you remember?' 'Wasn't that hysterical?' 'Who won that year?' 'Who painted that?' 'Who sang that?' hung on the air, all inextricably linked.

'Here's another gorgeous man,' sighed Marketa.

'That's Taggie's brother, Patrick O'Hara. He's a scriptwriter,' said Louise. 'That cross-looking brunette is his partner, Cameron Cook. She makes very good films.'

All the O'Haras, who included Declan, and Taggie's sister Caitlin, her husband Archie and their children, looked very cross on arrival, because they'd been held up by Taggie's mother Maud, one-time actress, addicted to making an entrance.

Now she swept in, her piled-up paprika-red hair set off by a sea-green satin dress.

'She's even more jealous of Taggie than Helen is,' Bas murmured to Gala.

'You look sensational, Mum,' said Taggie dutifully.

'I'd look even more sensational,' Maud took Taggie aside, 'in that emerald pendant of yours. Can you run upstairs and get it?'

And Taggie went as green as the necklace, because she'd sold it to pay for the party. Then even greener because the hunt had arrived, galloping out of the wood, across the fields, jumping fences; forty riders and twenty couple of hounds, stopping to drink out of the lake, sending Rupert's turned-out horses into a frenzy of excitement. Next moment, Quickly had leapt out of his box and joined in.

Hounds, all without collars, as though they were not wearing ties, catching divine wafts of roast venison, charged round relieving guests of filo-pastry baskets, chicken and mayo, goats'-cheese tartlets, eyes watering as they encountered hot sausages, wolfing up whole platefuls, until at Jan's roar of rage, the kennel huntsman called them more or less to order.

'He knows all their names,' said an awed Etta.

The field, mostly in black or in tweed coats, known as rat-catchers, were getting stuck into both food and drink.

'Why are hardly any of them wearing red coats?' asked Gala.

'Don't want to attract the antis,' said Dora, 'although the antis will be like a day in the country,' she burst out laughing, 'compared with Rupert when he sees who's rolled up.'

It was Dame Hermione, on a buckling dapple grey, her vast bottom, which Gala had last seen whipped crimson by Young Eddie, forced into white breeches.

'Where's Rupert?' she called out, grabbing a glass of champagne. 'My invitation still hasn't arrived. Must come and wish my favourite poster boy a happy sixtieth. Those look delicious.' She scooped up a fistful of goats'-cheese tartlets.

'Oh hell,' cried an utterly appalled Taggie as Hermione was followed by Damsire in ratcatchers on a bay mare: 'Come to wish my ex many happies,' and she also grabbed a large glass.

Taggie gazed imploringly at Jan who went off and had a word

with the Master about pushing off the moment they'd said a quick hello to Rupert.

'Course, old boy, thanks – just a top-up. Just saying, we were hunting near Rutminster woods at dusk the other day. Such a creepy place – hounds wouldn't go in there. Probably heard the ghost of Seeker howling.'

As Caitlin's children and Timon and Sapphire crowded round the hounds, hugging them, Dame Hermione had discovered the opera clique.

'Oh look, there's Tristan de Montigny, who directed me in the Oscar-winning film of *Don Carlos*, and Lucy Latimer who did my make-up and – coo-ee, coo-ee – there's my leading man, Baby Spinosissimo.' And she launched into their first duet: 'Di qual amor, di quant'ardor' which was so deafening that her horse bolted, and at first people couldn't distinguish the chug, chug rattle of a dark-blue helicopter. Over the loudspeaker, the showjumping music boomed out.

Let him be pleased, prayed Taggie, as Banquo, Forester, Cuthbert and Gilchrist, recognizing the helicopter, barking in hysterical delight, hurtled off to welcome Master, followed by Bianca, screaming: 'Daddy, Daddy!'

Looking down, Rupert saw Penscombe church spire and his beechwoods, a red fire flickering to welcome him. He noticed an inordinate amount of turned-out horses racing about to keep warm. After Melbourne, Heathrow had seemed bitterly cold. Suddenly he stiffened to see the large field to the right of the lake hidden by cars and at least ten helicopters, and the lawn, covered by a huge marquee and 'Happy Sixtieth Birthday Rupert' in green and blue, otherwise crowded with cheering people, the hunt milling around and hundreds of balloons bobbing up to meet him like a bright-blue bubble bath.

'What the fuck?' he howled to a terrified, trembling Bao. 'How bloody dare you not warn me?'

'It's a surprise party.'

'Well, I'm not going to any fucking party. Turn the chopper round now.'

'We haven't got a flight-path. Lots of guests arriving by

helicopter, we might crash with them. I promise Mrs Campbell-Black, I deliver you safe.'

'Don't be fatuous – don't you dare land.'

'Please, Mr Campbell-Black, please.' Bao was in tears. 'Mrs Campbell-Black, she work so hard for party, night and day for weeks and weeks. No one loves anything as much as she loves you. She make wonderful food and wonderful cake. You friends come from whole world, they bring wonderful presents.'

The chopper was hovering above the house and the yelling cheering multitude.

'I don't bloody care. Why are my horses out in the fields? What the fuck's the hunt doing? I expressly forbade Mrs Campbell-Black to have a party. She knew it was the last thing I wanted.'

'She want to please you,' beseeched Bao. 'Your dog miss you so much, see them barking.'

Rupert was relenting fractionally – perhaps bullets should be bitten – when Bao added, 'And Mr Jan too, he work night and day with Mrs Black Taggie, making wonderful lunch with whole reindeers, no one work as hard as Mr Jan.'

It was the final straw. 'Fucking Yansy Pansy. Turn the chopper round.'

'We might have no fuel.'

'Bollocks, we've got buckets. Tell flight control we're heading north. If we hurry, we'll catch Beijing Bertie and Jemmy at Nottingham.'

'We have to give Nottingham week notice.'

'Then we'll park nearby.'

It was terrifying, being in a small aircraft with a Sabre-toothed Tiger. London control were ringing through. 'What's going on?'

'We're re-routing to Nottingham,' Rupert told them.

At first everyone thought Rupert was just hovering to have a look. Then it became obvious the helicopter was heading north, and cheers turned to horrified screams.

'Come back, Daddy, come back,' sobbed Bianca. Back slunk the bewildered dogs.

'Bastard, bastard,' rose a great groundswell of rage. 'How could he do that to Taggie?'

481

'I've come fifty thousand miles for this party,' grumbled Baby.

Simmy looked at his phone. 'The helicopter's heading north.'

Jan discovered Taggie alone sobbing in the drawing room, oblivious of a porn DVD of Cindy Bolton romping with a goat, which was still playing and which he switched off.

'I should never have gone ahead with it,' she said. 'Rupert made it quite clear he didn't want a party.'

Jan took her in his arms, Lucy's make-up smearing his new jacket.

'Simmy's keeping track of the helicopter. We'll find him.'

'Oh God, how could he do that? All the children were so excited and all the people making an effort, coming all that way, all the presents, everyone here working so hard.'

'Hush, hush,' he stroked her hair. 'We've got all the guests here, lunch is ready. Let's get on with the party,' then dropping a kiss on her trembling lips, 'and show the bastard we can have a bloody good time without him. He's the one who'll be sorry.' Getting out a handkerchief, he wiped her eyes.

Quivering with mortification, Jan's arm around her, Taggie went out on to the lawn, as a gust of wind unleashed a shower of gold leaves. The roar of rage and speculation subsided as Jan clapped his hands.

'Mrs Campbell-Black wants to say how sorry she is to disappoint you all.'

An enraged Declan O'Hara was poised to take over: 'My daughter Taggie has done nothing wrong,' he roared. But Jan cut across him.

'I'm afraid the birthday boy's scarpered, but lunch is ready, and Mrs Campbell-Black hopes you'll all stay on for a great party.'

A huge cheer went up and carried on as everyone crowded round Taggie, patting her shoulder and comforting her.

'Why's he pushed orf?' asked Old Eddie.

'I'm afraid he can't handle being sixty,' sighed Helen.

'Naughty Grandpa,' said Sapphire.

'I don't like surprise parties either,' confessed Georgie Maguire. 'Guy gave one for me at midday on a Saturday; everyone rolled up to find me in trackie bottoms, with no make-up and dirty hair. Perhaps Rupert was worried his roots needed doing.'

People were starting to giggle. Gossip rose and fell as everyone swarmed into the marquee, exclaiming over the beauty of the displays and the flowers. The irony was the thousands of galloping horses in the videos: Rupert's horses winning Derbies, Grand Nationals, polo and showjumping championships.

'There's quite enough of your brother in this tent already,' said Baby to Adrian. 'Must say Taggie's found herself a beaut new man.'

Bianca, in floods, was being comforted by Feral.

'I wanted to see Daddy. I missed him in Australia, I haven't seen him for months.'

Gala was also devastated. She'd been so thrilled with her new dress. How could Rupert have done that to poor, poor Taggie?

But at least everyone was sorry for Taggie. No one's sorry for me, thought Gala, gulping down another vat of champagne and going off to waitress, only to be waylaid by Drew and Bas, insisting she sat between them with Gropius lying beneath her feet. How would Gav react to Rupert's defection, she wondered. He was due home today.

There was a moment of hope when the dark-blue helicopter returned, but only Bao jumped out. Traumatized and tearful, he sought out Taggie.

'I am so sorry, Mrs Taggie. I told him great party, but he was very, very angry. He ask me to drop him above village. I am so sorry.'

'Poor Bao.' Taggie hugged him. 'I'm sorry too. Did he say where he was going?'

'Perhaps Nottingham, but he have no coat.'

'Come and sit with us,' called out Etta. 'Valent can practise his Mandarin on you.'

Meanwhile, Rupert's son-in-law Wolfie and his sons, Marcus and Xavier, were having a council of war.

'Shall we fan out and look for him?' said Xav grimly.

'You've had too much champagne to drive,' said Wolfie. 'I'll go.'

'I'll come with you,' said Marcus.

'I haven't had that much,' protested Xav. 'I'm coming too.'

A rip-roaring party ensued, with guests well oiled from the long wait, as they helped themselves to Beef Wellington, venison and lamb, carved on a side table, roast potatoes, red cabbage, sweetcorn and asparagus, with a vast beetroot tart to each table.

Indignation meetings everywhere over Rupert's appalling behaviour soon gave way to wonder at the food.

'Who are your caterers?' asked everyone.

'Jan is,' said Geraldine. 'He's given everything a wonderful South African flavour.'

'And Taggie too,' reproved Dora, who was photographing the beetroot tart, 'they did it together. Hope the red's all right,' she whispered to Etta. 'Taggie gave me and Paris some bottles to try, but by the time we'd tested them all we were so plastered, we couldn't remember which one we liked best. Oh God, Dame Hermione and Damsire have sat down to lunch.'

'Ought to have your own programme, Jan,' called out Dame Hermione, taking a second huge helping of beetroot tart. 'You're just as good-looking as Paul Hollywood.'

Jan, worried that Taggie hadn't eaten anything, insisted she sat with her parents and a large plate of food.

'Please see she finishes it,' he said, adding, 'I'm just going to check things in the kitchen.'

Guests, having enjoyed second – even third – helpings were soon tucking into the puddings: cheesecake, sticky toffee pudding and a magnificent fruit salad steeped in sloe gin.

'What's this?' asked Dame Hermione, plunging her spoon into a lush cream concoction.

'Harrow Mess,' said Damsire, consulting the menu. 'Presumably because Rupert went to Harrow.'

'And made a mess of things as usual,' said his brother Adrian scathingly.

Adrian's father, Old Eddie, was talking to Helen, who he had forgotten had once been his daughter-in-law.

'I find a whole Viagra lasts too long, so I break each one into four.'

79

What had actually happened to Rupert was that flying north-ward, realizing he'd cut himself off from the yard and the stud, he had called Bas Baddingham to suggest lunch, only to be told Mr Baddingham had gone to a surprise birthday party. When he rang Ricky France-Lynch and then Drew Benedict, he was told the same story – bloody hell, all getting pissed at his expense. So he asked Bao to drop him off in a field on the north side of Penscombe.

'I'll be perfectly all right. You go to the party. I'll make my own way back, and I don't need an overcoat,' he'd told a distraught Bao.

It was actually so arctic after Melbourne and Santa Anita, Rupert bought a half bottle of whisky at the local off-licence and wandered down to Penscombe churchyard, where on Billy's grave he found a big bunch of white freesias, shuddering in the icy wind.

Darling Daddy, Best Father in the World. Missing you always. All love, Amber.

Rupert took a swig from his bottle; he ought to give the rest to Billy, who'd loved whisky – often rather too much.

The flowers looked new – Amber must have come over for the party. He wondered if that bitch Janey had crashed it; she had led Billy such a merry dance. Then suddenly he thought how horrified Billy, who'd endured all Janey's appalling behaviour, would have been at him boycotting the party. Billy was like darling sweet Taggie. With a shiver, Rupert realized what he'd done to her. How could he have humiliated her so? *And* cheated on her.

Taking another swig of whisky, hearing the distant roar of a party, he wandered into the church to find Constance Sprightly, who was always bullying Taggie and whose cat was always being treed by Forester, ramming bronze chrysanthemums into a large vase.

'Hello, Mr Campbell-Black, I thought you'd be up at the house. There's a big do going on.'

A bald man was strumming away on the organ: 'Dear Lord and Father of mankind, Forgive our foolish ways'.

Take a lot for God to forgive me, reflected Rupert, putting a tenner in the collection box. The next moment Constance gave a squawk of horror as an iron fist hoisted Rupert across the nave into a huge arrangement of yellow lilies, so that falling, he cracked his head on the corner of a pew.

'You ungrateful bastard,' said a voice. 'How dare you treat Taggie like that?'

Had he passed out? All Rupert vaguely remembered was being grabbed by his jersey and shirt and dragged to his feet.

'You're coming back to the house and bloody well apologizing.'

Back in the marquee, Louise and Marketa were getting off with the Carlisle twins, polo's golden boys. No better behaved in their forties, they were particularly taken with Gropius.

'We had a bull terrier called Decorum, so we could make jokes about exercising him.'

The party had progressed to cheese and a great deal more wine and liqueurs. Marcus, Wolfie, Xav and Jan had returned to the marquee.

Taggie, too upset to eat, had fled to the kitchen to supervise coffee, and on her return moved timidly along the tables, checking people were OK. At the end of the marquee, a little platform awaited any speeches. Mounting it, Taggie's brother Patrick took the microphone.

'God, he's gorgeous,' sighed Louise.

'As your hostess's brother,' Patrick had the same soft Irish accent as Declan, 'I'd just like to say a few words. Today is a bit like *Hamlet* without the Prince, but my brother-in-law doesn't have a very good track-record at parties. At his own wedding he was so anxious to be alone with my sister, Taggie, he only stayed at the reception for twenty minutes, sloping off into the sunset long before dinner, dancing, cake-cutting or any of the speeches.'

'We were there,' roared the Carlisle twins, 'the party-pooper.'

'To be alone with my sister,' repeated Patrick, 'who can't spell, by the way, so when it said "no presents" on the invitation, she actually meant "no presence" i.e. birthday boy wouldn't be putting in an appearance.' Which was greeted by howls of laughter.

'He's an absolute shit, my brother-in-law. CB stands for Complete Bastard but you can see from the marvellous display round the walls of this marquee, created by Tristan de Montigny, the great director, that Rupert has achieved a lot in his life.

'The food has been utterly amazing, and is almost entirely the work of my sister and Jan Van Deventer, who's supposed to be looking after Rupert's father, Eddie, but now seems more to be caring for Taggie.' Which was greeted by bellows of approval.

'No, Patrick,' begged Taggie.

'Everyone has worked ridiculously hard but it's most of all a shame for Taggie who's been slaving for months to celebrate Rupert's birthday.'

Whereupon everyone stood up and cheered her.

'I don't know where Rupert's got to,' went on Patrick. 'The chopper dropped him off near the village. The hunt's gone to look for him – I hope hounds tear him to pieces.'

'Couldn't agree more,' said a voice and there was a gasp as Rupert walked in, pausing in the gangway below the platform.

His slate-blue v-neck jersey and pale-blue shirt were splattered with blood, and drenched with water from Constance Sprightly's spilt flowers. His left eye was closing up, his suntan faded to a yellowing pallor. He was greeted by a hostile and deathly silence.

Taggie, about to race up the aisle to him, was grabbed by Declan, tugging her into a chair beside him. Next moment the silence was broken by barking and yelping as the dogs, led by Forester and Banquo in their blue and green bows, swarmed up the gangway throwing themselves on Rupert in ecstasy. This was followed by whickering and great snorts of delight as Safety Car trundled up, pushing the dogs to one side, nuzzling and nudging his master.

'At least someone's forgiven me,' drawled Rupert.

Then, in the silence that followed, Old Eddie could be heard saying: 'Who's that fellow with Safety Car?' which was followed by roars and roars of laughter, particularly from Rupert.

And like the sun creeping through the trees above the Penscombe and Cotchester Road and flooding the valley with light, his magnetism kicked in and everyone rose to applaud him.

'Rupert, Rupert,' said a voice. It was Dame Hermione, which nearly sent Rupert into reverse.

'What the fuck's she doing here?'

'Naughty, naughty,' chortled Hermione.

'Good par-eee, isn't it exciting?' cried Clover as Rupert raised his hand.

'All I can do,' he said, 'is apologize unreservedly to you all, but most of all to my darling wife. It was utterly unpardonable. My only excuse is I'd had a long flight, celebrating Dave winning the Melbourne Cup and Fleance coming second, pushing up Love Rat's winnings – and when I saw you all, I just bottled out. It's the wettest, most awful thing I've ever done. I'm so sorry, darling.' And watched with ambiguous emotions by Jan and Gala, he opened his arms and Taggie flew into them.

'I'm sorry, I'm so sorry,' they both gabbled, 'entirely my fault.'

Still hugging Taggie, Rupert went on, 'I want to apologize to all my children: Marcus, Xav, Bianca, Perdita and Tab, and to all my friends and guests who've come miles, and all my staff who've worked so hard to put on this amazing party.' Then, pausing to check his iPhone, he laughed, 'And the best birthday present, which should also please Bao, is that Beijing Bertie and Jemmy have just hacked up at Nottingham.'

'Roo-*pert*,' reproached his audience collectively.

'That's enough, Rupert, go and sit down,' shouted Dancer Maitland.

A little orchestra formed by Marcus on the piano, Bao and Abby on violins and Viking O'Neill on the horn then struck up.

'Happy birthday to you, happy birthday to you,' sang Dancer and Georgie Maguire. 'Happy birthday, Rotter Rupert, happy birthday to you,' with Hermione joining in, drowning the lot of them.

A beautiful cake was then wheeled in, decorated by a sugar model of Love Rat and sixty blazing red candles.

'Take a hurricane to blow that many out,' quipped Patrick.

But Rupert was glancing at his iPhone again, to check on Love Rat's latest nominations.

'Put that thing away,' thundered Declan.

'Cut the cake, make a wish,' shouted Bas Baddingham, then turning to Gala: 'We all know what that is.'

'Leading Sire for Love Rat,' said Gala.

Bleeding sire, she thought, noticing the blood all over Rupert's shirt and wondering who the hell had hit him.

Clutching a glass of red, Rupert toured the tables, trailing dogs, shaking hands, apologizing particularly to Bao, then reaching Baby and his brother Adrian.

'How the hell did you get here from Melbourne in time?'

'We took a private plane,' grinned Baby.

'I thought you were broke?'

'Couldn't miss your birthday.' Adrian smiled thinly. 'When are you going to reinstate my godson?'

Pretending not to hear him, Rupert moved on to Gala, sitting between Bao and Drew. He was jolted by how gorgeous she looked.

'Hi, you got back all right? Great dress.' He bent to kiss her, and was not amused when Bas and Drew chorused: 'Hands off, she's ours.'

'You'll have to help yourself to drink from now on,' Rupert told his guests, as he ordered his staff, before they got too hammered, to feed and settle for the night their horses, who might need extra rugs.

The horses were delighted as many of them got double and treble helpings. As Quickly had earlier jumped out of his box, it was no longer felt necessary to parade him. Beijing Bertie and Jemmy also received a rousing reception when they got home from Nottingham.

People had started dancing: Marcus with Alexei, his ballet-dancer boyfriend, his sister, Tabitha, wrapped round her husband Wolfie.

'I'm sorry I'm so jealous – I'm like Dad, but it's only because I love you, Wolfie.'

Looking round, Rupert saw Gala dancing with Drew, rather too closely.

'Gala,' he snapped, 'have you checked Quickly?'

'Killjoy! Come back,' Drew called after her as Gala fled from the marquee.

Reaching the yard, she found Quickly had turned the light on, and judging from his half-full manger, he had clearly enjoyed several suppers. Purrpuss-very-full was still tackling a pyramid of Whiskas. Louise had passed out in Delectable's box.

Glancing up, Gala saw a light on in Gav's flat, and felt over-whelmed with relief. What a comfort to have him back. She was about to nip up and knock on his door when the light went out.

Apart from his daughter Perdita bawling Rupert out for ban-ishing his grandson, and not accepting Eddie was going to become a father, then storming out followed by her husband Luke, the party ended without fights breaking out.

As he and Taggie fell into bed, Rupert said for the thousandth time how sorry he was for buggering off.

'My fault for giving a party. Your poor eye looks so sore, shall I bathe it?'

'It's fine.'

'Who hit you?'

'I honestly don't know. I must have cracked my head on something and blacked out.'

'Poor boy.' Taggie kissed him. 'Happy birthday, darling. I was wondering, as we've got the marquee up and there's buckets of food and drink, could all the lads have a party of their own tomorrow night?'

80

Rupert woke up next day with a blinding headache, a black eye and a huge bump on his head, to find the press having another field day. Half the papers had the headline CAMPBELL-BLACKEYE, and ran pieces that reaching sixty hadn't made Rupert behave any better: 'Sixty must be the new sixteen.' All of them speculating who had decked him for humiliating Taggie and 250 guests. Was it a jealous husband?

After thanking Jan profusely for saving the party from total disaster, Taggie, knowing she shouldn't gossip, couldn't resist asking him who he thought had blacked Rupert's eye.

Jan, who was taking glasses out of the dishwasher to return them to the marquee for the staff party, said nothing.

'Rupert hasn't a clue who it was, but they've given him a terrible bump.'

Still Jan said nothing, not meeting her eye.

'It wasn't you?' gasped Taggie in horror, and when Jan didn't deny it, 'Oh my God, it was you.'

'I couldn't bear him to get away with it, to see your heart breaking, after all you'd put into it. But please don't tell anyone. I only did it for you.'

'But how did you manage it?'

'Oh, I just nipped out after the main course . . . Hush, mam, Dora's coming.'

*

At the prospect of opening several wheelbarrowsful of presents, Rupert took four Zapains and summoned Gav to his office for a catch-up. He was delighted that, as a result of Quickly, Dave and Fleance's spectacular successes, Love Rat had received over a thousand new applications.

'We'll have to pick out the very best, don't want to wear the old boy out.'

'Penscombe yearlings sold very well in Keeneland,' said Gav.

'Good, we're going to need the money,' said Rupert. 'I've gotta find a fortune to buy Dave back from Baby, who'll screw every penny out of me. Lark's bringing him back – we need fresh blood. Love Rat's getting lazier, although you wouldn't think it to see him flying round his paddock this morning. All in all, we'd better pull in our horns. That party must have cost a fortune.'

'Don't worry about that,' said Dora, wandering in. 'Jan and Taggie did all the food themselves; Taggie would have trodden on grapes to produce the wine. In fact, you should make a profit. I took so many pictures and I've sold the lot to *Hello*.'

'Well, bloody well unsell them then!'

Having assured Taggie how much he adored his Love Rat cufflinks, Rupert settled down to opening his presents, watched beadily by Sapphire who couldn't understand why none of them were for her.

He loved the bronze of Banquo, the portrait of Taggie and the beautiful painting of Love Rat by Daisy France-Lynch. He was amused by the yearling called Jerry Hatrick from Drew, Bas and Hengist, but less so by the ton of Viagra and the Zimmer wrapped in red paper from the Carlisle twins.

A pair of red trousers were dropped straight in the bin, as was a made-to-measure gold bridle for Quickly, which Rupert said was the most vulgar thing he'd ever seen but which Sapphire bore off to try on her rocking horse.

Five minutes later there was a rattle of hooves and Quickly, wearing the gold bridle and ridden by a grinning Dora, appeared at the window.

'Look how dazzling he looks.'

'Bloody awful, take it off!'

Bao had given him three blue silk shirts. Helen, some huge fluffy bedsocks 'to keep you warm at night'.

'I've got Taggie, the stupid cow,' said Rupert irritably.

He had just opened in delight a first edition of an ancient biography of Eclipse from Gav, when the telephone rang. It was Lark in Australia, crying so much it was a few minutes before Geraldine could make out what she was saying. Having always resented Lark's popularity, she then hung up.

'Who was that?' demanded Rupert.

'Lark in floods, wanted to dump on you – I said you were busy.'

'Get her back,' snarled Rupert. 'At once.'

'Oh Rupert, oh Rupert,' sobbed Lark. 'Baby's sold Dave to Mr Wang.'

'W-h-a-a-at! You sure?'

'Quite sure. I've looked after him since he was a baby. I can't bear the thought of him going to China. I'm so sorry – I can't work here any more.'

'Course you can't – so sorry, angel, I'll send you your airfare. Don't give up hope, I'll talk to Baby.'

Gav had witnessed Rupert's rage on numerous occasions but never thought the telephone would catch fire.

'What the fuck are you playing at, Baby? How dare you sell Dave! You know I wanted him back. How much did Wang pay for him?'

'Mind your own business. I'm sorry, Rupert, but you couldn't have topped it. Means I'll never have to worry about money again.'

'So that's why you took a private plane over. Bet my brother's behind it.' Rupert looked up at a jauntily waving Rupert Black. 'Tell him he can have the fucking Stubbs if he wants it so badly – if you give me back Dave. You're retiring a great horse in his prime.'

'Who said anything about retiring him? We're going for the World Cup.'

After Rupert had hung up and was pacing up and down in fury, Gav said, 'I think this Wang is the same mafia thug who

494

killed Gala's husband. He was the reason why she fainted and
didn't bid for the red filly. I think he's Cosmo's backer. Don't say
anything to Gala – she's terrified.'

Opening the *Racing Post*, Rupert found a full-page advertise-
ment offering:

Congratulations to I Will Repay and Master Quickly in the
Breeders' Cup Classic and inviting them to take part in
the World Cup in Dubai in March.

And Dave as well, thought Rupert.

'When shall we three meet again?' he intoned.

'At least this should help Love Rat in the Global Sire awards,'
observed Gav.

81

The tensions and traumas of Rupert's surprise party had affected Taggie far more than she had realized. She couldn't understand why she continuously felt so exhausted. Even feeding the birds and the badgers tired her. Christmas with all the family pouring in would have wiped her out if it hadn't been for Jan. Now, nearly two months later, the prospect of them pouring in for Easter filled her with dread. How had she managed to cope with entertaining all Rupert's owners in the old days?

She was also fretting about Young Eddie, who'd been packed off to Australia to win races on Cosmo's horses. What was happening about his baby? Sauvignon must be at least four months gone now and Rupert still hadn't made it up with Eddie.

Rupert was away so much, and when he was home they weren't getting on. Thank God for Jan, who was so angelic and took so much pressure off her. And thank goodness for Forester, to whom she'd got closer and closer, who hadn't run away or killed or rolled in anything for weeks.

Then in February she'd become aware of him sniffing her a lot. One evening she'd been arranging a vase of yellow catkins on the kitchen table. The temporary carer was upstairs with Old Eddie and Bao had gone out to supper with Lark and Gala. Unable to be bothered to cook for herself, Taggie had collapsed on the kitchen sofa, trying to summon up enough energy to go to bed when Forester leapt up beside her, raking her left breast with his long claws.

'Ouch,' squawked Taggie. 'Stop it, Forrie, that really hurt!'

Putting up fingers to soothe the pain, she froze in terror as she encountered a lump. She must be imagining things . . . no, there it was again, the size of a large boiled sweet, hard beneath her trembling fingers as she squeezed it, her heart crashing, her breath coming in great gasps.

Rupert was in Dubai at a carnival running up to the World Cup. She longed to tell Jan but he was away seeing his family in South Africa. Thank God no one, except Old Eddie and Local Janet who were snoring upstairs, was there to hear her cry. She wanted to bury herself under the duvet. Upstairs, Forester jumped on to the bed and tried to comfort her, but when she tossed and turned, he retreated to the spare room in a sulk.

She wished he could accompany her on her first appointment with James Benson, the Campbell-Blacks' smooth family doctor, who'd handled multiple dramas over the years. He had allegedly been very keen on Helen, believing, as a young wife, Rupert had treated her appallingly. Taggie had always felt that James found her wanting by comparison, but today he was unbelievably kind, his good-looking, expensive, red-veined face unusually softened.

'Don't worry, darling, the lump's not very large. It's probably just a cyst.'

He arranged for her to see a specialist called Mr Minter at Cotchester Hospital, then urged her to tell Rupert immediately.

'You can't compare this, but look how he loathed having a surprise party landed on him. He'll want to know, he adores you. He'll want to look after you.'

'No, no!' Taggie was hysterical. 'Please not. He's abroad and he's got so much on, I don't want him worried.'

In the end James agreed to her pleas not to tell anyone. 'Let's see what Minter says.'

Taggie hardly took in James asking, 'How's that nice boy Gavin Latton getting on? Rupert said he had sex problems – waste of a good-looking bloke. Tell him to come and see me.'

Outside, a lovely day mocked her: the surgery lawns were white with snowdrops, their sweet drooping heads opening like parasols in the morning sun.

Pretending she was going to buy a dress for the Cheltenham Festival, the great jump-racing bonanza, next month, Taggie set off to see Mr Minter. In a waiting room surrounded by people accompanied by friends and with scarves and hats hiding their heads, she picked up a colour mag, which somewhat tactlessly had a piece celebrating the emergence of the cleavage. Would Rupert, who'd always adored her breasts, still love her if she lost one? Next moment, a girl came out of Mr Minter's consulting room in floods. Gazing into space, shaking violently, Taggie only responded when her name was called a third time. The other patients glanced at her. This must be the child bride of the notorious Rupert – awfully peaky, not a great looker.

Mr Minter, who had sleek grey hair and kind, very dark eyes behind horn-rimmed spectacles, was also interested in meeting the beauty who had allegedly held the love of the irresistible, once wildly promiscuous Rupert for twenty-odd years, and had worn his best pink silk tie in her honour. She looked about twelve, tall and leggy as a baby giraffe, her big grey eyes swollen and red.

Used to imparting bad news, he'd seldom been more reluctant than after feeling Taggie's breasts and subjecting her to a mammogram and then a scan, to tell her it was almost certainly cancer.

'I'm so sorry, Mrs Campbell-Black. We won't know what type it is until we do a biopsy.'

This involved plunging a needle deep into her breast to draw off a small sample. No worse perhaps than Forester's long claws, but very painful. After this, Taggie was told she'd have to wait three weeks for the results coming back on 5 March.

'Thank you,' stammered Taggie.

Was she planning to drive herself home? asked Mr Minter, who'd liked to have driven her himself.

'Yes.'

'Would you like us to ring your husband?'

'I'm fine.'

'Here are some leaflets,' said the breast nurse. 'Try not to worry.'

Taggie walked out into the street and was nearly run over, and as if sleepwalking, went to Cavendish House and bought a dress the colour of mango chutney and three sizes too large for her.

Both yard and stud at Penscombe were thrumming with gossip. Taggie had allegedly gone shopping in Cheltenham and returned as white as a shroud, growing increasingly thin and pale and most uncharacteristically biting the head off anyone who asked if she were OK. Bao had also confided that he kept hearing her crying at night. Gala felt riddled with guilt. Had Taggie sussed her and Rupert?

Rupert and Jan were still both away. Taggie confided in no one, but panicked inside. What would happen if she died? Who would look after Xav and Bianca, and Declan and Maud across the valley, and all the grandchildren, and the new great-grandchild when Eddie's baby turned up? Who would look after the dogs, and feed the birds and the badgers and visit the little foals on their wobbly legs? She had so many dependants.

On 5 March she went back to Cotchester. This time, Mr Minter was wearing a primrose-yellow tie decorated with black birds, and was even kinder.

'How are you, Mrs Campbell-Black? We've fixed up for you to have an operation on March the twenty-sixth. The good news is that as the lump is only about three centimetres, we should get away with a lumpectomy, so you may not have to lose your breast. But to discover if the cancer has spread to the lymph glands we'll have to locate them by injecting blue dye into your breasts on the twenty-fifth, the day before. This will flow into your armpit, so when I do the op I can identify and whip out from the armpit a couple of lymph nodes that have turned blue.'

'I see,' whispered Taggie. The twenty-fifth was the day before the World Cup. How could she disguise anything from Rupert if she had a blue breast?

'Will I turn blue for long?'

'Only where the injection went in. With luck all you'll have is a little scar under your arm and around the nipple.'

She looked such a baby to be married to that reprobate.

'You're not to worry. There are so many better ways of treating cancer these days and we've caught it early. Probably the biggest bore is all the forms you have to fill in.'

Jan was due back on 14 March. The same day, a fat envelope arrived from Cotchester Hospital containing pages and pages of forms. It was the last straw. Taggie could just decipher the title *Treating Breast Cancer* on a leaflet. How could she possibly fill everything in?

Hearing a step, she shoved the envelope into the drying-up-cloth drawer, then Jan walked in. He was wearing the brown cashmere jersey she'd given him, and had a tan almost as dark. But the huge smile lighting up his face vanished as Taggie burst into tears.

'Darling, what's the matter?'

'I'm OK, I'm OK.'

'You are not.' Leading her into the drawing room, he drew her into his arms.

'What is it? Rupert and Gala?'

For a second Taggie looked bewildered.

'No, no.' She was crying even harder. 'I found a lump. They say it's cancer. I've got to have a lumpectomy.'

'Cancer,' breathed Jan, the colour draining from his suntan, his eyes filling with horror then with tears. Nothing could have convinced her more that he loved her.

'Oh my darling.' Breathing in through clenched teeth, he gained control of himself, then gathered her back into his warm, comforting embrace. 'I'm so sorry, but it's curable these days. When are they going to do the op?' He was kissing her forehead and stroking her hair.

'The day of the World Cup.'

'Have you told Rupert?'

'No, no!' shrieked Taggie. 'He's got far more important things, the last chance of Love Rat getting the Global award. He might feel he had to stay here, and I don't want to stop him going. No one knows. Please Jan, you mustn't tell anyone. I don't want the press to find out – they were so vile after the surprise party.' She was almost hysterical.

Jan shook his head.

'You ought to tell him, he'll never forgive himself.'

'No one knows. But the hospital have sent me all these forms to fill in and I can't understand them; it's so shaming. Then there's this blue dye that turns my boob blue. I'll never be able to hide it from him.'

'Plenty of blue tits on the bird-table,' Jan sounded more like Rupert and when Taggie half laughed, 'Give me those forms. I'd better get upstairs and see to your father-in-law, but this evening we'll sit down with a pen and sort them out.'

Later, armed with two large gin and tonics, they got to work on the sofa. Forester insisted on wedging himself between them.

'I'll have to use you as a desk,' said Jan, settling the first form on Forester's brindle shoulder. 'Now what are you, Mrs Campbell-Black? Bisexual, homosexual, heterosexual, trans-gender or don't want to disclose? I wonder how many people put bisexual. Could form the basis of a dating agency. Cheer up, darling.'

He wrote in: 'heterosexual thank goodness'. 'Next, ethnic origin?'

'What's that?' asked Taggie.

'Nationality, goes on for half a page. Are you Black African, Black Pakistani, Chinese Asian or Black Indian?'

'I'm Campbell-Black.' Taggie took a slug of gin. She was beginning to smile slightly.

'So you are – probably a legit category; Rupert's fathered enough children to warrant a category of their own.'

'Oh, shut up.'

'What serious illnesses have you had?'

'I haven't really.'

'Marriage to Rupert?'

'Stop it,' protested Taggie, but she laughed.

'Here you are – White English.'

'No, I'm White Irish. Oh thank God you're home.'

'As I promised, I'm going to take care of you. Once we've finished these I'm off to make you a prawn omelette. You've lost far too much weight – and we're keeping on Local Janet to look after your father-in-law. You're my priority now.'

82

Rupert had a huge amount to occupy him. Apart from scouring the world to see his horses running, the covering season had begun on 15 February, with mega-star mares pouring in from equally far-flung places and the stud staff working overtime, eyes glued to the foaling cameras, waiting to deliver offspring.

Nor were matters helped by Love Rat being reluctant to cover even a couple of mares a day, when by contrast, Titus Andronicus had become so dangerously randy, he'd bitten a stud hand's finger off last week.

Even worse, Old Eddie, getting a new lease of life from Shannon, a buxom new carer who'd replaced Local Janet, and the approach of spring, kept wandering down to see Love Rat and leaving doors open . . . or was it someone else?

It was Bao's last week. Everyone was going to miss him, and he seemingly them as he toured yard and stud photographing staff and animals, particularly Love Rat, Safety Car, 'Quickry' and Forester.

Ivory and gold had lost popularity in China recently, with diamonds becoming the new vogue purchase. On his penultimate day, finding Taggie in the kitchen, Bao gave her a diamond necklace from which glittered more diamonds in the shape of a rose as a leaving present.

'I can't accept this,' gasped Taggie. 'It's far too beautiful.' And she started to cry.

Whereupon Bao led her to the sofa, handing her some kitchen roll, then sitting down beside her, he took her hand.

'Please Taggie Mrs, you of all peoples have made my visit in Britain Great a big joy. You are the loveliest woman in the world and the best mother, the kindest heart. I would like to have mother like you. You have taught me to love animals.' He stroked Forester's brindle head. 'I hope one day, I can show you China.'

'Oh Bao.' Taggie continued to mop up her tears. 'We will all miss you. You've worked so hard and you've been so kind teaching Timon and Sapphire Mandarin – such a good start for them. You'll be welcome back here at any time.' She squeezed his hands. 'But Bao, I can't accept this lovely rose.'

Taking it from her, Bao put it round her neck and did up the clasp, then he laughed. 'I have very good win yesterday on Sha Tin Cup in Hong Kong. Mr Campbell-Black also make nearly half million dollars.'

So Rupert, who was due back later in the day, would be happy, thought a relieved Taggie.

Leaving work on the same evening in the faint hope a returning Rupert might pop in, Gala chatted on the way to Gee Gee.

'How's Fleance getting on in his new role as a stallion?'

'Yesterday he mounted a French mare from the nearside,' sighed Gee Gee, 'and then from the right and ejaculated. This afternoon he got it right, sweet boy. Bloody Titus, however, ought to be in a straightjacket.'

Wandering on, Gala marvelled at the luminous pale-grey sky with a sliver of a new moon to the south, Jupiter in the east and Venus in the west, shining into each other's eyes. Surely spring must come one day. Then she heard terrible screaming, issuing from the stud behind her. Love Rat, having escaped from his box, was having an idle pick of grass when Titus, on his way to the covering barn, had broken away from his terrified young stud hand and flung himself on Love Rat, tearing him apart with his front hooves, plunging his teeth into, and leaving great gashes in, his gentle rival's shoulders and neck.

'Titus,' shouted Gala, racing back, ducking under the rail, seizing Titus' chain lead and trying to separate them. 'Titus, it's me!'

Next moment, Titus had wheeled round, knocking her to the ground, kneeling down on her, squealing furiously, about to bury his teeth in her face.

I'm going to die, thought Gala.

'Help!' she cried.

'You bloody fool!' yelled a voice.

The next moment, a heavy chain was being slashed back and forth across Titus' head until he was distracted enough for Pat to grab the maddened stallion's own lead chain, yanking at the agonizingly painful bit, dragging a squealing Titus back to his box while Gav tugged Gala to safety.

'You bloody fool!' he yelled again, seeing blood gushing from her cheek. 'Where else did he get you?'

'Nowhere – I'm fine. Love Rat's what matters. Get the vet,' she cried to the appalled stud hand.

Poor Love Rat lay on the ground, trembling violently, deep wounds everywhere, nostrils ripped, white coat drenched with blood which had stained the grass for yards around.

'Poor old boy,' sobbed Gala, crouching down, stroking his face. When Sammy Radcliffe roared up five minutes later, however, Love Rat, never a fan of vets, struggled to his feet, stumbled back to his box and collapsed again.

Even when Sam's father, Charlie, arrived it took hours to clean him up, both vets expressing great concern as they dressed his wounds.

'Thank God Titus didn't get his testicles. He's had a terrible shock – he's an old horse, shouldn't cover anything until he's fully recovered, if at all.'

Bleeding Sire. Pat was doubly devastated. He adored Love Rat but there would be all the hassle of finding replacement stallions to cover his mares.

Even when Gee Gee mopped up her cheek with Dettol and put on a big plaster, Gala refused to leave Love Rat.

'Sorry I yelled at you,' said Gav. 'You saved his life, but I think we should leave him to rest.'

'Let me stay a little longer,' pleaded Gala.

As she smoothed his bloodstained forelock, Love Rat pressed his head against her, then knuckered as Rupert appeared in the doorway.

When he heard the details, Rupert went ballistic.

'How the hell did Love Rat get out? Someone must have left his door open.'

'Your father was down here,' said Pat, 'and Bao was everywhere taking photographs. He's leaving tomorrow.'

No one was in the mood to hold a farewell party for Bao. Rupert, too preoccupied to notice Taggie's pallor, refused to leave Love Rat. His dogs, all fond of the old horse, slept huddled together for warmth outside his stallion box.

83

Gala felt totally ill-equipped for the coldest winter in years. Even smothered in six thermal vests with a roaring beech-log fire in the sitting room, she felt she would only be warmed by Rupert's arms around her. But he had been abroad so much chasing winners, and so frantic at home, worrying about Love Rat, she had hardly seen him. He was probably desperate to make his marriage work after all the appalling press following the surprise party.

Returning to Lime Tree Cottage later in the week, she was just lighting the fire and wondering whether there was more to life than a baked potato, *Holby City* and half a bottle of cheap white, when her mobile rang, and was in shock dropped in the log-basket.

'Hello, hello,' said a light clipped voice, then just, 'Shall I come over?'

'Yes.'

'Now?'

'Yes.'

She'd been too thrown to ask how long he'd be.

She'd been getting up so early, the place was a tip. The hyacinths Taggie had given her already had brewers' droop, their pink heads lying among a pile of unwashed clothes on the kitchen table. A mountain of washing-up waited to go into a full dishwasher. She was just frantically plumping cushions, chucking more logs on the fire, drawing curtains, gathering up abandoned bras and pants and Gropius' half-eaten breakfast, when she decided she herself was more important.

At least her hair was clean. Whipping off pants and jeans, she leapt into the bath, frantically directing the shower between her legs, sliding deodorant under her armpits, and then washing between her legs again in case he went down on her and tasted shower gel. Then she splashed herself in the lovely Mandarine scent Taggie had given her for Christmas . . . why did everything come back to Taggie?

She was just about to tear off her multi thermal vests when there was a thundering on the door – he was here. She tugged back on her jeans. Hell, she hadn't cleaned her teeth. She was just fishing a Polo out of a jacket pocket when she heard banging again.

'Coming, com-ing,' she shouted.

'Not quite yet,' mocked Rupert as she opened the door.

'Hi, how did you get here so quickly?'

'I sneaked out here so often in the old days, I know the way round every tree. This place used to be known as Knocking Cottage, particularly when Billy and I were showjumping and Janey entertained her lovers.'

There was snow all over his Puffa and his hair, proving he'd still be divine, even when he went white.

'I didn't know it was snowing.' Gala licked Polo chippings off her teeth.

'Sorry not to give you more notice – I'm off to Singapore tomorrow.'

There was a crackle and a flare as flames found a nail in a log.

'I suddenly couldn't bear not to see you. I missed you.' And as he drew her into his arms, kissing her on and on, she realized he tasted of toothpaste, reeked of English Fern and his hair was wet, not just from a scattering of snow so he must have showered specially. He must love her a bit to bother.

Next door they found Gropius on the bed, who totally ignored Rupert's order to get off and growled irritably when the Paddington duvet was tugged from under him.

'Good boy, to defend your mistress from everyone else but me,' said Rupert, chucking Paddington down in front of the still crackling, spitting fire.

'Aren't you worried about sparks?' asked Gala.

'Any sparks will come from us.'

'It'll take ages to undress me,' Gala warned as he delved under the layers of thermals and unhooked her bra, his fingers stroking her ribs before gathering up her breasts.

'Christ, these are gorgeous,' pulling off vests, bra and track-suit top, he buried his lips in her bare shoulder.

'Please take care of this Bear,' giggled Gala.

'Let me look at you – oh my God.' In the flickering firelight, her body was soft gold.

She gasped as his warm hands slid under the elasticated waist of her jeans, gold signet ring catching the light, as he fingered her belly button before creeping into the slippery cavern between her legs.

'Ker-rist, you do want me.'

And his smile of genuine delight, so seldom seen in the last few months, made the moment even more precious.

'Oh God, yes, I do want you.' She kissed his sleek muscular chest, then sliding her hand downward outside his trousers encountered a leaning tower of pleasure. 'Wow, you want me too.'

'"See! Antony that revels long o'nights is notwithstanding up."'

'Julius Seize him,' giggled Gala and had no difficulty unzipping, drawing down and finding her way in.

Kneeling down on Paddington, she languorously rotated her tongue down the whole legendary length, mumbling: 'Hail, cock of the West.'

'Careful, I don't want to come too soon.'

Next moment he'd stripped off in his full glory and pushed her down on the duvet, thinking how voluptuously cushiony and welcoming she was. Taggie had recently become so thin, pale and reluctant, showing no interest in sex.

Moving in, he licked her clitoris, then parted her labia, murmuring, 'I do like to make an entrance,' before plunging his cock deep inside her, hearing her laughter become gasps of joy.

'Oh buttercunt, buttercunt.' As her warm wet slipperiness gripped him he really had to battle not to come. Her cries grew louder as his long fingers crept down, gently stroking, until she stiffened, shuddered and came. They were both so out of it, they didn't notice a log falling out of the fire, or that someone was pounding on the door.

'Christ, it's the porter in *Macbeth*. Don't answer it,' hissed Rupert.

Gropius, however, jumped down and waddled past them, squeaking excitedly as the banging increased.

'Gala,' shouted a voice. 'It's Dora!'

At first, they couldn't stop laughing, then Gala said, 'Quick! Get in the wardrobe, next door. I'll pretend I was about to have a shower. Hurry! Dora'll tell half Penscombe and the world.' She gathered up Rupert's clothes and chucked them into the bedroom after him. 'I'll get rid of her.'

Wrapping herself in one of the big white towels that Taggie – again – had given her when she moved in, she answered the door. Gropius' squeaks rose, overjoyed to see Dora and his friend Cadbury, who after goosing Gala, discovered and wolfed down the remains of Gropius' breakfast.

'So sorry to bother you,' said Dora.

'I was just about to have a shower,' said Gala, whipping Paddington away from the fire and flinging him over an arm-chair. 'Sorry about the mess.' She kicked Rupert's underpants under the sofa.

'Lovely fire.' Dora put back a fallen log. 'I was looking for Rupert actually,' then as Gala froze, 'but I can't find him. I've got to get his *Racing Post* copy in before he leaves for Singapore tomorrow. I thought you might be able to give me a few pointers about Rupert. It's so hard when he's away so much.'

Well, he's a fantastic fuck, thought a dazed Gala then said, 'Not really. I haven't seen him recently.'

She noticed Dora looking longingly at the bottle of white on the table. Cadbury, meanwhile, had shoved his way into the bedroom. Very fond of Rupert, he was now wagging his tail and yelping excitedly at the wardrobe door.

'Come out of there!' yelled Gala.

'What on earth is he after?' asked Dora as the noises and scrabbling intensified.

'Probably a mouse – the place is crawling with them. I might borrow Purrpuss for a day or two. Get Quickers into training for when he goes to the World Cup. He misses Purrpuss more than Safety or Bitsy.' She was rattling on now. 'Could be the ghost, of course.'

'Didn't know there was one.'

'Goodness yes,' lied Gala. 'This cottage is eighteenth century, some keeper hanged himself. Gropius often barks at him.'

Dora shivered and looked at Jan's photographs of Ben.

'Wasn't he handsome? You must miss him so much.'

'Yes, yes I do. Cadbury, do come back. Dora, I must have that shower. I'm meeting a friend at the Everyman – another carer. We're going to *Miss Saigon*, a new production on its way to the West End. So I'd better get moving.'

'OK,' said Dora. 'Sorry to bother you, and if you can think of any other snippets of goss about Rupert . . .'

The moment Dora was out of the front door, Gala ran after her. 'You've left your torch behind.'

Only when she'd seen Dora disappear into the dark wood did she release Rupert from her wardrobe. He emerged, rubbing his neck. 'Midgets must have hung their clothes in there. I now know how horses suffered from bearing reins.'

'It's a First World Wardrobe.'

'Only compensation, your clothes smell of your scent. I thought that leopard dress was going to gobble me up.'

He must have remembered that from the party, thought Gala in wonder.

After that they attacked the bottle of white and got quite hysterical with laughter until he suggested they celebrate getting Gropius off the bed. What touched her in their second love-making was his gentleness yet determination to give her pleasure.

'I adore you,' she mumbled, lying in his arms afterwards. 'I'm trying so hard not to love you.'

'Please don't. I've tried so hard to stay away, to get you out of my system – it hasn't worked. I'll be back from Kringi next week and I'm definitely taking you to the World Cup.'

Returning to the stud, chided by hooting owls, Rupert admired a lovely filly Cordelia had just given birth to, watched Fleance covering a French chestnut mare – from the wrong side again – then checked on a worryingly listless Love Rat before retreating to his office to cool down.

Christ, he mustn't let Gala get to him, but she was so adorable and no one gave head like that – he must get her a Headmistress badge. He'd just switched on *At the Races* to watch one of Love Rat's offspring run at Wolverhampton when Dora wandered in.

'Absolutely riveting – I dropped in on Gala earlier, who behaved in a most extraordinary way. She was wearing only a towel and hastily kicked a pair of man's pants under the sofa. I'm sure she's seeing someone. She didn't even offer me a drink, and chucked me out saying she had to rush because she was going to *Miss Saigon* at the Everyman with a girlfriend. Well, I just Googled *Miss Saigon* and it doesn't start till next week. Sooo . . . I wonder who he is? I bet it's Gav. She pretends not to, but she's always fancied him rotten.'

'Don't be ridiculous,' snarled Rupert. 'And if you've nothing better to do than indulge in fatuous gossip, you can bugger off. I want to watch this race.'

'Oh,' said Dora, looking at the screen, 'isn't that one of Lester Bolton's horses going down to the post? He evidently paid Brute Barraclough a massive £300,000 for it.'

'The only way that horse will win a race is inside some greyhound,' said Rupert sourly.

'That is gross,' stormed Dora, going bright red in the face. 'There is nothing funny about horses going for meat and this week I think your column should attack the utterly atrocious transport of live horses.

'Did you know they cram thousands of horses, mares, little foals, randy unbroken stallions, delicate racehorses, donkeys, pony-club ponies past their sell-by date, carthorses so obese their fetlocks won't hold them up, all into lorries without partitions?

'Then horrible Eastern European travellers hurtle them across Europe without any breaks for food, water or rest, so they end up with broken legs or crushed to death on a floor running with blood and crap.

'And the drivers don't stop until they get them to the slaughter-houses in Italy, because the bloody Italians like their horsemeat fresh. It's an abomination, it's a bloody disgrace and once they dump the horses at the abattoir they turn round and hurtle back for another load. Are you listening to me, Rupert?'

'I've heard it all before,' said Rupert, looking up from the *Racing Post*. 'I know it's awful. Things are being done to improve it.'

'Not nearly fast enough. I'm going to write a real polemic in your name to shake things up.'

'And Animal Rights will say it's my fault because I contribute to the over-population with my stallions breeding hundreds of foals a season, like an assembly line.' Although Love Rat'll never get anywhere near that again, he thought sadly.

'Anyway, if people aren't allowed to sell horses for meat any more, they'll turn them out in a field to starve or freeze to death.'

84

Only a fortnight to go to the World Cup. With the lure of ten million dollars prize money and several other rich races on the same night, the best horses in the world would be flying into Dubai.

These included New Year's Dave, who'd been given another season by Mr Wang, To Die For, Simone de Beauvoir and Noonday Silence. An incredibly strong home side would be headed by Dubai's ruler the great Sheikh Mohammed – but the main interest was in a repeated clash between the two Breeders' Cup Classic superstars, I Will Repay and Master Quickly: whoever won would ensure his sire the Global Leading Sire title.

Brute Barraclough had also been invited to send Geoffrey, the bridesmaid horse who came second or third in everything. Rosaria, however, was panicking. Having learnt how much Mr Wang had forked out for New Year's Dave, Brute was determined to flog Geoffrey to Wang's great rival, Mr Tong, for a lot more.

Colin Chalford, Mr Fat and Happy, the banker whom Rosaria had liked and with whom she had danced at Cosmo's orgy, had persuaded Janey Lloyd-Foxe to bring him down to the yard to meet Geoffrey, and was clearly very taken with him.

Lark, despite missing New Year's Dave desperately, had been so happy to be back at Penscombe but found that everywhere reminded her even more desperately of Young Eddie. She half dreaded seeing both him and Dave again at the World Cup.

Would she find herself still hopelessly in love with both of them? And would Eddie even be there? After his great Breeders' Cup Classic victory, he'd won several races in Australia on Cosmo's horses – but Cosmo and Isa, who liked to keep jockeys on the jump, hadn't yet confirmed that Eddie would have any rides in Dubai.

Rupert meanwhile was increasingly worried about Love Rat, who had not recovered from his savaging, was not eating up or showing any desire to cover anything.

'Completely gone off sex,' sighed Pat.

Just like my wife, thought Rupert bitterly.

He and Taggie were not getting on. While he'd been off round the world, he had been increasingly wracked by desire for Gala. In fact, to lessen this he had ordered Taggie to come to the World Cup with him. But she had flatly refused and kept wriggling away from him. With her perched on the far side, their huge double bed was such a lonely place, he was tempted to send out search-parties. He was also worried in case she had found out about Gala. He didn't trust Jan. And who had let Love Rat out?

Suspicion was increasingly falling on Bao, particularly when Rupert saw the ravishing diamond necklace he had given Taggie – was he yet another man in love with her? The afternoon after she'd refused to come to the World Cup, he'd just wandered into the kitchen to make himself a ham sandwich when Lark walked in looking uncharacteristically furious.

'I don't mean to sneak, but Harmony, Repay's groom, just rang me to say Bao had lunch at Valhalla on Sunday.'

'He *what*?'

'Cosmo gave a lunch party. Zixin Wang and his beautiful wife, Bingwen, were there and Dame Hermione, who sang for Mr Wang – who evidently adores opera – and Bao played the piano accompanying her. Sauvignon was apparently there,' Lark's voice rose indignantly, 'all over Wang, when she's having Eddie's baby.'

'Christ! Wang's the bastard whose poachers murdered Gala's husband.'

'It seems he toured the stable admiring Dave and Repay, both of whom he now owns,' Lark's voice trembled, 'and is determined to win the World Cup with them. He's even based his silks on the Chinese flag.'

'My God,' said an outraged Rupert, adding an extra dollop of mustard to his sandwich, 'Bao must be our mole. All those leaks all summer going straight to Cosmo; the red chestnut filly at Tattersalls, me poaching Tarqui and firing Eddie. He was always hanging around the yard. He must have let out Love Rat.'

He took a bite of his sandwich and choked; it was a minute before he realized Jan was standing in the doorway.

'We're busy,' gasped Rupert, as Lark patted him on the back.

'I don't want to stir things,' said Jan, 'but I've always suspected Bao. I found your lucky shirt under the lining paper in his room and I discovered this in the inside pocket of the jacket, which he asked me to take to the dry cleaners.'

Jan handed over a photograph of a brutally handsome, granite-jawed Chinese man with his arm around a beautiful, also Chinese, woman.

'On the back of which Bao's written "Mother" in Mandarin,' said Jan.

'When did you speak Mandarin?'

'I don't, but when Bao was giving Sapphire and Timon Mandarin lessons, he made a card for them to send Tabitha, which is still in their rooms. Look – it's the same hieroglyph, "Mother".'

'Good God.' Rupert and Lark examined card and photograph.

'That's certainly the Wang who bought Dave,' said Lark with a shudder, 'and Mrs Wang.'

'I've been checking online,' said Jan. 'Zixin Wang is actually married to Bao's mother, Bingwen, who he stole from Mr Tong. The present Mrs Tong is Tong's second wife, Aiguo, and Bao's stepmother. No wonder Tong hates Wang and wants to beat him in the World Cup. Rumour has it he's trying to buy Geoffrey.'

'Also,' Jan went on, 'Bao's probably worried about his mother. Wang is suspected of having bumped off his first wife, who was in television, in order to marry her.'

'And assassinated Gala's husband – not a great track record,' said Rupert. 'Bao must be our mole, the little shit.'

'But he was so sweet,' protested Lark, 'and he really loved all the horses and the dogs. It doesn't add up. Perhaps he only went to Valhalla to check his mother was OK with Mr Wang. He so adores her. According to Harmony, vile Sauvignon was doing a real number on Wang on Sunday. Poor Eddie.'

'Wang, bang, thank you, Mum.' Rupert threw the rest of his sandwich in the bin. 'It's obviously Wang who's backing Cosmo, that's why he's been able to spend such billions on horses. I must go and ring Valent.'

Valent was equally appalled to learn of Bao's transgressions but reluctant to call the police because he was so involved with Tong on a business level; he and Rupert were also about to pull off a huge deal selling him hundreds of horses.

'I'll try and ring Bao,' said Rupert.

But Bao wasn't answering his mobile and had clearly pushed off back to China.

Worse was to come. With tragic irony, a fortnight after Dora's inflammatory column in Rupert's name, inveighing against the transport of live horses, Safety Car was found missing from his field, leaving his sheep friends racing around frantically bleating.

'He's probably in the pub,' said Roving Mike.

'Or been signed up to play football for Chelsea,' said Cathal.

'He'll go for meat, I know he'll go for meat,' sobbed Dora.

'Can't sell for meat without a passport,' said a shaken Rupert, then went cold when he discovered Safety Car's passport was missing from the office. It must be an inside job, somebody wanting to destabilize Quickly. Anyone armed with the passport could now spirit Safety Car across the Channel and on to a long-distance lorry rattling towards a bloody death.

'It must be Bao,' said Cathal. 'He was hanging around photographing Safety and Love Rat for hours on the day he left. He always made a point of cosying up to Safety, who probably went with him willingly, poor old boy.'

It was then discovered the CCTV had been switched off that night, so there was no evidence.

'I don't believe it,' said Taggie, fingering her diamond necklace in horror. 'Bao adored Safety – he thought he was so funny. He wouldn't do that.'

Marketa, who'd been so excited about taking Safety to Dubai, was inconsolable. 'Some windictive willain's stolen him.'

Equally inconsolable, but refusing to show weakness, Rupert called in the police and offered a £500,000 reward for Safety, not excessive when one appreciated Quickly was going to compete in a $10,000,000 dollar race.

'With his one ear, white face, scraggy tail and his photograph all over the press and internet, someone must recognize him,' said Lark hopefully. But as hammer blow followed hammer blow, it seemed that someone must really hate Rupert. On a pre-race canter the following morning, Bitsy got a leg treading on a pile of stones unaccountably thrown down on the gallops – so Quickly had no pacemaker with whom to go to Dubai.

Poor Taggie was just as upset about Safety Car, but at least it meant that people assumed he was the reason for her tear-stained unhappiness when, on the pretext of going shopping for Sapphire's birthday in Cotchester, she went to hospital for the blue-coloured dye to be injected into her breast. Jan had wanted to go with her but Eddie's buxom carer, Shannon, had a migraine so he couldn't get away.

Returning from hospital, Taggie was chucking out a pile of newspapers when she discovered on the features page of the *Scorpion* a picture of Rupert and Gala embracing after the King George. She was still fretting that, when Jan had found her crying a while back, he had assumed it was over Gala and Rupert.

On his last night before leaving for Dubai, Rupert was caught up with so many things in the yard, particularly a fading Love Rat, he was very late coming to bed. Taggie pretended to be asleep, but when Rupert woke her and tried to make it up, she shoved him away, petrified he'd discover the blue dye, refusing to let him touch her. Rupert had proceeded to walk out and have insomnia in the spare room with all the dogs.

In the morning, Love Rat was even more lethargic. He didn't even whicker when Rupert entered his box. Sapphire and Timon had spent the night in the straw beside him.

'He's not going to die, is he?' begged Sapphire. 'And Safety Car'll come home soon, won't he?'

'I'm sure he will, darling.' Rupert so loathed leaving them.

It was such a lovely day. Robins singing their heads off, woodpeckers laughing and rattling, custard-yellow sweeps of primroses, sticky buds on the chestnut avenue and a crimson blur on his beechwood. Rupert suddenly thought how nice it would be to stop chasing dreams and win the Lincoln Handicap, the first big race of the English flat season, rather than pushing off round the world. His dogs, knowing he was off, followed him around, all with sad 'suitcase faces'.

Going into the kitchen in a last attempt to make it up with Taggie, he found her sobbing in Jan's arms, toyed with the idea of hitting Jan across the kitchen . . . and then stormed out.

Thank God, Gala was going to be in Dubai.

85

Gala was already in Dubai but also in turmoil. On the eve of her departure, she had gone into the kitchen at Penscombe to check if she had any post and to rinse and return Rupert's favourite mug with Love Rat's picture on, which he'd left in the tack room. As she rummaged around for a drying-up cloth, an envelope fell out. Remembering this was the drawer where Taggie hastily hid any Valentines, Gala couldn't resist having a look – and went cold. Inside was a letter from Cotchester Hospital summoning Taggie to an operation on 26 March at 8.30 a.m. – that was the Friday before Saturday's World Cup. Also in the envelope were leaflets on treating breast cancer, including chemotherapy and radiotherapy.

Oh God – poor darling Taggie! That's why she'd been so red-eyed, wretched and up and down recently, and Gala had been riddled with guilt that she'd guessed about her and Rupert.

Not wanting to distract Rupert, Taggie was obviously having the op when he'd be safely in Dubai. This changed every goal post. Rupert had gone ballistic over the surprise party – how infinitely more so, if he discovered Taggie had cancer, particularly with Master Chef here holding the fort.

Taggie had always been angelic to her. How could she go to bed with Rupert knowing this? Yet she had to fight off an utterly shaming thought: if Taggie died, that would free up Rupert.

*

Janey Lloyd-Foxe was just typing another venomous chapter, mobbing up Rupert for becoming a great-grandfather in her *Billy and Me* book, which she needed to finish to pay lots of bills. She wouldn't have been so broke if bloody Rupert had allowed her to stay free at Lime Tree Cottage.

She was relieved to be interrupted by the doorbell – Colin Chalford, Mr Fat and Happy, dropping in with a bottle of champagne. As they were drinking it, even more excitingly, he took a little blue leather box out of his pocket and handed it to her.

'I'd like you to look at this.'

Inside was a huge and beautiful sapphire.

'Do you like it, Janey?'

'It's the loveliest ring I've ever seen,' gasped Janey.

'Oh good,' said Colin. 'I'm always unsure of my taste in women's things, but if you approve . . .'

'I do indeed.'

Janey flashed the sapphire on a dirty-nailed finger. If she married Colin, she reflected, she'd never have to sweat her guts out writing books any more. She was so delighted, it was a few seconds before she registered Colin saying, 'You see, I've met the loveliest woman in the world and I want to give her an engagement ring she really likes.'

Rupert landed in Dubai early on the Friday before Saturday's World Cup, moving into a suite in the Meydan Hotel, near the racecourse, where he could do business and pull off deals. Right in the middle of the desert, the hotel was attached to the end of a huge 600-metre-long stand which soared upwards like a multi-decked liner, topped from end to end by a roof shaped like a vast sickle moon. Meerkat, Tarqui, Gav and Cathal were staying in a nearby hotel.

On arrival, Rupert went straight to the deluxe quarantine complex half a mile from the racecourse where his horses, Blank Chekov, Delectable, Dick the Second and Quickly, were staying, with his stable staff accommodated in the rooms overhead.

Three overseas trainers were allotted to each barn, with

Penscombe ironically sharing with Valhalla and Tommy Westerham. For this reason, Gav had employed a nightwatchman to guard Penscombe horses and their tack. Everyone was giggling because at 5 a.m. the nightwatchman had been traumatized by Louise running downstairs in only her thong to shut up a whinnying Chekov with a bowl of nuts.

'He must have been kept awake finishing *The Cherry Orchard*,' said Gala.

Gav, however, had his head in his hands because Quickly, in addition to all his other setbacks, had come out worst with a coffin draw in the World Cup – right on the outside, fifteenth out of fifteen – while I Will Repay had drawn number three.

'But it's great here,' Lark reassured Rupert. 'So warm after Gloucestershire, and our rooms are lovely and there's a beautiful swimming pool and gorgeous food: lots of salads and kedgeree.'

Outwardly cheerful as usual, she was churning inside over whether Eddie would turn up. Knowing she shouldn't talk to the opposition, she hadn't been able to resist asking Harmony, who admitted Eddie was very out of favour, and that Roman and Ash were likely to take any rides. Horrible Sauvignon was evidently seeing a great deal of Wang, so Eddie was probably being kept out of the way.

Before he went back to his hotel, Rupert had a private word with Gav, who was pleased with the way Tarqui had limbered up Quickly with a half-mile work on the dirt that morning.

'He's in great form. Needs to be, to make up for this bloody awful draw.'

As Meerkat didn't have a ride in the World Cup, Rupert had agreed Rosaria could borrow him to ride Geoffrey. Aware that Gala seemed abstracted and unhappy, Gav then bravely warned Rupert not to hurt her and was told to mind his own fucking business.

'OK,' said Rupert, returning to take leave of the troops: 'I don't want any of you to go out on the razzle. I don't mind what you do tomorrow, but get some sleep tonight.'

He ignored the longing in Gala's eyes. But out of earshot, five minutes later, livid with Jan and Taggie, and with Gav for sticking his nose in, he rang her, telling her to come and spend the night at the Meydan.

'Are you sure it's safe?'

'Perfectly. *Gulf News* is hardly likely to lead on us and I need you. Bring your toothbrush.'

'What about Quickly?'

'Lark can keep an eye on him.'

It was terribly hot. As she blow-dried her hair, Gala looked back at Dubai, a vast distant huddle of skyscrapers, many of them wearing cranes like fascinators. Among the freebies beside her basin she found a little mending kit. Perhaps she should pass it on to Rupert to mend his marriage – and how could she put a deodorant called Sure under her armpits, when she was so unsure of everything? She felt shredded with guilt about Taggie, but couldn't help herself.

She fiddled with her make-up all the way in the taxi, worrying if her new lipstick entitled 'Passion' was too dark a red? On the glass behind the driver was a list of questions on how you rated your ride.

Have you been completely satisfied? asked the last one. I'm going to be that later, thought Gala with a shiver, but right now I'm going to be late, as the traffic was held up by an accident on the other side of the road and her driver jumped out to photograph it.

Rupert met her by the main stand. He was wearing jeans and a blue and white striped shirt. How was it that tiredness never dimmed his beauty?

Briefly he showed her the Hall of Champions.

'That room's called "the Horse Connections Lounge" – ghastly expression.'

To the right was a huge wall covered in glass moons, each framing the name of a previous World Cup winner. There was mighty Cigar, and Curlin and Dubai Millennium, a home win, and Victoire Pisa from Japan, whose victory had cheered up his country after a devastating earthquake. A few glass moons were still empty.

'That one's waiting for Quickly,' said Rupert.

'Oh goodness.' Gala's voice trembled. 'Wouldn't it be lovely?'

They dined in the Meydan Restaurant. Rupert had a rare steak and chips; Gala, Dover sole and a green salad. Trying to banish all thoughts of Taggie, Safety Car and Love Rat, they both drank a great deal more than they ate.

Rupert made no attempt to hide the fact they were together, calling her 'darling', holding her hand, waving to Tommy Westerham and Charles Norville and their wives across the room and blanking a furiously disapproving Roddy Northfield and Damsire, who were running Red Trousers in an early race.

Gala regaled Rupert with gossip: how Louise and Marketa had got off with two handsome Arabs and went round giggling, 'We'll be with you in a couple of sheikhs.' How Harmony had lost so much weight. How Tarqui was quite relieved to be away from his new baby because he hated being made to change nappies.

'It's not funny,' she went on, 'but Marketa's so miserable about Safety, she needed distracting last night and was complaining: "I've left my wibrator behind, so I'll have to make do with you", and dragged Meerkat off to bed.'

Rupert laughed and picked a fishbone from Gala's sole, then he said, 'Gav gave me a pep-talk earlier about not hurting you.'

Gala blushed. 'Did he really? That's very brave. He's been so good, putting aside his hang-up about Tarqui being Bethany's lover. He and Tarqui have almost made friends, and he's really helped Tarqui to bond with Quickly – two such wilfully strong characters letting Quickly think he's boss.'

'I don't want to talk about Gav,' said Rupert, drawing her leopardskin top over her black bra strap. 'My fifth leopard.' Then, running his fingers through her tawny mane of newly washed hair: 'You've got spanner eyes.'

'What's that?' stammered Gala.

'Every time you look at me, you tighten my nuts.'

I can't help myself, I utterly can't, she thought.

'Come on.' He took her hand. 'Let's go to bed.'

Upstairs he hung a Do Not Disturb sign on the door. Someone had turned down the sheets and put a chocolate on the pillow. Out of the window Dubai glittered like Taggie's diamond necklace in the darkness.

Rupert had stripped off first and lay on the bed checking results on his app. Seeing the Love Rat cufflinks given to him by Taggie on the chest of drawers, Gala was overwhelmed with sadness. This must be the last time she slept with him. Suddenly she thought of Browning's poem 'The Last Ride Together':

> Since nothing all my love avails,
> Since all, my life seem'd meant for, fails . . .
> Take back the hope you gave, – I claim
> Only a memory of the same . . .

Then how did it go?

Rupert patted the bed. 'Bit more comfortable than that Paddington duvet in front of your fire. Hopefully Dora won't barge in.'

The room was glitzy, with a gold-threaded counterpane and curtains, pictures of stallions, falcons and sheikhs on the walls and scores of silk cushions on the sofa.

'Wouldn't Forester love to chuck all those on the floor?'

Oh God, Forester, who'd be missing Taggie back in England.

I'll never go to bed with such a beautiful man again, she thought as she lay down beside him, kissing his smooth forehead, his long blue eyes, his high cheekbones and the tip of his Greek nose before moving down to his lips.

'I can't help it,' she breathed as his hand reached for her breast. 'I'm just crazy about you.' Kissing her way down his flat stomach, she took his soaring penis in her mouth, licking and teasing the tip.

'It's no good, I'll come too quickly,' said Rupert, tugging her up level with him and kissing her, before plunging deep inside her.

'Oh buttercunt, buttercunt.' A few frenzied thrusts and it was all over.

'That's the best thing that's happened to me in weeks,' Rupert told her with such tenderness. 'Definitely ride of the century.'

'And I adore you,' whispered Gala, wishing she could stay awake to prolong the joy, but she'd been up since five. As she drifted off, she suddenly remembered the last lines of Browning's poem:

> Take back the hope you gave, – I claim
> Only a memory of the same,
> And this beside, if you will not blame;
> Your leave for one more last ride with me.

Waking, not knowing where she was, murmuring, 'One more last ride with me,' she discovered a naked Rupert looking out of the window at the stars. He was shivering. There was something desolate about his hunched shoulders. Overwhelmed with love and pity, she got up and put a white towelling dressing gown around him, tucking his arms into the sleeves and doing up the cord as if he were a little boy.

Then, as though leaping into a waterless swimming pool from the top diving board, she made the supreme sacrifice.

'I know you love Taggie,' she whispered, 'and she loves you.'

'Funny way of showing it,' said Rupert bleakly.

'Well, as we speak, she's been having an operation today for breast cancer. She found a lump – that's why she didn't want you to touch her, in case you found it. And with Love Rat so ill and Safety Car missing she didn't want to worry you; she knew how important the World Cup and winning Global Leading Sire was to you,' floundered on Gala. 'She always said her breasts were the thing you loved most.'

'That's fucking intrusive, Tag would never have said that,' spat Rupert.

Then he went berserk, seizing Gala by the arms, shaking her as Cuthbert would a rat.

'Why the fuck didn't you tell me?'

'She didn't want anyone to know.'

526

'So who told you all this?'

'I found a letter summoning her to the hospital and some leaflets hidden in a kitchen drawer, then I overheard Jan comforting Taggie in the kitchen.'

'Jan,' exploded Rupert.

'Jan's a snake,' gasped Gala as Rupert's fingers nearly broke her arms. 'He's madly in love with Taggie, he'd do anything to break up your marriage.'

'Taggie's got breast cancer,' said Rupert slowly. Suddenly World Cups, and Global Leading Sires had faded into insignificance. 'I'm going home.'

Next moment, he'd telephoned and roused Sheikh Mohammed, the ruler of Dubai, and borrowed a jet to fly home.

'But what about the World Cup?' wailed Gala.

'Fuck the World Cup,' said Rupert, diving into the shower.

Oh God, what had she done? All she could think about was poor Gav, after all the work he'd put in, as she helplessly watched a still dripping Rupert tug on his clothes. He didn't need to pack because he'd never unpacked. Nor did he apologize to Gala, merely telling her to keep the suite herself.

86

Gloucestershire after Dubai was freezing. Arriving mid-morning, still in wet clothes, Rupert couldn't stop shaking. Reaching Cotchester Hospital, he found Taggie still asleep after the operation, and a hovering James Benson, looking a lot less smooth than usual, who when shouted at, replied that he'd wanted to tell Rupert, but Taggie forbade it.

Happily, they'd saved the breast, but had had to take quite a large lump out of it. 'We won't know for a week or so whether the cancer's spread to the lymph glands, but if the breast's too misshapen we can always insert a bit of lipo from off the stomach.'

'That's fucking immaterial.'

Taggie was wearing a hideous grey, yellow and red gown, with a label saying *for hospital use only* as if it could be for anything else.

Looking down at her, Rupert thought she had the longest, darkest eyelashes in the world, appalled that he hadn't realized quite how desperately thin and pale she had become. He was touched by a photograph of him and Forester on the bedside table. As she woke, she blinked, struggling to understand, gazing at him in wonder. 'I thought you were in Dubai.'

'When I heard, I had to come back. Why didn't you tell me? I can't bear to think you had to go through this on your own.' He stroked her face. 'Oh my poor angel, if you knew how much

528

I love you.' He picked up her hand, longing to take her in his arms but deterred by the drips and fear of hurting her.

'I'm so sorry,' mumbled Taggie. 'I thought if I lost a breast you wouldn't want me any more.'

'I'd still love you if your head was cut off.' Rupert's voice broke. 'Darling, I'm so sorry, I thought you were bats about Jan, when I found you crying in his arms. That's why I stormed out.'

'He was comforting me because of the cancer, and I thought you loved Gala.'

'Whatever gave you that thought?' said Rupert in outrage. 'I missed having Billy to talk horses with. You're the only thing that matters to me in the world. I love you so much,' and he kissed her wrist with the hospital band, on which he wanted to write *Mine*, rather than *Agatha Campbell-Black*.

'And I love you.' Taggie was drifting off to sleep again.

Next moment, a beaming Jan walked in clutching a big bunch of daffodils – and nearly had a heart attack to see Rupert.

'Yeah, I'm back.' Rupert grabbed the daffodils and with a crash shoved them into the pedal-bin. 'And you can fuck off and stop my father leaving stable doors open, which is what you're paid to do.'

'Poor daffies, not their fault,' said a nurse, fishing them out of the bin.

Leaving Taggie to sleep, promising to come back immediately, Rupert returned to Penscombe, having rung in and been told there was no news of Safety Car, and that Love Rat was fading.

Going straight to the stables, he was met by Old Eddie in his pyjamas and odd slippers, crying his eyes out. 'He's dead, he's dead. I went into Rattie's box and found him lying down. I said, "Come on, you lazy old boy, stop playing games," but he didn't move, he's dead, he's dead.'

Love Rat was lying in the straw, his dappled coat turned almost white with age, his big, dark, lustrous eyes still open. Rupert closed them and kissed him on the forehead, muttering, 'Rest in peace, Legend.'

'He so wanted to see you again,' Pat's voice trembled, 'but he couldn't wait any longer.'

Everyone in the yard was in tears, except Geraldine. 'What about his book of mares?' she grumbled.

Ignoring EU regulations that don't allow horses to be buried at home, Rupert said to Pat, 'Can you dig a grave for him in the graveyard?'

Outside, Old Eddie was sitting on a bale of hay, still crying his eyes out.

'He's dead, he's dead.'

Wincing to hear the desperate bleating of sheep calling for Safety Car, Rupert put his arms round his father. 'It's all right,' he said, making a superhuman effort not to break down too. 'He was such a sweet horse, he'll gallop up to heaven and jump straight over the Pearly Gates. We'll bury him beside Rock Star and Furious and Gertrude and Badger. He'll have loads of friends.'

But as he led his father back to his office and poured him a large glass of brandy, it sunk in that Love Rat would never be Leading Sire now, and even if Quickly won the World Cup later today, what would it matter if Taggie's cancer had spread to the lymph glands?

Purrpuss, who was missing his friend Quickly, wandered in and rubbed against Rupert's legs as if begging for news, then took a flying leap, claws out, on to Rupert's shoulder as the Penscombe dogs, just realizing Master was home, came barking joyfully into the office. Except for Forester who, finding no Taggie, crept dolefully back to the kitchen.

Me too, thought Rupert.

Back in Dubai on Saturday morning, desert-coloured mist swirled around buildings glittering in the rising sun, as excited crowds, revving up for the World Cup, gathered long before the first race at twelve noon.

Surprised that Gala hadn't turned up at the barn to join Marketa, Louise and Lark in taking Rupert's four runners for a gentle jog, Gav stood in for her and rode Quickly.

'Gala's obviously had too good a night with the Guv,' giggled Louise.

'Don't be bloody silly,' snapped Gav, gutted to be of the same opinion, but having to concentrate on staying on Quickly who, reaching a peak of fitness, was bounding all over the place and still yelling plaintively for Safety Car.

On Gav's return to the barn, however, he was stunned to receive a text from Rupert.

'Please take over, had to go back to England.'

Getting no answer from Rupert's mobile, he sprinted over to the Meydan. Here he discovered Gala alone and in pieces in Rupert's vast bed, and took her in his arms.

'I told the fucker not to hurt you. Oh baby, I'm so sorry. I know you loved him and he couldn't keep his filthy hands off you, the bastard.'

'No, he isn't – he loves Taggie.'

'Where the hell is he?'

'Flown home.'

'The fucker – Quickly's uptight enough as it is. In the middle of the fucking World Cup.'

'Taggie's ill.'

Gavin, with his passion for Quickly, was about to say, 'Fuck Taggie.'

'Very ill,' sobbed Gala.

'Right.' Gavin took over with total authority. 'Get up,' he ordered Gala, and pointing to Rupert's desk diary, 'Cancel all his meetings, tell people to get in touch next week. Then get yourself dressed and down to the barn. Quickly needs you.'

87

The World Cup's vast stadium, the biggest on the planet, had been built out in the desert by Dubai's ruler, Sheikh Mohammed, and consisted of endless stands and luxury boxes, now brimming over with people. In the middle was one small box behind curtains, into which all the Sheikh's wives and daughters were allegedly confined.

Before each race, the runners were stabled behind the stadium in the hope they would not be upset by massed bands and endless firework displays, with fairies or magicians on huge horses, exploding out of the sky. Every so often on the wide screen appeared one of Sheikh Mo's publicly admired poems, more Sheikhspeare than Shakespeare.

Glamorous non-Arab spectators from all nations abounded, mostly in lounge suits or cocktail dresses. The best-dressed man and woman would each be awarded a Jaguar car. The atmosphere was formal but intensely theatrical, the prize money astronomical. The winning World Cup jockey would get eight per cent of the ten million dollars, plus a gold whip.

Cosmo Rannaldini was in high spirits, offering to sell his mother Dame Hermione, who was very excited by the gold whip, for 1,000 camels. Cosmo himself, who had arrived with Mrs Walton, Sauvignon and Repay's new owner, Zixin Wang, was very excited by rumours of Rupert's defection. And Zixin Wang was very excited by his first colours – gold stars on a scarlet background – echoing the Chinese National Flag.

Meerkat was even more excited to be riding Geoffrey later in the World Cup. Rosaria had surprised everyone by turning up with Colin Chalford, Mr Fat and Happy, the banker she'd met at Cosmo's orgy.

'What's he doing here?' snarled Brute, who was in the process of selling Geoffrey for a vast sum to Mr Tong. 'Fat and Happy is Janey Lloyd-Foxe's boyfriend.'

Team Penscombe, meanwhile, was in tatters.

Everyone had noticed Gala's anguished face and Marketa kept bursting into tears every time anyone asked after Safety Car, so Gav gave them all a pep talk.

'Rupert's had to go back to London. Taggie's not well evidently, but I for one am not going to waste all the time we've spent working on our horses. Let's bloody well prove to Rupert we can win without him.'

Valent, not knowing the reason for Rupert's defection, was absolutely furious. After the World Cup, he and Rupert had intended to fly to China where Dubai were staging a similar meeting. He was only just realizing how in bed with China, Dubai was, and suspected that Wang, who couldn't resist an opportunity to make billions, was involved. Etta was sad for Valent. She knew he felt socially safer on occasions like this, when Rupert was around.

Cosmo was enchanted when it was confirmed Rupert had pushed off. 'Couldn't bear to witness any more defeats,' he told the press. Then, bumping into Gala and Gav outside the weighing room: 'So sorry your boyfriend's dumped you, Gala,' he said, before bursting into song. 'How could he treat a poor maiden in Meydan so.'

'Shut up,' snarled Gav.

'Don't get ideas above your station, Floppy Dick.'

'And you can shut up too,' yelled Gala.

Team Penscombe were further devastated by news of Love Rat's death. Gav, however, who had loved him from his days working in the stud, remained strong.

'He should have died hereafter; unfortunately, we've got work to do.'

All was not doom, however. Just before the first race, Louise raced into the barn.

'Glorious news,' she whispered to Lark. 'Sauvignon's not pregnant.'

Lark's hand stopped polishing Quickly. Her mouth fell open, but she couldn't speak.

'You know how Ruth Walton detests Sauvignon,' crowed Louise. 'They both came into the Ladies. Sauvignon was upstaging Mrs Walton with this phenomenally expensive bag Wang had just given her with her initials printed on it, and couldn't resist opening it to show off the beautiful rose silk lining. And quick as a flash, Mrs W squawks: "You've got Tampax in there. I thought you were pregnant".'

'Omigoodness,' gasped Lark.

'And,' giggled Louise, 'that phenomenally expensive old bag, Sauvignon, blustered a bit, saying, "Actually, I miscarried in January, but I was so traumatized I didn't tell anyone. I couldn't cope with the fuss if the press found out."

'"Having created all the publicity in the first place," says Mrs Walton, all disdainful. "And have you put poor Eddie out of his misery?" I left them shouting at each other and I've just texted Eddie the good news. Lark, Lark!'

But Lark had fallen to her knees in the straw, her hands together, her eyes closed.

'What are you doing?' asked Louise.

'I'm thanking God,' sobbed Lark.

As if determined to cheer them up, Chekov ran a blinder in the first race, the Dubai Gold Cup. This was on turf which stretched out in pale-green and dark-green stripes like a Harvie and Hudson shirt. Chekov was so laidback he even had a pick of grass at the start before trouncing the horses of Ash, Manu de la Tour and Hammond Johnson, and earning a massive £384,615.

Tarqui was in heaven and even more so when little Delectable, not distracted by anything, bounded up in the Al Quoz Sprint and was only just beaten by a Japanese horse. Almost as pleasing, Red Trousers came last. All the time the crowds were building up, then in the fading light, Dick the Second joined the runners in the Golden Shaheen.

'He's very much on his toes,' said Tarqui.

'Makes a change from standing on mine,' said Lou-easy.

Dick leapt out of the emerald-green starting stalls from a very wide draw. Hurtling across to grab a place on the inner, he collided – or was pushed – by Roman Lovell, and crashed into the rails, hurling Tarqui over his head. Staggering to his feet, Tarqui insisted he was perfectly all right. The doctors thought differently and bore a disconsolate Tarqui off in an ambulance to hospital, where it was confirmed he'd broken his shoulder.

'At least you won't be able to change nappies for a bit,' consoled Meerkat.

One blow after another. Safety Car stolen, Love Rat's death, Rupert walking out, Tarqui's shoulder.

'We're star-crossed,' wailed Gala.

'No, we're not,' snapped Gavin, not letting anyone disintegrate into self-pity.

Lark was desperate to see Young Eddie again. By now he must've got Louise's text about Sauvignon not being pregnant. But still not finding his name on the list of competing jockeys, she sidled up to Harmony and asked what was going on.

'Cosmo,' whispered Harmony, 'is playing games. When he thought Rupert would be out here, he wanted to irritate him by putting up Young Eddie to beat him on Valhalla horses. But the moment he learnt Rupert had gone home, he jocked Eddie off and gave his rides back to Ash and Roman Lovell. Even worse, Dave's been scratched from the World Cup, because if Dave won it, it would push Love Rat's earnings, even posthumously, above those of Roberto's Revenge. Cosmo's so obsessed with Roberto's Revenge winning Global Leading Sire outright. So Ash is riding Repay, who belongs to loathsome Wang.'

'Oh poor Eddie, and poor Dave,' cried Lark, seeing Isa and scuttling back to Quickly.

Overhead, a wistful jockey moon with a halo of gold looked down on the fireworks.

88

So, without Tarqui, who was going to ride Quickly in the World Cup – which was only two races and about an hour and a half away? Meerkat couldn't abandon Geoffrey at this late hour. The light had faded beneath a sooty black sky. The vast footprint-shaped course was lit up now like a Cecil B. de Mille film of the New Testament, as great waves of Arabs in flowing robes and keffiyehs swept after Sheikh Mohammed or his sons or other Eastern potentates. Many of them were on their mobiles discreetly ringing bookmakers in Hong Kong, because betting was forbidden in Dubai – which slightly took the edge off the occasion. In the parade ring, set aside on a table, vast gold cups and plates awaited the World Cup winner.

Meanwhile, a depressed Eddie had flown all the way to Dubai only to find himself jocked off. The one single blaze of sunshine was Louise's text that Sauvignon wasn't pregnant. A wildly relieved, no longer father-to-be Eddie had joined Etta and Valent in the ex-pat bar.

'Where's Grandpa, for God's sake? Is it true he's flown home because Taggie's unwell? She must be very ill.'

With no rides he might as well get plastered. He'd seen Lark leading up Delectable earlier and thought how adorable they both looked. Across the bar, he could now see Wang, his brutal granite face marginally softened as he smiled lustfully down at Sauvignon, who smiled lustfully back. Clad in a clinging cyclamen-pink dress and a fascinator as though pink rose petals had fallen on her glossy dark-brown hair, Sauvignon had just been awarded the Best Dressed Lady's Jaguar.

One carnivore deserves another carnivore, thought Eddie. Then, as though a great harpoon had been tugged out of his side, he realized he didn't give a damn about her any more. It was an ecstatic moment. He was about to down a quadruple gin and tonic when he became aware of the joyous notes of a hunting horn – the sound of his mobile ringing. It was Gav.

'Get your kit on,' he said. 'You're going to ride Quickly.'

'You sure?'

'Quite. I've been to the stewards and registered a jockey change.'

'What'll Grandpa say?'

'I'm calling the shots now. Go and get changed.'

Eddie had no time to be nervous or even daunted by the weighing room, which boasted four televisions, a vast restroom, a whirlpool, a huge Jacuzzi, two steam rooms, each big enough for a dozen jockeys, a twenty-foot sauna, fifteen washing machines, a dining room, lounge and gym. A Brobdingnag for Lilliputians. Here the greatest jockeys, fit from riding round the world all winter, wandered around naked except for their tattoos.

Rupert's blue and emerald silks, cut off Tarqui and hastily stitched together by a valet, were still drenched in sweat.

'That'll put on five pounds,' grumbled Eddie.

As he left the weighing room he was grabbed by Cosmo, who said it was beyond the pale for him to boost one of Rupert's horses in a stallion market, in which Valhalla was a direct rival.

'If you ride Quickly, you're fired,' said Cosmo.

'Good, I've resigned,' said Eddie.

About an hour before each race, the racing tack, which was kept in the barn, went over with the relevant groom and horse to the saddling boxes in the pre-parade ring.

As Gala and Lark left with Quickly, Harmony was setting out with I Will Repay.

'I know we're not allowed to talk, but you've lost so much weight,' whispered Gala.

'Cosmo's allowing me to ride out,' confided Harmony, 'and I've got a gorgeous boyfriend.'

'Not surprised – you look great.'

Meanwhile the nerves of horses, trainers, owners and jockeys were frazzled as more and more fireworks went off and more tales from *The Arabian Nights* were re-enacted by huge gold eyeless jockeys, galloping white ghost horses, whirling dervishes and dancing searchlights, whilst orange, red, green and yellow rockets exploded into the dark, symbolizing the speed with which buildings were shooting up in Dubai.

Even in the underground pre-parade ring, where the bangs were muted, for Gala, with Mr Wang around, they were too reminiscent of a Zimbabwe shoot-out. As she helped him saddle up Quickly, Gav put a hand on her quivering shoulders, saying, 'It's OK, they'll stop soon.'

Noticing he was wearing a pale-grey suit, white shirt and dark-grey tie, Gala said, 'I've never seen you in a tie before. You look lovely, just like a trainer.'

'Don't take the piss.' Gav punched her gently on the nose. 'To get beat, or not get beat, that is the question.'

Eddie was unbelievably touched when Quickly dragged Lark out of the pink and yellow saddling box, and with a thunder of whickering, rushed up and held his face against Eddie's.

'That's what Love Rat used to do,' said Lark in a choked voice.

'Hi, babe,' said Eddie, ruffling her hair. 'So good to see you again.'

'Great to see you,' gasped Lark. 'We're all knocked out that you're riding Quickly.'

'Don't know if I'm up to it. I was about to get hammered when Gav called me.'

'You'll be great.'

'Well, don't plait him up so I've got something to cling on to.'

The night was dark indigo now, the course surrounded by

huge square floodlights as though the stars themselves had come down to admire the beautiful gleaming horses.

Quickly, as a famous runner, led up by two such pretty stable girls, Gala and Lark, caused huge interest.

'Come on, Quickers,' cajoled Gala. 'You've lost your cat, your comfort blanket, your dad and one of your owners – now's your chance to show the world you can do it on your own.'

Quickly flapped his ears and listened, pretending to spook at all the white robes. With a change of jockey, he'd drifted to 25–1. Valent rang Ladbrokes in England, to put on another £10,000.

The owners and trainers stood in little groups as the horses circled. Gala had great difficulty hiding her loathing and terror as they passed Sauvignon and Wang.

'Isn't she beautiful?' sighed Lark. How could Eddie get over someone as gorgeous as that? 'But isn't *he* scary?'

'Terrifying,' shuddered Gala. But as she moved in to shield Quickly, for a second Wang turned and stared at her – giving her almost an eye-meet. He doesn't recognize me, she thought.

Standing beside his father Mr Tong, who'd made an offer for Geoffrey, Bao, in an off-white suit, was very aware of being blanked by the entire Campbell-Black team; they clearly suspected him of kidnapping Safety Car. Even kind Etta turned her back on him, as she and Valent waited with Gav for Eddie to come out with the other jockeys. It was 20 degrees in Dubai but Eddie was shaking violently and had gone as white as the Arabs' robes, all his cockiness gone.

'Sheikh Mo just asked me if I'd had any news of Taggie,' were his first words as he joined them. 'She will be OK, won't she?'

He looked so young and vulnerable that Etta hugged him, saying, 'Of course she will.'

'I can't do it. Grandpa will never forgive me. Why hasn't he rung already, jocking me off?'

'Because I've switched off my mobile,' said Gavin with the ghost of a smile. 'You'll be fine. Think Breeders' Cup, King George, Guineas.'

There were fifteen horses in the race, from all over the world.

Noonday Silence, the Japanese hope, had travelled over badly and lost a lot of weight. Geoffrey shuffled along, ignoring the ridicule, I Will Repay looked magnificent, ridden by Ash, as did Ivan the Terrorist, ridden by Roman Lovell, and Simone de Beauvoir, ridden by Manu. To Die For, whose career earnings were over $5.6 million, carried Hammond Johnson and American hopes, as local hopes were pinned on Sheikh Mohammed's great horse Dubawi Divine, and Irish hopes on a big chestnut called George Bernard Offshore.

The crowd had been delighted by a huge home win in the penultimate race: the Sheema Classic, triggering off the Dubai national anthem, tantivies from a vast local band, and lots of Arabs kissing each other and rubbing noses. Sheikh Mo did a little dance of delight.

It was time for the jockeys to mount. As Gala and Lark led Quickly over, Gav put two hands on either side of his face.

'Godspeed, little horse,' he said softly. 'You've travelled thousands and thousands of miles across the world to get here today, but the next mile and two furlongs are the ones that matter.' And he kissed Quickly on his pink nose.

God, Gav's sweet, thought Gala, fighting back the tears. Gav had written his notes on one side of an A4 page.

'Draw's awful,' he told Eddie. 'You won't be able to belt across and sit on the rail. Hammond and To Die For are going to grab that position anyway, so keep him wide. But you need to be prominent; don't linger and try to come from behind. Keep up with the pace, so he won't get kickback in his face. Relax him as much as you can, then use his turn of foot like a knock-out punch at the end.' As he legged Eddie up, he smiled. 'In a word, ride him as you've always ridden him – as if you'd stolen him.'

'Good luck, Eddie,' cried Lark, as the boy she loved joined the finest jockeys riding the most beautiful horses, except for Geoffrey who as usual looked ugly and half asleep.

'I think Geoffrey has much the most character,' said Mr Fat and Happy to Rosaria.

Quickly, who'd been behaving far too well, just to prove that fireworks were not just the prerogative of the Arabs, gave three terrific bucks, then going up on his hind legs, he walked a dozen paces. Eddie laughed and told him not to be silly. As he was riding out on to the course, he suddenly caught sight of Jan. What in hell was *he* doing here?

'Christ, I'm nervous,' piped up Meerkat, as together they cantered down to the start. 'I've just seen Lord Rutshire.'

89

Sheikh Mohammed had changed from snuff-brown to French navy, to match the indigo sky.

The fireworks had died out, leaving a smell of sulphur; the desert gleamed pale Labrador yellow. The lights of Dubai, in the distance, were another world. Eddie was suddenly terrified by the malevolence on both the faces of Roman Lovell and Ash, whose breath smelt like sour milk as he rode close.

'Don't try any funny tricks, pretty boy, or we'll get you.'

'Hell knows no fury like a faggot scorned,' snapped Eddie.

In sympathy, Quickly flattened his ears, and took a bite at Repay.

'No one should go near that brute without health insurance,' hissed Ash, lifting his whip.

Etta and Valent went up into the owners and trainers box to watch the greatest race in the world. Gavin and Gala stayed on the ground; any part of the track they couldn't see, could be watched on the vast screen.

Dear God, prayed Gala, let both of them come home safe.

Dubai was four hours ahead of Gloucestershire. With evening stables completed, all the staff including Old Eddie were gathered round the yard television. Most of the hospital staff, including James Benson, seemed to have squeezed into

Taggie's room to watch the race as the runners circled on the churned-up dirt.

'What the fuck's Eddie doing riding Quickly?' howled Rupert. 'Christ, he'd better not screw up.'

They could now see the horses jostling round in the gate . . . and then they were off, and Roman had surreptitiously knocked Eddie's whip out of his hand. Bumped on the other side by Ash, when he tried to go wide, Quickly took off, hurtling to the front. Without the moderating presence of a pacemaker Eddie was struggling to restrain him, when he felt the left rein give and come away from the bit. Next second he had lurched to one side and nearly gone out of the back door. Then he saw Geoffrey's big dirt-splattered face coming up on his right, felt someone grabbing him and with heroic strength tugging him back into the saddle. His saviour had been little Meerkat. He was aware of screams of consternation from the crowd.

'Thanks,' he yelled as the loose rein slashed his face. 'What the hell am I going to do?'

'Ditch the bridle,' yelled back Meerkat.

Only one end of the rein had contact with the bit. Even if Eddie leant forward and clutched at the bit rings, he couldn't steady Quickly and might any moment be catapulted over his head. As Quickly veered towards the rail, the offside cheekpiece gave way. Any moment, the reins might get terrifyingly tangled in Quickly's flying feet. The only answer was to pull the whole bridle off and fling it over the rails into the darkness.

As most of the field drew level, he must stay wide and not get trapped in the mêlée. All he could do was take hold of Quickly's blond mane, sit absolutely still and yell: 'Come on, Quickers, you'll have to look after me.'

And Quickly, realizing the vulnerability of the man on his back, for once agreed. Suddenly they were back among the buttercups on their first ecstatic gallop at Penscombe.

'He'll kill himself,' cried an anguished Gala, her hand slipping into Gav's.

Like a Red Indian hurtling across the prairie, raking up the cinnamon-brown dirt, Eddie and Quickly, hugging the far rail, passed the Japanese who'd travelled so badly, and without a side glance from Quickly, passed Manu on Simone de Beauvoir, passed the US ace Hammond Johnson, who seldom got beat on To Die For, passed Roman on Ivan the Terrorist and Ash in Wang's red and gold colours on Repay, passed the great horses of the Sheikhs and from Irish Ballydoyle, finally overtaking Meerkat trundling along on Geoffrey – and surged into the lead.

There was no way of putting the lid on Quickly. Eddie could only guide him by shifting his body.

'Dear God,' prayed Eddie, 'don't let him run out of gas.'

'He's going to do it!' yelled Rupert, sitting on Taggie's bed, watching in the grey five o'clock daylight and cheered on by most of the hospital. 'Don't let him – no, no, no, look out!' he shouted as I Will Repay sidled up on the left, stalking Quickly, hell bent on mugging him on the line.

Eddie could just hear Meerkat shouting, 'Watch out, Ash's coming up on your nearside.'

An exhausted Quickly slowed as Repay drew level – then, seeing his old enemy, he rallied; gathering all his strength, ears flattened to his head as they hurtled together, Quickly ahead, then Repay was moving closer, trying to rattle Quickly, but with a mighty last effort, Quickly hurled himself forward, past a winning post topped by a golden ball.

'Photo, photo!' cried the commentator.

The wait was everlasting. Then, out of a deafening roar of speculation: 'First Master Quickly,' by just an inch of pink nose.

'Good boy!' howled Rupert. 'Christ, he's good – that was the bravest piece of riding I've ever seen.'

On the screen they could see incredulity and wonder dawning on Eddie's desperately clenched features, as taking both hands off Quickly's mane, he raised them above his head, blowing a kiss to the sooty heavens.

'This one's for you, Love Rat,' he yelled. 'You're Global Leading Sire at last.'

By almost more of a miracle, with Quickly as a pacemaker, Geoffrey had come third. Taking Meerkat's hand, Eddie kicked his feet out of the stirrups and they cantered back together in front of a wildly cheering crowd, who although disappointed not to have a home-win for their revered Sheikh, recognized heroism.

Then a laughing, sobbing Lark came tearing up with a lead rope and a head collar to stop Quickly running away, hugging and patting him, and when a laughing, overjoyed Eddie leaned down and kissed her, she didn't even notice that Quickly was nipping her very sharply on the shoulder, to remind them who'd won the race.

Next moment, a plump girl in a black coat, her huge thighs emphasized by light-coloured breeches, cantered up on a chestnut, brandishing a microphone.

'What is going through your mind at this special moment, Eddie?'

'That I want to go on kissing the prettiest girl in the world.'

'And what was going through your mind when the bridle broke up?'

'This is it,' laughed Eddie. 'How the hell was I going to stay put.'

'How special is it to win the greatest race in the world without a bridle?'

'Quickly won it.' Eddie hurled his goggles into the crowd. 'He looked after me, he found and found, and he quickened twice, and Meerkat saved my life, but I'd like to know who fucked that bridle.' Then as he was wrapped in the American flag, the 'Star-Spangled Banner' rang out.

Meanwhile, on the grass outside the parade ring, Gavin and Gala had leapt in the air, screaming with joy, hugging each other. 'We did it, we did it . . .' Then as the photographers raced up the track to catch Quickly and Eddie, they paused and looked at each other. Gav's lean face was so transformed by happiness, his no longer sad eyes sparkling with tears.

'Yes,' said Gala in amazement. 'Oh yes, yes, yes, we did it.'

Unable to stop herself, she grabbed his head, burying her fingers in the thick black curls, drawing him closer and pressing her lips to his, kissing him harder and harder, until he responded and kissed her back even harder. Only when they began choking for lack of breath did they break apart, but still gazed at each other. Gala ran her hand down his cheek as if she were reading happiness in Braille.

'How stupid I am, oh my darling, I've been barking up the wrong tree.' And she kissed him again until they were tapped on the shoulder by a tearful overjoyed Valent.

'Hasn't your horse joost won a race? Shouldn't we go and congratulate him? And Rupert says will you switch on your bluddy mobile, Gav.'

90

Scenes of wild jubilation followed. Etta, as Quickly's only owner present, was ecstatic to receive the huge World Cup from Sheikh Mohammed, and water the vast accompanying bunch of flowers with her tears of joy. Rosaria and Mr Fat and Happy could be seen fox-trotting joyfully round the winners enclosure to celebrate Geoffrey's third place.

A spectator, meanwhile, had found the broken bridle chucked over the rails and returned it to the stewards. The stitches had been unpicked, and the prongs on the buckles, attaching the reins to the bit, had been unplugged. Sabotage must have occurred at the very last moment. So suspicion fell even more on Bao.

There would be an enquiry later, but there was no question that Quickly had taken the race. And it was generally agreed with Rupert that Eddie's had been the bravest piece of riding ever seen. Eddie agreed and now, brandishing his winning jockey's gold whip, was telling a vast army of tape recorders and cameras: 'We did it without a bridle or a whip, without a pace-maker and without Safety Car, Quickly's best friend. Quickly showed he is the greatest horse in the world.

'The tragic news is that Master Quickly's sire, Love Rat, died this morning.' Then, as a groan of surprise and sadness greeted this: 'But the great news is that by this awesome win, Quickly's earnings have pushed Love Rat posthumously to the top of the

Global charts.' Eddie flung his arms out and shouted so it echoed round the desert, 'You're Leading Sire at last, Love Rat.'

Over huge cheers, on a roll, utterly captivating his audience, Eddie went on to express gratitude to Meerkat for saving his life, and to Gavin and Gala who made Quickly great, and to Lark. Eddie searched round for her in the crowd. 'Where are you, Lark? She'll be back at the stables cherishing Master Quickly.

'Most of all,' somehow Eddie kept his voice steady, 'I want to thank Quickly's co-owner and my grandfather, Rupert Campbell-Black, who is simply the greatest trainer in the world. He had to fly home because his wife Taggie isn't well. Hope you get well soon, Taggie. Sorry I've been a piece of work in the past, Grandpa, but I hope you'll let me ride for you again one day.

'But I guess the one thing that will make Taggie and Grandpa happy is for Safety Car to come home. Safety's the kindest horse in the world, and he must be somewhere – and it's typical of Grandpa's generosity that he's offered £500,000 reward for his return. So please, guys, start looking.' Eddie brandished a large photograph of Safety Car. 'This is what he looks like.'

Watching back in Gloucestershire, Rupert was utterly choked. As Taggie was falling asleep, he went back to Penscombe to seek news of Safety Car, and to check on the yard and on Old Eddie. Jan had evidently vanished without trace, and a new carer had been bussed in.

'A gorgeous black lady called Bertha,' Pat told Rupert. 'Your father's in heaven – he's convinced he's in Barbados.'

Trailing dogs, Rupert crossed the garden, past the tennis court to the graveyard where the greatest, most loved animals were buried. No one had yet laid turf over Love Rat's grave but someone had put a vase of daffodils and a great bowl of primroses on the freshly dug earth into which a wonky wooden cross had been plunged. On it, Pat, who must have overheard Rupert yesterday, had scribbled: *Rest in peace, Legend.*

Oh Christ, why did everything hurt so much? His horse had won the World Cup, but he felt no elation.

They had still to learn if the cancer had spread to the lymph glands. It was as though he and the family were sitting in a room with a terrorist, bomb in his hand, peering in at the window. If Taggie went, everything would collapse.

The lawn was littered with white feathers. A buzzard must have taken out one of Taggie's doves.

He'd better go and be charming to Eddie's new carer. *Come Dine with Me* was on the television in the kitchen. Old Eddie was nosing around the vegetable rack, muttering: 'Must go and congratulate Love Rat, must be some carrots in here.'

Looking up and seeing Rupert, the sweetest smile spread across Old Eddie's face.

'Hello, how are you? Would you like a drink?'

'Probably,' said Rupert.

'Do you know my son Rupert?' enquired Eddie. 'You don't? I thought everyone knew Rupert. He's an awfully nice chap, awfully amusing. I'm sure you two would get on. I'd like you to meet him one day. He's a really nice chap.' And he turned back to *Come Dine with Me*.

Rupert went out on to the terrace, tears pouring down his face. What a mess he'd nearly made of his life. He hadn't been a really nice chap to Taggie. He'd spend the rest of her life, he shivered at how brief it might be, making it up to her. He hadn't been very nice to Young Eddie either. He must ring and congratulate him. But where the hell was Safety Car?

He was joined by Sapphire.

'Where's Ratty, Grandpa?'

'He's died, darling.'

'I know. But everyone says he's up there, in heaven. But Pat says he's down there, in the graveyard. How can he be up there and down there? I don't understand.'

91

Back at the World Cup, Mr Fat and Happy and Rosaria, who'd stopped fox-trotting round the winners enclosure, couldn't stop hugging each other. Geoffrey, coming third, had indeed out-raced his pedigree.

Vile Brute, thinking he was about to make a fortune selling Geoffrey to Mr Tong, had rolled up and bollocked Meerkat for tugging Eddie back on to Quickly.

'You could have won the race if you'd left the little shit to rot – and what a lousy finish you rode. You won't be riding Geoffrey again, he's off to China.'

'No, he isn't,' interrupted Mr Fat and Happy. 'I tracked down his owner Mrs Ford-Winters in Gloucestershire, nice old lady, happy to see him go to a good home, so Geoffrey's coming to live in Weybridge, Brute – and so's your lovely wife, Rosaria. And Meerkat can come and ride our horses whenever he wants to.'

Brute, utterly routed, was insane with rage. Even more maddened with anger was Mr Wang because Dave had been withdrawn and I Will Repay had only come second, and he wasn't going to be the first Chinese owner to win the World Cup.

Eddie was still giving interviews, euphoric because Rupert had just rung congratulating him and thanking him for a brilliant race. 'Come back to Penscombe straight away. Great, you saluted Love Rat.'

'I didn't have any reins to take my hands off this time.'

But bolstering his happiness even more was the thought of meeting up soon with Lark, who was probably still down at the stables, loving and cherishing Quickly, as he longed from now on to love and cherish her.

'Congratulations.' For a second Eddie thought the tall auburn-haired man shaking his hand was Jan, then realized it was Rufus Rutshire, the gay elder brother of frightful Roddy Northfield, and as lean and good-looking as Roddy was magenta-faced and portly.

Having no children, Rufus made no secret of how irritated he was that his title would pass to Roddy and Damsire's fat, pompous and charmless son Alfred who, unlike his royal name-sake, spent more time eating cakes than burning them.

Rufus now confided to Eddie, as he hemmed him into a corner, how glad he was that Red Trousers had come last in an earlier race, and could they have a word? Aware that people behind Rufus were still clambering to speak to him, Eddie glanced at his watch. 'I've gotta go soon.'

'Just wondering if you're free tomorrow fortnight,' said Rufus. 'It's the day after the National, so people will be in the mood for heroics. We're planning to create a James Northfield Memorial Race at Rutminster on the anniversary of his death. Your grandfather Rupert is the direct descendant of Rupert Black, who originally beat our James in the race. But you know all this, you spoke about it so well on *The Morning Line*.'

'I've truly gotta go.' Eddie drained his glass.

'We thought it would be a terrific idea,' persisted Rufus, 'if one of Rupert Black's descendants rode in a match race against one of our descendants. We could re-enact the race across the water meadows and through the wood.'

Then, at Eddie's raised eyebrows, 'No one's going to get killed this time. I'm going to clear the track through the wood so it's completely safe. Be great if you as a terrific rider could repre-sent the Campbell-Blacks.'

'I'd be glad to,' said Eddie. 'But what about Tabitha – she's brilliant – or Xavier? He used to ride point-to-points.'

'We need a big name like yours,' said Rufus, then with typical fundraising pushiness, 'And it would be wonderful if Mrs Wilkinson and Quickly could parade as well. They really pulled in the crowd last time.'

'Who's riding for the Northfields – Alfred?'

'Christ, no. Actually a rather marvellous distant relation's come out of the woodwork. Do think about it – could be very special. We could discuss it over dinner next week.' In Rufus's fox-brown eyes, the admiration was not entirely for Eddie's skills as a jockey.

'You'll have to ask Rupert. Not sure he'd like the idea or would regard me as a legit Campbell-Black.'

'I'll send him an email. Could raise a lot of money for the Injured Jockeys Fund.'

'Hardly appropriate, with James Northfield copping it. I've really got to go.'

Back at the quarantine barn, Lark was settling Quickly for the night, rinsing the last dirt out of his eyes, telling him what a champion he was and that tomorrow they'd return to Penscombe for a hero's welcome. Although Gav had employed a second security guard to watch Penscombe horses through the night, Lark wondered if she ought to sleep in Quickly's box. But she was so desperate to shower, and put on a rather daring zebra-print dress to go out on the town with the others. Eddie had been so lovely today . . . perhaps, perhaps.

She was just handing Quickly a carrot from a box which said *Made in China*, when he started and jerked up his head, hitting her in the eye.

'Lark,' said a voice.

Swinging round, Lark gave a scream and leapt in front of Quickly. 'Go away! Don't you dare come near him. Did you unstitch his bridle?'

'You have everything wrong,' protested Bao. 'It wasn't me doing the bad things. I never let out Love Rat and I love Safety.'

'I don't believe you.' Lark wanted to yell for help, but the place was deserted. 'What were you doing over at Valhalla, and where's Safety Car?'

For a terrifying moment, she thought Bao was going to strangle her. But he merely put a tape recorder to her ear.

'I am good at hacking, listen to message.'

The accents of the voices were unmistakable. Lark gave a shiver of horror.

'Oh my God!'

'I have Green Galloper at airport. I know where Safety Car is heading. If we hurry we might save him.'

'We must let Gav or Eddie know.'

But neither were answering their mobiles.

'There is not time, you know how to look after horse in bad way. I need your help.'

Upstairs was deserted. Team Campbell-Black had left the grooms' quarters for a celebratory dinner with Valent. Hurling her sponge bag into her overnight case, Lark wondered if she was crazy to trust Bao. Was she being ambushed? She scribbled a note for Marketa.

So sorry to bunk off. Look after Quickly for me. Apologize to Gav and Eddie. Bao and I are going to try and find Safety Car.

Bao was waiting outside in a Mercedes. As Lark joined him in the front, she opened the glove compartment, looking for a tissue to mop up her tears then shrieked as she discovered a gun.

'Is OK, we're going to need it,' said Bao, adding wryly, 'I am not stepson of mafia thug for nothing.'

92

Leaving Eddie, besieged by press and admirers, and Etta and Valent rhapsodizing with Rosaria and Mr Fat and Happy on the joy of homebred wins of such magnitude, Gavin and Gala sloped off.

'Shall we go to my room or yours?' asked Gala. 'Mine's nearer.'

In the end they went to Gav's because it had less history, and kissed all the way in the taxi.

'How can one be on earth and in heaven at the same time?' sighed Gala who was at least three drinks up.

Gav's room, with Thomas Wolfe's *Look Homeward, Angel* on the bedside table, was much smaller. It would have been nice to have got things going in Rupert's Jacuzzi, reflected Gala. On the walls were paintings of priapic, plunging Arab stallions. Out of the window reared up Dubai's tallest buildings.

'Too much competition,' said Gav, drawing the curtains. As he poured Gala some white, the bottle rattled against her glass. In a cardboard box on the floor were half a dozen little black camels with gold humps and hooves.

'I bought them for Dora, Gee Gee and Clover, et cetera. Did you know you can teach camels dressage?'

'I'm more interested in undressage,' said Gala, turning down the gold-flecked counterpane. 'Let's go to bed.'

Gav was silent for a minute, then he helplessly stammered, 'Look, I've got problems. "Floppy Dick" – you heard Cosmo. I tried to sort it, made an appointment with James Benson, but I bottled out. I simply can't get it up.'

'Hush.' Gala pulled him down on the sofa beside her. Putting her fingers to his lips, she said, 'We don't have to do anything, just lie in each other's arms. You are so beautiful,' she went on then, taking in his pale, tense face, his chattering teeth, his shaking shoulders. 'I've always wanted you. When I first came to Penscombe and said how attractive you were, only to be told you didn't put out, I was the one who was put out.'

Then, when he didn't even smile, 'There's no hurry, darling, we've got the rest of our lives to get it together.'

Gav looked up incredulously. 'What did you say?'

'The rest of our lives.'

'You mean that?'

Nodding, Gala took his sweating, trembling hands. 'Every word,' she said softly. 'To Gav and to hold, till death us do part. Gropius needs a father.' She had to joke, to stop herself crying. 'If you knew how gutted I was when I realized the Valentine I thought was from you was really from Eddie.'

'What about Rupert? He must have got three thousand Valentines.' How could he possibly measure up?

'I'm not a man-eating tiger whisperer,' said Gala. 'Taggie's the only person who can handle Rupert. I was always crucified with guilt because I love her so much.' There was a pause as she took a slug of wine. 'But I hope he'll give me a good reference.' Then when Gav half laughed: 'And what about Bethany?'

'She certainly won't give me a good reference.'

'I'll never be a millionth as beautiful as her.'

'You are.' Gav stroked her cheek with the back of his fingers. '"Your angel's face,"' he said, without the trace of a stammer, '"as the great eye of heaven, shines bright, and makes a sunshine in the shady place."'

'That's beautiful – who said that?'

'I just did,' he kissed her nose, 'and Edmund Spenser, more than four hundred years ago.' And he buried his lips in hers until they were both breathless.

'It's very hot in here. I'm going to undress,' said Gala, and was stripped off and into bed first.

As he joined her, she ran her hands over the Doberman-sleek hard shoulders and chest, the flat stomach and the thighs iron-hard from riding. 'You are divinely built,' she said and felt herself squirming with desire.

'Pity we're not going to do anything tonight except hold each other,' she added, but as his hands roved over her breasts, and hardening nipples, she cried: 'Oh that's heaven, perhaps we might.' Her hand slid down, but his limp penis didn't respond.

'Oh God, it's no good.' He rolled over, burying his despairing face in the pillow.

'You have the most gorgeous arse,' said Gala, wanting to keep things light. 'You sure it wasn't you had the bum implant, not Sauvignon?'

Lingeringly, she kissed first one buttock and then the other, gently running her finger up and down the cleft between them until Gav groaned with pleasure.

'Turn over,' she whispered, and when he did, she started kissing her way up his thighs, giving little puppy licks. Then, moving on to his penis, constantly murmuring words of love, she massaged the base, running her tongue round the tip, then taking the whole thing in her mouth, while reaching up to scratch his rigid belly with her fingernails.

'No, no,' he muttered.

'Stop it, I'm entitled to enjoy myself,' and she did, as miraculously, gradually, gradually his cock soared, growing and growing, until it was stabbing the back of her throat. Still she carried on licking and sucking.

'Go on, please go on, omigod,' gasped Gav, as he stiffened, tensed – and next moment had exploded into her mouth and joyfully, Gala swallowed every drop.

'That's the nicest drink I have ever had,' she mumbled. 'Much better than Pinot Grigio.'

'Penis Grigio.' They both shook with laughter, yet when Gala wriggled up the bed until she was level with him, she found his face wet with tears, and held him sobbing in her arms.

'Thank you, thank you, God, I love you.'

'That was a blown-away job,' giggled Gala. 'All this and Quickly winning by a short head.'

'You gave me very long head. We must stop making terrible jokes.'

After they'd lain giggling and entangled for a few minutes, Gav said, 'Your turn now.' He might not be able to go again, but he was desperate to give her pleasure.

He reached down to stroke her, and was so turned on to feel his fingers gripped by such wetness and warmth, he'd soon pulled her up on top of him.

'Oh, wow, oh wow!' gasped Gala, arching upwards in ecstasy, as his cock soared up inside her. 'You are amazing, Mr Latton. Dubai's tallest buildings have got nothing on you . . . aaaaaagh . . . they'll be landing helicopters and hanging flags from you soon.'

'Don't distract me, concentrate.' But she had made him relax. Next minute, he'd pulled out, rolled her over on her back and was on top of her and inside, driving and driving until he erupted into her a second time, yelling how much he loved her.

When they'd got their breath back, and the shuddering had ceased, he murmured, 'You've cured me of Bethany. I thought the disease was terminal,' and again his eyes filled with tears. 'Oh God, I love you so much,' then, 'What about Ben?'

'Ben was the past – the "blue remembered hills" – you're my future. I feel safe with you – I trust you.' Then after a long kiss, 'Sorry to lower the tone, but I must go and have a pee.'

Rifling through her bag in the bathroom, she found the dark-red lipstick called Passion.

'Come back, I miss you,' shouted Gav.

Returning to the bedroom, she was overjoyed how happy he looked.

'I need a pee too,' he said, getting up. In the bathroom he found scrawled across the mirror in dark-red lipstick: *Him Potent: To Gav and to Hold. I will always love you.*

As he returned, his happiness was interrupted by a thundering on the door, which he told to bugger off.

'Let me in, let me in, it's real urgent,' said a voice, as the thundering increased.

Grabbing a towel, Gav opened the door an inch to discover a distraught Eddie.

'You gotta come. Marketa found a note from Lark.'

'So?'

'Telling Marketa to take care of Quickly, because she's gone off with that crook Bao to find Safety.'

93

Safety Car had always adored jaunts and, seeing all the World Cup preparations in the yard, he had sussed a trip abroad was in the offing. So when, at dead of night, he was taken from his field and led up the ramp of a lorry, he went trustingly. Unloaded after a few hours, he could smell the sea. Tethered in a filthy stable, which reeked of petrol, he began to worry. Used to living outside, the confinement drove him crazy. Soon, Rupert, Marketa and Gavin would come and fetch him. When they didn't, his whinnying became increasingly loud and desperate, until the men who'd taken him, whose strange accents he didn't understand, clouted him with spades. Then when he tried to win them over, offering a hoof for a Polo, they hit him harder – and when he lay down and died for his country, they kicked him in the belly until he scrambled up.

For a couple of days they had tried to fatten him with an excess of food, but when he refused to eat, they loaded him up at night, took him across the Channel, then into a trailer jolting miles across country.

Where was Rupert? Where was Lark? Where was Marketa? Where was Quickly? And his sheep friends? By this time, he was dying of thirst. Weak from lack of food and hoarse from calling out, he was yet again unloaded, but nothing prepared him for the hell ahead of a big red lorry. He could hear moaning and banging and breathed in a terrible stench of blood and

559

excrement. But once again, hoping he was going home, he had trotted up the ramp where a scene of utter horror greeted him.

Horses of all shapes and sizes were rammed together – injured, diseased, exhausted, distraught: ponies, donkeys, terrified racehorses, massively stressed, violent stallions showing white eyes, trying to mount mares, who were in turn frantically trying to protect foals, before they were crushed underfoot.

Almost most pathetic were the horses who'd been deliberately fattened into obesity, their feet and fetlocks buckling agonizingly under their immense bulk. Some had gashes on their sides, some had broken limbs. Every so often, once they were on the move, a horse would have a panic attack, shaking the whole lorry, leaving more gashes and broken limbs until the entire floor ran with blood.

There were no stops for water or feed or rest. The gypsy drivers, mostly Eastern European, were paid to reach Northern Italy as soon as possible, dump their cargo of horses and drive back again to collect another load. There were meant to be border checks, but the drivers, warned in advance of these, were able to sail through without being stopped.

And all because the Italians liked to eat their horse and donkey meat fresh, and believed the lies on the packet that the animals had been reared locally. Anyway, nobody kicked up a fuss, because the live horse trade and the slaughterhouses were run by the mafia, and people were too scared to rock boats.

When the horses were finally unloaded, Safety Car was one of the few who could still stumble down the ramp, leaving a litter of corpses and groaning bodies behind him. Filthy, bloodstained coat coming out in handfuls, tail and quarters rubbed bald, his head, sunken between his shoulders, felt too heavy for him to lift. Then he heard even more hysterical neighing from a building ahead, smelled fresh blood, and violent trembling once again jolted his wasted frame. Dragged inside the building, more tortures awaited, as pints of blood were drained off for the plasma, needed for blood transfusions to combat equine diseases like swamp fever.

Hearing more groaning and crashing and terrified whinnying from the slaughterhouse ahead, Safety Car pulled back in panic. As the two slaughterhouse hands in charge of him swore and yanked him forward, the one who wasn't smoking clubbed him round the head.

'Stop that,' yelled a voice and in burst a dark man in a grubby off-white suit, followed by a slender, fair girl.

Recognizing them, Safety Car managed the faintest of whickers and pricking his one ear, staggered forwards.

'Give me that horse,' shouted the dark man.

Pretending not to understand, the first slaughterhouse worker was about to stub out his cigarette on Safety Car's shoulder when the cigarette was shot out of his hand, which was a language both workers understood, particularly when they saw that the dark man was brandishing a gun, and, in his other hand, waving a big handful of notes.

'Give us that horse,' he ordered, and only when the girl had taken hold of Safety Car's lead rope did he hand over the cash and didn't lower his gun until they'd both helped a tottering Safety Car to safety.

'Bastards, bastards,' screamed Lark, taking in the bloody moaning wreckage inside and out of the red lorries. 'We'll get you for this. We'll never give up until this never happens again.' Then, realizing she was frightening Safety Car, 'Poor old boy, we'll get you cleaned up and find you something to drink and half a ton of electrolytes – and then you're going home.'

94

Taggie came out of hospital on the Monday after the World Cup. She would later have to have chemotherapy and perhaps radiotherapy, and it still hadn't been ascertained if the cancer had spread to her lymph glands, but Rupert, petrified of her catching an infection, refused to let her stay in any longer.

Once the world learnt why Rupert had walked out of the World Cup, the family came storming in from all over the world and none of them demanded their airfares. Marcus cancelled a huge concert in Moscow. Tabitha was unexpectedly devastated.

'I'm sorry I've been so awful. I love you so much – you're the best stepmother anyone ever had.'

Equally devastated was Taggie's father Declan, who bit off the head of his wife, Maud, when she claimed Taggie had been selfish not to tell anyone she was ill.

Nor would there have been a daffodil left in the world as flowers poured in.

'An entire flora,' said Rupert proudly as vases ran out and yellow buckets had to be plundered from the yard.

'I hope you realize, Mum, at last, how much people love you,' chided Bianca.

Eddie had brought back Quickly's World Cup saddlecloth for Taggie, and when she praised him, replied that it was easy to get winners when a horse was gotten that ready.

Rupert's frightful press had in turn subsided overnight, particularly when people learnt of Love Rat's death. There was also huge praise for Gav: 'Small talk, but great victories', and how wonderfully he'd readied Delectable, Chekov and Quickly and how, when stepping into Rupert's shoes, he hadn't found them at all too large.

Rupert was the first to praise Gav, but appealed to the media to leave them alone: 'Taggie needs rest.'

Taggie was ashamed of feeling so cast down. It was lovely to be home, and Rupert was being so adorable to her. He'd told her not to worry about chemo or radiotherapy; he'd be with her every step of the way. She was so pleased about Gav and Gala, who couldn't keep their hands off each other and seemed so happy. But outside, the emerging spring was so beautiful, she couldn't shake off the dread it might be her last. She found it impossible to stay in bed, longing to get up and feed the dogs, who'd been banished from her bed, and the birds. Rupert had really lost it when he caught her sneaking out to feed the badgers.

She was heartbroken about Love Rat and worried stiff about Safety Car and Lark, who'd unaccountably vanished on the night of the World Cup, evidently with Bao who everyone said was an evil villain but who had given her such a beautiful necklace.

And what had become of Jan, who'd been so lovely to her and never shouted? Rupert, beyond saying he'd walked out, didn't elucidate and Taggie didn't want to upset him by appearing too interested. However, when Dora came to see her, bearing a big box of marrons glacés, she had, in a whisper, asked where Jan had gone.

'He walked,' said Dora. 'No one seems to know where. Rupert came back and told him to bugger off and he did.'

Later in the day, however, Constance Sprightly popped in to see Taggie, bringing a bunch of narcissi.

'So exciting about the World Cup,' she cried. 'Gavin Latton did so well. We were glued to the television. I must remind Gavin, he owes me a bunch of lilies.'

'Really?' said Taggie.

'Well, he hit your hubby across the nave on the morning of your surprise do, and Hubby sent a big vase of lilies I'd just arranged flying.'

'Gav?' said an amazed Taggie.

'Yes. He told your hubby he'd got to go to his birthday party in no uncertain terms, and evidently Hubby did.'

'But that was Jan,' protested Taggie.

'No, no, I know Jan, he's an occasional worshipper. It was definitely Gavin Latton. Very brave when he's so much smaller than your hubby.'

But Gav had never come to the party, thought Taggie. He must have got back from America, heard Rupert had gone missing and routed him out – and Jan had claimed it was him. Taggie felt a distinct sense of disquiet.

There was endless speculation about what had happened to Lark. Everyone was worried stiff – but Eddie was utterly demented. Suddenly he'd realized how much he loved her. Why couldn't Rupert offer £1,000,000 reward as well as the half million for Safety Car?

Quickly, the great World Cup winner, flew home on Monday, outraged to find no Safety Car and no Lark awaiting him. Safety's sheep never stopping bleating, driving everyone crackers.

Only the weather picked up, so lovely on Tuesday afternoon that Rupert and Taggie sat out rather self-consciously on the terrace and Rupert tried hard not to look at his iPad. There was a pale-green mist of young leaves on the trees, softened by white blackthorn blossom. A gentle breeze mingled wafts of wild garlic and balsam poplar, reminding Rupert of the Friars Balsam his old nanny had made him inhale for chest infections when he was a child. Why did everything make him cry? The birds were singing their heads off; what right had they to sound so perky when Lark and Safety were still missing? Clutching Taggie's hand, asking her for the hundredth time if she were warm enough, he heard the chugging of a plane.

They were then startled by a chorus of bleating as Safety Car's sheep hurtled across the field, to be greeted by hoarse whickering. Taggie and Rupert looked at each other, frantic with hope. Could it be?

Hearing the commotion, Quickly, throwing off jet lag and a squawking Purrpuss, jumped clean over his half door, clattering across the yard, leaping over the gate into the field.

'He'd better go chasing,' said Rupert, then gave a shout of joy as a still weak Safety Car, supported by Lark and Bao, tottered into view, trailing overjoyed sheep, and an ecstatically whickering Quickly.

Returning from jogging – to work off all the celebratory booze before the flat season began – an incredulous Eddie raced towards Lark yelling, 'Stable-lassie come home,' and despite her laughing that she was all dirty and scruffy, he kissed her almost unconscious, begging her never to leave him again.

Word hurtled round and Safety Car received a greater if more restrained welcome than for any of his thirty wins, as yard and stud poured out and gathered round. Every inch of him was stroked and patted, particularly by an ecstatic, incredulous Marketa.

'He could probably use a drink,' said Rupert in a shaken voice. Only after he had summoned Charlie Radcliffe to check every hair of Safety's emaciated body was the old boy bedded down in the barn. Here, jealously watched by Quickly and with a thunderously purring Purrpuss curled up between his front legs, Safety Car, counting sheep friends, fell into a deep sleep.

95

'Time for you and me to talk.' Rupert shook Bao's hand. 'You can have the £500,000 reward as long as you don't put it on a horse – and at least the Green Galloper will get worldwide coverage.'

Rupert gave Eddie's carer strict instructions to take Taggie straight back to bed, then took Bao into his office and poured him a vast vodka and tonic.

'I can't begin to thank you for saving Safety. I want to know exactly how you and Lark found him, but first I must apologize for totally misjudging you. We heard you were at Valhalla with Wang, and Jan claimed to have found one of my lucky shirts in your room, and a photograph of Wang and your mother in a pocket.'

Bao took a huge gulp, eyes watering at the strength, and then collapsed on the sofa.

'Mr Campbell-Black, you are very good kind man.'

'That's pushing it a bit.'

'But you have wicked enemies and they are very bad men. Wang is on bed with Cosmo Rannaldini. He give him many billions. He has spend forty million on stallion called Boo Sucks. He want to be big racing man. He kill anyone in his way.'

'My God,' said Rupert.

'He kill husband of Milburn Gala, because he try to save

rhino. My father is successful workaholic, my mother loved him but feel he should have stop adoption of my sister, so marriage in trouble. Wang hates my father for his success, and he wanted my mother because she is beautiful, so he murder his first television star wife and marry my mother and promise to find my sister, but he never did. My mother not happy with Wang. I worry stiffly for her. I went to Valhalla to check she was OK.'

Bao got up and started pacing the room.

'Wang was there, he much like Dame Hermione and opera. I play the piano for Dame Hermione, she sing Schubert Trout. That Chablis was there.'

Rupert smiled slightly. 'You mean Sauvignon.'

'Sorry, Sauvignon. I heard Wang ask her if she was having a baby. She say she miscarry in January, but I think she and Cosmo make whole things up to divide you and Young Eddie.'

'Well, we're back together now,' said Rupert, as Gilchrist and Cuthbert scampered in from their dog walk with Clover, and went into growling battle to be the one to sit on Master's knee.

'I hear Wang say he would help Sauvignon have baby,' went on Bao, 'and he much fancy her. This makes my mother sad, so I must rescue her, because Wang takes out wives when he wants to move on.'

'Christ, where does Jan fit into all this?'

Bao took another large gulp.

'I think Jan wish to destroy you. He know you love Safety and kidnap him to upset Quickry. Mr Old Eddie's loving horses give him chance to visit stud. Jan let out Love Rat. He hack into all your calls. He off tip Cosmo about red Filly and tell him moment you take on Tarqui and sack Young Eddie. He take lucky shirt. I'm sure he frighten Quickry in Leger. And Smith black, Marti Farrell, who put nail through Quickry's foot in Derby now works for Wang in China.'

'Jesus! Why aren't you working for MI5?' An outraged Rupert poured himself a vast whisky and topped up Bao's vodka. 'Are you sure?'

'I want to tell you these things but think I might imagine mistake like I gave Quickry too big water before Derby. Then I hack into call and hear Jan's kidnapped Safety, taking him to

Italy, and learn detail of lorry he is using. It was terrible there, poor boy. Horses must never travel like that. Lark was wonderful, she save his life, and gun you gave me.'

'You saved it too. Who sabotaged Quickly's saddle in the World Cup?'

'I do not know. Jan was in England. Could have been Chablis, I mean Sauvignon, but I do not think she know enough about horse. Difficult with much security, but someone from Cosmo's team in same barn could have done it.

'It go on. I think Jan give horses virus before Royal Ascot. Wang knew my father excited to come and wanted to spoil it. Jan put Russell Jack,' Bao smoothed Gilchrist's brown and white forehead, 'in horse walker and bugs in your bedroom.'

Bao, who also loved Taggie, wanted to broach the subject of her and Jan, but quailed seeing Rupert's narrowed eyes and drumming fingers. Stifling a yawn, Bao asked: 'You are good man so why Cosmo and Isa hate you?'

'That's very ancient history, but I'm not sure why Wang detests me so much.'

'Because women like you too much and you and my father and Edwards Valent have plans for racing in China. So does Wang. He has done too many bad things to stay in Zimbabwe, so he want power back in Beijing to join government and become first Minister of Racing.'

Rupert shook his head. 'OK, but why does Jan hate me so much – unless he's simply being paid by Wang and Cosmo to take me out?'

As Bao took another slug of vodka and a deep, deep breath, a flush stole across his face.

'I should not say but I think Jan is very, very madly loving of Mrs Campbell-Black.'

'Go on,' said Rupert and then, five minutes later: 'I'm going to call the police.'

Rupert then rang Chief Inspector Gablecross, with whom he'd had an on/off relationship when Gablecross had been tracking down the murderer of Cosmo Rannaldini's father during the filming of *Don Carlos*. The Chief Inspector was actually in the thick of another big murder hunt but promised he and his men would be over as soon as possible.

Having thanked Bao yet again, Rupert insisted that he must stay on and that his mother must use Penscombe as a safe house. He then checked on Taggie and found her asleep, a smile on her lips, Quickly's World Cup blanket spread over her as a counterpane and Forester lying beside her.

She looked so lovely yet so frail. His heart blackened against Jan. He didn't trust anything while the bastard was still free. He had better check on Safety Car.

He found Marketa sitting in the straw beside him.

'Safety is Wee-I-Pee now,' she whispered. 'Look at him on Facebook.'

The sun had gone behind dark-grey clouds; fog rose from the valley after a night of rain. Where was Banquo, normally his shadow? He hadn't seen him for hours. On the way down to the yard, he was accosted by Dora.

'We've got to organize a press release to announce Safety's return, and Quickly hasn't had his victory parade yet. He's won the World Cup, for goodness' sake. Penscombe expects.'

'Don't be so fucking stupid.'

'Well anyway. Gossip, gossip, gossip.'

'I haven't got time.'

'You will for this. You know Rufus Rutshire asked Eddie to ride in a charity race to commemorate the anniversary of James Northfield's death?'

'Eddie mentioned it. Frankly I've had more important things to—'

'Well, Rufus has discovered some long-lost relation who's a direct descendant of James Northfield and wants him and Eddie to re-enact the race through the woods and the water meadows in aid of the Injured Jockeys Fund.'

'Fatally injured, in James' case. Eddie mustn't touch it.'

'But Eddie's very keen – says it would make him feel he really belongs if he represents the Campbell-Blacks.'

'Not for much longer if he rides in that race.'

'Well, it looks as though we're going to have to put out another press release, about him and Lark and Gav and Gala, wedding bells ahoy. And, and, and – Sauvignon lost the baby in December, so you're not going to be a great-grandfather any more.'

'I know that – just bugger off.' Jolted and threatened, Rupert couldn't wait to hand things over to Gablecross.

Just then, there was a clatter of hooves and into the yard rode an ashen Roving Mike, who on his day off had gone hunting. A fine dog fox had run into Rutminster woods and once again hounds had halted in full cry and turned back whimpering. But, even stranger, from deep in the woods, Mike was sure he could hear the desperate howling of a dog.

'Sure it was the ghost of James Northfield's Seeker – it froze my blood.' Mike crossed himself before sliding down off his big horse.

A second later they were joined by a distraught Clover who'd been walking the dogs.

'Oh Rupert, I'm so sorry. I've lost Banquo. He's always so good, but Forester pushed off after a deer and by the time I'd got him back, Banquo'd gone missing. I brought the other dogs home and went back and looked for him for ages. He must have gone hunting. I'm so sorry.'

Banquo never went hunting. He was the sweetest, kindest, most undemanding dog, Rupert's shadow, who never complained if Forester or the Jack Russells hogged the limelight, but was the one who suffered most if Rupert were away.

'Perhaps the howling I heard in the woods was Banquo,' said Mike.

96

Leaping into his car, Rupert drove like a maniac, ringing Gav on the way.

'Can't find Banquo, going to check out Rutminster woods. Give me the opportunity to check the course. Eddie's riding in some crazy match race on Sunday week. Won't be long. Police are on their way. Can you and Bao wise them up about Jan, stall them until I get back?'

It was getting darker. Splashing across the water meadows, Rupert parked on the edge of the woods, already shrouded in mist. Trampling on primroses and wood anemones, effing and blinding, he clambered as fast as possible up to the original track along which Rupert Black and James Northfield had raced. Then he heard the spine-chilling howling of a dog.

'Banquo,' he yelled. Back came another howl. He raced up the track, slipping on wild garlic leaves, their green flames flickering treacherously, over twigs, stones, mossy roots, bramble cables and badger setts covered in leaves. There was no way Eddie was going to ride any horse over this course.

Rounding the bend into Seeker's Corner, on the right like black pillars reared up closely-packed trees, smothered in ivy. On the left, six feet down, was a narrow ledge and beyond that, treacherously filling up with fog, was the fifty-foot ravine into which James Northfield had plunged to his death.

On the ledge, tied to an ash sapling, crouched a terrified, trembling Banquo.

'Poor old boy.' Scattering stones, an outraged Rupert slithered down the cliff face on to the ledge and unknotted the rope. 'Who the hell's done this to you?'

Banquo's leg was at a nasty angle, probably broken. How could he possibly hoist him back on to the track? But typically, Banquo, while groaning, apologetically wagged his tail.

Next moment, the normally gentle dog went into a frenzy of growling and barking as a pair of green gumboots appeared above them. The mist swirled away to reveal a figure in a black Barbour, with a gun in his hands and madness in his eyes. It was Jan.

'How dare you steal my dog!' shouted Rupert, fury driving out any fear. 'How dare you! I think he's broken his leg and I've been talking to Bao. I know exactly what you've been up to. You came into my life to fuck up me and my marriage. What the hell have I ever done to you?'

Next moment, Jan had jumped down beside them, dislodging more stones and clods of earth, brandishing the gun in Rupert's face.

'Rupert Black,' he spat. 'Your great-great-great-great-great-great-grandfather,' the words came out like a funeral drum, 'murdered my great-great-great-great-great-great-grandfather James Northfield during a match race. Rupert Black was so desperate to win because there was so much money at stake, he pushed James and Spartan down this ravine.'

'Bollocks, you have absolutely no proof,' yelled Rupert. 'Black was just a bloody good rider.'

'Then the Northfield family chucked out James' young wife Gisela, my great-great-great-great-great-great-grandmother,' intoned Jan.

'The kitchenmaid,' drawled Rupert. 'The Northfields have always been frightful snobs.'

'You bastard,' hissed Jan, so close his acid breath was asphyxiating. 'She gave birth to a boy, who should have inherited the title. She loved James so deeply that after the birth – no one recognized post-natal depression in those days – she killed herself in despair.

'None of the Northfields gave a toss what happened to her or the baby, who was brought up in grinding poverty. But being Dutch, the Van Deventers worked hard and later migrated to South Africa where they prospered until the bastard colonial Brits came over and killed my great-grandfather in the Boer War.'

'I can hardly be held responsible for that,' said Rupert irritably, trying to calm a shuddering Banquo and pondering the best method of escape.

'You and all bloody Brits were guilty. So I decided to come over and avenge James and Gisela – and quite by chance I caught sight of you on TV at the preview of the Stubbs exhibition: such an arrogant bastard sauntering in followed by a black Labrador, where no dogs were allowed, and no one complained.

'I did my homework,' went on Jan. 'I'm actually a journo and discovered your father needed carers, which seemed the easiest way in, so I took a carer's course in Port Elizabeth and met Gala's sister.'

Rupert glanced up. 'Gala knew what you were up to?'

'I don't think so.'

Unnerved by Jan's crazy ranting, Banquo tried to crawl nearer the edge of the ledge and gave a groan.

'Look, I've got to get this dog to a vet.'

'Shut up, you're not going anywhere,' snarled Jan. 'Then I met you, pre-potent sire, and a total shit, just like Rupert Black. I was determined to bring you down by destroying you and your marriage. Having heard how insanely jealous you were, I pretended to be gay to lull your suspicions. Then I fell in love with your wife.' Jan's voice softened. 'You treated her so badly, it made me even more determined to ruin you.'

'So my lucky shirt went missing,' rapped out Rupert, 'and buckets of feed and water were left in stables before races and cats shut in drawers and new batteries taken out of torches and details about serious horses leaked again and again and stones chucked on gallops and bugs put in teddy bears,

573

and down you came to the yard with my father, which gave you the chance to leave gates and doors open and he got blamed. Love Rat would have been alive today if you hadn't let out Titus, who also very nearly killed Gala – and you accuse Rupert Black of being a murderer! You tried to frame Bao by putting my lucky shirt in his room, and if you loved Taggie you couldn't have sent Safety Car across Europe on a journey to hell.'

'I hacked into your phone calls,' interrupted Jan, his voice growing so raucous and loud that two nearby pigeons flew off with a clatter, 'but surprisingly I couldn't find any women.'

'There weren't any.'

'Except Gala, my trump card. She'd been hurt enough, for Christ's sake, but you had the raging hots for her and had to pull her in Santa Anita and Dubai. Taggie'll be so upset and I've got excellent footage of you both in Lime Tree Cottage.'

It was getting dark, the last red glow of the setting sun could no longer pierce the smothering mist. A barn owl like a rising ghost moon flapped past, making them both jump.

'I'd love to shoot you through the testicles and leave you to bleed to death but then I'd be done for murder, so you and that slug of a dog,' Jan gave Banquo a kick, 'are going over the edge, and everyone will think you lost your way on a walk. It's solid Cotswold rock at the bottom – no way you'll survive.' Jan's hideous, mirthless laughter echoed round the wood. 'Even if you shouted for help, anyone passing will think you're James' ghost and run like hell.'

Rupert was about to make a dive for the gun when Jan's voice became obscenely lascivious. 'And Taggie's so pretty she won't be a widow for a minute because I'm going to marry her and love and cherish her as you never did. She didn't even tell you she'd got cancer; instead she turned to me. She loves me, and as Rufus has made me his heir, she's going to be the loveliest Lady Rutshire of all.'

'She fucking won't!' howled Rupert.

Then suddenly Banquo barked, as a twig could be heard breaking and then another – and behind Jan's head, Rupert could see a bobbing torch approach.

'I repeat I'm going to marry Taggie and love and cherish her and she'll be the loveliest Lady Rutshire ever,' shouted Jan, then nearly fell off the ledge as a bulky figure loomed into sight and a panting voice yelled, 'No, she won't!'

Not daring to take his gun off Rupert, Jan glanced round.

'You bastard!' Unmistakably breathy, the voice was choked with tears. 'You swore it was me you loved, that I was the only one you longed to cherish. You promised to marry me and I'd be the next Lady Rutshire. And the loveliest.'

'Shut up,' screamed Jan, 'just shut up.'

As the mist swirled, Rupert suddenly caught sight of a big distraught face. God in heaven! It was Harmony.

'You promised me the Northfield family engagement ring,' she sobbed, 'if I sabotaged Quickly's bridle – which could have killed both Quickly and Eddie. Not to mention all the lies you persuaded me to tell about Bao, swearing you loved me so much. You even made me ring up Gala today to find out where Rupert was so you could trap him. I've never had a boyfriend before – how dare you deceive me?'

She had picked up a huge branch, brandishing it over them. Seeing Jan distracted, Rupert leapt forward, snatching the gun, which went off, echoing around the ravine. Next moment, slippery from Jan's sweating fingers, it had slid from Rupert's hand and he and Jan were wrestling on the ground, furiously landing punches, their only ambition to murder each other. Jan was bigger, younger and stronger, as *crash!* went one of his fists into Rupert's jaw, then *crash!* – another into his ribs. But Rupert was angrier and rage gave him strength to grab Jan's dark head and bang it on the stony ground as they scuffled, rolling over and over until they were both caked in mud.

Banquo growled helplessly, unable to crawl to his master's aid, even when Jan, landing on top, tightened his hands round Rupert's neck until Rupert jerked his knee upwards into Jan's groin, making him groan and loosen his grip.

They were both perilously near the edge, rocks giving way, when Rupert realized Harmony was on the ledge beside them. Slithering down the side in another shower of rocks, she had retrieved the gun from where it had disappeared into a clump of ivy, and shoved it into Jan's back.

'Let go of Rupert, you bastard.'

'Give me back the gun, Harmsie.' Jan had switched tack, his voice suddenly amorous. 'It's you that I love. I only said that I was going to marry Taggie to wind up Rupert.'

They were so near the edge, the ledge was giving way beneath them, about to precipitate them all into the abyss. Letting go of Rupert, struggling to his feet, Jan tripped over a bramble cable and before he could right himself and grab the gun from Harmony, Rupert had snatched it.

'Go and get help,' he snapped and with sudden superhuman strength, legged her bulk back on to the path. 'Get a vet – and for Christ's sake, *hurry.*'

Wailing in anguish as she lumbered down the track, Harmony rounded the corner slap into the arms of a large policeman.

'Please hurry. Rupert's taken Jan's gun off him,' she sobbed, 'but his dog's up there with a broken leg and Rupert'll shoot and kill Jan if anything happens to Banquo.'

Chief Inspector Gablecross had rolled up at Penscombe soon after Rupert had left. Typical cavalier Campbell-Black behaviour, he reflected, calling the police, stressing the urgency of the case, then buggering off to rescue some dog.

Comparing notes, however, with Gav, Mike, Bao, Lark and Cathal who, driving home, had seen Rupert's car parked on the edge of the woods, had spurred Gablecross into action, rustling up uniformed and CID men to raid the woods. Even so, it took eight of them to contain and handcuff Jan, who was now ranting and raving that Rupert had murdered his brother James Northfield and just tried to murder him by pushing him over the edge as well, and it was Rupert who must be arrested. Night was falling as they dragged him yelling out of the woods. Fortunately, an ambulance crew on standby had some morphine for Banquo.

As Rupert emerged, reeking of wild garlic, his face blood-stained and muddy, a heavily doped Banquo in his arms, a car splashed across the water meadows and Taggie in her nightie and blue striped dressing gown leapt out and came racing bare-foot towards him through the twilight.

'Oh Rupert, Rupert, my darling,' then, as she drew closer, 'oh my God, what have you done to yourself? Your poor head, your eye, and your poor lip.' She caressed his cheek with her hand. 'What happened?'

'I'm fine, honest, but Banquo's done a leg. I've got to get him to a vet and you back to bed or you'll catch your death.'

'More important, get you to a doctor.'

Doctor . . . How could a question of such enormity have skipped his memory! Crossing his fingers, he stammered, 'Did James Benson ring?'

'He did.' Taggie suddenly smiled. 'I'm OK, the cancer hasn't spread.'

For a second Rupert's head went back, his eyes closed and he took in a vast breath of relief.

'Oh thank God.' With no hands free he could only press his shoulder against hers.

Next moment Gav and Gala had raced up.

'Christ, are you OK? Give us Banquo.'

'He needs to go to the vet pronto. They'll probably have to plaster his leg.'

'We'll take him, poor boy – you two push off home,' said Gala.

The instant they had carefully relieved him of Banquo, Rupert took Taggie in his arms.

'It hasn't spread. Oh my angel.' His voice shook. 'If I'd lost you, my broken heart would never have mended, even if it had been in plaster for a thousand years.'

When Taggie, despite the sore and very swollen breast, clutched him back even tighter, he also wondered if Jan hadn't cracked a couple of ribs.

As, entwined, they walked through a crowd of police and onlookers back to Rupert's car, Taggie said, 'Gav told me a bit of what Jan's been up to. I'm so sorry. I mean, Jan told me it was him who blacked your eye and dragged you home to the surprise party, but Constance Sprightly swore it was Gav – and evidently Jan shopped Bao and often didn't pass on our messages.'

And the rest, thought Rupert.

'But why should he behave so appallingly? What was he up to?'

The poor angel had supped enough horrors in the last few weeks, thought Rupert. Time in the future for her to absorb the depths of Jan's iniquity.

'I guess he fell in love,' he said. 'I'm afraid it makes men behave very badly.'

97

Two mornings later, a battered Rupert, convinced cracked ribs were much worse than childbirth, having taken three Zapains, was drinking tea out of his Love Rat mug when Dora breezed into the kitchen, her arms full of flowers.

'Gossip, gossip!'

'Amaze me.'

'Zixin Wang has walked out on Mrs Wang. So two Wangs don't make a right (ha ha), but more dramatically, he has eloped to China with Superbitch Sauvignon, where Dubai are holding a meeting similar to the World Cup to encourage the Chinese government to embrace racing big time!'

'Valent's already there. I was meant to be going too.' Rupert handed Dora a cup of tea.

'Thanks. They're well suited, Wang and Sauvignon, two of the nastiest people on the planet. Mrs Walton'll be pleased. The only horrible thing is, they've taken darling New Year's Dave with them. Wang wants to show him off in some race.'

'That's appalling.' Gentle Dave was Love Rat's offspring most like him. 'Don't tell Lark.'

'I won't. Mind you, she's so blissful with Eddie. And did you know Chief Inspector Gablecross is at Valhalla cross-questioning Cosmo about Jan, who's gone completely off his handsome head?'

'I know that too. I had a four-hour session with Gablecross

yesterday, gathering evidence to charge Jan. Evidently he and Wang were inextricably linked. They met up back in Africa and Wang has poured billions into Cosmo's yard. Gablecross also had a long session with Harmony, who confirmed this.' He breathed out cautiously. The Zapains were beginning to kick in.

'How did Wang make his billions?' asked Dora.

'Poaching, mining, flogging arms to terrorists, telling them what building to blow up, then getting the contract to rebuild it. But Zimbabwe's got too hot for him – that's probably why he's moved back to China.'

'Taking Sauvignon as a guard bitch. I do hope they're kind to Dave.'

Dora was dividing her armfuls of flowers. 'These are for Taggie. How is she?'

'Still asleep. Sharing our bed with Forester and Banquo, whose leg's in plaster. I'm surprised Tarqui, with his broken shoulder, and Safety Car, haven't moved in to convalesce as well.'

'Poor Banquo,' stormed Dora. 'How dare Jan try to kill him and Safety, poor old boy. Safety's lost even more weight than Harmony.'

'He's still terribly jumpy,' admitted Rupert. 'Shivers out in the field, shakes whenever a gate slams, and totally ignores Cuthbert and Gilchrist when they try to play football with him.'

'And why did Jan have it in for you so much?'

'Generations of resentment. He must have arrived in England, gone to Rutminster, absorbed the ravishing beauty of Rufus' 2,000 acres and the stunning house, thought: This is my island in the sun, brought to me by my great-great-etcetera-grandfather's hand. Convinced he'd been denied such power and riches by Rupert Black shoving James Northfield down the ravine, he must have festered and festered and finally boiled over. He was also madly in love with Tag – another reason to dispatch me.'

'There was always madness in that family – look at Rodders,' said Dora. 'Hopefully Jan'll be inside for the rest of his life. The one I feel sorry for is Rufus: he was so excited about his new heir and his match race.'

'He can go and visit Jan in prison.' Rupert's voice hardened. 'That bastard tried to kill my dog, take my wife and he killed Love Rat – oh fuck!' His clenched hands had smashed Love Rat's mug.

'I'll get you another one,' cried Dora, gathering up and throwing the pieces in the bin. 'Cosmo'll be livid to lose Sauvignon, but Bao will be in heaven. He was so worried Wang was going to bump off his mother. Can we go and see Love Rat's grave? Oh, do look.'

Two doves, a robin and a blackbird had wandered in through the back door.

'I don't expect anyone's fed them,' said Rupert.

The animals' graveyard lay beyond the tennis court, under the shadow of a huge cedar, half an acre fenced off before the land rolled away into the fields. Cordelia and her final Love Rat foal, a lovely little grey, hung over the fence, whickering in sympathy. Love Rat's grave couldn't be seen for flowers.

Dora had brought a jug of water for her hyacinths and freesias. 'I hate seeing flowers without a drink.'

'Or anything else,' said Rupert.

'Such a sweet horse,' sighed Dora. 'When his stone's engraved, you must put: *Rest in peace, Legend and Global Leading Sire*, because he was. Nice that Gertrude the mongrel's grave is next door. She'll guard him.'

'Sapphire used to ride her tricycle through Love Rat's legs, and when she and Timon brushed him, he used to go to sleep.'

Realizing Rupert was having difficulty speaking, Dora slipped her hand into his.

'I'm so sorry you've had such a horrible time. Taggie's cancer, Love Rat, Banquo and Safety, Jan nearly murdering you . . . you must have done so much praying and bargaining with God.'

To lower the tone, Forester bounded up and lifted his leg on Gertrude's gravestone.

'That awful animal's jealous,' said Dora. 'He wants to be Taggie's all-time favourite dog.'

581

'I ought to be ecstatic Tag's OK,' Rupert confessed, as he stroked Cordelia. 'But I still feel as if I'm in a dark tunnel. It's stupid.'

'Not at all. You're beaten up. For yonks you've never stopped working, roaring around the world, allowing yourself about half an hour's sleep a night, forging an empire. You need a break, a holiday, but also you should realize what you've achieved, winning the World Cup, and if monstrous Jan hadn't let Love Rat out, he'd be outright Global Leading Sire. What you need is a victory parade to celebrate.'

'I bloody do not,' howled Rupert, so loudly Cordelia and her foal bounded away. 'We don't want to attract any press. Taggie doesn't need it.' And turning on his heel, he stalked back towards the house.

'Please, please,' Dora panted after him. 'You owe it to Eddie and Quickly. That was an historic achievement, like Fred Winter and Mandarin winning the National with a broken bit, and think of Tarqui and Delectable and Chuckoff winning those earlier races, and Meerkat and Geoffrey. Why don't you invite them to join the parade? And Mrs Wilkinson.' Dora's shrill voice was piercing his ears. 'She'll want to be part of it. People will be so pleased Safety's come home and we can celebrate Lark and Bao rescuing him and highlight the utter obscenity of transporting live horses, which you pointed out last month in your *Racing Post* column.'

'Shut up! I said bloody no!' Rupert was passing the tennis court, a salt-in-the-wound reminder of Jan's trouncing. 'Once Jan's charged with trying to kill me, the press will never leave us alone.'

'We needn't have it here,' Dora said breathlessly. 'The horses can parade down Penscombe High Street and convene, "that was a good word," at the Dog and Trumpet, and meet the press in the pub garden.'

'I'm not going to stress out Taggie,' exploded Rupert, 'and that's my last word on the subject.'

'We don't have to,' begged Dora. 'We just need to honour these great achievements.'

As they crossed the bridge over the ha-ha on to the big

lawn, Forester barged past, wagging his tail, jinking right to where Taggie, in her nightie, was topping up one of the bird-tables.

'I think we should have a parade, Rupert,' she urged him. 'The yard and the stud deserve the recognition. They need cheering up too, and so do you.' She raised a hand covered in breadcrumbs to stroke his furious face. 'Everyone agrees you're the King of Racing. You so deserve your crown. Please, please, Rupert.'

And so, Rupert caved in.

'And we've got so much more to celebrate,' added a delighted Dora, as a robin snatched a cornflake from the bird-table. 'Lark and Eddie getting married, Gala and Gav – I told you she was always bats about him.'

'You did.' Rupert raised his eyes to heaven.

'They're having such a lovely time, working their way through *The Joy of Sex*, Puccini pouring out of the cottage. Gav hasn't stopped smiling since the World Cup – and have you noticed his stammer's gone?'

Rupert had, and leaving Dora and Taggie, he tracked Gala down in the feed room.

'Congratulations, darling, Gav's a very lucky man.'

'So am I.' Gala kissed him on the cheek.

'I think,' Rupert added carefully, 'Taggie was scared I was in love with you, and I suspect Gav worried a little about us, and although it was lovely . . .'

'Lovely,' agreed Gala. 'We made a trip to the moon "on gossamer wings".'

'Exactly, but it might be better if Gav moved full-time into Lime Tree Cottage to give you both a bit of privacy, and Tag and Gav might find it easier.'

'I agree,' sighed Gala, 'but Gav would fret if he couldn't watch over his horses.'

'I've got a solution,' said Rupert.

Geraldine was appalled when she ushered Harmony Bates into Rupert's office later in the day. How could such a frump imagine gorgeous Jan was in love with her? She hadn't even bothered to smarten herself up today, and now the boss was giving her a large glass of white.

Harmony indeed looked wretched, deathly pale, with tear-stained eyes, and even more weight fallen off her.

Rupert, unlike Geraldine, felt so sorry for her. How could that bastard Jan have led her on and even proposed marriage? It was like entering a pig for Crufts.

Listening at the keyhole, Geraldine was outraged when Rupert immediately thanked Harmony for saving his and Banquo's lives.

'Look how grateful he is,' he went on, when Banquo wagged his tail as Harmony joined him on the sofa.

'I'm so glad he's OK,' she said.

'Forgive my asking,' went on Rupert, then weighed straight in: 'How did you hook up with Jan?'

'He came over to Valhalla to talk to Wang and Cosmo, then wandered down to the stud to admire Vengie. He was so good-looking – like a god – I couldn't believe it when he sent me flowers and asked me out. No one's ever asked me out before.' As she hung her dark head, the tears started to fall. 'Then he asked me out again, and again, said he loved me, then he proposed. Somehow, he bewitched me, said I owed it to Repay to sabotage Quickly's bridle.' Her breathy voice was coming in great gasps. 'I'm the one who should be in prison – Eddie could have been killed. I'm so desperately sorry.'

As Banquo nudged her in sympathy, Rupert came over and took her hand.

'Look, you've been horribly manipulated. You deserve a fresh start. You've got a lot of friends here. Tarqui's been pestering me to poach you since he joined us, Eddie's told me how you looked after him at Valhalla, and helped him at the Breeders', and Repay's success is a testament to you.

'Gav and Gala are getting married and they'll want to go on a honeymoon. Gav ought to move into Gala's cottage, which would mean the flat over the tack room will be empty. But Gav'd be terribly reluctant to move out, unless he felt someone who really loved and understood horses was taking over. How do you feel about moving in, as Assistant Head Lad?'

Harmony's mouth fell open, showing a white tongue. Rupert wondered when she'd last eaten.

'Are you offering me a job?' she gasped.

'I am.'

'Oh, I'd love it, there's nothing I'd like better. I don't deserve it. I promise I won't let you down.'

'You've lost so much weight, you can ride out. We're about to have a parade to celebrate Quickly's World Cup victory. So, you can kick off by helping to make the horses look spectacular. Penscombe expects.'

98

Penscombe expected and Penscombe got, helped by the most glorious day. Lambs raced across the fields, midges jived, celandines shone like little gold suns in the lush spring grass, birds singing their heads off nested in the hedgerows. Lit by chestnut candles all along Rupert's avenue, Eddie led the gleaming troop on Quickly, who was flaunting his red World Cup saddlecloth.

They were flanked by an equally beaming Lark on Delectable and Gala on Chekov, and by Meerkat on Geoffrey. Gav walked beside them, fleetingly resting a hand on Gala's thigh. They were followed by Louise riding Mrs Wilkinson with Chisolm bleating at their heels. The only sombre note was the black armbands worn by the riders in memory of Love Rat.

Swinging into Penscombe High Street, where he'd once kicked out wing mirrors, Quickly enjoyed the crowds thick on the pavements. There was Gee Gee cheering on Meerkat, and Colin Chalford, Mr Fat and Extremely Happy, looking much more attractive in a sharp blue suit than in his gorilla onesie. He was hand-in-hand with Rosaria, whose other hand showed off a beautiful sapphire. Both had been so thrilled Geoffrey had been invited to take part, and Colin had contributed three dozen bottles of Bollinger to liven up the party.

Past the village shop the troop clattered where Chisolm nicked more grapes, past the Easy Lay where punters, catching sight of the ravishing Delectable, hurried inside to back her in the Guineas.

As they reached All Saints, the vicar came out, blessed them and praised them and the Lord for their victories. Next moment, Constance Sprightly rushed out.

'Where's Gavin Latton? You still owe me a bunch of lilies, but well done.' Then, catching sight of Quickly, 'Oh, there's Little Mucker, that's Master Quickly's stable name. Well done, Little Mucker,' and Eddie and Lark couldn't stop laughing.

On to the garden of the Dog and Trumpet, where tulips, forget-me-nots and wallflowers were getting a bashing as a gratifying number of locals and press spilling out into a next-door field, were getting stuck into the Bolly and admiring a replica of the vast World Cup on the table.

Dennis, the landlord, had provided a splendid spread of quiches, sausage rolls and sandwiches, with baked potatoes and great beef and ale pies in the oven for later. Dora, jumping on to the table beside the World Cup, took the microphone to introduce the stars, starting with Eddie and Quickly, now in his World Cup Winners' rug.

'Quickly did it,' replied Eddie over the cheers. 'We had to ditch the bridle in the second furlong so it was a long way home. But he took care of me, running straight and true. Even when he was exhausted and overtaken at the end, he found another gear.'

'All without a bridle?' asked Channel 4's Alice Plunkett, putting her plate of quiche down on the table so she could pat Quickly, who promptly snatched up the quiche.

'We were a bridleless couple,' grinned Eddie, then reaching out for a nearby Lark's hand and kissing it, 'This is Quickly's stable lass Lark and she and I are going to be a bridal couple, because we're getting married very soon.' And the photographers went wild.

'What's happened to Sauvignon's baby?' called out the *Scorpion*.

Whereupon loyal Quickly provided a diversion by mounting Delectable.

'Stop it, Quickers,' chided Eddie. 'Why can't you save it for marriage like everyone else?'

And everyone roared with laughter.

'What sort of character is Quickly?' asked the *Cotchester Times*.

'Quickly is himself,' said Eddie philosophically.

Dora then introduced winners Delectable and Chekov, and Tarqui who'd ridden them so dazzlingly and who, despite a shoulder in plaster, proudly held up his enchanting newish baby to endear himself even more to the press.

Everyone was asking after Safety Car, to be told he was recuperating at home after his dreadful ordeal. Dora didn't add that Marketa had refused to join the party because she was still so worried about him. Lark and Bao, however, were interviewed about his rescue, until Lark burst into tears remembering the horrors, whereupon Eddie, in order to comfort her, handed Quickly over to Harmony.

It was then time for Dora to introduce Geoffrey, who was getting on so famously with Mrs Wilkinson he had to be dragged away to meet his ever-growing fan club.

Etta, Rosaria and Colin were also being much photographed as the owners of the first and third horses in the World Cup.

'I'm so sad Valent isn't here,' said Etta, 'but you must both come to supper when he gets back.' Then, as Geoffrey bustled back to Mrs Wilkinson's side: 'They really like each other. Perhaps Wilkie should have another foal.'

People were getting stuck into the beef and ale pies and asking where the hell Rupert was. Rumours were already circulating about Wang and Sauvignon, and that someone had tried to murder Rupert.

'A lot of us have wanted to do that,' quipped Matt Chapman.

But they all cheered their heads off and shouted, 'Long Live the King!' when he finally arrived.

'Poor man, he looks blasted,' whispered Rosaria, 'like some great proud tree whose leaves have been swept away by a hurricane . . .'

'Totally devastated at the thought of losing Taggie,' whispered back Etta.

Rupert took the microphone, thanked everyone for coming.

He then added how proud he was of his grandson Eddie, a true Campbell-Black, and Quickly, and how well Tarqui had done with Blank Chekov and Delectable, of whom they had very high hopes in the Guineas. He was, in addition, particularly grateful to Meerkat for tugging Eddie back on to Quickly when the bridle broke.

'How's Taggie?' shouted the *Sun*.

'She's getting on well, still a bit tired. I'm also lucky to have a marvellous stable staff. Dora's a great Press Officer,' another huge cheer, 'Lark and Bao were brilliant at rescuing Safety Car, but I particularly want to pay tribute to Gavin Latton, who when I had to go home during the World Cup, took over masterfully. He's the real deal.'

'Hear! Hear!' yelled Gala, who was holding Delectable and Chekov.

Gav had been perched on the little wall dividing pub garden and field, watching Gala and the goings-on, rejoicing in the fact that he wasn't terrified of parties any more. Raising his glass of Coke in gratitude at Rupert's tribute, he went back to blowing a dandelion clock.

'She loves me,' he was saying as each shiny silver floret whirled away. 'She loves me, she loves me, she loves me . . .' until the last one floated off. 'She loves me.' Then, looking up, he smiled across at Gala and her heart turned over, as she realized that with Gav's arms around her, she would never fear the chill of an English winter again.

The Editor of the *Cotchester Times* was chatting to Dora. 'You handled that presentation very well. Ever thought of coming to work on a local paper?'

Bao was talking to Etta.

'I am so happy, my father phone my mother this morning and I think they together get again, and perhaps they find my sister.'

'That is wonderful news,' sighed Etta. 'I hope he and Valent are OK. I hate thinking of them on that same continent as that beastly Wang.'

Happily, next moment her mobile rang and she moved out of the throng.

'Valent darling, how lovely, what time is it?'

Two minutes later, she came hurrying up to Rupert. 'Valent wants to talk to you – he has some very exciting news.'

Taking her mobile, Rupert also moved away from the crowd, amused to see Dennis the landlord surreptitiously knocking back a half pint of Bolly and Chisolm gobbling up Geraldine's blue silk scarf.

'How's it going?'

'Bluddy marvellous. Wang's been arrested. Got far too big for his jackboots. Seems he's been trying to muscle in on the government for weeks. His first wife's family have had the guts to come forward and expose him for bumping her off and, according to Tong, endless other skulduggery has come to light. Anyway, Tong and I were at the World Cup meeting when Wang rolls up behaving like the Great I Am, barged into the official lunch, demanding places at the top table for himself and Sauvignon, and was promptly taken into custody.'

'My God, Gala'll be pleased.'

'She will, and in China, when they fall, they really fall. Tong says he'll be stripped of all his assets – gold, houses, horses, warehouses crammed with tusks and rhino horns, the bastard. Tong's over the moon, doubts if Wang will ever come out.'

'Good. He can share a cell with Jan.'

'The best news,' crowed Valent, 'is that Wang brought New Year's Dave with him. Sauvignon convinced him she knew about horses, but she had no idea how to look after the poor animal and the Chinese had no idea what a valuable horse he is, so I bought him back dirt cheap.'

'Christ, that's fantastic. He can come back to Penscombe and be the next Leading Sire. Get Tong to sort out the Galloper at once and bring Dave home before anyone finds out. Christ, that is good news.'

'And a stallion Wang paid forty million for, called Boo Sucks, is evidently infertile.'

'Second sucks and so does Boo.'

Team Penscombe were delighted to see Rupert grinning from ear to ear for the first time in days, so delighted he actually hugged Etta as he gave her back her mobile.

Over at Valhalla, Cosmo was still lying through his teeth, trying to convince Gablecross that Jan had acted unilaterally.

'Guy was totally obsessed with bringing down Rupert. Isa and I aren't fans so we told him to get on with it.'

'Sabotaging the bridle?'

'That was Jan.'

'Sabotaging Quickly in the Derby and the Leger. Hacking into Rupert's phone. Stealing Safety Car?'

'That was all Jan.'

Cosmo was relieved when the telephone rang although there was no PA to answer it. It turned out to be Sauvignon, her voice for once conciliatory.

'How's China?' asked Cosmo.

'Hard to tell, the smog's so thick. Look, Wang's been arrested and is in custody.'

'So's Jan – it's the In place to be.'

'I misjudged the situation. My aim was to help you find out what Wang was really up to, meet the top people here, make the Chinese government realize how worthwhile it would be to deal with you and Isa.'

'How very kind of you.'

'But now Wang's inside, I need to get home. Can you organize a flight for me?'

'I'd hang in there, Sauvie,' purred Cosmo. 'There are more billionaires in China than anywhere else. You're in a really good place. Got to go,' and he hung up. 'I'm afraid that Sauvignon is corked,' he told Gablecross.

Having broken the news of Wang's arrest to an overjoyed Gala, Rupert headed for home, delighted how well Harmony seemed to be getting on, particularly with Quickly, who hadn't bitten anyone all day.

He was even more delighted when he got back to Penscombe, to find a perked-up Safety playing football with Marketa, Gilchrist and Cuthbert while his sheep friends dozed in the sun.

Taggie, on the terrace, was laughing at their antics, looking adorable in a pale-blue poncho.

Still carefully avoiding sore breast and cracked ribs, they hugged each other. They were interrupted by the telephone. It was Bianca, ringing from Perth.

'Oh Mum, Mum, wonderful news. We're coming home. Two Premier League managers are fighting to buy Feral for next season. Feral wants to keep an eye on his mum and I want to look after you and Dad.'

'How heavenly,' sighed Taggie. 'That is the best news.'

'What's more, Valent's son Ryan is also after Feral. He's desperate for Searston Rovers to go up to the Championship League and he needs Feral as striker to help him, so we'd be just around the corner.'

'That's even better. Gosh, how lovely, I must tell Daddy.'

'I know Dad's heartbroken about Love Rat so he needs a new interest. Why doesn't he buy shares in Searston Rovers? I think he'd be brilliant at co-running a football team, and he could help them buy some really good players.'

'Only if he can sign up Safety Car,' said Taggie.

Acknowledgements

Having finished a novel on jump racing six years ago, and loving the people and horses who inspired me so much, I was wondering how I could start another on flat racing, when I got an amazingly lucky break. At a riotous *Racing Post* lunch in 2011, I managed, by some fluke, to forecast the most winners of the afternoon's races. My prize was a trip for two to the Dubai World Cup at Meydan racecourse, owned by the great Sheikh Mohammed bin Rashid al Maktoum. Setting off with Felix, my son, who is even more bats about racing than I am, we met everyone from Frankie Dettori to the great late Sir Henry Cecil and after a conflagration of fireworks, watched a heroic race in the desert under an indigo sky. What better climax to any novel, so this ending became my beginning.

In Dubai, I was again lucky to meet marvellous trainers – first the wise, witty and forthright Mark Johnston, and his radiant wife, Deirdre, who invited me to stay in Paradise, their yard spread over a stunning valley in Yorkshire. Here I met their large, highly competitive and very happy stable staff and their super sons Angus and Charlie. I was particularly helped by Hayley Kelley, farrier Justin Landy and the prettiest major-domo, Mikaelle Lebreton, also a glorious photographer, who, with editor John Scanlon, produces Mark's marvellous monthly magazine, the *Kingsley Klarion*. During my visit, I was also nobly driven around by stable jockey, Joe Fanning, and Jock Bennett,

Mark's assistant trainer, winner of the immensely prestigious Godolphin Stable Staff of the Year award.

While staying with the Johnstons, I was especially charmed by an Irish terrier called Gnasher, who did high fives, and the video of one of Mark's horses, Hurricane Higgins, who, if he didn't feel like racing, lay down in the starting stalls, thus inspiring my hero horse Master Quickly in *Mount!*

In Dubai, Felix and I also made friends with silver-fox charmer Robert Cowell and his lovely wife Ghislaine who later invited us to stay at their gorgeous yard in Newmarket. Here we met their colt Prohibit, who got very up himself after winning the mighty King's Stand Stakes at Royal Ascot. Prohibit's rider, ex-jump jockey Jim Crowley, was particularly helpful explaining the rigours and self-control needed to transfer to the flat, which one of my heroes, Rupert Campbell-Black's grandson Eddie, endures in *Mount!*.

Also in Dubai, I made other lovely new friends. First, Diana Cooper, a passionate racing enthusiast, and for twenty-four years a stalwart of Godolphin, Sheikh Mohammed's international racing operation, and former star jockey Richard Hills, now racing manager to Sheikh Hamdan al Maktoum, and his wife Jackie, who have a parrot called Rodney, who is always urging Richard to ride faster.

Hospitality reaches such extremes of generosity in the racing world, I can only rename it Horse-pitality. Back in England, for example, another brilliant trainer, Hughie Morrison, and his ravishing wife Mary, entertained me at Royal Ascot and at home, where Hughie gave me an insight into the rights and wrongs of racing, and helped me with an inflammatory speech which enrages the great and good in *Mount!* Mary is a huge help to Hughie because she cherishes his horses and his stable staff, as does another ravishing and wonderfully funny friend, Yvette Dixon. Yvette is married to ebullient owner and breeder Paul Dixon, ex-supremo of the Racehorse Owners Association and ex-Chairman of the Horsemen's Group, who invited me many times to their joyful yard in Nottinghamshire, from which their immaculately tailored son Scott is making a name for himself as a trainer.

Other great trainers who inspired me were not only the legendary Peter Walwyn and Michael Dickinson but also Ralph Beckett, Brian Meehan, Andrew Balding and his marvellous parents, Ian and Emma, Luca Cumani, Gay Kelleway and the irresistible George Baker, who, incredibly kindly, offered for a couple of months to train a horse I had a share in, who wasn't performing, for nothing.

Another great favourite is Roger Varian, and his sweet stable lad Sheynets Vadym, who lit up the racecourse with his beaming smile every time the mighty Kingston Hill clocked up another win.

A trainer who lights up everywhere and who, with his lovely wife, artist Katie O'Sullivan, is particularly strong on horse-pitality, is the irrepressible Jamie Osborne. At his yard, I was enchanted to meet the great Toast of New York, winner of the UAE Derby, and only beaten by a whisker in the mighty Breeders' Cup Classic. After such exertions, Toast likes to lie in and often breakfasts on incoming stable staff's ankles.

A highlight of a visit to Newmarket was meeting a hero and achingly funny public speaker, Sir Mark Prescott, who sustained me with buttered toast before a lightning trip round his horses and yard with its narrowed starting stalls and intricate swimming pool, followed by the most delicious Pimms.

Another Newmarket hero is the hugely successful John Gosden, and his wise and wonderful lawyer wife, Rachel Hood. Anyone who doubts that racing people love their horses should have witnessed John's entire staff in floods when the great, sweet-natured Derby winner Golden Horn left the yard to take up stud duties.

Equally, when another great horse, Caspar Netscher, returned from stud having got only a handful of mares in foal, his owners, Charles and Zorka Wentworth, two of the nicest people in racing, insisted that thousands of pounds be spent rebuilding his new box, so he could look out straight into trainer David Simcock's office and not feel lonely.

Flat and jump racing often merge, and I'm so grateful for more advice, wonderful stories and ongoing horse-pitality from my jump trainer friends Richard Phillips, Jonjo and Jackie

O'Neill and Charlie and Rebekah Brooks.

Owning a racehorse needn't bankrupt you and provides colossal fun if you join a super syndicate like the ones Harry Herbert masterminds at Highclere, or the Hot to Trot Racing Club. This is run by the dashing Luke Lillingston and Sam Hoskins, who scour the top trainers for exciting horses and take their members on jaunts to visit the horses in their yards or to see them racing.

To experience owning a flat horse, I took a twelfth share in a lovely grey filly called Love Grows Wild in a syndicate set up by the irrepressible Henry Ponsonby. Broken in by Jamie Magee and trained by the handsome Michael Bell at Newmarket, the filly was looked after by Matt Johnson, who touchingly and regularly hand-wrote me letters about her progress. As an indication of how hard stable staff work, Matt fell asleep the moment any lorry left the yard. Travelling to Great Yarmouth, I was regaled with hilarious stories of yard life by other lads, Ian Smith and Martin Gleeson. My object was to watch Love Grows Wild being saddled up, but I was greedily side-tracked by an invitation to lunch by Great Yarmouth's Clerk of the Course, Richard Aldous.

I have been so lucky that my son Felix has looked after me and accompanied me not only to the Dubai World Cup, but to numerous other race meetings. We had a lovely time at Wolverhampton watching Love Goes Wild ridden by Hayley Turner come third and enjoying an excellent dinner with Clerk of the Course Fergus Cameron, Managing Director David Roberts and super starter Steve Taylor, who explained some of the intricacies of getting horses out of the stalls.

Whilst on this subject, another great inspiration has been the wonderful horse whisperer Gary Witheford, who seems able to sort out the trickiest horse, particularly those reluctant to start. Mention must be made of his lovely wife Suzanne and his charismatic rescued stallion Brujo.

Back on our racecourse tour we made many visits to Newmarket, where we enjoyed the company of past and present managing directors Stephen Wallis and Amy Starkey and their able executive assistant Lucinda McClure, and watched the great Frankel devouring the Rowley Mile. I'd also like to thank Lord and Lady March for a glorious lunch and day's racing at Goodwood, and Petra Gough for a fun day at Sandown Park.

Ascot is always an inspiration. Here manager Kevin Maguire showed me round the beautiful and tranquil stable block, which both Black Caviar and Frankel once glorified, and from where the mighty Yeats sallied forth four times to win the Gold Cup. I was also helped by my friend Becky Green, business development manager, and the gallant clerk of the course, Chris Stickles, who described the hardships of getting fit to ride in a charity race.

Another thrill on Champions' Day, at a marvellous lunch given by the then chief executive Charles Barnett, was announcing that my favourite horse was Gordon Lord Byron, and finding I was at the same table as his enchanting owners, Morgan and Mary Cahalan. Later they took me into the paddock to meet Gordon, and even more excitingly watch him hurtle home in the British Champions Sprint Stakes, followed by the bliss of welcoming him back into the Winner's Enclosure and drinking his health far too many times in the Winning Connections Room. Gordon is now starring in a film of his life.

Coming from Yorkshire, I adore Doncaster, particularly during the bustling fun of the St Leger's meeting and the Legends race earlier in the week, where champion jockeys such as Dale Gibson and George Duffield return from the past to raise fortunes for charity. The day organized by Kevin Darley also includes a great lunch and auction, brilliantly compered by journalist and broadcaster John Sexton and enhanced by the sartorially resplendent Tim Adams, one of the trustees of the Northern Racing College. I must also thank Sian Williams, former head of Racing Sales, for pointing out that the winner of the St Leger receives as a trophy a plate – beautiful, but not suited for drinking champagne out of at an orgy in *Mount!*

One shouldn't have favourites, but I always feel I'm coming home at York – the most beautiful course with wonderful racing, the loveliest flowers, even in the stable block, and the most friendly and welcoming of managements. Headed by Chairman

Lord 'Teddy' Grimthorpe, easily one of the nicest men in racing, they include Clerk of the Course William Derby, assistant Clerk of the Course Anthea Morshead, and Assistant to the Chief Executive Jane Richardson, who provided so much exciting detail for my several chapters devoted to York, which include the great Gimcrack dinner.

Again on the horse-pitality front, William De La Warr of De La Warr Racing, and his wife Anne, President of the Shetland Pony Stud Society, invited us to see their yearling parade at Wellington Barracks, and to lunch at Buckhurst Park during which Jenny Smith lyrically described riding out at dawn and scattering deer across a dew-laden park. Later we went racing at another lovely course, Lingfield.

We've also enjoyed Derby days as guests of Investec, and would like to thank Rupert Trevelyan, Epsom's manager director, and Kate Masters. My hero Rupert Campbell-Black however has always bet with Ladbrokes and I cannot imagine a more riotous way of spending Derby Day than in the Ladbrokes' box, in the company of serious punters, yelling encouragement to horses and players competing on different monitors round the room. For this, I'd like to thank David Williams, Ladbrokes' handsome media director, lovely Hayley Beaux O'Connor, the Irish PR manager, and the flame-haired Kate McLennan, the inspired director of Customer Relations. On another occasion, Kate wrapped a risqué mocked-up jacket entitled *Winners* round my book *Jump!*, which on the back flap thrillingly made me a member of Ladbrokes Elite, with whom I now register my own bets with delightful men in faraway places.

Talking of delightful men, few could be more charming than the bloodstock agents who advised me, headed by the divine Lord Patrick Beresford, who gives the most wonderful lunch parties during Royal Ascot. The legendary Charlie Gordon-Watson was another fund of information and great stories who, with his dazzling wife, Kate Reardon, editor of *Tatler*, also invited me to heavenly parties.

The beguiling Ed Sackville, who co-runs a thriving bloodstock agency, Sackville Donald, provided more hilarious anecdotes, particularly of selling horses in the Far East.

Another charmer, Richard Frisby, did me the truly good turn of introducing me to Nicky and Chris Harper, and their son Ed, who own Whitsbury Manor Stud in Hampshire. Here I had a magical visit and saw foals being born, mares covered, met great stallions Showcasing and Foxwedge and watched horses working on the glorious gallops, where Desert Orchid became a legend.

Other studs I was privileged to visit were Highclere, run by Harry Herbert, Sheikh Al Shaqab's racing manager, and Juddmonte Farm in Newmarket, another domain of dear Teddy Grimthorpe, racing manager to the great Prince Khalid Abdullah. Here, I would like to thank retired general manager Philip Mitchell, and express my delight when stable cat George ushered me across the gardens to meet the mighty stallion Frankel and his stable mate Oasis Dream, both looking happy and relaxed in the care of Rob Bowley.

Nearer home, I enjoyed an owners' day at Warren Chase Stud, and also loved visiting Tweenhills Farm and Stud, owned by David Redvers, also manager to Qatar Racing, who so generously sponsor the Qipco British Champion series. Here I was taken round and introduced to star handsome stallions Makfi and Harbour Watch by equally handsome stud groom, Ben Hyde, and showed some vital statistics by dashing form analyst Mikey Wilson.

My new friend Ed Harper later took me to a blissful open day at Dalham Hall Stud, Sheikh Mohammed's breeding HQ in Newmarket, where we watched more beautiful stallions, including New Approach, Raven's Pass, Exceed and Excel, parading in front of top breeders, who must find it almost impossible to choose the finest mate for their mares. Here I must also thank director of stallions, Sam Bullard, and Ali Rea and Richard Knight for showing me round backstage.

The parade was followed by an exquisite seafood and champagne lunch, after which Ed and I went racing at Newmarket, where we had a hilarious drink with owner and friend Jeremy Kyle, made a trip to Tattersalls, where Ed bought a lovely mare called Lady Macduff, and went to the best party in racing given by the Castlebridge Consignment. Finally, I tottered back to the marvellous Bedford Lodge Hotel, which has a splendid spa and in Noel Byrne the nicest manager in the world.

To cut the superlatives for a second, without owners, who carry on despite the often pitiful prize money, there would be no racing. For this and for their generous horse-pitality, I would like to thank Charles and Zorka Wentworth, Jane Meade, Piers Pottinger, Carole Bamford, Caroline and David Sebire, Laurence and Elaine Nash, Julia Langton and the utterly marvellous Lizzie Prowting and her dear husband Peter.

It can also only be vocation that makes jockeys starve themselves and drive endless miles for, if they are lucky, only a percentage of tiny prize money. I admire them so much and am grateful for inspiration from Jim Crowley, Joe Fanning, Hayley Turner, Harry Bentley, as well as great jump jockeys Richard Dunwoody, Sir Anthony McCoy and Noel Fehily. Stable staff, as I've said, work harder than anyone else, so I'd like to thank Jo Collinson, Leanne Brouder and many more for their input.

I was so lucky while writing *Jump!* that my friend Minnie Hall, a wonderful head lad who became a trainer, lived nearby so I could just wander out and bombard her with questions. Sadly, Minnie has moved to Bedford, but happily, while I've been writing *Mount!*, her place has been taken by two utterly wonderful friends. Firstly, the gorgeous Liz Ampairee, who works, among other things, on books at the *Racing Post* and is one of the most helpful and loved people in racing. Liz effected crucial introductions, drove me around, answered my questions on everything and even read through the manuscript for howlers.

Secondly, I have been constantly advised by the lovely Leanne Masterton, travelling stable girl for Andrew Balding and another worthy winner of the Godolphin Stable Staff of the Year Awards. Leanne is encyclopaedic on racing, has taken horses everywhere including the Dubai World Cup and, like Liz, gallantly read the manuscript.

One of the hardest parts of these acknowledgements is thanking the great and good and getting their titles right, because they're always playing musical chairmen. Simon Bazalgette is still COE of the Jockey Club, Paul Lee still Chairman of the Levy Board but stud owner Tony Hirschfeld is no longer

Chairman of the Racehorse Owners Association, and its last President, Rachel Hood, has been succeeded by Nicholas Cooper of the British Horse Authority, while yet another ex-chairman, Paul Roy, is now chairing ROR, namely the Retraining of Racehorses.

Tony Kelly of Arena Racing, who entertained me to yet another lovely lunch, has whizzed off to run the Hong Kong Jockey Club, while the Thoroughbred Breeders' Association, whose awards I thoroughly enjoyed, is now chaired by Julian Gordon-Watson. My thanks to all of them.

A huge incentive to owning a racehorse is that it entitles you to become a member of the wonderful Racehorse Owners Association, organized by the delightful Keeley Brewer, whose team keep one in touch with all owner events and who hold splendid lunches and award ceremonies with terrific speakers.

Nor can I express my gratitude too highly for racing's regulators, the British Horseracing Authority, who have been such a support that I have teasingly re-named a parallel organization BRA in *Mount!* Early on in my research, I had a fascinating lunch with Paul Scotney, former Director of Integrity. Later dear Adam Brickell, the present Director of Integrity, Legal and Risk gave me endless help, particularly into how an enquiry might be staged at the BHA. Details were provided by Danielle Sharkey, Compliance Adviser and Adam's sweet PA Fiona Carlin. The charming new BHA Chairman Steve Harman, and his Corporate Affairs Assistant Laura Bewick must also be thanked.

Another great friend Paull Khan, now Secretary-General of the European & Mediterranean Horseracing Federation, was invaluable with his advice when he was previously Racing Director of Weatherbys, the fount of all wisdom where racing is concerned. Also at Weatherbys, Ali Wade has been heroically patient checking whether my innumerable fictional horses' names have been used before. I cannot thank her enough. I'd like to thank Rachel Jones of Bloodstock Marketing Services for the glorious Weatherbys Stallion Book, and Nick Cheyne, Weatherbys jovial Client Relations Director, who invited me to the mighty King George VI and Queen Elizabeth Stakes at

Ascot, a crucial race in *Mount!* Best of all I have joined Weatherbys, who must be the wisest, most courteous bank in the world, and would like to thank its Chief Executive Roger Weatherby and Stephen Cannon and Simon Gardiner who advise and look after me so beautifully.

I am again so grateful to Diana Cooper, stalwart at Godolphin, for introducing me to her sweet sister-in-law Juliet Cooper, who invited me to a marvellous eventing weekend, the equivalent of Badminton, staged by Tattersalls in Ireland. This resulted in Juliet and Patrick, her glamorous husband, a leading light of BBA, the great Irish Bloodstock Agency, taking me to a blissful day at the Curragh, Ireland's greatest racecourse.

During my stay in Ireland, my great friend Jacques Malone, who seems to know everyone in racing, took me to another Paradise, Coolmore Stud in Tipperary, where no petals of the divine gardens were out of place. Here Mathieu Legars showed me round and I was ecstatic to shake hooves with gentle Galileo, the greatest stallion in the world, and equally thrilled to meet the mighty Camelot. For who in racing will ever forget the joy on the faces of his parents, trainer Aidan and Anne-Marie O'Brien, when their son Joseph in 2012 rode this wondrous colt to victory in the 2000 Guineas and the English and Irish Derbies?

Later, at Ballydoyle, Coolmore's racing arm, Polly Murphy drove us around endless tracks and gallops, enabling one to appreciate how Aidan prepares his horses for every eventuality. This was followed by a wonderful lunch for which I must thank spokesman Richard Henry and also Peter Steele, who took me round Coolmore's stunning museum, where an understandably rapturous thank-you letter from Her Majesty the Queen is proudly on show.

The following day, Jacques took me to visit awesome jump trainer Willie Mullins and his lovely wife Jackie. Willie's yard is a total contrast to Coolmore, bustling with dogs, hens, bantams with Christian names and utterly relaxed world-beating horses in every shape of box. Willie is so laidback, believing horses should get used to everything, he didn't miss a beat when on the gallops his Alsatian puppy ran through the legs of a hurtling stampede of horses. This pragmatic approach is clearly responsible for Willie's this year nailing the leading jumps trainer in Ireland and only by a whisker missing the English title.

Whilst in Ireland, I met another enchanting couple, Edmond Mahony, Chairman of Tattersalls, Newmarket and his wife Juliet, and back in England spent an excellent day at Tattersalls enjoying lunch and watching their stylish auctioneers at work. I was also most grateful to Property Manager John Morrey for taking me on a riveting tour of the stables and loading areas.

Although I was so lucky to go to the World Cup, I regretfully never made the Breeders' Cup in America or the Melbourne Cup, though they are essential to my plot. I therefore had to rely on television, DVDs and friends who'd been there. Here again, Leanne Masterton graphically described her journeys abroad with Andrew Balding's great horse Side Glance, while Jamie and Katie Osborne filled me in about those of Toast of New York.

Alastair Donald at the International Racing Bureau in Newmarket kindly and graphically unravelled the red tape surrounding the Breeders' Cup. The wonderfully funny James MacEwan of Janah Transport told me about flying at least six thousand horses a year round the world to race or take up stud duties, including one mare, for whom her solicitous owner begged a window seat. Kevin Needham of BBA Shipping also gave me great advice and it was marvellous to be able to call on Barry Preece of the Little Jet Company at Staverton for advice on flying planes and helicopters.

Racing people are not just generous in their hospitality, but also in the hours they devote to raising money for both horses and humans. Heading these are my great friends Andrew Parker Bowles, founder, and Di Arbuthnot, Chief Executive, of the marvellous Retraining of Racehorses (ROR), who find new careers for these brave horses once their days on the track are over. The indefatigable Paul Roy's recently becoming Chairman of ROR can only be to their good, whilst a lovely friend, Katie Dashwood, often rides rescued horses to victory.

Another pioneer in this field is dear Helen Yeadon with her sanctuary at Greatwood for retired and rescued horses, who often bond most touchingly with autistic children. I would also like to praise the Blue Cross, the Racehorse Sanctuary and in fact all the other sanctuaries everywhere who work so heroically to give these horses a better life.

As I pointed out in my acknowledgements to *Jump!* any horse's death is tragic, but I wish animal rights activists would direct their fire more towards the hideously long distances horses have to travel to slaughter houses abroad, or towards sadistic owners who, rather than fork out for a vet's bill, leave horses to starve or freeze to death outside. Thank goodness for World Horse Welfare and their CEO Roly Owers, and all the other organizations that prevent cruelty.

Equally, one cannot praise too highly the Injured Jockeys Fund, and its great-hearted former president, the wonderfully witty John Francome, his titanic successor, Sir Anthony McCoy, the indefatigable pioneering Vice President, Jack Berry, and Dale Gibson, Industry Liaison Officer to the Professional Jockeys Association.

I also have huge admiration for Michelle Bardsley, training co-ordinator of the Northern Racing College, and Gemma Waterhouse, formerly of the British Racing School at Newmarket, who are so crucial in enabling young people to embark on a career in sport. Three cheers too for the marvellous, much-enlarged Newmarket Racing Museum, which attracts so many thousands to the sport.

Racing is incredibly lucky that night and day, home and abroad, so many races are covered on television. Authors are lucky too. Goodness knows how Surtees and Somerville and Ross got off the ground without the beauty, information and entertainment provided by our three racing channels.

I would like particularly to express my gratitude to charming, unflappable Nick Luck, and all his team on Channel 4, including Alice Plunkett and Clare Balding, Sir Anthony McCoy and former participants John McCririck, John Francome and Mike Cattermole. Huge thanks too to *At the Races*, whose reports on racing throughout the night were particularly valuable and to their presenters Robert Cooper, Derek Thompson, Jason Weaver, Luke Harvey, Sean Boyce and the irrepressible Matt Chapman.

Nor can I ever express my gratitude sufficiently to the wonderful Diana Keen of Sunset and Vine, who let me come to production meetings, wander all over the set, hurtle in the cameramen's cars during the races and provided me with DVDs after she made beautiful heroic films of the Grand National and the World Cup.

Racing is also lucky to have such varied supporters from the great Sheikh Mohammed, the splendid increasingly svelte Sheikh Fahad al Thani and his brothers, plus Maurice Hennessy and Juan Carlos Capelli at Longines. And John Franklin, the engaging communications manager of Bollinger, the justifiably official provider of champagne at Ascot and Royal Ascot, adds a lovely sparkle to so many race days.

Racehorses are so swift and beautiful they inspire great copy at lightning speed. The sport again is incredibly fortunate to have the *Racing Post* chronicling every detail of every adventure. It seems invidious to single out anyone from such a great team, but I have been especially inspired by editor Bruce Millington, the evergreen Howard Wright, Alastair Down, Brough Scott, Steve Dennis, Lee Mottershead, Julian Muscat, Tom Kerr and Martin Stevens and Nancy Sexton on the bloodstock pages.

Equally, the joy as it flies is captured by their photographers, in particular the wondrous Edward Whitaker, who surely Uccello and Stubbs would have venerated. As they would George Selwyn, whose breathtakingly beautiful pictures appear in *Owner and Breeder*, another glorious magazine, published by ex ROA Chairman, Michael Harris, edited by Edward Rosenthal, and including great writers Emma Berry, Tony Morris, the ubiquitous Rachel Hood, and wonderful interviews by Tim Richardson. Terrific racing photographers also include Dan Abraham and Les Hurley.

Other inspiring authors number Robin Oakley, Marcus Armytage, Ivor Herbert, Bernice Harrison, David Ashforth, Lizzie Price, Marcus Townend, Richard Pitman, Dominic Prince, Felix Francis and Sean Magee, who worked so magically with that most lyrical legend, the great-hearted Sir Peter O'Sullevan. I'd also like to thank the authors of two great books: *Equine Stud Management* by Melanie Bailey and *The Last*

Resort, a memoire of Zimbabwe by Douglas Rogers.

Racing, in addition, inspires great equine painters: Katie O'Sullivan and Peter Curling, whose hilariously iconoclastic cartoon book *The Trainer* nearly got him chucked out of racing in Ireland, and Michelle McCullagh, whose drawings turn up in so much racing literature. Having read *Jump!* Michelle painted a hauntingly beautiful portrait of its heroine Mrs Wilkinson, mother of my naughty hero horse Master Quickly, which now proudly hangs in the drawing room at home.

So many other friends came up with great ideas. The former Home Secretary Michael Howard, over a blissful lunch at the House of Lords, was hilarious on racing in China, as was Robert Cole about China generally. Andrew Parker Bowles was brilliant as usual on racing. Judy Zatonski and Dr Mary Jane Fox were great on greyhounds. Michaela Galova and Marta Dostalova were great role models for my Czech Republic stable girls and dreamt up a lovely stable cat.

My great friends Bruce and Janetta Lee were endlessly helpful on racing in America. Freelance PR Kate Hills advised me on racing promotion, Colin Brown on race-day presentation and Lucy Cavendish on prepping young horses for the sales, Arthur Wade, Ian Minney and Sabina Marland on beautiful gardens, and Carole Adams, our Cotswold Hunt Secretary, on hunting. I also enjoyed a lovely lawn meet held by Toby Rowland and his wife Plum Sykes.

Dr Nattrass, from our Frithwood Surgery, advised me on medical matters, and on the veterinary front I had great guidance from our own vet Shane Jackson and his staff at Bowbridge Veterinary Group, from John McKenna, Shirley Bevin, Tom Austin, hilarious in Ireland, and Dr Jeremy Naylor, who was brilliant on racehorse illness and fertility problems.

My friends as usual provided endless support and input: they include Simon McMurtrie and Emma Devlin, Rupert and Ollie Miles, William and Caroline Nunneley, Rob and Sharon Morgan, Maria Prendergast, Jenny McCririck, Roly Luard, Lucy Lane-Fox, John McEntee, Katie Dashwood, Karina Gabner, Bernie Leadon-Bolger, Giles and Juliet Stibbe, Anthony Winlaw, Timmy Sim, Ingrid Seward, Barrie Foster, Marion Carver and

Nell and Carey Buckler. Carey in particular looks after sponsorship at Cheltenham Racecourse, and while on this subject I'd like to thank Cheltenham's managing director, Ian Renton, and his wife Jean for inviting me to magical racing during the winter months.

This must be the longest bread and butter letter ever written, but to my shame I took down the telephone numbers of so many other people but never followed them up. For this I apologize and even more for anyone who's helped me who I haven't included.

All the people who advised me were experts in their own field, but because *Mount!* is a work of fiction I only took their advice so far as it suited my plot, so any inaccuracies are mine. Equally all the characters are fictional, except those like Sheikh Mohammed, or Her Majesty the Queen, so renowned they appear as themselves.

With the help of Ali Wade of Weatherbys, I've truly tried to avoid the names of horses already taken but confess I've stuck with Safety Car, which seemed the perfect name for Rupert Campbell-Black's favourite and most endearing horse. I hope the *vrai* Safety Car, born in France in 2008, won't be too *furieux*.

The great Kenneth Tynan claimed that one should always write about things close to you. My main heroine in *Mount!* is therefore a Zimbabwean carer, widowed when her husband is gunned down trying to rescue a rhino from poachers. Moving to England, she lands a job caring for Rupert Campbell-Black's wayward father. After switching to working in Rupert's yard, she is replaced by a male South African carer.

I am in turn colossally indebted to the many marvellous carers who lived in and looked after my husband Leo in his last years, treated us both with such kindness and cheerfully endured the often long hours. A large majority were supplied by wonderful local agency Corinium Care, managed by Clare Janik. Many came from Zimbabwe or South Africa and provided me with crucial detail, inspiration, touching copy for my story and became huge friends. They include Lindy Botha and Ashleen McGovern from Zimbabwe, Lauren Holt, Louise Price, Susan Illing, Gorete Figueira, Norman Cilliers and Jen

Lombard, from South Africa, Lois Bell from New Zealand, Melissa Bathfield from Mauritius.

All had different invaluable takes on caring as did the numerous National Health carers, particularly Hazel John, who poured in in the various early stages and again treated both Leo and me with equal love and consideration.

I am particularly grateful to Jen Lombard and Hazel John, who were with me and such an incredible comfort when Leo died. Jen stayed on for several months and was so valuable advising me on South African catering.

Few diseases are slower and crueller than Parkinson's, few actions crueller and more violent than hacking off rhino horns or elephant tusks. We must find a cure for the first and totally outlaw the second.

A win at the races is hugely exciting, but I really screamed the house down when I learnt my marvellous publishers Transworld had won Publisher of the Year. It is so richly deserved. Led with great flair and kindness by managing director, Larry Finlay, every department is dedicated to cherishing their authors and selling their books.

I have the loveliest, wisest editor in Linda Evans. Greatly aided by the matchless Jo Williamson and the marvellous Bella Bosworth and Alice Murphy-Pyle, who have heroically dealt with getting a big rambling book to the printers and sewing the early seeds of publicity. I must also thank vigilant copy editor Joan Deitch, and the lovely desk editor Viv Thompson, who looked after the nitty-gritty of the process.

One of the incentives to finishing a book is to work on its promotion with my dear, charismatic freelance friend Nicky Henderson, who teams up so well with the serene and lovely Publicity Director Patsy Irwin, and her ace department at Transworld.

I'd also like to thank Bradley Rose for driving me around and being encyclopaedic on football, and Jean Kriek and Kathy Webb for always being so welcoming on the Transworld switchboard. Transworld is only one of the publishing jewels of the Penguin Random House group, so I was particularly touched that Tom Weldon, CEO of such a vast organization, found time to give me much encouragement.

In addition, I am hugely privileged to have an utterly marvellous agent in Vivienne Schuster, who inspires and protects me, sometimes curbs my silliness and always makes me laugh. She has in turn been helped by wonderful assistants Emma Herdman and Jess Whitlum-Cooper.

On the home front, it is impossible to describe how my life has been transformed by my PA, Amanda Butler. Kind, funny, warm, thoughtful, unbossily efficient, she spreads happiness wherever she goes. I must also thank her husband, 'Postman' Phil, for heroically delivering manuscripts and copy. Nor can I begin to thank Amanda and two other great friends, Annette Xuereb-Brennan and Mandy Williams, for gallantly deciphering my frightful writing; spotting howlers, making suggestions and miraculously producing a beautiful manuscript in just over a month. Nor would I last a day without Ann Mills, my divine housekeeper of more than thirty years and her joyful friend Moira Hatherall, who so cheerfully and uncomplainingly muck out my house and restore it to order and beauty. If I do any entertaining, they are also inspired party animals.

Since I had a hip operation a year ago and then gashed my other leg rescuing a ladybird, Celia Mackie and Julie Laws have been a source of fun and great comfort, dog walking and looking after me on different nights of the week. Phil Bradley has been equally swift and entertaining whilst driving me about, as has Simon Stroud.

My own family, as usual, have been beyond reproach. Laura Cooper, my stepdaughter, her son Kit and his girlfriend Lucille Cordell-Lavarack have been endlessly solicitous.

Emily, my daughter, a brilliant make-up artist, has been invaluable at de-croning me before smart racing parties. She and her husband Adam Tarrant and their three sons, Jago, Lysander and Acer, provide constant love and joy and marvellous copy, as do Felix and his wife Edwina and their daughters, Scarlett and Sienna. No family could be more cherishing.

The last three years have been tough in that as well as losing Leo, my beloved black rescue greyhound Feather and equally beloved rescued cat Feral both died. My darling remaining black rescue greyhound Bluebell misses them all too, but tries hard to fill the gap.

Finally, I'd like to thank Leo, wherever he is now, for fifty-two never dull years. I was so lucky to be married to a great publisher, whose kindness, stoicism and humour in the face of illness never failed him.